STRANGERS IN PARADISE

Four sizzling, sensual stories to heat up your summer.

Enjoy the fun with Carrie, Pam, Angel and Jo...
Visit Chicago and the Caribbean, Manhattan
and Montana, or Savannah and Florida.

The lilt of lazy, loving laughter is on the
breeze...and *somewhere* there's a strong, sexy
man with passion on his mind!

ABOUT THE AUTHORS

Kate Hoffmann graduated from the University of Wisconsin in 1977 with a degree in Music Education and went on to teach. She has also worked as an assistant buyer for a department store, an advertising executive, a copy writer and run a non-profit organisation. She sold her first contemporary romance in 1992 and from there it's been a whirlwind of deadlines, proposals and contracts. She thinks she now has the best job in the world.

Vicki Lewis Thompson was a journalist before she became a Mills & Boon® author, and believes she's probably a writer because her parents couldn't afford music and dance lessons, and pencils were cheap. She sold her first romance in 1983 and now nearly forty books later, with a few awards thrown in, she can't imagine anything else making her happier.

Stephanie Bond already has six novels to her credit. Her friends, family and fellow computer programmers are usually surprised when they discover she writes romantic comedy. After all, computers and comedy are an unusual combination. When Stephanie isn't in front of her computer, she's usually boating with her husband Chris or at home near Atlanta.

Lori Foster sold her first book to Temptation® in 1996 and her rise to stardom since then has been astronomical. Just four years and eight books later, she is a best-selling author with rave reviews to her credit. She lives in Ohio with her husband Allen and their three strapping sons, who inspire her to create exceptional heroes.

STRANGERS
IN PARADISE

KATE HOFFMANN
VICKI LEWIS THOMPSON
STEPHANIE BOND
LORI FOSTER

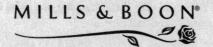

MILLS & BOON®

*First published in Great Britain 2000
by Harlequin Mills & Boon Limited,
Eton House, 18-24 Paradise Road,
Richmond, Surrey, TW9 1SR*

STRANGERS IN PARADISE
© by Harlequin Books S.A. 2000

The publisher acknowledges the copyright holders of the
individual work as follows:
NOT IN *MY* BED! © Peggy Hoffmann 1999
WITH A STETSON AND A SMILE © Vicki Lewis Thompson 1999
WIFE IS A 4-LETTER WORD © Stephanie Hauck 1999
BEGUILED © Lori Foster 1999

ISBN 0 263 82447 0

49-0006

*Printed and bound in Spain
by Litografia Rosés S.A., Barcelona*

CONTENTS

For Mary Bemis Raml, an old friend
who has become a new friend.

NOT IN *MY* BED!

Kate Hoffmann

Dear Reader,

With pages to write and deadlines to meet, it's always difficult to find time to schedule a real holiday. It seems I just finish one book and another hero and heroine are waiting for me to write their story. And when I do get away, my trips are usually for research and not for fun.

This year, I took a practical approach to holidays. I found a destination that required no air travel, no packing, no money. I decided to take my dream holiday in the pages of my manuscript. I had everything I needed—a warm climate, sunny beaches and a luxurious villa on a private island— even a gorgeous hero to do my bidding night and day. And I got a lot of writing done at the same time.

After I finished *Not in My Bed!*, I really felt like I'd been on a romantic getaway. I hope you feel that way, too.

Bon voyage,

Kate Hoffmann

Kate Hoffmann

1

AN ICY LAKE WIND whipped down the main street of Lake Grove, sending a bone-deep chill through Carrie Reynolds's limbs and stinging her nose candy-apple red. As she approached the storefront building that housed her travel agency, Adventures, Inc., she glanced up at the colorful posters she'd placed in the windows in the hopes of luring new walk-in clients.

Fiji. An exotic island getaway…sugar-sand beaches…suntanned men, bodies glistening…and women in bikinis so tiny that they could double as dental floss.

Winter was always the worst. Four endless months of leaden skies and numbing cold, punctuated by a few sunny days. And the ever-present wind screaming in from Lake Michigan, turning Chicago and its northern suburbs into metropolitan Siberia. Though winter was bad for the mood, it certainly wasn't bad for business. As Carrie peered through the plate-glass window, she noticed at least three clients waiting to be helped. And another at Susie's—

"It's him," she murmured, her gaze drawn to the man sitting across from her partner, Susie Ellis. She'd recognize Dev Riley anywhere. Even through a frosted plate-glass window from twenty feet away with his back toward her and her glasses fogged up.

Carrie reached up to the bulky knit hat she'd

tugged over her head before leaving the house. She hadn't even bothered with her hair that morning. And she'd skipped the makeup altogether. An over-size wool coat hid the worst of her sins: a dumpy green sweater and a pair of faded corduroys.

For a moment, she thought she might have time to run home and change. She only lived nine blocks away—a ten-minute walk if she rushed. But then Dev Riley stood up and shook Susie's hand. Before Carrie could formulate a new plan, he headed toward the front door, a familiar blue ticket folder clutched in his hand.

"Oh, God," she murmured, scanning the street for a place to hide. She pulled her hat down and her col-lar up, then spun around to cross the street. But the heel of her boot caught on an icy patch and, in a heart-beat, she lay sprawled on the sidewalk, her feet swept out from under her and a slow ache working its way from her derriere to her dignity.

Her hat had flown off and now tumbled down the sidewalk, blown by the wind. Her backpack lay near the curb, the bottle of grape juice she'd brought from home slowly seeping through the canvas to freeze in a purple puddle. And her glasses, knocked askew, had become tangled in her hair.

Carrie tried to scramble to her feet, but the lack of traction made the sidewalk treacherous. If she could just right herself, she might be able to—

"Are you all right?"

He had a voice exactly as she'd imagined: warm and rich, the kind of voice that could seduce with just a few simple words. Carrie had never heard him speak. Whenever he came into the agency, she always found some excuse to hide in the copy room or take refuge in the bathroom—any spot with a bird's-eye view. And considering that Devlin Riley traveled on business at least twice a month, she'd gotten quite adept at sprinting for cover and squinting through nearly closed doors.

"Can I help you?"

Carrie brushed the hair out of her eyes, knocking her glasses off in the process. Her breath froze as he held out his hand to her, long fingers gloved in elegant black leather. "No, thanks. I—I'm fine," she stammered.

"Please," he insisted, bending down and sending her a sympathetic smile. "Let me help you. Are you hurt?"

Carrie shook her head and was about to refuse his aid again, when he grabbed her hand and gently slipped his arm around her waist. An instant later, she was standing beside him, a slow flush of embarrassment warming her cold cheeks.

He was taller than she'd first imagined, his chin nearly even with her forehead. And his shoulders, emphasized by the fine cut of his cashmere overcoat, were impossibly broad. Carrie couldn't bear to look up into his eyes, but she just knew they were an intriguing shade of blue. She risked a glance—just one—but this time she couldn't look away.

"Green," she murmured beneath her breath. An intriguing and unexpected shade of green. How could she have imagined them blue?

His dark eyebrow arched. "Green?"

Her gaze dropped to her mittened hand, which now clutched his arm. "Seen," she corrected, hesitantly drawing away. "I—I should have *seen* the ice."

He nodded, then bent down and retrieved her

glasses. With careful hands, he replaced them, pushing them up on the bridge of her nose. "There, that should help."

"Thank you."

She watched as he grabbed her backpack, admiring the graceful way he moved, the way the wind ruffled his dark hair and the way the low morning light played over his perfect profile. "Gorgeous," she murmured.

Dev straightened and turned to her. "What?"

Carrie cursed inwardly. She had to learn to stop talking to herself! Living alone for the past eight years had turned her into a solitary chatterbox, giving voice to her every thought, just to fill her house with sound; carrying on extended philosophical conversations with her plants and her cat. "Gorgeous," she repeated, turning her face up to the gray sky. "I think it's going to be a gorgeous day."

He sent her another devastating smile, as she snatched the backpack out of his hands. "You think so? I heard it was supposed to snow. Five inches."

"I heard six," Carrie replied.

An uncomfortable silence grew between them, and though she wanted to drag her gaze away from his handsome face, she just couldn't. She wasn't sure when she'd get another chance to study him so openly. And looking at the real Dev Riley was so much better than her midnight fantasies and delicious daydreams.

He finally broke the stalemate, clearing his throat. "Well. If you're sure you're all right."

"I'm fine," Carrie said.

"Good. Then I'll be on my way." He gave her one last smile, then turned and headed down the sidewalk. She nearly sank to her knees in mortification, but then he turned back, and she quickly regained her composure. "You may want to stop in at the travel agency," he called, "and tell them about that icy sidewalk. They should put some salt down."

"I—I will!" Carrie cried, her voice cracking with forced enthusiasm. She hoisted her pack on her shoulder. "Yeah," she muttered. "I'll just walk right in and tell the owner what an idiot she is."

With a disgusted laugh, Carrie pulled open the front door and stepped inside. The warm interior fogged her glasses again, and when they cleared, she saw Susie standing in front of her. "You talked to him," she whispered. "You actually talked to Dev Riley." Susie shook her head in amazement. "I can't believe you finally worked up the courage. What did he say? What did you say?"

Carrie glanced at the waiting clients, then stepped around Susie and headed toward her desk. "I slipped, he helped me up, I thanked him. I looked like a complete klutz. Enough said."

She dropped her backpack beside her chair, then shrugged out of her coat and tossed her mittens aside. It was only then that she realized she'd lost her hat to the wind. "It was an ugly hat, anyway," Carrie muttered, avoiding her partner once again in her quest to get to the copy room and her morning coffee. "I need a doughnut."

High-fat bakery products always helped to soothe her nerves in the morning. French fries served as the tranquilizer of choice after eleven a.m. By late afternoon, she usually resorted to chocolate in any form. And before bed, there were those perfectly portioned pints of gourmet ice cream.

"I want to know what you said!" Susie cried, following hard on her heels. "You've been lusting after that guy for nearly two years, drooling and swooning every time he comes in the office."

"I never drooled!" Carrie said. "Now stop following me and go take care of your clients."

"I *am* taking care of my client—Dev Riley. Fantasy man. Hero of the hour."

Carrie groaned. There were times when she wished she'd remained a sole proprietorship. But Adventures, Inc. had grown too successful for one person to handle all alone. So Susie had gone from indispensable travel agent to aspiring partner, gradually buying into an equal share of the business. And along the way, she'd become Carrie's best friend—and tormentor.

In return, Carrie had been relieved of most of the more distasteful duties of a travel agent—like travel, for instance. Susie had also nagged and interrogated and lectured about her personal life until she had absolutely no secrets left anymore. "I don't lust after Dev Riley," she murmured as she poured herself a cup of coffee. "I admire his…" Carrie struggled for a word. His face? His body? His easy charm and smile? "His coat," she finished. "I—I think he has a wonderful fashion sense." She glanced up at Susie. "It was cashmere."

"And you couldn't be a worse liar." Susie studied Carrie thoughtfully. "Actually, it's good you finally talked to him. This is a big step for you. We both know, it's time you got a life. A real life with a real man."

Carrie took a bite of her doughnut. "I have a life," she said, her mouth full.

"You have a career," Susie corrected. She leaned against the counter. "You and I both know that you haven't had a life of your own since you were ten years old."

Susie was right. Carrie's life had been an idyllic picture of childhood happiness until her mother died almost twenty years ago. After that, as an only child, Carrie had become the woman of the house. She had cooked for her father and cleaned the house, ironed and shopped. And when she wasn't doing that, she lost herself in schoolwork. A straight-A student, Carin Louise Reynolds was the only person in the history of Lake Grove High School to win the geography prize four years in a row.

When it came time for college, she had turned down an academic scholarship at a prestigious east coast university, and chosen a small college within a half-hour drive of home. She didn't really mind caring for her father. Carrie loved him more than anyone, and enjoyed being needed. And it always gave her an excuse to avoid all the social pitfalls that came with high school: dates and dances...boys. She had to do the wash or pay the bills or iron her father's shirts for the next week.

In fact, she'd nearly resigned herself to a rather sedate future as a geography teacher, when her father did something completely out of character. The week of her college graduation, John Reynolds proudly announced his retirement, bought a condo in Florida, turned the deed for their house over to her, and presented her with a check for ten-thousand dollars. Basically, he told her that it was time for both of them to get a life.

So she had bought a little travel agency located in

the quaint business district of Lake Grove, a pretty bedroom suburb of Chicago filled with old brick houses on tree-shaded streets and populated with lots of disposable income. She created a niche for herself by booking adventure travel—trekking trips to the Himalayas, rafting trips down the Amazon, climbing expeditions to Antarctica—unique trips. It had brought in a young, upscale clientele and had been the key to Adventure, Inc.'s ever-increasing profits.

"Carrie?"

She looked at Susie and forced a smile, her mind already on a recent drop in airfare commissions and the effect on the bottom line. "I plan to get a life," she murmured. "I really do. Just as soon as I have time."

"Well, I suggest you begin this morning," Susie said, leaning forward. "You spoke to Dev Riley, your ultimate fantasy man. Now I think you should take the next step."

"The next step?"

"Call him up. Ask him out on a date. Lunch would be good. A little thank-you for picking you up off the sidewalk. I've got his number."

"He has a girlfriend. Isn't that what you told me? Besides, why would he ever accept a lunch invitation from me?" There was no use deluding herself. Dev Riley would never be attracted to her—a slightly klutzy, socially inept introvert with thick glasses and a perm from hell. She had a better chance of winning the Illinois lottery.

She glanced at her reflection in the coffeemaker, then ran her fingers through her tangled hair. Had she taken more care with her appearance this morning, she might have felt differently. But Carrie had always dressed in a fashion that made her nearly invisible to the opposite sex. Perhaps it was a way to protect herself, to rationalize any rejection she might experience. Of course men weren't attracted to her. Why would they be? "I couldn't," she murmured.

"You never know unless you try," Susie said.

Nervously, Carrie pushed her glasses up the bridge of her nose; powdered sugar from her doughnut smudged the lenses . "He'd say no."

Susie stood up. "Maybe he wouldn't."

"Oh, right. I'd be a welcome change from the gorgeous women he probably dates. From fashion models to flabby thighs. *Now* who's living in a fantasy world?" Carrie sighed.

"If you wait too long, you'll miss your chance," Susie warned.

"What is that supposed to mean?"

She smiled sympathetically. "I just planned a romantic vacation for two for him. He was here to pick up the tickets. This is the first vacation he's ever had me plan—it's always business trips. But this time, he led me to believe that he was about to pop the question to his traveling companion. Her name is Jillian. Jillian Morgan."

The name was like a knife to Carrie's heart. "He—he's getting married?" She turned away and tried to quell the unbidden flood of emotion that surged up inside of her. How could she feel this way about a man she didn't even know? He was nothing to her—just a silly fantasy! He barely even knew she was alive.

She took a shaky breath. "Let's be practical. A guy like Dev Riley would never look twice at me. Besides,

I made a fool of myself out there. I could barely put two words together. I just can't talk to men.''

Susie patted her on the shoulder. ''Making a fool of yourself is part of life—and love. We all do it.'' She paused. ''You just seem to do it more often than most people, but that's part of your charm.''

''My charm?''

''Carrie, you run one of the most successful travel agencies in the metro area. You're a well-respected businesswoman. You're smart and funny. And you're pretty, too, if you'd only pay a little attention to your appearance.''

''I'm also the most boring person you know,'' Carrie countered. ''What's worse, I'm the most boring person *I* know!''

Susie paused. ''Well, you can change that. Every day, you plan exotic adventure vacations for your clients. And yet, you've never really had an adventure—or a vacation—yourself.''

Carrie frowned, sipping her coffee. ''Traveling alone always seems so…desperate. So pitiful.'' She drew a deep breath. ''And a little frightening.''

''Then let me plan a vacation for you,'' Susie suggested. ''I'll make all the arrangements. I guarantee, when you come back, you'll be a different person.''

''I don't know, I—''

''Do it! Take the first step. I promise, you won't regret it.''

Carrie took another bite of her doughnut. Susie was right. How could she expect a man like Dev Riley to find her interesting when she didn't find herself interesting? He traveled the world. She read travel brochures. He lived life, and she merely stood on the sidelines and observed. He had sex on a regular basis.

She managed an intimate encounter with a man about as often as the nation elected a new president.

Maybe she did need to shake up her life a little. She was nearly thirty years old, and she'd spent the last year mooning over a man she could never have. It was time to step out of her safe little world and take a chance. There had to be at least one other man like Dev Riley out there…waiting for the woman of his dreams.

"So what's it going to be, Carrie Reynolds? Need I remind you that you turn thirty in two months? The world is waiting, and you're just getting older."

"I'll think about it," Carrie replied. "I'll let you know."

"This morning?"

"This week."

"Today," Susie insisted. "The rest of your life begins today! If you aren't on a plane by the end of this week, I'm giving up on you!"

Susie strode out of the copy room, leaving Carrie to consider her suggestion. To be honest, she'd been working on a few changes in her life. The perm from hell had been the first step in that direction—a spontaneous decision she had come to regret. She had really been thinking about a new coat of paint for the house or maybe a new car, but the pretty picture in the beauty shop window had muddled her common sense. In a secret corner of her heart, she had hoped that a new hairstyle might give her a boost in confidence, might make her more attractive to the opposite sex.

If she really wanted a man like Dev Riley—a relationship that was more than just a silly dream—then she'd have to turn herself into the type of woman he'd want. An adventurous, confident, worldly woman. A woman who could talk about more than just airfare wars, and group discount rates on hotels, and liability concerns for rental cars. A woman who didn't stuff herself with doughnuts every time she felt depressed.

"I'll do it," Carrie murmured, tossing her doughnut into the trash. "I'll do it! Or I'll make a fool of myself trying."

BY THE TIME THE TAXI pulled up to Carrie's resort, she was ready for a nap. The flight to Miami had been a white-knuckle affair. It was only the third time Carrie had been on a plane in her life. She had clutched the airsickness bag to her chest from takeoff to landing, and had tried to keep her mind off her nausea by focussing on Serendipity, the luxurious singles resort that Susie had booked for her.

It had taken a few days of cajoling, but she'd finally agreed with Susie's choice of destination. What better way to test the social waters? her partner had urged. There'd be plenty of available men to practice on, group activities that might mask her shy nature, and a relaxed atmosphere that was guaranteed to put her nerves at ease.

Carrie had studied so many travel brochures over the years that she could picture it so clearly: palm trees swaying in the south Florida breeze, the sound of the ocean, a balcony that overlooked the beach, a huge comfortable bed and a staff ready to cater to her every whim. She'd exercise and eat healthy food and pamper herself.

And maybe she'd venture out of her room once or twice to survey the singles crowd. She'd have to collect a few good stories to bring home, a few handsome men to describe, a few conversations to recount. Carrie moaned softly. Maybe it wasn't the travel that was making her nauseated, but the prospect of real social interaction with the opposite sex.

Or maybe it was the high-speed cab ride from the airport, weaving through traffic and tossing her around in the wide back seat. When she finally stepped out of the stifling car into the Miami heat and humidity, her knees nearly buckled beneath her. "There's a good reason I don't travel," she murmured, adjusting the straw hat on her throbbing head.

Airsickness, carsickness, a general sense of being out of control and out of her element. Visiting new and exciting places was now accompanied by the threat of another visit—from her last meal. If she could just conquer her nerves, she'd be fine.

The cabbie grabbed her bags from the trunk and set them beside her. Carrie rubbed her tired eyes, then looked around for a bellman. But there wasn't a bellman in sight…probably because there wasn't a resort in sight. They were parked at the waterfront, at the entrance to a brightly lit marina. "This isn't the Serendipity. There's supposed to be a resort, with lots of single—rooms."

The cabbie glanced at his clipboard. "This is it," he said. "This is the address you gave me. This is the Miamarina."

She turned to scan the opposite side of the street. "But there's no resort here. There must be some mistake."

The driver shrugged and pointed toward the fence.

"There's a sign over there on the fence that says *Serendipity*. Maybe that's a boat to the resort?"

Carrie groaned and slowly lowered herself onto her pile of luggage. "Oh, no. Not a boat. The plane was bad enough. I'm not getting on a boat."

"Well, lady, I have another airport run to make," the cabbie said. "I can take you back to Miami International, or you can stay here. Your choice."

Carrie gnawed on her lower lip. She'd come this far in the name of adventure. She couldn't quit now, defeated by a measly little boat ride. Susie would never let her forget it. "Go on. I'll be fine," she said, waving him off.

The taxi roared away, and Carrie cupped her chin in her hand and sighed. So much for her luxurious getaway. She was sick, she was hot, she had a splitting headache, and now, she had to get on a boat before she could even hope to take a shower and a nap. If most people handled travel as poorly as she did, Carrie realized, she'd be out of business pretty quickly. "People love to travel," she assured herself. "It's supposed to be fun. I'm having fun."

Carrie ran her fingers through her hair, then winced at the tangles. She'd spent most of the past three days getting primped and prettied for her big adventure. Her mousy-brown hair had been lightened to a sunny shade of blond and cut in an attractive shoulder-length bob. The girls at the salon had plucked her brows and pinched her cheeks, and when she left, she'd barely recognized herself.

She'd passed an entire day with Susie in a mad shopping spree at Watertower Place. They spent hundreds of dollars on fashionable warm weather wear, then went to Susie's condo and packed it all up in her partner's designer luggage, after adding a few choice items from Susie's wardrobe.

Carrie rubbed her eyes again. She'd even dug up the contact lenses she'd tried last year, hoping to show off the blue eyes that her hairdresser called "marvelous." But she knew better. All the stylists and best friends in the world would never be able to convince her that she was drop-dead gorgeous.

She was far too curvy to be fashionable. And too short to be considered statuesque. Her hair vacillated between mildly temperamental and downright belligerent. And her features were rather plain. All and all, she was what most men would consider ordinary—if a man ever took the time to consider her at all.

Maybe she was to blame for that. She always thought that when the right man came along, he'd recognize her positive attributes, and they'd live happily ever after. But after her silly infatuation with Dev Riley, she had been forced to conclude that if she ever wanted a chance at love and marriage, she'd have to make a few changes in her life. She'd have to stop hiding inside plain clothes and behind thick glasses. She'd have to learn to be charming and witty, to act confident even when she wasn't.

That's what this vacation was. A trial run in a place where she wouldn't have to risk running into someone she knew. She could make all her mistakes, swallow all her fears and confront all her insecurities. And when she went back home, maybe her life would become more than just her job.

"Ahoy there!"

Carrie looked up and saw a white-haired man, dressed in creased white shorts, a white shirt and a neat white cap, standing at the gate into the marina. He stood next to a cart loaded with coolers. An ice-cream vendor. God, she could go for an ice-cream cone right now. Maybe she'd have two, since her nerves were particularly frayed.

"Would you be Miss Reynolds, then?"

She shaded her eyes against the glare from his uniform. How would an ice-cream vendor know her name? Her stomach lurched. Right now, she really didn't care. Rocky road was all she could think about. Or maybe butter pecan.

"I'm Captain Fergus O'Malley," he said as he approached, his words thick with an Irish accent. He was a sturdy man with thick white eyebrows that nearly obscured his eyes. His skin was nut-brown and leathery from the sun, and though he was a complete stranger, Carrie immediately knew he'd be sympathetic to her plight.

"Captain Fergus?" She drew in a deep breath and wobbled to her feet. "Captain Fergus, do you have chocolate mint? Or rocky road? I'd even settle for plain old strawberry. Two scoops on a sugar cone."

A smile creased his weather-worn face. "Ice cream, is it? I can see what we have on board *Serendipity*, miss."

She frowned. Was this man sent to take her to the resort? "On board *Serendipity?* Don't you mean *at?*"

"No. On the boat. I'm Captain Fergus O'Malley, captain of *Serendipity*. And I'll wager you'd be one of my passengers: Carin Reynolds. Let me grab your bags, and I'll take you on board. Get you settled in."

"On board," Carrie murmured. "Then—then you aren't an ice-cream vendor? And Serendipity isn't a beautiful resort with soft beds and hot showers?" *And handsome single men,* she added silently, *in skimpy swimsuits.*

Captain Fergus chuckled as if she'd made a joke, and set off with her luggage tucked beneath his arms. "*Serendipity* is a fifty-four-foot ketch, one of the most luxurious bluewater boats to sail the Caribbean. We have a soft bed and a hot shower for you—that we do. And gourmet meals and fine wines. Did you not look at our brochure?"

Carrie shook her head and trailed along behind him, her legs feeling like limp linguini. "This whole vacation was supposed to be an adventure. The plane ride was an adventure and the taxi from the airport was an adventure. But a sailboat? That's too much adventure for me. You see, I'm not a strong swimmer and, I always say, if you don't want to drown, stay away from water. But that would be a little hard to do on a sailboat, don't you think?"

"There's no need to worry about your safety. And we won't be at sea all the time. We'll be putting in at pretty little spots almost daily, all along the Florida Keys."

She rubbed her throbbing temples. "But how am I supposed to practice?" she mumbled. "Susie knew I wanted to practice. Why would she put me on a sailboat where there's no one to practice with?"

"Practice?" Captain Fergus asked, stopping to look back at her. "And what would you be wantin' to practice?"

Carrie shook her head. "Never mind." She glanced up at the dock, a wave of nausea hitting her at the sight of the rocking sailboat. Carrie swallowed hard. "I'm going to kill you, Susie Ellis. I swear, as soon as I get home, you're going to pay for this."

"Well, here she is. I hope you'll have a fine voyage with us, Miss Reynolds."

"I'm sure I would have a fine time, if I were to get on your boat. But I can't. I'm afraid I'd get...ill."

Captain Fergus hoisted her luggage on board. "We can take care of that right away. You just wait there, and I'll get you some sea-sick pills. It'll set you to rights in a jiffy."

Carrie forced a smile. "That would be nice. I'll just sit here on this nice bench and contemplate my future. And the imminent murder of my business partner."

Captain Fergus gave her an odd look, then hopped on board and disappeared into the cabin. He returned a few minutes later with a huge fruit drink and a bottle of pills. "A welcome refreshment," he said. "No alcohol, but it will help wash the medicine down. You'll become accustomed to the motion after a short time. In a few days, you won't even notice it."

Captain Fergus proved to be right about the accommodations. After a half hour on the pier, Carrie managed to venture on board *Serendipity*, and found it all the captain had claimed. Her cabin was large and luxurious, with a huge sitting area that the captain called the "main saloon" and an equally large bedroom that he called the "forward berth." Even the tiny bathroom had a special name: the "head." *Serendipity* boasted all the amenities one would find in a fine hotel—except other guests.

Once she'd settled in, the first mate and chef—Captain Fergus's lovely wife, Moira—brought her a small tray of fresh fruit and a lobster salad, which she gobbled down.

As the sun began to set, the air grew still in the

cabin, and Carrie grew drowsy. Her clothes clung to her sticky skin, and she stripped them off, anxious to wash away the remains of a hectic day from her body and her mind. Wrapped in a towel, she headed for the bathroom. But she couldn't muster the energy to step inside the tiny coffin that served as a shower.

With a sigh, she returned to her cabin, tossed aside the towel and climbed into bed, too exhausted to search her bags for a nightgown. The crisp cotton sheets felt deliciously cool on her skin, and the medicine gave her a pleasant sense of lethargy.

Carrie had never gone to bed without her pajamas, but she was just going to lie down for a short nap. She was alone; what harm could it do? After a few hours' sleep, she'd get up, find a phone, call Susie and insist that she book a *real* vacation—in a hotel that didn't rock and creak and threaten to make her lose her lunch.

The gentle motion of the boat against the dock gradually lulled her into a deep sleep, the sound of the water against the hull soothing her ragged nerves. She awoke once and wondered where she was, but then allowed herself to drift back into a hazy dreamworld, satisfied that she was safe…and comfortable and…

The fantasy was not new. Dev Riley had invaded her dreams many times before. But he had always been a vague and unfocused presence. This dream was different. This time, he came alive in her imagination—the sound of his voice, the color of his eyes, the heady scent of his cologne.

Carrie sighed softly and wrapped her arms around a fluffy down pillow, stretching her naked body beneath the sheets. Dreaming of Dev was a wonderful vacation all its own. In her dreams, she was pretty and clever and sexy—exactly the type of woman a man like Dev Riley preferred. And he was passionate and commanding and completely enchanted by her charms.

They were in his bedroom—one of her favorite versions of the dream. He had a huge bed with filmy fabric draped like a canopy around them. Candles flickered in the darkness, bathing the room and his naked chest in golden light. He knelt over her, watching, waiting, the muscles in his shoulders and chest bunching and flexing, his hand hovering just inches from her skin....

But the bedroom dream never went any further. They never kissed or spoke; they simply watched each other...and waited. Carrie moaned and clutched the pillow in her fists.

Why did the dream always stall right before it really got good?

2

DEV RILEY WAS LATE. He'd nearly canceled this trip, but at the last minute, decided to go ahead with his plans anyway. To hell with Jillian Morgan! For that matter, to hell with women in general. It would be a cold day in the Florida Keys before he put his heart on the line again, before he trusted his future to a fickle female.

This trip was supposed to mark a turning point in his life. He'd been dating Jillian for nearly two years, and marriage had been the next logical step. Dev hadn't come to that conclusion without considerable thought. He'd weighed the pros and cons of a lifelong commitment and had decided to proceed.

After all, Jillian was beautiful, confident, intelligent, independent—the type of woman he'd be proud to call his wife. She loved her job, but more important, she understood his own obsession with work—the long hours and the late nights. And marrying Jillian was preferable to trying to find another woman who accepted his hectic life-style and his reluctance to start a family. Besides, he and Jillian spent most of their limited free time together. Why not make it official?

He'd given his travel agent a blank check. "Plan the most romantic getaway you can think of," he'd told Susie Ellis. "We want to be alone." And then he had surprised Jillian with the tickets. At first, she'd stubbornly refused to accompany him, begging off with excuses about work. But he'd worn her down, and finally she'd agreed that a vacation was precisely what they needed.

A bitter laugh burst from his lips. He'd been stupid enough to believe that Jillian had shared his plans for the future—until two days ago. He'd come home to find her gone—all her clothes and possessions missing—as if she'd never come into his life at all. He'd found a note of explanation, a businesslike missive— a resignation letter, of sorts—explaining that she'd decided to accept a promotion at work. A promotion that involved an immediate move to New York.

That news was followed by her sincerest wishes for his happiness. She'd wanted to break the news to him on their vacation, but then thought better of it. Never once had she mentioned love or commitment. Nor had she expressed any regret for her sudden decision. The words that she'd so blithely uttered during their moments of passion had meant nothing to Jillian, especially when they stood in the way of her precious career.

Dev slouched down and watched the lights of Miami's waterfront through the tinted limo window. Hell, even he'd been so obsessed with work, he'd chosen a destination that was just a short plane ride away from Chicago. He could have taken Jillian to Paris or Rome, but he'd thought about business first. He'd been a fool to think they could have a future together. The only common interest they shared—the single-minded pursuit of professional success—had doomed them from the start. But if he couldn't build a future with a woman like Jillian, who was left?

Maybe no one, Dev mused. Maybe he was destined to remain a bachelor for the rest of his life. All things considered, it wasn't a bad option. After all, he'd never had any problems getting a date when he needed one. And when a woman became too demanding of his time and energy, he'd just cut her loose and move on. He could go back to that life as easily as he'd planned to move forward into marriage, couldn't he?

Dev rubbed his forehead with his fingertips, trying to quell an ache growing there. So, that was the way his life would be. From now on, he was on his own. Women would have just one place in his world and that would be in his bed—on his terms! Once he got back from vacation, he'd throw himself into his work. But until then, he'd spend this next week alone, putting the bitter memories of Jillian into proper perspective. Putting women out of his life for good.

He'd learn the ins and outs of sailing. He'd get plenty of clean air and sunshine. He'd do a little snorkeling. He'd sleep late and waste time and teach himself to relax. And when he got home, his affair with Jillian would have become a distant memory.

The limo came to a stop at the entrance to the marina. As the driver opened the door, Dev could hear the clank of the rigging and the sound of water slapping against the sides of the yachts moored at the docks. Tall masts rocked back and forth against the night sky, creating wavering shadows on the sidewalk.

For a brief moment, he thought about asking the driver to take him back to the airport. This trip could turn out to be an excruciating bore—long days on the water, the only respite from sailing a private island retreat where he'd enjoy luxurious solitude... guaranteed to drive him crazy. And he could better use the time at the office, planning his next acquisition, while blotting the mistake called "Jillian" from his mind.

He'd never taken a real vacation—one that included complete isolation and relaxation. A few days off here and there were all he could spare, and he usually took his work along. "Come on, Dev," he muttered to himself. "You run a multinational corporation. Surely you can handle a vacation by yourself. It's time you learned to chill out."

What was he afraid of? Too much time to think? Too much time to examine the choices he'd made in his life? The mistakes? Too much time to get to know the man he'd become? He was thirty-seven years old. By this age, he should be comfortable in his skin. But since he'd taken over his father's business fifteen years ago, Dev had spent his days immersed in responsibility, loving every minute of it. It was only in the quiet moments of his day that he wondered whether there wasn't more to life than what he had.

With a soft curse, Dev stepped out of the limo and grabbed his bag from the driver. This was no time to examine his faults. A vacation was meant to be fun! He crossed to the gate and nodded at a uniformed man who waited there, warned of his arrival by a call from the airport. "Sorry to be so late," he murmured.

The captain smiled. "You'd be on vacation now, Mr. Riley. We don't watch clocks here."

Dev chuckled. "I'll try to remember that, Mr...."

"Captain Fergus," the older man replied with a thick brogue. "We're ready to cast off as soon as you're on board. Your companion arrived late this afternoon, and she's settled into your cabin."

Dev stopped on the pier and stared at the captain. "My companion?"

"She had a little problem with seasickness, but we took care of that. I believe she's asleep now. A pretty young lady, she is."

"My companion," Dev repeated. He drew a deep breath and let it out slowly. So Jillian had changed her mind. Her note had seemed so final. He'd canceled her half of the trip with his travel agent, and hadn't decided to go himself until a few hours before his flight took off.

If she'd had second thoughts, why hadn't she called him? Why just turn up in Miami without a word? Perhaps she didn't want to give him a chance to refuse her. Maybe she wanted the opportunity to apologize, to set things right. Dev sighed softly. Was he willing to forgive her? Could he ever trust her again?

"Would you care for some dinner, Mr. Riley? Perhaps a drink before we set sail."

Dev looked at his watch. It was nearly midnight. "Set sail? Now?"

"We sail at night so that you'll have your days for sightseeing. I know these waters like the back of my hand. No need to worry. With satellite navigation, it's no problem."

He shook his head wearily. "I think I'd like to get some sleep. You can take off right away. I'm sorry I held us up."

The captain showed Dev into the main saloon, then pointed down a companionway. "Your berth is forward. There's a tiny berth next to the head where you can store your luggage. We'll be in Elliott Key by early morning. You can have lunch on shore if you like."

"Great," Dev said without much enthusiasm. He wasn't even sure if he and Jillian would be speaking to each other by the next day, much less sharing a meal. Her sudden desertion spoke volumes about her feelings for him—feelings that he intended to fully understand before they docked tomorrow. "I'll see you in the morning, Captain."

The cabin was dark when Dev stepped inside; the only light was that filtering through the row of port-holes on either side of the bed. He reached for the switch, then paused before drawing his hand away. He really didn't want to talk to Jillian right now. His mind had been dulled by the effects of a long day of travel, and he wasn't in the mood for an argument.

With a deep sigh, he dropped his bags on the floor and shrugged out of his jacket. He'd wait and confront her tomorrow morning, when he felt sharper and his resolve was more focused. As Dev stripped down to his boxers, he stared at the unmoving form curled beneath the covers.

He fought a sudden urge to do away with the boxers and crawl in beside her, waking her slowly with his mouth and his hands. Perhaps if he made love to her first, he'd forget all his anger, and they'd be able to pass a tolerable vacation together. They'd always been good together, sharing a rather reserved passion in bed that they both found satisfying. And at the end of the vacation, they would go their separate ways. By that time, he'd have convinced himself not to care one way or the other.

In the end, Dev stretched out on top of the covers,

folding his arms behind his head. He'd settled on spending this vacation in solitary pursuits, and was even looking forward to some time alone. Now, he rather resented Jillian's presence. "It wouldn't be such a bad thing to be without a woman," he murmured, glancing over at her. "At least for a little while."

Jillian moaned softly, and he felt her press against him. Dev clenched his teeth and fought his impulses. So much for good intentions. Though he didn't want to wake her, just how was he supposed to resist her warm body curled against his, her breath soft against his bare skin? He turned toward her and stroked her cheek, her skin like warm silk.

With a groan, he slid down beside her and drew her body against his. His mouth found hers in the darkness, and he kissed her. For a brief instant, he hesitated, doubt niggling at his mind. She felt different in his arms, tasted different. His fingers tangled in her hair, and he wondered when she'd decided to curl it.

He brushed his thoughts aside as easily as he brushed the sheet from her body. Slowly, his hands found familiar flesh...familiar, yet unfamiliar to his touch. Where he once caressed hard muscle, he now enjoyed soft curves. The sweet fragrance of her perfume drifted around him as he bent to kiss her breast. Even her perfume smelled different...exotic... arousing.

"Mmm," she murmured, arching against him. "You're here. You're really here."

Dev froze at the sound of her voice, then pulled away. Stunned, he reached out and flipped on the bedside light, then looked down at the naked woman lying beside him. Her face was tipped up to the light, but her eyes were still closed. For an instant, Dev thought he recognized her, but then he realized the woman in his cabin—in his bed—was a complete stranger!

With a curse, he grabbed the sheet and carefully arranged it over her naked body. When his heart had stopped pounding and he'd gained control of his senses, Dev he reached out and grasped her shoulders. He gave her a gentle shake, but she didn't open her eyes. Then he scrambled out of bed and stood above her, not sure what propriety dictated in a situation like this. It certainly didn't allow for the growing desire evident beneath his boxer shorts.

Dev grabbed his trousers and tugged them on, leaving the button unfastened at his waist. Had another passenger stumbled into his cabin by mistake? He shook his head. That couldn't be! He and Jillian were to be the only passengers on *Serendipity*. That left only a member of the crew. He bent down and studied her face. For a person who spent her days on a sailboat, she was remarkably pale.

No, she couldn't be part of the crew. Captain Fergus had called her his "companion." Then what? She could have stowed away on this boat under false pretenses, claiming his bed as her own. Dev frowned. Who was she? And what the hell was she doing in his bed? Surely she wasn't one of the amenities that this charter offered!

He reached out to touch her again, then drew his hand away. She had the most incredibly soft skin, like nothing he'd ever touched before. Dev knelt down and studied her at eye level, his chin resting on his fist, his brow furrowed. On first glance, she wasn't what he'd consider beautiful. But upon more careful consideration, Dev had to admit that the woman in his bed was intriguing.

The differences between this woman and Jillian were like those between night and day. Jillian was cool and inaccessible. Her willowy body had been meticulously sculpted by a personal trainer, and she possessed a worldly attitude that came with the knowledge that her dark beauty was matched only by her intelligence and drive.

In contrast, this woman was all sunshine and light, from her curly blond hair to her fresh-faced looks. A scattering of freckles dusted her upturned nose and her pale cheeks. Her wide, lush mouth was curled up in what Dev suspected was a permanently impish smile. And from the curves that he could see hidden beneath the sheet, he doubted that she spent a lot of time pumping weights at her local gym.

She was everything that he'd never been attracted to. Yet Dev couldn't seem to take his eyes off her, couldn't shake the feeling that he somehow knew her. A cool salt-tinged breeze drifted through the cabin from the open hatch, and he watched as it fluttered a strand of her hair.

A sensible man would shake her awake and demand an explanation. A proper gentleman would at least search out the captain and find out how a stranger had ended up in his cabin. But Dev Riley was neither sensible nor a gentleman. Instead, he decided to crawl back into bed and get some sleep.

He would find out soon enough who this woman was. And until then, he wasn't going to give her a chance to jump ship before her explanations were deemed acceptable.

CARRIE GROANED and flung her arms out, pressing her palms into the mattress to steady the sway of the bed. For a long moment, she refused to open her eyes, certain that as soon as she did, her senses would be overwhelmed by the nausea. She felt sick, as if she had the flu or food poisoning. Or a really bad hangover—not that she'd ever had one. And then she remembered where she was.

"Oh, God," she cried. "I'm still on the damn boat."

"The question is, what are you *doing* on the damn boat?"

Startled by the unfamiliar voice, Carrie bolted upright. Her head snapped around, and her bleary eyes came to rest on a man lying next to her. She blinked and tried to focus. As soon as she did, the nausea doubled. Good Lord! Dev Riley was in her bed! And he was wearing nothing but silk boxers and a smile.

"I—I must be dreaming," she murmured, the room spinning around her, her mind whirling in the opposite direction. She rolled to her side and tried to convince herself that she was still asleep, pinching her eyes shut for good measure and taking a few deep breaths. "Oh, please. I have to be dreaming."

"This is no dream, sweetheart."

Sweetheart? Dev Riley was in her bed, in his underwear, and he was calling her "sweetheart?" Oh, this was definitely a dream. But her eyes wouldn't stay closed. And she could smell his cologne in the air, hear the water rushing against the hull of the boat. And this nausea! If this were really a dream, she would feel…well, she'd feel a lot better.

Slowly, Carrie pushed up to a sitting position and faced him at the very same moment that she faced her fears. *So let's say he is real,* she mused. What was he

doing here? And how did they end up on the same—
Susie! Susie had done this to her! Lured her down to
Miami under false pretenses and tossed her into bed
with Dev Riley.

"I'm not dreaming, am I," she murmured.

He grinned and shook his head, his gaze dropping
to her chest.

Carrie groaned again, then glanced down to see the
sheet revealing a little too much skin. With a tiny
scream, she snatched the sheet up to her chin and
wriggled to the edge of the bed, all the while keeping
her eyes on him.

Susie had arranged the whole thing: the trip, the
shared cabin, this forced intimacy with her fantasy
man…although it was hard to believe Susie had arranged those silk boxers he wore. If Carrie didn't miss
her guess, *Serendipity* was already underway, far
enough from land to make a quick escape impossible.
Susie had probably arranged for that, too!

"I think I'm going to throw up," she moaned, trying to struggle to her feet.

"Before you throw up, maybe you can tell me who
you are. And what you're doing in my cabin."

Carrie swallowed. "I can't talk right now."

She heard him curse, and a few moments later he
appeared beside her. "Here. Take this."

Her gaze drifted up his long, muscular legs to his
boxers, then stopped in the vicinity of his lap, riveted
to the faint outline of his… "Oh, my," she murmured.

Dev pushed the glass of water at her, and, with a
trembling hand, she grabbed it along with the dose of
medication, grateful for a momentary distraction.
"Take it," he ordered. "Then we're going to talk."

Carrie did as she was told, trying to sort out her

thoughts as she sipped the water. Susie had booked them on the same trip, in the same cabin. Yet Dev didn't know who she was. He didn't recognize her. So he couldn't possibly know this was Susie's idea of a setup. And what about his—? Carrie groaned again and buried her face in the twisted sheet. Had Susie found some way to get rid of his girlfriend as well? How could she possibly have arranged that?

Jillian—that was her name. His fiancée. Carrie moaned inwardly. Lying in bed next to him, naked, was humiliating enough. The only way matters could get any worse would be if his girlfriend walked in the door and caught them together. "Maybe if I just go back to sleep," Carrie said, rubbing her forehead. "This is all too confusing right now."

"Imagine how I felt when you curled up in my arms and kissed me," Dev said.

Carrie glanced up at him, her eyes wide. Kissed him? She'd kissed Dev Riley? How could she have missed such a momentous event? "You and I—" She drew a long breath. "We kissed…on the lips…in bed?"

His dark eyebrow quirked up, and he grinned one of those devastating grins that made her mind turn to mush. "On the lips," he confirmed. "In bed. It was very passionate. The earth moved, the angels sang."

Stunned, Carrie sat up and the sheet fell to her waist. With a soft cry, she snatched it up and tucked it under her arms. This was exactly why people shouldn't sleep naked! A person never knew who they might wake up with. "What else did I—I mean, we—do?"

Dev laughed. "You don't remember?" He clutched his hands to his naked chest. "I'm hurt. Usually, I'm very memorable. In fact, I'm so memorable that most women want to relive the moment—again and again and—"

"I get the picture," Carrie muttered, her heart banging against her chest. How could she have slept through it all? She'd made love to her perfect fantasy man, and she couldn't remember a single moment of the event. Unless... She glanced up at him again and caught a twinkle of amusement in his eyes. Could he be teasing her? Carrie cleared her throat and readjusted the sheet.

She couldn't just come out and call him a liar. And a secret part of her wanted to think that the dream she'd had the previous night was real. Even if she didn't remember it, it had to have been one of the most exciting events of her life. Still, she would have remembered, wouldn't she? Carrie cleared her throat. "W-was I good?" she asked.

"Good? You were incredible. So passionate and uninhibited."

She ground her teeth. Fat chance! He was lying, making fun of her. And for that, she wanted to make him pay. She wanted to wipe that smug little smirk right off his handsome face. "That's amazing," she said in a soft voice, "considering it was my first time. I always dreamed it would be perfect." She frowned. "I also thought I'd remember it."

His grin froze and his green eyes widened. "Your first time? You mean you're a..." He let his voice drift off, and she could see regret in his expression. Now whose turn was it to smile smugly?

Carrie sighed dramatically. "Umm-hmm. The very first time I've ever—" she drew a deep breath and narrowed her eyes "—ever met such a black-hearted, despicable, conceited, lying sonofa—"

He held up his hand. "All right, all right. Your point is made," he interrupted. "There's no need to disparage my mother. And I'm sorry for embellishing the truth. But you have to understand my surprise at finding you in my bed."

Carrie struggled to her feet, keeping the sheet wrapped tightly around her. "I might not know exactly what happened here, but I do know that we didn't make love."

Dev opened his mouth, then snapped it shut. "Well, we could have, if I hadn't been such a gentleman. And you hadn't been nearly comatose."

"And if I weren't a lady, I'd start screaming for the captain right about now."

"Hey, you're the one who's in *my* cabin." Dev backed away from the bed, then slouched down in a chair. "Why don't we start with your name?"

"It's Car—ah…" She bit back the rest, knowing that she shouldn't reveal her name. If he recognized it, then he might put two and two together and jump to the wrong conclusion: that *she* had deliberately planned this encounter just to get closer to him. But then, he'd always worked with Susie, and there was no reason for him to know Carrie's name. It wasn't painted on the front door or emblazoned across the company stationery.

"Cara? Cara what?"

"Carin," she quickly corrected. "Carin Reynolds." Such a boring name—not nearly as exotic and alluring as *Jillian*. "But my friends call me Carrie." *Cara* sounded much more sophisticated than *Carrie*, didn't it? *Carrie* sounded like a ninety-year-old maiden aunt. *Cara* sounded almost as good as *Jillian*.

She watched him carefully, waiting for some hint of recognition, but there was nothing. They'd come face-to-face on the street just a few mornings before, she owned the travel agency he visited at least twice a month—and he didn't have a clue! Carrie's heart twisted with indignation. So much for being memorable.

"And where are you from, Ms. Reynolds?"

She couldn't say Lake Grove, or even Chicago. Carrie searched her memory for an obscure spot on the globe, a place that Dev Riley couldn't possibly know intimately. "I'm from all over," she said. "My father was…a salesman. Mostly we lived in—in Anchorage. Alaska. Are you familiar with Anchorage?"

"I've been there a few times," he said.

"Well, we didn't live there long before we moved to Helena. Montana."

Dev shook his head. "I'm afraid I've never been to Helena."

Carrie breathed a silent sigh of relief. She knew all the places that Dev had visited—they were all on her computer. How had she missed Anchorage? So she'd be Carin Reynolds from Helena, Montana. As long as he didn't know her true identity, she could make her escape without being discovered. She could go back to Lake Grove and carry on as if she'd never agreed to this disastrous vacation. And when Dev Riley stepped inside her office again, he'd barely give her a second glance.

She twisted her fingers together in nervous knots. "Helena is the capital of Montana—did you know that? Although Great Falls should be, since it's more in the geographical center of the state. Montana is called The Treasure State. It's the fourth-largest state." Dev frowned at her as if she'd suddenly started speaking Greek. Carrie forced a smile and decided that it was a good time to stop babbling.

"Now that we've finished our little geography lesson," Dev said, "why don't you tell me what you're doing here?"

"Would you mind if we had this conversation fully clothed?" Carrie asked, tugging the sheet up on her chest.

"And give up my advantage? As long as you're taking cover beneath the covers, you can't avoid my questions. How did you end up in this cabin?"

Carrie drew in a deep breath, then gave him an innocent shrug. "It was obviously a mistake. I thought my travel agent was sending me to a resort. With lots of rooms…and more than one bed."

"And I booked this charter for two. That's all this boat carries."

"So where's your traveling companion?" Carrie snapped. "She wasn't in bed with us, too, was she?"

His jaw went tight. "She canceled."

"Well, that's it, then. They double-booked the cabin. It happens all the time in the travel industry. Perhaps Captain Fergus thought you intended to cancel as well, and that's why he took my reservation."

"But he was expecting me and my companion. In fact, he thought *you* were my companion. How do you explain that?"

Carrie felt her temper rise. "If you're implying that I tricked my way on board then—"

His eyebrow shot up again. "Did you? There are plenty of women who'd love to find themselves in bed with Devlin Riley for more reasons than I'd care to count. Are you one of those women, Ms. Reynolds? If that's really your name."

Of all the arrogant, condescending males she'd ever met, Devlin Riley took first prize! Could he be so egotistical as to believe that women—no, that *she*—would deviously weasel her way into his bed? How could she have even imagined herself attracted to someone so smug and self-absorbed? Even worse, how could such a creep still cause her heart to pound and her head to spin?

Carrie wrapped the sheet more snugly around her, then stalked across the cabin to stand at the door. "Get out of my cabin, Mr. Riley."

"This is *my* cabin, Ms. Reynolds."

"I was here first, and possession is nine points of the law."

He pushed to his feet, crossed to the door and bent perilously close to her. *"Possession,"* he murmured. "That's a dangerous word to be tossing around when you've got nothing on but a bedsheet."

Carrie ground her teeth, then spun around and grabbed his trousers from the end of the bed. She threw them at his head, and yanked the cabin door open. "Get out."

With a charming grin, Dev tossed his pants over his shoulder and sauntered out the door, whistling as he walked. "We're not finished this conversation," he said from the companionway, his back to her.

Carrie punctuated the slam of the cabin door with a caustic oath. "How could I have been so stupid?" she muttered. "My fantasy man? This vacation is a nightmare, and he's the boogeyman!"

Dropping the sheet, she bent down to retrieve fresh

clothes from her suitcases. She finally found a sundress that wasn't too wrinkled, and tugged it over her head. Her hair looked a mess, and she reached for her makeup bag, then scolded herself. After he'd disparaged her character, how could she still care what Dev Riley thought about her?

How had she managed to build him into such a paragon of manhood? All her fantasies and daydreams were built on nothing but pure imagination. Still, he was handsome and charming and undeniably attractive—and just looking at him made her breathless....

Carrie groaned and yanked a brush through tangled hair. She should hate him, but all she could work up was a mild case of righteous indignation. After all, he was quite gallant that day on the icy sidewalk. And he *had* been a gentleman in bed, even when confronted with a warm and willing woman.

"Don't make excuses for him!" she muttered, tossing her brush on the bed. He was a scoundrel, a cad with an ego the size of Switzerland. Insinuating that she'd put herself in that bed to seduce him! How dare he?

In an attempt to calm her anger, Carrie sat down on the rumpled bed and weighed all her options. She'd have to get off this boat. The last thing she needed was for Dev Riley to find out how she ended up on his vacation and in his bed. Or to realize how infatuated she was with him, in spite of his boorish behavior.

"I don't know where we are, but we have to be close to land," she murmured aloud. Carrie reached for the door. She'd explain the error to Captain Fergus, and he'd turn the boat toward the nearest port.

She'd ignore Dev Riley for the remainder of her time on board *Serendipity*. And if all went well, she'd be rid of her silly fantasies—and the man who had inspired them—by the time the sun set.

"THERE'S BEEN SOME MIX-UP," Dev explained.

Captain Fergus stood at the helm and stared out at the deep turquoise water, as Dev settled himself at a breakfast table set beneath a green-striped canopy. "Your accommodations aren't to your satisfaction?" the captain asked, squinting into the early morning sun. "If there's anything more you want, Moira will be happy to get it for you."

Dev savored a sip of freshly squeezed orange juice, then shook his head. "The accommodations are fine," he replied. "It's the woman sharing my cabin. She's a stranger."

A very entertaining stranger, Dev mused, but a stranger all the same. With a soft, lush body that she'd barely hidden beneath that bedsheet. All at once, she was sweet and vulnerable and stubborn and impertinent. A confusing mix of childish bravado and tantalizing allure. And she had a temper, too!

He'd come to the quick conclusion that her appearance in his cabin had been a simple mistake. She didn't seem the deceitful type. Still, he did find her piqued anger and stammered indignation amusing.

"A stranger, you say?" Captain Fergus chuckled. "Ah, lad. This happens all the time. The prospect of spending days in such close quarters. In my opinion, every couple should spend a week or two on a sailboat before they jump into marriage. It would certainly weed out the matrimonial weaklings."

Dev picked up his fork and cut into a thick omelette

filled with peppers and cheese. "You don't understand. Until last night, I'd never seen that woman before."

"A lover's quarrel. A romantic lunch for two at a secluded beach on Elliott Key will put everything to rights. I'll have Moira start the preparations."

Dev ground his teeth. He sure hoped Captain Fergus wasn't as obtuse about navigational matters as he was about matters of the heart, or they'd end up in Ecuador. "I don't *know* the woman in my cabin. My companion, Jillian Morgan, canceled at the last minute. I came on this trip alone."

"Then Ms. Reynolds isn't your—"

"That's what I'm saying. She's a stranger. We hadn't met...until last night."

The captain shook his head and clucked his tongue. "It's those damn computers. I told Moira that you can't trust a machine to do a first mate's work. Another mix-up, I'm afraid."

"You mean this has happened before?"

"This is what we get for signing on to a computer reservations service. The wife thought it would cut down on the paperwork, but I thought—"

"The point is," Dev interrupted, "I paid for that cabin in full. And she doesn't belong there. You're going to have to find her another cabin."

Captain Fergus scratched his chin. "Well, now. There's the problem. You see, she paid for her passage in full, too. And we only have one other cabin— the one we store the luggage in. It's not nearly as luxurious—just a few hammocks and a porthole. We use it for the grandkids when they're on board. It's not fitted out for guests. I suppose you and—"

Their conversation was interrupted by a commotion coming from the forward cabin. A moment later, a suitcase appeared in the main hatchway, followed by another. Dev heard a soft curse before an overnight bag tumbled out onto the deck. Carrie Reynolds followed, stumbling over the suitcases scattered around her feet. When she glanced up and noticed them watching her, she blushed. Then just as quickly, she regained her composure, smoothing her skirt and running her fingers through her tousled hair.

Dev couldn't help but smile. She looked so mussed, so skittish, as if she'd simply fly apart at any minute. He held out a glass of juice. "Breakfast, Ms. Reynolds?"

She scowled at him, then turned her attention to the captain. "I want to get off this boat! I need to get off this boat. How far are we from land?"

The captain smiled apologetically. "I'm terribly sorry, Ms. Reynolds. Mr. Riley explained the problem."

"I'm sure he did," Carrie muttered, sending Dev a sideways glare. "So, we need to find land so I can get off this boat. I need an airport, any place that has a plane to fly me back to Miami. This is not the vacation I signed on for. There was supposed to be a resort with room service and massages and a swimming pool and a—" her face suddenly went white and she pressed her fingers to her lips "—a place where the floor doesn't pitch and roll and…oh, my."

"Maybe some toast would help?" Dev suggested.

Carrie wobbled toward the table, then gripped the edge with a white-knuckled hand. Her fingers trembling, she snatched the triangle of toast from him and took a bite. "How—how long until we reach land?"

"About three hours," Captain Fergus replied, glancing over his shoulder.

She pulled out the bench and sat down with a soft moan. "Three hours." Carrie drew a long, deep breath. "Three hours. If I just sit right here and concentrate, I can make it for another three hours."

Dev watched as she closed her eyes, but a few seconds later, her face went pale again and her eyelids fluttered open. He held out another piece of toast, and she grudgingly took it. "It's better to keep your eyes open and fixed on the horizon," he suggested. "Seasickness is all an inner ear, balance thing. If you can get your bearings, you'll feel much better."

"I don't need your advice," she muttered, munching on the toast.

"I'm just trying to be helpful," Dev said. She looked so utterly miserable that he felt compelled to do something for her. Though he'd never been overly protective toward women before, Carrie Reynolds just seemed to be the type that needed someone to watch out for her. After all, if he wasn't keeping an eye on her, she might trip and fall overboard, knock herself unconscious with her luggage or—

Dev bit back a chuckle. She surely wasn't the picture of feminine grace. But he found her clumsiness quite endearing. After all, not every woman in the world was cut out for climbing mountains or trekking across the desert. Sitting on a sailboat was just about her speed—if it weren't for the seasickness.

Besides, a real woman shouldn't look perfect every minute of the day and night. Carrie Reynolds was a regular woman, and she wasn't afraid to show it. He had to admire that about her.

Her hair fluttered against her face in the salty

breeze, and he found his attention transfixed by a strand that caressed her pale neck. She watched the horizon, her profile outlined by the early morning sun. And then she turned…and caught him staring. For a moment, he thought she might smile. But then, she pressed her lips together and reached for her napkin. "Thank you," she said. "I do feel a little better."

"So would you like to try something else? This omelette is pretty good. And there's grilled ham."

A reluctant smile touched the corners of her mouth, and it warmed him as much as the tropical sun. "I am pretty hungry."

"Good," Dev said, cutting his omelette in half and placing it on her plate. "You'll feel much better after you eat."

Carrie dug into her breakfast with all the gusto of a starving sailor. He'd never seen anyone enjoy food quite as much as she did. Jillian ate like a bird and was always picking apart her meals, discarding anything that resembled a fat gram. But Carrie ate her half of the omelette along with what was left of his half, another piece of toast, two pieces of ham and half the pitcher of orange juice. By the time she finished, her color had returned and she looked almost content.

Dev leaned back in his chair and studied her. "Tell me about yourself, Carin Reynolds. Besides the fact that you enjoy a good breakfast."

"It's Carrie," she said. "Ms. Reynolds to you."

"All right, Carrie. Let's start with your personal life. Are you married? Engaged? Seriously involved?"

"That's none of your business."

"Ah, but it is. We spent the night together. I'm curious about the woman who warmed my bed."

"It was *my* bed," she countered. "I was there first. And—and we barely touched."

"All right. I'll concede those two points. As for the third, the touching part…well, you did touch me. There's no denying that."

A long silence descended over the breakfast table, the snapping of the sails the only sound. "There's not much to tell," she finally said, ignoring the bait. "I lead a pretty ordinary life."

"Yet here you are, taking an extraordinary vacation. Alone. This didn't come cheap. What do you do for a living?"

"This isn't the vacation I was supposed to have! My travel agent made a mistake. Once I get off this boat, I can have the vacation I paid for."

"You could stay if you wanted," Dev said.

She shook her head, more annoyed than surprised by his offer. "I'm sure some women would find that proposal irresistible, Mr. Riley—spending a few more days in your presence…in your bed. But—"

"I'm not suggesting we share a bed, Carrie. There is another cabin on board. It's not quite as nice, but—"

"No," Carrie said. "I appreciate your offer to move, but I—"

"*I'm* not offering to move," Dev said. "I meant that you could take the other cabin."

"B-but I was here first!" she sputtered.

"But your travel agent made the mistake, not mine. You said so yourself."

She crumpled up her napkin and tossed it on the table. "Whoever said chivalry was dead, was wrong. It's not just dead, it's buried under miles of the modern male ego." She pushed away and stood up, but she obviously hadn't completely gained her sealegs. Her knees buckled, and she reached for the table.

Dev stood and grabbed her by the shoulders before she lost her balance completely. "Hey! Are you all right?" He looked down into her wide eyes, and a wave of déjà vu washed over him. For an instant, he felt as if he knew her, and he swore he saw a flash of recognition in her gaze as well. But the feeling passed so quickly that he must have only imagined it.

"I'm fine," she said, twisting out of his grasp. "I just need to get off this boat."

"Maybe you should lie down. You can take the cabin—I don't care."

"No, I'll just stay outside." With that, she tiptoed through her luggage and found a spot on the forward deck. Gingerly, she sat down and turned her gaze toward the horizon.

Dev slouched back into his chair and wove his fingers together behind his head. To be honest, he was hoping that she'd decide to stay. He could use the company, and Carrie Reynolds wasn't at all disagreeable as a traveling companion. She didn't seem too impressed by his charm though; in fact, she was downright prickly toward him.

Hell, what did he care what she thought of him? He'd come on this vacation to get away from women. If he had to spend his time with one, she might as well hate him. That way he'd be able to avoid any thought of how he was going to get Carrie Reynolds back into his bed.

3

THE SUN BEAT DOWN on the narrow road that ran from the yacht club to the tiny airstrip. Carrie had convinced Captain Fergus that it was imperative that she get back to Miami, and he had bypassed their stop on Elliott Key and navigated to the northern end of Key Largo. She'd expected the town from the Bogart movie—a civilized spot—when she disembarked. But they were merely on the same island as Key Largo, and nowhere close to the real town that shared the island's name.

Key Largo was just a bump of land in the ocean, a mile-wide sandbar with lush vegetation. Outside the confines of the lavish yacht club, there was a small residential area with lovely homes and a few businesses. She'd managed to find a taxi, a battered car that offered rides to wheel-less sailors. Carrie had gratefully tossed her luggage in the trunk and directed the driver to the airport.

The landscape that flew by was probably quite lovely. But Carrie couldn't see much through the cloud of dust kicked up by the battered taxi. "Airstrip's just down this road!" Her driver was just a kid, barely old enough to see above the wheel. His long hair whipped over his eyes, and he drove with one hand, the other in constant use keeping his vision clear. Music blared from the radio, so loud she couldn't tell whether it was rap or Rachmaninoff.

Carrie moved to close the windows in the back, then realized the cab didn't have any windows. "I've died and gone to vacation hell," she murmured, coughing and waving her hand in front of her face.

She'd gotten off the boat as soon as it docked, scrambling onto the wooden pier, grateful to put solid, unmoving ground beneath her feet. Captain Fergus and his wife Moira continued to offer profuse apologies, but no amount of convincing would get her back on *Serendipity*. Dev Riley had watched her the whole time, his shoulder braced against the mast, his arms crossed over his bare chest.

If she'd still been a woman prone to fantasy, Carrie might have imagined that he was sorry to see her go. She might have dreamed that the firm set of his jaw, his implacable expression, his emotionless green eyes, merely hid his true feelings. But she knew better now.

That was the problem with fantasies. They faded quickly in the harsh light of reality. She'd built Dev Riley into some image of masculine perfection. And though, outwardly, the fantasy held up, she'd been forced to admit that the man was more than a gorgeous face and hard, muscular body. He was stubborn and opinionated and irritating.

The taxi careened around a curve, the back end fishtailing and tossing her to one side. She gripped the armrest and gritted her teeth. If she could just hold on for a few more hours, she'd be all right. She could settle into a nice hotel in Miami, she could get a good night's sleep, and then tomorrow, she could go home and forget this nightmare had ever happened.

An image of Dev Riley flashed in her mind—shirtless, his long, muscular legs and arms burnished by
the sun. Had she been braver, more confident, she
might have stayed. A week alone with a man like Dev
would have been a dream come true. But after just
one morning with him, she was honest enough to admit that he was well out of her league. Witty repartee
was not her strong suit, and Dev seemed to thrive on
sparkling conversation and sly innuendo. He'd bait
and tease her, then sit back and wait for her to rise to
the challenge.

When she got back home, she'd forget all about
him. And when he came into the agency, she'd barely
take notice. He'd be like any other client. Just another
guy in a cashmere overcoat...with gorgeous green
eyes...and the profile of a Greek god.

"Here we are!" the cabdriver called. The cab skidded to a halt at the end of a narrow clearing, and Carrie hopped out. "That's my uncle's plane over there.
He's usually not too far away."

Her luggage thudded to the ground, raising another small cloud of dust, and Carrie squinted as she
pulled her wallet from her purse and paid the cabbie.
"When is the next flight out?" Carrie asked.

The cabbie pointed toward the lone plane. "Whenever Pete takes off."

"There must be more than one airline here."

The kid shook his head. "Sometimes, if there's
more than one plane parked here. But don't worry,
Pete'll fly you anywhere for the right price."

"Fine," Carrie said, grabbing her suitcase and gathering her resolve. "I'm just going to go over there and
buy my ticket." *And get off this godforsaken sand dune*,
she added silently.

Carrie glanced around at the grass runway cut from the thick vegetation, and the tin shack that sat on one end. A wind sock with a hole in the toe was the only sign that this was a real airport. Except for that, the airstrip looked more like a farmer's field carved out of the dense underbrush.

She started across the scruffy tarmac, dragging her suitcases behind her, the wheels bumping along the hard ground. By the time she reached the plane, she was sweaty and dirty and out of breath—and close enough to get a good look at the transportation she'd chosen to take over a major body of water. The plane looked as if it was held together with chewing gum and duct tape. Dents and scratches marred the rusty fuselage, and one of the tires was noticeably flat.

A quiet mutter, the words indistinguishable, came from the other side of the plane. She bent down and saw a pair of battered sandals and saggy socks. "Excuse me!" she called.

"Third tee. Pebble Beach," was the only reply.

"I'm looking for a ride back to the mainland," Carrie said, circling the plane. "The kid who runs the taxi service said you can fly me back to Miami."

As she caught sight of the pilot, Carrie stopped in her tracks. The man, dressed in a loud Hawaiian shirt, paid no attention to her. Instead, he rolled a golf ball out in front of him, eyed it for a few seconds as he chewed on his cigar, swung his club back, then launched the ball down the length of the runway with a loud *thwack*. Each shot was followed by a muttered commentary.

His face, like those of many of the locals she'd seen, was weathered by the harsh Florida sun, permanent squint lines bracketing his eyes. The only thing that kept him from looking completely disreputable was the gray that peppered the closely cropped hair visible under his baseball cap. That and the gold wings that he had pinned crookedly to his shirt.

"Are you the pilot?" Carrie asked.

"Lieutenant Colonel Pete Beck. U.S. Navy. Retired." He studied another golf ball. "Seventeenth tee. Augusta." *Thwack*. He pointed to the ball. "Two hundred fifty-seven yards. Slight draw." He glanced back at her, carefully taking in her luggage. "There are other pilots roundabout this end of Key Largo. But I'm the only one here right now." *Thwack*. "This here plane is all mine. Bought and paid for."

Carrie looked at the plane again. She really longed to go to the Delta counter and buy a first-class ticket back home on a gleaming jet plane. She wanted pretty flight attendants and rubbery chicken, a little bag of peanuts and a seat cushion that could be used as a flotation device. But Lieutenant Pete was the only way back to Miami, short of getting back on another boat, or sticking out her thumb on the highway.

Carrie had already been through hell on this vacation. Hopping on a plane with a golf-obsessed aviator was infinitely preferable to another bout of seasickness—or facing Dev Riley at every turn. "Can you to fly me back to Miami?"

"I can fly you anywhere, if you've got the cash."

"How much?" she asked, mentally counting the money she had left in her wallet. Pete didn't look like the type to take American Express.

The pilot rubbed his whiskered chin, then gave her the once-over, silently calculating the depth of her wallet and her determination to leave the island. "Four hundred," he said.

Carrie gasped. "Four-hundred dollars? For a thirty-minute flight, one way? Florida Air runs a flight from Key West to Miami, and that's twice as far, for only $150.00. Round trip."

Pete chuckled. "Well, I'm not Florida Air, missy. And we're not in Key West, are we? And I just happen to need four hundred to buy my way on to eighteen holes at a pretty little country club in West Palm Beach. Take it or leave it."

Her temper snapped, hastened by the oppressive heat of the midday sun and the bead of sweat that trickled down her back. Carrie let go of her luggage and grabbed the man by his shirt. "Listen, mister," she said, trying to keep the hysterical tone from her voice. "I need to get off this island, and you're the only way off. You're going to fly me to Miami for a reasonable price, or I'm going to have a nervous breakdown right here on your damn runway. Do we have an understanding?"

For a moment, she thought he might relent, but then he set his jaw and narrowed his eyes. It was clear that she'd underestimated the pilot's tolerance for feminine hysteria. "Three hundred," he growled. "Cash. That's as low as I'll go."

With that, he turned back to his golf club, whacking another round of balls to the end of the runway. Carrie surveyed the plane, then the pilot, weighing her options. She had three-hundred dollars in her wallet, but her practical nature just wouldn't allow her to pay more for a flight than it was worth! And Carrie Reynolds knew better than any travel agent alive the precise value of travel between any two points on the planet.

For three-hundred dollars, she would spend another day with Dev Riley. Besides, upon further consideration, that choice was beginning to look like the lesser of two evils. At least she wouldn't crash and burn somewhere in the ocean with a pilot who was more concerned with his golf game than with the condition of his plane.

But then, she would make an idiot of herself with Dev, which would be much more painful than tumbling headlong into the ocean in a raging ball of fire. Carrie swallowed hard. "Three-hundred dollars is too much," she finally said, hoping he'd be willing to deal.

"Suit yourself," he replied with a shrug.

Carrie sighed, finally willing to admit defeat. "Well, then. I'll just be going back to the yacht club. My boat is waiting there. If I can use your phone to call the cab, I'd—"

"Can't call a cab," Lieutenant Pete said.

"You're not going to let me use your phone?"

He grinned. "I would if I had one—seein' as you're messin' with my concentration and gettin' on my nerves."

"Then how am I supposed to get back?"

"Suppose you'll have to walk."

"How do *you* get back to town?" Carrie asked.

He shrugged. "My nephew comes by every now and then, and I hitch a ride with him."

"When will he be back?"

The pilot shrugged again, a gesture that was starting to get on *her* nerves. "No tellin'. I 'spect if you need to get back to town, you might want to start walkin'. It's only about a mile, and it gets mighty hot in the afternoon."

With a vivid oath, Carrie picked up her luggage

and did her best to turn smartly on her heel and stride away. "This is not happening to me," she muttered. "I haven't really slipped into some alternative dimension where vacation is a form of torture. I'm just having a…bad day. A *really* bad day."

As she trudged down the middle of the road, she silently chastised herself for losing her temper. Had she been more charming, she might have been able to come to a deal with Lieutenant Pete. He couldn't be completely immune to feminine wiles, could he? But she was tired and dirty and just a little crabby. And the man was gouging her on airfare!

By the time she reached the main road back to the yacht club, her arms felt at least five inches longer. Her cotton sundress clung to her body, and a thin film of dust covered every inch of exposed skin. She'd walked three-hundred yards and was exhausted from the effort of dragging her body weight in baggage. But she knew that if she ditched her bags, she might never see them again.

She'd managed another hundred yards when the sound of an approaching truck stopped her dead in the middle of the road. With a joyous cry, she turned and waved to the driver, hoping against hope he'd stop before he flattened both her and her luggage. When he did stop, Carrie ran up to the driver's side and put on her most grateful tourist smile. This time, she'd put a little charm to work for her.

The man in the truck could have passed for Lieutenant Pete's brother, except that he wore a battered straw hat instead of an old baseball cap. A cloud of smoke surrounded his head, emanating from the cigar that he had clenched between his teeth. "Yer in my way," he growled.

"I need to get back to the yacht club. Can you give me a ride?"

The man gave her the once-over, then shook his head. "Got to take these chickens out to the airstrip. Air freight's pickin' the lot up in twenty minutes."

"I'll pay you if you turn around. Fifty dollars. Cash."

He scowled, and she thought he'd refuse. "Hop in the back," he finally said.

Carrie frowned. There was no back seat to the truck. And a huge dog occupied the passenger side in the front. It was then she realized that she'd be expected to ride in the pickup bed. "Beggars can't be choosers," she murmured, hefting her luggage over the side. Her overnight bag jostled a small crate, and as she climbed in after it, a pair of chickens voiced their disapproval with a great screeching and flapping of wings.

The entire pickup was stacked with chicken crates, all of them at maximum occupancy. The smell nearly knocked her over, and at any moment, Carrie was certain that a chicken would break loose and attack her. As it was, chicken feathers filled the air, sticking to her damp skin and tangling in her hair as the pickup gained speed.

The road was rougher than she remembered it, and she spent most of the ride frantically trying to keep the crates from tumbling. By the time they reached the yacht club, she'd taken on the distinct odor of her traveling companions. The truck skidded to a stop and, as if she hadn't been humiliated enough in one day, a crate came crashing down on top of her. Several well-dressed yachtsmen and their ladies gaped at her as she crawled out of the back of the pickup.

Considering her luck, Carrie expected *Serendipity* to be gone from its spot at the dock. But the boat was still there, rocking gently against the pier, its wooden decks gleaming in the sun. She grabbed her bags from the truck, then hurried up to the driver's door, determined to thank her savior. Carrie dug in her purse for a fifty-dollar bill, then shoved it through the window, but the only reply she got was a grunt and a squeal of tires, accompanied by more dust and chicken feathers.

Carrie didn't plan to be quite so happy to step back on *Serendipity*, but she was. Too exhausted to bring her luggage back on board, she left it on the dock for Captain Fergus to haul over the rail. A quick search of the deck revealed that Fergus and first-mate Moira were nowhere to be found. Nor was Dev Riley.

She went below and found the main saloon empty. With a sigh of relief, Carrie slowly made her way forward, then flopped down on the soft bed that she'd slept on the night before, brushing a chicken feather from her nose. She closed her eyes and smiled, her battered body finally finding a bit of comfort.

So what if she was in Dev Riley's bed again! He wasn't around, and she just needed a few moments to regroup. Then she'd find that taxi driver and have him take her to the nearest bus station. Or maybe, for a decent price, he'd drive her all the way back to Miami. But for now, nothing short of a nuclear detonation would get her off this bed. And as for Dev Riley, she'd deal with him later.

DEV STROLLED BACK to *Serendipity* along the waterfront, watching powerboats and sailboats as they headed out through the marked channel and into the ocean. The late afternoon sun was low in the sky, glittering across the turquoise-blue water.

After Carrie had made her abrupt departure, Fergus had suggested a trip to the crocodile refuge. Dev had caught one of the area's few taxis at the entrance to the yacht club and taken a quick ride out there. Though the refuge was closed to visitors, Dev could still watch the reptiles sunning themselves from a spot on the road, through a pair of binoculars provided by the driver. The young man informed him that the refuge sheltered about four hundred of the sharp-toothed beasts. He also told Dev to stay near the taxi, for there were rattlesnakes populating the ditches on either side of the road.

Dev had found the first sight-seeing trip of his vacation quite interesting, but not nearly as interesting as the conversation he'd had with the driver on the way back to the yacht club. The young man babbled on about a lady he'd taken out to the airstrip just before Dev's fare. This pretty young woman was so desperate to get back to Miami that she risked getting on a plane with the most notorious pilot in the Keys.

The driver found the entire incident quite amusing, then regaled Dev with stories about his uncle's exploits in the air. By the time the taxi reached the entrance to the yacht club, Dev had begun to feel guilty about sending Carrie Reynolds into the hands of such a disreputable man. But then, Carrie was an adult and she could make her own decisions. Besides, she was the one who wanted to leave. He really hadn't pushed her off the boat.

But then, he had teased and taunted her until she'd really had no choice in the matter. He should have seen how sensitive she was, and employed a more delicate approach in dealing with her. In all honesty, he'd taken out some of his anger toward Jillian on Carrie—something she really didn't deserve. After all, she was just looking for a comfortable place to sleep.

There was no use regretting his actions now. She was gone—probably back in Miami by now. He'd never see her again. Dev stared at the docks and caught sight of the flag that fluttered from the stern of *Serendipity*. He was alone now, yet somehow it didn't make him as happy as he had anticipated.

Rather than go back to the quiet solitude of the boat, Dev stopped at the yacht club's bar and restaurant and ordered one of the local specialties. The waitress brought him a cold beer along with a tasty dinner of fresh conch fritters. The patrons at the restaurant were a mix of bluewater sailors and locals, a colorful bunch that invited him into their conversations.

He shared a few more beers and a lively game of darts before he begged off and headed back to the boat. The sun had dropped below the horizon, and he waved at Captain Fergus as he approached, watching the man carefully fold a sail and stuff it into a bag.

His mind returned to Carrie Reynolds, and he realized that he'd half expected her to be on board when he got back. Though they'd only spent one night together—chaste by his standards—he couldn't help but feel a connection to her. She'd been so different, so intriguing. So damn difficult. Carrie Reynolds hadn't been his type, but she did possess a certain goofy charm that he found attractive. And she hadn't been hard to look at. In truth, she had been quite pretty, even to his jaded eye. He'd almost welcome another battle over the berth, but he'd have his bed all to himself tonight.

He kicked off his boat shoes and stepped on board. Captain Fergus called out to him, asking if he wanted dinner, but Dev waved him off. The conch fritters and the beer had been plenty. As he crossed to the hatch, he tugged his T-shirt over his head before stepping down into the cabin.

As his eyes adjusted to the dim light, he gasped in surprise. The main saloon was littered with his clothes. Shorts and shirts lay scattered around his overturned luggage. Towels from the shower she'd obviously taken strewn over chairs. With a soft curse, he crossed the saloon and shoved open the door to his berth.

She was curled up on the bed, a pillow clutched to her chest, and her mussed hair covering her eyes. For a moment, he thought she might be asleep, but then he heard a soft sniffle. "You're back," he said.

"You're observant," she replied.

"I suspected as much when I noticed someone had tossed all my stuff out of here," he said dryly. "I also noticed you're in my bed."

Carrie threw her arm over her face and groaned. "It's my bed now and I'm not leaving. Just go away. I want to be alone."

Dev closed the door behind him and leaned against it. He brushed aside an unbidden feeling of delight at seeing her. She'd decided to leave, and now she was back. He shouldn't have missed her, but he did, and that realization made him a little annoyed. He usually had such tight control over his feelings, but when it came to Carrie Reynolds, all his control seemed to vanish.

Now, looking at her in his bed, all he could think about was joining her there. He fought the urge to lie down beside her, pull her into his arms and kiss her long and hard. The taste of her lips was still fresh in his mind, and he craved that taste now. Dev drew a slow, deep breath. "I thought you wanted to get back to Miami."

"We don't always get what we want."

"I always get what I want," Dev said, his tone even.

"Just try to throw me out," she muttered, her voice muffled by the pillow. "I dare you!"

Dev crossed his arms over his chest. "Now there's an interesting suggestion," he teased. "I might enjoy tossing you overboard."

She pushed up in bed; her hair tumbled over her face. "Leave me alone. I'm tired and dirty, and I smell like chickens. I've got a sunburn and a headache and you're getting on my nerves. This is as much my bed as it is yours, and I'm taking a nap now."

He sniffed, then wrinkled his nose. "Chickens? Is that what that smell is? Chickens?"

She shoved her hair out of her eyes and glared at him. "I'm going to stay on the boat until we get to a bigger town—someplace with a real airport and real planes, and then I'll leave. But until then, this is my bed. Got it?"

"And where am I supposed to sleep?"

"You can lash yourself to the mast for all I care."

Dev frowned and then bent lower to peer into her face. "Are you all right?"

She threw the pillow at his head. "I told you, I'm tired and I'm sunburned and I—"

"Have spots," Dev said, pointing to her cheeks, a grin quirking the corners of his mouth.

Her fingers flew to her face. "Spots? What kind of spots?"

Dev shook his head and approached the bed. He sat down on the edge and hooked his thumb beneath her chin, tipping her face up to the light from the starboard portholes. "Looks like measles. Or chicken pox. Only bigger. And redder. Did something bite you?"

With a strangled cry, Carrie scrambled out of bed, crawling over him to grab a small mirror from her purse. She flipped it open and squinted at her reflection. "Oh—oh, my. I have…dots. Polka dots. All over my face. You can't get chicken pox from chickens, can you? No, that's not possible. Besides, I've already had chicken pox."

She looked over at him, and he could swear she'd turned a deeper shade of pink—if that was possible. He'd never seen a woman who looked more pitiful than Carrie Reynolds did right now. Dev stretched out on the bed and linked his hands behind his head. Even with the spots, she still had the audacity to look beautiful, too. Try as he might, he couldn't take his eyes off her.

But Carrie didn't appreciate his intent stare. A tear popped from the corner of each eye right before she buried her sunburned face in her hands. Though he knew he should comfort her, his first thought was of escape. He'd never been able to handle a woman's tears—not that he'd had much experience.

With a hesitant step, he rolled off the berth and stood in front of her. Her shoulders shook with her weeping, and he winced, then cursed silently. "It's not that bad," he said. "With a little bit of makeup—some of that powder stuff you women wear—you won't even be able to tell. And it's not like it's permanent. The spots will go away." He paused. "Won't they?"

His words didn't seem to have any impact. She continued to tremble, her weeping muffled by her hands. Gently, he reached out and pried her fingers from her eyes. Her fingertips were wet with tears, and her blue eyes were watery with those still unshed. "It looks like a reaction to the sun," he said softly. "Sun poisoning."

"I don't know whatever possessed me to agree to this vacation. I shouldn't have come! I should have stayed home, where I don't feel like throwing up every second of the day. Where the sun stays behind the clouds and where I don't have to worry about— about spots!"

"Don't cry," he murmured, his gaze fixed on hers. "It's really not that bad."

"You're just saying that."

Dev grinned ruefully. "Yeah, I am just saying that. Right now, I'd say just about anything to get you to stop crying."

She sniffled, then managed a wavering smile. "Well, thank you, for trying to make me feel better."

Dev wasn't sure what possessed him at that instant. Whether it was her watery blue eyes, wide with expectation. Or her damp mouth, soft and inviting. All he could think about was the kiss they had shared in their bed the night before; the heat and the passion that had bubbled in his bloodstream. He wanted to feel that way again, to taste her sweet mouth and pull her lush body against his. And to have her respond to *him*, and not some dreamy image floating through her slumber.

The moment he bent closer and touched her lips, he

was lost. His mind shut down, focusing entirely on the kiss. He expected resistance, but he encountered acceptance. Afraid to touch her, afraid to break the spell that had come over them both, he probed gently with his tongue. He groaned softly when she opened beneath him.

But when he grasped her shoulders, she drew back with a soft oath. He looked down to see pain in her eyes, and for a moment he thought she regretted what had just passed. Then he realized that she was in genuine pain—from her sunburned skin.

"I'm sorry," Dev said, backing away and holding his hands out.

She blinked, then frowned. "Sorry?"

His palms hovered over her shoulders, feeling the heat radiating from her skin. "You're in the tropics," Dev said softly. "Didn't you think to bring sunscreen?"

"Sure I did. I—I just didn't put it on. I just wanted to go home. That's all I was thinking of. And then the taxi drove off and left me at the airstrip with that awful pilot and his awful plane. And there were no phones. I had to walk to the main road and it was hot and—"

"You're not much of a traveler, are you?"

She frowned, oddly insulted by such an obvious observation. "I travel," Carrie said, a tinge of defensiveness creeping into her voice. "I've been all over the world. I—I was simply distracted."

Dev clasped his hands in front of him. "That's probably my fault. I feel partially responsible. After all, I'm the one who ruined your vacation."

"Thank you. I'm glad you've finally admitted that. This has been all your fault."

He grinned, then tweaked her red nose. "That still doesn't mean I'm going to give you my bed. For all I know, you got a sunburn on purpose just so I'd feel sorry for you."

With a scream of frustration, Carrie grabbed a pillow from the bed and swung it at him. He dodged it, then laughed. "A little too close to the truth?"

She cursed beneath her breath, then began to gather her things from the cabin in a fit of temper. "I should have known you couldn't be nice for too long."

Dev smiled apologetically. "Carrie, I was teasing."

"Well, now you won't have anyone to tease. You can have the damn bed. Sleep well. I hope all your dreams are nightmares."

Regret raced through him. He should have sensed that she was teetering on the edge of hysterics. She'd probably been through hell that afternoon, trying to find a way off the island. She was sunburned and exhausted. Just a few minutes ago, she'd been in tears. Dev couldn't begin to fathom the ups and downs of a woman's emotional state, but he knew that he'd pushed her too far. "Carrie, I—"

"I'm leaving," she muttered. "I don't know how I could ever have liked you. You are such a—a jerk." With that, she was out the door, leaving him standing in the middle of the cabin, utterly baffled.

"You are smooth, Dev," he murmured. "A real prince. Just kiss her and then insult her. The perfect way to make friends and influence people. And a great strategy to get a woman into your bed."

Why couldn't he just put Carrie Reynolds out of his head? Why was he so preoccupied with touching her and kissing her? Dev cursed inwardly. So much for putting women out of his life. That little resolution had lasted about as long as his solitary afternoon watching crocodiles. Well, he was not about to be drawn into another romantic relationship. Not now, not ever—and certainly not with Carrie Reynolds.

After the sting of Jillian's desertion, maybe he was simply using Carrie to soothe his bruised ego. It would be obvious to even the most casual observer that she wasn't his type. Jillian had been so self-assured, so ambitious and assertive. Carrie Reynolds was her polar opposite: nervous and needy and a little naive. Still, she was beautiful. And sexy as hell.

"Watch yourself, Riley," he muttered. "You certainly don't need a woman who needs you more than you need her."

CARRIE SHOULD HAVE KNOWN her vacation wouldn't be all smooth sailing. But she never expected to be caught in the midst of a hurricane of emotion and confusion. With every passing minute, she came to regret her decision at the airstrip. Why hadn't she spent the money to get back to the mainland? In some secret corner of her heart had she wanted to stay with Dev?

One moment, he seemed like the perfect gentleman. And the next moment, he was pricking her temper and driving her crazy with his arrogance. She didn't want to be attracted to him, but she couldn't help herself. She loved the way he laughed and the way he moved. She could spend hours fantasizing about the feel of his hair between her fingers, or the way his skin would feel against her—

With a soft cry, she braced her arms and legs against the edges of the couch and tried to anticipate the pitch and roll of the boat. Somewhere over the past hour, they'd hit rough seas. For the fourth time that night, she rolled off her makeshift bed in the main saloon and hit the floor with a thud. She silently cursed Dev, then Captain Fergus, then the entire Atlantic Ocean.

Dev was probably lying in the middle of his comfortable bed at this very minute, chuckling over her predicament. But she wasn't about to admit defeat. She'd make him regret his teasing accusations—or she'd die trying.

Carrie sighed. All of this was so unnecessary. After all, he had been teasing. But any suggestion that she might be manipulating him rubbed her the wrong way. Her temper, combined with the sunburn and the lingering effects of his kiss, had caused her to lose all common sense and storm out, leaving him with the comfortable bed. Had she been in a joking mood, she might be sleeping on a soft mattress this very minute, and *he* might be trying to keep himself off the floor.

Cursing quietly, Carrie sat up and tossed aside her blanket. If she didn't find a way to stay in bed, she'd never get any sleep. And she'd have pretty purple bruises to complement her sunspots in the morning.

"I should just sleep on the floor," she muttered. She stood up, then nearly fell down again as the boat pitched on a wave. Maybe she could try one of the hammocks strung in the small cabin across from the bathroom. At least she couldn't fall out of a hammock, could she?

She made her way forward, bracing her feet and hands where she could to keep from toppling over. At least she hadn't felt a twinge of seasickness all night. One bright spot in the midst of so many disasters.

Carrie opened the door to the tiny sleeping berth. It was little more than a closet with two hammocks strung from side to side. She frowned as she stepped up to the mass of loose rope netting, wondering how a person got into such an odd accommodation. She attempted to sit in it first, but ended up going over backward, her feet flying over her head. Then she tried to throw her knee over it and slide into the hammock. When that didn't work, she straddled the hammock, then slowly balanced against the rocking as she lay down.

Obviously, a hammock would not be a sailor's first choice for sleeping. Her feet were higher than her head, and her body was folded at a sharp angle. The rope rubbed at her sunburned arms, and she winced every time she tried to adjust herself.

Once she got settled, she took a long breath and closed her eyes, determined to get some sleep. But with each movement of the waves, the hammock swayed. An ever-increasing nausea clutched at her stomach, and she swallowed hard. Admitting defeat, she tumbled from the hammock after only five minutes.

"This is ridiculous," Carrie muttered. "I have every right to sleep in a real bed!"

With that, she grabbed her blanket and headed for the forward cabin. Carrie raised her hand to rap on the door, before deciding that arrogance was more important that etiquette. She turned the knob and stepped inside. Dev looked up at her from the bed where he'd been reading a magazine. He wore a pair of wire-rimmed glasses, and he stared quizzically at her over the rims. He didn't say anything; in truth, he didn't even look surprised.

"I'm reclaiming my half of the bed," Carrie said as she crossed the room.

A smile quirked the corners of his mouth, but he still didn't say anything. Instead, he reached across the bed and drew the covers down on her side—an obvious invitation. She felt her temper rise. Just because she was coming back to his bed didn't mean that he could take liberties!

Carrie grabbed the two cushions from the armchairs in the cabin, then pulled the covers back up, tucking them neatly under the mattress. She placed the cushions at the center of the bed, then bolstered them with a pair of pillows from her side of the bed, creating a sturdy barrier. "We're merely sleeping in the same room," she said. "As long as you stay on your side and I stay on mine, we shouldn't have any problems."

"I don't know," Dev said. "I toss and turn a lot in my sleep. There's no telling what I might do."

Carrie flipped her blanket out and then pulled it up to her chin. "It's late. I'd like to go to sleep now, if you don't mind."

Dev chuckled softly, then reached over to put out the light on his side of the berth. But Carrie didn't feel comfortable in the dark. She quickly turned on the lamp on her side of the bed.

"I can't sleep with the light on," Dev said.

"And I won't sleep with it off," Carrie replied.

Dev pushed up and rolled over the barrier as if it weren't there. His body lay across hers, and she could feel the warmth of his skin through the cotton pajamas she wore. He flipped the light off, but didn't make a move to return to his side of the bed.

She couldn't see him in the pitch-black of the cabin, but she could feel the soft caress of his breath on her lips. He was near, his body heavy on hers. Holding her breath, she waited, wondering if he planned to kiss her. If he did, she wouldn't refuse him. She craved that flood of desire that raced through her when their mouths touched.

"Sweet dreams, Carrie," he whispered, his voice coming out of the darkness.

Then he was gone, the delicious warmth disappearing, until she was left cold and alone on her side of the bed. Carrie drew a shaky breath and tried to banish the tingling warmth that raced through her limbs and pooled at her core. This was typical of her luck on this vacation. The first night she'd spent with Dev Riley, she'd slept through his kisses. And now, she'd lie awake wanting what she'd missed that first night.

She listened until his breathing grew slow and even. And then she turned to him and tried to make out his face in the dark. A feeble illumination from the boat's running lights filtered through the portholes, and she could almost see him.

Slowly, she reached out and touched his hair with her fingers, then drew her hand back. She'd spent such a long time fantasizing about this man. But now, even with all the troubles between them, she'd come to desire the reality much more than the fantasy.

4

CARRIE WASN'T SURE how long she slept, but the cabin was bright with the morning sun when she awoke. She held her breath and slowly worked her fingers out to touch the barrier she'd erected. But there was nothing on the other side except empty mattress and tangled sheets. She breathed a long sigh of relief and sat up.

She couldn't believe she'd spent another night in the same bed with Dev Riley! Fate had them crawling between the sheets for bizarre reasons. The first night—a mistake. The second night—necessity. Would there be a third night and a fourth? And what might transpire if there was?

A hazy fantasy drifted through her mind, and she closed her eyes and savored it for a moment. Though he could be an arrogant jerk at times, there was no doubt in her mind that he'd be a wonderful lover— strong and assured...masterful. She'd had lovers in the past, but sex had always frightened her a bit. She'd never known a man who could make her blood run hot and her body tremble in anticipation just at the mere thought of what might be.

That's what it should be like, Carrie mused, flopping back on the pillows. Heat and delirious need. Overwhelming passion. A frantic climb toward a shattering climax...and then perfect satisfaction. A sigh slipped from her lips. At least, that's what she'd read in all those magazine articles. Proper lovemaking required tossing aside all inhibitions. With Dev, she just might be able to do that.

After all, she had walked right into this very cabin last night and crawled into bed with him. The Carrie Reynolds she'd always known would never do something so bold and impulsive. But Carrie Reynolds, intrepid vacationer, bluewater sailor, and aspiring femme fatale was different. A little adventure had an intoxicating effect on her confidence.

A soft knock sounded on the door, and she pushed up, reining in her fantasy and wincing at the pain in her sunburned arms and shoulders. If she really wanted Dev, then why not make her feelings more apparent? She could be alluring and tantalizing—if she put her mind to it. Carrie tugged her baggy pajama top off one shoulder, revealing just a little more skin. Then she ran her fingers through her tangled hair and took a deep breath. "Who is it?" she called, expecting Dev to answer.

"It's Moira, dear. May I come in?"

Before Carrie could contain her disappointment, Moira had already stepped through the door, a tray balanced on her hip and a shopping bag hooked over her arm. "I brought you some breakfast," she said. "Mr. Riley said you might want to sleep late." Moira gave her a knowing look. "I hear you didn't get much sleep last night."

Carrie gasped. "He said that? Well, I can assure you that nothing happened here. We slept together, but we didn't *sleep* together. It was like...camping." She smoothed the sheets, then folded her hands in front of her.

"I'm sure it was. But I believe he was referring to your sunburn, dear," Moira said, her round face and sweet smile exuding motherly sympathy. "He said you were a bit uncomfortable and restless." She set the tray on the bed and held up a tube of ointment. "He had us radio to a doctor in Key Largo for this last night. It'll help those little spots on your face."

Her fingers flew to her cheeks. She'd forgotten the spots! Oh, how humiliating—trying to be sexy when she looked like a kid with chicken pox. It was lucky Dev hadn't been at the door. It would have been just another opportunity to make a fool of herself. "He sent for this?" she asked.

Moira took the tube and squeezed a bit on her finger, then gently applied it to Carrie's face. The ointment immediately salved the burn, cooling her skin to a tolerable temperature. "Then he hired a driver to bring it down to Tavernier, then a boat to deliver it out here this morning. I'd wager he paid a pretty price for that delivery. He also got you a few other comforts, dear. Some pretty creams and lotions, bath oil and a lovely nightdress made of the softest fabric."

"Dev Riley did that for me?" Carrie grabbed the bag and carefully examined the contents, baffled by his unexpected generosity. If he were willing to pay for these comforts, why was he so stingy about sharing his bed?

"He's quite worried about you, dear. I'd guess he's feeling a wee bit guilty over your little tiff. I'm so glad you two worked out your problems. You're a lovely couple."

Carrie groaned. "We don't have problems, Moira. We're not a couple. We don't even know each other. We're strangers."

"Strangers sleeping in the same bed," Moira countered, refusing to accept the truth. "Well, that boy has a fine way of treating strangers, I'd say."

"As soon as I can find a way back to Miami, I'm leaving," Carrie murmured.

With a long sigh, Moira stood and clasped her hands together. "I'd better be tidying up now. We've dropped anchor, and if you'd like to take a trip into town after lunch, we'd be happy to show you about. You can find that way back to Miami, if you're that set on leaving. You just let us know when you're ready."

She slipped out of the cabin, leaving Carrie to a delicious meal of crispy French toast and sausage. After she finished breakfast, she slathered her body with the creams Dev had bought her. Then she slipped into a loose and comfortable sundress and tugged a wide-brimmed sunhat on her head. She almost felt normal, well rested and…happy. And though she didn't want to admit it, she was anxious to find Dev and thank him for his thoughtfulness.

The balmy ocean breeze cooled her skin the moment she stepped into the forward cockpit. She waved at Captain Fergus, who stood in the aft cockpit, bent over his charts. Carrie looked up and her breath caught in her throat. They were moored in the most beautiful spot she'd ever seen: a tiny cove surrounded by a white sand beach. Mangroves ringed the beach and rustled in the wind and the water was so blue that it hurt her eyes. She glanced up and watched a pelican dive for its breakfast, then come to rest on an old piling near the shore.

"It's not nearly as beautiful as you are, but it will do."

The sound of his voice startled her, and she turned

her gaze to find him leaning against the boom, the breeze blowing through his thick hair, his naked torso gleaming beneath the sun. He'd been in the water, and his shorts clung to his skin, revealing narrow hips and muscled thighs. A shiver skittered down her spine, and she hugged herself.

"Where are we?"

He stretched his arms above his head and smiled. "It's called Bottle Key," he said, pushing his sunglasses up on his head. He met her gaze. "Are you feeling better?"

Carrie nodded, ignoring the current of attraction that sparked to life at the sight of him, the sound of his voice. "Thank you for the…the gifts," she said, shading her eyes as she stared at him. "It was very thoughtful of you."

She expected Dev to come nearer, but he maintained his spot on top of the forward cabin, his bare feet braced against the gentle rocking of the boat. Carrie swallowed hard, her mind searching for an appropriate topic of conversation. Finally, she conceded defeat. She couldn't think of a single thing that Dev Riley might find interesting. "It's a beautiful day." The weather was always a good topic. "Very… sunny."

"Did you sleep well?"

Carrie nodded. "Oh, very well. Like a rock. Out like a light. How about you?"

"I didn't think I would, but I did."

"Good," she said. "I—I'm glad I didn't keep you up."

"I'm not," he teased.

A long silence grew between them, and she shifted nervously, glancing back at Captain Fergus. What did

Dev mean by that? Had he wanted to do more than just turn off the light and fall asleep? And if he had, then why *hadn't* he?

"I'm glad you're up," Dev finally said. "I wanted to talk to you." He held out his hand and helped her out of the cockpit onto the forward deck. She followed him to the bow of the boat, her mind focused on the feel of their fingers laced together, the warm strength of his hands. How would it feel to have those hands on her body, his palms covering her—

She cleared her throat and banished such crazy thoughts from her mind. They'd spent the night in the same bed, and he hadn't made a single move in that direction. "If it's about the bed, I—"

He turned and pressed his finger to her lips, then drew his hand away, leaving a warm brand on her mouth. For a fleeting instant, she wished he would kiss her and put an end to their stilted conversation. A kiss she could handle much more easily than words.

He sat down on the deck and leaned back, bracing himself on his elbows and turning his face up to the sun. She took the opportunity to study his face, to memorize his features at close range and imprint them on her brain. When he glanced up at her, she quickly sat down beside him and fiddled with the wide brim of her straw hat.

"Do you think a man and woman can be friends?" he asked. "I mean, without sexual attraction getting in the way?"

Carrie shrugged, confused by a question that seemed to come out of the blue. "I guess so. Why not?"

"Have you ever had any male friends? Guys that you never wanted to go to bed with?"

"Sure," Carrie lied. The truth was, there had been so few men in her life she hadn't had the luxury of developing friendships with them. And she hadn't really enjoyed going to bed with any of the men she'd been with, either. It had all been so nerve-racking and clumsy and…disappointing.

"I've never had a woman friend," he continued. "Never even tried. I'm not sure it's possible."

"I'm your friend," Carrie said with a crooked smile. "Sort of. And if you haven't noticed, I am a woman."

He turned, his gaze fixing on her mouth. "I've noticed. Believe me, I have."

Carrie turned to look out at the horizon, secretly satisfied with his offhand compliment and his fascination with her lips.

"If we're going to spend the rest of our vacation together," he said, "it's good that we're friends, don't you think?"

"But we're not going to spend our vacation together," Carrie murmured. "I'm going into town this afternoon to see if I can find a way back to Miami. There's supposed to be a bus that—"

"But I want you to stay."

Carrie's heart stopped, and for a moment she forgot to breathe. Could he really mean what he said? She wanted to trust his words, but her instincts told her to maintain her distance. Reality rarely measured up to fantasy. Dev Riley had already proved as much.

"It'll be good for me. To be around a woman and not think about—you know." He paused. "Besides, you paid for this vacation. It's not your fault someone screwed up. You have as much right to enjoy yourself as I do. So I want you to stay. I'd enjoy the company. And you can have the bed. I'll find another place to sleep.''

Carrie felt her temper slowly rise. It was so nice to know that he could just put aside any attraction he might have for her! So reassuring to learn that she was so…forgettable. But then, next to the women Dev dated, she probably didn't stand a chance. That was the reality of Dev Riley. A reality she'd have to accept at face value.

''But you have a girlfriend,'' Carrie reminded him. ''How would she feel about…this?''

A long silence grew between them. ''Why would you think I have a girlfriend?'' he asked.

Carrie cleared her throat nervously. She knew because Susie had told her. ''I just assumed that…'' She took a deep breath. ''You booked a trip for two. You said so. And that first night, in bed. You thought I was someone else, didn't you? Someone more than a stranger. You thought I was her.''

''Jillian,'' he replied, his voice suddenly cold.

''And why isn't she here? Shouldn't she be sharing your vacation with you? Instead of me?''

She sensed him tensing beside her and she cursed her curiosity. Didn't she have a right to know what had happened to Jillian? After all, she and Dev had shared a bed two nights in a row. And he'd asked her to spend the rest of the week with him. If he was still seriously involved, she needed to know.

''She's not here because she valued her career more than she did our relationship. It's all over between us.'' His reply sounded so matter-of-fact, shocking her with its suppressed anger and bitterness.

Carrie pulled her knees up under her chin and tipped her face up into the breeze. Her heart skipped at this revelation, but she chose to ignore it. The news should make no difference at all. But it did cause her spirits to brighten a bit. "I'm sorry," she lied.

"I'm not. It's for the best. I don't need a woman in my life right now. Believe me, I'll be better off without her."

As quickly as her spirits had soared, they came crashing back to earth. He didn't need a woman in his life, yet he'd just asked her to spend his vacation with him. What did he think she was? Some sexless mutant alien? She was a woman with hormones, with normal needs, with passions and desires that could become inflamed by such close proximity to a handsome man!

"It's more ego than regret," he continued. "She wasn't ready to commit, and neither was I. I'm just angry that she realized it before I did."

Carrie glanced over at him. Had she been as sophisticated and worldly as Jillian, she might possess the techniques to make him see her as an object of desire rather than a—a traveling companion. But she wasn't Jillian, that much remained patently obvious.

"So will you stay?" he asked.

Carrie nodded and pushed to her feet. "Sure. No problem." She smoothed her dress and forced a smile. "Fergus and Moira offered to take me over to the village after lunch. Would you like to come?"

He shook his head. "Naw. I think I'll stay on board. Maybe take a swim, do some reading. Go ahead. Enjoy yourself." He leaned back and closed his eyes again. She waited for a few minutes, then silently moved along the rail to the cabin hatchway. When she regained the safety of her cabin, she sat down on the edge of the bed and tried to put some order to her confusion. After such a baffling conversation, she only knew one thing for sure.

It was much easier to hate Dev Riley when he acted like a cad.

CARRIE SAT IN THE BOW of the dinghy and stared at *Serendipity* as it rocked against its anchor in the secluded cove. When she'd emerged from her cabin before lunch, Dev had been gone. Captain Fergus had told her that he had ferried him over to town in the dinghy. Dev had promised to meet Fergus at the dock later that afternoon for a ride back.

Carrie spent the rest of the morning reading and waiting for him to return, but when it looked as if she'd be eating lunch alone, she decided to accompany Moira and Fergus into the small town of Tavernier on Key Largo. It was silly to waste time thinking about Dev, when she could be prowling the tiny shops that lined the harbor. To her surprise, she enjoyed her solitary explorations and reveled in her newfound confidence. Traveling alone wasn't nearly as awful as she'd thought it would be.

Tavernier was a bustling little village with a pretty harbor. When they arrived, Moira and Fergus set off to find a new halyard for the jib at a marina on the other side of the key. Carrie arranged to meet them at the dinghy in two hours, then set off on the narrow street that rose up from the waterfront.

The street was warm from the sun, and the soft ocean breeze fluttered the awnings over the shop windows. A scruffy little dog fell into step beside her, waiting patiently for her while she shopped. At Mississippi Mac's, an open-air tavern right on the waterfront, she found a table and ordered some deep-fried shrimp. She fed the little dog tidbits as she sipped a cool rum punch and watched the passersby—

A shrill whistle split the air, and Carrie turned to look out from beneath the awning.

"Aggie! You little tramp, where are you?"

She turned back to her dinner, uninterested in a stranger's domestic problems. But a few moments later, a shadow darkened her table. Carrie looked up from her food. Against the glare of the sun, she could see the silhouette of a man, broad-shouldered and shirtless, his long hair whipping in the wind. She shaded her eyes with her hand. For a moment, she thought it was Dev, until he spoke.

"Aggie, you know you're not supposed to beg." His Australian accent gave his words an odd cadence, and at first she didn't understand what he'd said.

"I'm afraid you've mistaken me for someone else," Carrie murmured nervously. "I'm not Aggie."

The man pulled out the chair next to her, flipped it around and straddled it. Her breath caught in her throat, and she swallowed hard as her gaze came to rest on the bronzed Adonis who sat next to her. His skin was golden brown, his hair streaked blond by the sun. His profile was startling in its perfection: a straight nose, high cheekbones and a strong jaw. Though he wasn't nearly as handsome as Dev, she had to admit that he wasn't hard to look at. He smiled and tipped his head toward the little dog. "Of course you aren't Aggie. But he is."

Carrie frowned.

"My dog," he explained. "His name is Aggie. And you must be Fergus and Moira's passenger." He reached over the table. "Name's Jace Stevens. Sydney, Australia."

Carrie hesitantly reached out and took his hand. "Carrie. Carrie Reynolds. Lake Grove, Ill—I mean, Montana. So, you know Captain Fergus and Moira?"

The man nodded. "We run into each other all the time in different ports around the Caribbean. I've know them for years. I saw them over at the marina, and Moira told me they had a charter. A pretty young lady, she said. And when I saw you, I knew that lady had to be you."

Carrie felt the heat rise in her cheeks and she dropped her gaze to her food. *A pretty young lady?* That was the second time in a day that a man had commented on her beauty. First Dev, and now this stranger. Did the spots on her face somehow make her irresistible to the opposite sex? Or were men in the Florida Keys particularly desperate?

"Thank you," she murmured, uneasy with compliments. Carrie swallowed hard and tried to think of something to say. After all, this is what she'd come on vacation for—social interaction with the opposite sex. Now was the time to practice! "Then you're a charter captain, too, Mr. Stevens?" she ventured.

Good question, Carrie thought, her mind racing to anticipate the next subject and her response. She'd just ask him to talk about himself. She'd read somewhere that men liked that. Carrie groaned inwardly. Why couldn't conversation come more naturally to her? She felt as breathless as if she were in the midst of a marathon.

He cupped his chin in his hand and shook his head. "No, just a boat rat. I spend winters down here, and summers on the racing circuit up north. What do you do in Lake Grove, Montana?''

"You race cars?'' she asked, steering the conversation back to him, and rather proud of her effort.

He chuckled, his white teeth gleaming in the sun. "No, sailboats. Big sailboats. Twelve-meter yachts. Like the kind they sail in the America's Cup.''

Carrie groaned inwardly. Twelve-meter yachts. Now there's a subject she knew absolutely nothing about. "It's hard for me to imagine racing a sailboat. Like racing turtles, isn't it? They don't go very fast.''

He leaned over and grinned. "You ought to try it sometime. There's nothing like it. The wind in your hair, the sails snapping overhead. It's better than sex.''

Carrie clasped her hands in front of her. If she didn't know better, she'd swear the man was intent on charming her! A perfect stranger comes up to her at a sidewalk café and starts a conversation—using his cute little dog to run interference! He was shameless—and sexy. And obviously interested. But why?

He didn't look that desperate. She studied him covertly as she took another sip of her drink. Maybe it was the new hair color or the sundress that revealed just enough cleavage to be enticing. Or did she somehow exude a newfound confidence with the opposite sex? Whatever it was, Carrie was enjoying the attention. And what harm could come of it? She was on vacation. And the man was a friend of Fergus and Moira, a couple she trusted.

"I'd probably throw up,'' Carrie admitted. "Fergus and Moira probably told you that I'm not much of a sailor.''

"That can't be true,'' he teased, reaching down to

pat his dog on the head. ''Aggie knows a good sailor when he sees one. Would you like to see my boat? I'm anchored in the harbor.''

Carrie shook her head, then glanced at her watch. ''I can't. I have to meet Moira and Fergus.''

''Why don't you stay and have another drink with me? I'll sail you back to *Serendipity* later.''

The brief flirtation had gone well, but Carrie wasn't sure that she was ready to move on to drinks and more intimate conversation, especially with a man she really didn't know. She placed her napkin on the table and slid back in her chair. ''They're expecting me.''

He stood and held out his hand. ''Then Aggie and I will walk you back down to the harbor.''

A familiar male voice joined the conversation. ''I'll walk her back.''

Carrie glanced over her shoulder to see Dev standing behind her. He wore a pair of baggy shorts and a pale blue T-shirt, the color of the sea. His hair was windblown, yet still damp at his nape, and his eyes were fixed on Jace Stevens and narrowed with suspicion.

Carrie cleared her throat, then quickly stood, uneasy with Dev's edgy mood. ''Dev Riley, I'd like to introduce a friend of the O'Malleys. This is—''

''We have to go,'' Dev interrupted. He reached down and took her hand, then tossed a few bills on the table. He gave Jace a curt nod before he led Carrie toward the street.

''I was just going to introduce you to—''

''We have to go!'' he repeated, more insistently. ''Moira and Fergus are waiting.''

Carrie turned back and gave Jace Stevens a little

wave. "It was nice meeting you," she called. "Bye, Aggie!"

"Don't talk to him," Dev muttered, tugging at her arm. "You'll only encourage him. Guys like that don't know when to quit."

"He's a nice man," Carrie countered.

"He's a stranger, and you don't talk to strangers."

"He's not a stranger. He knows Fergus and Moira."

"Maybe you talk to strangers in Helena, but not here. He could be a…a drug runner. Or a criminal on the lam. Or—or a pirate."

Carrie laughed, yanking her arm from his hand. "A pirate? Are you crazy? He races sailboats."

He gave her a sideways glance, his jaw tight. "Dammit, you know what I'm saying, Carrie."

She hurried to catch up with his long stride. "I know what you're saying, but I'm not sure why you're saying it. Who are you to tell me who I can and cannot talk to? Just because you're my friend, doesn't mean you can boss me around."

"I'm simply concerned for your safety," he said, his gaze fixed straight ahead.

"Maybe you're just jealous," she muttered.

He stopped in the middle of the street, grabbed her hand, and faced her. "What? What did you say?"

Carrie's gaze dropped to her toes and she kicked at a pebble. "Nothing."

"No, you said something. What was it?"

Planting her fists on her hips, Carrie tipped her chin up and met his angry gaze. "I said, maybe you're jealous."

"Of that bum? Ha! You're dreaming. I could buy and sell that guy a million times over."

Her eyebrow arched and she sent him her most disdainful look. "How nice to know that." She set back off toward the waterfront. "All I was doing was talking. He was quite charming. It was an enlightening experience."

"Is that what you call it? He was trying to pick you up."

"Listen, you may be blessed with an abundance of charm, but I haven't had much experience at this. That's why I came on vacation. To practice." As soon as the words were out of her mouth, she regretted saying them.

"To practice seducing strangers at a bar?"

"He wasn't a stranger, and I was sitting at a restaurant, not a bar. There was no seduction involved."

"Then what were you practicing for?"

Carrie drew a deep breath and tried to calm her temper. "It's none of your business what I'm practicing for."

"It's my business when you put yourself in danger," he insisted.

"That man was a friend of Fergus and Moira. I wasn't in any danger! Now can we stop talking about this?"

"You are too naive for your own good, Carrie," he muttered, starting toward the boat again. "You're not in Helena anymore. And it's plain to see that you don't have much experience with men."

Carrie gasped. "Well, maybe I don't. But I'm not going to get any experience if I don't practice!"

"Who are you practicing for?"

"I can't tell you," Carrie said, pulling away from him and quickening her pace.

He caught up to her in three short steps, blocking her way with his body. "Tell me," he demanded.

"We're supposed to be friends, aren't we? You can trust me."

Carrie nearly laughed at the absurdity of it all. What did he want to hear? That she'd come on this vacation to become the kind of woman *he* could fall for? That she'd been set on having a torrid tropical fling before heading home? "All right! There is this man," she finally said. "He doesn't even know I exist."

After a long silence, he tipped her chin up and looked into her eyes. "How could anyone not know you exist?" he asked, his voice soft.

Carrie shot him a sardonic smile, ignoring the tiny thrill that raced through her. "Hard to believe," she said. "But true."

"Do you love him?"

The question took her by surprise. Four days ago, Dev Riley had been nothing more than a fantasy. It had been so much easier to discount her feelings for him then. But now that she knew him, the feelings were so much more real. Whether it was love or not, she wasn't sure. But she was beginning to feel something, deep in her heart, something that stirred her soul and drew them closer.

Carrie took a shaky breath. "No," she said, her voice wavering. "I don't love him." She glanced up and met his gaze, his green eyes filled with concern. "All right. Maybe. A little."

"Then let *me* help you," he said. "Not some stranger you find in a bar."

"How can you help?"

"If you want to practice on someone, practice on me. And then I'll know you're safe."

Carrie shook her head. Safe? Practicing her seduction techniques with Dev Riley? "Thanks for the offer," she said. "But I don't think that would be such a good idea. Besides, why are you worried about my safety?"

"Because we're friends. And that's what friends do. They watch out for each other."

Carrie stared at him for a long moment, her eyes taking in the firm set of his mouth, his unyielding expression. This was all she needed: an open invitation to lust after her ultimate fantasy man. It was bad enough that they'd agreed to spend the week together, but now he was offering her the opportunity to hone her social skills on the very person she was practicing for!

This was not going to work, Carrie mused. It could only lead to disaster. But then, this whole trip had been a disaster, hadn't it? At least this particular catastrophe would be worth remembering once she got back home.

SERENDIPITY CUT SMOOTHLY through calm seas, her bow creating a white wake in the dark water. Dev braced his shoulder on the mast and looked up at the night sky, glittering with stars that he'd never seen before and a moon so bright that it lit the sails above his head. In the distance he could see lights from a village on the main highway; the inhabitants were obviously sound asleep, unaware of their silent passing.

He could almost imagine how these waters had been a few hundred years ago. Over dinner that night, Captain Fergus had regaled them with tales of pirates and wreckers, adventurers and settlers. He'd even told them a ghost story about a group of railroad workers who had been swept away during a hurricane, and now haunted the waters with their cries for help.

Carrie had listened raptly to all the stories, but had said little to Dev. She picked at her dinner of grilled snapper and made polite conversation, but Dev could tell that she'd been uneasy over her earlier revelations. His thoughts returned to their conversation on the street above the harbor. He hadn't meant to get angry with Carrie, but seeing her with another guy had just set him off. In any other man, it might have seemed like jealousy, but Dev knew he didn't have a jealous bone in his body. Instead, he brushed off his feelings as a simple need to protect a friend…a *good* friend…a friend he'd grown quite fond of over the past few days.

He'd tried to sleep in the small cabin, but after only a few minutes, he found himself on deck. Dev drew a deep breath of the cool night air and closed his eyes, pushing thoughts of Carrie—and the man she loved—out of his mind. But it was no use. An image of the guy flashed before his eyes, and it was an image that he found downright annoying. His imagination probably had nothing to do with reality, but he pictured the rugged cowboy type, the kind that populated a place like Helena, the type of man that all women found attractive—especially an innocent like Carrie.

He cursed silently. He couldn't begin to understand the attraction. What did some cowboy from Montana have that Dev didn't—besides a horse and a pair of well-worn cowboy boots? Did he have an MBA from Northwestern? Could he run a multinational corporation? Did he even know what a leveraged buyout was?

Dev's jaw grew tight. Obviously, Carrie had settled for the first man she'd been attracted to. She was too besotted to see the problems inherent in such an ill-advised liaison. After all, there were the long cattle drives and the rowdy evenings spent at the local saloon, not to mention the overpowering smell of sweaty horses and cow manure. A relationship like that was doomed from the start. And as her friend and confidant, it was his responsibility to convince her of this fact.

Dev cursed silently. Was he really concerned about her welfare? Or was he just using that as an excuse to ignore feelings that came perilously close to jealousy? He'd already resolved to keep his relationship with Carrie strictly platonic. But then, that was easier to accomplish in theory than it was in practice. In fact, everything became so much more confusing when he stared into her pretty blue eyes.

She had asked for his help, and as a proper friend, he was obliged to give it. Dev raked his hands through his damp hair. But was he really a proper friend? A friend shouldn't fantasize about kissing her. But he did. He shouldn't feel such an overpowering need to touch her. Yet he did. And more and more lately, his thoughts had turned to things much more intimate, much more passionate than just a simple kiss or a brief caress.

So why had he offered to help her "practice"? At every turn, his resolve would be tested. A smile curled his lips. He had to appreciate her naiveté. Carrie had no understanding of her own beauty. Her motives, unlike his, were entirely pure. Though he'd only known her a few days, he could be certain that she'd never resort to the typical feminine tricks, the manipulation and the flattery that worked on so many men.

No, once she set her mind to snaring her cowboy, it would take little more than a coy smile and a few soft words. After all, that's all she'd had to do to capture his heart. And Dev's heart had been well hardened by Jillian and her lot.

A movement caught his eye, and he turned to see Carrie walking along the rail to the bow of the boat. She wore the white nightgown he'd purchased for her. The breeze set it billowing around her legs, and for an instant, she looked like an angel floating to earth in the moonlight. At first, he thought she'd seen him. But when she passed without glancing his way, he realized she was oblivious to his presence.

He held his breath and watched as she looked out to sea, her face turned up to the soft spray that kicked up over the bow. She reached up and ran her fingers through her hair, then stretched her arms over her head. The bow light created a soft halo around her body, and he could see the outline of her form beneath the translucent fabric: her ripe breasts, her lush hips, the perfect curve of her backside.

His fingers clenched, and he felt himself grow hard with desire. He could imagine brushing the nightgown off her shoulders and letting it flutter down around her feet. Her skin would be warm and smooth, and his palms would explore every sweet inch of her flesh. She'd respond to his touch, and they'd lie down on the smooth deck, beneath the stars and the moon. They'd make love, the sea rushing past them, the warm salt air cooling their naked bodies.

He closed his eyes and drew a deep breath. What was it that drew him to her? What was this irresistible, yet unseen force that pulled him toward such a tantalizing prize? And why Carrie? Why now? The last thing he wanted in his life was another woman, another chance at confusion and frustration. He wanted things to be simple again.

But wanting Carrie *was* simple! She was sweet and pure and honest. Even though he'd known her only a few short days, he could trust her. Though she might attempt to hide her emotions, she was perfectly transparent, her every feeling and fear reflected in her pretty eyes.

He'd seen desire there, too, when he'd kissed her. He'd also detected confusion and regret. He wanted her in a way that he'd never wanted a woman before—total possession, complete surrender. But she loved another man. Was he willing to ignore that fact to satisfy his own baser needs?

Maybe the situation wasn't quite as clear as it seemed on the surface, he mused. She was in love, but the guy didn't know she existed. That meant there was no prior commitment. And Dev was free of any entanglements. They were both adults, both capable of making their own decisions. Why not let events lead where they might?

Lots of people had vacation love affairs, then went back home to their day-to-day existence without a second thought or a moment's regret. He'd go back to his work, and she'd go back to her cowboy—both of them content with the memories of their week together....

He frowned. Somehow, he sensed that forgetting Carrie would be far easier said than done.

He closed his eyes and leaned against the mast, letting the night wind buffet his body. Her image danced in his brain, teasing and taunting him, the nightgown slowly dissolving in his imagination until she stood naked before him, a sea siren drawing him into her domain.

When he looked over at the bow again, she was gone. Dev shook his head and rubbed his eyes. Had he only imagined her there? Had his addled brain manufactured her image to satisfy some unbidden desire? Or was he simply tired? With a silent oath, Dev made his way along the rail, then down into the main saloon. When he reached the door of his berth, he paused. The tiny cabin was close and airless, and he couldn't help but think about Carrie, lying in her big, comfortable bed, while just a thin bulkhead separated the two of them. Dev took a step toward the forward cabin, and then another.

He wanted to talk to her, needed to see her again before he slept. He listened at the door for a long moment, then pushed it open. The cabin was dark, and he could see her form on the bed, outlined by the moonlight that streamed through the portholes. Her soft breathing—slow and even—was the only sound that touched his ears. He fought the urge to walk over to the bed and crawl in beside her, to complete what he'd started that first night.

Would she respond to his touch? Or would she pull away? He wanted to make love to her, to possess her body and touch her soul. But he knew Carrie's heart was more fragile than most. She longed for true and everlasting romance with her cowboy, not a one-night stand with a virtual stranger.

She moaned softly and then mumbled in her sleep. Dev held his breath and listened, but soon she quieted. He crossed the cabin and stood beside the bed.

Her curly hair fanned out across her pillow, and he reached down to take a strand between his fingers.

"Dev," she murmured. "Umm, Dev."

He snatched his hand away and pressed his palm against his chest. His heart thudded beneath his fingertips. Slowly, she opened her eyes. At first, he thought she was asleep, still caught in the dream she was having. But then, Carrie frowned and pushed up on her elbow, brushing her hair out of her eyes.

"Dev?"

"I—I didn't mean to wake you," he murmured, stepping back. "I was looking for—for my—for something I lost. My book."

"Is everything all right?"

"I couldn't sleep."

She sighed softly, then reached over and grabbed the covers, pulling them back in a silent invitation. "Get the cushions," she murmured. "You can sleep with me."

Every instinct told him to walk out of the cabin right then. There was no way he could spend another night in her bed without touching her, without curling up against her soft body and burying his face in her fragrant hair, without peeling the clothes from her body and—

"It's all right," she murmured. "I don't mind. I trust you."

He grabbed the cushions and tossed them down on the bed, then stretched out beside them. For a long time, the cabin was silent, and he waited for her to say something, to give him an opening, a sign that she might share in his desires. Finally, he rolled to his side, took her face between his hands and kissed her hard on the mouth.

"Good night, Carrie." With a long sigh, he laid back and smiled, folding his hands on his chest. Now *she'd* have something to keep her awake the rest of the night, and he'd be the one to get a good night's sleep. And in the morning, he'd try to figure out just what the hell he was going to do about Carrie Reynolds.

5

CARRIE REYNOLDS STARED into the mirror, carefully evaluating her case of sun poisoning. The spots were gone and her complexion had taken on a healthy glow. The only remnants of another night spent in bed with Dev Riley were the dark circles under her eyes and the tingle that touched her lips every time she thought about his kiss.

As kisses go, it wasn't very romantic. He had taken her by surprise, so much so that she'd barely had time to react, and no time to evaluate his intent. She must have done something to make him want to kiss her, but she couldn't recall what it was. She hadn't said anything, or acted as if she wanted to be kissed. Had she known what precipitated the whole thing, she might be able to repeat it, because she surely did want Dev Riley to kiss her again.

Carrie reached for her lipstick and pulled off the cap, then stopped. Dev had made his feelings perfectly clear yesterday. They were friends—traveling companions and nothing more. But friends kissed each other on the cheek, not on the mouth. And friends slept in separate beds. The bounds of their "friendship" seemed to change at his slightest whim.

She carefully applied the lipstick and tossed it back in her bag, then ran her fingers through her tangled hair. If she'd had more experience with men, she might be able to read the signs a little better. "Whatever happens," she murmured, "will be good practice—for all those other men out there waiting for me." After all, that's why she'd come on this trip. To make herself more interesting. And what better way to do that than to experience all the delights the Florida Keys had to offer—including an occasional kiss from Dev Riley?

She rubbed her tired eyes. "I need some coffee," she said.

Carrie grabbed the blanket and wrapped it around her shoulders. She'd have her coffee in her cabin, as she dressed. But when she crawled out on deck, Moira and Captain Fergus were nowhere to be found. Nor was Dev. She glanced around the boat, then realized that they were no longer underway. The horizon wasn't moving, and the boat wasn't rocking.

Serendipity gently drifted with the wind, pulling against its anchor line. Over the bow, she could see the shoreline, with its narrow sand beach and thick mangrove forest beyond. Carrie called out, but no one answered. She made her way back to the rear deck where they usually enjoyed their meals, and found a carafe of coffee and a selection of pastries and fresh fruit.

As she munched on a croissant, she stared out across the azure water. It was a perfect day, the sky as blue as—

Her gaze landed on something in the water off starboard. A body! Floating face down in the water.

"Hey!" Carrie glanced around, then leaned over the rail. She recognized the blue shorts and the dark hair. It wasn't just *any* body in the water. "Dev!" He didn't move; his legs hung beneath the surface, his arms outspread. Her mind screamed with the possibilities. He'd drowned while she'd been sleeping the morning away. Or maybe he had been attacked by a shark, while she'd perfected the application of her lipstick. Or it could have been one of those poisonous fishes. Or he could have hit his head on a rock, or jumped in the water too soon after eating breakfast.

Carrie scurried around the deck, looking for something to toss into the water. She heaved a seat cushion over the rail, then another, then tossed out two of the rubber bumpers that protected the boat's hull from the edge of the dock. But her aim was off, and the body remained immobile, now floating away from her. By the time she grabbed the life ring from the stern of the boat, Carrie knew she'd have to jump in and swim out to him.

"If you don't want to drown, don't go near the water," she muttered, her voice trembling. She'd never been a strong swimmer, and the shore seemed so far off. But the water wasn't that deep, and if she held on to the life ring, maybe she'd be able to get to Dev in time. She dropped the blanket and slipped the ring around her waist. Drawing a long breath, she perched on the stern and gathered her courage, then began to crawl down the ladder.

Her nightgown billowed out around her, floating on the surface. The shock of the cool water creeping up her bare skin frightened her at first, but once she was certain she'd float, Carrie let go of the ladder and began to kick toward Dev. "You can do this," she murmured, her heart racing and her breath coming in soft gasps. But what would she do when she got to him? Would she have the strength to haul him back to the boat and drag him on board? Could she remember how to do mouth-to-mouth resuscitation? And what if he was dead? Oh, where were Fergus and Moira?

Carrie groaned and paddled faster. She was nearly there, her fingertips just inches from his head. Suddenly, he popped up out of the water so fast that she screamed. A scuba mask covered his eyes, and for the first time, she noticed the breathing tube tucked over his ear. Dev pushed the mask on top of his head and grinned. "Morning."

A vivid oath sprung from her lips, and she slapped her hand on the water, showering him with droplets. "I thought you were dead!"

He slicked his hair back and blinked in confusion. "What?"

Carrie couldn't control her temper. "How could you be so irresponsible? Swimming alone is dangerous. Where is Captain Fergus? And Moira?"

Dev wiped the water from his eyes, at first surprised, then amused by her futile flailing. He grabbed her around the waist and pulled her against him. "They took the dinghy and went across the channel to Little Torch Key. What are you so angry about?"

"I saw you from the boat and I thought you'd drowned. You were so still."

"You were trying to save me?" He glanced over her shoulder. "Is that why half the cushions are floating around the boat?"

Carrie pressed her hands against his bare chest, feeling the play of muscle beneath the smooth, sunburnished skin. She left them there just a few seconds longer than she should have before pushing him away. "You weren't moving. I didn't know what to do. I—I panicked."

"I was just snorkeling. There's a nice reef out here. I was watching a manta ray and didn't want to scare him off."

Carrie snaked her arms around his neck and wrapped her legs around his waist. "A manta ray? That's not poisonous, is it?"

He slid his hands along the outside of her thighs. "No. And it's long gone. You scared him off with all your flailing."

Untangling her legs from around him, she pushed away again. "You saw me swimming toward you, and you didn't come up?"

Dev chuckled. "I was enjoying the view beneath the surface. You have beautiful legs, Carrie Reynolds." He looked down through the crystal clear water and shook his head in mock amazement. "Incredible legs. And I like the lacy underwear, too."

Carrie reached down and pushed at the hem of her nightgown, but it kept floating up around her, exposing her legs and panties. "I could have drowned. I'm not a strong swimmer, you know."

"Are you saying you risked your life for me? A mere acquaintance? The guy who'd steal your bed the moment you let your guard down?"

She narrowed her eyes. "Next time I won't be so quick to jump in the water. I'll leave you to the sharks." He smiled at that, and Carrie realized that this had been that witty banter that she'd so admired in other women—a flirtatious little technique that she'd never been able to master. But suddenly, she was able to match him, word for word. And they were both enjoying themselves.

He reached out and brushed a strand of hair from her cheek. "You look pretty when you're all wet," he murmured. His hands moved over her body, around her waist, skimming her hips. Carrie trembled in anticipation. How could he touch her like this and not feel just a tiny flash of desire? She risked a glance up, and what she saw caused her pulse to jump.

He stared down at her, his green eyes dark with intent, his gaze fixed on her mouth. She willed him to kiss her the same way he had last night, only longer and deeper. A lazy kiss that would make her mind go numb and her fingers tingle.

Dev bent nearer, and she held her breath. Now she felt as if *she* were drowning, desire welling up around her until an uneasy panic set in. Carrie wasn't sure what to say, how to act. But once again, she'd sent him some silent signal, for a soft moan sprang from his throat and he pulled her into his arms.

They floated in the water; his mouth was warm on her wet skin. His lips traced a path along her jaw, down her neck to the angle of her collarbone, to the spot where her pulse fluttered. Heat seeped through her limbs, and she felt weightless, as the gentle waves pushed her against his lean, muscular body, then pulled her away.

Their hips met, then parted, then met again, hinting at what they might share if their passion overcame them both. The hard ridge of his desire branded her flesh through the fabric of her nightgown, and she wanted to touch him there, to wrap her fingers around his need.

His hands slid down along her hips, and he cupped her backside in his palms and drew her thighs up around his waist. Carrie had never felt so alive, yet so completely lost. Every sensation was new and impossibly arousing. His lips returned to hers and he explored her mouth with his tongue, gently at first and then with an intensity that threatened to render her unconscious. She groaned softly, and he drew away. "I could teach you," he murmured, tracing her lower lip with his thumb. "It's not difficult."

Carrie blinked. "W-was I that bad?"

"It's easier if you don't work so hard. Just relax."

"I am relaxed. Very...relaxed."

"I'm a certified instructor. I have been since high school. I've taught a lot of people."

She frowned. "To kiss?"

Dev laughed. He let go of her and began to stroke a lazy circle around her, splashing water at her playfully. "No, silly girl! To swim. I could teach you to swim. You already know how to kiss."

But she didn't want to practice swimming; she wanted to continue kissing Dev! How could he just switch gears so quickly, from swimming to kissing to swimming again? "I don't think so," Carrie replied. "I'm not very athletic. Every time I try, I sink like a stone."

He spread his hands around her waist. "Take off the life preserver. We'll have our first lesson right now. Payback for saving my life."

"I really can't." She paused. "I didn't bring along a swimsuit."

"You come to the Caribbean and you forget your swimsuit and your sunscreen." He sent her a devastating grin. "You don't have a clue how to travel, do you? What am I going to do with you, Carrie Reynolds?"

You could kiss me again, Carrie wanted to say. *You could touch me and make me feel like my skin is on fire. You could drag me out of the water and make love to me on the beach the way Burt Lancaster did with Deborah Kerr.*

"The truth is, I haven't traveled much," she finally said. "My mom died when I was young, and I took care of my dad all during high school and college. Then after I graduated, I worked at building my business."

"In Helena," he added.

"Helena?"

"Yeah. Montana. You told me the first night. Remember?"

Carrie forced a smile. "Oh, yes. Helena."

"The capital of Montana. The Treasure State." He winked. "See, if you can teach me the state capitals, I can teach you how to swim."

"I guess you could," she murmured.

"Trust me." With that, he carefully slipped the life ring over her head. As soon as it was gone, she felt herself sinking. Carrie slipped her arms around his shoulders and hung on. Her breasts pressed against his chest, the thin fabric of her gown now an unwanted barrier. She longed to feel nothing between them but the warm water, to put her lips on his chest and taste the salt on his skin. Had she been braver, she might have pulled the hem of her gown up and over her head, but the thought of such a bold move made her head spin and her confidence flag. She held her breath and tried to calm her racing heart.

"We'll start with floating," he murmured. "Tip your head back. Arch your neck." He held his hands in the small of her back, and she felt her body bob to the surface. "Point your toes. Now, take a deep breath and stick your chest out."

Carrie kicked her feet and sank back down into the

water, grabbing hold of his neck again. "What is this? You're not teaching me how to float! You are such a fiend."

He blinked in surprise. "I swear, that's what you have to do."

She glared at him suspiciously. "Are you sure?"

Dev nodded and pushed her away, slowly helping her back to where she'd stopped. "Put your arms out," he said.

His quiet and patient instructions lulled her into a relaxing sense of security. She stared up at the sky and listened to his soothing voice. His hands gradually drew away, and a tiny smile curled her lips as she floated on the surface of the water. She wasn't afraid, even though the water was over her head and the shore was a long swim away. Dev would save her if she started to drown.

As she relaxed, her mind drifted back to the feel of his hands on her body…so firm and sure. What would it be like to have him touch her with unbridled intent? He always stopped just as her own desire peaked; he was always in control. How would it be if just once he didn't stop? A delicious warmth worked its way through her limbs.

Just a few days ago, Dev Riley seemed so far out of reach—a fantasy man she could never hope to have. And now, here she was, so far from her day-to-day existence, talking to him, touching him, trusting him. What had happened to her? Had she become a different person the minute she stepped on board *Serendipity*? Or had she simply blossomed beneath the warm sun? She could talk to him the way she'd never been able to talk to a man before. And she felt a need stronger than she ever could have imagined.

Carrie closed her eyes and listened to the quiet, even sound of her breathing. Weightless, suspended in the warm water, all her doubts and fears seemed to float away. She sighed softly. It would be so easy to tempt him, to test his resolve. And what did she have to lose? Once she went home, she'd never have to talk to him again. If she made a fool of herself in the attempt, she could put it all behind her and go back to being the Carrie Reynolds she'd always been— mousy hair, bland wardrobe, boring life.

There was no risk, no downside…except that she'd probably destroy their newfound friendship. But was it friendship she really wanted to take away from this vacation? Or was it memories of a single passionate night with Dev Riley?

DEV SAT ON THE DECK of the boat, his legs hanging over the side. He took a slow sip of his beer and looked over at Carrie. She lay on the foredeck, protected from the sun by the canopy he'd draped from the mast to the bow rail. Her eyes were closed, and he suspected she was asleep.

She'd swum for nearly an hour, and by the time they had finished he'd turned her into a passable swimmer. It was nice to have something to offer a woman. Jillian had been so independent. She made her own money, her own decisions. Even when he had offered advice or an opinion, he got the distinct impression that Jillian wasn't really listening.

But the simple act of teaching Carrie to swim had brought him undeniable pleasure. She enjoyed little things—a shell he retrieved from the beach that she still held clutched in her hand, a drink he'd brought her when they came back on board, the canopy he'd put up to protect her delicate skin from the tropical sun. Any act of kindness was met with a sweet smile.

Dev's gaze drifted down from her mouth along the length of her body. She hadn't bothered to change out of her nightgown. Perhaps she might have, had she realized that it became nearly transparent when wet. The damp fabric still clung to her skin, outlining the perfect curves of her breasts, revealing the dusty-rose color of her nipples and the shadow of the panties she wore.

He drew a deep breath, then let it out slowly. A friendship with Carrie Reynolds had seemed like a practical goal for his vacation. But from the moment he'd made the suggestion, Dev had found good cause to question his sanity. How the hell was he supposed to keep her at arm's length when she kept falling into his arms at the slightest cause?

How odd that he found her so captivating. Had anyone told him he'd find himself attracted to such a simple and guileless woman, he might have brushed off the suggestion as absurd. But every time he turned around, she was there, unwittingly testing his resolve, tempting him with her sweet mouth and her lush body.

"Ahoy, there!"

Dev drew his eyes away from Carrie, and turned to see Fergus and Moira approaching the boat in the dinghy. He pressed his index finger to his lips and pointed to Carrie.

Fergus gave him a nod and Moira smiled as they quietly maneuvered the dinghy around to the stern. Fergus killed the outboard, tied up, then hefted a few bags of groceries up to Dev. He helped his wife back on board before nimbly jumping on behind her. "You've had a nice mornin' then?" he asked.

Dev nodded. "Very nice. I did some snorkeling, and Carrie learned to swim."

A knowing smile curled Moira's lips. "She did? And would you be her teacher then?"

"Moira McGuire O'Malley!" Fergus cried. "You stop that right now." He turned to Dev. "My wife fancies herself a bit of a matchmaker. You'll have to forgive her. I told her there was nothin' between the two of you, but she has other ideas."

Moira frowned at her husband, then grabbed the bag of groceries from his arms. "Had I waited for you to come callin', Fergus O'Malley, I'd be an old maid. I know a good match when I see one." With that, she sniffed disdainfully, then disappeared into the rear cabin. A few moments later, the sound of pots slamming against pans drifted up from the galley.

"She has it in her mind that there's something goin' on between you two," Captain Fergus explained. "I don't know where that woman gets her ideas, but I explained that you and Ms. Reynolds share no fond feelings for each other."

"No," Dev said distractedly. "We're just... friends."

"And I know Ms. Reynolds wants to get off the boat as soon as she can, so she can get on with that vacation she was promised."

Dev hesitated. He didn't like the direction this conversation was taking. "Maybe she does. I don't know. She hasn't said."

"I spoke with friends over on Little Torch Key. They're driving back into Miami this afternoon. I asked if they'd take Ms. Reynolds in to the airport, and they said they would." He glanced in her direction. "Or she can wait until tomorrow. We'll be in Key West, and there's an airport there. If she doesn't want to fly in a small plane, there's also an airport shuttle she can take back to Miami."

Dev shook his head. "Actually, I think she's decided to stay."

Fergus's eyebrow arched. "She has? But I thought she was—"

"No," Dev interrupted. "We've called a truce. There's no reason two adults can't spend a pleasant vacation together without it turning romantic. Right?"

Fergus's other eyebrow shot up, turning his expression to one of disbelief. He chuckled. "Have you ever been on vacation before, young man?"

"Yes. No," he amended, "not exactly. I've traveled, if that's what you're asking. But I've never really taken a vacation."

"I've been sailing folks around these islands for more years than I care to count," Fergus said. "And if I only know one thing, I know that these waters, these Florida Keys, have a way of changin' people. When a person forgets their troubles for a week or two, they leave room for more intriguing possibilities. Love, for one."

"We're not going to fall in love," Dev said, forcing a smile. "We barely know each other."

"I knew Moira was the gal for me the minute I first saw her. Love at first sight."

Dev considered his words for a long moment. Maybe if he were a sentimental fool, he might believe Captain Fergus. But he knew that love wasn't something that came quickly or easily. He and Jillian had known each other for two years before they'd even broached the subject. And then, their feelings for each other hadn't withstood the very first test.

"I'm not planning on falling in love with Carrie Reynolds," he insisted.

"Plans have nothin' to do with it," Fergus said, clapping him on the shoulder. "By the way, if you're so set on not fallin' in love, maybe you shouldn't spend a couple days on a romantic island with a pretty girl. Maybe you should be the one takin' that ride back to Miami before we get to Cristabel Key."

Dev watched the captain make his way through the hatch to his cabin, before turning back to Carrie. Maybe he should tell her about the ride back to Miami. Given the choice, she might want to leave. She'd tried once before. What made him think that she'd changed her mind?

He tipped his head back and sighed. He hadn't misread the desire he'd seen in her blue eyes. She'd wanted him to kiss her. But did she want him more than she wanted to go home? And did he have a right to keep her here?

Damn, he wasn't ready to let her go yet! Not until he'd figured out this strange fascination he had with her. Not until he'd decided once and for all that she wasn't the type of woman he wanted. Not until he'd stopped craving the taste of her, stopped aching to touch her.

And not until he was able to fall asleep without her pretty face drifting through his mind and invading his dreams. No, he wouldn't tell her about the ride. If she wanted to leave him, then she'd have to find her own way back home from Key West. Until then, he had one more day to figure out just why he wanted her to stay.

"GET YOUR SHOES. We're going out."

Carrie looked up at Dev from her spot in the forward cockpit, where she'd stretched out with a magazine and a cool drink. He stood near the mast, still shirtless and dressed in the shorts he'd been in since his swim that morning. With every day that passed, he looked less like the businessman from Lake Grove and more like a beach bum.

She glanced around. "Out where? We're in the middle of nowhere."

"Then don't take your shoes," he said, jumping down next to her. He grabbed her hand and pulled her to her feet. "You can go barefoot."

"But where are we going?"

"I've got something special I want to show you. We're taking the dinghy."

"But—"

He pressed his fingers to her lips and shook his head. "You wanted practice, didn't you? I want you to practice gracefully accepting my invitation. Then I want you to act like you're looking forward to spending time with me, that you're curious about my plans. Can you do that?"

Carrie nodded. "Yes, I suppose so."

Dev smiled, then dropped a quick kiss on her lips. "Very good. Lesson number one is going quite well, don't you think? You're a very good student, Carrie Reynolds."

Carrie smiled ruefully, then grabbed her shoes from the cockpit and followed him to the stern of the boat. She liked surprises, especially when they involved spending time with Dev. They'd spent most of the day together, sunning and swimming. Dev had shown her how to snorkel, and she found it as easy to float on her stomach as on her back—as long as Dev was holding on to her.

They saw a school of parrot fish and three different types of angelfish and an odd, four-eyed butterfly fish. Carrie was just getting comfortable with snorkeling, when Dev pointed out a school of small black sharks, each one barely longer than his arm. That put a quick end to her snorkeling adventures, as she quickly paddled back to the boat. A long nap was followed by a leisurely shower.

She'd taken special care with her hair and she'd chosen the prettiest sundress she'd brought along. When she emerged from the hatchway, she had found Dev waiting for her at the dinner table, along with a wonderful meal of spicy crab cakes and Caesar salad. Carrie indulged in a margarita, made with fresh Key limes. After dinner, she settled into the cockpit to read, while Dev did a little more snorkeling off the bow of the boat. But she'd had a hard time concentrating on her magazine and, instead, occupied her time with watching Dev swim.

He was completely comfortable in the water, diving and surfacing as naturally as the porpoises they'd seen earlier that morning. But Carrie preferred Dev out of the water, where she could admire his lean, muscular body, the way droplets clung to the light dusting of hair on his chest and his impossibly long eyelashes, the way water streamed off his chest and down his belly when he pulled himself up on the boat.

As Dev leaned into the galley and retrieved a basket and blanket from Moira, Carrie couldn't help but admire his shoulders, so broad and well defined. Though she enjoyed the fact that Dev rarely wore any more than a pair of baggy shorts, she still couldn't help but wonder what he looked like without them. She'd found a certain pleasure in watching him dry off after his swims, and always managed to be close at hand with a fresh towel.

How strange that it had been just over a week ago when she'd admired his cashmere overcoat. Now she was fantasizing about Dev in the shower, Dev getting dressed in the morning, Dev naked between the sheets of her bed. She'd never been a connoisseur of the male anatomy, but she had to believe that Dev was just as incredible out of his clothes as he was in them. He probably had the cutest little rear—

"Ready?"

Carrie drew in a sharp breath and forced a smile, pushing aside her errant musings. "I'm ready," she said. "Where are we—" She paused. "Never mind. I don't care where we're going. I didn't mean to ask."

"That's the spirit," Dev teased, as he helped her down the ladder and into the dinghy. He untied the line and hopped into the back, then started the outboard. They slowly pulled away from *Serendipity* and headed out into the deeper channel. Tiny islands surrounded them, lush with mangrove, their roots tangled at the shore. In the late evening light, she could make out one of the bridges that connected the "mainland" Keys, one after the other, like the string in a necklace of pearls. The headlights of cars drifted up and over, then disappeared where the bridge met land.

The air was soft and warm, and Carrie could taste

salt on the breeze as the dinghy skimmed across the water. A flock of seabirds wheeled overhead in the cloudless sky, diving and soaring as one. This truly was paradise. She found it hard to believe that the Keys they were seeing were the same as those packed with tourists. From the water, everything looked green and wild and perfectly deserted.

Dev had planned a wonderful vacation. Had Jillian come, she would have been witness to all this raw beauty. And she'd also have been the recipient of Dev's romantic attentions. But Carrie Reynolds was here instead, sharing his days and his nights, as if they actually meant something to each other. She glanced back at him, and he smiled. She should be happy for the time they did have together. After all, how many women got to live out their fantasies in such a wonderful setting?

Carrie stared out at the horizon and sighed. She hadn't lived out *all* her fantasies. At least not yet. There was one she'd been having that she liked to call her Robinson Crusoe fantasy.... She and Dev would visit a deserted island, much like the one they were approaching. And then, the outboard would break down, leaving them stranded. Of course, Fergus and Moira—or the Coast Guard—could come looking for them. Or as a last resort, Dev could probably swim back to *Serendipity* for help if he had to. And he might even be able to fix an outboard—but not in her fantasy.

Instead, they'd be completely alone. He would build a little house for them from palm fronds, and he'd catch fish and pick coconuts. And they'd spend all day together, swimming in a crystal clear lagoon and making love on the beach. They'd be wild and uninhibited, and they'd fall completely in love. And when they were rescued, there would be no doubt that they'd spend the rest of their lives together.

The dinghy jerked to a stop, the bow running up against the beach. Carrie watched as Dev hopped out and dragged the little boat up onto firmer sand. He held out his hand and helped her out.

"Are we here?" she asked.

He nodded. "This is it. Your very own deserted island. What do you think?"

She swallowed convulsively. Had he read her thoughts? Now all she needed to do was find some way to scuttle the outboard. "It's very...quiet."

"Exactly." He grabbed the blanket and basket and started down the beach. "Come on. The best spot's over here."

Carrie followed him, picking up her pace until she walked beside him. "How do you know about this place?"

"I came over here this afternoon while you were napping."

"What were you doing over here?"

"Just wait," he said, spreading the blanket out on the sand. "You'll see." He pulled her down next to him, then opened the basket and withdrew a bottle of wine and two glasses. When he'd filled her glass, he handed it to her, then raised his own. "To new friends," he murmured.

"New friends," she repeated. She touched his glass with hers, then took a sip of the wine.

They sat in silence on the sand, staring out at the horizon toward the sinking sun. Carrie wasn't sure what to say. Why had he brought her here? Had he enjoyed the same fantasy? "So," she finally said, turning toward him.

"So?"

"So why are we here?"

Dev took another sip of his wine. "Be patient. You'll see."

"We're just going to sit?"

"We could talk," Dev suggested. "That would be good practice. Why don't you tell me about that cowboy of yours back in Helena?"

Carrie dropped her gaze to her wineglass. "Cowboy?"

"That guy you're in love with," Dev said.

"He's not a cowboy," Carrie explained in a soft voice. "He's—he's a businessman." She hesitated, not sure how far to go with the story. "I'm not sure what he makes or sells. But he's very good at it."

Dev paused for a long moment, then he gave her a sideways glance and smiled. "Sounds like a real catch. The kind of guy every woman wants. Rich, powerful, successful."

"That's not all a woman wants from a man," Carrie replied, angry that he'd think that of her. She wasn't some mercenary out to snag herself a rich husband!

Dev took her hand, deliberately lacing his fingers through hers. "Then why don't you tell me what women want, Carrie Reynolds? Enlighten me."

Grudgingly, she stifled her anger and answered his question as best she could. "I guess most women would like to find a good man. Someone kind and honest. And some women want children. A family and a happy life."

"And is that what you want, Carrie?"

She wrapped her arms around her knees and

shrugged. "I think I'll know what I want when I find it. But until I find it, I'm not sure."

"But you're sure that you'll find it with this guy."

"Maybe. Or maybe with someone else." She felt his gaze on her, as if he'd touched her, and she turned to him. "What about you? What do you— What do *men* want?"

"Someone kind and honest," he said, recalling her own words. "Someone to love. Someone a lot like you."

Carrie felt a warm blush work its way up her cheeks. "You hardly know me," she said.

He grabbed her hand again and gave it a squeeze. "I know enough," he murmured. Dev drew a deep breath, then smiled. "There," he said, nodding toward the horizon. "That's why I brought you here."

Carrie turned to follow his gaze and her breath caught in her throat. The sky was on fire with orange and pink and lavender streaks. She'd never in her life seen a sunset so beautiful, so brilliant with color. Carrie turned back to Dev and found him staring at her. "It's perfect," she said. "I've never seen anything quite so lovely."

He nodded. "I thought you'd like it."

Carrie leaned over and pressed a kiss to his cheek. "Thank you for bringing me here. I won't forget it."

She turned back to watch the sun slowly sink over the Keys. They didn't say anything more to each other, just held hands and enjoyed the moment. And when the sun finally dipped below the horizon, Dev took them back to *Serendipity*, the dinghy cutting through the calm water under a deep blue sky specked with the first night stars.

They sat on deck for a long time, talking and laughing, until the moon had risen in the sky. When he made a move to turn in, Carrie expected him to share her bed again. But when she opened the door to her cabin, he stopped in the main saloon. She turned toward him and smiled. "It's all right."

Dev shook his head. "No. It's not."

"But you can sleep here. We did last night and there wasn't—I mean, we didn't—" She bit her bottom lip and waited for the hot flush in her cheeks to subside. "You're perfectly safe."

"There's nothing safe about sharing a bed with you, Carrie Reynolds," he murmured, pressing a gentle kiss to her forehead. "And don't ever think there is."

With that, he gently pushed her inside her cabin and pulled the door shut between them, leaving her alone. She sat down on the edge of the bed and rubbed her forehead where his lips had touched. A shiver worked its way up her spine, and she hugged herself and sighed.

There was nothing safe about sharing a bed with her? A tiny smile quirked the corners of her mouth. Did that mean she was dangerous? Carrie flopped back on the bed and pulled a pillow to her chest.

"Dangerous," she murmured. "Sharing a bed with me is dangerous." A giggle bubbled up in her throat. "I guess all this practice is starting to pay off."

6

DEV STOOD IN THE DOORWAY of Carrie's cabin, his shoulder braced against the bulkhead. She sat on the edge of her bed, unaware of his presence. This morning, she wore a pretty pink sundress that was cut tantalizingly low in the back. Her sunny blond hair tumbled over her shoulders in loose curls, and her arm was twisted behind her as she tried to apply the sunscreen between her shoulder blades. She turned toward him, and he watched as the soft fabric of her dress stretched tight against her breasts.

His fingers clenched as he remembered the feel of her beneath his palms, the lush warmth of her flesh, the tiny peaks of her nipples. He'd thought that she was Jillian that first night and had taken touching her for granted. Now he wished he could recall in more detail what it was like to caress her, to slide his hands along her naked hips.

He'd thought about that very thing for most of a sleepless night, swinging back and forth in that damn hammock. He could have followed Carrie through the door and crawled into bed with her. As she said, it was practical to share the only comfortable bed in the forward cabin. But he'd been tempted enough for one day.

Dev knew that if they shared a bed, he'd never be able to keep his hands off her. Not after sharing that sunset. She had looked so beautiful in the last light of day, and he wanted to see her by first light. But he'd been all noble and chivalrous, retreating to his own tiny berth to cool his desire.

He'd never thought twice about taking a woman to his bed—until Carrie. But then, the women he'd slept with in the past had been more interested in a night of passion than in a future together. He'd made sure of that before he even took off his shoes. But Carrie wasn't made for one-night stands. She had a tender heart—and he didn't want to be responsible for breaking it. No, Carrie was the kind of woman that a man married, not the kind that a guy used and then tossed aside. The kind of woman that he *should* want to spend his life with—if he were interested in a happily-ever-after.

Dev stepped into her cabin and smiled. "Are you ready to go?"

She glanced up at him. "Ready? For what?"

"We're in Key West," he said, peering out the starboard porthole. "Home of Hemingway. I thought we could go out. You know, have a date—just for practice." Practice with Carrie was becoming a convenient reason to spend time with her.

Carrie squeezed another blob of sunscreen into her palm and gave him a nervous smile. "A date?"

"Yeah. We'll do the tourist thing, and then we can find a nice little restaurant. We can have dinner, and then maybe we can go dancing. All the things people do on a date."

"Dancing?" she repeated. She continued to struggle with the sunscreen, preoccupied with her own thoughts. "Did you know that Key West is the southernmost point in the United States? The continental

United States, that is. Ka Lae, Hawaii, is much farther south."

"Did you read that in the guidebook?" Dev asked as he grabbed the bottle and squirted a good measure into his hand.

She shook her head. "I just knew it."

"And I suppose you know the northernmost point?"

"That's easy," she replied. "Point Barrow, Alaska, or West Quoddy Head, Maine." Her voice cracked slightly when he began to rub sunscreen over her shoulders, and a faint blush worked its way up her cheeks. "The—the highest point in the U.S. is Mount McKinley."

He smoothed the lotion across her back and shoulders. The instant he touched her, the warmth from her skin seeped into his bloodstream like a drug. He tried to focus on his task, but his mind drifted to the perfect curve of her shoulder, the silken skin at the base of her neck. His hands gentled to a soft caress, his fingers kneading and stroking, easing the tension he felt beneath them. "And the lowest point is Death Valley, right?"

"Umm," she said on a sigh. She closed her eyes and tipped her head to the side. "Two hundred eighty-two feet below sea level. The lowest point in the world is the Dead Sea. One thousand four feet lower than Death Valley."

Dev brushed her hair off her neck and applied the lotion to the skin below her jaw. "You know a lot about geography."

"I won a prize in high school," she said. "Four years in a row. It was my best subject."

Dev paused as he realized that this was another

rare tidbit of information she'd volunteered about herself. He knew that she was from Helena, that she was in love with a man she'd never met, and that her father was a salesman of some sort and her mother had died when she was young. But that was all he knew about her past. He and Carrie had been existing entirely in the present.

"So you were one of those smart girls," Dev murmured. "But I bet you had lots of boyfriends."

Carrie's eyes opened and she glanced over her shoulder. "Oh, no. I never had a boyfriend in high school. I was really…shy. Not pretty at all. I had thick glasses and braces, and I was a little…chubby."

Dev skimmed his fingers along her shoulders, then rubbed the lotion into her upper arms, leaning closer in an effort to cover every bit of exposed skin. His gaze fixed at a spot at the base of her throat. He became mesmerized, watching her quickened pulse beat beneath her skin.

Instinct overcame common sense as Dev bent to touch his lips to the spot. He felt her stiffen beneath his hands, but then, as he traced a path to her shoulder, she relaxed and sighed softly. Time seemed to stand still, the outside world fading into nothing more than the soft slap of water on the side of the boat and the distant cry of a seagull.

His fingers slipped beneath the thin strap of her dress, and Dev pushed it aside. He heard her breath catch, and he waited for a moment, then slowly turned her to him, shifting on the bed until she sat between his thighs. He wanted to kiss her, to cover her mouth with his, to continue this tender seduction.

The true impact of his desire slowly sank into his mind. He'd never needed a woman quite the way he needed Carrie. Every fiber of his being had become twisted around her until she'd become an undeniable need, an ache that wouldn't subside.

He didn't want her to refuse, and took away her opportunity by bringing his mouth down on hers. A soft cry fluttered from her throat as their lips met—a sound that he wanted to believe was more desire than denial. As if to convince her, he deepened his kiss, tasting and teasing her tongue. The moment spun out around them, full of possibilities. But Dev held back, knowing full well that he should stop. "I would have asked you to the prom," he said against her mouth.

She stared up at him, the color high in her cheeks. "No, you wouldn't have. Men like you never notice women like me. You walk right by us on the street and never even give us a second glance."

Dev scowled and cupped her cheek in his hand. "What are you talking about? Of course I'd notice you."

Carrie blinked, then cleared her throat. "Maybe we should go." She jumped up and smoothed her dress. "Have you seen my hat? I shouldn't go out without my hat."

Dev groaned inwardly, confused by her behavior. "Hang on a second."

"I don't need any more sunscreen," she said as she searched for her hat. "You got every spot. I—I'm sure."

"That's not what I'm worried about." He reached for her hand, but she sidestepped him and rummaged through a pile of clothes on the chair. "Just sit down for a minute. I want to talk to you."

"We don't need to talk. We need to get going. Key West awaits!" she said with forced gaiety.

Dev finally caught her arm and drew her back to the bed, then pulled her down to sit beside him. "Do you realize that's the first time you've talked about yourself this whole trip? I want you to tell me more."

She stared down at her lap, where her fingers lay twisted together. "Why?"

"Because I want to know you, Carrie. Is there anything wrong with that?"

She considered his point for a long moment, then shrugged. "There's really no reason. I mean, after this vacation, we'll never see each other again. Why would you want to know more about me?"

Dev tipped her chin up, forcing her to meet his gaze. "Dammit, Carrie, I'm not asking you to reveal any national secrets here. I just want to know a little bit about you. We're friends, aren't we?"

"Are we?"

"Yes! I thought we agreed on that point."

Her gaze dropped to her hands again. "Friends don't kiss each other the way you just kissed me. And—and when you touch me, you don't touch me like you'd touch a friend."

Dev let out a long breath. She was right. At every turn, he'd taken advantage of her sweet nature and her naiveté, assuming her desire had been as strong as his. Maybe he'd just hoped that was so. But from the strained expression on her face, he could tell he'd been wrong. She hadn't wanted any of this. "I'm sorry," he said. "I didn't mean to push you."

"You didn't push me," she said. "I—I liked it when you kissed me. It was nice."

"Nice?"

Carrie nodded, smiling ruefully. "What woman wouldn't like the attention? I mean, you're handsome and charming—a real catch. And I'm sure all the women you've kissed have enjoyed it. And you kiss quite well."

"So, what's the problem then?"

Carrie sighed. "The problem is that in a few more days, we're both going to go home. And we'll never see each other again. I don't want to do something we might regret."

"Who says we'll never see each other again?" Dev snapped. His jaw tightened. He'd been the first person to assume that they'd never see each other again. But now, he wasn't so sure. He didn't want to think that Carrie would just disappear from his life without a trace. But what did that mean? Did he want a long-distance relationship with her? Or would the memories of their time together fade once he got back home?

"Come on, Dev," she said. "You have your life. It doesn't include me."

"And you have your cowboy, right?" Dev muttered.

"My cowboy?"

Jealousy niggled at his brain, but he pushed it aside. "That guy in Helena. The guy you're in love with."

A tiny smile twitched at her lips. "My businessman," she corrected.

"How do you know you love him?" Dev demanded. "I mean, how can you be sure? You barely know him, right? I knew Jillian for two years, and I thought I loved her. But I was wrong. I don't even think about her anymore—she barely crosses my mind. How can *you* be so sure?"

"I'm not sure of anything," she said, a hint of defensiveness creeping into her voice. "I have no idea what's going to happen when I get home. Maybe nothing. Or maybe my life will change completely. But one thing I do know is that this isn't real life. This is some kind of temporary paradise, where everything seems perfect." She stood up again and glanced around the room. "Now, where is my hat?"

"I know one thing, too," Dev said, pushing to his feet. "I'm real. I'm here with you, and he's not. That has to mean something, doesn't it?"

"It means that we can spend a lovely vacation together," Carrie said, turning to smile at him. "It means that we can walk around Key West and share the sights. We can be friends, Dev. That's all." She pulled back the rumpled covers at the foot of the bed and discovered her straw sunhat underneath. "Here it is. Now can we go?"

Grudgingly, Dev nodded. "All right, if this is what you want."

"It's what I want," Carrie said. With that, she pulled the hat down on her head and adjusted the brim low over her eyes. He couldn't see the truth there, but he had to believe what she said. Carrie Reynolds wanted nothing more from him than friendship.

So why did that bother him? It certainly made his life simpler. He wouldn't have to worry about hurting her. She would never feel more for him than he felt for her. It was all perfectly platonic, Dev mused as he followed Carrie up on deck.

But if it was all so simple, then why was he so confused?

CARRIE SAT DOWN on a park bench and rubbed at her sore feet. She and Dev had managed to see most of the major sites in Key West in a single day, and had finally stopped at a pretty private garden filled with lush tropical plants. Above her head, a canopy of palms blocked the intense sun, casting her in cool shadow. Wispy ferns lined the pathways, and hanging orchids and vines tangled in strange trees called gumbo-limbos. The scent of green leaves and damp earth—like a perfume in the air—were so different from the salt breeze she'd become accustomed to.

She'd fallen in love with Key West, with its pretty Victorian homes and its bustling crowds, its noisy restaurants and narrow streets. The long-time natives, who called themselves Conchs, mingled freely with the tourists and vagabonds, creating a colorful group. Carrie and Dev had passed by the homes of Hemingway and Audubon on their walk. They'd visited museums dedicated to treasure hunters and wreckers—those 19th-century citizens who lured ships aground and then plundered them. And finally, they had climbed the stairs of a quaint white lighthouse and stared out over the town and the azure water beyond, searching the harbor for *Serendipity*.

A gentle breeze tugged at her skirt and tangled her hair, and she gazed down the path at Dev. He was intently studying an exotic flower, his head bent, his brow furrowed. She leaned back and sighed. All around her, colorful birds sang in a riotous chorus and insects buzzed, but all she could think about were the lies she'd told him earlier that morning.

If he'd just stop kissing her and touching her, she might be able to put their relationship in its proper place. But after their encounter in her cabin this morning, she wasn't quite sure what he wanted from her—

or what she wanted from him. Though he claimed that he just wanted to be friends, every time she looked into his eyes, she saw something more.

And then there were all the things that *she* wanted—the needs that bubbled to the surface every time he came near. She'd wanted him to push her down on the bed, to tug at her dress and to press his mouth on her naked skin. In truth, she wanted him to ravish her.

She'd never thought much about sex before, but since that first night with Dev, she'd been completely preoccupied with the notion. If his kisses were any guide, sex with him would be beyond incredible.

So what was stopping her? That's what she'd come on this vacation for, wasn't it? To collect a little experience. If she set her mind to it, she was certain that she could lure Dev into her bed again, and this time to do more than just sleep.

Carrie sighed. "Don't be ridiculous," she murmured to herself. "You've never seduced a man in your life." Besides, seducing Dev would not be like seducing some stranger at a singles resort. With Dev, her heart was at risk. She'd fallen in love with him without ever talking to him. How could she possibly fall *out* of love with him after sharing such a profound intimacy? Making love to Dev Riley would be the worst mistake of her life.

She watched him walk toward her, admiring his loose-limbed gait, his narrow hips and his muscular legs. Though she'd made her feelings quite clear, Carrie had expected him to test her again, to kiss her or to touch her sometime during their tour around Key West. But the closest he came was holding her hand as they strolled the streets. If he had any lusty thoughts, he'd hidden them quite well. And as the afternoon was waning, she'd convinced herself that their encounter had been so forgettable that it had slipped from his mind the moment after it happened.

"Are you ready for dinner?" Dev asked as he stood in front of her.

Carrie nodded, her eyes slowly drifting up his body. "It's beautiful here. Hard to believe we're still in the U.S. Everything is so...exotic."

Dev chuckled. "If the Conchs had had their way back in 1982, we wouldn't be in the U.S.," he said, grabbing her hand and pulling her up. "The Border Patrol set up roadblocks on the highway and tried to catch drug runners, but they only made the locals mad. So the citizens staged a mock secession and the Border Patrol backed off."

"Did you read that in the guidebook?" she teased.

He pulled her up to stand in front of him. "No," Dev said, acting insulted. "I read it on a sign outside the tourist center."

She slipped her arm through his. "I'm glad I got the wrong vacation," she said as they strolled down the pathway. "I can't think of any other place I'd rather be right now. Tomorrow, maybe we can see the aquarium."

"We're going to Cristabel Key tomorrow morning," Dev said. "It' going to be the nicest stop on the trip."

She sighed. "I keep thinking that I've just seen the most interesting place, and then the next day is better. I should go on vacation more often."

"And where would you go next?" he asked.

Carrie shrugged. "I don't know. It would have to

be someplace warm. In Chicago, everything is so gray and depressing. Here, it's so warm and green."

"Chicago is cold," Dev agreed. "But not colder than Helena, is it?"

She turned and looked at him, confusion muddling her brain. What had she just said? Had she mentioned Chicago? "Oh, yes," she finally replied. "Helena is much colder. I don't want to go back to Helena. *Helena* is definitely cold and gray."

"We could stay," Dev suggested. "We could quit our jobs and get ourselves a little hut on the beach. I could pick coconuts, and you could sell shells on the street corner."

Carrie giggled, relieved that she'd covered her little mistake. "You'd be so bored," she continued. "You love your work. I mean, you never take time off and this is the first—" She stopped short. What was she saying now? If she didn't know Dev, how could she possibly know these things? Unless, of course, Susie had told her—which she had. "I mean, you do love your work, don't you?"

He gave her another odd look and shrugged. "Of course I do. But until I took this vacation, I didn't realize what I'd been missing. I need to take more time off."

"There are so many interesting places to visit," she murmured, afraid to say anything else. All this easy conversation had caused her to lower her guard. If she wasn't careful, she'd say something that would give her away!

He squeezed her hand. "To tell you the truth, I'd rather be here with you than anyplace else in the world."

Carrie smiled. "That's very sweet," she said. When

he didn't reply, she looked over at him and found him staring at her.

"I came on this trip wanting to get away from women. After Jillian, I'd decided to write off the entire sex. But then you turned up in my bed and everything changed. That guy you love is a lucky man, Carrie."

"He doesn't know how lucky," she murmured, turning her gaze back to the path in front of her.

But would Dev really feel lucky if he knew that *he* was the object of her desire, that *he* was the man she was "practicing" for? Or would he feel betrayed by her lies, tricked by her deceptions? Carrie drew in a long breath. She'd just have to make sure that he never found out.

CARRIE TIPPED HER FACE UP to the starlit sky and spun around in a circle. The effects of too much rum made her legs a bit wobbly, and Dev caught her in his arms and steadied her. She was warm and flushed, and her lips were so tempting that he had to fight the impulse to kiss her again. With a giggle, she grabbed his hand and twirled beneath his arm in a fancy two-step that she'd learned just that night.

"I've never danced like that before," she said.

Dev chuckled and tugged her into his arms, swaying with the twangy country ballad that drifted out of Captain Billy's waterfront tavern. Her body was warm, her breasts soft against his chest, her waist circled by his arm. "And how have you danced?"

"By myself," Carrie replied. "In my pajamas with my cat. Eloise loves Madonna. But I'm partial to Motown. We've danced away many a Saturday night together."

Dev smiled and closed his eyes, inhaling the sweet scent of her hair. Not many women would admit to such a lackluster social life. The women he knew preferred to create an image of sophistication and power, completely indifferent to those who didn't share their stunning selection of male suitors. He'd always felt like the latest on a long list. But with Carrie, there was no one waiting in the wings—except her cowboy from Helena.

Dev slipped his arm around her shoulders, and they began to walk toward the marina. It was nearly midnight and Key West was just coming alive. Tourists and townsfolk had gathered to party away the night, sipping rum concoctions that raised the level of merriment with each little umbrella tossed aside. As they strolled past taverns and clubs, a crazy cacophony of music drifted out onto the street: country, rhythm and blues, reggae and a lot of Jimmy Buffett.

They'd begun the evening with dinner at a small café that specialized in Caribbean cuisine. While Dev wasn't as adventurous as Carrie in his choices, they both sampled each other's selections while they carried on an easy conversation. With each glass of wine, Carrie relaxed a bit more. Though she was always careful about what she revealed, she talked about everything from her childhood to her favorite flavor of ice cream: rum raisin.

By the time she had polished off her crème brûlée, Dev had decided that she was possibly the most beautiful woman in the world—not in the accepted sense of the world, but in a way he'd come to value more than a polished appearance and a perfect body. She radiated beauty from within, her sweet nature and sunny outlook lighting up the room around them.

And she was also the most mysterious and intriguing woman he'd known. At times, she was completely open, answering his questions without hesitation. And at other points in their conversation, he could sense a barrier between them, as if she were evaluating what she was about to say, editing it for his consumption. He could only believe that she wanted to hold a part of herself from him, protecting her vulnerability.

She'd asked him about his business, and he'd bored her with all the details. He usually glossed over his childhood with few words, but he told Carrie about it all. About living in a series of rundown apartments with parents who were forced to work two jobs each to support five children. About his father who'd scrimped and saved from his factory job to open his own electronics business. About how Dev had helped him turn that business into a multinational corporation before he retired to enjoy a life that had once been so hard.

They'd moved on from dinner to Captain Billy's, a rowdy bar with a bartender—Billy himself—who claimed a colorful background as a smuggler, gambler and all-around rogue. Billy talked Carrie into trying a Buccaneer's Delight, a wicked blend of rum and tropical fruit juice. It was served with two straws in a bowl shaped like a pirate ship, and by the time she lowered the level to the poop deck, she'd accepted Dev's invitation to dance.

"Where are we going next?" Carrie asked.

"Back to *Serendipity.* It's time to put you to bed.

Captain Fergus wants to leave for Cristabel Key in a few hours."

"But I don't want to leave Key West," she said. "I like it here. Nobody cares who you are or where you come from. I can just be me."

"You'll like Cristabel Key," Dev said. "I promise."

"But there's so much more to do here. Why don't we stay here until we have to go home?"

Dev hadn't bothered to tell Carrie about the last stop on their trip. And she hadn't questioned Captain Fergus about their itinerary. He wasn't sure she'd approve of Cristabel Key, and he didn't want to take the chance that she wouldn't. He wasn't sure why he was so determined to take her there. The private villa on Cristabel Key was supposed to be the most beautiful and romantic spot in all of the Keys, and he'd chosen it for one purpose—as the spot where he'd propose to Jillian.

But now, Jillian was out of his life. He wanted to share his last two days of vacation with Carrie—alone on their very own private island. Dev wasn't sure what he expected to happen on Cristabel Key. Did he hope that he'd suddenly understand his feelings for Carrie? Or did he want to put a pleasant end to their brief relationship before he went back home? Maybe deep down he was hoping that he and Carrie would figure it out between them.

But what then? With Jillian, he'd at least had a plan. And Dev was the kind of guy who always liked to have his strategy mapped out ahead of time. But Carrie wasn't some business objective that he could achieve. She was a mass of contradictions wrapped up in a body that drove him mad with desire. She was in love with another man, yet every time he kissed her, he felt her soften in his arms. And she had invited him into her bed, chaste as the experience had been.

So why was he so afraid to take a chance? Why not see just where a little passion might lead? He'd decided to be honorable when it came to Carrie, but Dev was beginning to believe that he was using honor as an excuse to avoid his real feelings.

If he didn't make love to Carrie, then he couldn't possibly fall in love with her. And she couldn't fall in love with him. And if they didn't love each other, then he'd have no problems leaving her. So that was that—no more kissing, no more desire, no thoughts of ripping her clothes off and making love to her until neither of them could think.

Serendipity bobbed gently against the pier as they approached. Dev held on to Carrie's hand, pulling her away from the edge of the dock when she came too close. She'd had a little too much rum that night, and would no doubt sleep well. When they reached the boat, he helped her on board and then down the steps into the main saloon.

"We need music," Carrie said, slipping her arms around his neck as if she'd done the same a million times before. "I want to dance."

Dev smiled and kissed her on the tip of her nose. "And I think you should sleep, Carrie."

She closed her eyes and swayed slightly, a smile touching her perfect mouth. "Maybe you're right."

"I am right," he said, his gaze fixed on her lips. Just one small kiss couldn't hurt. A good-night kiss between friends. He bent over her and covered her mouth with his.

But once she opened beneath him, all his resolve drained from his body and his mind focused on the taste and feel of her. She moaned softly, and he deepened his kiss, cupping her cheeks in his hands.

Carrie drew back and looked up at him, her eyes wide. "I thought we decided we weren't going to do that anymore."

"I can't help it, Carrie," he murmured. "Sometimes I just have to kiss you." He traced her mouth with his thumb. "How about if every time the urge strikes, I just ask? Would that be all right?"

"I'll say no," she warned, a pretty blush staining her cheeks.

He furrowed his hand through the hair at her nape and tugged her head back. His eyes bore into hers, and he watched the glint of humor slowly fade. "Can I kiss you again, Carrie?"

"No," she murmured.

He brushed his lips over hers. "All right, then this is the last time."

"The last time," she repeated.

He kissed her again, his tongue teasing hers, probing until she returned his desire in full measure. His hands slid along her rib cage, spanning her waist, then moving up to brush her breasts. But he stopped, suddenly aware of what he was about to do. A kiss was a kiss, but he'd been about to cross the threshold into something much more intimate.

Dev drew back and waited until she opened her eyes, hoping to read her reaction. She blinked, and he watched as the aftereffects of their kiss slowly faded from her eyes, only to be replaced by undisguised...pleasure. "That was—nice," she said in a hesitant voice. She swallowed hard and forced a smile. "Thank you."

"You don't have to thank me," Dev said.

"It was very good…practice."

"Practice?" he asked.

Carrie nodded. "Yes. Our date. The—the kissing. It was just for practice, wasn't it?"

Dev ground his teeth. Why did she deny the passion she felt? He saw it so clearly in her eyes, and she knew damn well why he'd kissed her. "I think we've had enough for one night." He grabbed her shoulders and steered her toward her cabin.

"Practice makes perfect," she said softly.

Actually, practice didn't make perfect. As far as Dev was concerned, Carrie was already perfect. The way she grew pliant in his arms, the way she opened so eagerly to his kiss—that was perfection. It was as if they were destined to be together, against all common sense, his need growing more intense with every passing hour, instead of subsiding with time.

But time was one thing they didn't have. In two days she'd go back to Montana, back to the man she loved. And he'd go back to his life in Chicago. Their vacation together would end…and real life would begin again.

She glanced back at him. "Do you want to sleep with me tonight?" she asked.

Dev stopped short. "What?"

"In my bed. That hammock can't be comfortable. I don't mind. I know you'll be a perfect gentleman."

"The hell I will," he muttered beneath his breath. He was growing a little tired of playing the gentleman with Carrie—especially when she responded so eagerly to his every touch, yet denied her response! There had to be a way to make her face her passion. To make her want him as much as he wanted her.

Dev was accustomed to getting what he wanted,

and he wanted Carrie. But he hadn't a clue how to go about getting her. And once he had her, what did he really want—one night of great sex, or many nights spent staring into her eyes and listening to her voice? Until he knew exactly what he wanted, it would probably be best to stay out of her bed.

He forced a smile, then turned and opened the door to his own tiny berth. "Good night, Carrie. Sleep well."

7

"WE'RE ALONE? Completely alone?" Carrie stood in the middle of the airy foyer, her luggage scattered around her feet. Her voice echoed from the cool Spanish tile floors up to the top of the staircase. She turned to Dev and frowned. "What about Fergus and Moira, and the rest of the guests?"

"Fergus and Moira are gone," he said. "And there are no other guests."

Carrie pushed her luggage aside and raced to the front doors. The view of the ocean was expansive, and she could see *Serendipity* slowly receding from the dock, skimming through calm water in the direction of Key West. "I don't understand. Why would they leave us?"

"A private island isn't very private when there's a crowd around," Dev murmured from over her shoulder. "Look at that beach. Isn't that beautiful? And can you believe this house?"

"There must be servants," she said, a hint of desperation creeping into her voice. "Where are the servants?"

"I asked that they come only in the morning. All our meals have been prepared. The refrigerator is stocked. We have everything we need right here. And if there's an emergency, there's a radio phone."

Carrie bit back a frustrated oath. "Why didn't you

tell me we were going to be here alone?'' she demanded.

"I didn't think it would make a difference,'' Dev replied with a shrug. "We've essentially been alone this entire vacation. We've slept in the same bed on more than one occasion. What's so different about this?''

Carrie scowled, then spun on her heel and gathered up her luggage. "It's different,'' she muttered. *Way different*, she thought to herself. On *Serendipity*, they had chaperones, boundaries, agreements. Here they had…the most romantic setting she could ever imagine. The villa looked like something out of a movie or *Lifestyles of the Rich and Famous*, it was so perfect.

The white stucco home was built just yards from the beach with a wide covered verandah spanning one entire side on both floors. The design combined Spanish and French influences with some elements of the Conch architecture that she'd seen in Key West. Ceilings were high and decorated with softly whirring fans. Sheer curtains billowed around shuttered French doors. The interior was decorated in soothing colors of salmon and cream, and potted palms rustled in the ocean breeze that filled the house. The atmosphere was peaceful and exotic—and very disconcerting.

"You're not angry, are you?'' he asked.

"We had an agreement,'' she said as she struggled up the stairs with her luggage. "Don't you remember?''

Dev followed hard on her heels, and she stumbled twice before he grabbed the largest of her bags and hauled it to the top of the stairs. He stood in front of her, blocking her way. "What agreement?''

"You're supposed to ask first," she said. "And if I want to say no, I can!"

"That's the kissing agreement. What does that have to do with this place?"

"Oh, don't play dumb," Carrie said, stepping around him. She strode down the hall and turned into the first bedroom. A huge mahogany four-poster bed dominated the room, with yards and yards of mosquito netting draped over it. She groaned. "Look at this! You planned all this. You brought me here to— to seduce me!"

Dev laughed out loud. "Actually, my travel agent planned all this a couple of weeks ago. And I planned to ask Jillian to marry me here. This was going to be the spot where I proposed." He glanced around the hallway, then pointed to the large bed. "That would probably have been the exact spot, if you must know."

Carrie felt the heat in her cheeks rise, right along with her mortification. Oh, Lord! What had she been thinking? How could she have forgotten Jillian? Dev hadn't brought her here on purpose. This had just been part of his original itinerary—a part bought and paid for, a part that had never included her.

She chastised herself in silence. Leave it to Susie to find a place like this for him. Her partner was a top-notch travel agent—after all, not every agent could find accommodations so luxurious. The villa reeked of romance, was positively perfect for seduction, and had every amenity a guest could desire. And it was the last place in the world she wanted to be with Dev Riley.

"I'm sorry," she said. "I jumped to the wrong conclusion. I just thought—"

Dev covered her lips with his finger in a gesture that had become so familiar. Why couldn't she just think before she spoke? Why did she have to blurt out the first thing that came into her head?

"Well, you thought right," he admitted. "Maybe I deliberately neglected to tell you that we'd be alone here. Maybe I did bring you here to seduce you. I'm not really sure myself. But I do know that I wanted to spend our last days of vacation here, with you. What's wrong with that?"

Carrie opened her mouth to protest, but he stopped her words again, this time with a quick kiss—so brief and fleeting and incredibly intoxicating.

"And you're also right about our agreement," he said.

"Our agreement?"

"The kissing agreement. It's also valid for other… pleasures. Nothing will happen here, Carrie, unless you want it to. Understand?"

She nodded, then forced a smile. Unless she *wanted* it to? That's all she'd been thinking about from the moment she'd found him in her bed! She'd weighed all the pros and cons and changed her mind a million times, and she still wasn't sure what she wanted. But now she knew that if she wanted her ultimate fantasy to come true, she'd have to ask for it!

How did one go about asking to be seduced? She'd always thought that it was an unspoken kind of thing. Something that both parties just sensed when the time was right. And when was she supposed to ask? Over dinner? Before retiring for the night? Oh, what difference did it make anyway? Carrie knew that she could never work up the courage to make such a request.

"So, is this bed yours or mine?"

She glanced over her shoulder at Dev. "What?"

"This place has five bedrooms," he said. "Is this the one you want?"

Carrie nodded. With that, Dev grabbed her luggage and stepped around her. She watched him set the bags on the bed, then walk over to the French doors and throw them open to the breeze. His dark hair fluttered as he looked out at the ocean. She imagined him in that exact spot, late at night, staring at the water, while she lay curled up in that magnificent bed. His skin would be slick with sweat and his eyes hooded with exhaustion. And she'd want him all over again.

Her throat tightened. Would that scene come to life before this vacation was over? Or was it just a silly flight of fancy to believe that this room might be the place where they would make love? If she wanted it to happen, it would have to happen soon. They only had two nights on this island before their vacation was over.

Carrie's heart twisted in her chest as she thought about leaving Dev. It wasn't as if she'd never see him again. He'd still wander into her life every now and then, when he came into the agency. But it wouldn't be the same. He wouldn't know who she was, or even that she was near. But she would be there, watching him and thinking about everything they'd shared, taking secret pleasure in the memories.

"I'm going to hit the beach," Dev said. "Want to come?"

Carrie shook her head. "No, I think I'll unpack and explore the house. You go ahead. Have fun."

Dev nodded, then walked out of the room, leaving her alone. She crossed over to the French doors and stepped out onto the terrace, then drew a long breath of the salt air. Maybe she should stop worrying about what *might* or *could* happen—and just have a pleasant time.

She returned to the bed and threw open her suitcase. Shopping in Key West had been a grand success. She'd bought a beautiful dress made of gauzy fabric. The flowing skirt and tight bodice made her feel so feminine, and the pale color set off the bit of tan she'd managed to acquire over the past week. She'd wear it to dinner tonight. And she'd bought some earrings made of hammered silver and polished rose quartz that dangled provocatively against her neck.

Carrie pulled out another bag, then dumped its contents on the bed. A riot of color spilled out in front of her: electric blue, sunny yellow, bright fuchsia. The swimsuit and matching *pareu* had been an impulse buy. She'd realized that she couldn't continue swimming in her nightgown, and there would probably be an opportunity to swim with Dev again before the week was over. She wanted to be prepared.

Carrie had never ventured inside a swimsuit, probably because she didn't have a very high opinion of her thighs. "Maybe it's time I took a chance," she murmured as she kicked off her shoes. Her sundress slipped down around her feet as she stepped out of it. Carrie held the suit up to her body. She hadn't had the nerve to try it on in the store; she'd just bought it in the same size that she wore in dresses.

Drawing a deep breath, she stripped off her bra and panties, then stepped into the swimsuit. In all of life's experiences, nothing could terrify a woman more than trying on a swimsuit, she mused—except maybe looking in the mirror afterward. She snatched up the sheer *pareu* and tied it around her waist, then hesitantly walked to the bathroom that adjoined her bedroom.

She found a full-length mirror on the back of the bathroom door, but for a long moment, she was afraid to open her eyes. "If it looks horrible, you can take it off," she said to herself. "If it's really awful, you can throw it away." But when she let her gaze drift down the length of her body, she was pleasantly surprised.

As a terminally single woman without prospects, she'd never spent much time looking at her body in the mirror. In fact, she usually avoided mirrors. But maybe she'd been wrong. With her new hair color and her sun-kissed skin, she looked pretty good in a bathing suit.

"All right," Carrie said, straightening her shoulders. "I put it on. Now the next step is going out in public." Actually, being in public would probably be a far sight easier than walking out on that private beach with only Dev Riley to see her. She hurried from the bathroom and looked out the French doors. She saw Dev on the beach below, wading through the surf.

"What's the worst that could happen?" she asked herself. Carrie fiddled with the knot on her *pareu*. "He could laugh. He could mistake me for a beached whale or a Russian submarine." But over the past week, Dev had seen her at her very worst—seasick and sunburned and sulky. Maybe it was time for him to see her as a real woman—a sexy woman. A woman he might want to seduce.

She ran her fingers through her hair and pasted a smile on her face. "Go for it," she said. "The only thing you have to fear is fear itself…and utter humil-iation and total embarrassment.'' But then, she'd al-ready faced both many times on this trip.

As she strolled down the terrace stairs and out onto the beach, she tried to concentrate on proper posture, attempting to walk casually. But her knees were wob-bly and her pulse was pounding and she could barely draw a breath for trying to hold in her stomach.

Dev had wandered down along the water and now sat in the sand, staring out at the horizon. She waited for him to notice her, but he seemed to be lost in his own thoughts. Carrie was nearly upon him, when he turned in her direction. Her heart skipped as she saw the look of appreciation in his eyes and the slow smile that curled his lips.

''Wow,'' he said, his gaze drifting down along her body.

Carrie smiled and took another step toward him. But he suddenly scrambled to his feet and held out his hand.

''Carrie, watch out for that—''

A vicious stinging sensation shot through her foot and up her leg, and she cried out. Dev was at her side in an instant. He scooped her up in his arms as she moaned in agony. A million needles of pain snaked up her limb and made her head swim. Tears came to her eyes. ''What happened?'' she asked.

''You stepped on a jellyfish,'' Dev said. ''God, Car-rie, you're a walking disaster.''

She groaned and buried her head against his shoul-der. ''I knew I shouldn't have put this damn swim-ming suit on. I should have stayed in my room and taken a nap.''

Dev chuckled and nuzzled her neck. "And miss that entrance? Not a chance."

"How's the foot?"

Carrie looked up from her bed to find Dev standing in the doorway of her room. He had a tray in his arms. "It still hurts," she said, wincing at the pain. "But I think I'll be all right. Thanks to you."

He had an uncanny knack for saving her when she found herself in distress. Dev had carried her all the way from the beach to the house, as if she weighed less than air. And then he'd retrieved a bottle of ammonia from the kitchen and dabbed a bit on her foot. Almost immediately, the pain had subsided, but he had insisted on using the radio phone to call a doctor. When the doctor had pronounced his treatment adequate, Dev had finally relaxed enough to tease her about her bad luck.

"I brought you something to eat," he said as he approached the bed. "I figured you might not be in any shape to walk to the kitchen."

Carrie pushed up in the bed, and Dev adjusted the pillow behind her back. "Why do I always seem to be at my worst when I'm with you?"

He placed the tray on the bedside table and sat down beside her. "How can you say that? I find your little exploits very entertaining. My vacation would have been boring without you."

"And here I was trying to be sexy," Carrie muttered.

He glanced down at her, an eyebrow raised in surprise. "Really?"

She forced a lighthearted giggle and tried to cover

her comment. "No. Not deliberately. I mean, I wasn't trying to—you know."

"Of course not," he said in a tight voice. For a moment, she thought he was angry with her, but then returned her smile, his gaze skimming her face. He took her hand and laced his fingers through hers, rubbing his thumb against her palm in a gentle massage.

Carrie risked a look up at him and found him staring at her with an enigmatic expression. Why not admit that she was hoping to catch his eye? Even better, why not just come right out and ask him to spend the night in her bed? How hard could it be? Not any harder than parading down a beach in a swimming suit for the first time in her life. Carrie marshaled all her resolve, ignored all her fears, summoned every bit of her courage and opened her mouth—but she couldn't do it.

After a long moment, he sighed, then stood up. "I'll let you get some rest now. I'm going to go for a swim before bed." He walked to the door. "Sleep well, Carrie. If you need anything—anything at all—just call me."

She wanted to call out to him that very moment, to ask him to stay, to tell him that she needed his lips on her neck, his hands on her body. But instead she leaned back into the down pillows, quelling the impulse. Maybe if she just relaxed and closed her eyes, she'd wake up in the morning completely refreshed and totally convinced that she really didn't want Dev Riley as much as she thought she did.

CARRIE WASN'T SURE how long she'd slept, or if she'd slept at all. Her foot ached and her leg had grown stiff from lying elevated on a pillow. She pushed up on her elbows and plucked at the damp fabric of her nightgown. The ocean breeze had stilled, and the room had grown quiet and close. She reached over and turned off the lamp, but the moonlight streaming through the windows was enough to illuminate her surroundings and keep her awake.

With a resigned sigh, she swung her legs off the bed and gingerly tried to walk. To her surprise, she was able to bear almost all her weight on her sore foot. She walked over to the French doors, hoping to catch a bit of a breeze to cool her skin. But the sight that met her eyes took her breath away, and made her heart lurch.

Dev stood on the sand, facing the ocean, the moonlight silhouetting his body. He no longer wore the shorts she'd seen him in earlier. He had discarded them and was now completely naked. Her gaze took in his broad back, his narrow waist, his long, muscular legs. Holding her breath, she slowly stepped out onto the terrace, grateful for the shadows cast by the stucco pillars.

Unaware of her, he slowly walked into the water up to his waist, then dropped down until he submerged. Carrie bit her lip and waited for him to appear again, and when he did, his body gleamed wet in the silver light. He looked like an ancient god sprung from the sea, fierce and untamed, stroking powerfully through the water, then diving beneath the surface.

Carrie watched him swim for a long time, wondering at the energy that he found. Perhaps he was as restless as she was. Maybe he was even thinking about her, contemplating what might happen between them if they shared a bed one last time. She moaned softly and turned away from the scene, leaning back against the cool pillar, trying to still her hammering heart.

But when she went to watch him again, she saw him striding up the beach, still naked, a towel hung around his neck. Carrie found herself transfixed, frozen in that spot at the top of the terrace stairs and unable to retreat. Dev looked up and saw her there, then stopped. For a long time, they just watched each other, their gazes locked, unwavering, unfettered desire burning a pathway between them.

"I—I want you to ask me," she said, her voice trembling. She gulped back her nerves. "Please."

Slowly, he slipped the towel from his shoulders and hitched it around his waist, regarding her with a wary eye. His hand gripped the railing as he ascended the stairs. "What do you want me to ask, Carrie?"

Carrie shook her head. "Don't make this difficult, because if you do I'm going to change my mind."

He nodded, approaching with silent steps, his bare feet quiet on the tile. His hand found her cheek and he gently caressed her face, tipping her gaze up to his. "I want you, Carrie. Do you want me?"

"I want you," she said, her hands splaying across his damp chest.

He sucked in his breath and tipped his head back, and she snatched her hands away, afraid that she'd made a mistake. But without looking at her, he captured her fingers again and put them back where they'd been. "You can touch me," he said. "I love the feel of your hands on my body."

She'd never been so bold with a man, but she needed to know him, to explore his body until it became familiar to her fingers and burned in her memory—the sharp angles of his shoulders, the rippled muscles of his belly, the soft line of hair that ran from his collarbone to beneath the towel. Every place she touched was hard and smooth, as if carved from marble.

Carrie had never felt such an overpowering need before. There had been other men in her life, but no one had ever possessed her soul like Dev Riley. He had begun as a fantasy and now he stood before her, so real and so alive. All the trepidation she should have felt had dissolved, and now she was fixed on her purpose—to love him fully and completely, to share every intimacy.

"I'm not very good at this," she murmured.

Dev bent closer, the warmth from his body seeping into hers. "You're doing just fine. Don't be afraid of me, Carrie. I promise, I won't hurt you." He drew her into his arms and molded her body to his, and she pressed closer until she could feel the hard ridge of his desire beneath the towel.

"Please, don't make me do this alone," she murmured. "Touch me."

It was as if he'd conceded all the power to her, and now she'd given it back to him, willingly and eagerly. When his hands skimmed her shoulders, brushing aside the straps of her nightgown, she shivered. Slowly, he pushed the soft fabric down along her arms, revealing her breasts to his touch.

Dev traced a line of kisses from her collarbone to her nipples, branding her skin. When his lips touched the hard nubs, electric shocks of desire pulsed through her body and she bit back a moan. For a moment, she thought her knees might buckle, but he clasped her waist between firm hands and held on tightly. Nothing before had ever felt so right, so perfect.

She'd held on to her passion so tightly, and for so long, that releasing all her inhibitions felt like soaring, rising and falling on currents of warm salt air like a seabird in flight. Carrie let herself drift, as Dev carefully peeled off her nightgown, caressing every inch of skin along the way, kneading and massaging her flesh. When she was completely naked, he stood and pulled off his towel.

Her breath caught in her throat at the sight of him fully aroused. She reached out to touch him, then pulled her hand back. Dev smiled and nuzzled her neck. "Come with me," he said, taking her hand.

He led her back down to the beach and into the water. Carrie expected the ocean to be cold, but a delicious warmth rose over her body as she walked in. Dev held on to her waist and tipped her back until her hair swirled around her head. The waves tossed them gently in the surf. She arched her back, and he drew his hand from the base of her throat to her belly, sliding frictionless over her slippery skin.

Every sensation was heightened by the water as their hands deliberately searched, their bodies pressed against each other. Dev hitched her knees up on his hips, and she felt him brush against her, hard and unyielding. She held her breath, wondering if he'd take her here, in the water. But instead, he carried her to the beach and gently laid her on a blanket.

Once again, his mouth played havoc with her body. Every nerve tingled at the touch of his tongue, and when his fingers found her core, she moaned out loud. Carrie raked her hands through his damp hair and pulled him closer. But when he moved lower to taste her, she let him go, sliding along with the languid passion that his touch evoked.

His mouth was sweet torment, teasing her until a knot of passion tightened within her. Carrie's mind screamed for release and her nerves hummed. All she could feel was him, between her legs. Slowly, he brought her closer, then drew away, taunting her with his power. But then, the warmth twisted inside her and she knew she'd break this time, rather than bend. Carrie urged him on with incoherent words, murmuring his name over and over until it matched the rhythm of her pulse.

The tension was exquisite and she cried out for her release. And then a wave broke on the shore, washing over her, drowning her, stealing her breath from her body. Nothing had ever prepared her for the power of her pleasure, the sheer awe of her need for him. As the shudders and shivers subsided, she pulled him up until he covered the length of her, warm and heavy.

With tantalizing patience, he slipped inside her. She watched his face as he moved, taking pleasure in the expression that suffused his handsome features. Hard and assured, he began to love her, first with great gentleness and then with a rising passion that threatened to carry them both over the edge, never to return.

He murmured her name once as he neared his peak, his body tensing above her. His breath was soft and warm against her ear as urgent sounds of passion slipped from his lips. And then, one smooth stroke and he was there, exploding inside her.

She'd never known anything that came close to

what they'd shared, the effect that it had on both her body and soul. She loved this man, more than she'd ever imagined. Her silly infatuation had transformed into a deep, soul-shattering realization. She wanted him in her body, in her future, in her life. Forever.

They made love again on the beach, wrapped snugly in the blanket, and she fell asleep in his arms. Carrie barely remembered him carrying her back up to her bedroom, barely noticed when he slipped into bed beside her and cradled her body against his. But when she woke up to his touch, she welcomed the feel of him on top of her, his hips nestled between her legs, the sweet sensation of him entering her again so slowly, and she knew that all her dreams had come true.

As he brought her to another climax, she realized that she'd found paradise in his arms. And as for reality—she'd leave that to the light of day.

HE WOKE UP ALONE, but as Dev rolled over in bed, he had to smile. Carrie couldn't have gone far. They were on an island with no way off. If he waited long enough, she'd come back to bed, and they could continue with all the pleasures they'd enjoyed the night before.

They'd finally fallen asleep in each other's arms in the very early morning, as the sky was beginning to turn from black to dark blue, and the birds were starting their morning songs. He'd wanted to watch the sunrise with her, but they'd both been too exhausted and had slept through it. No matter, though—they'd have the sunrise tomorrow morning.

He stared at the ceiling and let out a long breath. Why did the thought of tomorrow wrench his gut?

Dev still wasn't sure how they'd part, what he'd say, where he'd leave everything. He'd considered all his options; he'd even considered asking her to move to Chicago so they might find out if their relationship had a future. But his experience with Jillian made him leery of commitment.

Did he love Carrie Reynolds? For the moment, he did. His feelings for Carrie had grown way beyond what he'd ever felt for Jillian, and in only a short week together. But he was loathe to trust those feelings. He wasn't sure that they'd last outside the bedroom—or outside this paradise they'd found. He'd always heard vacation affairs were like a flash fire—hot and intense, but short-lived.

Dev rolled onto his side, then sat up and stretched his arms over his head. He planned to enjoy Carrie as long as he could. As for their future, he'd deal with that problem when it came up. He tugged on a pair of shorts and headed to the door. Right now, he needed coffee—and Carrie, not necessarily in that order.

The house was quiet as he left the bedroom, the only sound coming from the waves that rushed against the shore. The Spanish tiles were cool on his bare feet and a fresh breeze blew through the French doors. Dev slowly walked down the stairs, rubbing his eyes and yawning.

Maybe she'd gone looking for breakfast. The housekeeper would have arrived by now and probably had already started the coffee. But when Dev reached the foyer, he noticed Carrie's luggage sitting in front of the door. He was about to call out to her when she appeared from the rear of the house. She stopped short when she saw him, then forced a smile.

She was already dressed in a pair of neatly pressed

pants and a linen blazer. Her hair was pulled back and tied with a scarf that she'd bought in Key West. She looked as beautiful as she had last night, when she'd arched against him in her passion, her eyes dusky with desire, her breath coming in quick gasps.

"Good morning," she said in a quiet voice.

Dev stepped toward her, and almost instantly she took a step back. What was wrong with her? The warm and willing woman who had shared his bed was gone, and he was faced with icy indifference. He watched her for a long moment, then motioned to her luggage. "Where are you going?"

Carrie tipped her chin up as if he had no right to ask. "I'm going home. I'm taking the supply boat back to Key West with the housekeeper's husband in a few minutes. I'll get a flight back to Miami this afternoon."

His jaw tightened and his temper rose. "You were just planning to leave without saying goodbye?"

She gave him a halfhearted shrug. "I'm sorry. I—I didn't want to wake you."

Dev raked his hand through his hair and cursed. "You didn't want to wake me? That's your excuse? Dammit, Carrie, we made love last night. And it was incredible. You don't just sneak off after a night like that."

"I'm sorry," she said.

Dev cursed. "Well, sorry doesn't cut it, sweetheart—no matter how many times you say it. I think I deserve more than just 'sorry.' I deserve an explanation."

He waited for her to speak, refusing to let her off easily. Finally, she looked up from the floor and met his gaze. "You told me that nothing would happen if

I didn't want it to. I wanted last night. But I don't want to talk about last night. I just want to leave."

"What is it? Is it that cowboy? Do you feel guilty? You have nothing to feel guilty about. You haven't betrayed him."

"He's not a cowboy!" she cried in frustration, her fists clenched at her sides. "He's—he's no one. He doesn't make a difference. And I don't feel guilty. That's not why I'm leaving."

"Then stay," Dev said, reaching out for her. "We still have another day here."

She avoided his touch and stepped over to her luggage. "Dev, let's be practical. I—"

"The hell with practical! Why does everything have to be practical with you? We made love last night because we both wanted to. Practicality had nothing to do with it."

"We both knew we'd have to say goodbye sooner or later. I'm making it easier for both of us. I'm just saying that we shouldn't try to make this more than it is—was."

"And what was it?"

Carrie drew a deep breath. "Practice," she said. "I told you why I came here. And you know better than I do that this isn't real. What we shared was a—a fantasy. A vacation fling and nothing more."

Dev laughed bitterly. This is the speech he should be giving her! He'd planned it all out in his head, but now that he was hearing it, he didn't like it at all. "Is that it then? You're just going to walk away." He shook his head in disbelief. He should have known. She was no different than Jillian—just as fickle and coldhearted. What had made him think that she was special?

"Don't make this more difficult than it needs to be," Carrie said, gathering up her luggage. "Let's just leave it as a pleasant memory."

He reached out and grabbed her arm, pulling her to him. "I know you feel something, Carrie. I could see it in your eyes last night. I could sense it in the way you touched me."

"There's nothing," she said. "Nothing that won't go away with time."

Dev's jaw clenched and he tried to rein his temper. Anger would only drive her away. "Carrie, I don't want to forget you. And I don't want you to disappear from my life. Not this way."

"Then what way?" she asked, her question tinged with anger and frustration. "Do you plan to make promises you can't keep? Are you ready to tell me how much you love me? Dev, you don't even know me. You don't know who I am or what I am. We're strangers who shared a bed for a few nights. We don't have to make it mean anything."

But it did mean something to Dev! Until this moment, he hadn't realized how much. He hadn't thought about how he'd feel as he watched her walk away. And now, faced with her departure, he didn't know what to say, how to make her stay. "You're right," he finally said with a shrug. Bitterness welled up inside him, burning away his true feelings. "It didn't mean anything. Go ahead. Leave."

"I don't want you to be angry," Carrie said. "I had a wonderful time this week, and I'm glad I got to spend it with you. I'll never forget it."

"Me, too." With that, Dev picked up her luggage and carried it outside. The housekeeper's husband waited on the terrace. His boat was moored at the dock, waiting to take Carrie away from him.

She stepped out from behind Dev, then took one final look around. "It's beautiful here. I'm going to miss this place." She glanced over at him and sent him a regretful smile. "Don't worry. You'll forget all about me once you get home." Reaching up, she smoothed her hand over his beard-roughened cheek. "Take care of yourself, Dev Riley."

He turned and placed a kiss in the center of her palm, covering her hand with his. "I don't want you to leave," he murmured.

"I have to."

Dev gazed into her eyes one last time, then nodded. Carrie drew a deep breath, then turned and walked toward the dock. He waited for her to look back, but she never did. She climbed on board the supply boat and stared out at the ocean. He fought the urge to run down to the deck, to pull her off that boat and confess his love for her. To offer her marriage or money or anything that would get her to stay with him.

Dev watched the boat pull away. He watched a woman who he thought he loved sail out of his life for good. A painful emptiness settled around his heart as he realized that he'd never look into her pretty blue eyes again, never touch her soft blond hair and listen to her sweet voice.

Dev braced his shoulder on a pillar and stared out at the sea. "This is not over yet, Carrie. I'm not ready to give you up." He turned on his heel and stalked into the house, then took the stairs two at a time. The boat would be back this afternoon and by then he'd be packed and ready to go.

If his feelings for Carrie had to be tested by the real world, then he better get back to the real world as soon as possible.

8

"I WANT YOU TO PLAN another vacation for me," Carrie murmured. "Someplace far away from here. Someplace where I can forget everything that happened on my last vacation." She stood at the front door of Adventures, Inc., and looked out through the frosted glass at the busy main street of Lake Grove. Winter still held the Chicago area in its grip, and fresh snow had fallen overnight, turning the trees white and the streets slick.

She rubbed her arms and remembered the feel of the Florida sun on her skin, the bone-deep warmth she had loved, the bright skies and the blue water and the white sand. Since she'd returned, she hadn't been able to summon such pure contentment again. The weather seemed to hang oppressively over her, as gray and cold as her mood. And as her tan began to fade, she felt as if she was slowly losing that person she'd become in the Keys.

She'd colored her hair back to its mousy brown and thrown her contacts into a drawer in an attempt to set her life back to rights. But the more she tried to slip into the day-to-day life of Carrie Reynolds, travel agent, the more she realized that she couldn't completely go back. She was stuck in some strange limbo, between the person she'd been and the person she'd almost become.

Now Carrie wasn't sure who she was. All she really knew was that she'd left the best part of herself behind, in that bedroom where she and Dev had made love. Her mind flashed an image of him, lying naked, the sheets twisted around his limbs. She hadn't wanted to leave, but she couldn't face the goodbyes. She didn't want to see the end in his eyes, hear the regret in his voice. They had shared a vacation fling, and though it was wonderful, it couldn't last once exposed to the real world.

But then, she hadn't avoided the most painful part of all. She'd been forced to walk away from him, knowing in her heart that he was the only man she'd ever love. Her fantasy had come to life for one short week, and Carrie had to be satisfied with that. She'd carry the memories of her time with Dev forever. And the next time he came into the agency, her heart wouldn't beat faster and her mind wouldn't spin. She wouldn't gaze at him from afar and let her imagination take flight. Dev Riley was part of her past—and that's where he would stay.

"So, will you plan it for me?" she asked in a soft voice.

Susie sighed, then slipped her arm around Carrie's shoulders. "Running away won't stop you from loving him."

Carrie turned and faced her partner. "Who said I loved him!" she cried. "I never said I loved him." Maybe not out loud, but she'd said it so many times to herself over the past week. She wanted to believe that if the words didn't pass her lips, then the feelings wouldn't be real.

"You loved Dev Riley before you even knew him,"

Susie said. "Now that you've spent a week with him, you can't tell me that your feelings have changed."

Carrie drew a shaky breath. Susie could always see right through her. She swallowed hard and pushed back the tears that threatened. "I don't know what to do. He'll think I set it all up on purpose, that I went after him. I can't tell him the truth."

"Why not?" her partner asked.

She pressed her forehead against the door and watched as her breath clouded the cold glass. "When he finds out I own the agency that booked his trip, that I live right here in Lake Grove, he's going to think that I tricked him."

"If anyone should feel guilty, it should be me. Not that I do, but I probably should," Susie admitted with a smile. "I'm the one who set this whole thing up. You were completely innocent."

"He's not going to believe that. He told me he loved my honesty. And I'm the biggest liar of all. I could have told him the truth right from the start, from the minute I found myself in the wrong bed, on the wrong vacation."

"Sweetie, why would he be angry? You saw a man you liked and you went after him. He should be flattered."

"That sounds so mercenary. Like big-game hunting. Are the tigers and the elephants flattered?"

"Guys have bigger egos than elephants. I think they like being chased."

"But I didn't go after him," Carrie said, pushing away from the door. "I didn't even like him at first. He was so mean. But then I realized that he was angry because of Jillian. Then he started to be so sweet, and I couldn't help but fall in love with him for real."

"And how does he feel about you?" Susie asked.

Carrie hugged herself and pulled her jacket tighter, shivering despite the warmth of the office. "I'm not sure. We never talked about how we felt. Things just happened between us. We were on vacation. Nobody thinks on vacation."

"So you're going to slip back into your old life? And when Dev Riley comes in, you're going to hide in the copy room?"

"No," Carrie replied. "You're going to start delivering his tickets to his office. I don't have to run into him. Besides, he wouldn't even recognize me if he saw me."

"You didn't have to change your hair. You looked so pretty as a blonde," Susie said.

Carrie shook her head. "It wasn't me. I was pretending to be someone I could never be." She looked down at the drab clothes she wore: the baggy corduroys and the oversize jacket. "This is the real Carrie Reynolds. I'm comfortable with this person. I—I'm happy." She glanced over at Susie. "So, will you plan another vacation for me? Someplace quiet, where I don't have to talk to people."

Susie nodded. "When do you want to leave?"

"I need to catch up on a few things here at the office. I should be ready to leave by the end of the week."

"How long do you want to be gone?" Susie asked.

Carrie sighed and turned to stare out the window. "I don't know. I'll come home when I'm ready."

Susie stepped in front of her and drew her into a hug. "I'm sorry, Carrie. I never meant for you to get hurt."

Carrie rested her chin on her friend's shoulder and

distractedly watched a car park across the street. "I know," she murmured. "I know you didn't—" The words died in her throat and she shoved back and glared at Susie. "You did it again!"

Her partner frowned. "What are you talking about?"

Carrie grabbed her hat from a chair and tugged it down over her head. "That!" she said, pointing out the window at the dark BMW sedan. "You knew he was coming here and you didn't warn me. You wanted us to see each other."

Susie shook her head. "I didn't know he was coming! I swear, Carrie, I didn't set this up."

Carrie swung her backpack over her shoulder and grabbed the doorknob. "I have to go. I can't see him. Not yet." With that, she rushed outside. She risked a quick glance across the street, and for an instant, her gaze met Dev's. Then she ducked her head, pulled her collar up and hurried down the sidewalk without looking back.

When she reached a safe distance, she slipped into a shop doorway and tried to catch her breath. Her heart slammed against her chest and she felt faint. Carrie tipped her head back and cursed softly. "One look," she murmured. "And I can barely walk." She swallowed hard. "I can't do this. I can't risk running into him. I'm going to have to move."

She'd sell her house and start a branch of Adventures, Inc. in another town. Fairbanks, Alaska, or Amarillo, Texas. "Or Helena," Carrie said. "I'll just move to Montana. That would wipe out one lie, at least."

Carrie leaned out and looked down the sidewalk. Dev was just crossing the street, and she watched him. Her fingers twitched as she remembered the feel of his skin beneath her palms, the hard muscle that rippled beneath. For an instant, she was carried back to that room on Cristabel Key—the sea breeze blowing through the shuttered windows, the lazy whir of the ceiling fan, the melodious songs of the birds. She touched her lips and could almost taste his kiss. Every memory was so clear and intense that desire still welled up inside her.

How was she supposed to live without him? How could she go for the rest of her life without ever touching him again? She couldn't imagine feeling this passion for another man. Carrie pressed her mittened hand to her chest, trying to ease the ache in her heart.

There was one way to make things right with Dev. She could walk back into the agency and tell him the truth. Everything. That she'd watched him from afar, that she'd fantasized about him, that she'd deceived him at every turn. And then, once she'd taken in his reaction, she could tell him that she loved him.

"Do it," Carrie murmured to herself. "Tell him the truth. Go to him and ask his forgiveness."

She took a step out from the doorway, and the bitter wind slapped her in the face. In that instant, her courage and resolve vanished. She'd lived a dream with Dev Riley and if she gave him a chance to reject the person she really was, then that dream would be too painful to bear.

Maybe it was better to just leave things as they were, to go back to her life, happy in the knowledge that she'd known one week of true passion. She could live the rest of her days satisfied with that, couldn't she? She could separate the Dev she'd fallen in love with and the Dev that came into her travel agency on occasion.

Carrie turned and headed toward a coffee shop on the next block. She'd wait for a while and then go back to the agency as if he'd never been there, as if she'd never seen him on the street. Or maybe she'd go home and crawl into bed and eat a couple of dozen Twinkies. It was all for the better, keeping her secrets.

And if she told herself that again and again, maybe someday she'd feel it in her heart.

THE FRESH SNOW GLITTERED in the bright noonday sun and drifted with the wind. Dev squinted against the glare as he stepped out of his car across from Adventures, Inc. He shivered and clapped his gloved hands together, waiting for a break in the traffic. After nearly a week in the Keys, it would take more than a day or two in the north to become reaccustomed to the numbing cold and icy wind.

He glanced both ways before crossing the street, then stopped short as his gaze fell on a figure leaving the agency. The woman glanced across the street, and for an instant their eyes met. Then she turned and walked briskly down the sidewalk, her head bent to the wind.

Dev's breath froze in his throat and he blinked against the harsh light. His mind flashed an image of Carrie—her walk, the way she held her head, the easy swing of her arms as she moved. Though the woman wore a heavy coat and a hat, he still felt such a strong sense of familiarity that he took a few steps after her. But then he realized her hair was the wrong color and she wore horn-rimmed glasses.

He stopped his pursuit with a curse and raked his fingers through his hair. Good Lord, he was seeing Carrie Reynolds's likeness in a complete stranger now! Had he become that obsessed with finding her? Had she so totally stolen his heart that he couldn't go a minute without thinking about her?

Since the moment she'd walked away from him that morning at the villa, he'd been assailed by a maelstrom of emotion. He'd been stunned, hurt by her sudden and indifferent departure. Then, he'd grown angry and had managed to convince himself that her leaving was for the best. There'd be no tearful goodbyes, no doubts or regrets, no worries about what might have been. Just a quick and simple end to their vacation affair.

That feeling had lasted all of an hour—as long as it had taken him to pack and make plane reservations. Then a slow desperation set in, and any thought of forgetting what had happened between them was overcome by a need to find her. What he planned to do once he had her back, he wasn't really sure, but Dev couldn't let her go without seeing her one last time.

He didn't know what he was going to say when they finally came face-to-face. Something would occur to him in the moments before he looked into her eyes. Instinct told him to confess his feelings, to admit that he'd fallen in love with her. But he still couldn't put much faith in such an emotional reaction. They'd known each other for only a week, and love was supposed to take time. He'd agonized over his decision to propose to Jillian after a two-year affair, yet he was now ready to pop the question to Carrie without a second thought.

He wanted to spend his life with her, indulging his fascination with every passing day and every passionate night. They belonged together, in both heart and soul. The fact that he didn't know much about her made no difference. He could learn everything he needed to know to make her happy, and whatever was left, he'd spend a lifetime discovering. Nothing should keep them apart if they truly loved each other.

But there was the rub. He might love her, but did she love him? That was the question that had nagged at his mind during his flight back to Chicago. If she did love him, why did she leave? There was nothing calling her back home, except her love for a man she apparently didn't even know. What would possess a woman to brush aside the experience they'd shared for a relative stranger?

Dev sighed. He really wouldn't get his answers until he found her, which was turning out to be a lot harder than he expected. He'd contacted Fergus and Moira from the villa, assuming that they would have Carrie's home address. But oddly, they listed her hometown as Lake Grove, Illinois, and the agency that booked her trip as Adventures, Inc. Both he and Moira concluded that the bad information was due to another computer glitch.

Left without even the most basic lead, he'd decided to go to Helena. But after a Friday afternoon spent in Carrie's hometown, he was no closer to finding her than he had been in the Keys. Helena wasn't a big place, but short of scanning the phone book and visiting the nine travel agencies in the city, there was nothing more he could do. Carrie Reynolds had disappeared without a trace.

So he'd decided to ask for Susie's help. Dev pushed open the door to Adventures, Inc. and scanned the office for his travel agent. Maybe there was a way Susie could access airline records or track down the reservation that Carrie had made for *Serendipity*. Somewhere out there was another agent who'd made Carrie's arrangements. Maybe Susie could track that person down.

Dev tugged off his gloves and stuffed them in his coat pocket. If Susie couldn't find Carrie, then Dev had only one option left—an option that he was reluctant to employ. His head of corporate security was a former private investigator. Dev had never mixed business with his personal life, but if it came down to it, he'd break his own rules to find her.

"Dev Riley! You're back!"

Dev waved at Susie, then crossed the office and stood in front of her desk. "I'm back."

She pushed back in her chair and gazed up at him. "Sit down," she urged. "Tell me about your trip. I hope everything was as you expected? Very interesting, very relaxing?"

"Very," Dev said. "You planned a perfect trip."

She gave him a sympathetic look. "I'm sorry it wasn't as romantic as you'd planned. I was surprised to hear that your companion decided to cancel. I hope you weren't too lonely."

Dev frowned, then shook his head. There were times when he wondered what his vacation might have been like without Carrie. Even worse, what might have happened had Jillian accompanied him. By now, he could have been an engaged man, promised to a woman he'd never really loved.

But a silly mistake by some travel agent had changed his life, had turned it in a new direction. Maybe fate would prevail, and Susie could do the same all over again. "That's what I wanted to talk to you about," Dev said.

Susie laughed. "About loneliness?"

"No, I wanted to talk to you about a woman. A woman I met on vacation."

"But I thought you were alone," she said.

Dev leaned over her desk and shook his head. "By some strange mistake, *Serendipity* was double-booked. This woman was supposed to go to a singles resort and she ended up on my vacation—in my cabin and in my bed. I wanted to know if there was any way you could track her down. Her reservation was made through a computer service."

Susie blinked in surprise. "In your bed, you say? My, my, you *did* have a good vacation."

"It was wonderful. And that's why I need you to do this for me—why I need to find her."

"You shared a bed with this woman and you didn't bother to get her phone number? Not very good thinking on your part."

"It's not like that," Dev said. "She told me she was from Helena, but I went there and I couldn't find her. You have to help me on this."

"Well, I don't know," Susie said. "I really don't think—"

"You're just about my last hope," Dev said, an edge of frustration in his voice. "Short of hiring a private investigator or putting my corporate security team on her trail."

"You'd do that?" She cupped her chin in her palm and gave him a sly smile. "This woman must be very special."

"She is," Dev replied. "I've never met anyone quite like her."

"How special?"

He didn't anticipate having to explain his motives

or his feelings about Carrie Reynolds to his travel agent, but he was depending on Susie's help. "I think I love her," he said. Once the words were out of his mouth, he suddenly didn't question his feelings. "I do love her," he corrected. "I know it sounds silly. I mean, I never put much stock in love at first sight. But then, when it happens, well…"

"Well? Well, what?" Susie asked.

"Well, it's pretty incredible. So that's why I need you to track this woman down."

"So tell me," Susie teased, "is she beautiful? Let me guess. Tall, slender—a brunette with an attitude?"

"Not even close," Dev said with a smile. "She's small and not skinny. Curvy, just perfect. And she's blond with blue eyes. The most incredible blue eyes. And the sweetest smile."

"Doesn't sound like your type," Susie commented, leaning back in her chair.

"That's what I thought. But I guess I really didn't know what my type was until I met her. So, can you find her? I thought you might be able to check airline records."

"I can try," Susie said. "Why don't you give me a day or two and I'll get back to you?"

Dev nodded, then met her gaze squarely. "This is very important to me. *She's* important. I have to find her." He stood and rebuttoned his overcoat, then shook Susie's hand. "Let me know as soon as you find anything."

With that, he turned and strode out of the agency. When he got to his car, he sat behind the wheel for a long time, his breath clouding around his face and fogging the windows. Something nagged at his brain, something he'd forgotten. But Dev couldn't put his finger on it.

And then he remembered! He'd never even mentioned Carrie's name to Susie Ellis. And she hadn't even asked for it. He grabbed the door handle and pushed the car door open. How was Susie supposed to track Carrie down if she didn't know who she was looking for? Unless, she could get her name off the computer reservation on *Serendipity*.

Still, Dev wasn't willing to take any chances. He stepped out of the car and quickly ran across the street and into the agency. But by the time he got there, Susie was already occupied with another client. Dev tried to catch her attention, but she was too absorbed in her work to see him. Finally, he walked over to another agent.

"I'm wondering if you could give Susie a message," he said. "I don't want to disturb her when she's with a customer."

The agent looked up from her computer and smiled. "Sure," she said, grabbing a message pad and a pen. "What would you like me to tell her?"

"Tell her that I want her to find Carrie Reynolds."

"Oh, Carrie was in just this morning. In fact, she just called to say she'd be back in later this afternoon. Would you like to make an appointment?"

"No, no," Dev said. "Susie is looking for Carrie Reynolds for me. She doesn't work here. She's from Montana."

"Oh, no, Carrie is from right here in Lake Grove. She and Susie own the agency."

Dev shook his head, trying to make sense of the woman's words. Carrie Reynolds worked here, at the agency? But how could that be? Why would she have told him she was from—

Realization slowly dawned, and suddenly Dev understood everything quite clearly. There was no computer error with Carrie's reservation. It had been made from here at this very agency. And no wonder he couldn't find her in Helena. She didn't live in Montana, she lived in Lake Grove, Illinois! She'd come on his vacation, knowing full well who he was. Yet she'd kept her identity a secret.

Dev frowned. Those were probably the facts, but he was missing one very important bit of information— why? What had she hoped to accomplish by barging into his vacation? Surely Susie must have known, but why had *she* played coy with him? Were the two of them scheming in some way? He rubbed his forehead, trying to soothe away his confusion. "You say Carrie Reynolds will be in later this afternoon?"

The agent nodded. "She always closes. She's usually here until six-thirty or seven to handle the after-work walk-ins. Would you like an appointment?"

"No, I just think I'll stop by and see if she's free. Is Susie scheduled to work that late?"

The woman checked her computer, then shook her head. "Not tonight. Carrie will be the only one here. If you want to see Susie, she's got a one o'clock slot open."

Dev nodded. "No, I'd really like to talk to Ms. Reynolds." He pushed to his feet. "Thank you for all your help. It's been quite…illuminating."

The agent smiled brightly. "No problem," she chirped. "Have a nice day."

With that, Dev turned and headed back out the door. Oh, he'd have a nice day all right. And he'd have a nice week and a nice month and a nice life. Just as soon as he figured out what the hell was going on!

CARRIE STARED at her computer screen, comparing prices on first-class flights to San Francisco. A group tour of the California wine country for a local senior citizen's group had kept her busy for most of the evening, ticketing and making rooming lists. The tour was being led by a local wine merchant who'd promised colorful commentary on vineyards and winemaking.

She was tempted to go along, just to get away from Lake Grove and any chance of running into Dev Riley again. Moving was out of the question. Carrie had decided that earlier in the afternoon between the Twinkies and the Ben and Jerry's. She'd just have to learn to live with what might happen. And if she couldn't, then there was always the option of clearing the air with Dev. She could tell him the truth, and take her knocks. And after that, she could put her life back together and go on.

With a soft sigh, she went back to her ticketing. The front door squeaked, then slammed shut, and Carrie looked up from her task. Her heart froze in her chest, and a strangled cry worked its way out of her throat, as she watched Dev Riley stride toward her desk. Frantic, she searched for a place to run, a spot to hide—anywhere to get away from him.

Finally, she slipped down to the floor and crawled beneath her desk, hoping against hope that he hadn't seen her. From where she hid, she could see his feet, his expensive Italian shoes and argyle socks. He looked so different in a business suit and tie—not at all like the man she'd made love to. He was more imposing, more intimidating. She wished he were dressed the way he had been in the Keys: in shorts and a T-shirt. Carrie could talk to that man, but she couldn't talk to the stranger who'd walked into her travel agency.

"Hello?"

She decided to keep quiet, hoping he'd just go away.

"I can see you under there," he said. "Hello? Are you all right?"

"Hello," Carrie called. "I—I'm perfectly fine. Can I help you?"

He braced his hands on her desk and leaned over until Carrie could see the top of his head. She scrambled farther beneath the desk.

"I was looking for Susie," he said. "Is she in?"

Carrie coughed softly, trying to clear away the nerves in her voice. "No, no, she's not. She'll be in tomorrow. You can come back then."

His feet slowly circled around to the back of the desk, and soon she could see all the way up to his knees. He had nice knees, she remembered. And wonderfully long and muscular legs. In her mind flashed a memory of him walking from the surf, naked, his body glistening in the moonlight.

"What are you doing under there?"

Startled out of her brief fantasy, she sat up and bumped her head on the underside of her desk. With a soft oath, she rubbed the spot. "My pencil. I dropped my pencil."

Dev pulled a pencil from the cup next to her computer and held it out to her. "Here's a pencil."

"No, I want the pencil I dropped," Carrie said. "It's a…special pencil."

"Well, when you find it, will you come up here and talk to me?"

"I thought you wanted to see Susie. She's not here. If you leave and come back tomorrow, I'm sure she'll help you then."

"I'll settle for you."

"I'm afraid I don't have time," she called.

"You have time to search for a pencil you don't need, but you don't have time to help a customer?"

Carrie groaned inwardly. He wasn't going to go away. He'd stand over her desk and badger her until she came out. But as soon as he looked into her eyes, he'd surely recognize her. Drawing a deep breath, she slowly wiggled out. The choice had been made. There'd be no avoiding the truth now. She'd be forced to tell him everything. But maybe that was for the best. Maybe fate had stepped in to make the decision for her.

She hesitantly straightened, brushed off her corduroys, then looked up at him. Carrie expected an immediate reaction—recognition, surprise, confusion. But Dev simply stared at her with an impatient expression. She swallowed convulsively. Could it be that he didn't recognize her?

"Did you find your pencil?" he asked.

Carrie shook her head and quickly sat down, tugging her hair down to hide her face. He *didn't* recognize her! Her glasses had effectively hidden her eyes, and her hair was no longer a sunny blond. Still, she'd spent an entire week with the man—even made love to him! He'd seen her at very close range. How could he *not* recognize her?

She wasn't sure whether to feel relieved or insulted. He'd claimed that he'd never forget her, yet they'd been apart for two days and he couldn't recall the features of her face or the sound of her voice. Carrie ground her teeth. It would serve him right if she told him exactly who she was! Let him try to squirm out of *that* one.

Carrie opened her mouth—ready to speak her mind—then snapped it shut. Did she really want to explain her actions? Did she want to admit that she'd fallen in love with him over a year ago, before she'd even met him? That all her daydreams had come true when she'd found him in her bed on *Serendipity?* Because that's what she'd have to tell him if she told the truth. There were no other explanations.

"What can I help you with, Mr...."

"Riley," he said. "Dev Riley."

"Mr. Dev Riley." Lord, she loved the sound of his name on her lips. It had run through her head a million times since she'd been home, but saying his name out loud caused her heart to skip and her pulse to quicken.

"Susie was working on a project for me," Dev explained. "Maybe she told you about it?"

"I'm afraid I haven't talked to Susie since this morning. But I'm sure I can help you with any arrangement that you'd like made."

"Actually, I'm looking for a woman."

Carrie stared up at him and blinked in surprise. "A woman?"

Well, it certainly hadn't taken him long to get on with his life! They'd barely been apart for forty-eight hours, and he was already on the make. Oh, she was so much better off without him. And she was so relieved she hadn't revealed her identity. How humiliating would that have been?

"Her name is Carrie Reynolds," Dev said.

She gasped, all the breath leaving her lungs. "Carrie Reynolds?"

"I met her on vacation in the Keys. And I've been trying to track her down ever since. Susie was trying to help me find her."

"Susie knows that you're looking for—this woman?" She'd nearly said "me," but caught herself just in time. "You discussed this with her?"

"I talked to her earlier today. She's looking at airline records and computer reservation services to try to track her down."

Oh, Lord. Dev Riley was looking for her! Maybe he did care, maybe he regretted letting her walk away. Maybe he even loved her. Or maybe he wanted to see her for another reason. She recalled his description of his breakup with Jillian: how he had wanted to be the one to end it. Could that be why he searched for her? So he could reject her the same way she'd rejected him?

"I—I don't think she'll be able to find much," Carrie said. "Airline records are confidential." She paused. "Why do you want to find this woman?"

His eyebrow shot up, and he looked insulted by her prying inquiry.

"I mean, you're not a stalker, are you?"

"We left some things unsaid," he replied.

"Like what?"

Dev frowned and shook his head. "That's between me and Ms. Reynolds, don't you think?"

Carrie felt a flush creep up her cheeks, and she ducked her head down, worried that he might recognize that particular trait of hers. She had blushed a number of times in Dev Riley's presence. One in par-

ticular came to mind—when he'd come upon her on
the terrace steps...when she'd asked him to make
love to her.

"Of course it is," she said. "I just thought that—"

"That I'd confide in a complete stranger?"

He slid his hip onto the corner of her desk, and her
gaze fell to his lap, to thoughts entirely inappropriate
at the moment. "I'm not a complete stranger," she
murmured, her embarrassment rising. "I mean, I'm
Susie's partner. You can tell me anything."

He scowled at her. "I don't know much about her.
She ended up in my cabin on a charter sailboat. Some
mix-up with the reservations. Over the week we
spent together, we became...close."

"Close?"

"I don't think I need to go into detail," he said.
"She claimed she was from Helena, Montana. I went
there to look for her and she—"

Carrie twisted her fingers together in an attempt to
contain her surprise. "You went to Helena? To look
for—her?"

"As I said, it's imperative that I find her. I'm prepared to pay you for your time."

"You'd *pay* to find her?"

He pushed to his feet. "Whatever it takes. I'm not
going to stop until I see her again. Do you understand, Ms.—"

"I understand, Mr. Riley. And I can assure you that
we'll try our best."

"I don't want you to try, I want you to succeed," he
said. With that, he buttoned his overcoat and tugged
on his leather gloves. Then he walked to the door and
stepped out into the night, leaving her alone and
completely baffled.

Carrie rubbed her forehead. If he cared for her, why hadn't he recognized her? She yanked open her desk drawer and rummaged for a pocket mirror. She finally found an old compact in Susie's desk and flipped it open. "I don't look that different," she murmured, pulling her hair back from her face. "It's me— the same person he taught to swim, the person he kissed and made love to. If he cares enough to find me, then why can't he remember me?"

Unless…Carrie winced. Unless he really didn't care. Maybe all he wanted was to vent his anger, to settle some imagined slight. He could want to hurt her in the same way she'd hurt him.

Carrie plopped down in her chair and covered her eyes with her hands. How had this turned into such a mess? Dev was determined to find her, and, considering his financial resources, it wouldn't be long before he turned up here again, looking for answers.

Well, she wasn't about to wait in fear. She'd give him the answers he wanted right now! Carrie sat up in her chair and typed in a few commands on her computer. In an instant, she had Dev's client profile, a list of every trip they'd ever booked for him and his home address. She scribbled the address on a scrap of paper, then grabbed her jacket from the back of her chair and headed for the front door.

The weather had turned nasty since she'd arrived at the agency. Flurries had turned to a full-fledged snowstorm. The wind whipped the flakes into drifts on the streets. Carrie trudged down the sidewalk, squinting against the snow that clung to her hair and her lashes.

Dev lived in an old neighborhood on the edge of Lake Grove—a spot filled with beautiful brick homes

9

THE WIND RAGED OUTSIDE and snow pelted the windows of Dev's study. He poked at the fire he'd built to ward off the chill, then sipped at his scotch. As the liquor traced a line of fire down his throat, his mind drifted back an hour, to the very moment he'd set eyes on Carrie again. A flood of desire welled up inside him even now.

He might not have recognized her had he passed her on the street, but face-to-face, he knew her in a second. She'd changed her hair color to an unremarkable shade of brown, and she now wore glasses. But the eyes behind the glasses were undoubtedly the same eyes that had gazed into his when they'd made love.

Dev wasn't sure what he'd hoped to accomplish by confronting her at the travel agency. Maybe he hoped she'd explain how—and why—she'd ended up on his vacation and in his bed. And why she'd walked out on him with barely a goodbye. But she hadn't even admitted that she was Carrie Reynolds!

So he'd decided to play along with her charade. There had to be a good reason for her subterfuge. Maybe there was another man—or a husband. An unbidden flood of jealousy shot through him, and he pushed it back with another swallow of his scotch.

Wouldn't that be his luck, to find a woman he loved and to lose her to someone else?

He'd have his explanations soon enough. First, he'd wait to hear Susie Ellis's story: the results of her "search" for a woman who wasn't lost. And perhaps he'd pay another evening visit to the agency to test Carrie's nerves. Or maybe he'd run into her on the street and—

As Dev stared into the fire, watching the flames lick at the birch logs, a spark popped onto the hearth, red and glowing, then faded, and with it came a memory, just as quick and fleeting. That hair, those eyes. He had seen her on the street earlier in the day! The woman he'd noticed, with Carrie's walk, the tilt of her head. That had been her, leaving the agency.

Bracing his hand on the mantel, he closed his eyes and tried to picture the scene. How had she ever expected to keep her true identity from him? He visited Adventures, Inc. at least once a month to pick up tickets or make travel arrangements. And he and Carrie lived in the same town. For all he knew, they had run into each other many times before—in the post office, at the grocery store, at the train station.

The grandfather clock in the hall struck seven, and he downed the rest of his scotch. He needed some dinner before he sat down to catch up on all the work he'd missed. But as he headed for the kitchen, the doorbell rang. Dev frowned. Who would be out on a night like this? He peeked out the window at the shadowy form before he flipped on the outside light and opened the door.

A figure, bundled in a jacket, muffler and hat, stood on his porch. The person had snow stuck to every exposed surface like some Arctic explorer. He leaned closer and watched as the woman blinked her eyes, the only indication that she wasn't frozen solid. Beautiful blue eyes behind half-frosted glasses. "Carrie?"

She nodded, then shuddered with the cold. Dev grabbed her mittened hand and drew her into the house. The door slammed closed behind her, and he carefully began to remove her wet clothes. Layer by layer, the clothes and the snow fell onto the marble floor of the foyer, until Carrie was standing in front of him, her hair damp and her cheeks red.

He removed her glasses, wiped the fog from them with the cuff of his shirt, then returned them. "What the hell are you doing out on a night like tonight?"

Carrie's teeth chattered, and she stared up at him, wide-eyed. "You—you recognize me? You know who I am?"

"Of course I do," he said. He grabbed her hand and pulled her toward the study. "There's a fire in here. Let's get you warm."

"You know who I am," she repeated, stumbling along after him. "And you're not surprised to see me?

"Stop saying that. Yes, I know exactly who you are."

"But—but you were at the agency earlier. You walked right in and started talking to me as if you didn't know me. Did you know who I was then?"

Her questions were beginning to irritate him, and he ground his teeth. "Why do you think I was there? I came to see you."

Suddenly, she dug her heels into the oriental carpet and yanked her hand from his. "What kind of game are you playing?"

Dev turned to her, meeting her angry gaze. "I could ask you the same," he said in a deceptively even voice. "Don't you think I'm the one who deserves an explanation, Carrie? You told me you were from Montana. And here you are in Lake Grove. Living here, working here, right under my nose. And that's just the first of your lies."

"It's not like that!" Carrie said, crossing to the fire. She held out her trembling hands, then rubbed them together distractedly. He wanted to press her fingers between his, to draw them up against his chest and warm them against his body, but he clenched his fists at his sides and waited. Waited for her explanation. But she seemed intent on studying the flames.

"I suspect I know what the real story is," he said. "You and Susie saw an easy mark. A guy who'd just been dumped by his girlfriend. A guy with a little money, a business of his own and—"

"That's not it!" she cried. "I would never do that! How—how could you even think I'd be capable of something so…devious?"

A long silence grew between them. "You showed up at my door," he said softly. "You obviously came here for a reason. What was it?"

She pressed her lips together, as if she needed to contain her emotions. The fire cast her beautiful profile in light and shadow, and he couldn't take his eyes off her. "I came to explain." Her voice was so small and soft that he could barely hear her.

"I'm listening."

She still refused to turn and look at him. Dev stepped up beside her and she gave him a sideways glance, then turned back to the fire, as if looking at him made her explanations harder. "Remember when we were talking about the prom?"

"The prom?"

"You said you would have taken me to the prom if you'd known me in high school. That you would have noticed a girl like me. And I said I wasn't the kind of woman men noticed."

"I remember."

"Did you know that we met once?" she asked, glancing at him again. "Before the Keys. On the street in front of the agency. I slipped and fell on the ice, and you helped me up."

That's why he'd felt a spark of recognition when he'd first seen her on *Serendipity*. They had met and he'd remembered her—vaguely. "That was you? With the backpack and the grape juice?"

Carrie nodded, then stepped away from the fire and rubbed her arms. She took a seat on the leather couch and shoved her glasses up the bridge of her nose, then hugged her knees to her chest. Dev almost felt sorry for her. She looked so timid, not at all like the bright and confident woman he'd met in the Keys. He wanted her angry or frustrated or hysterical. He didn't want her quiet and complacent.

"Can you still say the same?" she asked, meeting his gaze. "Look at me. Can you honestly say that you would have noticed me? Would have been attracted enough to ask me out?" She held up her hand. "You don't have to answer. Those were rhetorical questions."

"I'll answer," Dev said. "No, I wouldn't have noticed you. And I wouldn't have asked you out. But then, I rarely take much notice of strangers, and I never ask them out. But we got to know each other in Florida and that changed everything. I got to know you, Carrie, and I—"

"That wasn't me," she interrupted. She pressed her

palms to her heart. "This is me. This is Carrie Reynolds. I'm shy and quiet and plain. I live in Lake Grove, and I own Adventures, Inc. And—and…"

"And what?"

She fixed her gaze on her tightly clasped hands. "And I've been in love with you for a long time. At least, I thought it was love. I didn't know what love was, so I guess you could call it a crush."

"A crush?"

A long breath escaped her tightly pursed lips. "You'd come into the agency, and I'd watch you from the copy room, or sometimes from my desk. You never noticed me. I used to think you were the most handsome, most interesting man in the world. You were everything I thought I wanted… and everything I knew I could never have."

"So you—"

She held up her hand to stop him. "Don't say anything. Not until I've told you the whole story." Carrie took another deep breath and continued. "For a long time, I kept my feelings secret. I thought they were silly…childish. But then Susie noticed me watching you and she realized what was going on. She took matters into her own hands and she sent me on that vacation, knowing that you would be there and Jillian wouldn't."

"Susie did all this?"

"The travel arrangements. But I could have told you the truth when you arrived. I could have left for home after that first night. But I stayed. And I kept up the lie." She sniffled, then wiped her damp nose on the cuff of her sweater. "I—I just thought you'd think I'd set it all up, to trap you or manipulate you or whatever it is women do when they see a man they want. Until you turned up in my bed, you were just a fantasy. I never meant for it to be anything more. I never meant it to be real."

He stared at her for a long time, confusion addling his brain. He didn't know what to say. Dev ran his hands through his hair and let out a tightly held breath. "Then it was real?"

She shook her head, then quickly stood up. "No. It was a fantasy, and now that fantasy is over." Carrie forced a smile. "I just wanted to clear the air. I'm terribly embarrassed about what happened. I never wanted it to go so far and I shouldn't have let it. You deserved the truth." Carrie turned on her heel and started out of the study. In three long steps, he caught up to her and grabbed her hand.

"Where are you going?"

"Home," she murmured in a tremulous voice. "I've said what I came to say, and now I can leave."

The hell if he was going to let her walk out of his life for a second time! "You can't leave," he said. "The storm is worse. And your jacket is all wet. It's too cold for you to walk home."

"I'll be all right," she said, hurrying back to the foyer. "Please, I've already humiliated myself enough for one night. Don't make it worse. Just let me go."

"What if I don't want to let you go? What if I can't?" Dev asked, following after her.

She looked back and into his eyes, pain etching her beautiful features. "You have to. We're back in the real world now, and there's no room for fantasies." She laughed softly. "Look at me. And look at you. We don't belong together. Never in a million years would you have come to me on your own. We met through a manipulation—a silly joke that a friend decided to play."

Dev wasn't sure what to say. On one hand, he was angry—about the lies, the scheming, her complicity in the whole thing. On the other hand, he ought to be flattered. She'd fallen in love with him without ever knowing—

"I'm the cowboy," he said, realization slowly dawning. "I'm the guy you were practicing for?"

Carrie nodded, two spots of color deepening on her cheeks. "I thought if I were more interesting, more confident...more experienced, that I might have a chance with you—with men. I went on vacation to practice."

"So the whole time it was happening between us, I was thinking you were in love with another man. And you were getting exactly what you wanted."

"I never meant to hurt you." She grabbed her jacket from the floor and tugged it on. "I was selfish. After a while I couldn't tell you the truth, even when I knew you might get hurt." She zipped up her jacket. "You didn't get hurt, did you? I mean, you're all right. I can tell you are. You'll be fine."

"I will?"

"You haven't lost anything. You were getting a woman who doesn't really exist, at least not outside the Florida Keys. This is the real Carrie Reynolds," she said.

"I don't see any difference," he said. "You've changed your hair, you're wearing glasses, but you're still the same woman I met on *Serendipity*."

Carrie shook her head. "No, I'm not. And I'm honest enough to realize that." She tugged her hat down over her ears, then wrapped her scarf around her neck. "Now that I've told you, I think I should be going." She swallowed hard, then forced a smile. "I really hope this doesn't jeopardize our business relationship, but I'll understand if you decide to work with another agency."

Dev cursed beneath his breath. After all this, she was concerned about keeping his business? What about the passion they'd shared? What about the need and desire he'd felt while holding her in his arms? Was she so immune to those feelings that she could turn and walk away from him? Hell, she was no different from Jillian!

Dev slowly shook his head as he stared at her, realizing she was right. The Carrie Reynolds standing in front of him *was* different. This wasn't the woman he'd fallen in love with—the silly, clumsy, smart-mouthed woman who drove him mad with desire. "Maybe you're right," he murmured.

Pain flashed in her eyes, and he saw her lower lip tremble. "I knew you'd realize that I'm not the woman you want—the woman you need."

Dev sighed. "I'm not sure what I need right now."

"Maybe you need things to get back to normal. What we shared in Florida was—nice, but it's over. You can go back to your life, and I can go back to mine." She paused, then held out her hand. "Goodbye, Dev."

He took her fingers in his, ignoring the current that shot up his arm and twisted at his heart. "Goodbye, Carrie."

With that, she turned and walked out of his home. Dev stood at the front door for a long time, the snow blowing in around him, the wind chilling him to his core. He wanted to run after her, to convince her that they could recapture what they'd shared in the Keys. But he wasn't sure she cared about him enough to make that happen. Or that she cared about herself enough to allow it to happen.

In all honesty, Dev wasn't sure about anything anymore. Except that he was in big trouble. For he was more in love than ever with Carrie Reynolds.

"YOU DIDN'T TELL ME why Dev came to the agency! And you didn't tell me that you told him who I was!"

Carrie stood in the middle of Susie's kitchen, dripping melted snow on her shiny linoleum floor. It had taken her nearly an hour to walk from Dev's place to Susie's apartment, fighting the snow and the wind and her tears the entire way. Colder and wetter than she'd ever been in her life, Carrie longed for the warmth of the Key West sun, the feel of the soft ocean breeze on her face. Right now, she felt like a drowned rat—a half-frozen, emotionally spent, heartsick drowned rat.

Susie sat at her kitchen table, munching on a handful of potato chips as she gazed up at Carrie. "I didn't tell him anything. And I didn't say anything to you because you said you wanted to put him out of your mind. Isn't that what you said?"

Carrie ripped off her mittens and threw them on the floor, where they landed with a splat. "I know that's what I said, but I expected you to tell me if he mentioned me to you."

"Run that by me again?"

"You know what I mean." She unwound her scarf. "He came into the agency looking for me. Looking for Carrie Reynolds."

"Umm-hmm," Susie said. "He's desperate to find

you. He asked for my help, and if I don't help him, he's going to hire a private detective to track you down. Isn't that romantic?"

"Well, he asked for *my* help in tracking me down, too. When he came in, he was looking for you. But he knew he'd find me."

"This is really confusing," Susie said, crinkling her nose and picking at the potato chips. "Besides, I didn't tell him where you were."

"He already knew! He was playing a game with me, hoping I'd admit the whole story."

"Why would he play games with you?" Susie asked, leaning back in her chair. "He loves you."

Carrie gripped the edge of the table with cold-numbed hands. "What? What did you say?"

"I said, he loves you."

"He said that? Dev said that he loved me?" She pulled the chair out and sat down. "He said those exact words?"

"Sure. Right out loud, right there in our office. Why else would he be so crazy to find you?"

Carrie combed her fingers through her wet hair. "I don't know. He didn't really say. I thought he wanted to get even. I thought he might be mad about what happened. So I went to his house and told him everything."

"Everything?"

"After all I said—humiliating myself that way—he just let me walk out. He didn't say anything about love. He must have lied to you." Her breath caught in her throat, and a stab of regret pierced her heart. "Or maybe, after seeing me, he changed his mind."

Susie reached across the table and covered Carrie's icy fingers with hers. "What did you say to him?"

A lump of emotion clogged Carrie's throat. "I told him everything. About the crush and the fantasies, about how I've loved him for a long time. And then I told him that we didn't have a future together," she said, rubbing her cold face with her hands. "I was giving him an easy way out. And he took it."

"You were avoiding rejection again," Susie said. "Only this time, you ran away from a guy who wasn't planning to reject you."

"He can't love me!" Carrie cried. "Not really. Look at me. How could he love someone like me? He thought he loved me, but now he doesn't. I was right all along."

With a frustrated sigh, Susie pushed up from her chair and grabbed Carrie by the hand. "Come with me," she said, dragging her to the bathroom. She flipped on the light, pushed Carrie in front of the mirror, and pointed at her reflection. "Look at you. Don't look at the details—the stringy hair and the red nose. Look at the total picture, Carrie. You're pretty. And you're just about the sweetest person I know. You'd never say anything bad about anybody. You know how to keep a secret. And you're loyal to your friends. And even you have to admit that you're funny. Why wouldn't he love you?"

Carrie stared long and hard at herself. Maybe Susie was right. She wasn't that unattractive, even with her mousy brown hair. And though her figure didn't come close to super-model status, she looked like a real woman, with curves in all the proper places. "But he's so…worldly. Experienced. Sophisticated."

Susie reached up and pulled Carrie's damp hair away from her face. "Terrific guys fall in love just the

same as ordinary guys. And they fall in love with terrific women—just like you."

"He loves me?" Carrie murmured. "He really said
that?"

"He loves you," Susie replied. "And I don't think
seeing you again, even in this condition, changed his
mind at all."

"But why did he let me leave?"

"Maybe because he thought you didn't share his
feelings," Susie suggested.

Carrie turned and hurried out of the bathroom. "I
have to go home. I have to think about this. I told him
that we didn't have a future. I thought I was making
things better…easier. Why didn't he tell me how he
felt?"

Susie dragged her back into the bathroom.
"Sweetie, we've got ourselves a blizzard here and
you're already freezing. Why don't you get out of
those wet clothes, take a nice hot shower, and I'll go
get you some pajamas. We can have a slumber party.
And we can talk about Dev and what you plan to do."
Susie plucked at Carrie's hair and winced. "And
maybe we can color your hair. This just doesn't do a
thing for you."

Carrie slapped her hand away. "I like my hair just
the way it is. It's me."

Her friend's eyebrow arched. "It would be you if
you were a rodent living in a hole in the wall. This is
not a color meant for a woman's head."

The mirror revealed the truth in Susie's words and
Carrie sighed. "It isn't very pretty, is it?"

Susie smiled. "I'll run out to the drugstore and get
everything we need. What do you think. Honey
blond? You could go red. Or a pretty brunette. New

hair will give you a completely new outlook on life—
and love."

"Changing my hair color isn't going to solve all my
problems."

"Maybe it will make you remember what's really
important. Who you *really* are. And after we color
your hair, we can talk about you and Dev and what
you're going to do. We'll get it all sorted out, you'll
sleep on it, and tomorrow morning you'll know exactly what to say to him to get him back."

"I'm not sure I can do anything," Carrie replied.

"You're going to have to talk to him again. You
can't let him go on thinking you don't care. He loves
you, Carrie! This is a big deal." Susie grabbed her
around the neck and gave her a hug. "Of course, I'll
be your maid of honor, as long as you don't make me
wear one of those frilly dresses."

"No! I mean, there won't be any dresses, frilly or
otherwise. We're not going to get married. He doesn't
want to get married—not after Jillian."

Susie reached into the tub and turned on the water.
"Take a hot shower. Then we'll color your hair, polish
your fingernails and eat a lot of junk food. Things always seem clearer after a junk food binge. I'll bring
you pajamas, and then I'll run to the drugstore." She
patted Carrie's back. "We're going to figure this out
before the night is over."

After Susie closed the bathroom door behind her,
Carrie slowly stripped out of her damp clothes, her
body numb. A shiver skittered down her spine, not
from the cold but from the raw emotion that raced
through her. Dev Riley loved her. But why hadn't he
told her? He'd admitted as much to Susie, but he
hadn't said the words to Carrie.

Would he say it again, if she gave him the chance? Could he put everything she'd said to him aside and reveal his true feelings? She'd tried her very best to convince him that she was a different person from the one he'd made love to at the villa. Maybe she'd tried too hard and had banished every bit of love from his heart.

Carrie stepped beneath the hot water, letting it wash over her body until it began to warm her blood. Her eyes closed, and exhaustion nearly overwhelmed her. Just a little more than a week ago, she might have described her life as normal—a little boring, but nothing out of the ordinary. Suddenly, everything she'd come to depend on had been thrown into chaos, and all because of Dev Riley. Nothing had prepared her for the power of her feelings, or the possibility he might return those feelings. What was she supposed to do? Could she trust his love? Or would he fall out of love, the way he had with Jillian?

Another stab of pain wretched her heart. She'd dreamed about loving him for so long, and now he'd professed to return those feelings. But would they last, or was he still infatuated with the woman Carrie had been? Carrie couldn't face the thought that she might lose him as quickly as she had found him. There were no guarantees they'd spend the rest of their lives together just because he claimed to love her now.

Bracing her hands on the tile wall of the shower, Carrie bent her head and let the water run along her spine. She couldn't work this all out in a few minutes or even a few hours. She needed time to think, time to weigh the risks of letting herself love Dev Riley—and of letting Dev Riley love her.

Carrie had always assumed that if—or when—she finally found love, it would all be clear to her. But it wasn't at all. Love was confusing and exhilarating and frightening and comforting. It stood before her like a wonderful dream that she was afraid would dissolve in the blink of an eye, as soon as she reached for it.

Closing her eyes, she turned her face up into the spray. Why couldn't she just grab that dream? She deserved to be happy, didn't she? "I'll take my time and think this over," she murmured. "And when I wake up in the morning, I'll decide what to do. If Dev truly loves me now, then he'll still love me tomorrow."

CARRIE SHOVED HER CARRY-ON into the overhead bin and wrestled a pillow and blanket out at the same time. She glanced around the first-class cabin at the other passengers, then sat down in her seat. Susie's seat next to her was empty, and Carrie wondered where her partner was. They'd planned to meet at the gate, but when she hadn't arrived by boarding time, Carrie had decided to wait on the plane.

When Susie had suggested they take a little junket, Carrie had jumped at the chance. After almost a week of mulling over her options, she had finally worked up the courage to call Dev. But he'd been out of town for the entire week, and his secretary refused to say when he'd be back.

Carrie couldn't help but feel relieved. She wasn't sure what she'd planned to say to him. Perhaps she might have been better prepared had she experienced love before. But Carrie had never been in love—not even close. All the emotions that spun inside her were completely new and unfamiliar.

How was she supposed to make a decision about something so serious, so life altering, without any understanding of what she felt? Time should have been her ally, each day crystalizing her feelings, until her decision was clear. But the longer she waited, the more she doubted herself—and doubted Dev's love.

She'd hoped that he might make the first move, make things easier on her. But obviously, he hadn't felt any urgency—he'd left town! All week, she'd waited for the memories of him to lose their intensity, to fade with each passing day. Maybe if she never saw him again, the images would someday disappear altogether. But it would take a very long time.

Carrie leaned back in her seat and sighed, hugging the little pillow against her chest. She needed to see him again, longed to look into his eyes, to reassure herself that he still wanted her. A girl just didn't toss aside a man like Dev, or procrastinate so long that he lost interest. She'd have to do something—soon!

A shadow fell across Susie's seat and a briefcase dropped down next to Carrie. "I'm afraid that seat is taken," she said, glancing up.

"I sure hope not. Because you're in *my* seat."

Carrie's heart stopped as she looked into Dev Riley's eyes. He slipped in beside her and tucked his briefcase beneath the seat in front of him. "First my bed and now my seat," he said. "I never considered you the desperate type, but this is getting a little out of hand, don't you think?"

"Wha—what are you doing here?" she demanded, heat rising in her cheeks.

"I'm taking a little trip," Dev replied. "And I'd assume you're here to tag along again?"

Carrie stood up and bumped her head on the overhead bins. She searched up and down the aisle. "Where's Susie? That's her seat, not yours."

"Oh, she's not coming. It's just you and me."

Carrie cursed softly. "I can't believe she's done this to me again. I didn't plan this. I didn't know you'd be here. And—and I'm not desperate!" She scrambled over him, out into the aisle, then grabbed her bag from above her head, nearly knocking him unconscious in the process. "I want to get off!" Carrie called to the flight attendant.

The attendant hurried toward her. "Ma'am, you can't get off. We've already closed the doors."

"Then open them. I can't stay on this plane."

She patted Carrie on the shoulder. "Please take your seat, ma'am. We're starting to pull back from the gate."

Carrie hefted her bag up and tried to push past the fight attendant. "Listen, sister, I'm a travel agent, and if you don't let me off this plane, I'm never going to book your airline again!"

"And if you don't sit down and fasten your seatbelt," the attendant said in an even voice, "I'm going to have to call the pilot. Now, please, take your seat!"

"I think you better do as she says. Threatening a flight attendant is a federal offense." Carrie glanced down to see Dev still smiling at her. He patted the seat beside him. "I'll let you have the window seat."

Carrie scowled, then reluctantly crawled over his legs and sat down beside him. "I'm going to kill Susie. How could she do this to me again? Aren't you angry?"

Dev buckled his seatbelt and cinched it tight, then leaned back and closed his eyes. "Susie didn't do this, I did."

Carrie gasped. "What?"

He opened one eye and then the other. "I figured if I was going to talk to you, I needed to get you alone first. There were no sailboats handy, so I took the next best thing. You can't get away from me on a plane—unless you have a parachute. You don't have a parachute in that bag of yours, do you?"

"I don't want to talk to you," she said.

"Too bad. We've got a four-hour flight and we are going to straighten this whole mess out. I was hoping you'd come to see me again, but—"

"I called your office, but you weren't there."

Dev blinked in surprise. "I never got the message."

"That's because I didn't leave one."

"Well, then, you can see why I had to resort to—"

"Kidnapping?" she finished.

"Not even close. You have a ticket for this flight, and you got on board of your own free will. Nobody forced you."

"I thought I was going on vacation with Susie."

"You *are* going on vacation. With me."

Carrie jumped up from her seat, but the flight attendant gave her a warning glare, and she sat back down again. "I—I can't go on vacation with you!"

"And why not? We spent a lovely time together in the Keys. We make good traveling companions. You do like traveling with me, don't you, Carrie?"

She narrowed her eyes. "Oh, you're exactly the kind of man a woman would want to spend her vacation with," she shot back in a sarcastic tone. "You're arrogant and selfish and egotistical and—"

"Now there's the Carrie that I know and love," he said with a soft chuckle. "I knew I'd find her in there somewhere, if I just pushed."

Her heart lurched at his simple confession. *The Carrie he knew and loved?* Over the past week, she'd dreamed of him saying those words, admitting his feelings for her. He reached out and tried to grab her hand, but she pulled it away. "I forgot to add *manipulative* to the list of your attributes," she murmured weakly, her indignation slowly dissolving.

Dev shook his head. "Carrie, what are you so afraid of? My feelings are perfectly clear, but I don't have a clue as to how you feel. Tell me so I can sort this mess out."

She turned and stared out the window, watching as the plane taxied to the runway. What was she supposed to say? She didn't know what frightened her, or why she was so reluctant. Putting her feelings into words had only brought a mass of confusion and doubt. But she had to try. This was her chance to make things right with Dev. Maybe her last chance.

"I'm afraid because I don't know what I'm doing," she murmured. She looked at him and forced a wavering smile. "I've never been in love before. I'm afraid I'll make a mistake, and then you won't love me anymore."

"That's not going to happen," he said, his words so resolute that she could almost believe him.

"How can you be so sure? You don't know me, Dev. I've been living my whole life afraid of rejection. One offhand comment from you, and I'll start doubting myself again. I'll start doubting your…love. I don't know if I can be the kind of woman you want."

"I think that's my decision, don't you?"

"You don't know me, Dev! How can you love someone you don't know?"

"I know that Carrie Reynolds is not two different

people. Our vacation in the Keys was the first time in your life you got a chance to be the real you. You let go of your past and responsibilities and all your worries—and someone very special came out. That's you, Carrie. And so is that bedraggled woman who showed up at my door the other night. And the woman with the sunburned face. And the woman I made love to at the villa. They're all you, and I love them all.''

"How can you be sure?''

Dev shrugged and smiled. "I just know." He took her hand and pressed it to his heart. "I know it in here.''

Carrie could feel his heart beating, strong and sure, as certain as the words he'd said. Then she pressed her other hand to her own heart. Her pulse raced and jumped.

"Just where did you get the idea you're not allowed to be happy?'' he asked in a soft voice. "Have you spent so much time taking care of other people, you feel you don't deserve to have a good life? Maybe no one has ever told you that you should have the best. I'm telling you now. You deserve all the happiness the world can offer.''

The plane began to accelerate, and Carrie closed her eyes and clutched at the armrests with bloodless fingers. Everything was out of her control. She couldn't stop her love for Dev anymore than she could stop the plane from hurtling down the runway and rising into the sky.

She swallowed hard and her ears popped. Higher and higher they flew, the roar of the jet rumbling in her head. But then Dev silently laced his fingers through hers and kissed her wrist. Suddenly, all the fear evaporated from her mind and her body—fear of the future, of rejection, even of flying. In one single instant, she felt completely safe. Just from a simple kiss.

If his kiss could make her feel this way, what could a lifetime with Dev Riley accomplish? She did deserve to be happy! To be loved and cherished. He was offering her a real life, with passion and joy and excitement filling every day and night. And she'd been too afraid to reach out and grab it.

Carrie drew a deep breath and opened her eyes. All the very best things in life came at a risk, didn't they? But if she spent all her time protecting her heart, then she'd never be able to truly love anyone. And she wanted to love Dev Riley, so desperately. She wanted to give her heart to him completely.

The seat-belt bell sounded. She glanced over at Dev and found him staring at her. Everything he felt for her was mirrored in those green depths and in his warm smile. A wave of confidence washed over her, and she stood up. "Come with me," she said.

He stepped out of his seat. "Where are we going? We're on a plane."

"We need some privacy," she said as she moved out into the aisle. She pulled him toward the bathroom at the rear of the first-class compartment. To her relief, it was unoccupied. Carrie opened the door and stepped inside, then dragged him after her. The door clicked shut behind him.

Airplane bathrooms were too small even for one person, and she found herself pressed up against Dev's body. He grinned and wrapped his arms around her waist. "We're alone now. What did you want to say?"

"It's what I want *you* to say," Carrie replied. "Tell me. Tell me how you feel."

He bent down and pressed his forehead against hers, gazing into her eyes. "I love you, Carrie Reynolds. I'm not sure when I fell in love with you, but I know my feelings aren't going to go away. Not in this lifetime." He paused and brushed his lips against hers in a sweet, but fleeting kiss. "I don't care how long I have to wait. I'll wait forever for you if I have to. But I want you to know, I'll never hurt you, and if you—"

"And I love you," Carrie said. "I thought I loved you before I even knew you. But now I realize that wasn't really love. This is love—what I feel in my heart right now. This is real."

A slow grin curled his lips. "You do love me?"

Carrie nodded. "I don't know what took me so long to say that. To truly believe it. I was just so afraid, so confused." She shook her head. "When Susie sent me on vacation, she promised me I'd come back a whole new person. And when I did, I wasn't sure what to do. I didn't know how to deal with the new Carrie Reynolds or all the feelings that she was having for you."

"And now you do?"

She wrapped her arms around Dev's neck and pushed up on her toes to kiss him long and hard. "I want you in my bed, Dev Riley. Not just for a week, but for the rest of our lives. I want to wake up with you every morning and go to sleep with you every night."

Dev spanned her waist with his hands and pulled her up against him, laughing softly. "Just think. All of this because you ended up in the wrong bed."

"*You* ended up in the wrong bed," Carrie teased. "That bed was mine."

"Well, I want you in the right bed from now on. My bed."

"Our bed," she corrected.

"Our bed," he agreed. He kissed her again, and this time, Carrie surrendered completely to him.

She had wanted an adventure in her life—exotic travel, exciting new places, glamorous people. She had wanted to be more interesting, more sophisticated—the kind of woman a man like Dev could desire.

It wasn't until this very moment, here in this rest room high in the sky, that Carrie realized adventure wasn't just found in the world around her—on planes and boats, in foreign locales and luxury hotels. Adventure was found in her heart and deep in her soul. And in the overwhelming love she felt for Dev.

She pulled back and gazed up into his eyes—eyes that were filled with all the love he felt. Carrie tipped her head back and laughed. If she knew anything about Dev Riley, she knew the greatest adventure of her life was about to begin right now.

For my sister Karen Santa Maria, and our first-ever
horseback ride many moons ago at
the River Road Stable

WITH A STETSON AND A SMILE

Vicki Lewis Thompson

Dear Reader,

By now, it's no secret that I find cowboys...appealing. God bless 'em, these guys don't see the logic in wearing baggy jeans. I'm fascinated by men born to the saddle as well as city slickers who finally let the cowboy inside them come out to play. Quinn Monroe fits into the second category. He also fits into a pair of jeans like you wouldn't believe.

Maybe because I also started life as an Easterner, I relate to Quinn's culture shock when he makes the transition from Manhattan to Montana. I was ten when my family moved to Arizona, and I still remember the jolt of trading cozy landscapes for majestic vistas. But I acclimated fast, and now I feel hemmed in if I can't see at least fifty miles in all directions.

Fortunately, within that fifty-mile radius, I can always spot a goodly number of lean-hipped, broad-shouldered, square-jawed cowboys to serve as role models for the heroes in my books. Out here in Arizona a girl doesn't have to try very hard to locate a Stetson and a smile. And that works for me.

Enjoy!

Vicki Lewis Thompson

Vicki Lewis Thompson

1

A SNAKE was loose in the cab.

Quinn swerved around a horse-drawn carriage parked in front of Tavern on the Green, whipped over to the curb and slammed on the brakes. He was out of the door and halfway across the street before he knew it. After several deep breaths, he finally worked up the courage to edge toward the car and jerk open the back door. Then he crept around to the passenger side and quickly opened both curbside doors.

He hated snakes. Come to think of it, he wasn't fond of lizards, either. One of the things he liked best about Manhattan was the absence of reptiles. If he'd known his fare was carrying snakes in that shoe box he wouldn't have picked him up. But the guy hadn't announced he was making a donation to the Central Park Zoo until they were almost there.

Quinn figured he'd been set up. It was too much of a coincidence that on the very day he'd accepted the challenge of driving one of Murray's cabs he'd be transporting snakes. Murray was convinced Wall Street had made Quinn too soft to handle a day driving cab, and it would be just like Murray to stack the deck and guarantee he'd win the bet.

Once Quinn had found out about the snakes, he'd almost gotten in a wreck twice on the way to the zoo. At last he'd let the guy off at the zoo entrance and pulled away with a huge sigh of relief. Then he'd looked down to find beady eyes staring at him from under the front seat. An escapee.

"Taxi!"

Quinn didn't turn around. He wasn't taking anybody anywhere until he got that snake out. The woman would have to find another cab.

"Taxi!"

Quinn realized she was coming over and turned to fend her off. "Sorry, I'm not..." He forgot what else he'd planned to say as he stared. Ogled. Lusted. Murray, always politically incorrect, would call her a babe. Tucked into a white silk shirt and red velvet jeans, with a red Stetson perched on glossy brown curls, she certainly produced a politically incorrect response in Quinn.

She adjusted her load of packages, which caused her silk blouse to shift and reveal a bit of cleavage. "I must get to the airport immediately."

"Airport?" Quinn struggled with the sad news that this fantasy cowgirl was leaving town.

"JFK. I'm in a hurry." She started toward the cab.

Watching her walk in those tight jeans and high-heeled boots was a treat. He also had a thing for long, curly brown hair after seeing *Pretty Woman* at an impressionable age. Taking this lady to the airport would be the highlight of his day—if it weren't for the reptile problem.

Quinn hated choices like this. The snake or the lady. "Uh, I'd better warn you about something. There's a snake in the cab."

She swung around. "Don't tell me you're one of those guys who keeps his pet boa constrictor near him at all times."

"No. My last fare left a snake. That's why I have all the doors open. I was trying—"

"Poisonous?"

Oh, God. He hadn't even thought about that. "How can you tell?"

"Folding fangs." She freed one hand and folded two fingers into her palm. Then she flicked them out, curving them to look like fangs. "They do that. Did this snake do that?"

"No." And if it had he would have fainted.

"Then let's go. On the way I'll coax him out for you."

"Oh, that won't be necessary."

"You look a little pale. You're not afraid of snakes, are you?"

"Me? Afraid of snakes? Nah. Not me." Quinn couldn't believe she could be so cool about the idea of a snake in the cab. She hadn't even asked what size it was. "I'm actually worried about the poor snake. He must be scared to death."

"I'm sure he is. Look, I really have to go. If I miss my flight my sperm will spoil."

Quinn almost swallowed his tongue. "Excuse me?" His voice broke like a sixteen-year-old's.

She rearranged her bundles and lifted a small cooler, the kind that could hold a six-pack. "Horse sperm."

Finally it dawned on Quinn that she, too, was part of this elaborate practical joke. "Okay, okay. You guys had your fun. First the snakes and now the horse sperm, just to throw old Quinn a curve. Murray's creative, I'll give him that. I'll bet that cooler contains the beer you're going to share with Murray while you celebrate winning the bet."

She looked confused. "Who's Murray?"

"Let me refresh your memory." He folded his arms and rocked on his heels. Now that he'd figured out what was going on he felt much better. "Murray's the guy you're in cahoots with, the one who owns the cab company, the guy who grew up next door to me in the Bronx, the guy who until today was my best friend, the guy I'm going to strangle once this shift is over."

"I don't know any Murray."

"Oh, sure. What did you two do, follow me from the zoo? You've probably been following me ever since I picked up the guy with the snakes, who was also a plant. Am I getting warm?" He smiled. Yes, he was in control of the situation now.

She stared at him and shook her head. "You're a crazy man, and I probably shouldn't trust myself to a crazy man. But the thing is, I always have trouble getting a cab in this city. Now that I've captured one, I'm not letting it go, even if it is driven by a guy who's missing a few rails from his corral. I have horse sperm that must get to Montana today, so I'm going to ask you again, very nicely, if we can get into your little cab and drive to that big place outside of town where they keep all the airplanes. Can you do that for me?"

Quinn sighed. "Murray sure knows how to pick 'em. You're very good. Okay, kiddo. If you can stand a ride with a snake, I can stand it." He gestured toward the cab. "After you, ma'am."

"Thank goodness." She walked forward, put her packages in the back seat and closed the door. Then she climbed in the front.

Quinn closed the street-side back door and paused before he got in the cab. He really didn't want to climb in there with that snake, but he didn't want Murray to get the upper hand, either. Besides, if Murray was behind all this, the snake was harmless. And maybe it had already slithered out. He rested his hands on the roof of the cab and leaned down to peer inside. "It's customary for the fare to sit in the back."

"I've never liked that custom," she said. "It seems downright unfriendly. Out west we—"

"Oh, yeah. That's right. You're from the wild and woolly west. Central Park West, most likely."

"Listen, could you continue weaving your fantasies while we drive? I'm running out of time to chat."

Quinn surveyed the floor in the front. "Did you, uh, notice the snake by any chance?"

"No, but if I sit up here I can protect you better."

That did it. Damned if he'd let this woman insinuate that he was a wuss. He slid into the seat with all the confidence he could muster. "A little snake doesn't bother me. I just wouldn't want you to be startled."

"I've faced timber rattlers with bodies as thick as your forearm."

Quinn laughed as he started the car. "That's a good line. Next you'll be telling me about the grizzly bear who lives in the hills up above your ranch."

"Actually there are two."

"Oh, I'll bet there are." Quinn pulled into traffic, noticing as he did that she filled the cab with a nice fragrance. "So what name are you going by for this caper?"

"The name I always go by. My own. Jo Fletcher."

"Short for Josephine?" Quinn didn't believe for a minute that was her name, but he decided to play along and see what sort of whopper she and Murray had dreamed up. It also took his mind off the snake.

"Well, yes. After my great-aunt Josephine. Which is why she left me the ranch, I guess. Well, that and the fact I'm the only member of the family who knows diddly about horses."

"You and Murray must have stayed up nights concocting this story. I'm impressed. Ticked off, but impressed. The guy will do anything to win a bet.''

''I don't know anybody named Murray and I certainly don't know anything about a bet.''

Quinn gave her a superior smile. ''Right.''

She cocked her head and looked at him strangely. ''Did anybody ever tell you that you look exactly like Brian Hastings, the movie star? Even the smile.''

''Only a couple of million people.''

''Ah. So you get that a lot.''

''Yeah. I'm pretty sick of it, which is probably why Murray asked you to bring it up, just to needle me.''

''I don't know Murray. But if you're sensitive about the Brian Hastings thing, we can drop the subject. It's just that you really do look like him.''

He swerved around a delivery van. The job took reflexes he hadn't used in years, and he liked knowing they were still there. ''But I'm taller than Hastings. You can't tell that on the screen because they use camera angles to make him look tall, and he stands on a box if he has a tall costar.''

''I'd heard that he was on the short side. So what? People are too hung up on how tall a guy is. Being taller doesn't make you a better man.''

''I didn't say that.''

''You sort of did, Quinn.''

''Aha!'' He thought he had her this time. His name had popped right out of that luscious red mouth of hers. ''How do you explain the fact that you know my name? Wiggle out of that little slip, if you can.'' He liked the mental picture of Jo wiggling. At least Murray had provided a beautiful woman as part of the joke. Quinn wondered if she was dating anybody.

''You told me your name.''

"Did not."

"Did, too. You said, 'just trying to throw old Quinn a curve.'"

"Oh."

"Anyway, I loved Brian Hastings in *The Drifter*. Did you see that?"

"Nope. I pretty much don't go to his movies. I pretty much boycott them, as a matter of fact." Two kids in purple hair jaywalked in front of him, and he gave them the horn. Except for the box of snakes, he'd had fun today. More fun than he'd been having recently planning investment strategies, to be honest.

"But why don't you go to Hastings' movies?" Jo asked. "He's a good actor, and now he's into directing. I think he's very talented."

Quinn recognized that tone of adulation. "Meaning you think he's sexy."

"Well, yes, I do. What, are you jealous because women find him sexy? Is that why you don't go to his movies?"

"No, I'm not jealous." It was more as if the guy had usurped his identity.

"Then why boycott his movies?"

"Think about it. I show up at a Brian Hastings movie looking like Brian Hastings. I've had women throw themselves into my arms, rip off pieces of my clothing, follow me for blocks."

"Poor baby."

"You think it would be fun, don't you?" He pulled over to let a fire engine roar past, siren screaming. "It's not fun. And besides that, they're not after me, Quinn Monroe, investment banker. They're after Brian Hastings, Hollywood star. So it means nothing."

"Investment banker? You must not be very good at it if you have to drive cab on the side."

Quinn glanced at her. She acted as if she had no idea he'd agreed to drive cab for one day on a dare. She just sat there gazing at him with an innocent look in those big brown eyes that would be hard to fake. For the first time he wondered if she was legit. "Either you're an incredible actress or you're telling the truth about this ranch in Montana."

"I can't act my way out of a paper bag."

"Would you be willing to show me your driver's license?"

"No, I would not."

He nodded, smiling. "Just as I thought. Your driver's license isn't from Montana, is it? I'll bet your name isn't even Josephine Fletcher."

"All right! I'll show you the damned license." She unzipped her purse and pulled out her wallet. "But you have to promise not to laugh at my picture. I look like an escaped convict." She flipped the wallet open and held it up.

He stopped at a red light and glanced at the license. Josephine Fletcher stared at him from the picture, unsmiling, grim, even, but still beautiful. The license had been issued by the Montana Department of Transportation.

Jo WATCHED amazement spread over Quinn's face as he glanced from her to the license and back again. He really was a cutie, with his laser-blue eyes and movie-star looks. She flipped the wallet closed and stuffed it in her purse. "Is that proof enough, or would you like to see my maxed-out Visa card, too?"

"If you're really Jo Fletcher, then I guess you have horse sperm in that cooler."

"Of course I do! Do you think I'd make up a thing like that?"

"If you were part of Murray's big plan, you would."

"But I'm not." They crossed the Queensboro Bridge, linking Manhattan with Long Island, and Jo glanced at the skyline. She might never fly here again, which was why she'd stocked up on extra souvenirs for Emmy Lou. No use crying over it now, though. She turned to Quinn. "Since I've proven I'm not part of some intricate plot, would you kindly tell me who this Murray person is?"

"My best friend since the second grade and the owner of a fleet of cabs. He's convinced I've turned into a stuffed shirt who couldn't handle a day in one of his cabs, so finally I bet him I could. When the guy showed up with a shoe box full of snakes I wondered if Murray had somehow engineered that. A cooler full of horse sperm was so outrageous I decided you were also in on the campaign to rattle me and make me lose the bet."

"I see." Jo had caught a glimpse of the little snake twice. It was just a harmless garter snake, but she'd suspected from the beginning of this adventure that snakes sent Quinn into a panic. She'd decided to try to catch the snake with a minimum of fuss so he wouldn't wreck the cab. Then she'd suggest they let it go in one of the open fields near the airport.

"Now it's your turn," Quinn said. "What's with the horse sperm?"

"It belongs to my friend Cassie's stallion, Sir Lust-a-Lot. Cassie was my college roommate, and I worked at her family's stable in upstate New York after graduation. Then I inherited the ranch, and we established a spring tradition—I take the red-eye to New York, shop all morning, meet Cassie for lunch at Tavern on the Green and leave with the sperm."

"Are you telling me you don't have horse sperm in Montana?"

"Sure, we do, but this is a connection with Cassie, and besides, Sir Lust-a-Lot has extremely viable sperm. Good little swimmers. My mares get pregnant like *that*." She snapped her fingers for emphasis, then glimpsed the snake easing out from under her seat. She kept an eye on it and said nothing.

"Is that what you raise on your ranch? Horses?"

"No. We try to raise cattle." Jo sighed as she was reminded of her heavy debt load, most of it accumulated since she'd inherited the Bar None. She might be good with horses, but she was financially challenged. She should have followed Josephine's advice and taken more accounting courses, but they'd given her a migraine, and she'd really had no idea Josephine would will her the ranch. "We lost quite a chunk of the herd this past winter. I'm already behind on my payments to the bank, so I'm not sure what the future holds."

"I guess it's tough to be a small ranching operation these days."

"It is tough. And when the ranch is such a little gem and has been entrusted into your care by your favorite great-aunt, you'd do almost anything to keep it going." She glanced at him. "I'm sorry you're not Brian Hastings. One of his advance men came by the ranch last fall and said they were looking for a location for his next film. If you were Brian Hastings, I'd fall to my knees and beg you to use the ranch in your movie."

He smiled at her. "And if I were Brian Hastings, I would use your ranch in my next movie."

"Thanks." She really liked that smile of his. Actually she thought it was sexier than Brian's, but she probably shouldn't say so. They were only going to be sharing a cab ride, after all. No point in starting anything, especially with a guy whose roots were in New York City. Despite her money problems, she'd discovered a kinship with Montana. Even losing the ranch might not force her to leave. But she intended to find a way to keep the Bar None. Somehow.

"I take it you haven't heard any more from the Hastings organization?"

"Nope. But I shamelessly told the bank that the movie deal was a sure thing. It's kept them off my back temporarily, but if Brian Hastings never shows, the bank will start demanding money again."

"I don't know if it's a good idea to stake everything on the whim of a movie star," Quinn said.

"Probably not." Jo watched the snake ease out a little more and poised herself to lean down and snatch it. To distract Quinn from what she was doing, she kept talking. "Considering the shaky condition of my finances I shouldn't have made the sperm run this year, but Cassie's decided to geld Sir Lust-a-Lot this spring, so this is my last chance to breed my mares to him, unless we get into freezing sperm, which is too complicated and expensive for me."

"Gelding. Is that where they cut off—"

"Let's just say he'll lose the ability to be a family man."

"Why would she do that?"

"Because he's a pain in the butt and useless as a saddle horse. Gelding should mellow him out. I don't blame her. She's the one who has to put up with his testosterone fits, not me."

"So you're carrying Sir Lust-a-Lot's last stand?"

Jo laughed. "I guess you could say that. The sperm's packed in dry ice, and it's always stayed fresh for the plane flight home, but I don't want to miss that plane and risk having it go bad.''

Quinn stepped on the gas. ''Then let's make sure you don't.'' He started weaving through traffic like a man on a mission.

Jo smiled. Some men took castration of male animals personally. Apparently Quinn was one of those who did. Maybe that was a good thing, because as long as he was thinking about Sir Lust-a-Lot's fate he might forget about the snake, which was almost within her reach. ''So you're really an investment banker?'' She leaned slowly down, straining slightly against the seat belt.

''Yeah, I really am.''

She made a grab for the snake and missed. ''Damn!''

''Sorry I'm not something more exciting, like a movie star.''

''It's not that.'' She tossed her hat in the back seat and unbuckled her seat belt as the snake moved quickly to Quinn's side of the car. ''Slow the car, get in the right-hand lane and hold still.''

''Oh, God. The snake.'' Quinn eased his foot off the gas.

''Yep. He's just a little guy, which makes him harder to catch.'' She got to her knees on the floor of the passenger side and reached toward Quinn's ankle.

''He's down there? Right by my foot?''

''Don't be afraid. He won't hurt you.''

''I'm not afraid, dammit! I'm just...'' He paused and made a strangled sound. ''What's that?''

''Hold still. He's trying to climb up your leg.''

''Up my *leg?* What for?''

''Maybe it's a girl snake, and she's curious.'' Jo clamped an arm around Quinn's thigh, noting he had great muscles, and reached under his pants leg.

"Oh, my God. What's happening?"

"Don't look down here! Watch where you're going, Quinn!"

"Holy sh—" Quinn's voice was drowned out by the loud thunk of metal against metal.

2

JO CLUTCHED Quinn's thigh to keep from being thrown against the dashboard as the cab lurched from the impact. The jolt dislodged the small snake, and she grabbed it behind its head. "Got him!"

"Jo!" Gasping, he clutched her shoulder. "God, I'm sorry. Are you okay?"

"I think so." She released his thigh and pushed herself upright. "See?" She dangled the snake in front of him. "Real small."

Quinn didn't look so good. In fact, he was breathing hard and looked ready to pass out.

"Quinn, are you hurt?"

"No." He kept staring at the snake. When someone started knocking on his window, he reached around and rolled it down without taking his eyes off the snake.

A man peered into the cab. "We got a problem here, buddy. You want to call the police?"

"Uh, sure." Quinn didn't move.

Jo figured if she didn't get the snake out of the cab he would stay frozen in that position forever. She looked around and discovered they weren't far from JFK. The vacant lot beside the expressway would have to do. She glanced at the man looking in the window. "Sir, I'm going to take this snake over to that field. In the meantime, Quinn, you can call the police and also call me another cab."

Quinn nodded, but he didn't take his attention off the wiggling snake in her hand.

Keeping a firm hold on it, Jo climbed onto the seat and opened the passenger door. As she got out she called to Quinn over her shoulder. ''Move my stuff over to the other cab while I'm gone, okay? I don't want to miss that plane!''

She climbed the knee-high metal railing beside the road and sidestepped down an embankment. ''After all this I want to get you far enough away from the road that you won't get run over,'' she said to the snake. ''This looks like a good field. There ought to be plenty of bugs, and when you're bigger you might even find a mouse or two.''

After hiking about thirty yards through clumps of wild grass, she slowly lowered the snake to the ground. ''There you go. Stay away from the road. Have a good life.''

The snake darted away without so much as a thank-you. But Jo felt immensely better as she walked toward the road. Holding the snake had been like a moment from home, where she'd learned to appreciate all creatures. She'd grown up in a city—her father and stepmother still lived in Chicago—but cities were no longer home to her. Maybe they hadn't been for a long time. Her summers with Aunt Josephine at the Bar None had probably ruined her for city life by the time she was ten.

When she reached the expressway, the police and a second cab had arrived on the scene. Quinn was standing beside the damaged cab waving his arms and looking upset. Even upset he looked damned good—broad shoulders, lean hips. He really was attractive, she thought. Too bad he lived in New York. She climbed the railing and walked to the group.

The man whose car Quinn had hit glanced at her suspiciously before turning to the police officer. ''There was something kinky going on in that vehicle, I tell you. I was riding along next to them, and they were going really slow, so I got curious and went slow. Then they started swerving all over the road, and then she got down and put her face in his lap, if you get my meaning.''

"She was trying to get a snake out of my pants!" Quinn bellowed.

The man glanced at the officer. "So who drives to the airport with a snake in his pants?"

"Nobody!" Quinn's jaw worked. "I'm sure my friend Murray is behind this snake thing. He probably paid the guy with the snakes."

The officer cleared his throat and gazed at Jo. "Would you like to tell us your version?"

She glanced at her watch and gauged the distance to the airport. "I would love to, but I'm warning you that unless I catch my plane, my sperm will spoil."

Quinn groaned.

Jo realized she should have phrased the sentence differently as soon as it left her mouth. "I was referring to horse sperm, Officer, which I am transporting, with all the necessary health department papers, to Montana. Quinn's previous passenger left a snake in his cab, and I was indeed trying to catch it when the incident occurred. I just released the little fellow in that field over there."

Quinn stepped forward. "Look, she really had nothing to do with the accident. I'll vouch for that. The cab company will assume all liability for this." He turned to the owner of the other car. "The sperm she's carrying is from a stallion that's being castrated, maybe right this minute. She has to get on that plane to Montana so the poor horse can have one last shot at immortality, okay?"

The man's belligerent expression evaporated. "Oh, well, in that case..." He turned to the officer. "Never mind the kinky thing. Just a routine fender bender. I'm sure the cab company will handle everything. This poor slob should be fired, though.''

"I'm sure I will be," Quinn said.

"So I'm free to go?" Jo asked.

"After I get some basic information," the officer said.

Jo gave him what he needed and turned to Quinn. "I guess this means you lose your bet with Murray."

"Afraid so. Jo, I'm sorry about this. It's just that—"

"You're petrified of snakes."

He flashed her a little-boy grin. "Yep."

"There are worse flaws," Jo said. "Listen, I gotta go. Is all my stuff in the other cab?"

"Bill transferred it as soon as he pulled up. I think he consolidated a few things so it'd be easier to carry up to the gate."

"That was nice of him."

Quinn stuck out his hand. "Good luck with the ranch."

"Thanks." She liked the feel of his hand—warm, strong, secure. "Good luck with Murray." With a smile she released his hand and hurried to the waiting cab.

Approximately thirty-five minutes later, as she was checking into the gate, she realized that the cooler of horse sperm was nowhere to be seen.

QUINN didn't find the cooler of horse sperm on the floor of the back seat until the tow truck arrived. Just before the cab was winched on the flatbed, Quinn put in a quick call to Bill and had him pick him up.

Bill grinned as Quinn climbed into the cab. "You're lucky you caught me. I was next in line for a fare at the airport."

"You're lucky I caught you, too." Quinn held up the cooler. "You forgot to transfer this. It belongs to Jo, the woman you just took to the airport. We have to try and catch her before she boards that plane.''

Bill gunned the engine and zipped into a break in traffic. ''I thought that was your lunch, man!''

''It's sperm from a stallion that is probably being castrated even as we speak.''

''Get outta here!''

''I know it sounds crazy, but she came to New York to pick this up and take it back so she can give it to her mares in Montana.''

Bill shook his head. ''Me, I don't believe in those methods. I know a guy who donated to a sperm bank. Now what fun is that?''

''Don't know. Never tried it.''

''Me, neither.'' Bill glanced at Quinn. ''How do you figure they do it with stallions?''

Quinn had been wondering the same thing ever since Jo had convinced him she was really transporting horse sperm. ''Let's not even go there. Listen, drop me at the airline where you let her off.''

''Good luck, but I really don't think you can make it. She was running behind. She thanked me for getting her packages all organized, and I guess she thought the cooler was in one of the bags.''

''Yeah, well, it's been a crazy day.''

''No kidding. Everybody knows about your little brush with the law, by the way. Murray's busting a gut laughing.''

''I knew it! I knew he was behind that snake thing.''

''No, he wasn't, swear to God! He said he couldn't have planned a better day for you if he'd tried.'' Bill maneuvered next to the curb. ''Should I wait?''

''Nope.''

''Yeah, but if you don't catch her, what are you gonna do? You can't follow her to Montana.''

Quinn stared at Bill as he considered the idea for the first time. He hadn't planned his next step if he missed the plane, but he'd been mostly to blame for this whole mess, and Jo would be bitterly disappointed to lose Sir Lust-a-Lot's sperm on top of all her financial problems. He didn't like to think about her being bitterly disappointed, especially if it was his doing. And it wasn't as if he couldn't get away from the office for a few days.... ''Sure, I can,'' he said.

DRIVING a back road miles from Bozeman, Quinn felt as small as a flea on the back of a woolly mammoth. The headlights of his rental car cast the only light for miles around, not counting the moon and stars overhead. The mountains loomed threateningly around him, pitch-black except for a pale topping of moonlit snow. There was so much *space* in Montana. If his rental car broke down, he could imagine waiting for days before another vehicle came down this two-lane highway.

Belatedly he wished he'd brought food and water, a sleeping bag, a...a *rifle*. He'd never shot a gun in his life, but this was the sort of country that seemed to require firearms. And it was Jo's country. His estimation of her grit and determination rose with every bend in the increasingly lonely road.

He hoped to God he was on the right lonely road. While he'd waited for his flight he'd asked his secretary to call every chamber of commerce in Montana until she found somebody who recognized the name Bar None. Fortunately she'd hit pay dirt within the first half hour of phoning. Unfortunately it was located near a town named Ugly Bug, on the banks of Ugly Bug Creek. After snakes and lizards, Quinn listed bugs as his third least favorite creature.

If he was on the right road he might miss the turnoff to the ranch, but at least he'd eventually get to Ugly Bug. If he was on the wrong road he'd probably drive until he ran out of gas, and then a bear would eat him.

He'd always been fascinated with the West, but he realized that his picture of it had been highly romanticized. Cowboys around a campfire, the comradery of a roundup, card games in the local saloon. His image of the West had been cozy, quaint and not nearly big enough. This country was enormous.

He rounded another bend and saw a spark of light nestled in a valley. Checking his odometer, he decided it could be coming from the Bar None. Maybe he'd defied the odds and found the place. Maybe they wouldn't find his bleached bones lying beside a dried-up watering hole.

A few more bends in the road, and sure enough, on his right stood a big wooden gate. Two upright poles supported a crossbeam, and from that dangled a sign. Quinn couldn't read it in the dark, but he'd bet it said Bar None.

He shone his car's headlights on the gate and got out to open it. The thing was wired together instead of padlocked, which was fortunate for him. The barbed wire fence on either side of the gate wasn't something he wanted to tangle with. He drove through and went back to hook the gate closed again.

Driving slowly down the dirt road toward the cluster of lights he assumed was the ranch, he noticed dark shapes scattered across the moonlit landscape. Either cows or bears, he concluded. He remembered Jo mentioning timber rattlers with bodies as thick as his forearm, and he shuddered. With luck, none of those would be hanging around the front porch of her house tonight.

Finally he arrived at a cluster of buildings and corrals. With his limited knowledge, he figured the two-story white clapboard one was the main house, the rust-colored structure was a barn and the third, also rust-colored, was probably a bunkhouse. Light spilled from the ranch-house windows onto the front porch with its wide swing and two rocking chairs.

The whole arrangement was right out of a Brian Hastings movie. Cowboys were making a comeback these days, and Hastings was cashing in on the new craze. Quinn hoped to hell Hastings would contract with Jo for the use of her ranch. Any woman who could keep her cool under fire the way Jo had today deserved a break.

Taking the cooler from the passenger seat, Quinn got out and closed the car door. A plump woman of about forty opened the door and peered out. Such a thing would never happen in the city, Quinn thought, remembering his triple-locked apartment door.

He smiled at the woman. "Hello, I'm—"

"Glory, hallelujah." The woman gazed at him as if she were witnessing the second coming.

Quinn figured she must have recognized the cooler he carried, but even so he was a little taken aback at the woman's worshipful expression. "Hey, glad to be of service. It's the least I could do, under the circumstances."

"You know about our circumstances?"

"Some of it. Listen, is Jo around? I'm—"

"I know who you are." The woman's grin put big dimples in both cheeks. "And I'm tickled spitless to see you. We'd about given up hope. Come in, come in. I'm Emmy Lou, the housekeeper. Have you eaten? I can warm up the leftover chicken."

It was a most gratifying welcome. Quinn decided he'd done the right thing. "Chicken sounds wonderful." He followed the woman into a small entry hall. "I figured Jo would be worried. I came as soon as I could."

"Jo has been worried, all right. Poor woman takes her responsibilities very seriously, although between you and me, I think she needs someone to give her good financial advice. Maybe you could recommend someone. But the main thing is, you're here. I wasn't sure you'd show up."

"Well, a lot is at stake. And a stud deserves to have his last shot count."

"Last shot?" Emmy Lou's smile was coy as she looked him up and down. "I hardly think so."

"Well, that's what Jo said this would be."

"How rude of her!" She peered at him. "When did you discuss this with Jo?"

"In New York." Quinn was becoming a little confused by the conversation.

"That little dickens. I need to have a talk with that girl. She may be getting a little too big for her britches."

Quinn thought Jo fit her britches just fine.

"Anyway, you're here now." Emmy Lou led him into a country kitchen filled with the scent of chicken and baked apples.

Quinn's mouth watered.

"Sit yourself down and take a load off," the woman said. "I'll run and fetch Jo. She's upstairs. She'll be *so* glad to see you."

"Okay." Quinn felt extremely pleased with himself. Maybe this sperm-delivery trip would improve his image after his sorry performance with the snake this afternoon. And if Jo truly needed financial advice, maybe he could help her there, too. He set the cooler on the floor beside his chair. After Jo got over the shock of seeing him, he'd bring it out as a special surprise. He wondered how she'd react. Maybe she'd hug him in gratitude. That was a nice prospect.

Emmy Lou left the kitchen and walked down the hall. "Jo!" she called up the stairs. "You'll never guess who's here!"

Quinn smiled with pleasure. Despite the snake, he must have made a decent impression on Jo if she'd told her housekeeper all about him. He'd planned to head straight back for New York, but with this kind of welcome he might be convinced to stay a little longer.

Jo CAME to the head of the stairs. "Who?"

Grinning like a politician at a barbecue, Emmy Lou motioned her down, and Jo descended the stairs, eyebrows lifted.

When Jo was two steps away, Emmy Lou leaned forward and delivered her news in a stage whisper. *"Brian Hastings."*

"You're kidding." Jo's heart rate kicked up a notch.

"Nope. Sitting right in my kitchen."

Technically it was Jo's kitchen, but she didn't correct Emmy Lou. If possession was nine-tenths of the law, Emmy Lou owned the kitchen. "He just showed up at the door? Nobody's with him?"

"He probably enjoys getting off by himself once in a while, away from all those screaming women. Why, I decided I wouldn't even ask him for a button off his shirt. At least not yet."

"Go slow on the button thing." Jo glanced toward the kitchen, and her chest tightened. As much as she'd prayed for this moment, she realized she'd never negotiated a movie contract. It probably wasn't a job for someone with math anxiety, either. She'd have to concentrate really hard and make sure she counted the zeros, although she had no idea how many there should be when someone wanted to rent your ranch. Lots, she hoped.

"It's really going to happen, Jo." Emmy Lou's voice trembled with excitement. "The Bar None will rocket to stardom, and we'll be able to pay the bank. Not to mention having Brian Hastings around for weeks. Do you think I should ask him for a part in the movie yet?"

"No!" Jo whispered. "And don't you ask about that darned button, either! This might still be a preliminary visit. We might have made the shortlist or something." She ran her fingers through her hair and glanced at the torn jeans and old T-shirt she wore. She could either meet a famous movie star looking like this or go upstairs and change, which would keep a famous movie star waiting. She decided to go with the outfit she had on and headed for the kitchen. A man used to starlets probably wouldn't give an ordinary woman a second look no matter what she had on.

She paused outside the kitchen door and took a deep breath. He was only a man, she reminded herself. But herself wouldn't listen. Her heart was leaping like a rodeo bronc at the idea of coming face-to-face with the very person commonly referred to as the sexiest man alive. And she couldn't blow this interview. The future of her ranch might depend on the impression she made in the next minute.

Closing her eyes, she counted to ten. Then she walked into the room.

Quinn Monroe smiled at her. "Surprise."

"Damn! It's you!"

His smile faded.

"Josephine Sarah Fletcher!" Emmy Lou said. "Is that any way to treat Mr. Hastings? Apologize this instant!"

"I'm sorry," Jo said. "In more ways than one. Emmy Lou, this isn't Brian Hastings."

"What do you mean, he isn't Brian Hastings? You're talking to a woman who saw *The Drifter* fourteen times! And *this*—" she gestured dramatically toward Quinn "—is Brian Hastings."

Quinn winced. "As a matter of fact—"

"I would know this man anywhere." Emmy Lou marched over to Quinn and took his face firmly in her hand. She lifted his chin. "Look at those sensuous lips." She brought his chin down again. "Look into those intense blue eyes. And the profile!" She whipped Quinn's head abruptly to one side. "There! Are you trying to tell me that's not the profile of Brian Hastings, love god?"

Jo sighed. "That's the profile of Quinn Monroe, investment banker. I couldn't say whether he's a love god or not."

"Only on alternate Thursdays," Quinn said.

Emmy Lou frowned and turned his head until she could look into his eyes. She fluffed his hair and stared at him some more. "Smile for me."

"I can't. You're digging your thumb into my cheek."

Emmy Lou released him. "Now smile."

Quinn obliged.

"You see? It's the Brian Hastings I'm-too-sexy-for-my-shirt smile! Only in real life it's even better." She patted him on the cheek. "You should make more public appearances. You look good close up. Not all actors do."

While Emmy Lou was talking, Jo's brain began working overtime. She was fascinated with the housekeeper's conviction that Quinn had to be Brian Hastings, despite Jo and Quinn denying it. Fascinated and intrigued. She might have been convinced herself if she hadn't seen him driving a cab, but logic had told her that Brian Hastings wouldn't get his kicks driving a cab in New York City.

"I'm here to deliver the sperm," Quinn said.

Emmy Lou gasped. "Young man, I know Hollywood's filled with sin and debauchery, but you're in Montana now, and we don't talk like that out here. You work up to that—a few dates, a few stolen kisses, a little fondling. And the term is *making love,* not *delivering sperm.*"

"You brought it?" Jo asked. Now that was something to be happy about.

Quinn reached beside his chair and lifted the cooler onto the table. "I figured you might still be able to salvage it if I caught the next flight to Bozeman. So I just came. On the spur of the moment."

"That's really...amazing. Thank you, Quinn. Let me stick it in the refrigerator." Jo's disappointment that Brian Hastings wasn't here to rent her ranch dimmed as she realized what a sacrifice Quinn had made. After putting the cooler inside the refrigerator she turned to Emmy Lou. "Remember the cabdriver who was afraid of snakes? This is him. I just forgot to tell you he looks like Brian Hastings."

Emmy Lou crossed her arms and surveyed Quinn. "Maybe Brian Hastings went undercover in New York City in order to get away from the pressures of making movies."

Jo shook her head. "Give it up, Em. He's not Brian Hastings, and all the wishing in the world won't make it so. But he's done me a very big favor, and I appreciate it." She glanced at him nervously as she thought about what a plane ticket had probably cost him. "I need to reimburse you for your ticket."

"No, you don't. I'm the one who made you lose the sperm."

''True. Then at least let us put you up for the night.''

''That would be great. And I'm...sort of hungry.'' He glanced at Emmy Lou. ''Does the offer of chicken still stand even if I'm not Brian Hastings?''

''Of course! I feed any poor hungry soul who comes through that kitchen door, no matter who it is.''

''Thanks, I think.''

''But I still can't believe you're—what was the name?''

''Quinn Monroe.''

''Any proof?''

''As a matter of fact, I have the chauffeur's license I had to get before I could drive one of Murray's cabs.'' Quinn reached in his back pocket and pulled out his wallet. Then he glanced at Jo. ''But you have to promise not to laugh. The picture makes me look like an escaped convict.''

''I'll bet it makes you look like Brian Hastings.'' Emmy Lou studied the license for a long time. Finally she handed it back to Quinn. ''Okay, so you're not him, but you could pass for him any day of the week.''

''Yeah, I know that.''

Emmy Lou stood and headed for the refrigerator. ''Come to think about it, I read that Brian Hastings is a vegetarian. Are you a vegetarian, too?''

''Nope. I'd be willing to bet there is almost nothing about me that is the same as Brian Hastings.''

Emmy Lou shook her head. ''What a shame.''

''Now, Emmy Lou,'' Jo said. ''You sound as if Brian Hastings sets the standard for all men. That's a little extreme.''

Emmy Lou pulled some containers from the refrigerator. ''Not for me.''

Jo sat at the table and smiled at Quinn. ''You'll have to excuse her. She's been a real fan for ten years.''

3

JO DECIDED to wait until Quinn had some of Emmy Lou's home cooking in his stomach before she hit him with her proposition. Still, she could do some preliminary spadework. "Is there a problem with you being away from your office for another day or so?" she asked.

"Not a huge problem. My secretary knows where I am. I thought I'd call her in the morning and see if anything major is going on I need to deal with."

"What time is your flight?"

He hesitated. "I didn't book a return because I didn't know exactly how long it would take me to find you. I can take care of it in the morning."

Excitement built within her. "Have you ever been to Montana?"

"Nope. First trip."

"Then as long as you've come all this way, how about staying for a few days? Spring is a great time of year in this country. You arrived in the dark, so I'm sure you didn't get the full impact. We have wildflowers galore, and all the trees are greening up. It's beautiful."

He looked interested, but cautious. "I'd hate to inconvenience you."

"No problem!" Jo liked her plan more and more. It might save the ranch and give her more time with this guy, and that was a good thing. Physically he appealed to her, but more than that she was charmed by his humanness. He might be afraid of snakes, but he'd traveled all the way to Montana to return a cooler of horse sperm. Although she wasn't bold enough to say so, Quinn interested her far more than the macho image projected by Brian Hastings.

Emmy Lou turned from the stove.

"Betsy and Clarise are fixing to foal any day now."

"The miracle of birth," Jo said. "How many Wall Street investment bankers have seen a mare bring a foal into the world?"

"Certainly not this investment banker," Quinn said.

"You just said he was afraid of snakes," Emmy Lou pointed out. "They're starting to come out now. It's snakes and more snakes this time of year."

Jo smiled at Quinn, who was looking doubtful at the mention of snakes. "Will you excuse me a minute?" She walked to the stove, put her arm around Emmy Lou and leaned down to murmur in her ear. "Will you work with me here? I have a stupendous idea. And besides, I think he's very cute."

"I can see that he's cute," Emmy Lou said under her breath, "but you need a greenhorn like him around like you need an alligator in the stock tank."

"Maybe I should go back to New York tomorrow, after all," Quinn said.

"Just taste Emmy Lou's cooking first," Jo said. "And then tell me if you wouldn't like to stay a few extra days. One bite of her chicken, and I promise she'll have you moaning in ecstasy."

QUINN COULD THINK of another scenario that would have him moaning in ecstasy. Not that Emmy Lou's cooking wasn't melt-in-his-mouth perfect, especially considering how hungry he was by the time he bit into her fried chicken, but it wasn't the housekeeper's skills at the stove that had him considering a stay on the ranch.

Of course there were the snakes to consider, and he still worried about how the town of Ugly Bug got its name. Maybe he could just stay inside a lot. Jo awakened basic urges in him, and basic urges were best investigated inside, anyway. He'd started fantasizing what it would be like to hold her in his arms, kiss those cherry red lips, touch her soft skin. But her physical attributes weren't the only draw. He was also a sucker for a woman in distress.

At first he'd only been concerned with getting the horse sperm to her on time, but now that he'd seen the ranch, he couldn't help thinking what a shame it would be for her to lose it. He didn't know a damn thing about ranching, but he knew a fair amount about money management. If he stayed a few days he might be able to suggest some things that would get Jo out of the bind she was in.

He doubted that she'd accept a personal loan, and he didn't have enough liquid assets to make that sort of gesture, anyway. But he might be able to arrange a new bank loan with one of his contacts or find her some investors. He mainly wanted to loosen the grip of this local guy and set her on a better course than the one that seemed to be leading her into trouble.

But he'd have to hang around a while and win her trust. The minute he'd seen her walk through the kitchen door, no matter how disappointing her reaction had been, he'd been inclined to do just that.

While he ate, he answered Emmy Lou's questions about New York. She'd never been there and had a fixation on the place, apparently. She proudly trotted out all the souvenirs Jo had brought her over the years, and Quinn made a mental note to send her something special when he got back to the city.

Finally he finished off the chicken and potato salad and pushed away his plate with a sigh of contentment. "That was delicious. Thanks."

Apparently his knowledge of New York and his appreciation for her cooking had warmed up the housekeeper considerably. "You have to have a piece of apple pie to top it off," she said.

He grinned at her. "Twist my arm, Emmy Lou."

She flushed and put a hand over her heart. "Land sakes, but you look like Brian Hastings when you do that. Makes my heart go pitty-pat."

"Maybe it'll also make you serve him some of your famous pie," Jo said.

Quinn had noticed that Jo was being terrifically friendly and obliging. He'd love to think it was his manly charm causing her to be so nice, but he also had the feeling she might be fattening him up for the kill. He just wasn't sure what sort of kill.

"Would you like ice cream on top?" Emmy Lou asked as she popped the slice of pie in the microwave.

"Sure, why not?" A piece of pie à la mode wasn't going to turn him into a mush brain, he decided. He'd navigated the tricky world of high finance without getting his butt kicked. Surely he could handle whatever this pair of women had in mind.

Jo watched him eat the pie with far too much interest. And every time she caught his eye she smiled a secret sort of smile. Something was definitely up.

He glanced at her. "Want a bite?"

"Oh, no, thanks. I just love to see a man enjoy his food."

Quinn polished off the pie. "I'm afraid the show's over. But I have to say that was the best piece of apple pie I've ever had, and I've eaten at some pricey restaurants. They could serve this pie with pride at the Waldorf-Astoria.''

Emmy Lou looked enraptured. ''I would love to see the Waldorf.''

''I've offered to take you on my sperm runs,'' Jo said.

''No, no, not like that. It would break my heart to fly in and out on the same day. I want to see the lights, feel the city's pulse, breathe in the rich aromas.'' She closed her eyes and took a deep, dramatic breath.

''You might want to give the rich aromas a miss,'' Quinn said. ''New York's rich aromas can be overwhelming, especially on garbage pickup day.''

Emmy Lou grinned at Jo. ''Spoken like a man who's never cleaned out a chicken coop. You'd better keep him away from shovel duty while he's here.''

''I had no intention of putting him on shovel duty.''

''Anyway,'' Emmy Lou said as she turned to Quinn. ''I don't want to give anything a miss. I want to hear the noise, taste a hot pretzel, mingle with the crowd in Times Square, give my regards to Broadway. I don't want a tiny bite of the Big Apple.'' She spread her arms wide. ''I want to have it all.''

Quinn curbed his impulse to immediately invite her there as his guest. It would be a real kick to watch her revel in the sights and sounds of the city. But he had no business inviting Emmy Lou Whatever to New York. He didn't even know her last name. The sugar must be affecting his brain for him to even think of doing such a thing.

Jo leaned forward, her dark eyes sparkling. ''So, Quinn, are you ready to extend your visit a few days? I think we're having pot roast tomorrow night.''

Logic warned him to use caution. She was a little too eager. But his libido reacted to that sparkle in her eyes in a very primitive fashion. And he did love a good pot roast. "I think it could be arranged."

"What about your job?" Emmy Lou asked.

"I can keep in touch by phone. With the help of Erin, my secretary, I can probably take care of anything critical from here." Quinn began to anticipate what it might be like living in the same house with Jo, or more appropriately, sleeping in the same house with Jo.

"Great," Jo said. "Because I have the most amazing idea. As long as you're going to be here, what if you told everybody you were Brian Hastings?"

Quinn groaned and buried his face in his hands as his fantasies dissolved. There it was. The catch.

Emmy Lou clapped her hands together. "Josephine, you're brilliant."

Quinn took his hands away from his eyes and leaned toward Jo. Damn, but she was beautiful. And treacherous. He lowered his voice. "But you see, I'm not Brian Hastings."

"You could fool them. You fooled Emmy Lou. And if everyone around here thought Brian Hastings was visiting my ranch, I could hold off the bank a while longer."

With a sigh of deep regret he leaned back in his chair. Like too many of the women he'd known, she was only interested in him because he looked like a famous movie star. "And then what happens when Hastings never shows up? You're in the same fix as before."

"But by the end of the summer I'll have some money, and I can make a partial payment. I need to keep the bank at bay until then."

"There may be other ways around this. It's possible I could arrange for a line of credit from—"

"No!" She held up her hand like a traffic cop. "I don't

want anyone else getting involved in my financial problems. If I go down, I'll go down alone.''

"That's very noble but totally unnecessary. Jo, this is what I do for a living. I don't know why I didn't suggest consulting with you about it before, during the cab ride.''

"Consulting?" She raised her eyebrows. "I'm sure you don't do that for free, Quinn.''

"Not normally. But we could work something out.''

"I'd rather struggle along on my own. If you'd just agree to be Brian Hastings for a week, that's all I ask.''

"All?" Quinn stared at her. "The guy's a movie star and a director, so he knows the Hollywood scene inside and out. Besides that he's a worldwide sex symbol. Do you realize how intimidating that would be for an ordinary guy like me?''

"Nonsense," Emmy Lou said. "You can do the sex symbol part with both hands tied behind your back. Just give the ladies that killer grin, throw in a wink or two, and they'll drop like flies.''

Maybe, Quinn thought, but he knew that when women found out for sure he wasn't really Brian Hastings they had a tendency to turn nasty, and he'd be in constant fear they'd find out. Besides that, he was sick of never being evaluated on his own merits, and he wanted no part of this scheme, no matter how nice it would be to spend time with Jo. As far as he was concerned, this wasn't the way to handle her money problems, either. It was only a Band-Aid when she needed a tourniquet.

"As for the movie lingo, we can fake that," Jo said. "Emmy Lou has seen every interview that Brian Hastings ever gave—Barbara Walters, Larry King, Oprah Winfrey. She can coach you on the show biz angle.''

Quinn shook his head. "Sorry. The whole idea goes against the grain. I've hated being mistaken for Hastings, and I sure as hell don't want to deliberately bring that kind of chaos down on my head. Listen, Jo, don't reject my financial advice out of hand. I might be exactly who you need. I could—''

''No, thank you. I appreciate the offer, but I have no guarantee I'll come out of this with the ranch intact. I don't want to risk your good name.''

''You won't ruin my good name, and even if you did, I'd rather involve myself that way than pawn myself off as some two-bit version of Hastings.''

''You're not giving yourself credit. You'd be at least a four-bit version,'' Emmy Lou said.

''That's what you think.'' The more closely Quinn evaluated this stunt, the more impossible it sounded. ''He's not only a Hollywood insider, he's a cowboy. I can't ride, I can't rope, and if you put boots and spurs on me I'd probably trip and fall down before I walked two feet into the local saloon. Let me do what I do best, which is manipulate money.''

Jo looked sad but determined. ''I can't let you get involved with my messy finances, Quinn. I just can't.''

''And I have no interest in masquerading as Brian Hastings.''

''Then I guess that's that,'' Jo said. ''But you're welcome to stay.''

He hated like hell to turn her down, but he could see that a few days at the Bar None would be a nightmare as people continued to mistake him for Hastings. He pushed back his chair. ''Thanks, but I'd better leave first thing in the morning. In the rush of coming out here to deliver Sir Lust-a-Lot's last legacy I forgot about your Brian Hastings connection. Chances are everyone would react the way Emmy Lou did. I'd rather not put myself through that.''

Jo nodded. "I understand. Emmy Lou, would you please show Quinn his room? I need to go out and check on Betsy and Clarise before bedtime."

"Come along, Quinn."

Under Emmy Lou's reproving glance, Quinn felt like a misbehaving schoolboy. He silently followed her up the stairs.

"I don't think it would kill you to do what Jo's asking," she said in a very schoolmarmish tone.

"That's because you've never been surrounded by a hoard of women who wanted to rip your clothes off."

Emmy Lou sniffed as she continued up the stairs. "I'm sure you're exaggerating. Why, I thought you were Brian Hastings up until recently, and I never once considered ripping your clothes off. All I wanted was a button from your shirt."

"See? It starts with the buttons. What harm's in that? Then we run out of buttons, so somebody wants a sleeve. Then somebody wants my belt. Then it's strip city. It only takes one person to start it off, and before I realize it I'm surrounded. I try to tell them they have the wrong guy, but do they listen? Not when they're in their Brian Hastings crazed mode. There are at least twenty women walking around this world with a button or a sleeve or a back pocket of my pants, and all of them think their souvenirs came from Brian Hastings."

"And I suppose this all happened in New York?"

Quinn followed her down the hall. "That's where I live."

Emmy Lou stopped in front of a doorway and turned to him. "Well, there you go. It's the too-many-rats-in-a-cage theory. They start eating their young or stripping their celebrities, whatever is handy. Out here we have room to stretch out. We're not so snappish."

"You just admitted you wanted one of my buttons!"

"Well, not now! Who wants the button off the shirt of an investment banker?"

Quinn was irritated. He couldn't decide which was worse, the loss of privacy when he was mistaken for Hastings or the blow to his ego when women finally accepted that he was *only* Quinn Monroe, investment banker. "I don't understand what women want with those trophies, anyway. Do they mount that button and shine a spotlight on it? Do they frame that piece of sleeve? Do they arrange my back pocket in a vase on the coffee table? I don't get it."

Emmy Lou cleared her throat and glanced at the ceiling. "Some might sew the button on a piece of velvet and embroider the person's name under it and frame it. If that someone really had a button from Brian Hastings' shirt, that is."

"Like you, for instance? I suppose your wall is full of framed buttons."

"No, it isn't. We don't get many celebrities out this way. And it was just dumb luck that Georgina Mason was in the ice cream parlor when Robert Redford came in. She claims he gave her the button, but it would be like her to pop it right off his shirt when he wasn't looking."

Quinn couldn't help smiling. "That'd be hard to do."

"Not for Georgina. She's the sneaky type. And she's such a showoff—has that framed button over the fireplace, where the whole world can see it." Emmy Lou gestured toward the doorway. "So here's your room, Benedict Arnold."

"Emmy Lou, nobody would believe me after the first five minutes! In New York it's different, because there are no horses for me to fall off of or cows for me not to rope."

"Cattle. Brian Hastings wouldn't say *cows*."

"That's my point!"

"We could teach you. Jo and I could whip you into shape in no time."

"Forgive me if I don't relish the sound of that."

"Okay. Be a coward. Bathroom's across the hall. If you were staying I'd hunt you up a change of clothes down at the bunkhouse, but I guess that won't be necessary."

Quinn vowed he wouldn't be baited into saying something he'd deeply regret. "Why couldn't you just take one of my buttons and claim it came from Brian Hastings' shirt?"

Emmy Lou looked shocked. "Because it would be dishonest!"

"Dishonest? You and Jo want to tell the entire town of Ugly Bug that I'm Brian Hastings, and you're worried about fudging on a button?"

Emmy Lou clucked her tongue in disapproval. "It's not worth lying just to spite Georgina Mason. But I'd lie from now until doomsday to save the Bar None for Jo." Her pointed stare indicated that she thought he should have the same missionary zeal. "Why, I—" She paused and cocked her head. "Somebody's downstairs with Jo."

Quinn heard the voices, too. Jo was talking to a guy, and from the sound of her voice, she wasn't too happy about the conversation.

"It's that Dick!" Emmy Lou said, almost spitting out the words.

"Would that be a first name or a description?"

Emmy Lou's eyes twinkled at him. "I do like you, Quinn."

"I like you, too."

"Dick Cassidy is Jo's ex. One of the worst things she ever did was marry him, and one of the best was to divorce him. All he wanted, besides the obvious, was access to Ugly Bug Creek so he could water his cattle.''

Quinn didn't like thinking about some guy enjoying the obvious with Jo. "The creek the town's named after is on this ranch?''

"Yep. At least the best stretch of it, and none of it runs across the Cassidy ranch next door. He put her through hell during the divorce proceedings while he tried to hang on to that water. We can't prove it, but we think Dick had something to do with so many of the cattle dying last winter. I think he was stealing the hay she put out for them. Besides that, he might have made off with some money, but Jo's not the best bookkeeper in the world, so she's not sure.''

Quinn's protective instincts surged to the fore. He tried to tamp them down, knowing they'd get him into trouble. "So why did she even let him in the door?''

"Oh, he always has some good reason he has to be let in. Last time, he came to report a break in her fence line, which I think he created. The time before that, his truck had broken down on the main road. The code of the west says you help out your neighbors, so Jo helped him. I say he's finding excuses to nose around and see how bad Jo's hurting. He's already offered her a lowball figure for the ranch.''

Quinn glanced through the door into his bedroom, taking note of sturdy oak furniture and what looked like a handmade quilt on the bed. "Okay, you've shown me where I'm sleeping.'' As the voices downstairs rose in volume, he glanced at Emmy Lou. "What do you say to a cup of coffee before I turn in?''

Emmy Lou beamed in approval. "I'd say that's a great idea.'' She led the way downstairs.

As they approached the kitchen, Quinn could make out the conversation much better.

"That section of fence was fine yesterday," Jo said, an edge to her voice. "Somebody's cutting that wire."

"Now who would do a thing like that? You think I want your bull trampling my cook's garden?"

"If it means I have to pay restitution for your specially ordered designer veggie plants, yeah, I think you'd love to have my bull running around in your cook's garden!"

Give him hell, Jo, Quinn thought. He stepped into the kitchen behind Emmy Lou, but the five-foot-something housekeeper didn't block his view of the proceedings. Dick Cassidy faced the door, while Jo stood rigidly with her back to it. Cassidy had soft, fleshy features that might have been cute when he was a kid and would look ridiculously juvenile in another ten years. Quinn hated him on sight.

Cassidy's reaction to Quinn was exactly the opposite, however. His eyes widened, and he broke into a goofy grin. "Well, I'll be damned. You're a sly one, Jo."

Jo turned toward the door and caught sight of Quinn and Emmy Lou standing there. Then she glanced at Dick. "It's not what you think. This is—"

"As if you have to introduce the guy." Dick pushed past her and stuck out his hand. "Dick Cassidy. I live on the neighboring ranch. I'd like you to come over and take a look. You might even like it better than the Bar None. The buildings are newer, and we've been able to keep up with painting and such better than Jo has. Well, you have to excuse her. A woman alone can't be expected to stay on top of everything."

"I like the rustic look." Quinn even hated Cassidy's handshake, which felt clammy.

"Then we can sand some of that paint off!" Cassidy said. "You name it, and we'll do it."

"Dick, let me explain," Jo said. "I know what you think, but this is—"

"Brian Hastings, of course." Dick pumped his hand. "I've seen all your movies. Damn good flicks, if you ask me."

Quinn had about three seconds to decide whether he could live with himself if he allowed this sorry excuse for a man to continue to ride roughshod over Jo. He decided in two. "That's good to hear," he said. "Which one did you like the best?"

4

JO HAD NEVER felt so much like hugging a man in her life. Thank God for Dick, jerk that he was. Apparently his appearance had tipped the scales in her favor and made Quinn decide to help her.

"It'd be real hard to pick a favorite movie," Dick said. "Which one did you like the best?"

"Couldn't say. Never see my own films."

Emmy Lou hovered nearby. "Except for the daily rushes, of course. I'm sure you see those."

"Well, yeah." Quinn gestured vaguely. "The daily rushes and sometimes the weekly rushes, but I don't bother with the monthly rushes."

Dick stared at him. "Monthly rushes?"

"Hollywood!" Jo threw up her hands. "Who can keep up with the funny little terms they use? Hey, I don't know about the rest of you, but I crossed two time zones twice today and I've had no sleep for twenty-four hours, so if you don't mind, I think I'll turn in." She glanced at Quinn. "Brian? You look pretty bushed, yourself. I'm sure you'll find the guest bed comfy."

Dick's jaw dropped. "He's staying here?" He turned to Quinn. "But where are the rest of your people? Your what d'ya call it...entourage?"

Quinn flexed his shoulders and looked bored. "I sent 'em off to Bimini, told 'em to relax, catch some rays. I need to be here alone, get in character."

"Wow. I never knew you guys were so dedicated. That's impressive, Brian. Is it okay if I call you Brian? You can call me Dick."

"I sure will, Dick."

"How many Oscars have you won, anyway?"

"You know, Dick, it's easy to lose track of things like that, after the first few." Quinn glanced quickly at Emmy Lou, who discreetly held up three fingers. "Three."

"Dick, I hate to be rude." Jo linked her arm through Quinn's. "But Brian's so polite he'd stay here answering your questions all night, when he really needs to get some sleep. I've appointed myself as his personal watchdog, to make sure he takes care of himself. Stars become so involved in their art that they sometimes neglect the essentials, like food and sleep."

She loved watching Dick try to hide his jealousy. He hated seeing her getting cozy with this movie star, but he also wanted to suck up to that same movie star. Jo hadn't counted on this little perk when she'd created her plan. It was a nice bonus.

The warmth of Quinn's body next to hers was a pleasant extra, too. She had an idea she'd enjoy working with him. He had lots to learn about being a Hollywood cowboy, and teaching him promised to be fun.

"Then I guess I'll be going," Dick said with obvious reluctance. He started toward the entry hall but paused. "Listen, I know people probably ask you this all the time, but seeing as how we're neighbors, in a manner of speaking, I was wondering if there'd be a part in this movie for me? I ride and rope real good."

Quinn took his time giving Dick the once-over. Jo caught Emmy Lou's glance and had to turn away and bite her lip to keep from laughing.

Finally Quinn nodded. "There might be," he said.

"Hey, that would be great. I really—"

"If..." Quinn said, and paused dramatically.

"If?"

"If you lose some of that flab. You're soft in the middle, Dick. Can't have that. I suggest lifting weights, an exercise bike, maybe a little jogging."

"Jogging? An exercise bike? Cowboys don't jog, and they sure as hell don't ride no exercise bike!"

Quinn shrugged. "Up to you. I'm just throwing out suggestions as to how you can become more acceptable for the role. You can do it or not."

Dick sighed. "Hell, I'll do it. I just hope none of my men see me. I'll be the laughingstock of the county. When will you start shooting?"

"When it's time."

"Huh?"

Jo choked back a burst of laughter.

"It's all about light, Dick," Quinn continued. "I have to wait until we have the perfect light. I'll know it when I see it. Might take months, might be in two weeks. Better buy that exercise bike and start jogging."

"Yeah. Guess so. Well, see you around, Brian."

"See you, Dick. Oh, and about your vegetable garden. Do you think, under the circumstances, that you could—"

"Hey, I don't really give a damn about the garden. I'm a meat and potatoes man, myself."

Quinn lifted an eyebrow. "And it shows. I'd suggest you switch to broccoli and carrots if you want to lose that spare tire."

Dick reddened. "I guess the cook can plant another garden. It was probably too early, anyway. No problem. Forget it, Jo."

"Don't worry. I will." Jo managed to contain herself until Dick closed the front door and headed toward his truck. Then she collapsed into a chair and clutched her stomach while she laughed until the tears came.

Emmy Lou joined her, stopping every now and then to pound on the table with glee.

Finally Jo glanced at Quinn, her voice choked with laughter. "You've just given me the best laugh I've had in months. Thank you."

He smiled. "You're welcome."

"If I ever get depressed, I'll just think of Dick pedaling away on that exercise bike to get rid of his spare tire. And forcing down broccoli."

Emmy Lou took off her glasses and wiped her eyes. "Or jogging in his boots. I'm sure that boy doesn't own a pair of running shoes." She chuckled. "Good thing Dick doesn't know any more about making movies than Quinn, here. Monthly rushes. I almost lost it." She shook her head. "Here's my first bit of advice, Quinn. Don't ad-lib. Before you go to bed I'll get you some of my back issues of *Premiere* magazine to study."

"I think your best bet is to keep me mostly out of sight. I can do mysterious."

"That's no fun!" Jo said. Then she gazed at him. "I really do appreciate this, you know. I realize you didn't want to do it."

"I still don't, but I couldn't resist going a couple of rounds with your ex. Don't take this personally, but if he's any indication, you have lousy taste in men."

"I like to think I was having an out-of-body experience when I agreed to marry him."

Jo felt a noble impulse coming. Try as she might, she couldn't sidetrack it. "Quinn, you can still leave tomorrow morning if you want. Now that at least one person believes you were here, I can use that to convince the bank the deal is on. I'll just say you were suddenly called away.''

Quinn rubbed the back of his neck and stared into space. Finally he met her gaze. "I'll stay a few more days."

"Spoken like a true hero," Emmy Lou said.

Jo had to agree. And heroes had been in short supply in her life recently. As she looked into Quinn's eyes her heart took on a jerky rhythm she hadn't felt in a long, long time. She wondered if she was risking more than she realized, if in the process of trying to save her ranch she was in danger of losing her heart. "I promise we won't be too rough on you," she said.

"Oh, I can take rough." He grinned. "The way this is shaping up, I'm just hoping I make it through alive."

QUINN WOKE with a start. The house was dark, but somebody was knocking on a door across the hall, which must have been what woke Quinn in the first place.

"Jo!" called a man in a loud whisper.

Quinn threw the covers back and got out of bed. He'd heard that locking the house wasn't always done out here in the neighborly west, so maybe neighbor Dick was back. Maybe Dick didn't know the meaning of the term *ex-husband*. Jo was probably out like a light after being up so many hours straight. Emmy Lou slept in a bedroom downstairs, but this joker had obviously slipped right past her. Jo's safety was in Quinn's hands.

Treading softly, he opened his door as quietly as possible and peered into the hall. Sure enough, a man was opening Jo's bedroom door. Talk about nerve.

Quinn crept across the hall and through Jo's bedroom door just as the creep leaned over Jo. "Oh, no, you don't, lizard breath.'' Quinn launched himself at the intruder's knees.

The guy let out a screech, followed by a loud yell from Jo as both men tumbled into bed with her.

''Don't worry, Jo!'' Quinn wrestled with the guy as best he could, considering it was very dark and he wasn't sure which arms and legs belonged to which person. ''I've got him!''

''I think you've got me!'' Jo yelled. ''How many of you are there? Let go! Ouch!''

''Help!'' cried the man, flailing wildly. ''Help, murder, police!''

''Murder sounds like a great idea,'' Quinn said, gasping. He made a grab for where he thought the guy was and encountered warm bare skin. Wonderful soft skin. ''Whoops. Sorry, Jo.'' He tried for the intruder again and caught the guy's leg.

''What in hell is going on?'' Panting, Jo struggled away from both of them.

''I'm protecting your honor.'' Quinn got hold of the guy's belt as he tried to squirm off the bed. ''And where do you think you're going, buster? What makes you think you can—oof!'' Quinn lost his grip as the guy kicked him in the privates. Groaning, he sprawled across Jo's legs.

The overhead light flashed on. ''Everybody freeze or I'll shoot!'' Emmy Lou bellowed.

''Go ahead,'' Quinn said. ''Put me out of my misery. But save a bullet for your friendly neighbor, here.''

''Don't shoot, Emmy Lou!'' the guy cried.

''She can't, Benny.'' Jo sounded thoroughly disgusted. ''That shotgun's not even loaded.''

''You're not supposed to tell anybody that,'' Emmy Lou said.

''It's okay to tell Benny,'' Jo said.

Quinn's pain subsided enough for him to lift his head and gaze at Jo. She wore a plaid flannel nightshirt, which had become sort of twisted around as he'd tried to save her, and the effect was rumpled and very sexy. "Who's Benny?"

"Me," the guy said.

Quinn raised himself on one arm and glanced to the other side of the bed where someone who was definitely not Dick lay half on, half off the bed, staring at Quinn apprehensively. "Who the hell are you?" Quinn asked.

The guy flinched. "Benny," he said again. "Emmy Lou, can I move now?"

"You can all move," Jo said. "I don't remember inviting a single one of you to join me in bed this evening."

"I thought Benny was Dick," Quinn said. "I was saving you."

"That's very sweet. But Benny is not Dick. Benny is my wrangler."

"And Fred's the foreman," Benny said. "He's got a beard."

"Thanks for the info," Quinn said. "If he happens to show up at your door tonight I'll know who he is."

Jo glanced at Benny. "So I've figured out that Quinn is here because you're here. But why are you—oh, my God!" She threw back the covers and jumped from the bed. "I'll bet it's Clarise!"

Benny nodded. "It's Clarise. Fred sent me. He said you told him to get you if it was time. I didn't know you had a movie star in your house."

"He's not a movie star, Benny. His name is Quinn. But I want to be with Clarise. Thank you for coming to get me."

Emmy Lou snapped into action. "Foaling time. I'll

make coffee.'' Shouldering the shotgun, she headed downstairs.

''I'll go help Fred,'' Benny said. He glanced at Quinn. ''You sure look like a movie star. Sorry I kicked you in the—''

''It's okay, Benny.'' Quinn had figured out the guy was somewhat of a lightweight in the brains department. Quinn almost felt bad for scaring him, except that he had a kick like a mule, which took the edge off Quinn's regret.

''I'll just go downstairs, okay?'' Keeping a wary eye on Quinn, Benny eased out the door and pounded down the stairs.

Quinn climbed off the bed, suddenly aware that he wore only his briefs. ''I, uh, really thought—''

''I'm sorry he kicked you.'' Her gaze drifted to that part of his anatomy. ''Are you…okay?''

''I'll live.'' In fact, as she continued to look him over, his injured parts became full of life.

''I imagine you will live, at that.'' She looked at him with amused tenderness. ''You thought somebody was about to do me wrong, didn't you?''

''Yeah.''

''So with no weapon, and having no idea what you might be up against, you came charging in here to protect me?''

''Yeah.''

Her gaze warmed even more. ''I haven't had a man risk his own safety for my sake in a long time. It feels nice.''

His pulse started to hammer.

She sighed. ''We'd both better put on some clothes. My mare is about to foal, and I want to be there.''

He was encouraged by that sigh and the interest in her brown eyes. ''Of course.''

"It's worth seeing, Quinn."

"I wouldn't miss it for the world." With one last look into those wonderful eyes of hers, he turned and headed out of the room. "Meet you downstairs in two minutes."

THE BIRTH of a foal always stirred Jo's blood, but with Quinn leaning over the stall door in rapt attention, the event seemed more emotional than usual. No doubt she was still affected by their encounter in her bedroom. The picture of Quinn standing there in his briefs would stay with her a long time. She'd never realized bankers could look like that. About her only experience with bankers was Mr. Doobie at First National in Ugly Bug. She'd never seen him in his briefs, but she could imagine it wouldn't be pretty.

Quinn, on the other hand, had made her tremble and quicken with desire. If she hadn't had Clarise on her mind…

"Get ready. I think we're close," Fred said.

"We're ready," Jo said. She and Benny stood behind the mare's rump, available to help deliver the foal, if necessary. Fred stood by her head, stroking her neck and talking to her in the gentle way he had with all animals. Some people were intimidated by Fred's size, his bushy gray beard and his gruff manner. Jo had known him since she was a kid, and when she'd inherited the ranch from Aunt Josephine she'd been thrilled when Fred had offered to stay on.

Unfortunately, his arthritis made riding painful for him, which left certain ranch chores strictly to Jo and Benny. That was how she'd ended up accepting help and advice from Dick, who'd even loaned her a couple of his men during roundup. But there had been strings attached. Actually more like steel cables attached. She'd felt shackled by Dick for way too long. Having Quinn step in tonight and torque Dick around had soothed her soul.

A couple of times in the past half hour she'd glanced up and caught him watching her. She wondered if he could soothe other parts of her, too.

The thought filled her with trepidation, because of how Dick had made her feel about herself sexually. Dick's method of intimidation was to subtly belittle a woman until she began to doubt her worth. She'd divorced him before he could do a thorough job on her, but she still felt insecure about a few things. Like whether she was any good in bed.

Clarise snorted and shifted her hindquarters.

"Here it comes!" Benny said.

"Yep." Jo's heart pounded with excitement as the mucus-covered nose and forelegs of the foal poked out between Clarise's haunches. "Good girl, Clarise. Keep pushing."

The mare groaned and sank to her knees as more of the shimmery foal emerged.

Fred groaned, too, as he knelt beside her. "You and me both, Clarise. After this I'm having a shot of whiskey."

Jo watched anxiously as the process seemed to stall. She clutched Benny's arm. "Do you think she needs us to pull?"

"I think she's doin' fine. Just fine." Benny's eyes shone.

Jo loved Benny like the little brother she never had, even though he was a few years older than she was. His mental slowness made him seem forever young, but when it came to ranch duties, Benny knew his stuff.

Sure enough, Clarise gave another mighty heave, and the foal slipped out.

Benny leaned forward to clean its nose so it could breathe. "It's a colt," he announced proudly.

"Wow," Quinn murmured.

"Wow is right." Jo couldn't take her gaze away from the new baby.

"What do you do about the glop it came in?" Quinn asked.

"Watch," Jo said. "Do your thing, Clarise."

The mare turned and began to lick her baby clean.

"Ugh," Quinn said. "I'll never eat oysters Rockefeller again."

Jo laughed. "Yeah, I know. If human mothers had to do this, I'd probably opt out of having kids."

Benny gazed at her with worship in his gray eyes. "You'd make a real good mommy, Jo."

"Thanks, Benny." She gave him a smile.

"So when are you gonna be one?"

Fred snorted as he got slowly to his feet. "Benny, you ask too many questions."

Benny looked troubled. "I don't mean to. But it'd be fun to have some little kids around."

"Yeah, it would." Jo stretched her stiff muscles. Too many hours on a plane and not enough sleep had taken their toll. "But a mother needs a daddy."

Benny grinned and jerked a thumb at Quinn. "How about the movie star? I'll bet he'd do it."

5

QUINN had joined in the laughter following Benny's remark, but under cover of the joking that followed, he'd checked out Jo's pink cheeks and the sparkle in her eyes. He decided she didn't hate the idea, no matter how embarrassed she was.

He didn't hate the idea, either, which was amazing. As the child of divorced parents, he was wary of the whole marriage and fatherhood thing. He'd promised himself he'd live with a woman for a long time before he even proposed, and as for kids, he hadn't thought he wanted any.

Yet watching Jo serve as one of the midwives for her mare, he'd had some very unfamiliar yearnings. Murray had two kids, and he'd raved about the delivery room scene. Quinn hadn't been able to relate...until now. Maybe it was the sugar in the apple pie still affecting his brain, but he'd found himself wondering what it would be like to be a proud father at the moment of birth. He'd probably imagined Jo in the role of the mother because she was handy.

"Stand back, everybody," Fred said. "She's going to get that little fella on his feet."

"No way." Quinn surveyed the colt's spindly legs and couldn't picture it. "I don't think he has the engineering for it yet."

"He has to," Jo said. "It's the only way he can nurse."

"He's not up to it, I tell you." Quinn grew agitated as the mare hauled herself to her feet. "Make her lie down and drag him to the right spot."

Jo walked to the stall door and stood near Quinn. "You can't interrupt nature like that," she said gently. "In the wild, a horse's survival depends on getting upright as soon as possible. This has been going on for centuries."

"Well, I don't like it." Quinn folded his arms across the top of the stall door and frowned as the mare started pushing the colt with her nose. "She's expecting too much, too soon."

"She's acting on instinct," Jo said.

"She's pushy, is what she is." Quinn breathed in the sweet scent of Jo's hair. It looked as mussed and tangled as it had in the bedroom. She probably hadn't bothered to comb it in her rush to get to the barn. When she shifted her weight, tendrils of it brushed his bare forearm. If he moved his hand a fraction, he'd be able to wind a lock around his finger.

But he didn't want such a tame experience. He wanted to grab handfuls of her hair and let the rich silkiness flow between his fingers. He wanted to comb her hair over her naked breasts so that she looked like a brunette version of Lady Godiva. He wanted—

"See? He's up."

"I'll be damned." To Quinn's astonishment, while he'd been fantasizing about a sensuous experience with Jo's hair, the colt had somehow balanced itself on those four matchstick legs and was sucking vigorously on his mother's teat. "He's going to fall, I tell you. You should prop something under him. A stepladder would probably work."

Emmy Lou walked over and patted Quinn's arm. "Relax. These folks know what they're doing. We've had lots of foals born on the Bar None, and not a one of them ever needed to be propped up with a stepladder. Now if you'll all excuse me, I'll bring us some coffee.''

Benny turned from his inspection of the colt. ''And chocolate chip cookies?''

''Of course. What would foaling be without a batch of my chocolate chip cookies? Before we came down here I took them out of the freezer.''

''Good thing.'' Quinn grinned at her. ''I can't stand a foaling without chocolate chip cookies, myself.''

Emmy Lou gazed at him and sighed. ''Are you *sure* you're not Brian Hastings?''

''Matter of fact, I am. Until somebody blows the whistle on me.''

''That reminds me.'' Jo turned to Fred and Benny. ''I need to let you two in on what's happening. In spite of what you might think, this man is not Brian Hastings.''

Fred stuck a plug of tobacco under his lip. ''Who's Brian Hastings?''

Quinn smiled. He'd found a friend.

Benny pointed to Quinn. ''He is.''

''No, he's not,'' Jo said.

''Makes no never mind to me.'' Fred put his can of tobacco in his back pocket. ''He can be Donald Duck for all I care. A man's name's not important. It's how he conducts himself.''

Jo glanced at Quinn. ''Fred doesn't go to the movies, and he hates TV.''

''I gathered.''

She turned to Benny and Fred. ''Remember when that guy came by the ranch last fall looking for a place to shoot a movie?''

Benny looked blank.

Fred scratched his beard and finally shook his head. "Guess he didn't make no impression on me."

"He was an advance man for Brian Hastings, who is the top box office draw in the country."

Fred spit tobacco juice into a can. "Whoop-de-doo."

Quinn was liking this guy more every minute.

"The thing is," Jo continued, "I told Mr. Doobie at the bank that Brian Hastings definitely would use the ranch, and we'd be able to make a big payment on our loan soon, so he gave me an extension. Only Brian Hastings hasn't ever come here."

"But he did," Benny said. "We were all in your bed together."

Fred almost swallowed his chaw. "What did you say?"

"Benny, this is not Brian Hastings. He just looks a lot like him." She glanced quickly at Fred, who had developed a dangerous gleam in his eye. "Now don't look like that, Fred. This very nice man is Quinn Monroe, from New York."

"I don't give a damn where he's from. He'd better stay the hell out of your bed. Benny, you and me need to have a talk. You ain't ever been to the big city, and these city slickers got some tricky ways about them. You gotta be on your guard."

Judging from Fred's expression, Quinn was afraid he'd just lost his new best friend. And if he valued his life, he'd shelve his fantasies about Jo. "I was only trying to save her," he said.

"Yes, that's true," Jo said. "He saw Benny coming into my room tonight, and he didn't know it was about Clarise. He thought Benny was Dick, up to no good. So he tackled him, and we all ended up rolling around on my bed until Emmy Lou arrived with the shotgun."

Fred glared at Quinn. "Likely story."

Quinn tried to salvage Fred's goodwill. "Would you believe I've agreed to impersonate this Brian Hastings character so the bank will get off Jo's back?"

Fred pointed a gnarled finger at Jo. "Don't you be getting too grateful, Josephine Sarah. You see what gratitude got you with a Dick Cassidy type."

Benny jumped into the conversation and pointed at Quinn. "But he's not a Dick," he said brightly.

Fred scowled at Benny. "Go up to the house and help Emmy Lou bring the coffee and cookies down."

"Okay." Benny opened the stall door, and Quinn stood aside to let him out. Benny peered at Quinn. "Who are you, anyway?"

"Benny, I'm losing track of that myself."

Benny nodded as if he understood the problem completely and sauntered out of the barn.

Jo turned to Fred. "I haven't wanted to worry you, but we're not in good financial shape."

"I could figure that out on my own. If I coulda done more riding this winter I mighta been able to catch Cassidy doing some of his dirty work. We shouldn'ta lost all them cattle. But the only way to catch him would be sneak up on horseback. The truck makes too much noise, and that's all I was using this past winter."

"I tried to catch him," Jo said. "Never could. But that's water over the dam. Right now Quinn is my best hope. If Mr. Doobie believes Quinn is Brian Hastings, then he won't heckle me for money. If I could get Doobie signed up as an extra in the movie, he might not ever heckle me again."

"So I'll sign him up," Quinn said.

Fred held up his hand. "Wait a minute. You're not a movie star or director or nothin', but you're gonna sign Doobie up for a movie?"

Quinn shrugged. "Sometimes movies don't get made. The money dries up. I don't know much about it, but I figure a lot can go wrong when you're trying to raise a few million dollars to make a picture."

Fred's eyes widened. "A few *million?*" He turned to Jo. "If this Hastings really rented the ranch, how much would you get?"

"I don't know. The important thing is that Doobie doesn't know, either. He's willing to let my note ride until after the movie's shot."

"But Hastings never came back." Fred shifted his wad of tobacco to his cheek. "There might never be a movie."

"I know, but Quinn's agreed to buy me some time. So for the next few days, if anybody asks if Brian Hastings is staying on the Bar None, say yes."

"I can do that, but this may be way too complicated for Benny to figure out."

Jo nodded. "I realize that now, but I can't lie to Benny. If I'd told him Quinn was a movie star and Benny found out later it wasn't true, I'd feel awful."

Fred patted her shoulder. "Yeah, we all feel that way about Benny. I'll see if I can explain it to him."

"Oh, and Fred, I have a favor to ask."

"Yeah?"

"The real Brian Hastings is a cowboy star. He knows how to ride and rope and everything. Quinn's the greenest greenhorn you'll ever run across."

Quinn stood up straighter. "Hey, I wouldn't go that far."

"I'm telling you, Fred, he doesn't have the foggiest idea about that stuff. He doesn't even have the right clothes. I'd like to turn him over to you for…" She smiled at Quinn. "For cowboy school, I guess you'd call it."

Quinn's stomach felt as if he'd eaten cement, and he

didn't trust the gleam of relish that flashed in Fred's eyes. Didn't trust it one bit. Fred looked Quinn up and down like he might be sizing him for a coffin, Quinn thought.

Finally the big man spoke. "I think he'll fit into Benny's duds. As for the rest—" He grinned, showing tobacco-stained teeth. "Leave him to me."

A shiver of dread ran down Quinn's spine.

"Now if you'll keep an eye on Clarise, I'm gonna head down to the bunkhouse and get my whiskey."

"Could you bring an extra glass?" Quinn asked. He had a feeling he needed some fortification.

Fred smiled again. "Real cowboys don't need no glass," he said. "They drink straight from the bottle."

After Fred left, Quinn leaned against the stall door, which still separated him from the delectable Jo. Jo the turncoat. "I thought you were going to teach me how to be a cowboy."

"I was." She looked disappointed. "I was really looking forward to it."

"You weren't the only one."

"But then, while Clarise was giving birth to her foal, I started thinking."

"Yeah, me, too."

"About what?"

"You first." This didn't seem like the time to tell her he'd started thinking how nice she'd look pregnant.

"Here's the deal." She moved a little closer to him. "I like you. I like you a lot."

"Is that why you're turning me over to Grizzly Adams? Because, gosh darn, you sure do like me?"

"Yes." She trailed a finger along his forearm. "Because if I did all the teaching I'm afraid we'd get involved."

"And what a disaster that would be." So what if her

touch affected his breathing? He could work around that. The one bright spot in this whole episode had been wiped out, almost as if Fred had hit it dead center with a stream of tobacco juice.

"It would be a disaster." Jo's expression was sweet and serious as she continued to draw imaginary lines over his arm. "Now that you're going to be Brian Hastings, you have to play your part and hightail it out of town before anybody's the wiser. You can never set foot in these parts again. It'd be too risky."

He was beginning to get her point. He didn't like it, but he was getting it. He captured her hand. She had strong hands, but warm and so soft. She must slather them with lotion to keep them that way, he thought. "And you're not the kind of woman who wants a fling with a guy who can never set foot in these parts again."

"I wish I could be, Quinn. If I could be that kind of woman, you'd be the very guy I'd choose to have a fling with."

"That's such a comfort." He brought her hand up to his lips and kissed her knuckles one by one.

Her eyes darkened to the color of chocolate. "Are you the kind of guy who would have a fling with a woman you could never see again?"

Under the glow of that gaze he began to fidget. He looked away. His conscience wasn't as clear on this score as hers apparently was. There was that time in Rio, when both he and the woman had known the relationship would go nowhere, yet they'd had a damned good time for a few days. And then there was the woman he'd met on the subway. She'd come to New York for a convention and had flown home to Paris three days later. Even though the time together had been great, neither of them had felt committed enough to uproot their lives to be with each other. Both times he'd suspected the women were pretending he was Brian Hastings, but that was another matter.

"I guess you are that kind of guy," Jo said quietly. She tried to pull her hand away.

He held it tight and met her gaze. "Okay, I'll admit I've been willing to do that in the past. Not often, but it's happened. I'll also go out on a limb and say that I wouldn't want that sort of arrangement with you."

"Because you think I would get hurt?"

He stroked the back of her hand with his thumb. "Because I think we could both get hurt."

Her gaze softened. "Thank you. You're a kind man, Quinn."

Not kind, he thought. Right now he wanted to come into that stall and push her down on the fragrant hay at her feet. "Just telling it like it is. I hadn't thought this through as completely as you have. You're right. Now that I'm going to impersonate Hastings, we really shouldn't let anything develop between us." He hated saying that, but it was true.

Jo sighed wistfully. "You sure look good with no clothes on, though."

Quinn's body tightened even more. "You sure felt good—whatever part of you I got a grip on when I was wrestling with Benny."

"My thigh. You grabbed my thigh."

"Mmm." Probably another spot she slathered lotion on. An ache began to build in the vicinity of his groin. He should end this conversation while he could still walk. "I said I was sorry. I wasn't really."

"That's okay." She sounded breathless. "Maybe we should get all these comments out in the open, now that we're not going to…do anything. I think you look lots sexier than Brian Hastings. It's just my personal opinion, of course.''

''That's the opinion that counts.'' He kissed her palm and felt the shiver that ran up her arm. ''I've been wishing I could run my fingers through your hair. I love your hair.''

She drifted closer, until they would have been nestled against each other if they hadn't been separated by the stall door. ''And I love your eyes.'' Her voice grew husky. ''Such a deep blue. I've heard Brian Hastings wears contacts.''

''How do you know I don't?''

''Do you?''

God, but he wanted to kiss her. ''No. Do you?''

She shook her head. ''No contacts, no capped teeth, no breast implants.''

He glanced down and noticed she'd skipped putting on a bra under her T-shirt. Her nipples pushed at the soft material. He looked into her eyes. ''I wanted to comb your hair over your naked breasts.''

Her breath caught. ''And I wanted to feel your chest muscles flex. Do you...work out?''

''Not much.'' Desire thickened his vocal cords. He sounded as if he had strep. ''Mostly I go out to Murray's house on Long Island and help him with his projects.'' Only one project interested Quinn at the moment, and that was finding a quiet place where they could both get naked. ''He's always adding a room or something.''

''You can do handyman stuff?'' Her breasts touched his chest as she leaned closer.

''Hey, I'm very macho.'' He ached to kiss her, but he didn't dare. Instead he ran a forefinger gently over her lower lip until she closed her eyes and sighed, surrendering to the caress. ''Forget teaching me to ride and rope,'' he murmured. As he eased his finger between her slightly parted lips, his erection pressed against the rough wood of the stall door. "I'll impress the population of Ugly Bug by hammering a couple of boards together. Then for an encore I'll saw a plank in half."

"Coffee and cookies, anyone?"

Quinn and Jo leaped away from their respective sides of the stall door. Then Quinn quickly plastered himself to the door again, grimacing at the impact of the wood against the body parts most affected by Jo.

"Hi, there, Emmy Lou. Hey, Benny." Jo blushed furiously. "We were just—"

"Were they kissing?" Benny asked Emmy Lou.

"Not quite." Emmy Lou set a wooden tray on a leather trunk in the aisle between the rows of stalls.

"We were talking," Jo said.

Emmy Lou poured a mug of coffee and handed it over the stall door to Jo. "Honey, no explanation necessary. You already told me you thought he was cute." She filled a second mug and gave it to Quinn.

Quinn's embarrassment turned to delight. "She did?"

"I just meant in a general sense," Jo said, blushing.

"But you did say it."

"Yes, she really did." Emmy Lou patted him on the arm. "I think you're cute, too."

"Well, I don't think he's so damned cute," Fred said as he walked into the circle of light by the stall door carrying his bottle. "How're momma and baby doing?"

"Sleeping," Jo said.

Quinn glanced guiltily at the mare and foal. They could have been dancing the tango for all he knew. Once everyone had left he'd forgotten the horses and become completely immersed in Jo.

"Whatcha gonna name him?" Fred asked.

Jo gazed at the little foal curled up against his mother. "Well, if people hear that Brian Hastings was present for the birth, they'll expect this colt to be named Brian, probably."

"Aw," Fred said. "Don't do that. That don't sound like a horse name. And don't be calling him Hastings, either. That sounds like a butler."

"Then I guess I'll call him Stud-muffin," Jo said.

Fred groaned.

"I think it's clever," Emmy Lou said.

"What's it mean?" Benny asked.

"Never mind, Benny," Fred said. "So is that it, Jo?"

"That's it."

"Then if it's official, I can drink to it." He uncorked his bottle. "Here's to—" He grimaced. "Stud-muffin. Long may he live." He took a swig and wiped the top on his sleeve. Then with a rascal's glint in his eye, he handed the bottle to Quinn.

Quinn took it. "I'll bet you think I've never swigged whiskey from a bottle before, don't you?"

Fred nodded. "That would be my guess, city boy."

"You'd be wrong." It had been a few years, but he'd done it. Once. "Here's to Stud-muffin." Quinn took a big swallow from the bottle and choked, spilling coffee on himself in the process. The whiskey burned its way to his stomach. The coffee on his shirt seared his chest. He whimpered.

"Give me that!" Emmy Lou grabbed the bottle out of his hand and sniffed it. Then she glared at Fred. "What do you think you're doing, giving that boy some of your hundred-and-fifty-proof home brew? You want to kill him before he has a chance to do this Brian Hastings thing?"

"Jo said I was supposed to turn him into a cowboy!"

"She didn't tell you to turn him into a lush, now, did she?"

Fred stuck out his chin. "A real cowboy can hold his liquor!"

Quinn had recovered enough to set his coffee mug on the wooden tray. "Give me that bottle, Emmy Lou."

"Nope."

Quinn knew his smile could accomplish most anything with Emmy Lou, and he used it. "Come on, Em. Let a guy salvage his pride."

Jo leaned over the stall door. "Forget your pride, Quinn. That stuff would burn a hole right through the floor of this barn."

"You're all a bunch of pansies," Fred muttered.

Quinn motioned for the bottle. "Give it here."

"Don't drink it," Benny said. "It rots your innards."

Quinn glanced at Fred. "He's still standing."

"You can't go by him," Emmy Lou said. "His insides are galvanized steel."

"Emmy Lou. The bottle."

"Oh, give it to him," Jo said. "It's a guy thing. Might as well get it over with."

Emmy Lou surrendered the bottle with obvious reluctance. "Just so you know, we don't have a very up-to-date medical clinic in Ugly Bug."

"I won't need a medical clinic." Quinn met Fred's piercing gaze. Then he slowly raised the bottle to his lips and took another drink, a slightly smaller one this time. Damn, but it was strong. Tears sprang to his eyes, but he lowered the bottle and smiled at Fred. "Good stuff," he said hoarsely. "You make this yourself?" His whole chest was on fire.

"I do."

Quinn wiped the bottle on his sleeve and handed it back. ''Thanks.''

''Any time.''

''I'll remember that.'' Quinn looked into Fred's eyes and was rewarded with a gleam of exactly what he'd been hoping for—respect.

6

Jo woke at six-thirty, which was late for her, and heard rain drumming on the roof. She flopped back on the pillow. Rain was good, making the hay grow that she'd use to feed her cattle next winter. If she still had the ranch next winter. But rain meant mud as she went about her chores. Mud wasn't so good.

Jo turned her head and looked at the picture of her great-aunt Josephine sitting on her dresser. Aunt Josephine had believed in past lives, and she claimed that Jo was a reincarnated pioneer woman, which Aunt Josephine said explained everything.

Jo's mother had died when she was thirteen, and her father had married a woman who didn't seem to like Jo much. Aunt Josephine had been Jo's salvation, and she'd dreamed of helping run the ranch someday. But her great-aunt had insisted she go to college instead of moving directly to the ranch after high school, and there Jo had met lovable, bossy Cassie.

Jo smiled. When Cassie got an idea in her head, most people went along, including Jo. So after graduation she'd worked with Cassie at her family's stables for a year, always thinking she could eventually join Aunt Josephine in Montana. Then an unexpected heart attack claimed her seemingly ageless great-aunt, and suddenly the Bar None belonged to Jo.

"Heels down! Back straight! Grab some mane! That's it!"

That sounds like Fred. Jo threw back the covers and hurried to the window. Her breath fogged the glass, and she rubbed a clear place to look through.

Sure enough, Fred had somebody up on Hyper, and from the way the rider was bouncing around Jo knew who it had to be. God, what had she done?

As she pulled on her jeans, she hopped one-legged to the window to see if Quinn was still aboard Hyper. Trust Fred to give him the acid test, just like he had with the whiskey. And in the rain, no less. Everything was slippery in the rain, including saddles.

Still buttoning her shirt, she took the stairs at a rapid clip.

Emmy Lou was in the kitchen frying bacon. "Fred came to get Quinn at five-thirty," she called as Jo headed for the door.

"Why the hell didn't Quinn tell Fred to get lost?" Jo clamped her hat on her head and grabbed a yellow slicker from a peg by the door.

"I think he wants to be your knight in shining armor," Emmy Lou said.

"I don't know what to do with one of those," Jo said. "I never had one before."

Emmy Lou came to the door. "You were on the right track last night in the barn."

Jo shook her head. "That would completely louse up the plan."

"Then maybe you need a new plan."

Jo flung open the door. "Can't think about that now. I have to go save Quinn before Fred breaks every bone in his gorgeous body."

She ran toward the corral, splashing through puddles

along the way, but she wasn't in time. As she arrived, Hyper slid to an abrupt halt, haunches down, and Quinn popped right out of the saddle. The corral was a sea of mud, so there was no question he'd land in it. Fortunately it was butt-first instead of headfirst.

Jo stormed up to Fred, who was leaning against the top rail, the brim of his hat creating a mini waterfall in front of his face. He didn't turn. "Mornin', Jo."

Jo would never publicly chastize anyone who worked for her, but it took an effort for her to keep her voice down so Quinn couldn't hear her. "It's raining, Fred. A real trash mover."

"I did notice that."

Jo nodded. "Okay. I guess we'll move on to my next point. Quinn's riding Hyper."

"I noticed that, too."

"Why is he riding Hyper, Fred?"

"That was the horse he wanted."

"Of course he did!" Jo heard herself getting loud and lowered her voice. "That's the horse everybody wants, because he's beautiful. I'll bet you didn't tell him that horse is a spoiled brat, did you?"

"'Scuse me a minute, Jo." Fred made a megaphone of his hands. "Your hat's over yonder!" he called to Quinn. "Grip harder with your thighs next time."

"I don't want there to be a next time," Jo said.

Fred turned to her at last, a challenge in his gray eyes. "Wanna take over?"

"No, I want you to take it easy on him! At this rate he'll end up in the hospital, which is not fair considering he's only doing this as a favor to me."

"I don't think he'll end up in the hospital."

"No? I've already seen him take one tumble. The next one could be—"

"He's hit the mud four times already." Fred sounded proud of the fact.

"Four?"

"Whoops. Make that five."

Jo whipped around to take stock of the newest disaster. What she saw made her go cold. Quinn lay facedown in the muck. "God, Fred, you've killed him." Jo ducked through the rails of the corral and ran toward Quinn. "Are you okay? Please be okay!" She crouched beside him. At least he seemed to be breathing. "Quinn! Speak to me!"

Slowly he rolled to his back and glanced at her, his face grimy with mud. He grinned. "Well, damn. I thought I'd have this riding thing figured out before breakfast. It may take a little longer than that."

"Don't move." Jo wiped a glob of mud from his chin with a trembling hand. If he was really hurt she'd never forgive herself. "You may have a concussion. A broken back. Broken neck. Broken ribs."

"Nah. Besides, I can't just lie here. The way the rain's coming down, I'll drown."

Jo leaned closer, her conscience kicking her six ways to Sunday. "You don't have to do this," she said in an undertone. "I'll tell Fred I've changed my mind about having you impersonate Hastings. Go get cleaned up, have Emmy Lou's famous ranch breakfast and drive out of here."

His blue gaze, usually so easygoing, slowly took on the look of tempered steel. "Nope. Can't do it."

"Why not? Surely you're not trying to prove something to Fred. I could have throttled you last night with that stupid posturing about the whiskey."

Quinn smiled and eased to a sitting position. "It did taste a lot like the muck in this corral." He turned his face away and spit.

"Go back to New York, Quinn. Please."

He looked at her. "You don't want me around any-more?"

"I didn't say that."

"Then I'm staying." He jerked a thumb at Hyper. "Is it true that horse slept in your bed?"

So Fred had explained that she was the one who had spoiled Hyper. "He was tiny. Premature, and an orphan. So cute and lonesome. Fred told me I'd be sorry."

Quinn gave her a sly grin. "You said I was cute, and I'm feeling kinda lonesome."

She tried to ignore the leap in her pulse rate. "I don't make those mistakes anymore. You see how Hyper turned out." She stood. "Come on, I'll help you up, and we'll go inside."

He ignored her outstretched hand and got to his feet by himself. "I told you I'd do this, and I'll do it."

She noticed him wince and caught his arm. "You were never supposed to learn to become a real cowboy! I thought you could pick up a few things and fake it."

He leaned down and retrieved his muddy hat, obviously a loan from Benny. The mud-spattered jeans and shirt looked like Benny's, too, and the worn boots. Mud-spat-tered or clean, Benny had never looked so good in these clothes. Quinn might be a lousy rider, but he was born to dress in snug jeans and broad-shouldered Western shirts.

He settled the hat on his head and glanced at her. "There's something I forgot to tell you. Faking it isn't my style." He tipped his hat. "Excuse me, ma'am." There was a definite drawl in his voice. "I need to go catch your spoiled-rotten horse."

As he ambled away, Jo stared at him with her mouth open. "What's with the drawl? You're from New York! New Yorkers don't drawl."

Quinn laughed. "I bit my tongue on that last go-round. Drawling feels better than talking fast."

"And where'd you get that bowlegged walk? That's not your normal walk, either."

He kept going, headed for the dark bay standing in a corner of the corral. "I always wondered why cowboys walk this way. After banging around in that saddle a few times, I get it."

"Quinn, stop this!"

He kept walking.

Jo stalked to Fred. "We have to make him quit."

"Now, Jo, have you ever known a cowboy you could talk out of something once he's set his mind to it?"

"Read my lips—*he's not a cowboy.*"

Fred shrugged. "I wouldn't be so sure. I thought he shouldn't ride this morning on account of the rain. But he wanted to."

"You're kidding."

"Nope. He just asked if rain would be bad for the horse."

"But you should have talked him out of riding Hyper."

"I tried. He said if he could ride Hyper he'd know he'd really learned how to ride. Said he'd keep at it until he could stay on. And look at that. Damned if he don't have old Hyper figured out."

Jo gazed across the corral. Hyper started out with his usual crow hops, but Quinn gripped with his thighs and held on. Jo could tell that he was gripping with his thighs because of the way the wet denim moved. Not that she was looking at his thighs on purpose. And she was definitely not looking at the spot between his thighs, the place that had taken so much punishment from the saddle this morning. He'd probably appreciate an ice pack for that area. She cringed as Quinn's butt came partially off the saddle and slammed down again.

But, God, he had a great butt. And he was keeping it mostly in the saddle this time. He dug his heels into Hyper's ribs, and the gelding took off at a lope. Quinn's hat flew off, and for a second Jo thought Quinn would tumble into the mud again, but he corrected his position by using those spectacular thigh muscles.

As Hyper and Quinn rounded the curve of the corral, Quinn let out a whoop. "Coming through," he yelled. "I still can't steer worth a damn!"

Jo scrambled through the fence barely ahead of the thundering hooves.

"Yee-haw!" Quinn shouted as Hyper made another circuit, flinging mud everywhere.

Jo turned to stare at Fred. "Yee-haw?"

"We'll work on that," Fred said. "He probably thinks that's what you're supposed to say at a time like this. Can't expect him to get everything right at first. He's from New York."

Jo gazed at Quinn sailing around the corral in the rain, a big old grin on his face. "Let me get this straight. This whole circus this morning was Quinn's idea, not yours?"

"I've seen how you look at him, Jo. I wouldn't deliberately do the boy wrong."

Jo pulled her slicker closer around her. "I don't look at him any certain way."

"Okay. Whatever you say. And he don't look at you no certain way, either. I'm an old coot and I don't know what I'm talking about."

Jo sighed. "You sound like Emmy Lou."

"Well, she's an old lady, just like I'm an old coot. Our eyesight's no good, and besides, we can't remember what it's like to have them feelings, so don't pay us no mind."

Jo had a sudden flash of insight. She began putting together isolated incidents and finally decided she had a case. "Fred, are you sweet on Emmy Lou?"

The part of Fred's cheeks not covered with his bushy gray beard grew red. "Now what makes you say a darn fool thing like that? Emmy Lou and me have been working on this ranch together for years, been giving each other hell for years, too. We've known each other too long, and we're too danged sensible for such goings-on."

Jo grinned. "I'll be damned. You are sweet on her. Does she know?"

"She don't know because there's nothing to it!" Fred turned abruptly and made a megaphone of his hands again. "Hey, Quinn, how about finding the brake on that nag? I need me some breakfast!"

"You go ahead. I'll be fine."

"You will not be fine. Don't go getting cocky on me. In case you hadn't noticed, you're on a runaway horse. Hyper's got the bit in his teeth, and if you weren't in this here corral, he'd be taking you on a trip to the high country, and you wouldn't have any say about it at all."

"I'll bet I could stop this horse whenever I want."

Fred exchanged a glance with Jo and sighed. "Ain't that just like any other cowboy in the world? A little success, and he gets to bragging on himself."

"Fred, he's not a cowboy."

"He sure as hell acts like one." He raised his voice. "Let's see this control you've got over that horse, cowboy. And don't go jerking the reins and hurting his mouth. Go easy."

"Okay." Quinn started pulling as he rounded the curve coming toward Jo and Fred. Nothing happened. He frowned and pulled harder.

Fred folded his arms. "We're waiting on you, cowboy. Try yelling *whoa.*"

Quinn put more muscle into it. "Whoa!" he yelled. When Hyper still didn't respond, he leaned back on the reins. "Dammit, stop!"

"I'll get him not to say *dammit, stop* when I mention the *yee-haw,*" Fred said.

"Good idea. Look out, here he—"

Hyper slid to a stop right in front of Jo and Fred, spraying mud all over them.

"—comes," Jo finished, holding out her arms and surveying her yellow slicker, now polka-dotted with mud. At least her clothes were protected by the slicker. Fred would have to start over before he appeared at the ranch house.

"Wow. Just like a New York street sweeper." Quinn sat in the saddle staring at them. "Sorry about that."

Jo glanced at him and saw the sparkle of mischief in his blue eyes. "Funny, but you don't look sorry," she said.

"Oh, but I am." He leaned on the saddle horn and grinned at her.

Amazing, Jo thought. At this moment every obnoxious, sexy, devilish inch of him screamed out *cowboy.* But he wasn't quite cowboy enough to know he should keep his feet in the stirrups until he was ready to dismount.

Taking note of that, Jo slipped through the rails of the corral. "Let me help you get off that beast."

"Oh, that's okay." He patted the horse's neck. "Me and Hyper, we're getting along fine. You have to know how to deal with him. He just needs a firm hand."

"I'm sure you're right. What was I thinking? Thanks for telling me." She hoped Hyper remembered the trick she'd taught him when he was still a colt. She grabbed his reins and gave a soft, low whistle.

On cue Hyper reared, and Quinn slid neatly down the horse's rump into the mud.

"It's a good idea to keep your feet in the stirrups when you're sitting in the saddle," she said with a sweet-as-pie grin. "You never know what might happen if you don't." She led Hyper out the gate Fred held open.

"Good job," Fred said, smiling in approval as he took the reins from her. "I'll walk him a little and give him a rubdown." He glanced at Quinn, who still sat in the mud as if he couldn't quite believe he'd ended up there after his grand finish. "Come on down to the bunkhouse for a shower before breakfast, cowboy," he said. "You're not fit to sit at Emmy Lou's table looking like that." He walked Hyper toward the barn.

Quinn continued to sit in the mud with the rain pouring down on him.

Jo stood by the open gate. "Are you coming out?"

"You did that on purpose," he said, a note of surprise in his voice.

"Somebody had to. You were getting way too big for your britches." She stepped a little closer, hoping her little maneuver hadn't been too rough on him. "Are you okay?"

"What if I'm not?"

Instantly she regretted her impulsiveness. She hurried toward him. "Oh, Quinn, I didn't mean to hurt you. I only wanted to prick a hole in your pride before it got out of control." Anxiety twisted in her stomach. "Can you stand?"

"I don't know."

Dammit, why had she allowed herself that moment of revenge? "Where do you hurt?"

His head drooped. "All over. I don't think there's a single inch of me that doesn't hurt."

"Oh, Quinn." She dropped to her knees in the mud beside him and put her hand on his mud-caked shoulder. "Did you twist your ankle? Is that why you're afraid to stand up? What can I do?"

His head lifted slowly. She had the space of a heartbeat to see the wicked gleam in his eyes before he grabbed her and wrestled her to the mud. She shrieked and fought, but he unsnapped her slicker and started smearing mud down the front of her shirt.

"Stop that! I'll kill you, Quinn Monroe!"

"Devil woman," he said, laughing as he rolled with her in the muck. "How dare you make that horse rear? You turned him into a regular water slide."

"How dare you tell me how to handle him? Let me up!"

He pinned her to the ooze and proceeded to rub mud all over her. "Not until you're as covered with this goo as I am. Dump me in the dirt, will you?"

"You were getting too cocky!" Her breathing became labored as she struggled to free herself. Or maybe it was the other sensation, the one of having his hands all over her, that was causing her to gasp for breath.

"I deserved to be cocky." His chest heaved as he gulped in air. "I got up at the crack of dawn and busted my butt, literally, on that spoiled horse of yours. And, by God, I rode him."

"I think it was more like he took you for a ride!" She continued to squirm away from his touch, but her heart wasn't in it. In fact, the squish of the mud was beginning to feel sort of good. And she was feeling a bit warm and oozy inside as well as outside.

"That horse knew who was boss." His hand grazed her breast as if by accident. "I was in control the entire time."

"Were not."

"Was, too." He grabbed her wrists and held them as he rolled on top of her.

Surely she hadn't meant to make a cradle of her hips. Surely he hadn't meant to ease himself between her thighs. Surely neither of them had intended to end up in the perfect position for her to discover that he was fully aroused.

"Were not," she whispered, looking into his eyes.

"Was, too." His eyes darkened as his gaze searched hers. "Jo…"

Her heart beat like a rabbit's. "Don't kiss me, Quinn."

"Okay, I won't." He lowered his head.

"You are." She was quivering. "You're going to kiss me."

"No. Brian Hastings is going to kiss you. Think Brian Hastings."

When his mouth found hers, she didn't think at all. She sure did feel, though—cool lips that quickly warmed against hers and shaped themselves into the soul of temptation in no time, a tongue that told her exactly what Quinn would be doing if they didn't have two layers of denim between their significant body parts. She liked everything about this kiss, even the mud that squished between them as he eased his chest to press against her breasts.

The only thing she didn't like was that he stopped kissing her.

"More," she whispered, keeping her eyes firmly closed.

"Can't."

"Can so."

"If I kiss you some more, I'm liable to unzip your jeans and start getting serious about this maneuver."

Reluctantly she opened her eyes. At least he looked as

7

"TARNATION, boy, don't they feed you in New York City?" Fred stared at Quinn as he served himself a second helping of biscuits and gravy.

"Not like this." Quinn dove in while Emmy Lou beamed. He'd never been a breakfast eater in New York. Coffee and toast did the trick. But he wasn't in New York anymore, and he polished off enough bacon, eggs, biscuits and gravy to make him embarrassed, except that everyone else ate almost as much. None of the people sitting around the table was plump except Emmy Lou, and on her it looked nice.

Nobody was rude enough to mention the ice pack Quinn had positioned against his crotch. Emmy Lou had noticed the way he was walking and had suggested it. After a few minutes the ache had gone away and he just felt numb down there, which was probably a good thing considering the direction his thoughts took every time he glanced across the table at Jo.

The topic of conversation turned to Quinn's impending move to the bunkhouse. Jo didn't say much, just got pinker and pinker as the discussion continued. Her hair was damp from her shower, and she wore no makeup. Quinn had always loved the stage in a relationship when a woman became comfortable enough to appear in front of him fresh from the shower without doing her hair or putting on makeup.

Of course this didn't count as a stage, because he wasn't involved with Jo. Wouldn't be involved with Jo. Dammit. Maybe he should strap an ice pack permanently to his crotch.

"People will think it's terrible if we make Brian Hastings sleep in the bunkhouse," Emmy Lou said. "I think you should stay up at the house, Quinn. The bunkhouse is grungy."

"No, it ain't!" Fred said. "Just because I won't let you clean it every five minutes and put doilies around on whatever don't move, you—"

"It's a pit," Emmy Lou said to Quinn with a smile. "Fred and Benny act like it's their clubhouse or something. All I did was try to vacuum one day and rearrange a few things, and you'd think I'd burned the place to the ground."

"You Hoovered the ace of clubs out of my lucky deck of cards, woman!"

Emmy Lou leaned over and patted Quinn's hand. "Stay up at the house. Don't you agree he should, Jo?"

"Well, I—"

"Emmy Lou," Fred said, pointing at her. "Don't be forgetting that Jo's a divorcée."

"So what?" Emmy Lou said.

Fred acted as if he were explaining a simple fact to a three-year-old. "People think a certain way about divorcées. They'll think there's hanky-panky going on between him and Jo if he sleeps in the house."

And they would be right, Quinn thought. But it had nothing to do with her being divorced. Jo would tempt him single, divorced, even virginal.

"That might be the way your mind works, Fred," Emmy Lou said. "But everybody doesn't automatically think like that."

"Wanna bet?" Fred pointed at Emmy Lou. "Try hanging out in the Lazy Bones Saloon sometime."

Emmy Lou glared at him. "I've been meaning to try that. But first you'd better teach me how to chew and spit. Honestly, Fred. As if I care about what a bunch of old booz—"

"Watch yourself, woman," Fred said.

Benny's eyes widened. "You're gonna learn to chew and spit, Emmy Lou?"

"Not really, Benny." Emmy Lou smiled at him. "I think it's a perfectly disgusting habit, don't you?"

Benny glanced uncertainly from Fred's scowl to Emmy Lou's smile. "I think…I want some more biscuits."

"Well done, Benny," Jo said. "It doesn't pay to get in the middle of a lovers' quarrel, you know." Then she looked stricken. "Oops. I didn't mean to say that. I really didn't. Must be the stress getting to me. I'm sorry."

Quinn stopped chewing as silence descended over the table. He looked at Jo, who sat gazing anxiously at Fred and Emmy Lou. Then he glanced at Fred, who had a murderous gleam in his eye, and Emmy Lou, who had turned the color of the tomatoes ripening on the windowsill.

Finally Emmy Lou cleared her throat. "I have no idea what you're talking about, Josephine." She stood and started collecting dishes. "I wouldn't take up with that old goat for all the tea in Japan."

"It's China!" Fred muttered. "And that goes double for me." He pulled his napkin from where he'd tucked it into his shirt and tossed it on the table. "I got chores to do."

"You don't have to hide it!" Jo cried. "I didn't mean to spill the beans and embarrass you both, but I think it's wonderful if you two have something going!"

"Me, too!" Benny said. "What do they have going, Jo?"

"Not a dad-blasted thing," Fred said. He started out of the kitchen just as the doorbell rang. "I'll get that."

Jo walked to the sink and put her arm around Emmy Lou. "Em, I'm sorry. I didn't even figure it out until this morning, and then—damn, I just opened my mouth and out it came."

Emmy Lou squirted a large stream of dishwashing liquid in the sink and turned the faucet on full blast, creating mounds of foam. Then she began washing furiously. "If that man said anything to you I'm going to hang him by his…thumbs."

"No! It was just the way he made a certain comment, and I asked if you two were sweethearts, and he got all red, like you're doing now. Em, you and Fred are like parents to me. This feels perfect, the two of you in love."

In her agitation Emmy Lou slopped water and soapsuds on the floor. "Who said anything about love?"

"It's perfectly obvious, the way you two fight, that you're in love."

Quinn sipped his coffee and watched in fascination. For so many years he'd lived by himself in Manhattan. Sure, he had buddies, and twice he'd had a live-in girlfriend for a few months, but aside from occasional trips to Murray's house, he hadn't been in a family setting in a long time. That's what this morning felt like, and he was loving the hell out of it.

Fred appeared in the kitchen doorway. "It's that fool Doobie and his scrawny wife, Eloise. I parked them in the living room. I imagine they want to get a look at Brian Hastings."

Quinn tensed. Last night's performance with Dick had been a reflex action, and Dick hadn't been inclined to be skeptical. Quinn remembered that Doobie was president of the local bank. In his experience, bankers were born skeptics. He glanced at Jo.

"It's up to you," she said. "You don't have to see them. In fact, you don't have to see anybody. You can be as reclusive as you want."

"Yeah, but this is your banker. I'm supposed to offer him a part in the movie, remember?"

"You don't have to." Ever since they'd squirmed together in the mud this morning she'd had a captivating shyness in her eyes whenever she looked at him.

Quinn smiled at her. Hell, didn't she know he'd do just about anything for her? Only a guy who was wrapped around a woman's little finger would voluntarily suggest that he move to the bunkhouse after she'd announced that they shouldn't become sexually involved.

"I'm sure we can find a part for him somewhere," he said. He'd never wished that he could be Brian Hastings, but at the moment he almost wanted to be, just so he'd have the power to shoot a movie here and help her cause. He set down his mug and pushed back his chair. "Come and introduce me." He stood up, and the ice pack dropped to the floor.

Jo blushed as she glanced at the ice pack and at his crotch. "Um, are you better?"

Quinn leaned down and picked up the ice pack. "Good as new."

"I'm glad. I mean, that's good. I mean…"

Fred coughed. "Maybe you should drop that particular topic, Jo."

"Good idea." Jo swallowed. "Come on, Quinn. Let's go meet my banker."

"I'll come in with some coffee and arsenic in a little

bit." Emmy Lou continued washing dishes without turning.

Fred snorted with laughter. Then he snuck a look at Emmy Lou and glanced quickly away again. "Benny, you and me got stuff to do. Let's get a move on."

Emmy Lou kept her back to Fred while she washed and rinsed dishes with a vengeance. "I was hoping you men would clear out of my kitchen and let me get my pot roast in the oven," she said. "Can't accomplish a dad-blasted thing when you're underfoot."

Jo winked at Quinn.

He winked back and followed her out of the kitchen. "How long do you think it's been going on?" he said in a low voice.

"Probably years. I was just too wrapped up in my own problems to notice, but when Fred started talking this morning I got this flash, and all sorts of things began to click in my brain." She walked into the living room, where a skinny man and his wife sat on a worn leather sofa. "Mr. and Mrs. Doobie! May I introduce you to Brian Hastings?"

Doobie popped up from the sofa and came forward, hand outstretched, but Mrs. Doobie looked as if she might pass out.

Her mouth opened and closed several times, but she made no sound.

"Mr. Hastings," Doobie said in an unfortunately high voice. The few strands of long hair he'd combed over his bald head quivered as he pumped Quinn's hand vigorously. "This is quite an honor."

Definitely not a speaking part, Quinn thought. "I feel lucky to be here," he said. "This is the perfect location to film *The Brunette Wore Spurs.*" Yeah, that was a good title. Amazing what he could come up with on short notice.

Jo stared at him in astonishment. "That's a working title, right?" She gave him a slight nudge with her foot.

"Guess so. Works for me."

"It sounds a little like a film that would be in the adult section at the video store." Jo chuckled and nudged Quinn again. "But, as we all know, film titles get changed all the time."

"They do?" Quinn had never thought about that. "I mean, yes, they certainly do. Why, Julia told me—you all know Julia Roberts, right?"

Jo looked wary, but Doobie and his wife nodded enthusiastically.

"Well, Julia told me that *Pretty Woman* was almost called *Pretty Prostitute.* And the other day I was talking to Bob Redford, and he said that—"

"Coffee!" Emmy Lou announced. "Hello there, Doobies! So good to see you up so bright and early this morning. What do you think of our celebrity guest, Eloise?"

Eloise licked her thin lips and twisted her hands in her lap. "Mr. Hastings, was that really your fanny in that nude scene?"

"Eloise!" Doobie blanched.

Quinn gulped. He hadn't seen a Brian Hastings movie in years. He didn't know the guy had shot a nude-fanny scene. He wished he had known before he'd agreed to impersonate the guy.

"Of course it was him." Emmy Lou calmly poured coffee from a silver urn into a china teacup. "You think anyone else would have a tush that cute? Here you go, Eloise. Sugar and cream's on the coffee table there."

"I've always wondered," Eloise said. She took the coffee but continued to stare at Quinn as if she might ask him to strip down and prove it was his fanny in the scene. "The lighting wasn't very good. You were mostly in shadows."

Thank God, Quinn thought. Even though he hadn't been the one naked in front of the cameras and half the free world, he was pretending to be that guy. He hoped there had been *lots* of shadow.

Doobie turned to his wife. His face had gone from pale to quite pink. "You told me you closed your eyes at that part."

"I lied, Cuthbert."

"You know I don't approve of a married woman seeing another man's naked...parts."

Eloise sat up straighter. "And I've obeyed you all the years of our marriage, until I found out there would be a nude scene in *Rogue's Reward*. When we saw it at the Lyric Theater I closed my eyes to please you, but I left them open a little slit, like this." She demonstrated her peeking technique. "Then I bought the video," she added bravely.

"And watched that scene again without me?" Doobie looked scandalized. "Eloise, how could you?"

"Brian Hastings is the only man who could tempt me to break my vow to you, Cuthbert." Eloise gazed adoringly at Quinn. "Two hundred and six times."

Doobie made a little choking sound.

"Well, that certainly must be a record!" Jo said brightly. "I don't know how many people watch the same movie two hundred and six times. You should be very flattered, Brian."

"Oh, I didn't watch the whole movie." Eloise took a dainty sip of her coffee. "Only the nude-fanny scene. I keep the tape permanently rewound to that section."

Quinn couldn't look at Doobie. The poor little man

seemed about to have a fit, and Quinn couldn't say he blamed him. He wouldn't be too happy to discover such a fact about his wife, if he had one. He glanced at Jo. "What did you think of that scene?"

"It was pretty hot, Brian. Some of your better work." She looked as if she might burst out laughing any minute.

He didn't think it was so damn funny, and he didn't much like the idea that she'd been drooling over Hastings' butt, too. "Did you buy the video?"

She pressed her lips together, as if that was the only way she could keep from laughing. She shook her head.

"I did," Emmy Lou said. "And since you never watch your own movies, you might like to take a look sometime."

"Yeah. Yeah, I'd like to see that, uh, scene."

"It's wonderful," Eloise said with a sigh. "All the girls think so."

"Girls?" Doobie squeaked. "What girls?"

"The Ugly Bug Garden Club. We always close the meeting with a showing of that scene."

"Oh, my God," Doobie wailed. "My wife's peddling porn in the sanctity of our home."

"Get a grip, Cuthbert," Emmy Lou said. "It's one scene, for crying out loud. And it's not pornography, it's art."

"We're all hoping you'll do another," Eloise said to Quinn. "Any chance of that in *The Brunette Wore Spurs?*"

"No."

"That's too bad." Eloise set down her cup and saucer. "Mr. Hastings, the ladies of the garden club would consider it a great honor if you would—"

"*What?*" Quinn wasn't aware he'd backed up until he

bumped into a leather wing chair in the corner of the room.

"—speak to our group," Eloise said. "Goodness, what did you think I was going to ask?"

"Uh, nothing." Quinn cleared his throat and took a deep breath. "I'd love to do that, of course." Not. He couldn't imagine speaking to a bunch of women who ended every meeting ogling his bare butt. Or Hastings' bare butt, which nearly amounted to the same thing. "But I'll be pretty busy investigating the area and figuring out..." He racked his brain for what a filmmaker might need to know about a location. "I have to decide where we can plug in our lights."

Jo turned to him with a puzzled expression.

But he'd hit upon a way to work in something he knew about, which was home improvement, and he decided to go with it. "Yep, electricity's a big concern with these things. I look around at Jo's ranch, and I like what I see, but I have to ask myself, are there enough outlets? When you're filming, you can never have too many outlets."

"Or *generators*," Jo said, rolling her eyes.

"Well, there's that option, too," Quinn said casually. "Personally I like lots of outlets."

"So I guess the Brian Hastings town festival is out of the question," Doobie said, sounding relieved.

Jo turned to Doobie. "What Brian Hastings town festival?"

"Dick Cassidy brought it up last night when he was buying rounds of drinks at the Ugly Bug Saloon. I guess he's pretty set up about getting a part in the movie. Word got back to the town council, and the mayor asked me to come out this morning and ask about it, considering that I have a close relationship with Jo, here."

"Do you?" Quinn asked. From what he'd heard, Doobie could hardly wait to foreclose on the Bar None.

"Absolutely." Doobie smiled at Jo. "She's like the daughter I never had."

Eloise bounced out of her seat. "Cuthbert Doobie, you *have* a daughter, and she's given you nine lovely grandchildren. It's not her fault that none of her husbands have been able to hold a job."

Quinn decided it was time to stroke old Cuthbert's ego. "I've been thinking about something ever since I walked in here." He pointed a finger at the skinny banker. "You're the perfect Pierre."

Doobie blinked. "Pierre?"

"A French character in the movie. You have that same worldly look, that same sophistication."

Doobie preened. "Maybe so, but I don't speak French."

"No problem. It's not a speaking role."

"Then how do we know that he's sophisticated and worldly if he never says anything?"

"Trust me. The minute you walk in front of the camera, everyone will know the kind of person you are."

Doobie nodded and looked wise. "I see your point. Then certainly, I'll do it. How about a dance?"

Quinn's jaw dropped. "You want to dance with me, Cuthbert?"

"No, no." Doobie laughed, and his dentures slipped a little. "I meant we could have a dance, just a simple dance on Saturday night, instead of the town festival. Or say, even better, a small rodeo in the afternoon, followed by the dance. If you could possibly see your way clear to participate, the people of Ugly Bug would be very appreciative."

Quinn glanced at Jo, and she shrugged, letting him

know it was up to him. A dance sounded relatively harmless. He was a decent dancer. But a rodeo would expose him as a fraud, for sure. "You don't want me to perform in the rodeo," he said. "The liability, you know. If I got hurt, the resulting suit would bankrupt the town."

"Oh! Then of course we don't want you to be *in* the rodeo. You can be the guest of honor."

"All right."

"Wonderful! Then—"

"Cuthbert, if we hold these events, we have to make a rule," Emmy Lou said. "Women are not allowed to grab at Brian's clothes or pinch his tush. No button popping, no pocket ripping. None of that."

"Certainly not!" Doobie looked offended at the very idea. "Well, then, I guess our mission is accomplished, Eloise. Come along."

Eloise didn't move. She stood gazing at Quinn, a dreamy smile on her face. "Save me a dance," she said.

"Sure."

"Oh, *thank you.*" She sighed and clasped her hands together. "I'll be counting the hours."

Doobie snorted and took his wife's arm. "Don't make such a big deal out of it, Eloise. It's just a dance."

"Just a dance? Just a *dance?* I think not, Cuthbert." She kept her gaze fastened on Quinn as her husband dragged her to the entry hall. "Why, dancing with Brian Hastings is more important than winning best garden of the year, more important than giving birth to our darling Primrose, more important than our *wedding night.* Which reminds me. I know you think you're a great—"

"Thanks for the coffee!" Doobie called as he hustled his wife out the door.

After they left Jo grinned at him. "You've done it

again. First Dick, and now that weasel Doobie. Thanks, Quinn.''

''I loved it, Eloise's tush fetish and all.'' Emmy Lou gathered coffee cups.

''Don't remind me about that part,'' Quinn said.

''Oh, she's harmless,'' Emmy Lou said. ''But he's not. Can you believe he had the nerve to say you were like a daughter to him? Just last week when you asked for an extension on your loan he said you might as well sell out and go back east, where you belong. Quinn, you were magnificent.'' She smiled at him. ''Brian Hastings couldn't have done it better. Well, he might not have spouted all that nonsense about electrical outlets, but otherwise, good job.'' She left the room carrying the tray.

''Doobie really said that to you last week?'' Quinn wished he'd been a little rougher on the guy.

''Well, to be fair, I am pretty far behind on my payments.''

''Listen, Jo, I—''

''Nope.'' She held up both hands. ''I shouldn't have brought it up. Forget I said anything.''

Quinn gazed at her. ''If you say so.'' Quinn longed to get his hands on her books. Okay, he'd rather get his hands on her, but she'd put the skids on that program. But if he could look over her accounts and have her explain the ranching business to him, he knew he could help.

''Don't you need to call your office?''

''Guess I do.''

''While you're doing that, I'll go down to the barn and check on Clarise and Stud-muffin. See you in a little while, then.''

''Right.'' Quinn noticed she hadn't suggested he use her office phone, probably because she didn't want him in there, period. So he made his call on the phone in the hallway.

As he was hanging up, Jo came in and hooked her slicker on a peg by the door.

"Everything okay at the barn?" he asked.

"Great." She looked damp, pink and very kissable. "How's your office?"

"No problems. What's next on the schedule?"

Jo shook her damp hair. "It's still raining. I called the vet before breakfast, and she can't come out to inseminate Lullabelle and Missy until tomorrow." She looked at Quinn. "We're sort of at loose ends today."

"What do you usually do when it rains like this?"

"Oh, paperwork in my office."

Exactly, he thought. "Jo, don't be so damned stubborn. Let's go into your office and you can give me a rundown on your financial situation."

"Nope, nope, nope."

Emmy Lou appeared in the doorway with a tape in her hand. "Here's *Rogue's Revenge* anytime you want to take a peek. I have some others, but it sounded like this was the one you were interested in."

"Hey, we can watch that!" Jo seized the opportunity. "You really should see one of your—I mean, Brian's—movies and get an idea of his personal style before you show up at the rodeo and dance on Saturday."

He couldn't argue with her reasoning. And he'd be dumb to turn down a chance to sit on the sofa with her and watch a movie. "Okay. We can do that."

She walked into the living room and opened the oak cabinet that housed the television set. "Sit down, sit down. You're about to be able to see yourself without hordes of screaming women interfering with your viewing enjoyment."

"I can hardly wait." He wouldn't mind one particular woman interfering, he thought as he sat on the sofa.

After shoving the tape into the VCR, she picked up the remote and started toward the sofa.

Okay, he thought, wondering how close she'd sit.

At the last minute she veered toward a wing chair. "Maybe I'll sit over here, for good measure."

"Hey, Emmy Lou's right in the kitchen. What could happen?"

"I suppose you're right." She sat on the sofa, but put a good three feet between them.

The movie started, and Quinn had to admit it was eerie how much Hastings looked like him, except that he seemed completely at home in a Western setting. "He's a good rider."

"You'll be fine with a little more practice. If all you do is attend that rodeo and dance, you might not ever have to demonstrate your riding to anyone."

He looked at her. "You mean I tortured my privates for nothing?"

She glanced at his crotch, and her cheeks grew pink. Then she looked at the television screen. "Watch the movie, Quinn."

He'd rather watch her, but he dutifully turned his head toward the TV.

Emmy Lou appeared in the doorway pulling on a raincoat. "The pot roast's in the oven, and I have to run into town for a few groceries."

Jo grabbed the remote and hit the pause button. "Want some company?"

"No, thanks. I'm taking the truck and I need the space for the bags. I'll be back in a couple of hours."

Quinn's heart began to pound. *A couple of hours.* He glanced at Jo.

8

ON HER WAY to the chair, Jo glanced out the window and saw Fred climb in the truck with Emmy Lou. So that's what Emmy Lou had in mind, Jo thought with a smile.

"What's going on out there?" Quinn asked.

"Emmy Lou's taking Fred to town."

"No wonder she didn't want you along."

"Yeah." Still smiling, Jo sat in the chair and punched the remote to restart the movie.

"But Benny's still around?"

"Oh, sure, and he's great with the horses, if you were worried about Clarise and Stud-muffin being alone down there. And if Betsy goes into labor, I'm sure he'll come up and get us."

"Glad to hear it."

"Now watch the movie, Quinn." Her pulse wouldn't settle down. She didn't think for a minute that he was worried about who was watching Clarise and Stud-muffin or whether Benny would alert them when Betsy went into labor. He wanted to know exactly how alone they were and how much temptation lay before him.

She wasn't about to explain that although Betsy was due any day, she showed absolutely no signs of going into labor. Benny wasn't the type to pop into the house for no reason, and Jo was sure Fred had told him to stay in the barn and keep an eye on the new baby. The chances of Benny showing up before lunch were practically nonexistent. She knew how alone they were, and it made watching the movie very difficult.

"I don't sound exactly like Hastings," Quinn said after a while.

"No, you sound better." Whoops. She hadn't meant to say it like that.

"What do you mean, better?"

Now she'd done it. "I happen to like a deeper voice on a guy, that's all."

"Oh." He sounded pleased with her answer.

"I don't think it's a problem that your voice is a little deeper than his. Nobody's mentioned your voice being different. In fact, they're all so gaga they don't notice anything different. They're prepared to believe you're him."

"I guess so."

But Jo could already tell big differences, and the advantage was in Quinn's favor. His eyes were a deeper blue, and his mouth had a more sensuous curve to the lower lip. And she liked Quinn's hands better. The fingers were longer, the back of his hand broader. Of course that was probably because Quinn was taller, bigger all over. And then she wondered if he was bigger *all over*. Her mouth grew moist.

The movie was quickly approaching the famous scene in the mining shack, the one that had made Eloise Doobie break her promise that she wouldn't look at another man's naked parts. The heroine, played by superstar Cheryl Ramsey, had already taken refuge in the shack while a terrible storm raged. She was conveniently in the process of taking off her wet clothes by candlelight while sitting on a cot.

"He's going to show up, isn't he?" Quinn said.

"Yep." Jo was becoming embarrassingly aroused being in the same room with Quinn during this sexy movie. She was so glad she wasn't a man. The poor guys couldn't hide their sexual interest at all.

"We're getting down to it, aren't we?"

"Yep." She didn't dare look at Quinn to find out if his sexual interest was beginning to show, but she'd bet it was. She could hear him breathing, and he kept shifting on the seat cushions. She wondered if getting an erection was painful after the punishment of his morning ride. "Are you okay?"

"How do you mean?"

"Um, are you…uncomfortable?"

"Yeah." His voice was dry. "Any suggestions?"

"I could get another ice pack for your—"

"No, thanks."

Jo tried to concentrate on the movie instead of the state of Quinn's private parts. Cheryl Ramsey was quite beautiful and quite naked. Jo really didn't like Quinn looking at her, but it couldn't be helped.

Brian Hastings opened the door of the shack. The woman glanced up. The look that passed between the two of them made Jo quiver. Then, without saying a word, Hastings unbuttoned his shirt.

Jo remembered thinking he looked pretty damned good when she first saw the scene, but that was before she'd been treated to Quinn Monroe in his briefs last night. Still, watching Hastings peel off his shirt and reach for the buckle of his belt reminded her of the joy of watching a well-put-together man undress. Quinn had been right about Dick's physique—he was soft in the middle.

She gripped the remote as Hastings, standing partially in shadow with his back to the camera, took off his jeans and his underwear in one movement. No wonder the Ugly Bug Garden Club closed out their meeting with this scene, she thought, her gaze riveted to the screen. But she'd wager that Quinn's behind looked even better than this.

Hastings walked over to Cheryl and sank to his knees before her. That simple, knightly gesture was the sort of thing that had made Brian Hastings number one at the box office, in Jo's estimation. She held her breath as Hastings kissed Cheryl—her mouth, her throat, her breasts. Jo's breasts felt tight and feverish.

As the music swelled, Hastings guided Cheryl to the cot, and the soft light illuminated their bodies as he moved over her.

Jo moaned softly and gripped the remote.

The scene froze in place.

"Did you mean to do that?" Quinn's voice was strained.

"No!" Jo glanced at the remote and punched it, but her hand was shaking so much she kept missing the play button.

"Fast forward through that scene, dammit," Quinn ordered tightly.

"I'm trying!" She stood and pointed the remote at the VCR while she stabbed at the buttons with trembling fingers.

"I'll do it." Quinn half rose from his seat and made a grab for the remote in her hand.

"I've got it!" She backed up and stumbled. The remote flew out of her hand and plopped between the cushions of the sofa.

"Oh, for crying out loud." Breathing hard, Quinn dropped to one knee and started fumbling for the remote.

"I've got it, I've got it." Jo sat on the sofa and shoved her hand in the space.

He pushed her hand aside. "Get out of there and let

me. This cushion is the deepest—'' The VCR clicked and whirred.

"You must have hit something. I think it's rewinding!"

"We're sure as hell not going to see that again!"

"Whoops, now it's going forward. Whoops—"

"Move your tush so I can reach under here and—damn, but leather is slippery. You paused the tape on purpose just when they were doing it, didn't you? You're just like those garden club ladies."

"No, I swear! It was an accident!"

"Quit jiggling around. Okay, I've got it." He leaned forward, and his cheek bumped her breast.

"Oh." She couldn't help it. She was on fire.

Quinn went very still. Slowly he lifted his head and looked into her eyes while the movie rewound behind him. "Don't look at me like that," he murmured.

"How?" She drifted closer to him as if pulled by an invisible string.

"Like you want me to rip your clothes off."

"Oh." She was breathing hard. "Okay, I won't." She closed her eyes.

"Dammit, that's worse. Open your eyes."

She did as he asked.

He groaned. "No help there."

As her gaze shifted to his sensuous mouth, she couldn't seem to help the downward tilt of her head, bringing her closer and closer. "It's because of the movie. We're just worked up because of the—"

"Speak for yourself." He cupped the back of her head and kissed her.

But she couldn't speak for herself when he kissed her like that. She couldn't even think for herself with her heart pounding so loud. Vaguely she heard a click and whirr as the movie surged to fast forward again. Quinn must have abandoned the remote, leaving it to fend for itself. As if she cared.

A girl couldn't be worried about remote controls when being kissed by a man who knew how to use his tongue the way Quinn did. When he started unbuttoning her blouse she let him do it. She even helped with a button or two. When he fumbled with the front catch of her bra she pushed his hand away and unhooked it herself.

After all, a man who could kiss like that would know what to do when presented with a woman's aching, needy breasts.

Quinn knew.

Jo arched her back and moaned as he showed her the full extent of his knowledge. After stroking her for several delicious moments, he slid up on the sofa and leaned her back over the armrest. She'd never been caressed so fully or with such murmured appreciation. She barely noticed as the movie switched from rewind to fast forward with every abandoned movement she made. She began to respond in other ways, becoming very moist at the point where the denim seam of her jeans started to pinch. The tender spot cried out for his attention.

He was panting by the time he kissed his way back to her mouth. He plunged his tongue in deep, letting her know what he wanted, and then slowly drew back. "I'm in agony," he said, gasping. "We need a decision, here. Either unzip my jeans or button your blouse."

She cradled her face in his hands. "I'm in agony, too."

His smile looked strained. "Yeah, but you weren't bouncing on a horse for an hour this morning."

"Oh! Poor Quinn."

"Poor Quinn is right." He slid his hands under her bottom and fit his erection tight against her. "I'm being tortured here, Jo."

"Oh, Quinn." She pressed closer.

He pushed back with a groan. With a whirr and click the VCR reversed direction.

She rocked against him and closed her eyes. *Whirr, click.* "I don't know if—"

"I know I'll be permanently impaired in another minute. God, Jo." He shoved harder. Another click from the remote was followed by a loud snap and a frantic spinning noise from the VCR.

Quinn turned his head toward the television. "What the hell?"

Jo stared at the snow on the screen. "I think we killed the movie."

"We didn't touch it!"

"But we bounced on the remote, Quinn. We pushed its little buttons, back and forth, back and forth, until snap! It came apart."

He gazed at her. "You are certainly pushing mine back and forth, back and forth, Josephine, and I am definitely ready to come apart."

She didn't let many people call her that, but she had a feeling Quinn had become one of the select few. "I'm getting scared, Quinn. This has the potential to be bigger than both of us."

"That's what the bulge in my jeans feels like."

"Do you want some ice?"

"No." He looked at her with frank admiration. "I want you. I want to take off your jeans, undo mine and finish what we started."

Her heart hammered as she pictured them doing exactly that. "I want you, too. So I guess there's only one solution."

His hand went to the buckle of his belt. "Live for today and to hell with tomorrow?" he suggested hopefully.

"No. I'll tell Dick and Mr. Doobie that you're not really Brian Hastings. I'll say we were playing a practical joke and they should forget the whole thing."

He sighed and took his hand away from his belt buckle. "Nope. Absolutely not. Those two would never let you forget it. Doobie would probably foreclose on this ranch immediately, and Dick would snap it up so he could have Ugly Bug Creek." Looking very much in pain, he eased slowly to the end of the couch.

"Quinn, I'm sorry." She pulled her blouse together, not wanting to make his condition worse. Or hers. But his sounded more critical.

"No, you're right," he said. "It's either tell everybody the truth or stop fooling around." He sat on the end of couch and rested her booted feet on his knees. "Be careful with your feet. One of these pointed toes in the wrong place would probably kill me."

"Maybe I could find you some sweats. That would give you more room."

"And maybe I should just stay away from you and Brian Hastings movies. Can we replace the tape?"

"We could have bought a new one at the video store yesterday, no problem. Today—big problem. I'll bet now that the word's out on you there's not a Brian Hastings movie for sale in the entire town of Ugly Bug."

He shifted position and winced. "Then I'll just call my secretary and ask her to overnight a copy of the tape."

"That would be wonderful."

"Yeah, I can autograph it for Emmy Lou."

"Oh, my God. Autographs. We need to find a copy of his signature for you to practice on."

"Or sprain my writing hand."

"A fake sprain, you mean."

"Oh, no, I want a real sprain. Something major to take my mind off my...other problem."

"Quinn, we're not going to deliberately injure you. I'm sure Emmy Lou has something with his signature on it. You can practice. I can't believe I didn't think of autographs. The trouble is, I keep forgetting that you're supposed to be Brian Hastings."

"You do?" He turned to her, and his gaze was steady. "I thought that's what was going on just now. You had me confused with him."

"You thought that?" She tightened her grip on her blouse to keep it together. "You thought I was like those women who rip your clothes off because they think they're getting a piece of Brian Hastings? You thought I'd parked my brain somewhere?" She *had* parked her brain somewhere, which explained her rash actions, but she'd never for a minute fantasized that Quinn was Brian Hastings. Quinn was powerful enough for any woman's fantasy.

"Well, we were watching one of his movies, and you were getting turned on."

"So were you! Does that mean you imagined I was Cheryl Ramsey?" she asked, suddenly worried.

"No." He propped a hand on the back of the sofa and leaned over her. "It means that the movie inspired me to think of what we might be doing. Power of suggestion. And to be honest, when I'm in the same room with you I need very little of that. This movie was overkill."

"So it wasn't seeing that beautiful naked woman that got you worked up?"

"Not by a long shot. It was the thought of seeing this beautiful naked woman."

Her pulse raced as his gaze traveled over her. "And for

the record, it wasn't seeing Brian Hastings' butt that got me worked up, either,'' she said.

He looked into her eyes. "Thank you." He gave her a wry smile. "But I would have taken that. I want you so much I don't care who you think I am if you'll let me touch you."

"Me, too," she murmured. "I don't care if I'm substituting for a glamorous movie star."

Desire flared in his eyes. "You're not. She wouldn't be a fit substitute for you."

"That's sweet. I don't believe it for a minute, but—"

He leaned closer, and his hand went to his belt again. "Want proof?"

"Oh, Quinn, I—uh-oh, I hear the truck coming up the road."

Quinn moved to his end of the sofa and grimaced as his jeans tightened across his crotch. "Better go upstairs and put yourself back together."

Jo sat up. Under her cushion the remote clicked again, and snow crackled on the television screen.

"Easy." Quinn gently lowered her feet to the floor.

"Would it help if you stood up?"

"Yeah. I'll do that in a minute. Go on."

"I hate to leave you to explain the broken tape to Emmy Lou."

"I'm a big boy."

She couldn't resist. "So you said."

His gaze was challenging. "Looks like you'll have to take it on faith."

"Yep." Jo couldn't help glancing at his crotch and remembering what he'd felt like pressed against her. She had some idea of what she was giving up, which didn't make the sacrifice any easier. A little bit of knowledge could be a terrible thing, she thought as she stood on rubbery legs. "I'm sorry I put us in this position," she said, starting past Quinn. "It won't happen again."

He reached up and gripped her thigh. "I'm not sorry," he said, gazing at her. "I love this position."

"Okay, so do I."

He gave her thigh a squeeze. "If it happens again, I'll make no noble guarantees about my behavior. I'd take you on any terms. Any terms at all."

Warmth rushed through her. "I'll keep that in mind."

"See that you do." He released her.

She wanted to stay, wanted to make love to him more than she'd ever wanted that with any man. The slamming of the truck's door propelled her reluctantly up the stairs.

QUINN'S EMOTIONS were in a shambles, but he could pick one truth out of this mess. He should never make Jo choose between him and the Bar None. Maybe in a moment of sexual weakness she'd choose him and hate him forever for causing her to lose this ranch.

Emmy Lou made a lot of racket coming into the house. Quinn suspected she was giving notice in case he and Jo were in the middle of…exactly what they'd been in the middle of.

"I'm back!" the housekeeper announced in a loud voice as she closed the front door with a bang and bustled into the kitchen with a paper sack in each arm.

"Need any help?" Quinn called. He was almost in shape to render aid. Almost.

"I've got it, thanks." She sounded breathless.

Quinn flashed on an old memory—coming home from a hot date and discovering his mother still up watching a movie on television. He'd responded to her greeting in that same breathless way before hurrying to his bedroom to see whether his shirt was buttoned up wrong or he had lipstick smeared across his mouth. Sure enough, once Emmy Lou dumped her bags in the kitchen she scurried down the hall toward her bedroom. Apparently everyone had some repair work to do.

Quinn took his time standing, then turned his back to the door to adjust himself. He'd had uncomfortable erections before, but nothing to compare with the pain of being saddle sore and aroused at the same time. He had new respect for cowboys who could ride all day and make love all night. They must be tough in places he'd never considered needed toughening.

Finally he was able to crouch and lift the seat cushion to retrieve the remote. As he reached for it, he noticed a movement next to his foot. He leaped back, knocking over the coffee table in the process.

"What on earth is going on in here?" Emmy Lou appeared in the doorway, her plump cheeks flushed.

"Stay back!" Quinn glanced around for a weapon and settled on the shovel from the fireplace tool set. By the time he had it in his hand, the creature had scuttled under the sofa.

"What is it?" Emmy Lou put her hand to her throat. "A rattlesnake?"

"It's not a snake." Quinn's insides were flipping around, but he was the only man in a house with two vulnerable women. It was up to him to protect them.

"Then what is it, for heaven's sake?"

Quinn thought of Jo lying on the sofa, her soft skin exposed, and shuddered. Then he thought of what might have happened if he'd unzipped his jeans, and he nearly passed out.

"Quinn, tell me what you've found."

"I don't know." He gripped the shovel and raised it over his head as he crept slowly toward the sofa. "But it's a monster," he said, his voice quivering.

9

"A RAT?" Emmy Lou asked.

"You have rats out here, too?" Quinn wondered how anybody in Montana slept at night.

"Well, of course."

"Well, it's not a rat or a mouse. It had a bunch of legs."

"Oh, a bug." With a chuckle, Emmy Lou took off her shoe and walked to the sofa.

"Stay back!" Quinn warned. "I'm the man around here. I'll handle this."

"If you whack that bug with the fireplace shovel you'll spray soot from here to kingdom come. Put that thing down and I'll take care of this, whatever it is."

"It had fangs."

"Really? How many legs, exactly?"

"Too many."

"Probably a wolf spider," Emmy Lou said.

"A *wolf* spider?" Quinn's hands grew clammy. "It attacks wolves?"

"No, no." Emmy Lou looked as if she was trying hard not to laugh, for which Quinn was grateful. "They just look ferocious. They're not poisonous or anything, and they keep the other insects under control."

Quinn got a bad feeling in the pit of his stomach. "What other insects?"

Emmy Lou gazed at him, a twinkle in her eye. "You

know, it's really sweet of you to offer to defend me, considering you're so scared of bugs.''

"I'm not, either! That's no bug. Bugs are things like flies and mosquitoes and ladybugs. Moths, butterflies, caterpillars. This is…prehistoric.''

Emmy Lou smiled. "How did you think the creek and town got named?''

"I tried not to think about it, if you must know.'' He had a horrifying thought. "You mean these things are *common* around here?''

"Sure. You get used to them.'' A wicked little gleam appeared in her eye. "You're more likely to find them down at the bunkhouse than up here.''

Quinn caught his breath. For one wild minute he thought of reconsidering his sleeping arrangements. Then Jo appeared in the living room doorway, and he knew he'd have to stay in the bunkhouse, ugly bugs and all. She'd combed her hair and fastened her clothing so she looked perfectly proper, but he remembered all too well how she'd helped him unbutton her blouse. And how she'd unhooked her bra for him. And then lifted those spectacular breasts, pressing them into his waiting hands.

"What's going on?'' Jo asked, gazing at the sofa cushion tossed aside, the coffee table capsized and the fireplace shovel in Quinn's hand. "Spring cleaning?''

"Sort of,'' Quinn said. "Don't come in here, Jo. Wolf spider.''

"Really? Cool! Where is it?''

He couldn't believe her reaction. "Under the sofa,'' he said ominously. "You know, under the *sofa*.'' He wondered how long it would take her to realize the monster could have attacked while she was lying there exposed.

"Then let's move the sofa,'' Jo said, totally nonchalant about the whole thing.

"Don't, Jo. You'll faint when you see it. It's huge."

"They usually are," Jo said, walking toward the sofa.

"Suit yourself, Red Riding Hood." Quinn folded his arms, but he kept hold of the fireplace shovel. "Move that sofa and take a look at that big old wolf spider. Don't blame me if you start screaming your head off. I warned you."

Emmy Lou started out of the room. "Hold on. I'll get a glass and see if we can catch it and put it outside."

Quinn almost dropped the shovel. "You're going to *what?*"

"Try to catch it. You know, put a glass down on top of it and then slide a piece of cardboard underneath."

"Are you crazy?"

"No. I've done it before."

Quinn rolled his eyes. "Then you'd better bring a punch bowl and a piece of plywood! We're not talking about Charlotte here, ladies. We're talking big. Very, very big. Spiderzilla."

Emmy Lou smiled at him. "I've discovered that men tend to exaggerate the size of things." She left the room.

Jo let out a very unladylike snort of laughter, and Quinn glared at her.

She tried to compose herself but was obviously having trouble. "Did you tell her about the tape?"

"Not yet. I—"

"Well, this should work." Emmy Lou came in holding a water glass and the back of a cereal box.

"For one leg," Quinn muttered darkly. "But if you women are determined to do this reckless thing, I'll ride shotgun. If it starts to attack, I'll be here."

"They don't attack," Jo said. "Okay, Em. I'll move the sofa just a bit, and you stand ready with that glass."

"Right."

"And I'll stand ready to whack it when you two run screaming out of the room," Quinn said, raising the shovel over his head.

Jo moved the sofa a few inches, and the spider ran right at Quinn.

The women didn't scream, but he was afraid he might have as he started banging the shovel everywhere, stirring up clouds of soot as the spider raced around the room.

"Quick, over by the door, Em!" Jo cried.

Emmy Lou pounced with her glass. "Got him!"

"Or her," Jo said. She crouched as Emmy Lou slid the cardboard under the glass and expertly flipped the whole thing over. "Nope, it's a him."

Quinn stared at the two women in horrified fascination. "How can you tell? And why would you want to?"

"Spiders are fascinating," Jo said. "His sex organs are right by his mouth, an arrangement certain people might envy. Want to see?"

"That's okay." Quinn was sweating like crazy. Sure enough, the monster fit in the glass, but he wouldn't have bet on it. "I'll take your word for it."

"This is a pretty big one," Emmy Lou said. "That body looks almost two inches across, so with the legs and all, it's—"

"Gigantic, like Quinn said," Jo finished, giving Quinn an understanding smile. "Bigger than his fist."

"I'll take him outside and let him go," Emmy Lou said.

Quinn tried to sound casual. "Uh, where would that be, exactly?"

"Out in my veggie garden. He'll like it there. He'll probably stay."

"Oh." He rolled his shoulders and made a mental note

to never, ever offer to pick vegetables for Emmy Lou. "I'll, uh, pick up around here, then."

"I'll help," Jo said.

Quinn replaced the shovel in the fireplace tool holder and turned to find Jo looking at him with great tenderness.

"What?" he asked.

"It's just that you're so adorable," she said.

"Adorable?" He preferred words like *virile* and *manly*, himself. *Adorable* was for kids.

"A big strong man like you who's afraid of snakes and bugs," she said. "And trying so hard not to be. It's very sweet."

Quinn felt his face heat up. He set the coffee table on its feet to avoid looking at Jo. "I had an older cousin who used to tease me, shoving wiggly things in my face."

"Shame on him," Jo said.

"It was a girl," Quinn said, growing even redder.

"Then shame on her." She walked over to touch his arm. "But you know, it's possible to get over things like that."

"I doubt it. Been that way ever since I was four."

"You can desensitize yourself. It would be easy around this place, because you'll always be coming in contact with creepy-crawlies. Soon you'd barely notice them."

He glanced at her hand. His arm already tingled where he felt the light pressure of her fingers. He looked into her eyes. "Think that would work with you, too?" he asked in a low voice. "Because I'd sure love to try."

She jerked her hand away and stepped back.

"If the concept works, it should work for anything," he said, closing the gap between them. "Maybe if I kiss you enough, eventually I won't get so aroused when I do it."

Jo swallowed. "I don't think…we have that much time."

"I don't think we'd ever have that much time," he murmured.

"So," Emmy Lou said from the doorway, "how did you two enjoy the movie?"

Quinn cleared his throat and glanced at Jo. "I broke it."

"No, we broke it together." Jo turned toward Emmy Lou. "We're both to blame."

Emmy Lou looked confused. "Broke it?"

"Yeah," Quinn said. "The tape snapped. Don't worry. I'll have my secretary send a new copy right away."

"How much did you get to see before it broke?"

Jo tapped her chin. "Let's see. Was it before the train robbery? Or was it after that scene in the miner's shack?"

Quinn didn't dare look at her. "The miner's shack scene, I think. Anyway, a new tape's practically on the way. I'll make a—"

"Oh, don't buy me a new one." Emmy Lou blushed. "I know why it broke."

"You do?" He wondered if she'd somehow figured out what had been going on.

"It's all that pausing and rewinding."

"How did you know about that?" Quinn asked before he could stop himself.

Emmy Lou's eyes widened, and then she clapped a hand over her mouth. A smothered giggle slipped out anyway.

Jo's cheeks grew pink. "You mean *you* paused and rewound the tape a lot at that spot."

Emmy Lou nodded, her eyes bright. "Plus it was a rental tape I bought on sale at the video store. I'm sure it was already weak right there. I guess you two weakened it a little more.''

Quinn's ego had suffered enough. First he was revealed as bugophobic, and now Emmy Lou thought he was some sort of voyeur who'd had to replay a nude scene over a hundred times to get his kicks. ''It was by accident that we kept rewinding it,'' he said. ''The remote fell between the sofa cushions, and…'' He realized the quagmire he'd stepped in about the same time he caught the dismay in Jo's eyes.

''You know, that pot roast smells a little too good,'' Jo said. ''Maybe you should check on it, Emmy Lou. I think you might need to turn down the heat.''

Emmy Lou put her hands on her hips and glanced from Jo to Quinn and back to Jo again. ''I believe I could say the same thing to you.''

''The thing is,'' Quinn began, determined to find a way out of this, ''I lost my balance and—''

''Did I hear the dinner bell?'' Fred asked, coming through the front door.

''We don't have a dinner bell,'' Emmy Lou said.

''Well, I didn't think we had one, but then I was out in the yard and I heard all this clanging and banging that sure sounded like a dinner bell. So I figured I'd just wash up and come in to find out if it was time for lunch yet.''

''Why, as a matter of fact, it is,'' Jo said. ''I'm starving. How about you, Quinn?''

''Starving,'' Quinn agreed.

Emmy Lou glanced at them both with a smile on her face. Then she picked up the remote, pointed it at the television and flicked off the power. ''Then let's eat.''

''What was that clanging sound, anyway?'' Fred asked as they headed toward the kitchen.

Quinn wondered if Emmy Lou would tell on him. Fred

could make his life a real hell if he knew about Quinn's fear of bugs and snakes.

"You must have heard me banging around with my cast iron pans. I got in the mood to rearrange them," Emmy Lou said.

And with that single statement, Emmy Lou won Quinn's loyalty forever.

THE RAIN LET UP that afternoon, and Jo spent the hours between lunch and dinner riding the fence line with Benny, checking for downed wire, while Fred kept watch on the new foal and taught Quinn something about roping. Jo wasn't pleased to admit it to herself, but she also spent the afternoon missing Quinn.

She wanted to be the one to teach him how to rope, although that would be a disaster in the making, and she knew it. Whatever time she spent with Quinn was filled with danger, and she wanted to be with him twenty-four hours a day. She had a gigantic crush on the guy.

She had plenty of time to analyze why Quinn affected her so deeply, and she nearly had it nailed down. Any woman would be attracted to a guy who looked like Quinn, which explained the physical draw he had for her.

But what had really hooked her was his ability to make bold, generous gestures coupled with his very human weaknesses. He'd flown all the way from New York on impulse to return the horse sperm, yet he was so frightened of creepy crawlies he'd wrecked the cab. He'd gallantly decided to move to the bunkhouse to keep a safe distance between them, but when faced with temptation, he'd crumbled, just as she had. Crumbled in a very delicious way. She still tingled at the thought of those moments on the sofa.

"Say, what's that yonder?" Benny asked, pointing to a far hillside.

Jo squinted into the distance. "It looks like a man running."

"Then somethin's wrong," Benny said. "People don't run out in the middle of nowhere. Unless they lost their horse or somethin's after them."

"I'll check." Jo reached to her saddlebag and pulled out a scarred pair of binoculars that had belonged to Aunt Josephine. She focused on the small figure running up the hill and grinned. "It's Dick. I think he's jogging."

"Jogging? I wanna see."

Jo handed the binoculars to Benny and leaned over to rest her forearms on her saddle horn while she gazed at the tiny figure pumping madly up the hill. In jeans and boots. She loved it.

"I can't figure out what he's tryin' to catch. There ain't no horse around, or cattle, neither." Benny seemed totally mystified by the concept of a man running for no visible reason.

"Actually he's trying to lose something."

"Ain't nothin' chasing him, neither. No bear or nothing." Benny continued to stare through the binoculars. "He looks plum possessed. I ain't never seen him so red in the face."

"Let me look again." Jo knew that revenge was a mean-spirited emotion, and she shouldn't be indulging in it. Well, she'd have to get saintly some other day. Watching Dick jog was too damn much fun to miss.

She adjusted the focus so she could see Dick's red face. He was panting like a freight engine, too. Unlike Benny, she'd seen him that red in the face before—during the divorce proceedings when the judge had upheld her right to fence off Ugly Bug Creek so Dick's herd couldn't water there as they had been during the two-year span of Dick and Jo's marriage. At that point old Dick was back to hauling water, and he hadn't liked it much.

"Do you reckon we should go over there?" Benny asked. "Somethin' could be wrong."

"I think something's finally right," Jo said. Her heart lifted at the knowledge that Dick could be bested that easily, and she vowed she'd no longer be his victim. "Thanks to Quinn Monroe."

"Are you sure that's his name?"

"Yes." Jo tucked the binoculars away. "That's his name. Did Fred explain our plan?"

"He tried, but I got mixed up. You know I get mixed up."

Jo's heart squeezed at the forlorn look on Benny's face. "I know you're the best wrangler a gal could have."

"I wish I was smarter."

"You're smart where it counts, Benny. Now let me try and explain this situation as best I can."

All the way home Jo did her best to untangle Benny's confusion regarding Quinn Monroe and Brian Hastings. She thought she'd succeeded until Benny asked if he could be in the movie.

"There may not be a movie, Benny."

"But Dick and Mr. Doobie are gonna be in it."

"Quinn was only pretending about the movie when he told them they could be in it."

"If there's a movie, I wanna be in it," Benny insisted stubbornly.

"Okay," Jo said at last. "If there's a movie, I'll do my best to get you in it."

"But I ain't running up no hill."

"No, Benny." Jo smiled again at the memory. "That's a special thing only Dick has to do."

Benny grinned. "He looked like a dork, didn't he?"

"Yep, he looked like a dork." Jo was in an extremely good mood as she rode toward the ranch buildings in the light of the setting sun.

And the catalyst for her good mood stood in an empty corral, twirling a loop over his head. With a beat-up Stetson shading his eyes, leather gloves on and a rope in his hand, he looked a lot like a cowboy. Jo's heart picked up the pace. She wondered if buried under all that Wall Street conditioning was a man who could learn to love wide-open spaces and tolerate bugs and snakes.

Then she remembered why that was a dumb thought. No matter how much Quinn adapted to life as a cowboy, he couldn't stick around, even if he had a notion to. The person everyone believed to be Brian Hastings couldn't very well take up permanent residence in Ugly Bug.

Fred was nowhere to be seen, and Jo decided he must have coached Quinn on the basics and left him to practice. Quinn twirled the loop one more time, and with a snap of his wrist he let it go. It floated out in a beautiful arc and settled nicely over the post he had been aiming for.

"Yes!" he shouted, cinching it tight. "Finally!"

"Nice throw, cowboy," Jo called.

He glanced over, shoved his hat to the back of his head and grinned at her. "Thanks, ma'am."

Jo gulped. Damn, but he looked good. Almost like he belonged here. She nearly tripped dismounting because she couldn't stop staring at him. "Of course that post isn't moving," she said. "Most things don't stay still when you try to rope them."

"That's a fact."

He'd even started sounding like a cowboy, she thought.

"I'll put the horses up, if you want to go talk to Mr. Hastings," Benny said.

Jo groaned. Apparently she hadn't gotten through to Benny on this double identity deal. "No, that's Quinn over there, Benny."

"His name's Quinn Hastings?"

"No, it's—" She decided if she kept this up pretty soon she'd be as confused as Benny was. She handed the reins to him. "Never mind. Thanks for taking care of Cinnamon for me."

"No problem. I love it."

"And that's why you'll have a place here as long as I own the Bar None."

"I know." With a shy smile, Benny tipped his hat and led the horses away.

Benny was another reason she needed to hang on to the ranch, Jo thought. A new owner might only notice Benny's mental deficiencies and not give enough credit to his instinctive bond with the animals. And then there was Fred, who was getting too crippled with arthritis to do as much as he once had. If Fred was fired, then Emmy Lou would leave the ranch. All three of them depended on her to keep the place going.

Jo looked at the corral as Quinn neatly roped the post again. The golden light from the setting sun touched his broad shoulders as he coiled the rope for another try. He was learning that skill for her, just as he'd been determined to ride Hyper this morning so that he'd do a credible job as Brian Hastings. If she managed to hang on to the ranch, much of the credit would go to Quinn for agreeing to her wild idea.

He'd abandoned his own work so he could get saddle sore, plagued with giant spiders and probably mauled by the townspeople during Saturday's rodeo and dance. All to help out a lady in distress. Other than the satisfaction of a good deed, he wasn't getting anything out of the deal.

A girl should be grateful when a man put himself out like that, Jo thought as she watched Quinn form a loop and twirl it over his head. Unfortunately, gratitude had landed her in hot water once before, when she'd been stupid enough to think she owed Dick the favor of marrying him after all the help he'd given her running the Bar None. But Quinn wasn't asking for her hand in marriage or a chunk of the ranch. All he wanted was to make love to her.

God, that would be tough to take, she thought with a wry smile. But it wasn't the lovemaking part that worried her. That would be glorious. No, what kept her from rushing into his arms and into his bed was not the loving. It was the leaving.

10

QUINN had loved watching Jo ride in. She'd tied her hair back with a scarf and worn an old brown hat that gave her a rough-and-tumble tomboy look he thoroughly enjoyed. She sat straight in the saddle, her tummy in and her breasts thrust forward as she laughed and talked with Benny. Nice.

Years of riding had obviously made her feel completely at home in the saddle. He doubted she was the least bit worried about falling off. He'd spent a little more time on Hyper this afternoon, and he'd been constantly worried about falling off. With good reason. He had bruises on top of bruises.

Wondering if he'd ever achieve that relaxed look on a horse, he studied the way Jo sat and how she gripped with her thighs. Then he had to stop studying Jo. Focusing on her while her thighs were open and her hips rocked gently in response to the horse was not a good idea.

He'd really done himself in this time. He couldn't back out of his agreement because Jo might lose the ranch and he'd feel guilty for not helping her. Yet the longer he stayed at the Bar None the more desperately he wanted to make love to her. Tomorrow was the rodeo and dance, and by Sunday he'd probably need to hit the road. His head understood perfectly that he should keep his hands off of her until then. The rest of him wanted to argue.

Thinking about Jo had screwed up his usually excellent

concentration on the task at hand. Consequently, as she'd returned to the ranch, he had yet to rope the post. Fred had told him not to quit until he lassoed that sucker at least once, and he'd begun to wonder if he'd be out here after dark with a flashlight, still trying after everyone else had turned in. He wanted to have some roping ability in case something came up during the rodeo, but he seemed to have no talent for it.

Then he had an inspiration. Squinting at the post, he imagined it was Jo standing there, daring him to throw a loop around her. The concept took some effort, because Jo had interesting curves that the post lacked and a waterfall of fragrant hair and...okay, so the concept took *tremendous* effort. But finally he stared at the post so long it became Jo—saucy as you please, head thrown back, a taunting look in her brown eyes, a smile on those full lips.

Quinn took a deep breath. Now this he could get into. Twirling the rope over his head, he concentrated on the image of settling a rope around those lovely shoulders and pulling Jo closer and closer and... Flick. He sent the rope sailing as he'd done a hundred times this afternoon. And he roped the post.

Better yet, Jo had seen him do it and had called out some encouragement. Of course she also had to mention that the post wasn't moving, a fact he knew very well. He had to perfect this stage before he could advance to moving targets.

He decided to try again. This time he added an embellishment and imagined Jo standing in the corral, impudent as hell, with no clothes on. He roped the post even more competently than before. Apparently all he needed was the appropriate goal. Smiling, he loosened the rope from around the post and coiled it again.

"Looks like you made some progress this afternoon."

Quinn turned to see Jo walking into the corral. In a few seconds she'd be the same distance from him as the post, but a little to the left of it.

"I'm learning." He built his loop and swung it over his head again. "It's harder than I thought it would be."

"Chances are nobody will expect you to perform tomorrow."

"I know, but I'd still like to have the basics down." He twirled the rope and thought about his next move. If he missed he'd look really stupid. So he wouldn't miss.

"I hate to tell you, but the basics won't do you much good if somebody wants you to demonstrate your roping skills. They'll expect you to rope something alive, not a post planted in the ground."

"Maybe all I need is a little more practice." He turned toward her, took a split second to gauge the distance and tossed the loop.

She stared at him, openmouthed, as the loop dropped over her head.

Using every new skill he'd gained, plus some instinct he didn't know he had, he pulled at exactly the right moment, and the rope tightened around her arms, pinning them to her body. With a quick movement he cinched it.

"Quinn!"

Keeping the line taught, he went hand over hand toward her, watching her intently the whole way. She did her best to look indignant, but the effect was spoiled by the eagerness in her eyes. Finally he stood next to her. "How's that?"

"Very clever, Monroe." Her breathing was quick, urgent. "You can let me go now."

"I guess I could." He kept the rope taut with one hand while he pulled the glove off his other hand with his teeth. He loved the way her eyes darkened and flashed as she watched him. He tucked the glove in his belt. "Then again, I've never roped a woman before. Shouldn't I get a prize for that?"

"I've never heard of one. In Montana the men don't generally go around roping women."

"Maybe they should try it." He'd acted on impulse, not realizing how secluded the corral was. Benny and Fred would have no reason to pass on their way to the house for dinner. "It gets the women hot." He took off her hat and set it on the post. Then he took off his and dropped it on top of hers.

"Does not."

He loosened the scarf from her hair, pulled it over her curls and stuffed it in his back pocket. "Does, too." He brushed his knuckles over her throat and down the V in her blouse, taking great satisfaction in the shiver he produced. "You want me to kiss you so bad you can hardly stand it."

"Listen to you." She sounded breathless. "One lucky toss and your head's swelled up like a balloon."

"That's not the only part of me swelling up, honey bunch." He tunneled his fingers through her hair and cupped the back of her head. "But I have the feeling you're getting mighty stirred up, too."

Her lips parted in anticipation. "Your macho routine doesn't do a thing for me."

He leaned closer, keeping his grip firm on the rope. "Oh, I think it does."

"Wrong," she whispered.

His lips hovered over hers. "Let's see," he said softly, and took his prize.

If every roping session ended with this sort of reward, he'd give up his banking career. He took everything her ripe mouth offered, and she was offering plenty. She wasn't just hot, she was steaming. He shifted the angle of his mouth, then shifted again, trying to get deeper, trying to touch the essence of her.

She responded with a hunger that took his breath away. With a groan he tugged on the rope, snugging her against him. As he pressed his body to hers, he remembered how her hips had moved rhythmically as she rode in this afternoon. He remembered her passion this morning—the velvet of her breasts, the erotic taste of her. And he wondered if not making love to her, not ever making love to her, would drive him crazy.

Fear of that prompted him to finally lift his mouth from hers and loosen the rope. It dropped to the ground at her feet. "I've tried not to want you, Jo." He gasped for air. "It's not working."

She lifted her arms and wound them around his neck as she rested her head on his shoulder. "I've tried, too. I thought about you all afternoon."

"Good." He continued to cradle her head as he stroked her back with his gloved hand.

"Not good. This can go nowhere, as you very well realize. Unless, of course, I blow your cover."

"Don't do that. Just make love to me. I'm developing a condition."

"A condition?" She lifted her head to look into his eyes. "What condition?"

"Denim-tightis. It's fatal if left untreated."

A smile twitched at the corners of her mouth. "I offered you sweats."

"Cowboys don't wear sweats." He cupped her bottom and brought her tight against him. "They take care of the problem so their jeans fit right again."

Her voice grew husky. "Do you think it's that simple?"

"Probably not." His aching erection sought her heat. "My jeans may never fit when I'm around you. But it's worth a try. I really don't think Brian Hastings would wear sweats to a country dance, do you?"

"No." Amusement and desire flared in her eyes. But gradually her expression grew serious. "What I meant was that making love is not a simple solution to the problem in any sense. Just suppose we make love tonight."

"I like supposing that." His heart hammered as he rocked gently against her hips. "Let's do suppose that. Let's seriously suppose that."

"Quinn, quit joking around. I'm—" She paused and cleared the huskiness from her throat. "I'm trying to make a point."

"So am I. Going to bed may not be a permanent cure for my condition, but I'm willing to settle for symptomatic relief."

"And then what? Tomorrow's Saturday."

"Fortunately followed by Saturday night." He leaned forward and nibbled on her earlobe. "Another opportunity to treat my potentially fatal problem." He ran his tongue around the pink inner shell of her ear.

She moaned. "The point is—"

"Yes?" He loved the way she turned into a rag doll in his arms, so supple, so willing. He considered scooping her up and carrying her into the barn, except that Benny and Fred might still be in there, and what he had in mind required privacy.

She took a deep breath and attempted to push him away, but it was only a halfhearted effort. Her words came out in a determined rush. "The point is that Saturday's your big coming-out party, which means it would be very advisable for you to leave on Sunday, before people get suspicious."

He had no wish to think about the leaving-on-Sunday part. "Tonight could be the granddaddy of all coming-out parties, with your participation."

"Quinn, will you stop thinking about your...problem and listen?"

"It's hard." He lifted his head and waggled his eyebrows at her. "Very hard."

Breathless laughter trembled on her lips. "Honestly, you act as if you'd never been sexually frustrated before in your life. Has every woman except me tumbled directly into your bed?"

"Not by a long shot. But this is not mere sexual frustration. This is sexual torture. To be more specific, I could represent my previous sexual frustrations by, say, a gnat, and my present one by, say, a wolf spider."

"Really?" She looked sort of pleased with the news.

"I'm afraid so."

"Why do you think that is?"

"I've asked myself the same thing, Josephine. I don't know. All I know is that if I'm forced to drive away from here on Sunday without ever making love to you, I might have to throw myself off the top of the Empire State Building."

Her cheeks grew pink, and her eyes sparkled. "How you exaggerate. Besides, they've put up barriers so people can't throw themselves off the Empire State Building."

"Then I'd have to tie a cement block to my feet and jump off the George Washington Bridge. And I'd probably land on a garbage scow and sink over my head into the muck, like Luke Skywalker in *Star Wars,* only I wouldn't ever come up again. I'll die covered in slime." He kneaded her firm bottom with his gloved hand. "I'm sure you don't want that on your conscience."

"You sure know how to treat a girl, Quinn." Her chin

had a saucy tilt, but her bedroom eyes gave her away. "First you rope her and then you whisper sweet nothings about garbage scows and slime."

"It's a gift." He smiled. "Take pity on me, Jo. I'm a desperate man."

"But this is all we'd ever have."

"I know." His smile faded. "And I know that's a problem for you. It could be a problem for me. If I could find the off switch on this obsession I'd use it. That was my plan, to shut down that part of me. Turns out I'm not as strong as I thought I was."

"I need some time to think."

Quinn glanced around. Dusk was upon them. After dusk came night, and it might be the longest, most frustrating one of his life if Jo shut him down. She thought he was kidding about the Empire State Building and the George Washington Bridge. And he was, sort of. But he'd never wanted any woman like this, and he wasn't sure life would be worth living if he'd never know the ecstasy of holding Jo's warm, responsive and totally naked body in his arms. "How much time?"

"You can see my bedroom window from the bunkhouse."

"I guess. I never checked."

"Well, take my word for it. You can. By eleven tonight everyone will be asleep."

"Not everyone."

"Everyone *else,* then. I'll turn my light out at ten-thirty. If I flash it twice at eleven, meet me at the barn. I'll bring a blanket."

"We're doing this outside?" Quinn got a quick picture of all sorts of creatures slithering around and decided he'd have to deal with it. "Hey, outside's fine. Outside's terrific. I love outside."

"I was thinking the hayloft."

That was only marginally better in Quinn's estimation, but he smiled, trying to demonstrate extreme confidence. "Fine. The hayloft it is. Sounds great. A roll in the hay. I'm there. I'm—"

"But if I don't flash my light twice, then that means I think it would be better if we stay with our original plan and not make love while you're here."

Quinn had temporarily forgotten that she hadn't committed to the plan. The realization hit him like a medicine ball in the gut. "Oh." He was afraid he looked like an abandoned cocker spaniel as he gazed at her. This craving was turning him into a pathetic shadow of his former self. "Please flash."

"I still think we'd be making a terrible mistake, Quinn. You're thinking short-term."

"Very short. Like from now until eleven tonight. What if you fall asleep and forget?"

"No chance." She stood on tiptoe and brushed her lips across his. "Watch my window," she whispered. Then she eased out of his arms, retrieved her hat and headed in the direction of the house.

Quinn stood in the shadows and knew exactly how Samson must have felt when bewitched by Delilah. Marc Anthony when captivated by Cleopatra. A woman had never wielded this much power over him, had never turned him into a beggar.

He picked up the rope and walked away from the post. He could barely see it in the darkness, but that made his new technique easier. He hardly had to squint to mentally turn the post into Jo. *Rope me, and I'm yours for the night, cowboy.* He twirled the rope, let it sail and neatly roped the post.

SITTING ACROSS the table from Quinn and contemplating her decision regarding the evening ahead, Jo could barely eat Emmy Lou's delicious pot roast. Quinn appeared to have no trouble, though.

"You sure seem to be enjoying your meal," Jo commented with some irritation as he forked up a second helping of meat. She thought it was highly unfair that nothing ever seemed to take away a man's appetite, while women's stomachs were affected by every little bit of stress.

"I love pot roast." He gave her a dazzling smile before tucking into the meal once again.

Emmy Lou beamed from the end of the table. "It's a pleasure to watch you eat, Quinn."

Fred snorted. "Why, I'm covered with goose bumps at the sight, myself."

"You are?" Benny stared at him. "I don't see nothin'."

"Oh, Fred, you're just jealous," Emmy Lou said, "because you can't put away food the way you used to when you were younger."

"Who says I can't?" Fred held out his plate. "I'll take another helping of that pot roast."

"I'm not serving you seconds." Emmy Lou pushed his plate aside. "You'll be up all night with heartburn and you know it."

Quinn glanced up in alarm. "Yeah, and the rodeo and dance are tomorrow. I'm sure we all need a good night's rest."

"Oh, we certainly do," Jo said, covering a smile with her hand.

"I damn well know what's happening tomorrow, and I'll have another helping, Emmy Lou." Fred thrust his plate in her direction again.

Emmy Lou rolled her eyes. "Okay, you stubborn old goat." She placed more meat and vegetables on his plate. "Don't blame me when you're walking the floor at three in the morning."

Quinn gripped Fred's arm. "You know, Fred, I'll bet that would taste even better for lunch."

Fred glared at him. "Listen here, greenhorn. I was eating Emmy Lou's pot roast while you were still in diapers, so don't be telling me the time of day when I can enjoy it. Now take your mitts off my arm."

"Well, I'll tell you what, my eyes were bigger than my stomach." Quinn pushed his plate away. "I'm stuffed. Couldn't eat another bite. Just one more mouthful and I'd have heartburn for sure. I'm saving this for lunch. And you know, Fred, if we put cellophane over our plates, we could heat them in the microwave and save Emmy Lou the trouble of making us lunch tomorrow before we leave for the rodeo. What do you think of that?"

Fred shrugged. "Suit yourself. Emmy Lou knows she don't have to bother about my lunch if she's too tired. I'm capable of building a sandwich."

"Is that a fact?" Emmy Lou gazed at him. "I'm glad you told me, Fred. And when was the last time you built yourself a sandwich? When Nixon was president?"

Fred looked down the table and winked at her. "I do believe Johnson was in the White House at the time. Now if you'll excuse me, I have a meal to eat."

Now that she understood the true nature of it, Jo was fascinated by Fred and Emmy Lou's relationship, which could turn from gruff to lighthearted in a split second. She assumed that was the mark of an enduring partnership, but she'd never been around a couple who'd had such a long and apparently loving association. She hadn't known either set of grandparents well, and Aunt Josephine had stayed single all her life.

How sweet it would be to know someone that well, she thought with a pang of longing. Irrationally she thought of Quinn, the man she was destined to know for less than a week. Funny, but he was exactly the sort of man she could imagine creating a long-term partnership with. She could picture them thirty or forty years from now, sparring with each other the way Emmy Lou and Fred did, with a deep respect and love underlying every teasing word.

Love. Oh, my God. Jo glanced quickly at Quinn, as if he might have been able to read her thoughts. She couldn't love him. She hadn't known him long enough. She'd never met his family, his friends. She didn't know if he had a dog, or maybe a cat, or precisely what he did for a living, except that it had to do with money, a subject that had always confused her.

Of course she hadn't been thinking that she *did* love him, only that she *could* love him, in some other circumstance, after they'd become friends and spent lots of time in each other's company—years, maybe. Love was a tricky emotion. She'd talked herself into loving Dick, and that hadn't worked at all.

Now it seemed she was talking herself out of loving Quinn. She hoped that worked a little better. Quinn was definitely the wrong man for her to fall in love with, unless she wanted to give up her ranch and send Emmy Lou, Fred and Benny into the street. Good thing she'd had this little mental chat with herself, so she didn't allow her heart to do something really, really stupid.

''Who wants dessert?'' Emmy Lou asked.

Quinn patted his flat stomach. ''Couldn't possibly.''

''What is it?'' Benny asked.

''Cherry cobbler.''

"I'll have some," Fred said, finishing the last of his pot roast. "Warm, with ice cream on top."

Emmy Lou shook her head. "Frederick, I do hope you have a good book to read, because you aren't going to be doing any sleeping tonight."

"Ah, I'll sleep like a baby," Fred said.

"Babies wake up constantly," Emmy Lou replied.

"I could run into town for some sleeping pills," Quinn said. "Or those tablets that fizz, or maybe that pink stuff that coats your stomach, or maybe it's white. I don't know. I'll buy it all. Whatever you need. I think sleep is important. Very important."

Fred gazed at him. "You seem mighty interested in getting me to sleep tonight. Any particular reason?"

Quinn reddened. "Just looking after your health, Fred."

Fred nodded, but there was a gleam of mischief in his eyes. "That's what I thought."

11

AFTER DINNER Jo excused herself from the table and headed for her study to figure out which bills she should pay and which ones she could stuff back in the shoe box. She'd never completely understood Josephine's bookkeeping system, so she'd come up with one of her own, but even she had to admit it wasn't adequate. She should have stuck with those accounting classes, but it was a little late to worry about that now.

The process of bill paying always left her stomach in knots, but it was her responsibility. After an hour of figuring and refiguring, she kept coming to the same conclusion. She needed some quick cash, and one of her best mares had produced an outstanding foal. She had to sell Clarise and Stud-muffin.

She wrote down the decision so it felt irreversible. Sherry, the vet who was coming out early the next morning to inseminate the mares with Sir Lust-a-Lot's sperm, had mentioned she had a buyer for Clarise once she'd foaled successfully. Sherry knew Jo's financial problems well—the vet had let bills slide many times in the past. Keeping Clarise and Stud-muffin was selfish and financially irresponsible, Jo decided, and she couldn't afford either behavior.

With the decision made she got up from her desk and paced the small room while she tried to come to grips with losing one of her favorite mares. Aunt Josephine had taught her not to get sentimentally attached to the cattle, but even tough-minded Josephine had hated selling a horse, including the ones who misbehaved or who were too old and swaybacked to carry a rider.

Someone tapped on her study door. Drawing an unsteady breath, she walked over and opened it.

Quinn took one look at her and reached out a hand to cup her cheek. "What is it?"

She forced a smile. "Nothing. Ranch business."

He combed her hair over her ear. "I thought you were probably in here wrestling with your finances. I wish you'd be willing to discuss the situation with me."

"I did." Her emotions lay close to the surface, and his gentle touch threatened to bring tears. She stepped out of reach. "I told you I needed to stall Doobie until September, when I could make another payment on my loan."

He allowed his hand to fall to his side, and there was a flash of hurt in his eyes. "I'm sure there's more to the problem than that." His glance flicked to the shoe box. "If you'd tell me what's going on, I might be able to help you work through it."

"Quinn, you can't be my financial adviser, even if I wanted you to, which I don't. You're leaving on Sunday."

"So what?" He motioned toward the telephone sitting on her desk. "That's the connection I have with my clients, for the most part."

She stared at him for several seconds. Then she lowered her voice. "Quinn, you can't have it both ways. You can't beg me to make love to you one minute and offer to provide long-distance financial counseling the next. The two just don't go together."

He studied her. Finally he shook his head. "You're right, dammit. If we make love tonight—"

"Shh." Jo glanced into the hall before pulling him inside the room and closing the door. "For heaven's sake. It's an old house. The walls have ears."

"Then let's stop talking." He pulled her into his arms and kissed her thoroughly. "Mmm. That's better," he said, lifting his head.

Well, at least he'd taken her mind off her troubles, she thought as warmth surged through her. "Are you..." She stopped to catch her breath. His kisses packed a wallop. "Are you trying to influence my eleven o'clock decision?"

He studied her face for several long seconds. "I don't know what I'm doing."

"Could have fooled me."

"I came in here to see if I could help you with your books."

She wound her arms around his waist and fit herself against the jut of his obvious erection. "Uh-huh."

"Honest. And now you tell me the only way I can possibly help is if we don't make love tonight." He stroked her cheeks with his thumbs. "You sure know how to hurt a guy."

"I don't want you to help me with the books." But he could help her forget that she'd soon be selling Clarise and Stud-muffin.

"You should want me to. I'm very good at it."

"Yeah, well, maybe I'm more interested in finding out what else you're very good at." She rubbed sensuously against him and kissed the hollow of his throat. What she'd never admit to him was that she was embarrassed to have him look at her books and discover they were in total disarray. A professional like Quinn would probably go into shock if he could see the mess she'd made. She'd rather shock a stranger, if it came to that.

No, she didn't want Quinn's financial advice, but if

she'd allow him to, Quinn could certainly get her through this rough patch. By impersonating Hastings, he was postponing her financial crisis, and by making wonderful love to her he could make her forget her worries, at least for a little while, and that was worth quite a bit.

Quinn groaned. "Damn, but you make it tough to be noble." He took her by the shoulders and gently pushed her away. "But I'm going to give it a shot. Show me your ledgers."

She couldn't admit that she wasn't sure what ledgers were, exactly, so she reached for the top button of her blouse. "I'd much rather show you my—"

"No." He gripped her hand and closed his eyes. "I can't believe I'm stopping you from unbuttoning your blouse. I must be out of my mind." He held her hand tighter and opened his eyes to gaze at her intently. "Jo, this is for your own good. Forget sex."

"Have you been drinking?"

"Not yet. I may start on Fred's rotgut after this conversation. Listen, forget everything I said to you out in the corral. Think about your commitment to the ranch. I can help you keep that commitment. Use my services. Please." He released her hand and stepped away from her. Although a muscle in his jaw twitched as if the effort was costing him, he kept his arms at his sides.

He was magnificent, she thought. As much as he wanted her, he'd deny himself in order to help her achieve her goals. "Why are you doing this?" she murmured.

For a moment he looked confused. "Because I—because that's the best thing for you."

"But not for you," she said softly.

"My needs aren't as important as yours right now."

She wondered if he knew he was falling in love with her. Just as she was falling in love with him. Their relationship would be short and intense, but at least it would exist. She wasn't going to squander this chance at a moment of happiness for the possibility of straightening out some dry old ledgers, if she even had ledgers, which she doubted.

She took a long, shaky breath. "I absolutely refuse to allow you to get involved in my financial affairs," she said.

"Jo, don't—"

"But I'm looking forward to our brief but significant love affair. Never mind all that signaling nonsense. I'll be at the barn at eleven with a blanket. Now go on out to the bunkhouse before Emmy Lou begins to wonder what we're doing in here so long with the door closed."

He shook his head, but his ragged breathing indicated he was greatly tempted by her offer in spite of his noble intentions. "You're making a mistake. Please reconsider."

She shook her head. "You don't have to show up at the barn, though, if it would compromise your principles."

His laugh was dry as he gazed at her with fire in his eyes. "Sweetheart, I'm not that strong. I'll be there."

QUINN didn't intend to give up the idea of helping Jo create a workable financial plan before he left. But obviously the straightforward approach wasn't going to work. He'd have to be more devious.

He walked into the bunkhouse to find Benny and Fred playing a game of what Quinn used to call War when he was a kid. It was a simple game, the kind Benny could probably understand, and Quinn thought it was decent of Fred to play it with him.

Fred glanced up. "Hey, Quinn."

"Hey, Fred."

"Hi, Mr. Hastings," Benny said before returning his attention to the game.

Quinn decided not to correct Benny about his name. Instead he faked a huge yawn. Yawns were supposed to be contagious. "Aren't you guys tired?"

Benny yawned, right on cue. "Guess so. You tired, Fred?"

"Nope." He glanced at Quinn. "Go on to bed if you want. We'll be quiet."

"Okay, believe I will."

"I'm going to bed, too," Benny said.

Fred shrugged. "Okay. I'll play solitaire."

One down and one to go, Quinn thought as he sat on the bunk assigned to him and pulled off his borrowed boots. The bunkhouse reminded Quinn of the cabin he'd been assigned to at Camp Washogee twenty years ago. He experienced no nostalgia—for a kid who hated wiggly things, summer camp had been a nightmare.

The metal beds looked exactly the same as the ones at camp. There were four of them lined up against opposing walls, two on a side. A scarred dresser topped by a mirror was against the end wall between the beds.

A table and four captain's chairs took up most of the opposite end of the bunkhouse, and a door in the far wall opened into a small bathroom. Nails driven into the walls held jackets, hats, a rope or two and a bridle Fred was repairing in his spare time.

Fred wasn't working on the bridle at the moment, Quinn noticed as he shucked his pants and shirt and pulled back the blanket on his bed. Fred's belt was undone, and the guy looked uncomfortable. Emmy Lou obviously knew Fred's digestive system well.

Quinn's stomach felt fine, but the rest of him was a

little beat-up. He groaned softly as he climbed into bed. Between bruises and sore muscles, he could be pretty well crippled by tomorrow, especially considering the activity he had planned for tonight. He took off his watch and set it on the windowsill next to the bed, where he could see the time by turning his head. An hour and a half before he was supposed to meet Jo.

His groin tightened. In less than two hours, assuming he could sneak past Fred, he'd have Jo in his arms. He wondered what she'd wear to their rendezvous and if she'd bother with items like underwear. Underwear could be very erotic, but getting it off might take up valuable time. Quinn decided he'd rather she didn't wear any.

Maybe he wouldn't wear any, either, although you had to be damn careful with the zipper in a case like that. Too careful, come to think of it. He'd wear his briefs. Considering how much he wanted Jo, he'd be shaking like a leaf, and sure as the world, he'd get something important caught in the zipper.

Then he wondered if he should wear his hat to the barn. Of course he didn't *need* that Stetson on his head, considering it would be dark and he was planning to climb to the hayloft and make love all night. But in another way he did need the hat. Wearing it made him feel more like a cowboy, and damned if that didn't seem to add a certain something to his self-confidence.

He also liked the idea that he'd meet Jo looking like a seasoned ranch hand, a devil-may-care stud of a wrangler. Maybe he ached all over from today's activities, maybe he couldn't sit a horse like a pro or rope a wild bull yet, but he could project the image darn well when he put on that Stetson. He knew because he'd checked it out in a mirror.

Yeah, he'd wear the hat, maybe even keep it on while

he took his other clothes off. He hoped Jo would keep her outfit simple. A pair of pull-on shorts and a T-shirt sounded perfect to him. He could strip those off in no time, leaving Jo lying on the blanket, waiting....

And then Quinn went cold. He had no condoms. He had no reason to expect Jo to be using any form of birth control, and besides, a stud didn't show up at the appointed place with no protection for his lover. Dammit, what to do? Benny wouldn't have any, but Fred…Fred might. But he couldn't ask. He'd have to snoop, and if he hit pay dirt, he'd have to swipe. Normally he wasn't a swiper, but this was an unusual situation.

"You asleep, Mr. Hastings?" Benny whispered from across the room.

"Not yet, Benny."

"I can't sleep from thinking about the movie."

Quinn sighed. "I don't think there will be a movie, so just relax and go to sleep, okay?"

"I think there will be a movie. And I want to be in it."

"Benny, I'd give up the idea if I were you. Chances are—"

"Will you promise me, if there is a movie, I'll get to be in it?"

Quinn hated to make a promise like that to a guy as trusting as Benny. What if the real Brian Hastings showed up some day? What if the damned movie actually got made? Dick and Doobie could go hang, but Quinn didn't want Benny to be disappointed. "I don't think I can make that kind of promise."

"Yes, you can. Jo did."

"She did?" Quinn thought about that for a minute. All along he'd been hoping that Hastings would come back and make the movie so Jo would get the money. Yet he suddenly pictured Hastings hanging out at the Bar None, interacting with Jo and granting her favors like giving Benny a part in the movie. If Jo was attracted to Quinn, who was a poor woman's version of Hastings, then she'd probably fall head over heels for the real thing. Quinn felt a little sick to his stomach imagining Hastings putting the moves on Jo. With a guy like that, it would probably be an automatic reaction to a beautiful woman.

"So can I be in it?" Benny asked again.

"I guess so," Quinn replied, feeling depressed. "If there is a movie."

"There will be," Benny said with complete confidence.

Quinn grimaced. Damn, he really wanted that movie to be filmed at the Bar None, for Jo's sake. Of course he did. This morning she'd insisted that looking at Hastings' bare butt hadn't been the reason she'd jumped Quinn's bones. Quinn wanted to believe her, but Hastings was America's sexiest leading man. *People* magazine had said so. Quinn wondered why every single thing that would be good for Jo turned out to be the worst thing that could happen to him.

"Night, night." Benny yawned. "Sleep tight."

"Thanks, Ben."

"Don't let the bugs bite," Benny added in a sleepy voice.

Quinn stiffened. "What bugs?"

Benny's reply was barely audible. "Dunno. People just say that." Soon afterward he began to snore.

Quinn lay rigid as a corpse and tried not to think about wolf spiders as big as his fist creeping under his bed, on his bed. Finally he cleared his throat. "Fred?" he called softly.

"Yeah, Quinn."

"You get many of those wolf spiders in here?"

Fred chuckled. "Ugly sons of bitches, ain't they?"

"I guess."

"That's how the creek got named, they say. Then the town after that. I picture some old prospector waking up in the middle of the night with one of those suckers sitting right by his nose. Musta scared the crap outta him."

Quinn swallowed. "Yeah, probably. I bet you don't see them much anymore, though. Like in the bunkhouse and stuff."

"Oh, sure, we do. This place was built in nineteen-ten, and it's not real tight. We get all kinds of critters in here. Last week it was a small rattlesnake."

"No kidding?" Quinn realized his voice had squeaked and deliberately lowered it. "That's interesting."

"You're turning into a regular chatterbox, aren't you, Quinn? I thought you said you was real tired."

"I am. Good night." Quinn didn't want to discuss critters with Fred anymore. He lay there wondering what he was doing surrounded by poisonous snakes and ugly bugs. In Manhattan he could swim with the sharks, or face a bear market without blinking. In Manhattan he could be a hero.

But Jo wasn't in Manhattan. She was in Montana, and so, for the moment, he had to do his best to be a hero in Montana.

He stared at his watch and willed Fred to go to sleep. Not only did he want to slip out of the bunkhouse so he could meet Jo, he also wanted to spend the night somewhere besides a place with cracks big enough to drive a truck through, or at least a herd of wolf spiders.

After what seemed like eternity squared, Fred began to snore in his chair. Quinn leaned over and checked the floor before swinging his feet down. He dressed in record time but left his boots off. He took the blanket off the spare bed and rolled it up before arranging it under his own blanket to approximate the bulk of a person lying in the bed. Then he padded to the dresser.

The top two drawers belonged to Fred. Quinn figured the top drawer was his best bet. He eased it open and felt cautiously among the socks, briefs and T-shirts. Nothing. Finally, in a back corner, his fingers closed over some foil packets.

He counted four. Decided to take two. If and when Fred discovered the loss, he might chalk it up to losing track of his inventory. Feeling like a seventeen-year-old raiding his dad's supply, Quinn shoved the condoms in his pocket with a little prayer that they were the right size.

There was just enough light from the lamp on the table for him to see a shadowy version of himself in the rippled old mirror over the dresser. He put on his Stetson, gave it a rakish tilt and headed out carrying his boots. He would have given his best Armani suit for a flashlight.

JO CHANGED clothes eleven times between ten o'clock and ten forty-five. Quinn was probably used to fancy lingerie and soft little dresses that came undone with a quick pull on an invisible tie. At least that was the way Jo imagined a Manhattan woman dressed for a late-night meeting with a lover.

She didn't have anything like that. Cotton underwear made sense when you lived in jeans and Western shirts. In winter she wore thermal long johns, even less romantic. She had exactly two dresses, one full-skirted for dancing and the other a sedate linen thing that buttoned up to her neck. Neither of them qualified for a secret rendezvous.

Dammit, when Quinn looked back on this episode she didn't want him to think of it as the night he spent with the hayseed. She rummaged through all her drawers, tossing things on the bed. Then she went through her closet one more time, swishing hangers along the rod in her impatience. At the far end of the closet she found a box she couldn't remember putting there. She opened it and started to laugh. Perfect.

In an abortive attempt to put some romance into her relationship with Dick, she'd bought herself red silk boxers and a chemise. But before she'd had a chance to try them out, Fred had seen Dick kissing a waitress at the Ugly Bug Tavern and forced him to confess he was having an affair. Jo had filed for divorce and had forgotten all about the sexy outfit.

The silk felt good against her bare skin. She'd have to wear something over the outfit, of course, or she'd freeze to death walking to the barn. The slicker hanging by the front door would work. She stood in front of the mirror and admired herself in the red silk while she imagined Quinn's reaction. Her breath quickened.

Smoothing the material over her breasts, she closed her eyes. She craved his touch so desperately it scared her. Maybe meeting him tonight wasn't the wisest thing she'd ever done, but logic wasn't in charge at the moment. Deep in her heart she knew that if she didn't make love to him before he went back to New York she would regret it for the rest of her life.

She slipped on a pair of sneakers and picked up a folded quilt before creeping downstairs. As she made certain to avoid the steps that squeaked, she shivered as much from excitement as the chill in the air. The house was dark and quiet as she made her way to the front door and took down the slicker. She picked up the flashlight they kept on the entry hall table and reached for the knob of the front door.

As she started to turn it, she felt resistance, as if...as if someone was turning the knob from the other side.

Heart pounding, she stepped away from the door. Maybe Quinn had become impatient and decided to come to the house to get her. After the incident with Benny, he knew they didn't lock doors at the Bar None.

The door opened, but the man silhouetted by the glow from the porch light wasn't Quinn. He squinted in the darkness. "Jo, is that you?"

Jo pulled the slicker tight around her and swallowed. "Hi, there, Fred."

12

JO DIDN'T KNOW who was more embarrassed, she or Fred.
She was glad the light wasn't very good, because she was
sure her face was bright red. They both started a sentence
of explanation at the same time, then stopped and stared
at each other.

"I, uh, thought I'd get something for my upset stomach," Fred said, his usual bluster completely gone.

"I...wanted to go check on Betsy." It was a transparent fib. She'd checked on Betsy two hours ago, and the
mare had shown no signs of going into labor. Fred knew
that as well as she did.

But he nodded as if that was a brilliant idea. "Sure."

"There's...there's probably some of that pink stuff in
the downstairs bathroom," Jo said.

"I figured." He glanced at the blanket. "How long you
planning to, uh, spend time with Betsy?"

"Well, I wasn't sure." He probably knew what the
blanket was for, she decided, but she wondered what he
thought of her slicker. It wasn't raining. "A couple of
hours?"

"Sounds about right."

"Then I guess I'll be getting on down there." She had
no idea if Quinn would be waiting. With Fred prowling
around, Quinn might have decided to stay put until the
coast was clear.

"Yeah, might as well get on down there. Check on Betsy," Fred said.

"Fred, you're blocking the door."

"Oh!" He came all the way into the house, and they sashayed around each other in the narrow hallway like two people do-si-doing at a square dance.

"See ya," Jo said as she hurried out of the house.

"Yep." Fred closed the door quietly behind her.

Once she was headed down the porch steps, Jo began to grin. Shoot, those folks had probably been carrying on like this for years. Josephine might have known about it but couldn't find a good way to inform her young grand-niece. Jo wondered why they'd never made their romance public and gotten married.

But she could guess. Fred might enjoy having Emmy Lou nearby, and she no doubt felt the same, but Jo couldn't picture Fred becoming domesticated enough to live in the house, which would probably mean giving up his chewing tobacco and his occasional trips to the Ugly Bug Saloon.

Jo swept the ground with her flashlight, checking for snakes. She didn't expect to find any. The nights were still too cold for them to be out and about at eleven o'clock. Finding nothing, she started around the house toward the barn and glanced quickly at the entrance lit by a dusk-to-dawn light.

No Quinn.

Although Jo told herself he was probably waiting until he was sure Fred wouldn't see him, her self-confidence slipped a notch. Maybe he'd reconsidered and wasn't coming, after all. Or even more humiliating, maybe he'd fallen asleep, his ardor for her forgotten once his head touched the pillow. She'd rather be rejected outright than forgotten like some dentist's appointment.

The more she considered it, the less she liked the idea
of hanging around the front of the barn for God knew
how long before Quinn decided to show up, assuming he
would show up and wasn't sawing logs at this very minute. Quinn wasn't following the script. He was supposed
to be so excited that he'd arrive early. Eager and nervous,
he would then pace back and forth until the appointed
time. When he first glimpsed her, he'd rush to meet her,
and she would drop the quilt and flashlight (gracefully)
and run to meet him, except the moment would be drawn
out in slow motion, with appropriate background music.

Instead Quinn was late. He would arrive, if he arrived
at all, to see her standing in the unflattering glare of the
dusk-to-dawn light wearing her yellow slicker and clutching an old quilt. She probably looked like a refugee. Or
a flasher.

On impulse she stepped into the shade of a large oak.
When she saw him coming, she could hurry forward as if
she'd just arrived, as if she'd lost track of the time and
had suddenly realized that it was past eleven. Yes, that
was a good line. She'd say she'd been reading a wonderful book and hadn't realized how late it was. That should
put Mr. Quinn Monroe in his place.

Assuming he showed up at all.

If not she'd have to stay here for two hours because
she'd subtly promised Fred she wouldn't interrupt him
and Emmy Lou any sooner than that. From Jo's perspective Fred and Emmy Lou had the ideal relationship. It sure
beat marriage, from what Jo had seen of that institution.
She envied their comfortable, no-strings arrangement.
This standing out in the cold waiting for some guy to meet
you was for the birds.

She used to play in this tree when she was a kid, she
remembered. The trunk branched off about three feet from

the ground, providing a crotch that was a perfect place to put your foot and heave yourself into the tree for a good climbing experience. The oak had leafed out in the past couple of weeks, and it provided dense enough shade to camouflage her until Quinn arrived or…he didn't. If the rat didn't show, she'd find some way to get revenge.

Strong arms came around her from behind, and she yelped. The quilt and flashlight plopped to the ground.

"How come you didn't come over to the front of the barn, where you said you'd be?" Quinn murmured in her ear as he pulled her hard against him.

"Because you were late!" she whispered hoarsely, her heart going like crazy. "I decided to wait here until you managed to get yourself out of the bunkhouse!"

"I wasn't late." He nibbled her earlobe as he held her tight and began unsnapping her slicker with one hand.

"Were so." Even through the slicker she could feel his erection pressing against her, rock hard and ready.

"Was not. I stayed in the shadows so there was no chance Fred would see me. I watched you coming toward me and decided I'd wait until you got right to the door of the barn before I showed myself, in case anyone was watching." His teeth raked the lobe of her ear as he slipped his hand inside her slicker. "Except for some reason you changed your mind and decided to hide under this tree. So I had to come and get you."

She gasped as he reached under the silk chemise and cupped her breast. Cool air touched her skin through the open slicker. She should suggest they go into the barn, but his hand felt so good she didn't want to move just yet. In a minute they could move. He kneaded her breast with his strong fingers. In another minute. "I…met Fred coming in the house as I went out," she said.

Quinn's breath was warm against her ear, his voice

husky and deep. "And what did you tell him?" He rubbed his thumb back and forth across her nipple until the ache inside her became almost unbearable. Perhaps it was knowing that they would finally make love tonight that had touched some basic chord, making her vibrate so she could barely stand.

"I told him I was…oh, Quinn, I can't think when you do that."

"That's okay." He continued to knead her breast while he slid his other hand beneath the elastic of her boxers. His words rasped in the darkness. "I don't really care what you told Fred." Boldly he tunneled his fingers through her moist curls. "I just—" He caught his breath as he probed deeper.

She moaned and leaned back in his arms.

"Ah, Jo." He caressed her with a gentle, rhythmic motion that soon had her quivering. "You're drenched, sweetheart," he whispered. "Why did you hide from me?"

This was crazy, she thought, letting him touch her this way with only the darkness to conceal them. But for the life of her she couldn't ask him to stop.

He kissed her neck, then nipped playfully as he slowed his strokes, drawing out the exquisite pleasure. "Why, Jo?"

She could barely breathe as she reached for the summit. Almost there. Just a little more. "Playing it…cool."

"Oh."

She could feel his smile against her skin as he paused, his finger lightly touching her throbbing flash point. She thought she'd go crazy. "But I'm not cool," she said, her words a breathless plea.

"No?"

She trembled on the brink of ecstasy. "Quinn, have mercy. Do something."

"Like this?" He pushed deep and pressed down on that aching, needy spot with the heel of his hand.

Her world came apart, and the rest of the world would have known all about it if he hadn't taken his other hand from her breast and gently covered her mouth, muffling her cry of release. She arched in his arms as the quakes took hold of her. She felt tumbled about like a pebble in the rapids of a stream, and through it all Quinn held her, supported her, whispered sweetly in her ear.

At last she shuddered and was still, drooping in his arms as she gasped for breath. "Wow."

"Good?" His voice sounded hoarse.

"Oh, yeah."

He eased his hand out of her boxers and slowly turned her to face him, holding her firmly by her shoulders as if he realized without his strong grip she'd fall flat on the ground. "I'm glad."

She gazed at him. "I feel as if I've had too much to drink."

"I know the feeling. I'm pretty high myself."

"Yeah, but you're still standing. You may have to carry me to the barn."

He gave her a lopsided grin. "I'm not sure I can walk that far." He guided her a couple of steps backward until she felt the trunk of the oak against her back. "Let's rest a minute before we decide." He took off his Stetson, hung it on a nearby twig and leaned down and covered her mouth with his.

She didn't find his kiss at all restful. One thrust of his tongue and the ache began to build again as if he hadn't just given her the most dramatic climax of her life. She'd never experienced lovemaking like this. There seemed to be no quenching the fire inside. When she thought it had burned itself out, Quinn breathed the embers to life again.

His hands found their way under her chemise, cupping her breasts, coaxing her nipples to quivering tautness. Then he lifted his mouth from hers, pushed the chemise up and leaned down to draw one nipple into his mouth. Without the tree's support she would have definitely crumpled to the hard ground as he lavished her breasts with attention.

She was guilty of pulling the chemise higher, so it wouldn't flutter down and get in his way. And she arched her back to make it easier for him to do all those marvelous things with his mouth and tongue that she remembered from their session on the couch.

"Oh, Quinn, I want you so much," she cried softly.

"Undo my jeans," he murmured against her tongue-dampened breasts.

"Here?"

"Right here, sweetheart. I need your hands on me in the worst way."

She gasped as he resumed fondling her. "Then you'll have to stop…doing that."

She wondered if he'd heard her, but he must have, because eventually he kissed his way to her throat and nuzzled the sensitive skin beneath her ear as he continued to stroke her breasts.

"And that," she said breathlessly.

"What can I do?" He squeezed her breasts gently. "I want to touch you. I need to touch you."

She moaned with pleasure. "But I can't concentrate when you touch me. So stop. Just stand there."

With a husky sigh he drew back and braced his hands on the tree's two main branches.

Taking a long, shaky breath, she leaned forward and

unfastened his belt with trembling hands. As she started to ease the zipper over his rigid shaft, she looked into his shadowed face, her heart pounding with anticipation. "You're sure you want me…to do this here?"

"Oh, yes."

"But—"

His voice was tight with desire. "No one can see. I wouldn't have known you were under this tree if I hadn't watched you slip back here. And I'll never make it to the barn, Jo. I'd wreck myself trying."

She unzipped his jeans carefully. His harsh breathing drowned out the crickets as she followed his lead and slid her hand beneath the elastic of his briefs. Her hand closed around enough warm, rigid male to make any woman very happy. Her body reacted with an intense, hollow ache and a rush of moisture.

She caressed him and he groaned, but it was muffled, as if he'd clenched his teeth to keep from crying out. That low, desperate sound made her heady with her own power to please. And the quilt was almost within reach. "Stay here."

"I couldn't move if you shoved a stick of dynamite up my—"

"I'll be right back." She released him, ducked under his arm, grabbed the folded quilt and dropped it at his feet. "There."

"What are you doing?"

"This." She knelt on the quilt and wrapped her fingers around his sizable erection once again. Damn, he was impressive. And he was all hers. When she took him into her mouth, a massive shudder went through him.

"Jo…I didn't mean…that you…oh, Lord." He began to quiver.

She lifted her head and gazed at him while she stroked

his sensitive tip with her thumb. "Want me to stop?" She barely recognized her voice, which had become throaty and seductive.

He struggled for breath. "No."

"Good." She replaced her thumb with her tongue. The more she loved him, the more insistently her body demanded his presence deep inside her. She'd never felt this way, as if the world wouldn't make sense anymore unless she received that elemental connection with this particular man. Only with this man.

Quinn gasped and trembled. "Jo. Jo, stop now. Please."

She took her time about releasing him and gave him one last sensuous stroke before rising to her feet. "I need you now," she said, her voice thick with longing. "Right here, right now. On the quilt, in the dirt, I don't care. Now, Quinn."

His laugh was shaky. "I hate it when you're indecisive. Get off the quilt a minute."

She stepped aside, and he picked up the quilt. She thought he'd spread it on the ground and pull her down with him, but instead he kept it folded and settled it into the crotch of the tree. Excitement rose in her, hot and wild.

He turned to her and guided her close to the tree. Then he slipped his thumbs under the elastic of her silk boxers. "I like these," he murmured, tugging them down. "But they gotta go."

Impatient and aching, she started to help him.

He pushed her hands away. "Oh, no. My job."

He went to his knees in front of her as he pulled the boxers down. He kissed her navel, flicking his tongue inside the indentation. Need shot through her, and she cried out.

"Shh," he whispered, drawing her boxers over her knees as he kissed her damp curls.

She could barely breathe from the pressure of wanting him, yet he was moving at a snail's pace. "Are you... going to make a big...production out of taking those off?" she asked.

"Yep." Steadying her with one hand, he grasped her ankle and lifted, so that she stepped out of one leg of the boxers. Then, before she quite realized his purpose, he'd cupped her behind and tilted her pelvis so that he could give her a very intimate kiss indeed.

She gasped, and her knees buckled as pleasure surged through her. She felt the quilt brush the small of her back. Trembling, she leaned weakly against the padded crotch of the tree as he had his way with her. She was helpless against the onslaught of his tongue as he urged her pulsing, tightening body to enjoy, enjoy, enjoy.

Gripping the rough branch arching beside her, she pressed the back of her other hand to her mouth as the explosion came, rocking her against the tree. Her muffled cry sounded like the keening of a wild creature—the wild creature he had set loose within her.

And she wanted him still. Even as the shock waves continued, she wanted him. She took her hand from her mouth. Her plea was choked with emotion, but he couldn't possibly mistake what she needed.

He didn't.

He eased her gently against the tree and steadied her with one hand as he reached in his pocket. She made a real effort and managed to stay upright when he released her so he could put on the condom. Slipping it over his erection, he made a noise low in his throat, as if even that contact challenged his control.

Then he was back, his hands under her bottom, lifting

her to the wide crotch of the tree, holding her there. She braced her hands against the outstretched branches, leaned into the cradle of his cupped hands and opened her thighs.

With her slicker draped protectively around them, he stepped closer and probed gently, his breathing ragged. "Don't let me hurt you."

She moaned in frustration. "I want all of you, Quinn. Every last rigid inch."

He eased inside a little more. "Okay?"

Oh, he was big, but she wanted big. She wanted to be filled, at long last, with everything this man had to offer. She panted with need. "Not enough."

He pushed slightly deeper.

"More," she whispered.

He gave her a fraction more, but he was obviously holding back, obviously had a hangup about being too big.

"Oh, Quinn." In one swift motion she wrapped her legs around his hips and pulled him in tight. "Oh, *Quinn.*"

Apparently he couldn't control his growl of satisfaction, but then he went right back to being the soul of concern, although his voice was a little rough around the edges. "I'm hurting you."

"That was not hurt you heard in my voice," she said breathlessly. "That was heaven. My body is singing, Quinn, singing the praises of your big beautiful—"

"Okay. I get it." He covered her mouth with his.

His kiss might be all it would take, she thought, her heart pounding as he explored thoroughly with his tongue while still locked against her. He might not have to move that astounding equipment at all, since it filled her so totally, making contact in all the right places.

Then he began to move, and she decided moving might

be a good thing. Moving might be a great thing. Moving might be a really spectacular thing.

He lifted his mouth from hers. ''Ah, Jo. I've never… this is so good.''

''So very good.'' She absorbed another soul-filling moment as he buried himself deep, eased back and pushed home again.

''As if this is what we're meant for.'' He nibbled at her lower lip.

''Oh, yes.'' She welcomed another thrust, treasuring each and every one.

''We fit.'' He kissed her chin, the hollow of her throat, all the while holding her steady as he eased his hips back and forth, bringing her joy with every stroke.

''Like a sword in a sheath.'' The quickening that had started with the first glorious full contact had intensified with each rhythmic motion. She wanted it to last forever, but knew they had only seconds to go, knew from the subtle way Quinn increased the pace, the slight change in his breathing.

Faster still. Exquisite friction. So right. There. Yes. Now. Quinn. Oh, Quinn. Love me. Love me, love me, love me.

He kissed her hard, forcing the cry into her throat, smothering the groan rumbling from his chest. Holding her tight and deeply impaled, he absorbed her convulsions and drank her whimpers of delight until his own release gripped him.

For the first time in her life, she felt the joy of another's climax as if it were her own. And as he shuddered helplessly in her arms, gasping her name, she knew that no matter how much heartbreak it brought her, she would never regret this night of loving Quinn.

13

QUINN had decided to make love this way because he'd figured that lying on the ground was just asking for interference from snakes and bugs. However, the experience had turned out to be much better than he could have imagined. He'd go so far as to say he'd never known anything to equal making love propped against an oak tree on a chilly spring night in Montana.

With Jo, he quickly added. Jo, the most perfect sexual partner he'd ever known. The funniest, sweetest, sexiest woman he'd ever known. He kissed her eyes, her cheeks, her hair. Gathering her close, he savored the recent ecstasy of being enclosed by her warmth.

If this wasn't love, then he didn't understand what love was all about. He not only wanted to spend the rest of the night with her, he wanted to spend days, months, years with her. "Maybe I could dye my hair blond," he murmured, nestling her head against his shoulder.

"*What?*" She roused herself and stared at him. "Quinn, you make love like no man I've ever known, but your after-the-loving conversation needs work. This is not the time to discuss hair treatments."

He chuckled, and as he gazed at her he felt as if someone had poured warm melted butter over his heart. Yeah, he probably loved her, loved her strong enough to last clear into doddering old age. "Or I could shave my head. That's popular these days."

"I'm not wild about that look, if you're really determined to discuss this now. And blond won't go with your skin tones as well as dark brown does. What's this about?"

"I'm trying to figure out how I could sneak back to see you again after I leave town. I think the blond hair would work. And maybe a mustache and glasses."

She cupped his face in both hands. "Let's just tell everybody you're not Hastings."

"No. I can't let you do that."

"Well, I can't let you dye your hair. Your friends and clients would wonder what on earth was going on. I don't want to be responsible for making you look dumb in front of everybody. Let's tell."

"No. I'll dye my hair."

"No." She combed her fingers through his hair. "I love it this color. That's partly what makes your eyes look so incredibly blue—your skin is a nice bronze color." Her voice grew soft and wispy. "The contrast is wonderful," she murmured, drawing him down to her waiting lips.

Incredibly he began to get hard again. He deepened the kiss and kneaded Jo's firm bottom, just to see where that would take him. Sure enough, it took him right back to where he'd been when he'd first lifted her to the perfect level for this activity. Maybe it was the wildness of making love to a woman sitting in the crotch of a tree that was causing him to feel randy as a seventeen-year-old who'd just lost his virginity. Or maybe it was simply Jo, the scent of her, the taste of her, the feel of her.

And judging from the way her breathing had changed and the hungry way she opened her mouth to his kiss, she also wanted him again, and that was another small miracle. Heart soaring, he gave thanks for his foresight and prepared to enter paradise a second time. How he loved the supple feel of her muscles beneath his palms as she moved in response to his thrusts.

He longed to see her face, but even though he lifted his head to gaze at her, the shadows were too deep. "I wish I could look into your eyes," he murmured, his voice already rough and trembling, his climax hovering near.

"Do you?"

"Yes." He heard the quiver in her voice and knew she was on the edge, too. How quickly they could excite each other. Like lightning.

"Why?"

"Because." He pushed in again, listening for the catch in her breath that meant she was ready. When it came, he slowed, wanting to draw the moment out this time. "I want to see how your eyes change when you're close, like now."

"Are you…?"

"Yes." He drew back ever so slowly and slipped in with practically no force at all. Easy, easy. "Very close."

She trembled in his grip. "I want to see your eyes, too."

"It's too dark." He held back, but even his lazy strokes were going to get them there very soon, no matter how much he wanted to draw out the process.

"I know how your eyes look." She gasped as a tremor shook her. "Like blue flames."

"And yours are like warm chocolate." She was there, and he couldn't keep himself from going with her, moving faster, pushing deeper, trying to touch that part of her that would make her his. "So rich…so hot."

"Quinn." His name was a moan on her lips. "Kiss me, or the world will hear how I feel right now."

He took her mouth with some regret. Maybe the world shouldn't hear just yet, but he'd like to. When he carried her once more into the whirlwind, he wished he could listen as she moaned and cried out his name. He wanted all the sounds he'd helped create as she trembled in his arms.

Because those sounds might include the words, "I love you."

JO CLUNG to Quinn for many long moments, savoring the closeness and the incredible pleasure. But at last he eased back and lifted her gently to the ground. She leaned against the tree, feeling weak and just the slightest bit bowlegged, while he turned and got himself together.

When he turned back to her, he had picked up her silk boxers from the ground. "Want some help putting these on?" he said with a smile in his voice.

Incredibly, considering all she'd experienced, a shiver of desire went through her. "No, thank you." She took the boxers from him and put them on. If she let him help, he might begin to think she was insatiable. Which she might be, but she still didn't want him thinking she was. Besides, as it was she'd have trouble sitting a horse tomorrow. Much more of Quinn's loving and she'd be crippled. Happy, but crippled.

"Stay there," he said. "I think I heard Fred leave the house. I'll go make sure." Quinn left the shadow of the tree and crept around the house.

Once he was no longer holding her, kissing her, making her forget everything but his loving, she had the unwelcome chance to think about their situation. He sounded really serious about disguising himself so he could come back and see her. The trouble was, she didn't want him to be an occasional visitor, she wanted him to be a fulltime, old-fashioned husband. There, she'd finally admitted it to herself.

She loved him, and not only because he was, as the saying went, hung like a horse. That was a nice bonus, but she'd fallen in love before she discovered that pleasant reality. She'd fallen in love with his courage, his generosity and his sense of fun. To have him drop in once in a while would break her heart.

It could very well break his, too. The man she loved wouldn't be happy with that arrangement for long, but he was an investment banker, not a cowboy. He might want her, in fact he obviously wanted her very much, but he didn't want this life-style full of creepy-crawlies, belligerent horses and saddle sores. She couldn't ask him to sacrifice his career to live with her in Montana, but if she didn't cut their relationship off right now, he might get in deep enough to consider such a move only to regret it later. She hated the thought of hurting him, but it was the only way.

Quinn walked to the tree. "He's gone back to the bunkhouse," he said. "The coast is clear." He slipped his arms beneath her slicker and pulled her close, resting his cheek against the top of her head. "But I don't want to let you go. Listen, maybe I could use colored contacts and glasses. And a beard."

She drew back and gazed at him. Maybe it was just as well she couldn't see his face in the darkness. That made it easier to say what must be said. "Forget the disguise idea, Quinn. It wouldn't work."

"That's what you think. You'd be amazed what facial hair can—"

"No, I mean it wouldn't work for me. I don't know if I'll ever find another man to love, but if I do, he needs to be somebody who belongs in this country, somebody I can share ranch life with. If you keep showing up, I'll naturally keep wanting you, but you belong in New York, not out on some remote Montana ranch. We both need to cut our losses, Quinn.''

He gasped and stepped back as if she'd slapped him. He seemed to struggle with his breathing for a moment, and then he finally spoke. ''Okay, if that's the way you see it.'' His voice was raw with hurt. ''I guess I thought we'd created something worth hanging on to.''

''I will hang on to it,'' she said softly. ''I'll never forget this night as long as I live.''

''But you never want another one?''

She braced herself against his agonized plea. ''Not when it means I have to keep watching you head to New York when it's over. And you have to do that, Quinn. We both know it. That's what you're trained for, what you're used to.''

He turned away from her. ''Yeah. That's me. Wall Street or bust.''

She touched his arm. ''Please understand how much you mean to me. How much what we've shared means to me.''

''Yeah.'' His voice was thick with sorrow.

Oh, God. If Quinn started getting emotional, so would she. She'd be bawling her eyes out in a minute if she didn't get out of there. ''I'd better get back to the house.''

''Okay.''

She gave his arm one last squeeze, grabbed the blanket and ran to the house. The quick movement told her she would indeed be very sore tomorrow. But it would be nothing to equal the pain in her heart.

QUINN STOOD in the shadows feeling as if somebody had come after him with a bullwhip. He knew he wasn't much of a cowboy, but she didn't have to be so brutal about it. Apparently he was so bad that she never even considered he might someday be of use on this ranch. She thought he was so hopeless that even she and Fred couldn't teach him enough to make his sorry ass worth something around here.

Nope, she was sending him right back to New York where he belonged. And she would look for a real cowboy. Like Hastings. Quinn gritted his teeth. He'd never met Hastings, and the guy was probably a decent human being, but Quinn was really beginning to hate the bastard.

He started to the bunkhouse and tripped over something. He picked up the flashlight she'd dropped when he'd grabbed her from behind. Damn, but her breasts were silky, and her…no. He couldn't think about any of that or he'd go crazy.

He glanced at the flashlight and remembered seeing it on the table in the hallway. Maybe he should quietly return it so it wouldn't become a topic of discussion. Tomorrow would be weird enough without having to explain the mysterious roving flashlight.

When he reached the porch he took off his boots so he wouldn't make noise. The unlocked door still amazed him, but with all the nocturnal comings and goings around the place, a key would be a nuisance. And he supposed being surrounded by all these acres of rangeland kept the threat of crime very low.

He stood in the darkened entryway and battled temptation. Despite what Jo had said, if he went up those stairs and climbed into her bed, she wouldn't refuse him. He might be out of condoms, but there were plenty of other ways to find mutual satisfaction, and his hunger for her still raged. But that plan wouldn't come to pass as long as he had a shred of pride left.

He started to set the flashlight on the small table by the door when another thought occurred to him. He had a flashlight, so he wouldn't have to turn on a lamp and risk having Fred or Benny notice it. Okay, so he wasn't a cowboy, but he was a hell of a good hand with figures. If Jo didn't lock her front door she sure as hell didn't lock her desk.

He had a few hours before daybreak. It might be enough time to work some magic with Jo's books.

QUINN DIDN'T show up for breakfast, which was fine with Jo. Despite the open kitchen window that Emmy Lou had raised to let in a warm spring breeze, the air was thick with tension as Emmy Lou and Fred exchanged looks, and Benny, clueless, chattered away about the day's events. Finally Fred suggested that Benny go polish the tack in preparation for the rodeo, and Benny breezed happily off to do his chores.

"I'll be getting down to the barn, myself." Jo pushed back her chair. "Sherry will be here for the insemination any minute." She'd never blushed when she'd talked about such matters before, but she blushed now. Dammit.

"Hold on a second, Jo," Fred said.

Jo sat down. "Listen, if it's about last night, that's none of my business. I'm happy for both of you. I—"

"It's about last night." Emmy Lou cradled her mug of coffee. "But not what you think. We're not kids, and we won't ask for your permission. If our behavior isn't to your liking, then we'll hire on somewhere else, right, Fred?"

Fred stared at her. "You'd leave this place on account of me?"

"Amazing, isn't it?" Emmy Lou grinned. "Don't let it go to your head."

"I just never thought…" He shook his head, a smile lifting the corners of his gray mustache.

"We were going to broach another subject, weren't we, Fred?" Emmy Lou prompted.

"Yeah." Fred hunkered over his coffee. "Yeah, we were. Jo, you know we didn't think much of Dick."

Emmy Lou cleared her throat. "Except to imagine him swinging by his—"

"Em." Fred sent her a look of warning.

"I'll bet Jo's thought of that, too," Emmy Lou said a touch defensively.

"I have."

"Anyway," Fred continued, "we think you should hang on to this one."

"This one?"

"The greenhorn," Fred said. "He has heart, Jo. More'n Dick ever dreamed of. I know he can't ride a lick or rope worth a damn, but he's got guts, and that's what counts. We could teach him—at least, I think we could. He's not real talented, but he's determined. And I have to say I was impressed because he had sense enough to...uh, use protection last night." Fred gulped his coffee and choked.

Emmy Lou pounded on Fred's back while Jo sat there getting very red and wondering how Fred could possibly know such an intimate thing. Surely Quinn hadn't left evidence lying around.

Once Fred calmed down, Emmy Lou glanced at Jo. "Quinn borrowed from Fred's supply," she said gently. "Fred noticed because he was down to four, and two were missing."

"Oh, my God." Jo buried her face in her hands. "I can't believe I'm having this discussion with you two."

Fred still sounded a little wheezy, but he seemed to want to get his message across. "It ain't always easy to talk about. But Emmy Lou and me saw you make one mistake by takin' up with Dick, and we don't want to see you make another one by lettin' the greenhorn go.''

Tears pushed at the back of Jo's eyes. ''That's the sweetest, most considerate and wonderfully protective attitude, and I thank you both. But there's a tiny problem. Quinn doesn't want to live here and be a cowboy.''

Fred looked astonished. ''Why not?''

''Because he's a New York investment banker. He chose that, the same way you chose to work on ranches. He wouldn't mind coming to see me once in a while, but he's not interested in moving to the Bar None.''

''He said that?'' Fred scratched his head, still not comprehending.

''Not in those words, but it's very obvious. I think it's a bit too primitive for him.''

''What's primitive?'' Quinn asked from the doorway.

Jo glanced up and couldn't seem to remember what she'd been saying. He looked tired, but still gorgeous. Despite everything she'd told herself, she wanted to walk straight into his arms.

Fred stood. ''I got business at the barn. Sherry'll be here soon.''

''And I have to check on something in my garden,'' Emmy Lou said, leaving the table on Fred's heels. ''There's coffee and toast and a few hash browns left. I'm sure Jo could scramble you some eggs.'' She hurried out of the room.

Quinn glanced after them as the front door closed. ''I sure know how to clear a room.''

''I need to get going, too.'' She pushed back her chair.

''Before you do, I have something to talk to you about.''

''What?'' Her heart began to pound. Maybe he wanted to make some sacrifices so they could be together. She couldn't imagine how it would work, but then she didn't know exactly what investment bankers did. Maybe he could investment bank in Bozeman.

"Well, I—"

"Yo, Brian!" The shout came from the front yard.

Jo groaned. She did not feel like facing Dick this morning.

Quinn walked over to peer out the window. "He's riding a bike."

"You're kidding." Jo got up to look. Sure enough, Dick was riding back and forth in front of the porch on— Jo could hardly believe it—a pink girl's bike that was too small for him.

"Hey, Brian! Got a minute?" Dick called. "My heart rate's up, and I need to keep it elevated, buddy. It ain't time for my cooldown, or I'd stop riding and come on in. But I gotta talk to you."

"Coming!" Quinn called through the window. "I'd better go or he's liable to ride around out there forever."

"He might," Jo agreed. "He functions on about a sixth-grade level."

"Come with me?"

When he gave her that look she couldn't deny him anything. "Okay."

Quinn walked out on the porch, and Jo followed. "Nice bike, Dick," Quinn said.

"Found it at a garage sale. It'll do until the Nautilus equipment arrives."

"Nautilus?" Jo asked. "You're getting a home gym?"

"Sure am." Dick grinned at her as he pedaled across the yard, his knees sticking out awkwardly. "After people see me in this movie, I might be getting other offers. Gotta stay buff, you know. 'Course, I don't ride this thing where my men can see me."

"Of course not," Quinn said. "What's on your mind, Dick?"

"Me and Doobie got to thinkin'."

"There's a scary thought," Jo muttered.

"Yeah?" Quinn said. "About what?"

"We understand you can't be in the rodeo and all, on account of you being such a valuable property, but we figured it wouldn't hurt for you to lead off the grand parade."

Jo remembered Quinn's wild ride on Hyper and smelled disaster in the air. "Oh, you know, Dick, that's a wonderful idea, but Brian really shouldn't be on a horse right now."

"Why not?"

Jo thought quickly. "Well, he recently spent some time in the tropics and went swimming in questionable water that gave him a real bad case of jock itch."

"I'll do it," Quinn said, glaring at her. "I'm completely cured."

"Don't be a hero," she said, glaring back at him. "You know you're not a hundred percent."

"Close enough," Quinn said.

"You're sure?" Dick asked. "That's nasty stuff. I remember one time I got it, and I tell you, I scratched till I thought my—"

"I'll be fine," Quinn said. "Plan on me doing it."

"Great. Well, gotta get on down the road. Still got my lifting program to do. Until the Nautilus stuff comes I'm using a broomstick with a six-pack strapped on each end. Oh, and I drink a glass of raw eggs every morning."

Jo grimaced.

"Good idea," Quinn said.

"I thought so. See you." Dick pedaled off, humming the theme from *Rocky*.

Quinn gazed after him. "So you don't think I can ride well enough to lead the grand parade?"

"Maybe. Depending on the horse you choose. But you're taking a big chance, Quinn. I think you'd be better off if you—"

"Said my jock itch flared up again?" He sounded testy.

"I'm sorry. It was the first thing I thought of, and I couldn't very well say you were saddle sore, could I?"

"And what makes you think I am?"

"The way you walked out on this porch."

"You're walking with a certain amount of care yourself this morning," he said.

Her cheeks warmed.

"Will you be riding in this grand parade?" he asked.

"Yes. All of the contestants ride in it, and I always do the barrel racing event."

"Barrel racing, huh? And how will that feel after…last night?"

She couldn't look at him. "I admit that I'm a little tender."

"Then I guess we'll suffer together. Because I'm going to lead that grand parade regardless of my delicate condition."

"Okay, then I'd recommend riding Butternut. He's—"

"Thanks, but I'll pick my own horse."

Jo groaned. "Don't tell me."

"Yep. I'll be lookin' good. I'm riding Hyper."

14

HIS CROTCH hurt like hell. Quinn sat atop a restless Hyper at the entrance to the small rodeo arena outside Ugly Bug and wished he'd used the jock itch excuse, after all. But when Jo had automatically assumed he couldn't even lead a sedate little parade, he'd taken offense. He'd decided he had something to prove to her before he left on the red-eye tonight.

Besides, after watching people steer horses down Fifth Avenue during parades in New York City, he figured there was nothing to it. This would be even easier because it was contained inside a fence.

He hadn't counted on the fact that the leader had to carry an American flag big enough to wrap a body in. And he hadn't counted on wind.

Hyper jumped sideways with every snap and billow of the massive flag. And with each jump, Quinn was painfully reminded of his manly attributes. Jo was somewhere behind him in line, along with Benny, Dick and a bunch of other real cowboys and cowgirls. Mostly they'd behaved themselves, and only a couple had asked for autographs, which he'd politely postponed until after the parade. With luck he'd sprain his wrist in the next twenty minutes, because he'd never gotten around to practicing Hastings' signature.

The other residents of Ugly Bug, however, weren't behaving themselves. Whistling, stomping and calling out his name, or rather Hastings' name, they jammed the modest bleachers. Camera flashes popped constantly, even though it was the middle of the day. At least ten home-made signs waved in the crowd. The more conservative ones said things like Brian Hastings for President, or We Love You, Brian, but one held by a rowdy band of high-school-age girls was covered in huge lipstick kisses with red, glittery letters that spelled out Take Me, Brian! Take Me Now!

A couple of Western lawmen types had positioned themselves at either end of the bleachers. Quinn appre-ciated having them there, but if the mob decided to rush him, even Marshal Matt Dillon wouldn't be able to control this crowd.

Quinn swallowed. If he survived the parade, he was supposed to sit in a special section smack-dab in the cen-ter of those bleachers. The roped-off area already held Doobie and his tush-fixated wife, along with several other middle-aged couples. Jo had wangled a place in that sec-tion for Fred and Emmy Lou, thank God. Maybe they'd help protect him.

As Quinn waited for the gate to open, sweat dampened the black Western shirt with pearl buttons that Benny had insisted he wear. Benny had also donated his best black Stetson, and Fred had brought out silver spurs that winked in the sunlight. Hyper's coat shone like polished mahog-any, and his mane and tail were braided with red ribbon. The horse looked great, just as Quinn had imagined. All Quinn had to do was stay on him.

A wizened old cowboy swung open the arena gate, and members of the Ugly Bug High School Band swung into a fast-paced march. Quinn mentally reviewed his instruc-tions. Once around the arena, then straight up the middle to face the grandstands. The other riders would fan out on either side of him, forming a line facing the bleachers as the band played the national anthem. Then he'd lead the riders around to the exit. Taking a firm grip on the flag, he nudged Hyper in the ribs with Fred's silver spurs, and the crowd surged to its feet, applauding loudly.

With a piercing whinny, Hyper reared.

Quinn grabbed at the saddle horn with his free hand and by some miracle hung on, but by the time Hyper's front feet hit the ground, the horse had the bit in his teeth.

Quinn felt the gelding's muscles bunch. "Whoa!" he yelled.

Hyper wasn't listening. He shot through the gate and in three strides was in a dead run. Quinn's hat sailed off, and he lost his stirrups, but he kept his grip on the flag, which streamed dramatically over his shoulder. The grandstands, filled with cheering people, passed in a blur, then passed in a blur again as Hyper turned the arena into his private racetrack.

As Quinn whizzed past the gate, the other riders waved their hats and whistled. Quinn would bet Jo wasn't whistling. And if Hyper kept up this merry-go-round much longer, she might even ride out and pull him to a stop. God, how humiliating.

"Whoa, dammit!" he yelled. He was afraid to let go of the saddle horn to pull back on the reins, and if he dropped the flag so he could grab the reins, then everyone would know he was involved in a major screwup instead of the dramatic flourish they were giving him credit for. Worse yet, they might begin to wonder if he was really Brian Hastings.

He tried to remember what Fred had taught him. Oh, yeah. Grip with your thighs. You could even steer with your thighs, assuming your thighs didn't feel as if somebody had set fire to them, which Quinn's pretty much did.

He gritted his teeth as he flashed by the stands again. Hyper was young and strong. He could probably run for quite a long time, especially when he had the impression he was being chased by an American flag. So Quinn couldn't hope the horse would get tired. And he definitely didn't want Jo to ride out and save him.

The only solution was to get the horse through the gate somehow. After that Hyper would probably continue to run, but maybe they'd get far enough away that Quinn could safely drop the flag and try to establish control. Then again, maybe he and Hyper would see a great deal of the Montana countryside together.

Quinn figured that if he shifted his weight and used his tortured thigh muscles, he might be able to get Hyper to swerve through the gate instead of sailing past it. Bracing himself against the pain, he started leaning and squeezing as Hyper went into the straightaway and headed in the direction of the gate. Twice before the horse had veered left and continued around the arena. Quinn vowed he wouldn't do it again.

Apparently Hyper didn't care where he ran as long as he could keep doing it. He stampeded right through the gate as riders waiting beside it scattered in front of his pounding hoofs. Ahead was the parking lot, and beyond that, open country.

Quinn hung on as Hyper veered headlong between rows of pickup trucks. Once out of the parking lot, Quinn figured he'd drop the flag and try to put an end to this wild ride. Then he heard hoofbeats behind him and looked over his shoulder. Sure enough, Jo was in hot pursuit, with Benny behind her. Maybe it was just as well, he thought. He was nearly at the edge of the lot, and he really didn't want to ride this nag all the way to Idaho.

As he faced forward again, a long white vehicle pulled

across the empty space at the end of the lot. Quinn squinted, not quite believing what he saw. A limo? In Ugly Bug? Hyper didn't slow his pace as the limo stopped, blocking the horse's path.

Quinn dropped the flag and seized the reins in both hands. "Whoa, you sorry nag! Whoa, goddammit! You're gonna hit the car, you idiot horse!" When Hyper didn't respond, Quinn braced himself for one hell of a collision.

Instead, Hyper gathered himself and sailed gracefully over the limo. Unfortunately Quinn didn't make the trip with him. Falling sideways, he hit the roof of the limo and rolled down the windshield, coming to rest facedown on the hood.

In seconds, Jo was leaning over him. "Don't move! Did you hit your head? Where are you hurt? Oh, Quinn, speak to me!"

He was having trouble drawing a breath, but he was at least able to register the concern in her voice. Well, good. She cared for him a little. "Don't call me Quinn," he muttered. "I'm Brian Hastings."

"That's funny," said another voice. "So am I."

"NOT YET, you're not," Jo said, barely giving the man a glance as she leaned over Quinn, her chest tight with fear. So Brian Hastings was here. So what? "Talk to me, my darling. Does anything feel broken?"

"I don't think so. Where's Hyper?"

"Benny went after him."

"Boss, you need anything?" said the uniformed driver as he climbed out of the limo.

"Not right now, Sid," Hastings said. Then he turned to Jo. "What do you mean, *not yet?* I've been Brian Hastings ever since the studio changed my name from Bernard Hilzendeger. I made it legal ten years ago. Listen, do you want me to call 911?''

''Yes,'' said Jo.

''No,'' said Quinn. ''I'm okay.'' He pushed himself slowly to his hands and knees. ''But I dented the limo.''

''It appears you did,'' Hastings said.

''Call 911,'' Jo said as she gazed into Quinn's beloved face. Fred had said the greenhorn had heart, and Fred sure knew what he was talking about. ''He's in shock.''

''No, don't call 911,'' Quinn said, looking at Hastings.

''My God.'' Hastings stared at Quinn. ''It's like looking in a mirror.''

''Don't you wish.'' Jo didn't spare the movie star a glance as she stroked Quinn's cheek. ''I'm so sorry I put you through this, sweetheart. Please forgive me. I should have found a better way to raise the money than having you impersonate this guy. If you're seriously hurt I'll never forgive myself.''

''Hold it.'' Hastings frowned at Quinn. ''You've been pretending to be me? Trading on my fame? Well, I hope you have a damned good lawyer, mister, because you have a lot more to worry about than a dented limo hood.''

Jo whirled toward him, glad to be able to focus her anger on someone besides herself. ''Don't you dare threaten him! He nearly killed himself for me, and all because you wouldn't get off the dime!''

Hastings' square jaw dropped. ''This is my fault?''

''It certainly is.'' She shook her finger in his handsome face. ''Your advance man came by my ranch and was so enthusiastic he got my hopes up that you would actually use my ranch in your movie!''

Hastings adjusted his sunglasses. ''Actually, I was thinking I'd—''

''But did you show up to close the deal?'' Jo barreled

on. "No, you did not. Well, you may have millions, but some of us struggle along from one payment to the next, trying to live the American dream, while our ex-husbands sabotage us at every turn."

"But, you see, that's why I'm—"

"And then, when we finally find a decent guy who's willing to go that extra mile for us, willing to risk life and very attractive limb to make our dreams come true, along comes some millionaire movie star threatening to sue the pants off him!"

"And these aren't even my pants," Quinn added.

Hastings propped his hands on his hips and gazed at Quinn. Then he looked at Jo. "I still don't get it."

Jo took a deep breath. "It's very simple. If my banker thought Brian Hastings was staying at my place, he'd assume the movie deal was on and that at some point in the future I'd be able to make a sizable payment on my loan so he wouldn't foreclose."

"But then, if the movie never gets made...?"

"By this fall, especially if the price of beef goes up, I should be able to make a payment that will satisfy him."

"I have a couple of other ideas, too, Jo." Quinn climbed off the hood and came to stand beside her. "You don't have to sell Clarise and Stud-muffin. Instead you should shop around for a better insurance rate, for one thing. What you're paying is outrageous."

She turned to him, her eyes wide. "You snooped in my books?"

"Yeah, as a matter of fact, I did. I set up a basic book-keeping system you should have no trouble following, and in the process found some cost-saving—"

"I can't believe this!" Jo cringed at the thought that he'd seen the chaos of her financial affairs. "That is extremely private!"

"Dammit, Jo, it's my area of expertise. And I thought we'd arrived at a point where I could—"

"You think because of what happened in that tree you now have the right to invade my private financial records and make all sorts of recommendations? Well, let me tell you, Mr. Quinn Monroe, investment banker, that I—"

"Excuse me, Jo," Hastings said. "That is your name, right?"

"That's my name." Jo still glared at Quinn.

"Jo, I have a comment to make. I'm not sure what went on between you and this Hastings look-alike in the tree, but if he's willing to give you some free financial advice as a result, I suggest you take it. I hate to tell you what I pay my accountant, but it's worth every penny. I'm not good with numbers, and obviously, neither are you."

Jo lifted her chin. "I've been managing."

"Oh, yeah? Then what was that speech about the American dream and loan payments and sabotaging ex-husbands all about?"

"I got...carried away."

"Okay, but it's hard-won advice I'm passing out. And these guys hardly *ever* work for nothing. That tree experience must have been something else." Hastings folded his arms and glanced across the roof of the limo. "Here comes the horse you rode in on, Monroe."

Jo looked over to see Benny leading Hyper toward them. Then she glanced toward the arena and noticed a small contingent of people, led by Emmy Lou and Fred, coming toward them. She had to find a way to stall them until she figured out what to do.

Benny reined in his horse and stared at Quinn and Hastings. "Separated at birth," he said in an awed voice, shaking his head.

Jo hurried to him. "Not quite. Listen, Benny, I need

you to do something for me. See Emmy Lou and Fred coming over here with all those people?''

Benny nodded.

''I want you to ride over and tell them that Brian Hastings has a big surprise planned, and everyone has to remain in their seats, or it will be ruined.''

Benny frowned. ''Okay. But the flag's on the ground.''

Jo snatched it up, shook it off and handed it to him. Benny had always longed to carry that flag. ''You take it back, Benny. You're the flag bearer and the messenger, okay? I'm counting on you.''

Benny grinned. ''You bet.'' He kicked his horse into a fast trot to make the flag ripple as he rode toward the approaching crowd, and Hyper followed docilely behind.

Jo heaved a sigh and turned to Quinn and Hastings. ''Now, where were we?''

Hastings gazed at her. ''I was about to ask if you want to negotiate the terms for my use of your ranch, or are you going to be smart and turn it over to Mr. Investment Banker, here?''

Jo's heartbeat quickened. ''You really want the ranch?''

''Yep. I drove out there just now, and it's perfect. But nobody was home, so I came into town, saw all the commotion and decided to investigate.''

Jo glanced from Hastings to Quinn. ''That's great. Really great. But we have this tiny problem.'' She looked at Hastings. ''People around here think Brian Hastings has already arrived.''

Hastings stroked his jaw and looked at Quinn. ''Think we could make the switch?''

''Maybe,'' Quinn said.

Jo shook her head. ''No way.''

''Why not?'' both men said at once.

"Because you really don't look anything alike," Jo said. "Quinn's eyes are much bluer, and he's taller, and his shoulders are broader. His hair's thicker, and he's got that cute little freckle on his cheekbone, and everyone may not notice, but when he smiles, one of his eyeteeth is *slightly* crooked, which gives him a rakish air you can't get with caps."

"I don't have caps," Hastings said stiffly. He glanced at Quinn. "But maybe I need the name of your stylist. To be honest, I haven't been all that happy with Antoine recently."

"My barber's in New York."

"No problem. Maybe he'd like to relocate."

Quinn's expression turned belligerent. "If you're going to steal the first decent barber I've found in six years, I'm not telling you his name."

"Guys. Could we get back on track? I don't think it will work to switch one of you for the other, so what else have we got?"

"We could say it was all a joke," Quinn said.

Jo looked doubtful. "But you promised people parts in the movie."

Hastings groaned. "Oh, boy. Here we go. Not speaking parts, I hope?"

"No," Quinn said. "I wasn't specific, except I told this one guy, Jo's banker, that he'd be perfect for this French character."

Hastings shook his head. "I'll get with the scriptwriters. The last thing I want is bad publicity because some local guy thought he'd be in the movie and he's not." He hesitated, as if afraid to ask the next question. "Did you...tell them what it was about?"

"No," Jo said.

"That's a relief."

"I only gave them the title," Quinn said.

"The title?"

"Yeah. *The Brunette Wore Spurs.*"

"Ye gods and little fishes. That's *awful.*"

Quinn looked hurt. "I sort of liked it."

Hastings gave him a disparaging look. "Which is why you're in investment banking and I'm in filmmaking. Okay, we can deal with that. I'll tell them we had some fun with that title, thought of turning this into a Mel Brooks type spoof, but the producers didn't think it would suit my image. You didn't know that when I sent you out to Ugly Bug."

"You sent me? Wait a minute, you didn't—"

"Work with me here, Monroe. I'm trying to get you out of trouble, sport. Now, picture this." Hastings glanced around to make sure they weren't being overheard. "I met you in New York. That's where you're from, right?"

"Yep."

Hastings nodded. "Good. I go there all the time. So I met you and noticed the striking resemblance." He sent Jo a challenging look, but she only shrugged. "I've been looking for a stand-in, so I asked you if you were interested. You agreed to give it a try, so I sent you to Ugly Bug as a test, to see if people would believe you were me. It worked. I'm ready to hire you."

"But I don't want the job."

"I'm not really offering you the job! Hell, you probably can't even act!" Hastings shook his head. "Damn, but bankers can be literal. So I offer you the job, you turn it down, and we go on from there. Do you love it?"

Quinn nodded. "It might work."

"Might work?" Hastings threw his hands in the air. "It's brilliant! Improv at its finest! It's so hard to get any honest appreciation these days."

"I appreciate it," Jo said. "You've just found a way to save my reputation in Ugly Bug. Thank you."

"That reminds me," Hastings said. "Where'd that dumb name come from?"

"You don't even want to know," Quinn said.

"Maybe not. We're sure not using it in the script, that's for sure. I even hate to put it in the credits, but I guess we'll have to." Hastings motioned to the limo. "Shall we?"

Jo eyed the limo dubiously. "Where are we going?"

Hastings smiled his perfect smile. "Straight into the arena, my friends. If there's one thing Brian Hastings knows how to do, it's make an entrance."

Jo glanced at Quinn. "You'll have to go some to top the last one."

15

QUINN WATCHED Hastings maneuver his way through the rodeo festivities and the dance that evening, and by the end of it he had to admit Hastings was a hell of a guy. He handled crazed fans with a finesse Quinn envied, but of course he'd had plenty of practice. For the first time Quinn understood that being a star in the spotlight required boundless energy. Hastings was on the go constantly from the moment he stepped out of the limo in the middle of the rodeo arena to his late-night tour of the Bar None ranch buildings.

Quinn used the time Jo and Fred were showing Hastings around to change into his city clothes and lay his borrowed ones in a neat pile on his bunk. He hadn't told anyone about reserving a seat on the red-eye, figuring he'd make his goodbyes short and sweet when the time came. Finally he walked to the house, where a light shone from the kitchen window and he could see people gathered around Emmy Lou's table, probably swapping stories of the day and sampling one of her pies.

Quinn felt very sorry for himself. Not long ago he'd sat in that kitchen enjoying the same treatment Hastings was getting, being fed like a king and hailed as Jo's savior. Now she had a new hero. Come to think of it, she'd never really needed Quinn. Salvation had arrived only a few days after he was pressed into service. If Hastings hadn't turned out to be an understanding guy, Quinn's presence even might have ruined the movie deal. He'd been worse than useless—he'd been in the way.

At least he wouldn't make the mistake of hanging around. He walked up the steps to the porch just as Jo came out the front door.

"There you are! I've been wondering where you—" She paused and surveyed his outfit. "Why are you dressed like that?"

"I'm taking the red-eye, Jo."

"Tonight?" Her face paled. "You're leaving right now?"

He nodded. "I was coming in to say goodbye to everyone."

"I see." She swallowed. "Well, let me say, while we're out here by ourselves, that I'm very grateful for all you've done." She twisted her hands in front of her. "I can't...thank you enough."

Gratitude, he thought, was beggar's wages. He wanted love from her, not a polite thank-you. But she needed a cowboy to love. "It turns out I didn't do a damn thing. Hastings was on his way."

"We didn't know that. You stepped into the breach, Quinn. I'll never forget...that."

He figured she would forget it, and him, eventually. He wasn't part of her world and never could be. But standing here and not reaching for her, no matter how dumb the gesture would be, was the most difficult thing he'd ever done.

"I, um, guess you need to come in so you can get going," she said.

"Yeah." His voice was husky with sadness.

"I'll...I'll be right down. I need to...check on something." She turned and fled, letting the screen door bang after her as she ran upstairs.

With a heavy sigh Quinn walked into the house and entered the cheerful kitchen, the kitchen he'd never see again.

Conversation stopped, and Fred glanced up from his plate. "Where've you been, boy? I know how you crave Emmy Lou's cooking."

"It's been one of the best things about this trip," Quinn said, smiling at Emmy Lou. "Thank you for feeding me so well."

Emmy Lou frowned. "That sounded like a goodbye thank-you, to me."

"And you got your own clothes on for a change," Benny said.

"I'm catching the red-eye for New York tonight," Quinn said.

Benny leaped from his chair. "I'll be right back. Don't leave yet."

"I've got a few minutes left," Quinn said. Funny how emotional he felt at this moment. Like he was leaving his own family.

"Does Jo know?" Emmy Lou asked.

"Yeah. I met her on the porch."

"So that's why she pounded up those stairs like a skunk was after her," Fred said.

Quinn cleared his throat. "I wanted to say that you've been great, all of you." He glanced at Hastings, who sat at the table with his chauffeur, Sid. Hastings had a button missing from his shirt. Emmy Lou had scored her trophy, after all. "You, too, Brian," Quinn said. "You could have nailed me for this little stunt. Thanks for letting it go."

Hastings grinned and leaned back in his chair. "Hey, I love a challenge. Figuring out how to explain you to the good folks of Ugly Bug was the most fun I've had in years. Just don't go trying to be me anymore, okay?"

Quinn returned his smile. "I never wanted to be you in the first place."

"You *didn't?*" Hastings pretended great shock. "Who wouldn't want that?"

"I sure as hell wouldn't," Fred said. He got up to come over and shake Quinn's hand. "It's been a pleasure."

Quinn's conscience nagged him about the swiped condoms. "Uh, Fred, I—you might notice sometime that you—"

"I already did." Fred winked at him. "Forget it."

Not likely, considering what I used them for. Quinn nodded. "Thanks."

Emmy Lou pulled Quinn into a big hug. "Come back, you hear?"

"I...we'll see."

Emmy Lou stood back and gazed at him with tears in her eyes. "How about a button off your shirt?"

Quinn laughed in surprise. "I'm no celebrity."

"You are to me. I've never known a New York investment banker before. Can I have one?"

Quinn shrugged, more touched by the request than he wanted her to know. "Why not?" He stood patiently while she found some scissors and snipped off the button nearest his collar.

Then she patted his chest. "I mean it. Come back."

He was sure she knew that wasn't going to happen, or she wouldn't be fighting tears. "I'll try."

Benny came charging into the kitchen, his black Stetson in his hand. He shoved it at Quinn. "Here."

"Benny, I couldn't take this. It's your best hat."

"It looked good on you today. Well, until Hyper started running and it fell off. Wear it in New York. Go on. Take it."

Quinn recognized the gift as a gesture of friendship that

meant as much to Benny as it did to Quinn. "Thank you. I'll wear it with pride." God, it would be tough leaving these people. He put on the hat and adjusted the brim while Benny beamed at him. Another couple of minutes and Quinn was afraid he'd be bawling. "Well, folks, I'd better get on the road."

"I'll walk you out," Hastings said, pushing back his chair.

Uh-oh. Quinn wondered if Hastings was as laid-back as he'd seemed about the impersonation thing. Maybe he wanted Quinn to sign an affidavit promising never to repeat the stunt. Or maybe he was planning to press charges after all. "Okay."

After a last round of goodbyes, handshakes and hugs from Emmy Lou, Quinn walked to his rental car with Hastings, his eyes moist. It took him a few seconds before he trusted himself to speak. "So, what's on your mind?" he asked as they reached the car.

"The more appropriate question is, what's on yours?"

Quinn stood by the driver's side of the sedan and turned to Hastings. "What do you mean?"

"Are you really as stupid as you're acting right now, or do you have some master plan you're not telling anyone?"

Quinn stared at him.

Hastings sighed and shook his head. "So you're stupid. So stupid you're going to leave that woman, even though she loves you to pieces."

"Jo?"

"No, Meg Ryan." Hastings snorted. "Yes, Jo! Lord love a duck, but you're dense. I was thinking of hiring you for a couple of financial deals I'm working on, but if this is how you are, forget it. Jo is crazy about you. Genuine crazy, not the starstruck stuff I get most of the time.

She loves you deep down to the bone. A guy finds that maybe once in a lifetime, if he's lucky, and you're walking away from it. You're an idiot, Monroe.''

"She wants a cowboy. She said so."

"Oh, my God. So be a cowboy."

"I'm no good at it."

"Trust me, she won't care. All you really need to pull it off is a Stetson and a smile. Benny just gave you the Stetson, and according to Jo, and I quote—'' Hastings slipped into falsetto ''—when he smiles, one of his eyeteeth is slightly crooked, which gives him a rakish air.'' Hastings rolled his eyes. "That's love talking, sport. L-U-V, love. She looks at you as if you're the most expensive thing on the menu, something she'd give anything to have, but she's afraid she doesn't have the money to pay for."

Quinn's brain whirled as he wondered if he dared believe what Hastings was saying. "But if she really wants me—"

"She's scared to say, because of your big important job. Are you married to that hotshot position in New York, or could you see yourself moving to Montana? Montana's not so far from California, and if you can convince me you have at least a few brain cells working, I could probably scare you up some Hollywood clients. They're flaky, but they're rich. But then, you're flaky. It should work out."

"I'm not flaky."

"Oh, sure. I've heard enough to think otherwise. You hop on a plane to bring the lady horse sperm, and then you parade around here pretending to be a big star when you're clueless about the film industry, and then you climb on some spoiled-rotten horse and go tearing around a rodeo arena in front of the good people of Ugly Bug when you can't even ride, let alone ride and carry a flag. I'm gonna hook you up with Steve Martin. You two are soul mates.''

"You've got me pegged wrong." Maybe he used to be like that when he was growing up in the Bronx with Murray, but he'd changed.

Hastings grinned at him. "Have it your way. I've spent years studying how character is revealed, and I know this cold. You're a wild man. I'm not even going to ask what went on in that tree, but news flash, Quinn, baby—tight-assed guys don't make love in trees."

"I was just trying to stay away from snakes!"

"Are you kidding? Snakes can climb trees!"

Quinn could have lived without that factoid. "Okay, okay. What do you think I should do?"

"I have to tell you? Put away your car keys and go upstairs!"

"But everybody's in the house. It's an old house. I don't want—"

"I see your point. Okay. Especially considering your wild streak. Sid and I will take everybody for a moonlit limo ride. I can give you an hour, maybe an hour and a half. But if you can't get your business done in under sixty minutes, you're not the banker for me."

Jo KNEW she was being cowardly, but she couldn't go back downstairs and watch Quinn leave. Besides, no amount of makeup or eyedrops would be able to disguise that she'd been crying buckets. She'd closed her door and muffled the sound with pillows so they wouldn't be able to hear her downstairs, but with all those people in the house talking and laughing, they probably couldn't hear her, anyway.

Through her sobs she listened to everyone filing out of

the house. No doubt they'd all gone to wave goodbye as Quinn drove away. He'd been a popular guest. The sound of a car engine drifted up to her window, and a fresh wave of tears engulfed her. He was really gone.

When she heard her bedroom door open, she moaned. "Go away, Em. And don't tell me I'm stupid to cry over him." She sniffed. "I already know that."

Footsteps approached the bed.

"Please, Emmy Lou. There are some things a girl has to get through alone. I should never have allowed myself to care about him, but I did, so now I get to pay the consequences."

The bed sagged.

"Dammit, Emmy Lou. I don't need mothering, I need—" She lifted her head and stared into Quinn's blue, blue eyes.

"Loving?" he murmured, smoothing her tousled hair from her damp cheeks.

She buried her face in the pillow, mortified that he'd heard her babble about him and especially that he saw her like this, weeping like a dope because he'd left. "What are you doing here?" she mumbled into the pillow. "You'll miss your flight."

"Guess so." He stroked her hair.

"Why are you wearing Benny's hat?"

"He gave it to me. He likes me."

"Well, I don't. And don't you dare stay here because you feel sorry for me! I'm not crying over you, anyway."

"You're not?" He kicked off his shoes, took off his hat and scooted down next to her on the bed. "Then what are you crying for?"

"None of your beeswax."

He curved his arm around her waist. "I haven't heard that since fourth grade."

"Don't touch me, either."

"Why?" He nestled closer and pushed her hair back so he could nibble at her ear. "Because I have cooties?"

"Exactly." She didn't want to like his arm around her, or his warm breath on her ear. Maybe he wasn't leaving tonight, but he would leave tomorrow. And she'd have to go through this all over again.

"But you like bugs."

Apparently she'd cried so hard she'd sapped her strength. That was the only explanation for why she allowed him to roll her onto her back. And before she knew it, he'd plastered himself on top of her. And her stupid body was getting all hot and bothered about it, too. "Go away." The words came out in a croak.

"No." He began to kiss her eyes and her cheeks.

"Don't kiss me. I probably look like hell."

He grinned. "No, you don't. Just a little red and puffy."

"You missed your plane just so you could tell me that? What a guy."

His grin faded. "No, I didn't miss my plane so I could tell you that. I missed my plane so I could tell you this. I love you."

The world stopped. She stared at him, her mouth open.

"Breathe, Jo."

She gasped.

"That's it. Now keep breathing. In, out, in, out. That's a good girl."

She struggled to do as he asked, but it wasn't easy. "Sorry," she said in a strained voice. "But that's not the sort of thing I hear every day."

He gazed at her with loving concern. "I sure hope not."

She looked into his eyes. She'd suspected he was falling in love with her, but she'd never in a million years expected him to say so. "Why are you telling me this?" she asked.

"In hopes I could get you to say the same thing back to me."

"And then what?"

He nudged her gently with his arousal. "We have an hour before the group comes back from their moonlit limo ride."

"No."

The light in his eyes dulled. "No, you don't love me?"

"Yes, I love you, but no, we won't be frolicking in the sheets for the next hour."

The gleam returned to his eyes. "Why not?"

"Because this love talk is bad enough, but if you throw in a session with your talented and very large equipment, I won't be able to survive your leaving tomorrow, that's why."

He leaned down and brushed his lips across hers. "Which means I have to stay."

Her breath caught at that sweet contact. "Don't be ridiculous. You can't stay. You'll ruin your career."

"My career will be fine." He feathered a light kiss on her mouth. "I'm just afraid I'll be in the way around here. I can handle your ledgers like no one you've ever seen, but as you know, I can't ride and I can't rope and I'm scared of snakes and big ugly bugs."

"You think I care about that?"

He lifted his head to gaze at her. "I thought you did, yeah. I thought I wasn't cowboy enough for you."

"Oh, *Quinn*." She pulled his head down and proceeded to kiss him until the press of his arousal became very prominent indeed.

Gasping, he levered himself away from her. "Is that a yes?"

"I don't recall you asking a question."

"I didn't? Damn. Okay, let's make it a two-parter. First part—will you marry me? And second part—can we get rid of these clothes and get to it before that limo pulls up in front of the house?"

She smiled at him, her heart brimming with happiness. "Here's a one-part answer to your two-part question. Yes."

"Hallelujah." Quinn began unbuttoning her blouse at a furious pace.

"Oh, Quinn, we haven't talked about children!"

"Do we have to right now?" He tugged off her jeans and panties in one motion. "We only have about forty-four minutes left." He pulled his shirt over his head without unbuttoning it.

"We certainly do have to talk about children, unless you came prepared for this encounter, which I seriously doubt, because I happen to know Fred's supply was nearly exhausted last night."

Quinn paused, his pants half off. "He told you I swiped?"

"Yes, and he's about out by now. So, are we having kids or not?"

"That's up to you." Quinn pulled a foil-wrapped square from his pocket before letting the slacks fall to the floor.

"Are you taking Fred's last one?"

"Nope. He has a backup stash. And this time I didn't have to swipe it. He offered."

Jo's cheeks heated. "So everybody knows what we're doing up here?"

"Pretty much. So what'll it be?" He leaned down and

wiggled the packet in front of her face. "I happen to like kids, myself."

Jo's embarrassment lost out to a powerful surge of desire. "I like kids, too," she said, her voice husky.

Quinn straightened, tossed the packet over his shoulder and took off his briefs.

Jo looked at him standing before her in all his glory. He was perfect, but one little detail would make him even more perfect. "Quinn, do me a favor?"

"Anything."

She picked up the Stetson from where he'd laid it on the bedside table. "Humor me and put this on."

Quinn chuckled as he took the hat. He set it on his head and pulled it low over his eyes. "Damned if Hastings wasn't right."

"About what?"

"Nothing, sweetheart. Nothing at all." Then he smiled that heart-stopping smile, the one that made her knees weak and her pulse race.

Her heart brimming with happiness, Jo opened her arms. "Come here, you big, beautiful cowboy."

This book is for Rita Herron,
who insisted that Pamela have her own story.

Many thanks to the Girl Scouts,
whose cookies arrived the week of my deadline.

WIFE IS A
4-LETTER WORD

Stephanie Bond

Dear Reader,

Take one uptight computer boffin who was just jilted at the altar, add one flamboyant blonde bombshell who has a penchant for finding trouble, and you've got one calamity after another! Alan and Pam are the most unlikely pair imaginable, which only make their romance more...*climactic*.

I adore writing romantic comedy and I had a blast writing this story in particular. I hope *Wife is a 4-Letter Word* gives you many hours of enjoyment.

Drop me a note and let me know how I'm doing:

Box 2395, Alpharetta, GA 30023, USA.

Stephanie Bond

1

ALAN PARISH DREW BACK and kicked the aluminum can high in the air, mindless of damage to his shiny formal shoe. Hands deep in his pockets, he watched the can bounce and tumble on the deserted rain-soaked sidewalk in front of him, gleefully imagining it to be John Sterling's head each time the metal collided with the pavement.

His mouth twisted with the ballooning urge to curse, but he couldn't think of an appropriate expletive to describe the basically nice guy who'd just happened to steal his fiancée—at the altar. Right now the only adjective for the man that came to mind was…smart.

Glancing around, Alan looked for something else to kick, suddenly wishing it were physically possible to make contact with his own backside. He should have asked Josephine to marry him months ago—no, years ago. Instead he'd taken their relationship for granted and she'd fallen in love with one of her clients, then canceled her marriage to him before his mother, perched on the front pew, had time to work up a good cry.

At this very moment, his friends and business associates were no doubt toasting the happy impromptu couple, at Alan's expense—literally. He winced, remembering that he'd made sure a case of his favorite champagne would be sitting behind the bar in the reception hall.

The sound of a speeding car approaching behind him, along with a telltale beeping horn, made him turn just as the vehicle zoomed through a curbside puddle and showered him from head to toe. Alan raised his arms in a helpless, deep shrug as the cold, muddy water seeped under his white shirt collar and dripped down his back. An aged white Volvo sedan jumped the curb a few feet in front of him and lurched to a lopsided halt, with one wheel up on the sidewalk.

Oh, well, he'd actually seen *worse* parking out of Pamela Kaminski.

"Sorry," she yelled, fighting and tugging her way out of the death trap she drove. "The hem of this damned lampshade dress got tangled in the pedals." She slammed the door and limped toward him. "Broke a heel, too," she reported.

Alan rubbed a finger over the lenses of his glasses to remove the water blurring his vision. Pamela should have looked ridiculous in the peach organza bridesmaid dress with the armful of stiff chiffon around her bare shoulders, but she didn't. With her typical irreverent air, and her remarkable good looks, she carried off the eighties prom-dress knockoff with panache.

From her alarmingly low-cut neckline, she dragged out a handful of white handkerchiefs. She then shoved back a strand of dark blond hair that had escaped her topknot, and began to swipe at the water streaming from his chin. "Sorry 'bout that," she murmured.

"No problem," he said tartly. "I needed to cool off."

She grimaced. "I was talking about the wedding."

"Oh." Trying to keep his eyes averted from the bosom of his ex-fiancée's best friend, Alan decided he'd never been more miserable in his life than at this moment. He stood completely still and allowed Pam to continue a woefully inadequate job of soaking up the water. "I can't

believe Jo actually selected that dress for you to wear,"
he said sourly.

"She didn't," Pam said, painfully sticking the end of
a hankie into his ear before moving on to swab his forehead none too gently. "Someone mixed up the order, but
when it arrived, Jo seemed so stressed-out, I didn't want
to bother her with it."

Alan scowled. "Since she only had eyes for John
Sterling today, I'm sure she didn't even notice."

"It appears she did have a lot on her mind," Pam
agreed.

Inhaling, then expelling his breath noisily, Alan said,
"I suppose they got married."

Pam kept her eyes averted and nodded. "I heard Jo
breaking the news to her mother just before I left."

"And you didn't stay?"

She pressed her full, brightly painted lips together and
shook her head. "Between Jo, the groom and his three
kids, I figured there were already enough people at the
altar."

Grunting in frustration, Alan sputtered, "I can't believe
after all these years of saying she didn't want children, Jo
just up and marries a man with so much baggage!"

"Mmmnn," Pam said sympathetically. "*Three* carry-
ons." She tossed the ruined handkerchiefs into a nearby
trash can and pulled out her neckline, presumably to look
for more.

Alan swallowed hard. He'd never thought about Pamela
Kaminski romantically, but he was in the same pool as
the rest of Savannah's male population when it came to
admiring her generous physical gifts. The glimpse of a
wildly inappropriate black strapless bra beneath the in-
nocuous dress was enough to dry his tux from the inside
out. When she plucked out two more hankies, he pulled

a finger around his suddenly too-tight shirt collar. "Were you planning to shed a few tears, Pam?" he asked wryly.

She frowned and waved a hankie. "They were for Jo. The poor girl was crying like Niagara all morning."

"Thanks."

Pam glanced up and smiled sadly, her hands stilling. "I'm sorry, Alan. I didn't mean to hurt your feelings. I know how much you love Jo."

Anger, hurt and frustration welled up anew, so he cleared his throat and changed the subject. "Why did you follow me?"

She tossed the last two soiled handkerchiefs. "Thought you might need a friend. Where's your best man?"

"My guess is he's two choruses deep into the Electric Slide."

"Where were you headed?"

"To the airport."

She angled her head at him and laughed. "That's quite a walk."

"My flight to Fort Myers doesn't leave for four hours." He smiled tightly. "I allowed us plenty of time to celebrate at the reception."

"You're not serious," Pam said cautiously, as if she wasn't sure she was dealing with a sane person. "You're still going on your honeymoon?"

"Sure." He shrugged, then lifted his chin. "Why not? It's paid for. I'll drown my sorrows in buckets of margaritas on the beach. I plan to eat enough limes to stave off scurvy for a lifetime."

Pam stared at him, the blue of her eyes startling against the wide whites. Then she blinked and looked up as a large raindrop dripped down her cheek. Within a few seconds, the rain was pelting down.

Which Alan didn't mind since his day couldn't possibly get any worse.

Suddenly a bolt of lightning streaked through the sky and struck a stand of trees several hundred yards away. On the other hand, perhaps he shouldn't tempt fate.

Pam was already tugging him toward her car. "I'll give you a ride. Where's your luggage?"

"In the back of the limousine at the church. I'll buy everything I need when I get to Fort Myers." He opened the passenger-side door, lifting it out and up at its awkward angle, then gingerly lowered himself onto the dingy sheepskin-covered seat. Once inside, he turned to look at Pam, who barked, "Buckle up," as she started the engine.

With a teeth-jarring jolt, they descended from the curb in reverse. Then Pam peeled rubber on the wet pavement, and made an illegal U-turn. As they sped toward the highway, Alan winced at the sound of her stripping gears, then braced an arm against the cracked vinyl dashboard. A dislocated shoulder was the most minor injury he could hope for when the rescue team extracted them with the jaws of life.

"Uh, Pam."

She glanced over at him, turning the steering wheel in the same direction. He gasped as the car ran off the shoulder, then sighed in relief when she jerked it back to the pavement. "What?" she asked, oblivious to his alarm.

"Never mind," he said hurriedly. "We'll talk when we get to the terminal. Do you know where you're going?"

She scoffed and made a heart-stopping weave across the yellow line, then yanked the hem of her dress above her knees. She was barefoot. "Alan, you know I practically live in my car. It's my *job* to know where I'm going."

Alan now realized why Pamela was the most successful

real estate agent in Savannah—after a ride with her, prospective home buyers were probably too rattled to refuse.

To his horror, she reached over to tune the radio, and after enduring a full fifteen seconds of her not once looking at the road, Alan lurched forward and offered to find a station. He tuned in to some light rock and eased back in his seat, trying to relax.

Pam made a disapproving sound. "Is that all you can find? My *dentist* plays that stuff, as if the sound of a drill isn't torturous enough."

Alan sighed and found a more trendy station, assuming Pam was satisfied since she began singing along—badly. Suddenly he focused on the windshield wiper on his side and pursed his lips. "Is that a man's sock?" he asked.

"Yeah," she sang, weaving and shrugging. "The wiper blade fell off and the sound of that metal arm scraping against the windshield wore on my nerves."

Alan shivered.

She turned a dazzling smile his way. "The black sock is hardly noticeable and it works great."

He begged to differ, but he didn't dare. He briefly wondered which of Pam's admirers had left the handy souvenir, then pushed the thought aside. Instead, he closed his eyes and conjured up visions of sandy beaches and unlimited quantities of alcohol. He'd buy and finish the entire set of a new science-fiction series he'd been yearning to read. And Mrs. Josephine Montgomery Sterling, mother of three, would be far, far away…wiping runny noses.

Pamela respected his silence, humming and singing along with the radio, but not pressing him into conversation. After several minutes, he opened his eyes and glanced at her. Her profile was almost classically beautiful—the tilt of her nose, the curve of her pronounced cheekbones. Except Pam's upper lip protruded slightly over her lower lip, giving her the appearance of having an upside-down mouth. Combined with large blue eyes and a mane of dark gold hair, she was stunning to the point of being intimidating. She had the braver half of Savannah's bachelors running to her bed, and the smarter half just plain running.

He'd heard the stories in the locker room at the club— Pam's exploits in bed were legendary. But he'd often wondered how many of the rumors were rooted in fact and how many were pure conjecture based on Pamela's background. She'd grown up in the Grasswood projects, the black eye of Savannah's otherwise beautiful downtown face. Grasswood was notoriously populated with several generations of dopeheads, prostitutes and petty thieves.

The first time he met Pamela, he'd peeled her off another girl's back in the hallway of his private high school and she'd rewarded him with a sharp kick to his shin. In response to public pressure, Saint London's Academy had extended scholarships to a handful of families from the projects, and Pamela's was one of the lucky ones. He remembered her two brothers being hoodlums and she herself being garish and unkempt, mouthy and irreverent, courting fights with girls, boys and teachers alike. One by one, the Kaminskis had all been expelled.

When he'd started dating Jo several years later, he'd been amazed to learn the girls were best friends, and more stunned still when he discovered that dirty-faced, sparring Pamela had become a top-producing agent for Savannah's largest realty company. Jo took Pam's flamboyance and reputation in stride, and soon Alan had grown more relaxed with Pam's company, despite her unpredictable and scandalous behavior.

The first time Jo had asked him to accompany Pam to a charity benefit as a favor, he'd been slightly uncomfortable, hoping desperately his high-bred mother didn't get wind of it because he didn't want to listen to her reproof. But he'd watched with fascination as Pamela the sexy siren had morphed into a sleek and charming conversationalist as she worked a roomful of potential clients. As a bonus, she'd even procured him a few introductions that had proved beneficial in advancing his computer-consulting business.

She was as different from his reserved, proper ex-fiancée as night and day. Jo was a quiet reading bench, Pam was a tousled bed. Jo was a contented house cat, Pam was a prowling lioness.

Alan frowned. The woman *was* a little scary.

"I'll wait with you," she announced as she veered into long-term parking.

"That's not necessary," he said, hanging on while she took him on a harrowing ride through the parking garage.

They lurched to a crooked halt one-eighth of an inch from a four-foot round concrete pillar. "I'll buy you a drink," she said, and lifted herself out of her seat with the force of putting on the emergency brake. "Let me get some decent shoes."

Hiking up her skirt, she walked around to the trunk in stocking feet. Alan got out of the car and followed her. She unlocked and lifted the lid to reveal an unbelievable array of footwear—pumps, sandals, boots, tennis shoes— he guessed there were fifty or more pairs scattered to the far corners of the trunk, no doubt from her perpetual careening.

"Do you moonlight as a traveling shoe salesman?" he asked.

She laughed. "I never know what kind of terrain I'll be showing a house in—I try to be prepared."

Alan reached in and withdrew a thigh-high red-patent leather boot. He lifted an eyebrow and asked, "Where's the matching leash?"

She smirked and yanked the boot away from him. Pam hastily rummaged through the pile and came up with one light-colored high-heel pump and slid her foot into it, then stood on one leg while she searched for its long-lost mate. "Aha!" she said, finally retrieving it, then tossed in the pair with the broken heel and slammed the trunk with vigor. It bounced back up and she slammed it twice more before it held. "The catch is tricky," she informed him, slinging her purse over her shoulder. "Let's go."

They garnered more than a little attention as they made their way through the airport and settled into a booth at a tacky lounge. To send him off right, Pam ordered a pitcher of margaritas on the rocks, then poured one for each of them. She licked the back of her hand and sprinkled salt on it. He did the same and lifted his glass to hers.

"You make the toast," she said, her eyes bright.

Her beauty struck him at that moment, and his tongue stumbled slightly. "Uh, to being single," he said, clinking her glass heartily.

"I'll drink to that," she seconded, then downed half her drink, licked the salt from her hand and sucked on a lime wedge.

He followed her lead, squinting when the sour juice drenched his tongue. "I really didn't want to get married anyway," he mumbled.

"So why did you propose?" she asked.

Alan shrugged. "It sounds silly now, but at the time it seemed like the thing to do."

Her look was dubious, but she didn't question him further. Instead, she laughed. "You're a mess."

Alan glanced down at his wet, disheveled tuxedo and chuckled, then scanned her rumpled appearance and grinned. "So are you."

They both laughed and he loosened his bow tie, letting the ends hang down the front of his stained, pleated shirt. "What a hell of a day," he said, shaking his head and cradling the frosty glass of pale green liquid.

"Yeah," she agreed. She swallowed the rest of her drink, licked her hand and sucked a fresh lime wedge. "Did you have any idea she was hung up on John Sterling?"

He frowned. "I knew he was hung up on *her,* but I never suspected she'd even consider a man with so many kids." He finished his drink, licked, then sucked. "Did you know?"

She shook her head and refilled their glasses. "I knew something was bothering her, but I assumed it was just prewedding jitters." She lifted the glass and downed a good portion of the margarita. He watched with interest as her tongue removed more salt from her hand. She sunk small white teeth into the lime and her cheekbones appeared as she drew in the juice.

"I feel like a fool," he announced, swallowing more of the tangy drink and performing the same ritual. "I know everyone is laughing at me."

She shook her head again, dislodging another strand from her stiff hairdo. "They probably feel sorry for you."

"Oh, thanks, that makes me feel *tons* better."

"Everyone will forget about it by the time you return," she said in a soothing tone as she topped off their glasses again.

The alcohol was beginning to take effect on his empty,

nervous stomach. His tongue and the tips of his fingers were growing increasingly numb. He pushed his water-spotted glasses back up on his nose. "I hope so, but I doubt it. Maybe I should move."

She scowled, an expression which did not diminish the prettiness of flushed cheeks and flashing eyes. "That's ridiculous—you've lived in Savannah all your life. Your parents would be hurt. And your consulting business—" she lifted her glass again and squinted at him "—you can't leave before you get old Mr. Gordon's computer account. I went to a lot of trouble linking up the two of you at the children's benefit."

"I know," he said mournfully, swirling the liquid in his glass before taking another deep drink. "You're right, of course. But let me wallow a little—my ego is pretty tender at the moment."

"You'll bounce back," she said with confidence. "There'll be debutantes lined up at your door by the time you return from your trip."

Her words were slightly slurred—or was his hearing becoming somewhat warped? "Nope." He sat up straight and jerked his thumb to his chest awkwardly. "I'm never getting married. As of today, *wife* is a four-letter word."

"Alan," Pamela said, leaning forward, "*wife* has always been a four-letter word."

He frowned. "You know what I mean."

Feeling a little tipsy herself, Pamela looked across the sticky table at her drinking companion and a feeling akin to envy crept over her. She wondered what it would feel like to have a man so in love with you that he'd swear off marriage completely if he couldn't have you. Pam bit her bottom lip. She'd known Jo Montgomery for years, and her best friend had always demonstrated remarkable good sense—until today.

What could have possessed her to abandon her faithful boyfriend of three years at the altar to marry a widower with three kids? Granted, Jo had confided that her and Alan's sexual relationship left a little to be desired—and personally, Pam found Alan quite bookish and dull, but even a boring man didn't deserve to be jilted. But she knew Jo felt bad because she'd asked Pam to go after him. Even though she didn't say it, Pam knew Jo feared Alan might do something impulsive and self-destructive.

She watched as Alan tilted his head back and emptied his glass. In high school, Pam had triumphantly dubbed him "the Ken doll", a nickname she still used in conversations with Jo, much to Jo's consternation. His fair hair was cut in a trendy, precision style, and his round wire glasses were like everything else in his wardrobe: designer quality.

The man was painfully clean-cut, his skin typically scrubbed within an inch of its life, his preppie clothes stiff enough to stand in a corner. She perused his slim, chiseled nose and squared-off chin, complete with an aristocratic cleft. He was handsome in an Osmond kind of way, she supposed, but everything about him screamed predictable.

Alan Parish came from thick money, as her mother would say. She doubted if he'd ever experienced belly-hurting hunger, missed school because his shoes had finally fallen completely apart, or scraped together money to post bail for three family members in one week. The worlds they came from were so far apart, they were in separate dimensions.

Then she bit back a smile. Right now, with his hair mussed, his glasses askew and a narrow streak of mud on his jaw, he looked more like one of her stray lovers—disorderly and disobedient. Only she knew better. Alan was an uptight computer geek—she'd bet the man had a flowchart on the headboard of his bed.

"What's so funny?" he asked, his expression hurt.

"Nothing," she said as fast as her thick tongue would allow while waving for the waiter to bring them more drinks. Then they spent the next half hour extolling the virtues of being footloose and commitment-free while they drained the second pitcher.

At last, Alan tossed a spent lime wedge onto the accumulated pile and looked at his watch, moving it up and back as if he was trying to focus. "Time to go," he said, standing a little unsteadily.

Pam stuck out her hand. "I think I'll stick around and sober up for the drive home."

"With your driving, who could tell?"

She scowled. "Have a great time, Alan."

"Yeah," he said dryly. "I'm off on my honeymoon all by myself." He bowed dramatically.

"Maybe you'll meet someone," she said.

Alan straightened, then frowned and pursed his lips.

"What?" she asked, intrigued by the expression on his face.

"Go with me," he said.

Pam nearly choked on her last swallow of margarita. *"What?"*

"Go with me," he repeated, giving her a lopsided smile.

"You're drunk," she accused.

He hiccuped. "Am not."

"Alan, I'm *not* going on your honeymoon with you."

"Why not?" he pressed. "My secretary booked a suite at a first-rate hotel, and it's all paid for—room, meals, everything." He pulled the plane tickets from inside his jacket and shook them for emphasis. "Come on, I could use the company and you could probably use a vacation."

A week away from Savannah was tempting, she mused.

His smile was cajoling. "Long days on the beach, drinking margaritas, steak and lobster in the evening." He wagged his eyebrows. "Skimpily dressed men."

At last he had her attention. "Yeah?"

He nodded drunkenly. "Yeah, you might get lucky."

But she couldn't fathom spending a week with Alan, and she'd *never* share a bed with the man, no matter how roomy. She shook her head. "I can't."

"I'll sleep on the pullout bed," he assured her.

She set down her drink. "But what will people think? What will *Jo* think?"

"What do you mean?" he asked.

Pam squirmed on the uncomfortable bench seat. "Well, you know—us being together for a week."

His shocked expression didn't do much for her ego. "You mean that someone might think that we're…that we're…*involved?*" His howl of laughter made her feel like a fool.

Of course no one would jump to that conclusion—a high-bred southern gentleman and a trashy white girl from the projects—it was ludicrous.

"And as far as Jo is concerned," Alan continued, "if she ever thought there was a remote possibility we'd be attracted to each other, she'd never have trusted me to escort you to your business functions."

Pam's fuzzy brain told her an insult was imbedded in his rambling. "I suppose you're right, but a few people might jump to conclusions."

Alan shrugged. "It's not like the whole town of Savannah is going to know, Pam."

She glanced down at the horrid peach-colored dress. "But I don't have any clothes."

"We'll go shopping when we get there," he said simply. "Come on, will you go or won't you?"

She had accrued vacation time. And only one deal in progress that she could probably handle over the phone. And Jo *had* asked her to keep an eye on Alan. She pressed a finger to her aching temple. It hurt to think too deeply.

Pamela emptied her glass and wiped the back of her hand across her mouth, then looked up at him and smiled. "Well, I could use some new sandals...why the heck not?"

2

ALAN SALUTED the head flight attendant, then dropped into his seat, wincing when the jolt threatened to scramble his furry brain. He felt as if he was forgetting something, but the answer hovered on the fringe of his memory, eluding him. His neck suddenly felt rubbery. Laying his head back, he closed his eyes and slowly reached up to pat the wallet in his breast pocket. That wasn't it. Hmm, what then?

"Ex-schuse me," came a loud female voice. He opened his eyes a millimeter and Pamela Kaminski slowly came into focus, just as her purse whacked some poor businessman upside the head. "Sorry, sweetie." She leaned over to place an apologetic kiss on the man's receding hairline.

Alan smiled and tried to snap his fingers, but missed. Pamela! He'd forgotten Pamela.

"There you are!" Pamela said, her eyes glassy. "When I came out of the ladies' room, you'd disappeared. Thank God, my middle name is Jo. Then all I had to do was convince a woman at the gate that the last name on my license and the name on the ticket were different because I'd just gotten married." She giggled. "Whew!" She swung into the seat next to Alan, then leaned against him and squealed. "I've never flown first-class before."

"Unlimited drinks," he informed her, rolling his head.

Her grin was lopsided. "No fooling? I'm up for another pitcher."

"You'll have to settle for one drink at a time—and they don't serve margaritas."

She pouted, sighing at the inconvenience, then noisily fumbled with her seat belt until Alan lifted his head and offered to help. "It's twisted," he announced, reaching across her lap to straighten the strap. The chiffon ruffles at her plunging neckline tickled his jaw. He valiantly tried to concentrate on the silver buckle, but his eyes kept straying to her cleavage. The tiny embroidered rose front and center on her black bra made an appearance every time she inhaled. After three clumsy attempts, he finally clicked the belt together, then settled back into his seat heavily.

The flight attendant eyed them warily when they ordered bourbon and water, but served them promptly enough. They finished the weak drinks before takeoff, and Alan found himself beginning to doze as they taxied down the runway. An iron grip on his arm startled him fully awake.

Pamela's left hand encircled his right wrist so tightly her knuckles were white. Her long peach-colored nails were biting into his flesh. And her face was turning as green as the many limes they'd sucked dry.

"What's wrong?"

"Remember when I said I'd never flown first-class?"

"Yeah."

"Well, I've never flown before, period."

"No kidding? Why not?"

"I just remembered—it's a phobia of mine." She put her fingers to her mouth. "Oh, dear."

He leaned forward and twisted in his seat. "What?"

"I'm going to throw up."

Alan panicked. "Oh, don't do that."

Still holding her mouth, she nodded in warning, her eyes wide. Alan fumbled for the airsick bag, and jerked it under her mouth just as the plane banked. She unloaded, missing the bag more than hitting it, although Alan accepted some of the blame for holding the paper bag somewhat less than stone still. He heard a groan go up from surrounding passengers.

When her retching gave way to dry heaves, Pamela slumped back into her seat, frightfully pale. A flight attendant was at their side as soon as the plane leveled off, extending a warm, wet towel to Pamela. "I'm going to need more than one," Pam muttered, eyeing the mess she'd made.

Organza was more absorbent than it looked, Alan decided, fighting the urge to vomit, himself, as he handed the bag to the attendant. Insisting she was too weak to make a trip to the lavatory, Pam cleaned up as well as she could sitting in her seat. The attendant, obviously at a loss, murmured the two-hour trip would pass by quickly.

"Oh, God," Pam breathed, laying her head back. "It's an omen—I should have never gotten on this plane."

"Relax," Alan said, reaching forward to pat her arm, then decided it would be more sanitary to pat her head. Her hair was stiff and had pulled free from the clasp that hung benignly above one ear. "It'll be a smooth flight— I travel all the time and I've never had any problems."

Suddenly the plane dipped, then corrected, then dipped and banked again. The Fasten Seat Belt sign dinged on, and the pilot's voice came over the intercom. "Ladies and gentlemen, we have encountered some turbulence." The attendant was thrown out of her fold-down wall seat, but she recovered and continued smiling as she fastened her own belt. ''Please bear with us while the captain climbs to a higher altitude.''

It was the worst flight Alan had ever experienced. The plane continued to pitch and roll, eliciting gasps and moans from the passengers. A cabinet door in the small galley gave way, sending trays of food into the aisles.

Alan felt terrible, willing his stomach to stay calm, and pressing his throbbing head back into the seat to keep it as immobile as possible. He felt terrible, too, for inviting Pam to come along. She'd probably be traumatized for life. He heard others seated around them getting sick, and he glanced anxiously at Pam to see if she would lose it again.

Her eyes were squeezed shut, and her lips were moving. ''Hail Mary, full of…full of gr-grace…'' She opened one eye and whispered to Alan, ''I've never said my prayers while I was loaded—do you think it cancels out?''

Alan pursed his lips and considered the question, then shook his head and she continued to stumble through the prayer, finishing with ''Pray for us s-sinners now and… and at the hour of our death. Amen.'' Then she crossed herself.

''Hey,'' he whispered soothingly. ''We're going to be fine. It'll level out here in a few minutes.''

On cue, the plane made a sickening dip. Pam swallowed and jerked her head toward him. ''Are you crazy, Alan? We're all going to die and I'm going to be buried in this horrid dress—*if* they find our bodies.''

He sighed. ''Of course they'll find our bod—'' He stopped and shook his head to clear it. ''Wait a minute— we're not going to die, okay? I refuse to die in a plane crash on my wedding day.''

Her eyes widened and she gestured wildly with her

hands. "Oh, Mr. Moneybags, I suppose you're going to buy your way out of this?"

Alan frowned. He'd spent his entire life trying to make his own way, only to be frequently reminded he was a Parish, and therefore was forced to share the credit for his accomplishments with his family name. He crossed his arms, closed his eyes and refused to be provoked. "I'm not going to argue with you because I'm drunk and tomorrow this conversation won't matter."

"Does anything affect you, Alan?" Pam asked, her voice escalating. "You got jilted today and you still came on this honeymoon like nothing happened. Now we're getting ready to crash and you sit there like a dump on a log."

"That's lump," he corrected, his eyes still closed. "A lump on a log. Or is it bump?"

"I meant what I said," she retorted. "I'm drunk, but I'm not incoherent…I'm…I'm…oh, God, I'm going to be sick again."

His eyes snapped open. He reached for the airsick bag on his side and thrust it under her chin. "Arrgghhh!" he cried when she missed the bag again. He looked away and tried to reach the attendant bell with his elbow. Once the remaining contents of her stomach appeared to have been transferred to the bag, the floor and all surfaces in between, she fell back into her seat, completely exhausted. At last the pilot located a more comfortable altitude, and the turbulence ceased. The passengers cheered, and within seconds, Pam fell into a deep sleep.

Alan surveyed his traveling companion and winced. If his head didn't hurt so much, he'd probably be laughing. Pam Kaminski, the perpetual playmate, looked like a rag doll in her stained, smelly, ugly gown. Her hair was lank and damp, her mouth slack in slumber. He flagged the busy attendant and quietly asked for more towels, then carefully leaned toward Pam, trying not to wake her.

With fierce concentration, he delicately wiped her face, admiring the fine texture and translucence of her creamy complexion, and the long fringe of lashes on her sleep-flushed cheeks. She never once stirred, not even when he dabbed at the corners of her upside-down mouth. But for the first time ever in the presence of Pamela Kaminski, Alan felt *himself* stir.

He shifted in his seat, trying to stem the rush of inappropriate feelings for his ex-fiancée's best friend. But sitting there in her mussed gown with her mussed hair, she looked like the grubby little tigress she'd been in high school, all piss and vinegar, and she made his blood simmer.

Passing a hand over his face, Alan blamed the lapse on his own lingering drunkenness. He hadn't made a big enough fool out of himself already today—why not make a pass at Pam and watch her laugh until she vomited again.

PAM WAS A BIRD flying over a landfill, dipping and diving, the stink of rotting trash permeating the air. She started awake and blinked, disoriented at first, then realized with a jolt that she was on a plane hurtling toward a shared honeymoon with Alan Parish, and that the stink was *her*.

"Ugh." She wrinkled her nose in disgust, and pulled herself straighter in the seat, flinching at the explosion of pain in her temples. She turned her head oh-so-slowly to see Alan zonked out, snoring softly and leaning against the wall. His expensive black tux was probably beyond cleaning, but his mottled jacket still lay folded neatly across his lap. Embarrassment flooded her when she remembered how he'd held the airsick bags as she filled them. She smiled wryly. Alan had surprised her.

A ball of white fuzz dangled in his hair, and she reached forward impulsively to remove it. Awareness leaped through her when she touched the silky blond strands, which was almost as alarming as the feeling of warmth that flooded her as she watched his chest rise and fall. Awake, he was Alan the Automaton. But relaxed in sleep, he looked downright sexy. A memory surfaced... she'd had an absurd crush on him for the short time she had attended the private school his family practically owned.

Before she had time to explore the amazing revelations, the attendant who had earlier emptied the linen closet on Pam's behalf, touched her arm and murmured, "Are you feeling better, ma'am?"

Pam nodded gingerly.

The woman smiled gently. "I'm sorry, Mrs. Parish— this flight wasn't a very promising start to a honeymoon."

Confusion clouded her brain. "But I'm not—" She glanced up at the woman and smiled tightly. The situation was too convoluted to explain. "It'll be fine once we get to Fort Myers."

"Congratulations—was it a long engagement?" the woman pressed.

"N-no," Pam stammered, suddenly nervous. "This was all quite sudden. Could you direct me to the bathroom, please?"

The blue-suited attendant pointed and smiled, then walked back down the aisle.

Pam slowly pulled herself to a standing position, but the movement stirred up a fetid smell from her dress. Swallowing her urge to gag, she gathered her skirt in her hands, hiked her dress up to her knees and sidled her way to the lavatory.

Not sure what she expected, she was nonetheless disappointed by the cramped booth. "People actually have sex in here?" she mumbled. A glance in the mirror evoked a shocked groan. Her makeup had disappeared, except for mascara that rimmed her eyes. Her hair was a sky-high rat's nest of tangles. Miserable, she looked down at her dress and shuddered—nothing much she could do there.

After washing her face with cool water, she opened her makeup bag to repair as much damage as possible. At the last minute, she held up a perfume bottle and gave her dress a couple of squirts. Too late, she realized she'd only intensified the stench. Cursing under her breath, she exited the cubicle and made her way self-consciously back to her seat, aware of passengers recoiling in her wake.

Alan was still dozing when she lowered herself into the seat. The pounding in her head had lessened, making room for reality to ooze into the crevices of her brain. In her occupation, vacations were hard to come by because time off meant missed commissions on home deals that were possibly months in the making. She'd passed up a week in Jamaica with Nick the All-Nighter, and a long weekend in San Francisco with Delectable Dale.

Only to squander seven days in close, romantic quarters with Annoying Alan.

The captain's voice came over the intercom and announced they were beginning their final descent to Fort Myers. Beside her, Alan roused and started to smile, then his nostrils flared. "Oh my," he said, his eyes watering.

Pamela frowned sourly. "You're no fresh breeze yourself."

"A shower would feel pretty good right now," Alan

agreed, then touched his forehead. "Not to mention a couple of aspirin. We really tied one on."

Pam nodded. "Tequila will make you say and do strange things." She caught his gaze and studied his eyes, wondering if he was having as many misgivings about his hasty invitation as she was about her impulsive acceptance.

But his ice-blue eyes gave away nothing. "Better buckle up," he said, pointing, then smiled shyly. "Need a hand?"

Inhaling sharply, she shook her head. She could handle the guys who thought they were macho, the self-assured lady-killers—they were safely shallow. What she couldn't handle was Alan's Mr. Nice Guy persona...it threw her off balance.

It was six-thirty when they emerged from the airport, and dusk appeared to be converging. With only a few wrong turns, they found the car rental where Alan's reservations had been made.

"I'm sorry, sir," the clerk said, smiling sympathetically. "We're all out of full-size luxury cars. We'll have to step you down—with a sizable discount, of course."

Alan sighed and pinched the bridge of his nose. "Okay, I'll take a midsize."

The man tapped on the keyboard, then made a clicking noise with his cheek. "No, sorry."

"Utility vehicle?"

More clicking. "Nada."

Alan pursed his lips. "What *do* you have available?"

The man smiled and pointed out the window to a row of tiny white compacts.

Alan shook his head firmly. "No way."

Pam frowned. He was exhibiting typical Parish behavior. "Alan," she whispered loudly. "What do you mean 'no way'? It's a lousy rental car—what do you expect?"

He looked at her and mirrored her frown. "The best."

She crossed her arms impatiently and tapped her foot. "I'm tired, sick and cranky—get the stupid car and let's go."

His mouth tightened in displeasure, but he nodded curtly to the clerk.

"*I'll* drive," Alan announced firmly a few minutes later as they approached the little car.

"Fine," Pamela said, not missing the dig. "I hope this resort is close by—I'm beat."

With a lot of cursing from Alan, and frustrated mutterings from Pam, they finally managed to wedge themselves into the car. Alan unfolded the map he'd purchased, taking up the entire interior of the car. "Looks like about a twenty-minute drive." Then he spent fourteen minutes rattling the map, trying to refold it.

Pam leaned her head back, forcing thoughts of the coming week from her mind. She'd just roll with the punches, as always. Why was she letting a few days with Alan rattle her? She was safe—the man wasn't the least bit attracted to her. But it was his uptight idiosyncrasies that were going to drive her crazy. He was still rattling that damned map. She reached over and tore it from his hands, wadded it into a ball and tossed it in the back seat. "Let's go."

ALAN SQUINTED at a sign as they drove by. "Did that sign say Penwrote or Pinron?"

"We're lost, aren't we?"

He scoffed and pushed up his glasses. "Of course not."

She sighed dramatically. "Oh, yeah, we're lost, all right."

"'Lost' is a relative term."

"And I guess you're one of those guys who'd rather run out of gas than stop and ask for directions."

"Well, if you hadn't destroyed the map—"

"Forget the map—pull off at the next exit."

Suddenly the car wobbled. At a thumping sound on the back right side of the car, he slowed. "Darn it," he mumbled as he steered the lame car to the shoulder of the road. "We've got a flat."

"Beautiful," Pam said, throwing her hands up in the air. "We're lost *and* we have a flat."

"Well, it's not my fault." He shoved the gearshift into park. "You're the one who insisted we take this, this… matchbox car to begin with!"

"So call them to bring us another car."

"My cell phone is in my suitcase in Savannah."

She reached into her purse and pulled out her own mobile phone, but frowned. "The battery's dead."

"Great. This is just great!"

She pointed down the highway. "There's probably a phone off that exit."

Exasperated, Alan said, "I'm sure there is, but by the time I've walked that far, I could have the tire changed."

She sighed mightily once more, then opened the passenger-side door and stepped out. Alan did the same and walked back to the tiny trunk, swaying as vehicles passed them at terrific speeds.

"Are you sure you know how to do this?" Pam asked suspiciously.

"Sure," he said with false confidence. He'd once read a roadside manual, and he was sure the information would come back to him. Men just knew these things, didn't they?

Thirty minutes later, he was on his back, still trying to

position the jack, when he looked over to see Pamela standing with her skirt hiked up to her thighs, and her thumb jerked to the side.

"What the heck are you doing?" he shouted.

"Getting us a ride," she yelled matter-of-factly.

"Would you please cover yourself? You'll attract every serial killer in the vicinity."

"I don't care, as long as he'll give us a ride to the resort."

"I've almost got it," he lied.

"Sure," she said, unconvinced, then smiled wide into oncoming traffic.

He heard the sound of a large vehicle slowing down and glanced over to see a big rig edging onto the shoulder in front of their cracker-box car.

"It worked!" she squealed, trotting toward the truck.

Alan heaved himself to his feet and took off after her, grabbed her by the elbow and pulled her to a halt. "Are you crazy? Didn't your mother ever tell you not to accept rides from strangers?"

Pam angled her head at him. "Alan, there's no one stranger than you." Then she yanked her arm out of his grasp.

He frowned at the tire iron in his hand, then tested its weight and hurried after her. At least he could break the serial killer's knees if he tried anything funny.

The burly, bearded murderer was already climbing down from his rig, doffing his cap to his vivacious victim. The man hadn't yet noticed him, Alan observed.

"Howdy, little lady, having car trouble?"

He couldn't hear Pam's response, but from the tilt of her head, he assumed it was something pathetically feminine and appropriate. She did at least gesture back to Alan, and the man looked up at him, frowning at the tire iron in his hand. Alan swung it casually as he stepped up beside Pam, slapping the metal bar against his left palm as if he wielded the weapon often—and well.

"Name's Jack," the man said cautiously as he extended his grubby hand to Alan.

Alan sized him up. *Jack the Ripper, Jack the Jackal, Jugular Jack.*

Shifting the bar to his left hand, Alan firmly shook the paw the man offered, then spit on the ground in what he hoped was a universal he-man gesture.

"I'm Pamela and this is Alan," Pam said cloyingly, her eyes shining.

Jack looked them over. "You two just get married?"

"No," Alan said.

"Yes," Pam declared.

The trucker looked between them, and took a tentative step backward.

Pam shot Alan a desperate look. "I mean, yes," Alan said, conjuring up a laugh. He shrugged and winked at the man. "Still can't get used to the idea."

"We just need a ride," Pam said quickly. "To the…" She looked to Alan for help.

"The Pleasure Palisades," Alan said, somewhat self-consciously. Pam raised an eyebrow and he felt his neck grow warm.

Turning back to the man, she asked, "Do you know where it is?"

"Yeah," Jack said, tugging at his chin. "Y'all ever been there?"

"No," Alan said. "My secretary moonlights as a travel agent—she made all the arrangements. I hear it's a very nice place."

The trucker pursed his lips, then nodded slowly. "Yep."

"Can we get a ride?" Pam pressed. "We'll be glad to pay you for your trouble." She dug her elbow deep into Alan's rib. He gasped, then nodded.

"No bother," Jack said, turning to walk toward his truck. He swept his arm ahead of him. "Climb on in."

"What're you hauling?" Pam's new drawl and buoyant step were evidence she'd already bought into the little adventure.

"Hogs," the man said proudly as he climbed up to open the passenger-side door.

"Hogs?" Alan parroted as Pamela clambered inside. She was barefoot again, carrying her shoes in one hand.

"Yep." The man grinned as he waited for Alan to get in beside her. Still gripping the tire iron solidly, Alan glanced over his shoulder uneasily.

"You'll need to put down that tire iron, son," the man said bluntly.

Alan straightened and puffed out his chest. "And why is that?"

Another grin. "So you can hold Barbecue," the man said, pointing inside.

"Oh, it's a baby!" Pam cooed.

Letting down his guard slightly, Alan slid one eye toward the cab. Pamela was sprawled in the seat, leaning over to fondle a tiny pig on the floorboard.

"That's Barbecue," the man said, laughing. "Born a few days ago. The rest of the litter died, so I figured I'd keep him up here till the end of the run."

"He's adorable," Pam said, squealing as loudly as the nervous, quivering pig.

"Get in, son," Jack said, giving him a slight shove.

Alan spilled into the deep seat. The door banged closed behind him. "We're goners," he said to Pam.

Her forehead creased. "What?"

"The man's probably got all kinds of butcher tools on him, and a meat hook for each one of us."

"You're paranoid," she scoffed. "We're lucky he stopped."

Jack opened his door and climbed up behind the huge steering wheel, effectively halting their conversation. He pulled down the bill of his cap, then started the truck. It rumbled and coughed, then lurched into gear. "To the Pleasure Palisades," he crowed, slapping his knee. "You folks will have a dandy wedding night there."

Alan's heart pounded and he didn't dare look at Pam. He glanced at his watch and almost laughed out loud. Less than eight hours ago, he was ready to walk down the aisle to marry Jo Montgomery, hoping the act of commitment would put a new spin on their lackluster sex life. Instead he was sitting in the cab of a big pig rig with a woman who smelled almost as bad as the cargo, with only the promise of a lumpy sofa bed to sleep on—*if* they ever made it to the resort.

Pamela chatted with Jack, while Alan sank deeper into the seat. He felt moisture on his foot and looked down in time to see Barbecue squatting over his shoe. Alan didn't have the energy to pull away, so he simply lay his head back on the cracked vinyl. He'd officially sunk to the level of piglet pee post. What a poetic way to sum up the day.

3

"ARE YOU SURE this is it?" Pamela peered out the window at the four-story structure. Half of the sign's neon letters were unlit.

"Yep," Jack said.

"Linda said it was an older resort, but with a lot of atmosphere." Alan said, frowning slightly. "It's beach-front, though—I think I can see the water from here."

"Well, it's hard to tell much in the dark," Pam said agreeably, allowing Alan to help her down from the truck. His hands were strong around her waist, and he set her only a few inches in front of him. Surprised at her body's reaction, she quickly stepped back.

They looked up and waved to thank the trucker. Jack leaned out of his window and yelled, "Wish I were you tonight, son. She's a looker!"

Pleased, Pam grinned, then glanced at Alan. He'd turned beet red and his smile was tight as he nodded at the man, speechless. Pam felt sorry for Alan being put on the spot, so she scrambled for something to smooth over the moment. "Well, let's get checked in. I can't wait to get out of these clothes."

Too late, she realized she'd only added fuel to the fire. Alan cleared his throat, then turned toward the entrance. Without the lights of the truck, the parking lot was plunged into darkness. She took a step, then stumbled and grabbed the back of his jacket on the way down, very nearly taking him with her. He straightened and reached for her, his hands moving over her in search of a handhold. She felt him latch on to her shoulder and heard the rip of fabric as he came up with a handful of chiffon ruffles. He cursed and pulled her to her feet with an impatient sigh. "Do you think we can manage the last hundred yards without another catastrophe?"

She nodded, shocked at the sensations his hands were causing. It was the alcohol, the hunger, the exhaustion, the darkness—all of it combined to play games with her mind. What she needed was rest and daylight to remind her he was only uptight, dweeby Alan.

He grasped her elbow and steered her in the direction of the hotel. Pam suddenly had a premonition about the place and the week to come, but she kept her mouth shut and tucked her torn ruffles inside her bodice.

Flanked on either side by two gigantic plastic palm trees, the front entrance was less than spectacular. A dank, musty smell rose to greet them when they stepped onto the faded orange carpet of the gloomy reception area. To their right, stiff vinyl furniture so old it was back in style and more plastic plants encircled a portable TV set with an impressive rabbit-ear antenna. A home shopping channel was on, and two polyester-clad, middle-aged couples sat riveted to the screen. To their left, the gift shop was having a clearance on all Elvis items. Pam pursed her lips—maybe she could expand her collection.

She glanced at Alan to gauge his reaction. He was frowning behind his glasses, clearly ready to bolt. "This isn't exactly what I expected," he mumbled. She bit down on her tongue, suddenly annoyed. She doubted if he'd ever spent a night in less than four-star accommodations.

The reception desk stood high and long in front of them, dwarfing the skinny frizzy-haired clerk behind the half glass. She was snapping a mouthful of chewing gum. "Can I help you?" she asked disinterestedly, not looking up. She was surrounded by cheap paneling and sickly colors. In a word, the decor was garish. Alan's ex-fiancée, an interior designer, would have fainted on the spot. Yet for Pam, the place had a certain…retro charm.

"Hello," Alan said tightly. "I'm not sure this is the right place. Are there any other hotels named Pleasure Palisades in the area?"

Twiggy glanced up, her eyes widening in appreciation as she scanned Alan. She completely ignored Pam. "Nope," she said, sounding infinitely more interested. "This is it."

Alan gave Pam a worried glance, then looked back to the clerk. "Do you have a reservation for Mr. and Mrs.—" He coughed, then continued. "For Parish?"

"Parish?" She flicked a permed hank of dark hair over her shoulder, turned to a dusty computer terminal and clicked her fingers over the keyboard. "Parish… Parish…yep, Mr. and Mrs. Alan P. Parish, the deluxe honeymoon suite through next Friday night." She glanced up and added, "With complimentary VCR and movie library since it's almost Valentine's Day."

Alan's eyes widened in alarm. "We're in the right place?" Twiggy didn't answer, only blew a huge pink bubble with the gum, sucked the whole wad back into her mouth, then smiled.

"I'm sure the room is nice," Pam whispered, trying to sound optimistic. As long as it had running water, she couldn't care less.

He held up his finger to the girl. "Just one moment." He curled his hand around Pam's upper arm and pulled her aside. "There must be some mistake. I'll call Linda and get this straightened out *immediately*. I saw a Hilton a couple miles down the road—we'll get a room there tonight.''

Pam was shaking her head before he finished. ''I don't have 'a couple miles' left in me or in these shoes.'' She stamped her foot for emphasis.

''We'll call a cab,'' he said, frowning.

She stabbed him in the chest with her index finger. ''*You* call a cab, and *you* go down the road to the Hilton. I'm tired and I'm hungover. As long as this place is clean, I'm staying!''

He took a step back and poked at his glasses. ''You don't have to get nasty about it.''

She swept an arm down the front of her dress. ''That's the point, Alan. I *am* nasty.''

Holding up his hands, he relented. ''Okay, okay—we'll stay one night.''

Two minutes later, the clerk swiped his credit card, then handed them two large tarnished keys. ''Room 410 in the corner, great view, cool balcony. But the elevator is out of order, so you'll need to take the stairs.'' She smiled tightly at Pam this time, and snapped her gum. ''Have a pleasant stay.''

Alan moved in the direction she indicated, but Pam grabbed his arm. ''I'll need to purchase a few things to change into,'' she reminded him, nodding toward the gift shop.

''You need something in the gift shop?'' the girl asked. She didn't wait for an answer, just reached under the counter and pulled out a piece of cardboard that read, ''Back in a few,'' and propped it against a can of cola. ''I'm the cashier, too.'' She snapped her gum and emerged from behind the wooden monstrosity.

Pam followed the girl into the gift cubbyhole, rubbing her tired eyes. ''Alan, what does the 'P' stand for?'' She quickly surveyed the dusty merchandise on the cramped shelves, searching for items to help her get through the week.

Alan moved to the other side of the store, intent on his own shopping. "What 'P'?"

She stacked toiletries in her arms, then moved to a wall rack of miscellaneous clothing. "Your middle initial, what does it stand for?"

He was silent for several seconds, then said, "Never mind."

She turned around and grinned, her curiosity piqued. "Come on, what's your middle name?"

The frown on his face deepened. "Forget it, okay?"

"Well, it has to be something odd or you wouldn't be so touchy."

He looked away.

"Parnell?"

"No."

"Purcell?"

"No."

"Prudell?"

"Pam." His gaze swung back to her, his voice low and menacing. "Don't."

She made a face at him, then turned her attention back to the shelves. She'd need shorts and a T-shirt, not to mention underwear. Pam spied a single package of men's cotton boxer shorts and picked it up, then stopped when she realized Alan also had a hand on them. They played a game of mini-tug-of-war, with each tug a little stronger than the last.

She yanked the package. "I didn't figure you for a boxer man, Alan."

He pulled harder. "And I didn't figure you for a boxer woman, Pam."

She jerked the package. "You don't know me very well."

"I *have* to have underwear," he protested, then nearly stumbled back when she abruptly released the package.

Pam acquiesced, palms up. "Since underwear has always been optional for me, they're all yours."

His Adam's apple bobbed and he looked contrite. "M-maybe we can share."

Perhaps it was the timbre of his voice, or his boyish, disheveled appearance, or Elvis's "Blue Christmas" playing softly in the background, but Pamela suddenly felt a pull toward Alan, and it scared her. "I don't think so," she said more haughtily than she meant to.

Alan shrugged. "Suit yourself. Do you have everything you need?"

Nodding, Pam yanked an Elvis T-shirt and a pair of pink cotton shorts off the rack, then heaved her bounty onto the counter.

Alan piled his items on top. "I'll get these things," he said, opening his wallet. She started to protest, but he held up his hand. "It's the least I can do," he said, then raised an eyebrow when the clerk lifted a package of rub-on tattoos from Pam's things.

Pam grinned. "I always wanted a tattoo."

Five minutes later she lifted her skirt, shifted her packages and tilted her head back to look up the stairwell that seemed to go on and on. She was exhausted and again her decision to share a room with Alan for a week seemed ludicrous. On the way up they had to stop several times to rest, then walked down a dimly lit outdoor walkway, past several doors to reach the last room, 410.

Pam could hear the ocean breaking on the beach below them, and she leaned over the railing to get a better look. Suddenly Alan's arm snaked around her waist and dragged her back against his chest. The length of his body molded to hers, and Pam gasped as her senses leaped. After a few seconds, he released her gently, then admonished in a low voice, "I don't trust that railing, and I don't want to make a trip to the hospital tonight."

Her heart still pounding in her chest, Pam laughed nervously and listened while he fidgeted with the key in the dark. "You'd think they could put up a few lights," Alan muttered. He pushed open the door, reached around the corner and flipped on a switch.

They stood and stared inside the room in astonishment.

"They obviously saved all the lights for the *in*terior," he added flatly.

Pam nodded, speechless. The room's chandelier was a dazzling display of multicolored lights, multiplied dozens of times by the room's remarkable collection of mirrors.

"It's a disco," he mumbled.

And the bed was center stage. Huge and circular, it was raised two levels. A large spotlight over the padded headboard shone onto the satiny gold-colored comforter, and Pam doubted the light was meant for reading.

"At least the carpet is new," she said, stepping inside.

"Yeah," he said. "And I'm sure they paid top dollar— brown shag is really hard to find."

She glanced around the room, at the avocado-green kitchenette, the makeshift living room consisting of a battered sofa—presumably the pullout bed—and two chaise-size beanbag chairs. The sitting area was "separated" from the sleeping area by two short Oriental floor screens. The wide-screen TV was situated to be visible from the bed or from the sofa.

"It's spacious," she observed. "And functional."

"Yeah—for orgies."

She scoffed and set down her bags, crossing the room

to inspect the bed. She poked at the comforter and watched the bed ripple. "It's a water bed," she said, grinning. "And look." She held up a small bottle lying on the pillow. "Complimentary body liqueur—cinnamon." She twisted off the lid, then dipped her index finger in and tasted it. "Mmm, I'm starved."

Alan rolled his eyes, then looked around the room as if plotting how to get through the night without touching anything. "It's a dump," he pronounced.

Pam replaced the liqueur. It was a repeat of the car rental—nothing but the best was good enough for Alan Parish. "Lighten up, Alan, this is fun."

"Speak for yourself," he muttered, shaking his head.

Straightening, she put her hands on her hips and threw back her shoulders. "Why don't you come down from your high horse and see how the other half lives?"

"What the hell is that supposed to mean?"

"It means life isn't always first-class, and you have to learn to roll with the punches."

He squared his jaw. "I can roll with the best of them."

"Hah! You can't even *bend*, Alan, much less roll. You're just a spoiled little rich boy."

"I resent that," he said, his eyes narrowing.

"Go ahead—it's still the truth." She jerked up the bag that contained her new toiletries and headed in the direction of what appeared to be the bathroom. She opened the door, then breathed, "Wow."

A large red sunken tub dominated the room, appropriately set off by pale pink tile. It appeared that the sink, shower and commode had been miniaturized to make room for the tub, which could easily accommodate three adults.

"Hmm," Alan said behind her. "Another novelty." His voice was still laced with sarcasm.

"But not the last," Pam said, pointing out the picture window over the tub.

Their room was the last one set in a U formation, giving them a perfect view over an open plaza of the brightly lit room on the opposite side. Though not as spectacular as theirs, the room was furnished in the same style and occupied by an elderly couple who clearly had a disdain for clothing. Pam stared, fascinated, as the couple moved around in the kitchen, completely nude—with no tan lines. "It's like watching a car crash," she murmured. "You don't want to look, but you can't help yourself."

The woman turned her gaze directly toward them, then nudged her husband. Pam and Alan stood frozen, like two animals caught in headlights. Then the couple smiled and waved.

Alan reached forward and yanked the curtain closed over the tub. "Unbelievable," he muttered. "Those people are old enough to be my parents."

Pam leaned over and turned on the hot-water faucet. The first few trickles of water looked a little rusty, but it ran clear within a few seconds, so she stopped up the tub and poured in a handful of scented salts from a gold plastic container.

"Not everyone loses interest in sex when they get older, Alan." Then her best friend's comments about her drab intimate relationship with Alan rattled around in her head. "Assuming a person was ever interested in sex in the first place," she added dryly.

She reached around the back of her dress to capture the zipper in her fingers, and began to ease it downward. Suddenly, she remembered Alan was still in the room, and stopped. Holding up her neckline, she sighed. "Alan, I don't have the energy to throw you out, but I'm warning you—these clothes are coming off in the next few seconds, so if you don't want to be embarrassed twice in one evening, you better vamoose.''

He paled, then groped for the doorknob and bolted out of the room. Pam giggled, then slid the zipper down and escaped from the hideous, rancid dress. After ripping off her shredded panty hose, she unhooked her bra and stepped into the heavenly, hot bubbles.

''Ahhhh,'' she breathed, sinking in up to her neck. Leaning her head back, she closed her eyes, her hands moving over her body to dislodge the day's grime. She automatically lapsed into a series of isometric exercises she always performed in the tub or shower for toning and relaxing. After a few minutes, her limbs grew languid, but her skin tingled.

Gingerly, she lifted her head and looked toward the closed door. Scooping up a handful of bubbles, she trickled them across her raised leg. Alan Parish was the most conservative, stuffy man she'd ever met under the age of sixty. Of course, he did have a lot to live up to, being the oldest son of such a prominent Savannah family. A subdivision had even been named for them—Parish Corners. He was a regular pillar of the community, unlike herself, who had nowhere to go in the world but up.

And here they were, two opposing forces, thrown together in a tacky hotel room. Paper and matches. Roses and switches. Uptown and downtown.

She smiled wryly. Inviting her to come on the trip was no doubt the most spontaneous thing Alan had ever done in his life. How ironic that he was probably the only man in Savannah who would invite her to spend a week with him, without having anything sexual in mind. Pam eased her head back. She could relax—Alan Parish's relationship with her was even less than platonic.

ALAN PASSED A HAND over his face and paced the length of the room. He wouldn't have believed it possible to be so tired and yet so awake at the same time. His hungover head was screaming for sleep, but the rest of his body was rigidly aware that Pamela Kaminski, a woman who had a sexual position named for her—the Kaminski Curl—was in the next room, naked…and lathered.

He swore and ripped off his bow tie, then tossed it across the room. When he caught a glimpse of himself in one of the many mirrors, he came up short, surprised at the anger he saw in his face. He prided himself on always remaining calm, regardless of the situation, but today— he sighed and shoved his fingers through his hair—today he'd been put through the wringer by two different women. His laugh was short and bitter. If he didn't know better, he'd suspect it was a conspiracy.

His empty stomach rolled, prompting him to call the front desk. Twiggy's bored drawl was instantly recognizable. "Yeah?"

Alan bit back a tart comment, and instead mustered a pleasant tone. "My—uh, *our* package includes meals, and I was wondering if the hotel restaurant is still open."

"Just closed," she said cheerfully.

He groaned. "We're starved—can we get room service?"

Twiggy sighed dramatically. "What do you want?"

"A couple of steaks and a bottle of wine."

"I'll see what I can do."

"Thanks." He hung up and frowned sourly at the phone. How had his secretary found this place? Remembering he still needed to find accommodations for the rest of the week, he called Linda's voice mail and left her a message to call him. Then he contacted the car rental agency who promised to have another car delivered to their hotel first thing in the morning.

Trying mightily to forget the events of the last few hours, Alan removed the black studs from his buttons, shrugged out of his wrinkled shirt and folded it neatly over the back of a stiff kitchen chair. He slipped off his shoes and socks, then lowered himself to the dreadful carpet and performed fifty push-ups. Breathing heavily, he pulled himself to his feet, wincing at the odor of his own sweat. A shower before dinner would feel terrific. Glancing at his watch, he frowned and hesitated, then went to the bathroom door and rapped lightly. Steam curled out from under the door, warming his bare toes. Alan swallowed. "Pam?"

He heard her moving in the water, splashing lightly.

"I ordered room service and it should be here soon."

She didn't answer. Alan shifted from foot to foot, wondering if she'd fallen asleep in the water. Suddenly, the door swung open and Pam stood before him, holding the ends of a dingy white towel above her breasts, her hair dripping wet. His breath caught in his throat, and the room seemed to close in around them.

Pamela smiled benignly. "I left my new clothes out here," she said, pointing to a bag on the floor. She brushed by him, her clean, soapy scent rising to fill his nostrils. He watched with blatant admiration as she walked over to retrieve the articles. Her long, slender legs were glowing with bath oil and speckled with water. His heart skipped a beat when the towel sagged low enough in the back to expose her narrow waist and the top of her—

"Astringent," she mumbled, rummaging in the bag.

"Wh-what?" he croaked.

"Remind me to buy astringent tomorrow when we go

shopping,'' she said, bending over, the towel inching up to reveal the backs of her thighs.

Alan felt his knees weaken, and averted his glance to the ceiling as he cleared his throat. ''Okay.'' The plastic bag rattled.

''And a hair dryer.''

''Sure.'' He sneaked another peek. Her back was still turned, and she was still standing butt up, the towel barely covering her. Squeezing his eyes shut, he suppressed a groan.

''Are you okay?''

His eyes snapped open. Pam was staring at him, squinting.

''Uh, tired and hungry, same as you, I suppose.''

She nodded toward the bathroom. ''You'll feel better once you shower.''

Gratefully, he escaped to the bathroom, where he leaned heavily against the closed door for a few seconds to compose himself. But he was still muttering to himself a few minutes later when he stepped under the cold spray of the cramped shower. Any other man would have ripped off that towel and carried Pam to the bed...so why hadn't he? Sighing, he massaged his tired neck muscles. Because Pam would have welcomed it from any other man. But he'd been around Pam enough to realize she saw him as little more than a big brother—completely asexual. Why else would she have sashayed into the room practically naked, as if he wasn't there? She hadn't acknowledged his masculinity enough even to be modest around him. It was downright insulting. Just because he wasn't like the Neanderthals she typically dated didn't mean he wasn't alive.

A tapping sound on the shower glass startled him. "Alan?"

He froze, then whirled, instinctively crossing his hands over his privates.

4

PAM BLINKED. She'd seen so-so bodies and she'd seen good bodies. But who would have thought this magnificent specimen had been walking around Savannah all this time disguised as Alan Parish? Wide, muscled shoulders, smooth chest, washboard stomach...now if only he'd move his damn hands out of the way.

Through the steamed glass of the shower door, his face was screwed up in anger. "Pam!" he yelled. "Do you just walk in on a person no matter what they're doing?"

Pam gave him a wry smile. "Don't get your bowels all twisted, Alan. Unless yours is green, you don't have anything I haven't seen before. Your secretary is on the phone."

"Linda?" he asked, talking above the noise of the water.

"How many secretaries do you have?"

"Has she found another place for me—us—to stay?"

Pam sighed impatiently. "I didn't ask, Alan. I think she's still recovering from the fact that a woman answered the phone."

His eyes widened. "Did you think to disguise your voice?"

She planted her hands on her hips in annoyance. "Sorry, I was fresh out of helium, but I think we're safe."

Alan nodded, the water streaming down his face.

"You're probably right—she'd never suspect you were here with me."

"No one would," Pamela agreed dryly. "Not in a million years."

He stared at her, nodding and dripping, then sputtered, "Well?"

"Well, what?"

"Well, hand me a towel!"

Pam grinned, enjoying his self-consciousness, then reached for the remaining bath towel folded not so neatly on the toilet tank. She dangled the flimsy cloth in front of the shower door and watched as he considered uncovering himself to retrieve it. Thirty seconds passed.

Alan shifted and blushed deep pink. "Just drape it over the top of the stall, will you?"

Pressing her lips together to control her smirk, Pam tossed the towel over the top of the shower door and Alan grabbed it just as it passed his waist. She laughed and exited the room shaking her head.

Imagine, she thought as she collapsed on a yellow beanbag chair and began to untangle her wet hair, Alan was *modest*. It was actually kind of…refreshing in an attractive man, quite the opposite from the chest-pounding antics of her transient lovers. Then she frowned. Maybe Alan was more than just a "lights off" kind of guy— maybe he harbored a host of hang-ups that kept him from enjoying sex. Her friend Jo had never gone into specifics, and even though Pam had been dying to know details, she'd respected her friend's privacy.

The sound of the bathroom door opening broke into her thoughts. Alan emerged in a pair of navy sweatpants and strode over to the phone. He was polishing his glasses with the bath towel and didn't look at her, but the set of his shoulders told her he was still ruffled by her invasion.

He shoved aside the wet hair hanging in his eyes, yanked up the handset and turned his back to Pam.

"Hello, Linda?"

Unabashed, Pam used the opportunity to more closely scrutinize his startling physique. His skin was damp and glowing, golden and sleek, like a swimmer's.

"You just got back from the wedding? They must have had a blowout reception."

His shoulders were wide and covered with knotty muscle that rolled under his skin as he paced around the nightstand, gripping the phone.

"No, Linda, don't feel bad—I'm glad you enjoyed the champagne...well, thanks for the condolences, but it's probably for the best."

She could smell the clean, soapy scent of him even at this distance, stirred up every time he pivoted on his bare feet.

"Yeah, I decided to take the trip anyway."

Pam squinted at the length and width of his feet, made a few mental calculations, then pursed her lips in admiration.

"Let's just say this place is not exactly what I expected."

The baggy sweatpants dipped low to reveal the top of his hard-won boxers and a narrow waist. Being a computer nerd must be more physically demanding than she thought.

"Actually, Linda, it's a dump."

Now that she thought of it, she *had* passed him going in and out of the workout club a couple of times.

"What do you mean, this is the only room available?"

His butt was narrow and hard, like a greyhound's...aerodynamic...built for speed. Desire struck low in her abdomen, shocking her.

"The woman who answered?" Alan glanced at her over his shoulder, then quickly back to the phone. "Uh, nobody…that is…nobody you'd know." He laughed nervously. "A m-maid."

Pam frowned, but a knock at their door and thoughts of food distracted her. She scrambled up and swung open the door, then practically snatched the covered food tray from Twiggy's hands. When the girl stuck out her skinny foot to prevent Pam from shutting the door, Pam smirked, set down the tray and shoved a five-dollar bill into her bony hand.

She slammed the door with a bang and motioned for Alan to get off the phone. He nodded, his face a mask of frustration. "Just keep checking, Linda, and let me know when you find something."

By the time he hung up, Pam was already sitting cross-legged on the water bed and lifting the lid from their meal.

"Bad news." He sat on the edge of the mattress and triggered a small tidal wave.

"I know—no pickles," Pam said, staring down at a platter of grilled-cheese sandwiches.

"Linda says it's the height of the season, and with Valentine's Day only a few days away, everything is booked."

"Damn," she mumbled, sinking her teeth resignedly into the surprisingly good sandwich. "I really wanted pickles."

"She's going to call if something opens up."

"Mmphh," Pam said, licking gooey orange cheese from her finger.

Alan stared at the food tray. "I ordered steak. That is not steak."

"But it's good," she mumbled, cracking open a can of cold soda.

"And that is definitely not wine."

She glanced up at him. "You ordered wine?"

He blushed, then stammered. "W-well, you know, the meals are already paid for."

"I thought I was too tired to eat, but I was wrong." She stuffed in the last bite of her sandwich.

Alan picked up a sandwich by the corner and sniffed it. "Cholesterol city."

"My hometown," Pam said with a smile, then she tore off a huge chunk of a second greasy sandwich. "Live a little, Alan."

He wrinkled his nose and took a tentative bite, then chewed slowly. "Linda said the wedding was a big hit."

At the serious tone of his voice, Pam stopped munching and searched for something comforting to say, but nothing came to mind.

"I thought Jo really loved me," Alan said without self-pity. He seemed genuinely perplexed.

"She did," Pam quickly assured him. "She told me so many times."

"Then she fooled us both."

Pam shook her head, then finger-combed her wet bangs. "That's not true—Jo doesn't have a deceitful bone in her body. Look how close she came to marrying you because she thought it was the right thing to do."

Alan gave her a wry smile. "Pam, don't ever go into motivational speaking."

"Okay, that didn't come out just right, but you get the gist—she really does care about hurting you."

His blue eyes darkened. "I knew John Sterling was trouble the minute I laid eyes on him."

Pam chose her words carefully. "It takes two to tango, Alan." Then she muttered to herself, "Three in France."

He sighed heavily. "You're right. She certainly fell hard for him."

Sympathy barbed through Pam—the man *had* been robbed of the future he'd planned. She felt compelled to say something. "Well, if you ask me, Jo missed out." Pam leaned sideways to give Alan's shoulders a friendly squeeze, but she was unprepared for the electricity beneath her fingers when she made contact with his smooth skin. Alan jerked his head around and their faces were mere inches apart.

For a few seconds, neither one spoke. Pam swallowed audibly.

"Do you really think she missed out?" Alan asked, his voice barely above a whisper, his gaze locked with hers.

Sirens went off in Pam's head. She fought the waves of awareness that flooded her—his scent, his warmth, his incredible physique. Her body softened and hardened in response. Sexual energy flamed to the surface and singed the fringes of her mind. Incredibly, a message was delivered to her brain amidst the smoke and fire. *It's Alan. Alan—who's still in love with your best friend.*

Pam inhaled sharply and pulled back carefully, not wanting to make the moment even more awkward. The fluid mattress bumped them up and down. She laughed nervously. "Yeah, I do," she said brightly, then swept her arm out toward the room. "She missed all of this on her wedding night."

To her relief, Alan smiled and looked around. "Something tells me she wouldn't have appreciated all this, um, atmosphere as much as you do. Jo would never have climbed into that ridiculous tub."

"It was fun."

"And she would never have sat on a beanbag chair."

"The most underrated furniture on the market, in my opinion."

"And this bed…" He laughed, smacking the shiny comforter, then bobbing up and down with the waves. "She would *never—*" He stopped midlaugh and glanced up, then blushed.

Pam grinned and shrugged. "She might have surprised you. Water beds aren't so bad."

With one eyebrow raised, Alan reached for another sandwich. "You speak from experience, I take it."

She nodded amiably. "My first experience, as a matter of fact. Which was so unremarkable, it's a wonder I don't have a bad association with water beds."

He laughed again. "My first time was less than memorable, too. To this day I have an aversion to spiral stairs."

Surprise shot through her, and she couldn't keep it out of her voice. "Spiral stairs? *You*, Alan?"

His smile was sheepish. "I seem to remember that was also my first introduction to Kentucky bourbon."

"Ah," she said knowingly. "Been there, done that." She dropped her half-eaten cheese sandwich onto the platter and stifled a huge yawn. "I think the day is catching up with me, but it's scarcely ten-thirty."

He glanced toward the television cabinet. "How about a movie before we, um, turn in?"

"Sure," she said, shifting on the bed, flashing forward to their sleeping arrangements. She felt restless and uncomfortable with her newfound attraction to Alan, and grateful he didn't share her momentary indiscriminate horniness. But the thought of sleeping with Alan and then returning to Savannah to face her friend Jo was enough to have her begging her guardian angel for strength.

She watched out of the corner of her eye as Alan removed the food tray and slid it onto the dresser. He moved with casual elegance, running a hand through his drying hair, separating the glossy strands. Pam groaned and crossed her arms over her saluting breasts, squeezed her eyes shut and whispered, "Oh Holy Angel, forsake me not…"

At the sound of his moan, she peeked. Alan leaned over and arched his back, cracking and popping the stretched vertebrae, flexing his well-toned upper body. Sweat broke out on her upper lip. "…give no place to the evil demon to subdue me…"

"I hope this free video library has something decent to offer." He straightened, then walked over to the cabinet and swung open the door. When he knelt down to finger the row of black video cases, his baggy sweatpants inched even lower, revealing more of the new pale blue boxers.

"…take me by my wretched and outstretched hand…"

"Oh, great," he scoffed, his back to her. "*Denise Does Denver, Long, Dark, and Lonesome,* and the soon-to-be-classic *Tripod Man.*"

"…and keep me from the front—I mean, every affront of the enemy…"

"Did you say something, Pam?"

Her eyes widened. Alan was squinting back at her over his shoulder. She straightened and smiled, her mind racing. "N-no, just reciting my to-do list for tomorrow."

He frowned. "To go shopping?"

"No, I, uh…I have a big home deal in the works that I have to check on." Which was the absolute truth, although she hadn't given it any thought until now.

"Anyplace I'd know?"

"The Sheridan house."

He whistled low. "That should be quite a commission."

"That's why I need to check on it."

After reshelving the tapes, he retrieved the remote control and pushed himself up from the floor to sit at the foot of the bed. With his back to her still, he asked, "Isn't the Sheridan house haunted?"

Pam felt the wave he'd started ripple beneath her rear end. "*Please* don't add fuel to that rumor—the house has been on the market for nearly two years and I finally have an interested buyer." *And please don't come any closer.*

"Hey—'X-Files' reruns." He turned and clambered up to join her on the bed, a happy grin on his face. After stacking the slippery, bumpy pillows behind his back, he scratched his bare, flat stomach and crossed his long legs at the ankles.

Pam held her breath, rattled by his nearness. Her head bobbed from the rolling mattress. "I've seen this episode," she said, exhaling.

He turned his head toward her and pushed his glasses higher on his nose. "Really? You like this show?"

"Never miss it—I'm a big science-fiction fan."

His eyebrows rose. "Me, too."

Pam sat perfectly still, her thigh a mere eight inches from Alan's elbow. "So, do you think Mulder and Scully will ever get together?"

Alan made a clicking sound with his cheek and shook his head, his fair hair splaying against the shiny gold pillows. "I hope not."

"Why?"

"Because they're great just the way they are. Sex would...would—" He waved vaguely into the air. "Well, you know—"

"Complicate things," Pam offered, trying to relax.

He nodded. "Cloud the picture."

"Muddy the waters."

"Yeah, I'd hate to see them backslide to the 'X-*rated* Files.'" Alan smiled and forced himself to take his eyes off Pam and concentrate on the television show. His skin tingled from her proximity and he had to keep his leg bent in order to hide the other physical reaction she provoked. "Of course it's obvious that Mulder thinks Scully is really hot."

"You think?"

"Sure," he said, sneaking another peek up at her from his reclined position. He was eye level with her chest... and she wasn't wearing a bra. She glanced down at him, twisting a lock of dark blond hair around her finger. His bent leg began to tremble. "Can't you tell by the way he, um, looks at her all the time?"

She squinted at the screen. "Does he?"

"Yeah, and haven't you noticed that they're always invading each other's personal space?"

"How can you tell?"

"Eighteen inches. Americans like to keep a private space of eighteen inches around them." He started to draw an imaginary arc around him, but stopped when he realized the line would encompass Pam. His leg was practically jerking now. "Th-that space is reserved for, uh—"

"Intimacy?" she prompted, looking completely innocent.

His pulse leaped. "Or k-keyboards," he croaked.

Her finely arched eyebrows drew together. "What?"

He shrugged, suddenly feeling foolish. "Computer humor—most of us spend more time with our PC's than with any one person."

"Agreed—more than with any *one* person," she said, smiling wryly, then breaking out in a huge yawn.

Great, Parish. Not only is your conversation putting her to sleep, but you come off looking like some kind of freak who's turned on by his mainframe. And he hadn't missed her unnecessary reminder that when it came to sex, she liked to experiment. Which was an even bigger slap in the face considering they were in bed together and she was fighting to keep her eyes open.

He turned his attention back to the television, trying to lose himself in the fantasy on the screen. His wedding night was turning out to be somewhat less exciting than he'd hoped for. Not that he'd invited Pam along as a substitute for Jo—sleeping with her hadn't entered his mind.

Well, okay, so it *had* entered his mind, but not seriously. Not any more than when he saw a gorgeous model or movie star on TV. To him, Pamela had always seemed just as distant, just as untouchable. And even though the long expanse of her bare leg beckoned to him just a few inches away, she might as well have been still in Savannah for all the good it would do him.

He bit the inside of his cheek, his frustration mounting. One half roll of his body would put him face-to-breast with the most beautiful, sexual woman he knew. Maybe all he needed to do was make the first move. Maybe she'd rip off her clothes and he'd get to see what half of Savannah was raving about. Maybe they'd be great together and he'd give her a blinding orgasm.

His confidence surged, and he made a split-second decision. For once in his life, he would seize the moment and let the chips fall where they might. Before he could change his mind, he drew a quick breath and rolled onto his side, realizing the instant his chin met soft, pliant skin that he'd underestimated the distance *and* the size of her breasts. Her light floral scent filled his lungs, and his mind spun. His eyes darted to her face as he scrambled to think of something witty to say. Panic exploded in his chest…until he saw that she was sleeping.

He pulled himself up and expelled a small, disappointed sigh as he studied her lash-shadowed cheeks and the eternal pout of her fuller upper lip. He allowed his gaze to rove over her slender neck, then down to her breasts. The dark crescents of her nipples were barely visible beneath the thin fabric of her T-shirt. Elvis smiled at him, obviously happy to be stretched over Pam's ample bosom.

Alan's body hardened and he fought back a groan. He lifted his free hand and let it hover over an area where her shirt had risen high on her thigh. Was she wearing panties? Did he dare peek? After all, she'd seen him all but buck naked.

No, he decided. He wasn't a voyeur—he wanted anything that transpired between them to be consensual. "Pam," he whispered, his voice scratchy.

She moaned and moved down on the pillows and slightly toward him, but didn't rouse.

"Pam," he repeated a little louder.

He held his breath as her eyelashes fluttered for a second and her mouth opened as if she was going to speak. His desire for her swelled even more and his heart thumped in anticipation.

"Alan?" she murmured, her eyes still closed.

"Y-yes?" he whispered hopefully.

She wet her lips, and he thought he might go mad with wanting her. He moved toward her open mouth, intending to kiss her awake, but the sound emerging from her throat stopped him cold.

She was snoring…loud enough to shake the mirror on the ceiling above them.

5

PAM'S LEG itched. Trying to ignore it, she floated deeper into the pillow, enjoying the last fuzzy minutes of sleep. But the itch persisted until at last she reached down and scratched her knee vigorously. The thought that she needed to shave skittered across her mind, but was obliterated when she realized she hadn't even felt her fingernails against her skin.

Her eyes flew open, and she froze at the image in the mirror ceiling. Alan, stripped down to his boxers, lay wrapped around her like a koala bear in a eucalyptus tree, his arm resting comfortably across her chest, his bent leg heavy upon her abdomen. She could feel his warm breath upon the side of her neck. Her mind spun and panic welled within her. The last thing she remembered was watching television—had she…did they…oh, God, what was that stabbing into her side?

She pushed at his arm, dragging him with her as she attempted to roll away from his body. The fluid mattress surged, grabbed her, then slammed their bodies back together, abruptly rousing Alan from his slumber.

"Huh?" he muttered, lifting his head.

His glasses sat askew on the top of his head and his hair had finished drying in every direction but down. "Get off of me," Pam said, enunciating clearly.

Squinting, he appeared not to have heard her. "Alan," she repeated more loudly. "I'm not Jo—get off of me."

She knew the precise second her words registered because he stiffened and his nearsighted eyes rounded. "Pam?"

Throwing him a smile as dry as her mouth, she said, "Afraid so."

He wasted no time disentangling himself from her, but floundered a few seconds before propelling himself off the bed. Pam followed him with her eyes, averting her glance from the bulge straining at the front of his underwear. To avoid aggravating her mushrooming headache, she lay still until the waves stopped.

Patting furniture surfaces, presumably searching for his glasses, Alan walked into the half-unfolded sofa bed. Flesh collided with metal in a sickening thunk. "Son of a—" He broke off and bit his lower lip, wincing.

"They're on the top of your head, Einstein."

Alan fumbled for his glasses, jammed them on and looked back to the bed as if he still hadn't seized the situation.

She lifted her hand and fluttered her fingers at him. "I trust you slept well," she said in a sarcastic tone.

Patting down his hair, he scowled and bent over to scoop up his sweatpants. "How could I, with you snoring loud enough to rattle my teeth?"

Annoyance bolted through her, and she shot up, grimacing at the pain exploding in her temples. "Do you always curl into a fetal position when you're in agony? Our deal was *you* would sleep on the sofa bed!"

He reached down to massage his shin. "I tried to pry open the damn thing, but it wouldn't budge."

She rubbed her forehead, glancing around the sunlit room. "What time is it?"

He held the sweatpants in front of his waist with one

hand and picked up his watch with the other. "Almost ten o'clock."

She sighed, pushing tangled hair out of her eyes. "At least the stores should open soon."

"Forget the stores, give me a restaurant."

"Fine. We'll have a bite to eat, then I can go shopping." Thankfully, the awkwardness was dissolving. "Wonder what the weather will be like this week?"

Alan picked up the remote and found the weather channel, then tossed the control on the bed. Without another word, he turned and limped into the bathroom.

Pam frowned after him. He didn't have to be so snotty—after all, *he* had invited *her*. He wasn't being a very gracious host.

Oh, well, at least Mother Nature was smiling on them. According to the chipper weatherwoman, they had arrived smack in the middle of a February heat wave: temperatures in the low nineties, and sun, sun, sun.

Pam gingerly pulled herself out of bed and walked to the far end of the room, away from the bathroom. In the light of day, the kaleidoscope room really was horrid. Groaning, she reached overhead in a full-body stretch, wriggling her toes in the chocolate shag carpet, then drew aside the yellow brocade curtain covering a sliding glass door. The balcony Twiggy promised was a tiny wooden structure about the size of a refrigerator enclosed by worn railings. Despite the slight pain caused by the morning sunlight, she unlatched the door and stepped out into the cool air, feeling her spirits rise along with the gooseflesh on her arms.

A set of questionable-looking narrow stairs descended to a pebbly path that disappeared into palm trees and sea grass. She took a step forward, then stopped, rubbed one bare foot over the other, and decided not to chance it. If she fell and broke a leg, Alan might shoot her to put her out of his misery.

Without the wide sign from the neighboring Grand Sands Hotel, they might have had a very good view. Despite the obstruction, a slice of the white beach was visible, dotted with morning walkers and shell-seekers. The air, full of sand and salt dust, blew sharp against her bare arms and legs. Inhaling deeply, she drew in the tangy ocean breeze and was suddenly very glad she had come. Maybe the circumstances weren't ideal, but she loved the ocean and Savannah's beaches were a bit too cold to enjoy this time of year.

Humming to herself, she turned and reentered the room, closing the sliding door behind her. Then her gaze landed on the bathroom door and her smile evaporated. Obviously, Alan already regretted the invitation to share his honeymoon. She was a poor replacement for the woman he loved. But she was here, and she'd promised Jo she'd keep an eye on him. She blushed guiltily—the amount of time she'd spent eyeing him since their arrival probably wasn't what her friend had had in mind. Lifting her chin, she gathered her willpower. She could keep her lust at bay for a lousy week, but darn it, she wasn't going to let him mope and ruin the only vacation she'd had in over a year!

She took in her appearance in one of the many mirrors at her disposal and groaned out loud. As if he'd be interested, anyway. Her friend Jo rolled out of bed looking great. She, on the other hand, looked as if she'd been dragged backward through a hedgerow.

Dropping onto the unmade bed, she grabbed the phone. She needed to check her messages and see if old Mrs. Wingate had made up her mind about buying the Sheridan house, haunts and all. She retrieved her answering service with a few punched buttons. The message from Nick the All-Nighter was wicked enough to fry the phone lines. And Jo had called, concern in her voice—had Pam seen Alan and was he all right?

She shot a look toward the bathroom door just as it opened. *Speak of the devil.* Swallowing, she scanned the tempting length of Alan in black running shorts and a tight touristy sweatshirt. He offered her a small smile, apparently in a much better mood. She lifted her finger, then turned away from him and tried to concentrate on Jo's rambling, heartfelt message. With a sigh, Jo thanked Pam for going after Alan and asked Pam to call her at John's house—Jo laughed—make that *her* house. Pam smirked into the phone, happy for her friend, but disturbed by the sticky mess she'd left behind.

She felt contrite as she replaced the handset. It wasn't Jo's fault that she was having these inappropriate feelings for Alan. "Jo left me a message."

Alan's handsome face remained impassive—perhaps a little *too* nonchalant. "What did she say?"

Pam hesitated, then said, "She was wondering if I'd seen you and how you're doing."

He exhaled loudly and cracked his knuckles in one quick movement. "What business is it of hers?"

"She's just worried about you—"

"Well, I'm not suicidal," he snapped.

Pam stood, jamming her hands on her hips. "You don't have to shoot the messenger."

"Sorry—I'm not feeling very well."

"Join the crowd," Pam yelled back, then touched a hand to her resurrected headache.

His expression softened a bit. "You don't look too bad—I mean, uh, you look…fine."

She smiled wryly, then turned toward the bathroom. "Nice try. I'll be out in two shakes."

Alan watched her retreat into the bathroom, the curves of her hips tugging at the hem of her T-shirt. A little more than *two* shakes, he amended silently, making fists of frustration at his side.

"This is insane," he said to the frantic-looking man in the mirror.

"Why are you worried about it?" his image asked. "Just *bed* the woman, for heaven's sake."

"I can't—she's my ex-fiancée's best friend."

"Even better."

Alan squeezed his eyes shut and cursed, then slowly opened them to address his argumentative reflection. "This is a fine mess you've gotten us into." Oh, well, maybe his secretary would come through with less evocative accommodations.

True to her word, Pam showered quickly, emerging like a ray of sunshine, her skin glowing, her golden hair caught up in a high, swishy ponytail. He groaned inwardly. She was even gorgeous in running shorts and a baggy white jersey sporting a multicolored parrot. "Ready?" she asked.

"And willing," he mumbled, picking up his wallet.

At the last minute, they both shoved their feet into hard, ill-fitting plastic thongs, then stumbled downstairs to find the reservation desk deserted. A fiftyish woman sprawled in one of the lobby chairs, smoking a long cigarette and watching a church program on television. She was happy to nod in the direction of the restaurant, and as soon as they smelled food their clumsy steps quickened.

Alan's stomach rumbled when he saw how packed the restaurant was. Grasping Pam's elbow, he pointed to the buffet line. "If you'll get us something to eat, I'll try to find a table.'' She nodded and he cased the area, his eyes lighting on a family of four wiping their chins over emptied plates. He scrambled toward the table, arriving at the same time as a busboy and an older couple holding laden plates.

The silver-haired man smiled. ''Share?''

''Sure,'' Alan agreed.

''We're the Kessingers,'' the man supplied. ''I'm Cheek and this is Lila.''

Alan introduced himself as he pulled out the older woman's chair. ''Another person will be joining me.''

''We're from Michigan,'' Lila offered.

''Savannah,'' Alan told her, as he took a seat opposite her. The Kessingers seemed nice enough, divulging they were devoted snowbirds who migrated south every January until spring.

''There you are,'' Pam said, precariously balancing two plates piled high with food. Alan relieved her of half her burden, then introduced the senior couple.

''Hi,'' Pam said cordially as she swung into her seat.

Alan frowned down at the plate in front of him. Every single item was fried. ''I see you got plenty of the *brown* food group.''

''Eat,'' Pam said pointedly, stabbing a sausage patty with her fork.

With visions of whole-wheat bagels and fresh fruit dancing in his head, Alan ate, stopping frequently to sop the grease from his food with paper napkins. Lila Kessinger proved to be quite chatty, which gave Cheek plenty of time to ogle Pam, he noticed, surprised at the needle of jealousy that poked him.

''Are you newlyweds?'' Lila asked.

Pam glanced at him. ''No, we're just...uh...''

Alan's stomach fluttered. ''Buddies,'' he offered.

"Pals," Pam affirmed.

"Oh," the woman responded. "I assumed you were married since you're in the honeymoon suite."

Alan stopped. "How did you know we're in the honeymoon suite?"

Lila grinned. "We're right across the plaza from you, in room 400. Remember—we waved."

He frowned, trying to recall, then grunted as Pam kicked him under the table. One look at her raised eyebrows and his memory flooded back. The naked couple! He dropped his fork with a clatter and a burning flush crept up his neck. "Oh, I didn't recognize you—"

"Because we're both nearsighted," Pam cut in. "We couldn't see much." She looked at him for reinforcement. "Isn't that right, Alan?"

"Y-yes," he said, a picture of the wrinkled nude couple emblazoned on his mind. "In fact, we didn't see anything at all. You waved, did you say?" He brought a glass of room-temperature water to his mouth for a drink.

Lila beamed and nodded. Cheek leaned forward, his eyes devouring Pam.

Lifting his wrist, Alan pretended to be shocked. "*Look* at the time. We have to go," he said, eyeing Pam.

"But I'm not finished," she protested.

"We'll get a stick of butter for the road," he said through clenched teeth, casting his eyes toward the door.

"Okay," she relented sullenly, wiping her mouth and standing. "It was nice to meet—"

Alan pulled on her arm, and nearly dragged her back through the restaurant.

"Let go of me," she said angrily, then jerked away from him. "What the devil is wrong with you?"

He stared at her and exclaimed, his frustration high, "That's the thanks I get?"

"Thanks? For what?"

"That dirty old man looked like he was getting ready to have *you* for breakfast!"

Pam tilted her head and laughed. "You're jealous!"

"What?" Alan scoffed, embarrassment thickening his tongue. "That'z we—ridiculous!"

"Weally?" Pam teased.

Grunting, Alan sputtered, "I thought you wanted to go shopping."

She grinned, looking triumphant. "I do."

"Then let's go see what the car rental agency delivered." He pivoted as quickly as the stupid sandals would allow, then flapped back toward the lobby, fuming. Damn, he hated her teasing, filing him in the same category as her bevy of besotted suitors.

Twiggy had returned to her post, and looked as bored as usual when he asked about the car. Without a word, she held up a key and pointed to the parking lot.

"Finally," he breathed, taking the key. "*Something* is going right."

He walked stiffly across the lobby and out into the parking lot, unable to look at Pam, still smarting from her taunt. He knew she was behind him, but he didn't know how close until he spotted their car, stopped dead in his tracks and felt her body slam into his.

"What's wrong?" she asked, stepping up beside him. Then she gasped. "A limo?" She whooped, then laughed until her knees buckled.

Alan, however, did not share her mirth. "This is unbelievable." He removed the letter tucked under the windshield wiper and read aloud. "Dear Mr. Parish, please accept this upgrade vehicle as our apology for your unfortunate breakdown—" He broke off and glanced at the powder blue stretch limousine. "They sent me a damn pimpmobile!"

Pam laughed even louder, clapping her hands. "What a blast!"

He stood paralyzed in shock as she swung open the back door. "Ooooh," she breathed, her eyes shining. "A television and everything!"

I'm in the twilight zone. "We're taking it back."

Her head jerked around. "What? We can't!"

"Oh, but we can."

Pam's eyebrows crumpled, and she pulled out her secret weapon: the pout. Damn! Surely she knew what that mouth did to him. He wavered. "Maybe we'll keep it just for the day."

She brightened and tumbled inside, then stuck her head back out. "I'll ride in the back." He felt the vacuum of air as she slammed the door.

Feeling like a colossal fool, he glanced around, opened the front door and slid behind the wheel. Pam had already found the button that operated the divider between them and was zooming the panel up and down.

"This is amazing," she squealed.

He glanced in the rearview mirror at her smiling face, watched her pressing buttons and exploring, and felt a strange tug at his heart. As exasperating as she could be, Pam's unflagging enthusiasm was undeniably charming. Somewhere between childhood and yuppiehood, he'd lost his zest for simple things...now he wondered how many wonderfully pure pleasures he'd overlooked the last several years.

"There's a refrigerator!" she exclaimed. "And olives!"

He pulled onto the highway, keeping one eye on Pam. She reclined in the back seat, propping her long legs on the bench seat running up the side. Then she unscrewed the lid from a slender jar and popped green olives into her mouth like a squirrel eating nuts. For some reason, he found the whole scene provocative.

"Hey, Alan, have you ever gotten naked in a limo?"

He weaved across the centerline so far he might have hit the oncoming car if the guy hadn't blared his horn and punctuated it with a hand gesture.

Breathing deeply to stem the charge of adrenaline through his body, he said, "I, uh, no, I can't say I have."

"Me neither."

Although her admission surprised him, he didn't say so. For a fraction of an instant, he entertained the idea of sharing Pamela's first sexual *something*. The way he figured it, the only new variable he could possibly add to her experience equation was location. Shaking the thought from his mind, he kept his dry mouth shut and his eyes peeled for signs indicating a mall.

Once he found a shopping center, it took several minutes to find a place to park. At last they were inside the mall and Alan felt some sort of normalcy returning at the sight of regular people in smart, upscale surroundings. He made a beeline for a well-known department store.

"We can split up," Pam suggested.

Alan shook his head. "I'll go with you, I'm paying."

"Wait a minute—"

"Don't argue. I talked you into coming, and it's my responsibility—"

"I can take care of myself!"

He drew back at the change in her mood, the vehemence in her voice. He'd obviously hit a nerve, so he gentled his tone. "I know you can take care of yourself, Pam, but I'd feel bad if you spent money on top of taking time from your job. Let me do this—make me feel good."

Immediately, he felt his skin warm at the implication of his own words.

She chewed on her lower lip, considering his words, then smiled slyly. "I think this may be the first time a guy has offered to do something for *me* to make himself feel good."

Glad her mood had lightened, he crossed his arms and mirrored her smile. "Maybe you've been hanging around with the wrong guys."

Her smile dissolved and her gaze locked with his. "Maybe you're right," she said, her voice barely above a whisper.

Alan studied her face and inhaled slowly, sure his chest was going to explode. This woman was driving him crazy. One minute she made him feel like an inept teenager, the next minute she made him feel as if he wanted to take care of her. Which was nuts because she'd made it perfectly clear she intended to take care of herself.

His fingers curled tighter around his biceps, itching to smooth the stray lock of hair back from her soft cheek. To hold her pointed chin and tilt her porcelainlike face up to the sun. To kiss that lopsided, upside-down, top-heavy pink mouth.

"Okay, go ahead," she said, shrugging.

He actually took a half step toward her before he realized she was talking about the clothing tab. "Where to first?"

"Men's shoes."

"What?"

She pointed to his red, thong-pinched feet and grinned. "You're going to need comfortable shoes to keep up with me."

Good idea, he decided three hours later as he shared a

bench with an older gentleman outside the women's dressing room.

"Birthday?" the guy asked, obviously bored.

"No."

"Anniversary?" The man tapped out a cigarette and
put it in his mouth, unlit.

"Uh-uh."

"Ah—you're in the doghouse."

"Well, not really."

"Oh, God," the man said, rolling his eyes. "Don't tell
me you love her."

"Pam," he said loud enough to carry into the dressing
room, "I need to eat something nourishing for a change.
Can you hurry up? I'm getting light-headed."

"I think I found a swimsuit," she sang, then burst
through the swinging doors. "What do you think?"

"Good Lord," the man muttered, his unlit cigarette
bobbing.

Alan swayed, then gripped the side of the bench to
steady himself. Pam's curves were stunning. Metallic
gold, the top of the string bikini barely covered the tips
of her generous breasts, the veed bottoms arrowed low to
her bikini line and high on the sides, emphasizing the
opposing curves of her waist and hips. His throat closed
and perspiration popped out on his upper lip despite the
chilling air conditioner.

Her pale eyebrows furrowed. "You don't like it."

"He loves it!" the man next to him shouted, his cigarette bouncing off the carpet. Then he punched Alan's
arm so hard, Alan fell off the side of the bench.

Flat on his back, Alan wet his lips carefully, then
croaked, "It will do."

6

"AREN'T YOU COLD?" Alan asked for the eleventh time.

Pamela jerked her head toward him, then lowered her ninety-nine-cent white sunglasses. "No."

"You look cold."

"Then stop looking." She leaned her head back against the plastic chaise lounge that suspended her several inches above the wet, white sand of the beach. "And stop talking."

After spending the day shopping with him yesterday and sharing an awkward dinner last night, she was ready to scream. They'd been at each other's throats all evening, culminating in an argument over finding someplace else to stay because he refused to sleep on the broken foldout bed. In the end, she had won separate sleeping arrangements, but he had complained about his back all morning.

Although quiet at the moment, he was driving her bananas, hiding behind those mirrored designer-prescription shades, reminding her every few seconds that she lay nearly naked within touching distance, yet he had no intention of doing so. Which was a good thing, she fumed, because she'd cuff his chiseled jaw if he laid a hand on her.

She harrumphed to herself. As if she would stoop to fooling around with her best friend's ex. Pam winced and concentrated, desperately trying to dissolve the sexual pull radiating from him.

After all, once they returned to Savannah, Alan might run into Jo at an odd party or two, but Pam saw her at least a couple of times a week. Jo had been a true-blue friend, and Pam wasn't about to risk their relationship for a beach fling—no matter how pulse-poundingly gorgeous Alan looked lying glistening in the sun.

It was a glorious day, the sun as high as it could climb in a February Florida sky. As promised, the air temperature hovered in the mid-nineties, although she suspected the water temperature would be a bit more sobering. Still, it hadn't stopped several families from romping in the foamy waves, some with floats, some with masks to protect their eyes from the brine.

The beach was much more crowded than she'd expected. Portable stereos blared and the nutty smell of suntan lotion mingled with the salty air, barely masking the underlying scent of fish. Striped umbrellas populated the sloping stretch of pale sand and waitresses threaded their way through bodies to deliver drinks and hot dogs from the oceanside grill. The whole spring-break atmosphere was just another in a long series of surprises this trip had brought, she thought wryly, sneaking a sideways glance at Alan.

Bent over a book he'd bought at the mall, he looked relaxed and untroubled. Pam frowned sourly. *She* was wrestling with lewd and inappropriate thoughts, and *he* was reading a book.

"What is it now?" he asked, raising his head. "Is my breathing bothering you?"

Her gaze flicked across his oiled chest, watching defined bone and muscle expand and contract every few seconds, the sun dancing over every ripple. She could see her twin reflection in his gray lenses and wondered if he had any idea what he was doing to her. Unable to withstand the strain and confusion any longer, she swung her feet down, then stood, wrapping a short black sarong around her hips. "I'm going to stretch my legs."

Alan closed his book, keeping his place with one finger. "Want me to go along?"

Noting his uninterested tone, she shook her head. "I'll be back in an hour or so."

The strip of beach where fingers of water rolled in offered the clearest path for walking. She picked her way down to the front, ignoring a couple of low catcalls, then dug her toes in the cool, silky sand. Water hissed over her feet and frothed around her ankles, sending chills up her legs.

The beach snaked ahead of her, the people growing increasingly tiny in the distance, the shoreline curving left, then right again and disappearing about a mile away. Pam inhaled deeply, then set off at a brisk pace. Nothing cleared a person's head like the wind, water and sky.

As she made her way down to the water's edge, more than one good-looking man passed her, jogging or walking the other way, and more than one looked interested. A small smile curved her lips. One way to fight her ridiculous distraction with Alan was to find another man to distract her. A Robert Redford look-alike ran by her and grinned. Pam turned to watch him run away from her. A little on the short side, but he was definitely a looker. He had turned around and was running backward, scanning her figure up and down. After plowing into a group of teenagers, he saluted and went on his way.

"Don't tell me you're alone," a deep, accented voice said behind her.

Startled, Pam turned and looked up into the glinting eyes of a dark-eyed, dark-haired stranger. He looked to be of Latin American descent, his deep brown skin set off by gleaming gold jewelry at his throat, wrist and left earlobe. He grinned, exposing amazingly white teeth. Pam shivered. Dark, dangerous, good-looking…just her type.

"Uh, yes," she said, then added, "at the moment." A girl had to be careful in strange surroundings.

The man extended his long-fingered hand. He wore a diamond-studded horseshoe ring on his middle finger. "Enrico." The "r" rolled off his tongue seductively.

Pam smiled and put her hand in his. "Pamela."

"Ah, Pamela. Do you live here or are you on vacation?"

"Vacation."

"Then surely you have just arrived—I could not have overlooked such a beauty."

Enrico massaged her fingers between his. "I flew in from Savannah yesterday."

"A southern belle. I thought I detected a slight, how do you say—*drawl?*"

"Yes," she said, then gently extracted her hand. "Where are you from?"

"Puerto Rico, originally, but I have lived in the United States for several years."

Pam nodded congenially. "In Fort Myers?"

"No, I am vacationing, same as you." He leaned toward her and lowered his voice to a husky whisper. "And I was becoming *very* bored."

Odd, she felt nothing but indifference as he looked into her eyes. Not a sizzle or a zing. Not even a stir. "Well, I'd like to finish my walk," she said pleasantly, stepping around him. "It was nice to meet you, Enrico."

His eyes devoured her. "Until next time, Pamela."

She gave him a shaky smile, then trotted away. Pumping her arms to elevate her heart rate, she kept her eyes averted from passersby and walked two miles, past rows of resorts that ranged in appearance from posh to worse-than-the-Pleasure-Palisades. Finally, the crowds thinned and the sand became coarse and strewn with sea debris.

Pam waded into the waves up to her knees to cool off, watching a group of wet-suited windsurfers in the distance. It looked like fun—maybe she'd try it before they left. Sighing, she wondered if she'd be able to find enough entertainment to fill the hours between now and Saturday. Anything to keep her mind off Alan.

Anything but Enrico, that is—the guy gave her the willies. Turning to retrace her steps, she felt a surge of anticipation at seeing Alan again, then instant remorse. So much for clearing her head. She spotted him while she was still several hundred yards away—he was hard to miss since he stood at attention smiling down at a willowy brunette.

Absurd barbs of jealousy struck her low, but she squashed them. The woman was striking, thin and elegant in a simple black one-piece, wearing a large hat that shaded her face. The thought struck Pam that the woman might have been Jo's sister, she resembled her friend so closely. Regal, demure, classy...definitely Alan's type. Pam bit her lower lip, wondering if he wanted privacy, but knowing she needed sunscreen. Oh, well, she'd just swing by to pick up the lotion, then perhaps she could find the Robert Redford runner again.

Alan smiled and nodded to the lady, his book abandoned, Pam noted wryly. Above the music and the general din of the crowd, his voice floated to her in snatches as she approached the couple. "Show companies...become more productive...automation...accessibility."

The woman looked very impressed, nodding thoughtfully and lifting her expressive eyebrows. Her voice was lilting and definitely *interested.* "Client-servers… centralization…remote stored procedures."

Aha—a she-nerd. Out of all the people on this beach, how had they found one another? Pam sighed. Just like Enrico, the tongue-rolling Romeo, had found her—birds of a feather, yada, yada, yada. Oh, well, if Alan was occupied, the temptation to jump his bones would definitely be removed…or at least reduced. "Hi," Pam said cheerfully as she approached the computer couple.

"Oh, hi," Alan said, smiling awkwardly.

"Don't mind me," Pam said, waving a hand. "I just came back to get sunscreen."

"Um, this is Robin," he said, gesturing to the woman, who pursed her lips at the sight of Pam.

"Hiya, Robin," Pam said, nodding to the woman. "Nice hat."

"Thanks," Robin replied slowly, then turned to Alan. "I guess I'll be going."

"Don't leave on my account," Pam assured her, holding up her lotion triumphantly.

"No, that's all right," the woman continued. "My friends will be wondering where I've gone." She smiled at Alan and swept his figure, head to toe. "I certainly hope we run into each other again."

Alan's tongue appeared to be tied, so Pam stepped in. "I'm sure you will—he'll be here until Saturday." She leaned toward the woman and lowered her voice conspiratorially. "He's available, you know."

The woman smiled awkwardly, then glanced from Pam to Alan.

"Pam—" Alan protested, but she waved her hand frantically to shut him up.

"And you are…?" the woman asked with a small laugh.

"Alan's sister," Pam said without missing a beat. "I'm Pamela." Alan made a small choking noise, but she ignored him.

"Oh." The woman nodded agreeably. "Well, it's nice to meet you...Pamela." She winked. "And I'll see *you* later, Alan."

"Don't be a stranger," Pam sang as the woman walked away.

"What was that all about?" Alan demanded when she turned around. His arms were crossed over his broad chest, his pale eyebrows high over his shades.

Pam shrugged, her movements mirrored twice in his dark lenses. "It's plausible—we have the same coloring. Besides, who's going to believe the real story?"

Alan threw his hands up in the air. "I give up trying to follow your logic."

Falling into the chaise, Pam smeared sunscreen all over, down to the crevices between her peach-lacquered toes. Alan reclaimed his chair and his place in the book he was reading. She glanced at the cover and smiled. "Hey, *Dr. Moonshadow*. I thought it was the best book in the entire series."

He glanced over. "You've read the Light Years series?"

She nodded enthusiastically. "Have you gotten to the part where the Light Knights return with the king's head in a box?"

He dropped his head back on the chair, looking mortified. "That would be, I take it, *the ending?*"

Pam bit her lip. "Oh...yeah, I guess it would be."

Tossing the book in the sand a few feet away, Alan cursed and pushed himself to his feet. "Now *I'm* going for a walk."

Pam watched him stride off, admiring his defined hamstrings and calves. And she didn't miss the head-turning that spread through the women on the beach like "the wave" as he walked by. Oh, well, she decided as she fished in her purse for her cellular phone and a pad of paper, maybe he'd run into Robin the RAM/ROM woman.

Pam pulled out the phone's antenna, then stabbed in a number with the end of a pencil. Then maybe *she* could stop thinking about how much she enjoyed teasing Alan, how many interests they shared, how sexy— "Hello?" she responded to the voice on the end of the line, then realized her client, Marsha Wingate, had updated the message on her service.

"Hello, this is Madame Marsha, psychic in training, Monday, February twelfth. If this is Ronald, son, wear your guardian pendant today. I communed with the weatherman this morning through the television and the winds today in Syracuse are *definitely* unfriendly. If this is Sara, dear, don't talk to any Aries men today, and don't drink the tap water. If this is Lew, give me a trifecta twenty-dollar bet on the number three, four and seven greyhounds in the fifth race. And if this is Pamela, I drove by the Sheridan house last night precisely at midnight, and the bad vibes coming from that place—jeez, Louise! I want an expert's opinion, though, so I arranged to have a crystal reader from Atlanta drive down tomorrow. If this is anyone else, I have nothing to say, so don't bother to leave a message."

After the tone, which sounded vaguely like the theme from "The Twilight Zone," Pam left an upbeat message telling Mrs. Wingate she was out of town for a few days, but could be reached through her cellular phone if she decided to scoop up the Sheridan house before someone else got wise to what a steal it was. Smiling wryly at her own transparent sales tactic, Pam then checked into the office to let them know she didn't have her pager.

When she had exhausted every nit-picking phone call she could think of, she winced at the still-strong recharged battery light on her phone, then sighed and dug out the scrap of paper on which she'd written her friend Jo's new phone number. With her heart pounding guiltily, Pam punched in the numbers and prayed no one would answer.

"Heh-wo?" said a young voice.

"May I speak to Jo, please?"

"Jo-mommy?"

Pam blinked. Boy, did that sound weird—her friend Jo, a mommy. The littlest one must have picked up the phone, she decided. And although she was no expert on kids, he seemed way too young to be answering the phone. "Yes, Jo-mommy," she said carefully. "Go get Jo-mommy."

"Hello?" another voice said, this one slightly older. "Who is this?"

Pam frowned. "Who is this?"

"This is Peter Pa—I mean, this is Jamie Sterling. Who do you want?"

The middle one, she decided. "I need to speak with Jo."

"What for?"

Taking a deep breath, Pam forced a soothing lilt into her voice. "Just to talk—I'm a friend of hers." Then she heard the sound of the phone being ripped from his hand, followed by a scuffle and at least two raised kid voices as they tried to claim ownership of the phone, which was being bounced around the room.

"Hello?" A girl's voice came over the line. Jamie was still yelling something in the background.

The oldest one, Pam remembered. An owlish-looking little thing. "May I speak with Jo, please?"

"May I ask who's calling?"

At least she was polite. "This is her friend Pamela."

"She's indisposed at the moment."

Pam pulled back and looked at the phone. Indisposed? Quite a vocabulary for a tyke. "I'm calling long distance—are you sure she can't come to the phone?"

"She and my daddy are upstairs jumping on the bed."

With pursed lips, Pam nodded to herself. Of course. Where else would they be? Before she could think of an appropriate reply, Jo's voice came on the line. "Hello?" she asked breathlessly.

"Gee, Jo, can't you guys control yourselves at least until the kids go to bed?"

"Pam!" Jo laughed. "It's not what you think—John is testing the springs on the new mattress."

"Oh, is *that* what married folk call it?"

Jo laughed again, this time harder. She sounded almost giddy, Pam thought irritably, despite the clatter in the background. "Oh, never mind, Pam. I called your office this morning and they said you were out of town. Let me guess—Nick the All-Nighter?"

Pam squirmed on the lounge chair. "No."

"Delectable Dale?"

Sweat beaded on her upper lip. "Uh, no."

"Someone new?"

After mustering her courage, Pam muttered, "I'm with Alan in Fort Myers."

"Excuse me? Hang on a minute." Jo put down the phone, then Pam heard the sound of a police whistle peal shrilly, followed by, "QUI-I-I-I-I-ET!" The clatter ceased, then Jo picked up the phone. "Sorry. Now, what did you say?"

Pam tried again. "I'm with Alan in Fort Myers."

"You're with Alan in Fort Myers?" Jo asked, her voice richly colored with surprise.

"Yes, I'm with Alan in Fort Myers." It was getting easier to say, but she still felt as if she was going to have a stroke. She took another deep breath. "He decided to take the trip anyway. I gave him a ride to the airport, and he talked me into coming along. I haven't had a vacation in over a year, and he was acting a little desperate—"

"Pam," Jo cut off her rambling. "You are the best friend a woman could ask for."

Swallowing guiltily, Pam ventured, "I—I am?"

"I've been so worried about Alan. Now I can relax because I know you're looking out for him. How is he?"

Pam paused, thinking of all the just plain looking *at* him she'd been doing since they arrived. "He's a little depressed, which is normal, I guess."

"I'm sure his ego is bruised," Jo said mournfully. "I feel terrible. Can you try to cheer him up?" she pleaded. "Maybe take him dancing or do something fun?"

Pam's hands were so sweaty she nearly dropped the phone. Manufacturing a little laugh, she said, "Well, I'm not so sure the words *Alan* and *fun* can coexist, Jo, but I'll give it a shot."

"Make him extend himself a little," Jo urged. "Maybe he'll meet his soul mate while he's there—or at least have a little beach fling."

"He's certainly getting a lot of female attention," Pam agreed, failing to mention how much of it had derived from her.

"Good. Eventually Alan will realize we weren't right for each other, and that our marriage would never have worked. But for now, he could probably use a diversion."

"Right," Pam said as if she were receiving an assignment. "So, how's married life?"

"Wonderful," Jo said. On cue, a hellacious howl erupted in the background. "Oops, gotta run. Thanks again, Pam—you're a savior. Bye!"

Pam frowned at the silent phone. Savior? Sinner, perhaps, with all the wicked thoughts about Alan spinning in her head. She bit her lower lip—she should have gone to mass yesterday morning.

"What's wrong?" Alan asked as he dropped into his lounge chair, his body gleaming with perspiration. He picked up a towel and wiped his face. "Did the FDA issue a moratorium on fried foods?"

She smirked. "No. I talked to Jo."

He stilled, then pressed his lips into a straight line. "You mean, Jo *Sterling?*"

"Um, yeah."

Alan lay his head back and Pam's heart twisted at the hurt on his face. "And how are the newlyweds?"

"Busy, from the noise in the background."

"Did you tell her where we are?"

Pam studied her nails. "Yeah. She seemed relieved."

He made an indignant sound. "You mean that I haven't self-destructed?"

"Well, she didn't use those words."

"She wouldn't have."

"I think she really does feel bad about what happened, Alan."

A deep sigh escaped him. "I'd rather not talk about it."

"Fine," Pam said, also eager to drop the subject. She glanced toward the water, then noticed a young man had set up shop on the beach, guarding a half-dozen Wave Runners bobbing in shallow water.

He picked up a megaphone and yelled, "Rent a Wave Runner, by the hour, by the half hour."

"Let's do it," Pam said, clambering out of her chair.

"Do what?"

"Rent a Wave Runner," she said, tugging on his hand.

"They look dangerous," Alan said with a frown.

"Can you swim?"

"Yes," he answered indignantly.

"Then come on, take a risk for once in your life."

He pushed himself up slowly, then followed her at a leisurely pace. "I'm a risk-taker," he defended himself tartly.

"Oh, sure, Alan," she said over her shoulder. "You're a regular daredevil."

Alan bit his tongue. She was the most infuriating woman! He wanted to shake her, but he suspected that putting his hands on her and giving her breasts an excuse to jiggle would probably undo him in his current state. She strutted away from him, giving movement to the rub-on flower tattoo he'd watched her apply to her hip this morning in the room—a performance he'd been able to endure only by virtue of much teeth-grinding. His jaws still ached.

The young rental man was so bedazzled by Pam and her little bikini, he could scarcely speak. Amidst the boy's nods and a dancing Adam's apple, Alan halfheartedly negotiated a price for a Wave Runner and two wet suits, still unconvinced he would relish the ride.

Pam poured herself into a full-length neon pink wet suit with a built-in life jacket whose front zipper simply could not accommodate her chest. But leaving the zipper down a few inches only lifted her breasts higher and further emphasized her deep cleavage. Alan pulled on his own rubber suit, which was about six inches too short in the arms and legs. He performed a deep knee bend to loosen the material.

"I'll drive," Pamela announced, grabbing the handle-bars and floating the Wave Runner out a few feet into the shallows.

"Oh my God," Alan gasped when he waded into the bracing cold water. "Are you sure this is going to be enjoyable?"

She scrambled up on the bobbing machine, straddling the bright yellow vinyl seat and plugging in the ignition starter. After slipping the stretchy key ring over her wrist, she turned around and held out her hand. "Would you stop complaining and get on?"

"What's that for?" he asked, pointing to the wristband that connected her to the machine.

"It's like a kill switch," she said with a grin. "If I throw us off, the engine dies."

"Oh, that's comforting," he said as he gingerly climbed up on the back and settled behind her on the long padded seat.

She pushed a button and the engine purred to life. "Better hang on," she warned over her shoulder as she turned the handlebars quickly and revved the engine, sending them into a sideways spin.

Alan grabbed the strap across the seat and managed to hang on, barely. "Have you ever done this before?" he shouted into the wind.

"Too many times to count," she yelled, leaning low and feeding the gas until they were hurtling across the waves at a breathtaking speed. They caught a wave, rode off the edge into the air, then landed with a teeth-jarring—and frigid—splash. Pam squealed in delight, then shouted, "You're throwing us off balance. Hang on to me!"

Too shaken and waterlogged to refuse, he wrapped his arms around her waist, twining his fingers into the buckles of her wet suit. She was going to kill him. Was drowning a painful way to die? In this case, he'd probably have a heart attack first. The air whooshed from his lungs as they landed hard and a wave of freezing water swelled over the back and drenched him. At this rate, he might suffer both tragedies in the space of the next few seconds.

Several hundred feet offshore, they zigzagged the water many times, and Alan could feel her confidence growing with each pass. He could have simply let go to escape the frenzied ride, but he had to admit the experience was rather thrilling. He jammed his body up behind hers, holding fast to her waist and pressing his face into her wet hair, giving in to the sexual zing that pierced his abdomen at holding her so close and bumping against her with every jump and spin.

She drove faster and faster, jumping higher and higher, landing with belly-flipping spinouts. When they caught the underside of a particularly deep wave, Alan sensed impending doom. Pam screamed in delight, and they were airborne for what seemed like a minute, when Alan decided they would be safer to land separate from the Wave Runner. He lifted his arms to clasp her, harness-style, then twisted off to the side, taking her with him, but releasing her before they hit the water.

He plunged in, bubbles fizzing around his ears, his senses temporarily clogged with the glug, glug of enveloping water. With two powerful kicks, he reached the surface, then slung water from his eyes and immediately looked for Pam.

Alan spun all around, treading water, frantically searching for a flash of neon pink, but he saw nothing except the silent wave runner several yards away and endless foamy green-gray waves.

7

ALAN'S HEART SLAMMED against the wall of his chest and panic coursed through his veins. "Pam!" he shouted, "Pam, where are you?" He swam toward the Wave Runner using long strokes, swallowing great gulps of cold, salty water as waves pushed and pulled at him, elevating his terror. She could have hit her head on the machine when he pulled her off…she could have hit the water at an odd angle and broken her silly neck…she could have been dragged down by an undertow…she could have—

"Of all the…stupid…things…to do!"

Alan stopped, then went weak with relief as he realized her voice came from the other side of the Wave Runner. She coughed fitfully until she gagged, then coughed more, wheezing, cursing him with every breath. He swam around to find her clinging to the side of the water bike, her golden hair molded to her head and neck, her mouth open to take in as much air as possible. She confronted him with wide, blazing blue eyes.

"Were you trying to kill me?" she croaked, then another coughing spasm overtook her.

"*Me?*" Alan yelled. "I was trying to keep you from killing us *both!* We would have been thrown off for sure on that last kamikaze maneuver!"

"Would not!"

"Would too!"

"Would *not!*"

"Would *too!*"

Pam stuck her tongue out at him, then reached up to climb back on the Wave Runner. "Next time I'll leave you on the beach with your book."

Alan shook with fury. First she'd given him the scare of his life when he thought she'd drowned, then she yelled at him for spoiling her fun! "Wait just a minute," he said, grasping her arm and pulling her back into the water.

"Let go of me!"

"I'm driving back."

"Oh no you're not!"

He squeezed her upper arm and pulled her face near his. "Oh yes," he said with finality, "I am."

Her eyes widened slightly in surprise, then her mouth tightened, but she didn't argue. A drop of water slid off the end of her nose and Alan once again marveled at the smoothness of her skin. The thought crossed his mind that she was close enough to kiss, but he was pretty sure she'd drown him if he tried. Her chest heaved with her still-labored breathing, straining the already taxed wet-suit zipper to near bursting. His body leaped in painful response because there was nowhere in his wet suit to expand. But the flash of pain brought him back to reality and he released her slowly, then moved away to a safer distance.

His brain had been scrambled from Pamela's joyride, Alan reasoned as he pulled himself out of the water to straddle the Wave Runner. He took a deep, head-clearing breath before turning around to offer his hand to help Pamela climb up. Her mouth quirked left, then right, but finally she let him help her up. She slipped a couple of times, which made him laugh, then she went limp with giggles and sank back into the water.

"You," he said, shaking his head, "are wearing me out."

"Then you," she said, heaving herself up far enough for him to pull her onto the seat, "don't have much endurance." She handed him the wristband.

"I never needed it with Jo," he said as she slid behind him. He bit the inside of his cheek and turned over the engine, immediately regretting mentioning his ex.

But Pamela simply reached around his waist and laced her hands together, then said close to his ear, "But I'm not Jo, am I, Alan?"

Her breath felt warm against his cold, wet ear, and her words swirled round in his head, taunting him. *I'm not Jo, am I, Alan?* An understatement of gigantic proportions. *I'm not Jo, am I, Alan?* As if he weren't electrically aware of the fact. *I'm not Jo, am I, Alan?* And he realized with a jolt that he was having fun, more fun than he'd had in a long time—and he was very glad that Pam was, well…just Pam.

His heart strangely buoyed, he tossed a mischievous smile over his shoulder and said, "Hang on." Then he leaned low over the handlebars and mashed the gas with his thumb, sending them lunging forward. Pam squealed in surprise and delight, ramming herself up against him, which tempted Alan to squeal with delight. He mimicked her earlier technique, driving fast, catching waves and landing with a spin, drenching them with walls of water that surged over the back. Adrenaline pumped through him and, combined with the sheer physical thrill of being close to Pamela, for the first time in his life he felt blatantly cocky.

Alan threw back his head and whooped, reveling in the pressure of Pam's thighs squeezing his. For several minutes, he sent them skimming and jumping over the sun-drenched water, slowing at last as their time remaining slipped to less than ten minutes.

Hating to see the ride end, he adjusted the speed to idle and guided them toward the rental stand several hundred yards away. All sorts of strange and inappropriate emotions were running rampant through his body, and they were all directed toward Pam, who hadn't relaxed her hold around his waist. Waves slapped against the sides of the Wave Runner, and the sounds of beach music rolled out to meet them. Although sunset was still hours away, the beach was emptying rapidly as the locals packed up their families to go home for the evening meal.

"Did you have fun?" she asked, resting her chin on his left shoulder.

For a split second, Alan considered lying—he had an uneasy feeling that admitting he enjoyed Pam's company was not in his immediate best interests. But for the past hour, he had laughed more than he would have thought possible only a few hours ago, and for that, he owed her the truth. "Yeah, I did have fun. Thanks for taking my mind off...you know."

"What are friends for?" Pam asked lightly, closing her eyes and swallowing her guilt. She'd promised Jo she'd make sure he had fun. But at some point during their outing, she had forgotten she was supposed to be entertaining Alan because she was having such a good time herself. And now, putting back toward shore, she felt deflated and angry with herself for even thinking there wouldn't be too many excuses this week to hold Alan so close.

"Maybe we can take it out again tomorrow," Alan suggested, turning his head and inadvertently bringing his smooth cheek next to her mouth.

"Sure," she said casually, already looking forward to the ride. "Unless you'd rather take Robin."

"Who?" he asked, his tone innocent.

"My, what a short memory we have," she noted dryly. "You know, the smart woman in the hat."

"What makes you say she's smart?"

"Well, she works with computers, doesn't she?"

"The computer industry has its share of incompetents."

Pam brightened. "So she isn't smart?"

"Oh no, she's smart," he corrected, evoking a little stab of jealousy in her. "But don't assume anything just because someone talks in acronyms."

"You're getting sunburned," she said irritably.

He laughed and they pulled up next to the rental stand. "Are you sure it isn't the reflection from your suit?"

The young rental man had walked out into the shallows to meet them. Pam reluctantly relinquished her hold on Alan and dropped into the water up to her knees, already tugging at the confining zipper. By the time she reached the warm sand, she'd only managed to peel the rubber suit from one shoulder and she was already exhausted. She fell to the sand, knowing the grit would only make things worse, but she didn't care.

Lying on her back, she squinted against the sun and watched Alan extricate his magnificent body from his too-small suit with great sucking sounds as the rubber relented. Her breasts tightened in awareness and desire struck her low as he dragged the suit down, yanking his conservative navy trunks low on his hips. Standing in the sun with gleaming wet skin, his fair hair dry and tousled, he looked healthy and sexy, and Pam acknowledged for the first time that she was very attracted to him. And in more than just a physical sense, although simply looking at him had become a favorite pastime.

Today when he'd driven the Wave Runner, she had seen a side of him she'd never glimpsed before: carefree and spontaneous. He was actually fun to be with.

"Need a hand with your suit?" he asked, standing over her and grinning.

Pam nodded and took the hand he offered her, allowing herself to be pulled to her feet. She tugged at the opposite shoulder of the suit and succeeded in budging it an inch or so. Alan reached for the collar. "It's harder now that your skin is wet and the suit is heavy."

His fingers felt like branding irons against the cold flesh of her collarbone. He gripped the thick material and peeled the suit down her arm, turning the sleeve inside out. With both arms free, Pam was able to work the suit past her hips with some self-conscious wriggling, but had to admit defeat at her thighs. Then she lost her balance and sat down hard in the sand. Alan howled with laughter, but before she could get her breath to chew him out, she was thrown to her back because he had yanked her legs in the air to finish stripping off the stubborn suit. Sprawled in the awkward position and at his mercy, Pam felt like a too-big toddler being changed, and bristled at the hoots and laughter of the sparse but rapt audience staked out under umbrellas in the sand around them.

Alan also appeared to be enjoying her discomfort. At last he held up the pink garment as if it were a trophy and said, "I don't think this suit will ever be the same," then gestured to the deformed top of the fatigued-looking rubber suit. The comment brought him cheers from the members of the male gallery within earshot.

Pam scrambled to her feet, not sure if she liked this new, cocky side of Alan. "Well, while you strut for the other roosters," she said with a deceptively sweet smile as she brushed the sand from her bottom, "I'm going to find a beer."

Then she turned to march back to their blanket and chaise lounges they had rented for the day.

"Better go after her," some guy yelled to Alan behind her back.

"I'll go," another male voice piped up, triggering more laugher. But Pam had to acknowledge a little thrill that everyone assumed she and Alan were together.

"Hey," Alan said, jogging up beside her with a sheepish grin. "I'm thirsty, too."

Pam glanced at him, increasingly alarmed at the pull she felt toward him. "You need sunscreen."

He scrunched up his face and rubbed his cheek. "My skin does feel a little tight."

"Uh-oh," she warned. "Wait until after sundown."

He stepped in front of her, stopping her in her tracks. With eyebrows raised, he asked, "What will happen after sundown?"

Pam's pulse skipped and, not without a certain amount of panic, realized Alan was also feeling the sexual pull between them. His eyes searched her face, and she sensed that, ever the gentleman, he was waiting for a signal. They had reached the sticky point where everything they said to each other could be stretched, warped and misshapen to mean something else, an unstable area that might lead them to ruin unless one of them took control. And since Alan was freshly wounded from Jo's rejection, he was vulnerable to sexual revenge, even if he wasn't conscious of his motivation. And it was Pam's job to make sure that she wasn't a physical party to his retaliation for being dumped at the altar.

She forced lightness into her tone, ignoring his invitation to prolong the flirtation. "Sunburns are always worse after sundown," she said quietly, glad they had reached their chairs. She tossed him a bottle of sunscreen and pulled a short mesh cover-up over her head. Pointing up the sandy incline, she said, "I'm going to get a beer."

"Sounds great," he said, grabbing a T-shirt, but Pam held up her hand.

"Stay here and I'll bring them back," she said, desperate to escape his proximity. She practically ran up the stone path to the grill, but told herself she'd have to find a way to steel herself against the magnetism that had materialized between them—they would be here another four days!

The grill turned out to be a charming little outside eatery comprising a long bar and three weathered multilevel decks covered with latticed-wood "ceilings" that allowed the sun and wind to filter through. Pam glanced over the crowded tables, then walked to the bar and ordered two draft beers.

"Ah, Pamela, we meet again," came a deep, rolling voice behind her. Pam turned to see the handsome Enrico standing with an umbrellaed drink in his bejeweled hand.

"Er, yes," Pam said, offering him a small smile. As dangerous as the man appeared, at the moment he seemed the safer of two choices.

"Have you been enjoying the afternoon?" he asked conversationally, straddling a stool next to where she stood. His chest was well-developed and covered with dense, black hair. Pam made a split-second comparison to Alan's sleek physique, then bit the inside of her cheek when she acknowledged her preference.

"Sure," she answered casually, as the bartender slid two beers toward her.

"A two-fisted drinker?" he asked, his dark eyes dancing.

"For a friend," she explained, lifting one of the cups to her mouth with a shaky hand. Her revelations about Alan had her completely rattled.

"A male friend?"

Pam nodded.

Enrico formed a pout with his curvy mouth. "Is he jealous?"

Pam pressed her lips together, stalling. "I don't know," she said, licking the bittersweet liquid from her lips.

He made a clicking sound with his cheek. "Silly man." Then he leaned forward and wrapped a long blond lock around his forefinger. "I would never let you out of my si—iiiiIIIIEEE!" Enrico jerked back as a large arm descended between them on the bar with a resounding smack.

Pam swung her head up and gasped to see Alan standing between them, nursing a smirk. "I was getting thirsty," he said.

Anger flashed through her. How dare he show up while she was trying to forget about him! "Alan," she protested, "what are you doing?"

He nodded at the dark man he towered over. "Is this guy bothering you?"

"No!" she snapped.

"Excuse me," Enrico said, pushing away from the bar slowly. "Perhaps I'll see you later," he said, lifting his bronzed hand in a wave. Then he walked away, sipping his drink.

Alan watched him, then muttered, "Someone should tell him his back needs a trim."

"What the heck was that all about?" Pam demanded.

"I was defending your honor," Alan declared hotly. "*Again.* And a lot of thanks I get—again."

"Well, I guess I'm finally getting a glimpse of the real you, Alan P. Parish," she said through clenched teeth. "Tell me, does the 'P' stand for 'prehistoric'?"

He glared.

"Or 'paternal'?"

He glared.

"Or just plain 'putz'?"

He straightened and picked up his beer. "I can take a hint—if you want that...that gorilla with all his gold chains, then who am I to stand in your way. But if you start choking on a hairball, don't come crying to me."

A shrill ringing stopped him. Pamela reached inside her purse and pulled out her cell phone, then flipped down the mouthpiece. "Hello?"

"Pam?" Jo asked.

"Oh, hi, Jo," she said for Alan's benefit.

He frowned and took a huge gulp of beer.

"I was hoping I could talk to Alan," Jo said. "You know, explain what happened."

"Alan?" Pam asked, raising her eyebrows.

He shook his head no and waved his arms frantically, mouthing the words "No way."

"Uh, you just missed him," Pam said. "He went to get a beer."

"Are you both having fun?" Jo asked.

"Oh, yeah," Pam said, laughing merrily. "Fun, fun, fun."

"Oh, good," her friend answered. "Would you tell Alan I called and that I hope we can talk when he gets back?" She hesitated. "And that I'm really sorry for how things turned out?"

"Sure thing," Pam said, giving Alan a tight smile.

"And Pam," Jo said. "Thanks again for being such a good friend to me and to Alan."

"Don't mention it," Pam answered, then folded up the phone. "Jo said she hopes the two of you can talk when you get back, and that she's really sorry for how things turned out."

Alan downed the rest of his beer, then slid the plastic

cup across the bar for a refill. "On second thought, I think I'll stay right here and get drunk," Alan said, settling on the stool Enrico had vacated.

Pam rested one hip on the corner of the neighboring stool. "I don't know if that's such a good idea," she warned with a half smile. "The last time you got drunk, you invited me to go on your honeymoon."

One corner of his mouth lifted. "This is one for the record books," he said, shaking his head. "Do you suppose I'm the only man in history who won't get laid on his honeymoon?"

"Well," Pam said slowly, "it doesn't have to be that way." When his eyes widened, she stammered, "I m-mean, there are lots of women on the b-beach…" Flustered, she swept her hand in the air. "Take what's-her-name in the hat."

"Robin," he said, then began draining his second beer.

"Robin!" she seconded, nodding. "Nice teeth."

"Cute figure," he said.

"If you go for the boyish look," Pam agreed, still nodding.

"Nice legs," he said.

"Thick ankles," she murmured.

"Pretty hair."

"Sloppy dye job."

"Are we talking about the same woman?" Alan asked, angling his head. "I talked to her for twenty minutes and you saw her for what—twenty seconds? How did you notice all those things?"

Pam shrugged. "A woman knows."

"I thought she was nice."

"She was nice," Pam agreed. "*If* you're going to settle for nice."

"What's wrong with nice?" Alan asked.

"It's boring."

"One person's boredom is another person's reliability."

She sighed, exasperated. "We're talking about a beach fling, Alan. Reliability doesn't even make the list." She turned and gestured to the crowd around them, deciding she'd have to get the ball rolling for him. "Look—women everywhere—just pick one."

Alan turned slowly on the stool. "You make it sound so, so..."

"Spontaneous?"

"I was going to say cheap."

"What about the redhead in the corner?" she asked, pointing her pinkie.

"She's cute," Alan agreed with a halfhearted shrug.

"Well, don't get too excited," she warned sarcastically. "I suppose you prefer brunettes."

"Not really," he said, draining his beer and smiling. "It's been a while since I went looking for a woman, but I don't think I discriminate."

Pam finished her beer and accepted a refill. She was already getting a buzz since she hadn't eaten much all day. "How about the one in the green bikini?"

He looked and squinted. "She's kind of skinny, don't you think?"

"I thought men liked skinny women."

"Slender, great. Curvy, even better. But skinny, no way," he said, shaking his head.

"The yellow shorts and piled-up hair?"

"A definite possibility," he conceded slowly.

Pam frowned and gulped her beer. "She laughs like a seal, though. I can hear her barking from here."

"Wow, look at the one in the red suit," he said, leaning forward slightly.

Pam squinted, then dismissed her with a wave. "They're fake," she said with confidence.

"How do you know?"

"Can't you tell? They don't move."

"Well, she isn't on a trampoline. Besides—" he turned a wolfish grin her way "—I hate to break it to you, Pam, but most men don't care if they're real or not."

"You don't have to tell *me* about men," she said.

He adopted an expression of mock remorse. "Sorry— I forgot I was talking to the source." He frowned. "I'm curious—is there a straight man in Savannah who isn't after you?"

She grinned. "Two Baptist reverends, and you."

Alan saluted her with his drink. "Gee, thanks—you do wonders for my ego. Ever been married?"

"Nope."

"How have you managed that?"

Pam ran a finger around the rim of the plastic cup and pursed her lips. Then she gave a little shrug and said, "I've never fallen in love."

He scoffed. "I think falling in love is a vicious rumor that was started thousands of years ago by the world's first wedding director."

She giggled, then sighed as memories washed over her. "I came close once—I was seventeen and looking for a way out of the projects. He was nineteen and had the world by the tail."

"What happened?"

"He also had two other girls by the tail."

"Oh."

"That's when I decided it was much safer to play the field rather than risking it all on one horse. And I've been hedging my bets ever since."

"Hey," he said, holding up his hand. "Forget the horses—I don't want to hear about the kinky stuff."

Pam giggled.

Alan polished off another beer. "What's your secret for staying single?"

"It's easy," she said. Leaning forward, she whispered, "Don't close your eyes."

"What?"

"When you kiss—don't close your eyes."

He looked dubious. "That's your secret weapon?"

She nodded emphatically, and noticed the room still bounced slightly even when she stopped. "When you close your eyes during a kiss, your mind starts playing all kinds of games. You start to imagine a make-believe world where love conquers all. And you forget that most marriages end in divorce—or worse."

"My parents seem pretty happy," he said.

"That's nice," she said, and meant it. "My dad split when we were little, so I barely remember my folks together."

"I'm sorry."

She smiled sadly. "Me, too. That's why I'd rather stay single and childless than risk dragging kids through a mess."

"I'm for the childless part," Alan noted wryly. "A toast," he said, lifting his cup to hers, "to keeping your eyes open."

"Hear, hear," she agreed, touching her cup to his, then giggled when beer sloshed over the side. A gust of cold air blew over them and Pam shivered. Dusk was approaching, and the temperature had dropped dramatically. "I think I'll go back to the room and change."

Alan climbed down from the stool slowly. "I need to

check in with my secretary and see if she found us a room. I'm not anxious to spend another night in Hotel Hell.''

"It's not so bad," she said as they walked, picking their way carefully back down the unlit path. The clear night and bright moon made the going easier, and the now-deserted white beach stretched below them like a wide satin ribbon. "Ooh, look at all the stars," she said, waving her hand overhead. "Let's go for a walk."

"Anything to avoid going back to the room," he agreed, falling in step behind her.

She pulled loose pants from her canvas bag and stepped into them, then decided to carry her sandals. "The sand looks like snow," she said, digging in her toes. The tide was coming in, eating away at the beach and forcing them to choose a higher path. The air felt cool and invigorating and Pam tried hard to focus on anything but the romantic atmosphere as they headed down the beach toward their hotel. Millions of stars twinkled overhead and, as always, simply thinking about the distances their mere existence represented left her breathless. And coupled with the sight of Alan's handsome face silhouetted in the moonlight, she was left downright light-headed. "Alan, do you really think there's life on other planets?"

"Sure," he said without hesitation. "I think it's pretty arrogant to think the entire universe was created just for us."

She tingled in appreciation of his honesty—she could never broach this subject with any of the men she dated. "I agree—but it's a little scary, don't you think?"

He shook his head. "Nah, if they were going to harm us, they would have done it by now." Then he grinned. "Besides, with all our societal and environmental problems, Earth is probably the laughingstock of the universe."

"What you're telling me," she said with a chuckle, "is that I clawed my way out of one slum simply to exist in a larger one?"

"In a manner of speaking," he conceded with a laugh.

"Okay, the 'P' stands for 'pessimistic,' right?"

He laughed again, something she was beginning to look forward to. "So I'm not the most upbeat person, especially this week." He brushed against her accidentally and her arm burned from the contact. They walked past several tall dunes, which cast tall shadows over them, throwing them into almost complete darkness.

"What doesn't kill you will make you stronger," she said, wondering for whose benefit she was speaking— Alan's or hers? She stumbled on a clump of glass and yelped, grabbing Alan's arm on the way down. But she caught him off guard and he fell with her. Pam grunted when she landed, then was struck with the thought that being horizontal felt pretty good. She gingerly lifted her head and saw Alan sprawling face first next to her. When he raised onto his elbows, his face was covered with a layer of white sand. Pam burst out laughing.

"You," he said with mock fierceness, "are dead meat."

She shrieked and tried to scramble to her feet, but he grabbed her bare ankle and yanked her down to the sand. Weak with laughter, she tried to crawl away from him, but he dragged her back and rolled her over, pinning her arms down.

Her laughter petered out at the closeness of his face to hers in the darkness, and a warning siren screamed in her head. He lay half on top of her, his chest against hers. His T-shirt had worked up and she felt the warm skin of his stomach through the flimsy cover-up she wore. Every muscle in her body tensed and her pulse pounded in her ears. "Alan—" she said in a shaky voice.

"Pam," he cut in with a hoarse whisper, his breath fanning her lips. "Please don't tell me to stop, because then I'll have to."

She couldn't see his eyes, but she could hear the loneliness, the desperation in his voice. "Alan," she croaked with as much strength as she could muster.

He sighed slowly and lifted his head a few inches in resignation. "What?"

Seconds stretched into a minute as the waves crashed behind them and the love scene in *From Here To Eternity* passed before her eyes. God, Alan was so sexy and so...so...so *here*. Who cared about eternity? "Kiss me," she said breathlessly.

For a while, he was completely still, and she wondered if perhaps he hadn't heard her. But then he lowered his mouth with such sweet slowness, she was able to anticipate the feel of his lips on hers and ready herself for his taste. His lips were like velvet, she thought, as her mouth opened for his. When his mouth met hers, Pam moaned at the surge of desire that swelled in her chest. If she had expected tentativeness, those expectations were banished immediately. It was as if his lips knew hers, as if they had explored the surface and depths of her mouth many times. His tongue boldly tangled with hers in a slashing, grinding dance and he shuddered, offering a deep groan that echoed down her throat.

The urgency of their kiss increased and he released her arms to seek out more forbidden areas. He caressed her collarbone, then blazed a trail south to cup her breast and thumb the beaded nipple, practically the only skin her bathing-suit top covered. She arched her body into him, and slid her hands under his shirt to feel the hard wall of muscle across his back. He kneed her legs open, then shifted to lie cradled between her thighs.

Longing pulsed through her body and moisture gathered at her core where he pressed the hard ridge of his erection against her. Slipping her hands below his waistband, she gripped the smooth rounds of his hard buttocks, her mind spinning with the responses he evoked from her body. He lifted his head and gasped, ''Not here. Someone might—''

She cut him off with a deep kiss, then whispered, ''The beach is deserted, no one will see us. Besides,'' she murmured, yanking his T-shirt over his head, ''I think it's kind of exciting.''

In a flurry of sand, she pushed down his trunks and dragged them off with her feet. He lay naked on top of her, kissing her deeply and kneading her covered breasts with a slow intensity that told her he planned to take his time undressing her, enjoying her. She writhed beneath him, urging him on with her wandering hands, anxious to explore his body.

Then a blinding light flashed over his shoulder, directly in Pam's eyes. ''Hold it right there, mister,'' said a gruff male voice.

Alan stiffened, then lifted his head and swung to look over his shoulder. He raised his arm to shield his eyes. ''What the hell?''

''Police,'' the man boomed, thumping his badge unnecessarily since the uniform said it all. ''Stand up slowly and put your hands in the air.''

Alan scoffed. ''You can't be serious—''

''I said, on your feet!''

Pam's heart pounded in her chest and she squeezed her eyes shut, unable to watch. When she finally chanced a glance, Alan stood squinting into the cop's light with his arms in the air, hosting a monster erection.

"God," the cop said, wincing.

"I hope that means you'll let me find my pants," Alan snapped, outraged.

"Make it quick," the officer said. "I'd hate to haul you in naked."

"What?" Alan barked. Pam sprang up, her heart in her throat.

The cop gave him a sneering smile and pulled out a pair of handcuffs. "This is a family beach, you pervert. You're under arrest for indecent exposure."

8

"I'VE NEVER BEEN so humiliated in my life," Alan declared as he followed Pam out of the city jail and squinted into the late-afternoon sun. She looked chipper in her crisp white shorts and red silk blouse. He, on the other hand, still sported the sand-crusted swimming trunks and T-shirt he'd been wearing last night when the cop hauled him into jail like a common criminal. Between the cot he'd slept on and the realization that he and Pamela Kaminski had been minutes away from sharing carnal knowledge, he hadn't slept a wink.

"No one will find out," Pam said in a soothing voice.

"Oh, really?" he asked. "Is that like, 'It's deserted, no one will see us'?"

She frowned. "I said I was sorry a hundred times—didn't you hear me?"

"One hundred thirty-six times," he corrected. "I heard you during the entire walk to the squad car last night, *and* as you ran alongside the police car when we drove away, *and* this morning in the courtroom while the judge was lecturing me—" He stopped and stared toward the street in disbelief, then pressed his palms against his temples. "Pam, are you nuts?"

"What?" She pushed the cheap sunglasses high on her forehead and unlocked the door to the powder blue limo.

"You left this pimpmobile parked in a fire zone in *front* of the jail for two hours?"

She shrugged her lovely shoulders. "I turned on the hazard lights."

"Oh, well," he said with as much sarcasm as he could muster. "I didn't realize you'd turned on the *hazard* lights." He summoned a dry laugh. "After all, everyone knows that hazard lights cancel out every broken law. Mow down a pedestrian? No problem, just turn on your hazards."

"Well, it's still here, isn't it?" she demanded hotly.

"Who the hell else would want it?" he cried, feeling on the verge of hysteria.

She pointed to the passenger side. "Just get in, will you?"

"Oh, no," he said, holding out his hand for the keys. "You are *not* driving."

"I drove here without any problems!"

"Oh, really?" Alan crossed his arms, then nodded toward the front fender. "And I suppose that telephone pole–size dent just appeared from nowhere?"

She bit her bottom lip, and handed over the keys in silence.

"Thank you," he said, then opened the driver-side door just as a police car pulled up behind the limo with its siren silent but flashing. When the young cop stepped out, he had already begun writing the ticket.

"Sir," he said in a pleasant voice. "Do you have any idea what the fine is for parking in a fire lane in front of a government building?" Alan closed his eyes and counted to ten.

A few minutes later, Pam studied the pink carbon copy the police officer had given him and whistled low. "A hundred and forty-five dollars?"

"Do me a favor," he said calmly, gripping the steering

wheel so hard his hands hurt. "Just sit over there and don't talk."

"Look, Alan, I know you're upset—"

"Upset?" he crowed. "Just because I'm now considered a sex offender? Why would that upset me?"

"It's not as bad as you make it sound."

"Before yesterday, I'd never even received a speeding ticket."

Pam lay her head back. "Do you realize you can re-arrange the letters in your name to spell 'anal'?"

He scowled in her direction. "I'm not going to apologize for being a law-abiding citizen."

"Your secretary called last night."

His stomach twisted. "You talked to Linda?"

"Relax, I told her I worked for the hotel and all your calls were being routed to me. She found you a room."

"Finally, some good news," he said, his shoulders dropping in relief.

"I told her you changed your mind."

He weaved over the centerline. "What?"

"She needed an answer immediately, and I didn't know how long you'd be in jail..." Her voice trailed off and she raised her hands in a helpless gesture. Her manicured nails had gone from peach to bright red during his incarceration.

"I'll call her later to see if the room is still available," he said. "Right now, even the broken couch in Hotel Hell sounds good." Then the thought struck him that Pam might think they'd be sharing the same bed, after what nearly transpired last night. Except now that he'd had a few idle hours to ponder their lapse, he realized what a huge mistake it would have been. No matter how much he *wanted* to sleep with Pam, only a jerk would have rebound sex with his ex-fiancée's best friend. Besides, he admitted begrudgingly, as infuriating as she could be, Pam was starting to grow on him, and he didn't want to tread on their burgeoning friendship, didn't want to be relegated to her bottomless dating pool. "I'll call and see if the pullout bed can be fixed."

"Done," Pam said with a little smile. "This morning I slipped the maintenance man a twenty and he fixed it in no time."

"Great," Alan said, nodding.

"Yeah," she said.

After a pregnant pause, they both spoke at the same time.

"About last night—" she said.

"I want to apologize—" he said, then stopped and they both looked away and laughed awkwardly.

"It was the moon and the stars—"

"—and the beer and the ocean," she added.

"I was still feeling a little rejected over the wedding—"

"—and I was feeling lonely."

"What a big mistake it would have been," he said, attempting a casual laugh.

"Huge," she agreed.

"Gigantic—"

"Colossal—"

"What with you being Jo's best friend—"

"—and you being Jo's ex-fiancé."

Feeling relieved, Alan inhaled deeply. "So we're in agreement." Then he glanced over and realized with a sinking feeling that despite his new resolve, he still wasn't immune to her remarkable beauty.

"Completely in agreement," she assured him with a bright smile.

SHE HAD DONE a lot of stupid things in her relatively short life, Pam decided the next day as she lay in a rental chaise on the beach and watched a kidney-shaped cloud move across the otherwise clear sky. But all of them rolled into one wouldn't have compared to the absolute brainlessness she would have exhibited if that cop hadn't shown up the night before last.

Luckily, Alan seemed to agree with her and they had touched on, danced around and sidestepped the issue of their sexual attraction while somehow agreeing that the sex act itself would have been a grievous error. The logical side of her brain had no problem going along with that argument, but the emotional side of her brain kept remembering the feelings raging through her that night when Alan kissed her—after all her bragging, she had actually closed her eyes! And though she had definitely responded to him on a physical level, he had also stirred something deep inside her. Alan had accidentally managed to blaze a trail where no man had gone before, and the realization saddened her because a relationship between them was impossible. Unthinkable. Inconceivable.

He was still in love with her best friend, for God's sake. And she wasn't about to return to Savannah arm in arm with Alan and have Jo think they had been carrying on behind her back all these years. Besides, Alan P. Parish came from Savannah's most prosperous family, while she came from Savannah's most pros*ecuted* family. He wouldn't be interested in anything other than a sexual relationship with her. Typically, such a revelation wouldn't bother her, but she was starting to feel a weird sort of affection for the man, striking a memory chord from when she'd first known him in high school. Warning bells chimed in her head and some untapped part of her soul telegraphed increasingly urgent distress signals.

SUBJECT IS DANGEROUS STOP HEART IN JEOPARDY STOP PROCEED WITH CAUTION STOP

"Our paths keep crossing." Enrico's undulating voice wafted above her. Pam opened her eyes to see him standing over her, surveying her new red two-piece suit with open admiration. He wore a straw hat and snug little bikini swim trunks that Europeans seemed fond of wearing. Pam pressed her lips together in amusement at the recollection of Alan's scoffing reference to the shiny, elastic garments as "nut-huggers."

"It must be destiny," the dark-skinned man continued with a charming grin.

"Or just a small beach," she offered, making no movement to encourage him to stay. She had enough on her mind, and she felt her patience dwindling.

"Could I interest you in dinner tonight?" he asked. "I know a restaurant where the lobster is fresh and the drinks are strong." He wagged his dark eyebrows and Pam wondered where he or any other man had gotten the idea that women found the gesture provocative.

"I already have dinner plans," she lied. "Thanks anyway."

Enrico's expression grew sultry as he dipped his head. "And do you also have plans for dessert?" he asked, his meaning clear in the husky timbre of his voice.

"I'm on a diet," she said, smiling tightly. "Thanks anyway." Then she retrieved a book from her canvas bag and opened it.

"That man in the bar yesterday, he is your boyfriend?" Enrico pressed.

Pam glanced up from the book, suddenly at the end of her fuse. "No," she said with quiet authority. "He's my husband."

"Oh?" He looked surprised, then pulled a sad face. "And he has left you alone yet again."

"I wore him out," she said evenly, then looked back to her book.

Enrico must have taken the hint because he moved away after a tongue-rolling farewell, but she felt his dark gaze linger over her and shivered.

The book was one that Alan had purchased, one she'd devoured years ago, but it was worth another read. Especially if it took her mind off Alan, who lay spread-eagle on the water bed where he'd slept since returning from jail yesterday afternoon. She had eaten dinner alone last night and crawled into the lumpy pullout bed where she'd lain awake for hours thinking about the man only a few feet away.

She sighed and immersed herself in a world of fantasy and science fiction, caught up in interstellar wars, life and romance in the next millennium.

In the early afternoon, she gave in to hunger pangs and walked up the path to the grill. After ordering a messy hot dog, she sat down at a table overlooking the beach to sort through the last few days' disturbing turn of events.

The crowds had thinned a bit since the locals had resumed their midweek work schedules, leaving behind vacationers and snowbirds who seemed to group almost exclusively by twos. With a start, she remembered that today was Valentine's Day, so no wonder everyone was paired off—lots of folks were probably here for their anniversary since February fourteenth seemed to be a popular date for weddings. The bartender confirmed her theory by announcing a couples' sand castle–building contest for the remainder of the afternoon, with the winning pair to receive a romantic dinner at a local seafood restaurant.

Her mind wandered to Alan and she hoped he was resting. As if on cue, he emerged from the trees that hid the pebbly path below their balcony. To her dismay, her pulse kicked up as she watched him move with natural athleticism down the slight incline and out onto the white sand. A towel lay around his wide shoulders, and he carried a small gym bag, which she surmised was full of books. His head pivoted as he scanned the area. Was he looking for her? she wondered with a little smile. Then he waved to someone farther down the beach and Pam forgot to chew the food in her mouth as she spotted Robin the Computer Lady and her big floppy hat.

Swallowing painfully, she watched as Robin stopped and waited for Alan to walk to her, which he seemed eager to do, she noted wryly. Today Robin wore a high-necked tank suit of boring brown, but Pam conceded her legs were long and slim. From a distance, the woman's resemblance to Jo was uncanny. She held on to her hat with one hand as she tilted her head back to smile up at Alan. Pam stabbed her chili dog with enough force to snap the plastic fork.

And Alan seemed to have recovered from his ill mood, she noticed as he offered the woman a broad smile. Robin gestured in the direction from which she'd come and Alan nodded happily, seemingly anxious to follow her… where? To her blanket? Pam sank her teeth into her bottom lip. To lunch? She shredded the paper napkin in her lap. To her room? Pam felt something akin to gas pain in her stomach. At least if he had a fling with Robin, she reasoned, the sexual tension hanging between herself and Alan would be relieved. And maybe they'd be able to get through the rest of the week and arrive back in Savannah with all friendships intact.

The computer couple stopped after a few steps and Robin squirmed, pointing to her shoulder. Alan stopped, investigated and brushed away the offending object. *Oh, brother—the old "something's on me, will you get it off, you big strong he-man" trick.* Pam rolled her eyes. *Amateur.*

But Alan must have been convinced because he inched closer to Robin as they strolled away. When Pam could no longer see them from her chair, she stood up. When they disappeared past tiptoe level, she walked to the corner of the deck. "Go for it, Alan," she muttered as she hung out over the edge with her back foot hooked around the railing to keep from falling. "I couldn't care less."

THE POOL AT THE RESORT where Robin was staying glimmered blue and white, interrupted only by a few adults who lounged in one corner, with firm grips around their drinks. Alan sat next to Robin, bored with shoptalk and hoping something conversational would pop into his head. Accepting her invitation to join her at the pool had seemed like a good idea an hour ago, but now he was feeling restless. For some maddening reason, Alan couldn't keep his mind off where and with whom Pam had found entertainment for the afternoon.

"What's wrong?" Robin asked cheerfully.

"Nothing," he assured her. She was very attractive, and had pulled her chair so close to his she'd pinched her fingers between the two arms. And if he had any doubts she was interested in him physically, they were banished when he felt her bare foot caress his leg from calf to ankle. Startled, he stiffened.

She flashed him a flirty smile. "Want to take a swim? The pool is heated."

"Sure," he said, pushing back from the table, suddenly wanting to escape. He followed her into the shallow end, then swam the length of the pool, not at all surprised when she surfaced near him at the other end. With the concrete wall at his back, he closed his eyes and raised his face to the sun.

"Great day," she said, allowing her body to graze his beneath the water.

"Mmm." He really should find Pamela and apologize for being so cross yesterday.

"I always stay in this resort when I'm in town," she continued.

"Nice," he murmured.

"My room has a fabulous view," Robin said near his ear, and several seconds passed before her meaning sank in. She rubbed her breast against his arm and his eyes popped open.

Her mouth curved provocatively. "Want to go up for a look?"

Alan glanced at her and realized with a sinking feeling that she reminded him of Jo—in more ways than one. Although Jo had never been as forward as Robin, he experienced the same mild stirring of sexual interest when he looked at the slim woman in her sensible brown bathing suit. All the time he had dated Jo, he'd hoped their relationship would become more sensual, but now he had to admit that their chemistry had never been quite right. And while he had loved Jo from the beginning, he had never been *in* love with her...had never craved her company so much that he experienced physical pain when he was away from her...had never been tempted to get naked with her on a dark beach.

"Alan?" Robin whispered, moving in for a kiss. Her mouth shifted against his pleasantly and Alan tried to conjure up some level of desire, especially in light of his new revelation. He absolutely couldn't be falling for Pam....

Robin's mouth became more insistent and Alan awkwardly pulled her against him, running his hands over her slight curves and waiting for his body to respond.

She lifted her head, breathing heavily. "How about that view?"

Alan's mind raced. *Do it, Parish. Get Pam out of your head and out of your system.* "Um, sorry," he said, withdrawing and pushing himself up and out of the pool. "I promised Pam I'd...take her shopping."

Robin stared at him from the water. "You'd rather go shopping with your sister?"

"No," he said hurriedly, grabbing his towel and gym bag. "It's just that I promised...I'll see you later, Robin."

"Count on it," she said pointedly, as if next time he would not get away so easily.

Alan trotted off in relief, then slowed to a walk when he reached the beach. He made his way back up the shore, keeping on eye on the horizon for a Wave Runner rider in an overflowing neon pink wet suit and wrestling with the bombshell of the feelings he harbored for his ex-fiancée's best friend.

Along the way, he noticed several sand castles, some simple, some intricate, and realized a contest was under way. A few hundred yards later, he noticed a loose knot of men had gathered to watch a work in progress. But as he approached, he recognized the fake flower tattoo on the firm hip of Pamela Kaminski. She crawled on all fours and stretched to add yet another tower to the elaborate castle she had created. He smiled wryly at the realization that although her sand fortress was by far the most impressive he'd seen, *Pam's* turrets were gaining far more attention than her castle's.

Seemingly oblivious to the attention, her head was bent in concentration, although she kept brushing back a strand of golden hair that had escaped the high ponytail. The red bikini was a masterpiece, he acknowledged, marveling at the way she filled it to bursting yet managed to keep everything safely in place as she moved around. His body began to harden at the memory of her lying beneath him in the sand. But knowing that train of thought led to a dead end, he forced himself to squash the provocative vision. Uncomfortable with the thought of being a part of the ogling crowd, he stepped forward and announced, "There you are!" in a loud voice.

Pam glanced up and smiled, then sat back on her heels, offering a mouth-drying view of her cleavage. Her breasts were confined by two tiny triangles of cloth that had to be much stronger than they looked. "Hi," she said, and Alan could almost hear the groans of dismay as the men realized their up-close perusal had come to an end. One by one, they drifted away.

"Are you alone?" she asked, peering around him.

"Yeah," he said, suddenly wondering how he could have been so angry with her yesterday.

She turned her attention back to the sand castle. "Have you been in bed all this time?"

"Pretty much," he said, shrugging. "But I feel much better."

"That's nice," she said tightly, but she didn't look up.

She was probably still miffed at him for the way he'd behaved yesterday afternoon, he reasoned. "I'm sorry I was so grouchy when you came to pick me up," he said, not sure why he felt the need to get back into her good graces. "I did appreciate it."

"It's okay," she said in a tone that didn't sound okay. Then she glanced over her shoulder. "You got it all out of your system, right?"

"Right," he said, hoping he looked properly contrite. "Truce?"

"Truce," she said with a suddenly cheerful smile, then stood and dusted sand from her knees.

"Hey," he said, studying her design. "You need a moat." He took one of the buckets she'd been using as a mold and filled it with water, then fed the small channel she'd dug around the perimeter of the castle. After several trips, the moat was filled, and she nodded, satisfied with his contribution.

"That's quite a spread, little lady," the bartender from the grill said as he made his way toward them. "Nice castle, too," he muttered to Alan with an envious wink as he walked by. The chubby fellow shook her hand and gave her an envelope. "The best sand castle by far—you two have a real nice Valentine's Day dinner." Then his expression turned serious. "Be careful after dark, though—I hear we have a pervert on the loose, some naked guy scaring women and little kids."

Alan frowned, but at least Pam managed to restrain herself until the man had walked away. "Pervert?" She threw her head back and laughed. "Is that what the 'P' stands for?"

"Ha, ha, very funny."

"Here," she said, handing him the envelope and wiping her eyes. "You and Robin have a nice evening."

"Robin?" He shook his head. "I've spent all the time with her today that I want to. What about Enrico?"

"Somehow I don't think he'd be much of a dinner companion," she said, and Alan got her meaning loud and clear: the man was a lover, not a talker. He tried to stem the jealousy that flooded his chest, but the thought of Pam with another man was crushing. Had she rendezvoused with the hairy horndog last night or this morning—or both?

"Looks like we're stuck with each other, then," he said

with a casual shrug that belied the emotions raging through him.

"Looks like it," she said, falling a little short of looking happy at the prospect herself.

PIER TWENTY-EIGHT was bustling with couples celebrating Valentine's Day. Boasting a large bar, a roving Italian quar tet and a great oceanside view, Pam could see why. As they waited at the bar for their table, she noticed Alan's gaze lingering on her again. Although she had hoped his little diversion with Robin would ease the situation, she had felt more on edge than ever while they were getting ready for dinner.

Just to be safe, she had emerged from the bathroom already dressed in a simple deep pink sleeveless sheath, but she'd felt him watching her while she piled her hair on her head with various combs. And she had to admit she struggled to keep her attention elsewhere while he applied lotion to his reddish shoulders before donning a dress shirt.

He did look fabulous, she decided, and allowed herself a bit of pride to be on his arm tonight. When they had attended functions together in Savannah, it had been different—everyone knew he was devoted to Jo, so Pam had never entertained thoughts of what kind of couple she and Alan might make. But now she knew they were garnering a fair share of attention, and she conceded they looked like a classic "match": tall with blond hair and glowing tans. But looks could be deceiving, she noted with a little twist of her heart.

"Well, if it isn't the newlyweds," a man's voice said behind her. Pam registered Alan's slight frown before she turned to see Cheek and Lila, the senior-citizen couple who, thankfully, they hadn't seen naked in a while.

"Cheek," Lila said with a motherly smile. "They're not married, remember? They're just friends, right?"

"Right," Alan and Pam said in unison.

"Wasn't it a lovely day?" Lila continued, waving vaguely toward the beach.

"Great dress," Cheek said bluntly, talking to Pam's breasts.

"Er, thanks," Pam said as Alan cleared his throat.

"You're getting a nice tan," Lila commented.

"I was on the beach all day," Pam told her.

"This beach?" Cheek asked in amazement. He leaned forward then glanced around as if he were about to divulge military secrets. "There's a nude beach about twenty miles away," he said in a conspiratorial tone. "It's five bucks a head, but it's worth it," he finished with an emphatic curt nod.

"We'll keep that in mind," Alan said tightly.

The man turned to Pam and said, "If you decide to go, we'd be glad to give you a ride."

"I said," Alan said, his tone louder and his expression harder, "we'll keep it in mind."

"Great," Cheek said, completely missing the rebuff. "You want to see if we can get a table for four?"

"No!" Pam and Alan nearly shouted together.

"Uh, it's a very special occasion for us," she said with a smile, leaning into Alan.

He put his arm around her waist and nodded. "We really wanted to be alone tonight."

"Oohhhhhhh," Lila sang, her eyes twinkling and her finger wagging. "Friends indeed! Do I hear wedding bells?"

Pam scrambled for something to say to get rid of the couple without embarrassing Alan further. "I guess you could say it was the idea of wedding bells that brought us to Fort Myers, right, Alan?''

He hesitated only a few seconds. ''Oh…right.''

Lila laughed delightedly. ''Dingdong, dingdong.'' Her head bounced left, then right.

Pam tingled at the intimacy and awkwardness of the conversation. Thankfully, their name was called and they said a hasty goodbye.

''*Talk* about dingdongs,'' Alan muttered as they followed a waiter to their table.

''They're harmless,'' she said, waving off his concern.

''They should be somewhere playing shuffleboard instead of scaring up entertainment for a nude-beach matinee,'' he said as he held out her chair.

The waiter handed them their menus, took their wine order and left.

Pam laughed and opened her menu. ''Percy,'' she said.

''What?''

''Your middle name—Percy?''

He scoffed and rolled his eyes. ''No.''

''Pendleton?''

''No.''

''Pernicious?''

He laughed. ''No. Forget it—I'm not telling you.''

''Will you tell me if I guess it?''

He dropped his gaze to his menu. ''Sure, because you'll never guess it.''

''Pembroke?''

''No—and that's enough.''

''Who knows it?''

''Only my parents and siblings—and they're sworn to secrecy.''

''Jo doesn't even know?''

''Nope. What looks good?''

Pam bit her tongue to keep from saying that he looked mighty tasty. "Probably the orange roughy."

"Fried, of course."

"Of course."

"How about lobster?"

Pam winced at the price. "I don't think the gift certificate will cover lobster."

"Screw the certificate—last night I slept through dinner, and the night before I had a roll of breath mints in jail." He folded the menu and gave it a light smack. "I'm having lobster."

She watched as Alan craned his neck, looking all around. "Our waiter said he'd be right back," she reminded him.

"I know—I'm making sure they didn't seat us near a bunch of kids. I specifically asked for no kids."

"Relax—I don't see any kids."

"They can hide," he assured her, lifting the tablecloth for a peek.

"The 'P' stands for 'paranoid,'" she declared.

"Would you stop with the 'P' stuff already?"

"Alan, kids have to eat, too."

"Fine—as long as they're not sitting near me. Nearly every time Jo and I—" He stopped and a strange look came over his face. "There I go again."

Pam's heart twisted at the hurt that flashed in his eyes. "Alan, you have a lot of history with Jo—you can talk about her. Nearly every time you and Jo what?" Jo had divulged that her and Alan's sex life had been practically nonexistent, so she was relatively sure he wasn't going to say something too personal. Because of Jo's comments, Pam had always labeled Alan as a wet fish, but now she was doubting her best friend's judgment.

He straightened, but his cheer seemed forced. "Nearly

every time Jo and I ate out, it seemed like some spoiled kid would ruin it—screaming, throwing food.'' He passed his hand over his face and a dry laugh escaped his mouth. ''Now I'm wondering if things were going sour between us, and I was simply looking for any excuse to explain the awkwardness.''

''What's so bad about kids anyway?'' she asked.

He opened his mouth to answer, then looked puzzled. ''I don't know—they're loud—''

''I'm loud.''

''And messy—''

''I'm messy.''

''And the diapers—''

''Okay, you got me there,'' she said with a grin.

''Do you like kids?'' he asked, his eyebrows raised in surprise.

Pam shrugged. ''I practically raised my kid sister.''

''I didn't know you had a kid sister.''

Pride swelled in her chest every time she thought of Dinah. ''She's ten years younger—twenty-two. I sent her to *your* high school, except I made sure she finished,'' she added with a laugh.

''Where is she now?''

''Finishing up at Notre Dame,'' she said with satisfaction. ''But she'll probably start law school this fall.''

Alan whistled low. ''Not bad.''

''Well, I wanted to make sure one of the Kaminskis ended up successful and on the right side of the law,'' she said, thinking about her thuggy brothers.

''You're doing all right for yourself,'' Alan said. ''Top sales producer for the largest realty company in Savannah.''

Pam tingled under his praise, but knew that no matter what her achievements, she was, and would always be, a

Kaminski. Dinah had informed her she would not be coming back to Savannah to practice, and Pam suspected the blight on the family name had influenced her decision. Looking across the table at a man whose name alone put him out of her reach, Pam suddenly felt queasy.

"Will you order for me?" she asked, then excused herself to the ladies' room, telling herself she had to banish the ridiculous thoughts that galloped through her head every time she looked at Alan.

In the rest room, she splashed cold water on her neck, then pondered the wisdom of leaving Alan in Fort Myers and returning to Savannah early. Once she was back in her normal surroundings, these crazy feelings for Alan would evaporate. She could fabricate something about being needed at her office, and make her getaway. The fact that she didn't want to leave him was frightening enough to cinch her decision. She left the ladies' room feeling sad but resolute.

On the way back to the table, a male voice stopped her. "We *must* stop meeting like this, Pamela."

She turned to find Enrico dressed in black slacks and a shiny red shirt. Annoyance fueled her temper. "I can't stop to chat—I need to get back to my table."

His smile was slow and syrupy as he fell in step beside her. "Did your husband bring you or has he abandoned you once again?"

"No," Pam said through clenched teeth as she walked. "We're having a quiet, romantic dinner." But he followed her around the corner, where she came up short.

Alan stood by their table, sharing a deep kiss with Robin the computer lady.

9

SEVERAL SECONDS PASSED before Alan registered the fact that Robin, who had appeared from nowhere, was kissing him very hard and very invasively. After he managed to untangle his tongue from hers, he clasped her arms and gently pushed her away. Her eyes held the slight glaze of drunkenness. "Robin," he said with a little laugh, "I don't think this is the place."

"Oh? Then how about here?" she slurred, yanking his waistband hard. The button on his fly popped off and flipped up in the air.

A gasp sounded behind him. "Alan, how could you?" He wheeled to see Lila and Cheek standing near him, being led to a table. Lila stood with her hand over her heart. "I thought you were going to propose to Pamela tonight."

"Prrrropose?"

Alan turned the opposite direction, toward Enrico's rolling voice. The dark-haired man stood just a few steps away, with a possessive hand on Pamela's waist. Alan frowned. Where had *he* come from?

Enrico's expression was black as he stared at Pam. "I thought the two of you were already married!" Pam looked at Alan. Her mouth opened and closed, but no sound came out.

"Married?" Robin yelped, jerking his attention back to her. "I thought she was your sister!"

"Sister?" Lila shrieked, and he swung his head back to see the older woman's face twisted in distaste. "That's disgusting."

Cheek appeared slightly less distraught. "Well, it's illegal anyway."

Everyone started talking at once, and Robin advanced on him, her eyes narrowed, and her steps wobbly. "Alan, what the hell is going on?"

Alan held up his hands. "Wait a minute. *Wait a minute!*" The group quieted. He took a deep breath and a step backward, then fell over a potted fern, landing on his tailbone hard enough to set his glasses askew. The waiter hurried over to help him up, but Alan, clawing the air in frustration, brushed him off. He scrambled to his feet, straightened his clothes, then made chopping motions in the air to punctuate his point.

"Look...you...you *people!* Pamela and I came to have a nice, quiet Valentine's Day dinner." He felt a vein bulging at his temple. "The nature of our relationship is nobody's business!" He yanked up his pants by his sagging waistband. "Now, I'll thank everyone to move along!"

Lila and Cheek were the first to bustle away, then Robin and Enrico slipped off in the same direction. Alan had the brief thought that the two of them should get together, then he looked at Pam and swept an arm awkwardly toward the table. "Shall we?"

She nodded, then stooped and picked up his wayward button. She handed it to him, then moved stiffly to her place at the table. After pulling out her chair, Alan reclaimed his seat, snapping the napkin before settling it over his lap. For several long minutes, they toyed with their wineglasses and fingered the silverware.

Although he couldn't fathom why, Alan felt as if he owed Pam an explanation. When he could stand the silence no longer, he cleared his throat. "I wasn't kissing her, you know."

"Not that it matters," she said, sipping the wine that had been served in her absence. "But the lipstick on your mouth, nose, ear and eyelid proves otherwise."

He swiped the napkin across his face, frowning at the reddish stain that transferred. "I mean I wasn't kissing her *back*."

"Like I said, it doesn't matter."

"I guess not," he conceded with a wave, "since you were skulking in the hall with your Latin lover."

She frowned. "My lover? Where on earth did you get that idea?"

His heart lifted a notch. "You haven't been messing around with him?"

Pam rolled her eyes. "If I wanted to mess around with him, why would I have told him you and I were married?"

Unexplained relief flooded through him. "And he believed it?"

"Crazy, huh?" she asked with a little laugh. "That someone would think we were husband and wife?"

"Yeah," he said, joining her laughter. "Ridiculous."

"I mean, you and me—" Pam's giggles escalated.

"Right," he said, laughing harder. *"Mr. and Mrs. Alan Parish."*

She roared. *"P-Pamela P-Parish!"*

Alan wiped his eyes and took a big gulp of wine. "The way the last couple of days have been going, I suppose anything seems possible."

"It's been an adventure," she agreed.

He sighed and glanced across the table, struck anew by her glowing beauty. Pam looked like a movie star, her hair and skin wrought with gold, her mouth wide, her eyes shining. Her gaze met his and Alan's ears started ringing. He felt as if he were teetering on the edge of a precipice, in danger of falling into a pit so deep he might never return. The notion skating through his mind, the emotion blooming in his chest was nothing short of insanity. He was falling for Pamela Kaminski.

Pam's smile evaporated and she squirmed in her chair. Looking into her glass, she said, "I was thinking about leaving tomorrow."

Alan stopped and choked on the wine in his throat. "Leaving? You mean, going back to Savannah?"

She nodded.

He experienced the panicky feeling that something wonderful was about to slip through his fingers. "B-but why?"

Pam abandoned her glass and rolled her eyes heavenward, counting on her beautifully manicured fingers. "A bad flight, a flat tire, a dilapidated hotel, a powder blue limo, a police record..." Her voice trailed off. "You came to the beach for a week of R&R," she said. "And so far it's been more like a week of S&M."

"Well, it hasn't been your fault," he offered generously.

But she simply smirked.

"Not totally," he added weakly.

"Lying is not one of your talents."

Spotting an opening, he leaned forward with eyebrows raised. "Is that a concession that I have talents elsewhere?"

"No."

Deflated, he sat back. "Oh."

Surprised at the wounded look on his face, Pam scrambled to soothe his hurt feelings. "I mean, I wouldn't know if you had talents elsewhere..." She swallowed and searched for firmer footing. "It's not like Jo and I ever discussed your, uh…anything."

He shifted in his seat. "Well, I should hope not."

"Oh, no," she assured him hurriedly. "Jo and I never talked about what you and she did—or *didn't* do."

Alan pursed his lips. "Didn't do?"

A flush burned her neck on its way up. "I didn't say 'didn't.'"

"Yes, you did."

Panic fluttered in her stomach. "Well, I didn't *mean* 'didn't.' I meant…oh, damn."

He closed his eyes and downed the rest of his wine. After setting his empty glass on the table with a thunk, he inhaled deeply. "So, Jo wasn't happy with our sex life."

Pam shook her head. "She *never* said that."

He flagged the waiter for more wine, then gave her a dry laugh. "Well, I have to admit we didn't exactly keep the sheets ablaze."

She held up her hands. "I don't want to hear this."

"I can't explain it. Jo is a beautiful woman, but when it came to—"

Pam put her hands over her ears and started to hum, but she could still read his lips, and what she saw made her squeeze her eyes shut. "I'm not listening," she sang. "I'm noooooooooooooot liiiiiisssstennnnniiiiing. I'm noooooooooooooot liiiiiisssstennnnniiiiing. I'm noooooooooooooot liiiiiisssstennnnniiiiing." When she opened her eyes, Alan sat staring at her, along with two waiters who stood by the table, their arms loaded with trays. She smiled sheepishly, straightened her napkin, then gestured for them to serve.

During dinner, neither she nor Alan mentioned the subject of her returning to Savannah early. They talked about their respective jobs, mutual acquaintances and state politics. They talked about the Braves and the Hawks and the Falcons, one advantage of having sports-minded brothers, she noted. They laughed and argued and laughed some more, and Pam hated to see the pleasant meal come to an end.

For dessert, they decided to split a rich, velvety cheesecake with cinnamon topping, which reminded Pam of the unused bottle of body liqueur in their room.

She picked up her utensil and with every luscious bite, she imagined devouring him—biting, licking and swallowing him whole. She savored every succulent bite, allowing the sweetness to melt on her tongue before letting it slide down her throat. The more she ate, the more moist her flimsy panties grew until she nearly moaned aloud. At the sound of Alan's chuckle, she glanced up, afraid she had. Instead, he was simply watching her.

"Was it good?"

"Wonderful," she said, smiling to herself.

"You're killing me," he said, shifting in his seat.

She frowned. "What do you mean?"

"Pam," he said, leaning close and lowering his voice. "Do you always eat dessert with a knife?"

With a start, she stared at the huge, blunt dinner knife in her hand. She glanced up with a sheepish smile, enormously relieved to see the roving Italian musicians were approaching their table.

The men were dressed in brilliant costumes of red, black and gold, with snow-white shirts. The violinist nodded to Alan and kissed Pam's hand, then put his instrument to his shoulder and began to play a sweet, haunting melody, accompanied by the other musicians.

It was almost too much for her—the great food, the good wine, the beautiful music...and Alan's company.

She glanced over at him and inhaled sharply at the desire she saw in his blue eyes. He abandoned his napkin, stood and swept his hand toward the tiny vacant area by their table. ''May I have this dance?'' Then he leaned forward and whispered conspiratorially, ''Of course, I'll have to hold you close to keep my pants up.''

She grinned, then accepted his hand and allowed him to pull her into his arms for a slow waltz. He was a surprisingly good dancer, with natural rhythm and perfect form. It was a good thing he could lead, she decided with her chin resting on his shoulder, because she was too weak-kneed to do little more than follow. He smelled wonderfully spicy and she ached to taste the skin on his neck. He melded her body to his until she felt every muscle beneath his clothing. They might have been the only two people in the universe. When the music ended, she sensed his reluctance to part was as strong as hers, but with an audience, they had little choice. While the other diners applauded, Alan raised her hand and kissed her fingertips.

''Happy Valentine's Day,'' he whispered.

Later, on the way back to the hotel, Pam was quiet, consumed by raging desire for the man next to her, yet lamenting the ramifications of her actions. Conversely, Alan seemed downright cheerful, whistling tunelessly under his breath and fidgeting with all the gadgets on the limousine panel until she was ready to scream. The walk from the parking lot to their door seemed interminably long to her.

''Couldn't get that room Linda had reserved, huh?'' Pam said, laughing to hide her nervousness as she stepped through the door onto the familiar shag carpet.

''Actually,'' Alan said with a smile, ''I told her I'd

changed my mind since we only have two more nights. Want to go down to the beach for a walk?''

Remembering the disastrous results of their last moonlit stroll, she shook her head.

"How about the hot tub?" he asked.

"I'm not fainthearted, Alan, but even *I* am not brave enough to climb into that algae-infested wading pool. Besides, Cheek might be in it, naked."

"Which could account for the algae," he said. "Then let's make our own hot tub."

She laughed. "What?"

He gestured toward the bathroom. "That ridiculous tub in there—it's plenty big enough if we fill it up with hot water."

Amazed at the change in his demeanor, she reached up and lifted his glasses. "Who are you and what have you done with Alan P.—the-'P'-stands-for-tight-as-a-pin— Parish?"

His mouth quirked to the side. "You better get your bathing suit before he comes back."

Pam looked into his blue eyes and studied his boyish face. He was so incredibly handsome…and had turned into such a surprise. Ignoring the warning flags that sprang up en masse at the periphery of her brain, she grinned and said, "I'll meet you in the deep end."

She grabbed her suit, went into the bathroom, then turned on the hot water, unable to ignore the pounding of her heart. Biting her lip hard, she stared at herself in the mirror as she tucked her curves into the gold bikini that had sparked a light in Alan's eyes at the department store. Beneath the harsh illumination of the bare bulb in the room, she looked raw and vulnerable. Her eyes stung from indecision. She wanted Alan so much her chest hurt. "If this is wrong," she whispered, "send me a sign."

The bulb popped, then went dark with a sizzling sound.

She stood in the dark for several seconds, then said, "I need to be really, really sure. Would you mind sending another sign?"

"Pam?" Alan knocked lightly on the door. "Who are you talking to?"

"Uh, no one," she yelled. "The light went out."

His chuckle reverberated through the door. "I'll get the Elvis candles you bought."

Pam looked heavenward. "I gave it my best shot."

He was back within a few seconds, wearing trunks and bearing matches. She placed "Love Me Tender" candles around the room strategically, growing increasingly alarmed at the romantic atmosphere they were creating. She lowered herself into the hot water just as Alan reappeared with a bottle. "Ta-dah!"

"Champagne?"

He uncorked the bottle, spilling foam on the pink tile. "Since I didn't get a drop at the wedding reception, I gave Twiggy fifty bucks to find a bottle of my favorite. Happy Valentine's Day." Alan handed her a full glass, then stepped into the water, only to jump back out. "Good Lord, Pam! Are you cooking shrimp in there?"

Already light-headed at the sight of the candlelight dancing on his sleek, muscled chest, she sipped the champagne and giggled as the bubbles went up her nose. "Ease in, Alan, you'll get used to it."

He tried again, gasping and wincing, sending her into fits of laughter as he squatted into the water inch by inch. "It's a good thing I don't like kids," he muttered as he settled in up to his armpits. "Because my sperm have been parboiled."

"Is that what the 'P' stands for?"

"Cute, real cute."

"Is it 'Parker'?"

"No."

"Preston?"

"No."

"Palmer?"

"No! Enough already. Either turn on the cold water or the egg timer because I'll be done in a few minutes."

Pam turned on the cold water to let it drip. "What's the big deal about your middle name?" She started as his leg brushed against hers beneath the water.

"It's private," he said with a smile. His leg brushed hers again, and she nearly groaned with the desire that welled within her. "Don't you have something private, something you don't share with everyone?"

She manufactured a laugh. "Private? You forget who you're talking to. My life has been public property in Savannah since I was sixteen. Don't tell me you haven't heard the stories."

"I have," he admitted, raking his gaze over her. "But I'm not sure how many of the stories are true and how many of them are pure fantasy on the part of the men who told them."

Her neck felt rubbery, so she laid her head back and looked at him through slitted eyelids. "Alan, have *you* ever fantasized about me?"

His eyes widened and he cleared his throat, then drained his champagne glass. Pam's skin tingled in anticipation.

"I've always thought you were beautiful, Pam," he said finally, moving lower in the water and settling his leg against the length of hers. "But I've never fantasized about you."

She pressed her lips together in disappointment. He wasn't attracted to her, after all. The sexual current she'd felt between them had been a figment of her teenage imagination, dating back to the time when she'd dreamed that Alan P. Parish would notice her, ask her out, take her to his fine home—

"Until this week," he added quietly.

Pam lifted her head.

"I know what you think of me, Pam—that I'm an automaton, a computer geek—"

"A tight-ass," she added with a smile.

He smirked. "Thanks." Then he moved closer, and set her glass aside with his. He floated inches over her in the water before lowering himself against her, setting the warm water into motion. "But I'm not a machine, Pam."

His face was only inches from hers, and she felt his breath fan her cheek. The water lapped around them, warming her skin, then falling away to leave her covered with goose bumps. Her nipples hardened. His proximity crowded her senses and she had never felt so close to losing control. "Are you sure? Because I—I can certainly feel your hard drive."

"I want you."

Pam closed her eyes, trying to recall any shred of relief she had felt the morning after their near lapse on the beach, any rationalization that she shouldn't be feeling like this. But now his hands on her obliterated all doubts, negated all concerns, neutralized all complications. And her hands moved of their own volition to the nape of her neck to loosen the ties of her bikini top. She allowed the water to float the material away from her breasts, and Alan crushed her against him, claiming her mouth in a plundering kiss.

Pam raised her body to meet his and he clasped her urgently, squeezing her hips against his, whispering her name into her throat. After a thorough exploration of her mouth, he set aside his fogged glasses and drew back to view her breasts.

"You are magnificent." The sheer wonder in his voice sent waves of desire flooding her limbs. He dragged her breath from her lungs by pulling a puckered nipple into his mouth.

"Oh, Alan." She pushed her fingers through his hair and arched into him, urging him to take as much of her into his mouth as possible. His erection strained against her thigh, and she ran her hands down his neck, over his muscled back, and under the waistband of his trunks.

Their moans echoed off the walls of the small room and Pam had never felt so aroused. The combination of the heated water, the candlelight and the man were incredibly erotic. Every nerve ending, every muscle, every sense burned and throbbed with raw desire and she raked her hands over his body. His name emerged from her throat over and over, as if some part of her suspected their time together was short and she wanted to experience as much of him as possible.

He devoured her, drawing on her breasts one at a time, rolling her sensitized nipples between his finger and thumb. His hands skated over her body, assuming the rhythm of the water until their movements became so frenzied, the now-lukewarm water splashed over the edges and onto the tile.

Alan felt his body growing more engorged, yearning for release. The feelings she had unleashed in him were so staggering, he prayed he could maintain control long enough to please her. "Let's go to bed," he said thickly against her neck and she moaned her agreement.

He drew back and tried to stand, fell, and succeeded in dunking them both before they gained their footing. Pam stopped long enough to grab a towel for her sopping hair.

The sight of her standing bare-breasted was enough to make him grit his teeth.

"We'd better hurry," he said, tugging on her hand.

They slipped and slid across the tiled floor, laughing and cursing until they crossed the threshold of the bedroom. They tumbled onto the bed, launching a small tidal wave. Alan kicked off his trunks and rolled down her bikini bottoms, groaning when he uncovered the nest of wet blond curls between her firm, tanned thighs. He raised himself above her, pushing her wet hair back from her face. "You are so beautiful," he whispered hoarsely. "I need to make love to you now—are you protected?"

She nodded, her blue eyes luminous, her luscious upside-down mouth soft and swollen. With utmost restraint, he lowered himself, rubbing his straining shaft against her. Oh so carefully, he probed her wetness, then sank inside her slowly, capturing her mouth with his and absorbing her gasps as their bodies melded.

Heaven. She felt like pure heaven around him, pulsing, kneading, drawing his life fluid to the surface much too quickly. He slowed and clenched his teeth, wanting their lovemaking to last, postponing the moment she would pull away from him. For now he wanted to be inside her, wrapped around her, smelling her, tasting her. When he found a slow rhythm, she began to pant beneath him, clawing as his back. He was so stunned at the level of her response, he was momentarily distracted from his own building release and concentrated on making her climax powerful.

He laved her earlobe and whispered erotic words he'd never uttered before, phrases loosened from his tongue by the fantasy woman writhing beneath him. He moved with her, responding to every moan and gasp with more intense probing until her cries escalated and she climaxed around him, her contracting muscles finally breaking his restraint and unleashing the most intense orgasm he'd ever experienced. They rode out the vestiges of their explosive pleasure, slowing to a languid grind. At last they stilled, but the water mattress bumped them against each other, eliciting gasps as their tender flesh met.

He gingerly lifted himself from her and rolled to spoon her against him, half to hold her close for a while longer, half to avoid facing her until he had time to sort out a few things for himself. The regrets, the remorse, the self-recrimination had not yet set in, and for the time being, he simply wanted to enjoy the intimacy of lying with this wonderful creature, however fleeting the time might be.

Alan sighed and closed his eyes, pushing his nose into her damp hair, inhaling her scent. He couldn't remember feeling more content, but he blamed his thoughts of spending the rest of his nights like this on the fog of sleep that ebbed over him. His dreams were restless, fraught with stress-packed, nerve-shattering days of living with Pamela Kaminski.

10

WHEN PAM'S EYES popped open, the first light of dawn had found its way between the heavy opaque curtains over the window and sliding glass door. Despite the sunny warmth, a cold blanket of dread descended over her. She craned her neck slowly toward the mirrored ceiling, muttering words of denial until she was faced with the naked truth.

"Oh…my…God," she murmured, groaning at the tangle of bare tanned arms and legs they presented. They'd *done* it—the deed, the wild thing, the horizontal bop—they'd had *sex*. She and Alan. Her and her best friend's ex. Panic ballooned in her chest and she pushed herself up, frantically whispering, "Oh my God, oh my God, oh my God."

Alan stirred and rolled to his back, displaying a puptent erection beneath the thin sheet. She averted her eyes, cursed the erotic scenes that kept replaying in her head and began to extricate herself from his grasp as gently as possible.

"Hey," he mumbled in complaint, pulling her against him.

She punched his arm. "Let me go," she protested, scrambling to get out of the rolling bed.

"You really should work on that morning disposition," he muttered with a yawn.

She bent and scooped a towel from the floor, which she

wrapped around herself. Astounded at his nonchalance, she bounced a pillow off his face. "Get up! Can't you see we're in big trouble here?"

He blinked and sat up, shaking his head as if to clear it, then swung his feet to the floor. "Excuse me?"

"Alan, we had sex last night."

"I was there—or don't you remember?" he asked wryly, standing for a full-body stretch.

That was the problem—she remembered his mind-blowing participation all too well. Pam glanced down at his raging morning erection, then expelled an explosive sigh. "Put a towel on that rack, would you?"

She tossed him a pillowcase they had somehow managed to work free during their lovemaking, then jammed her hands on her hips. "*What* are we going to do now?"

Holding the crumpled cloth over his privates, Alan scrubbed his hand over his face, then ventured, "Go to Walt Disney World?"

"That's not even remotely funny," she snapped.

"Could I have a few seconds to wake up? And maybe relieve myself?"

It had meant nothing to him, she realized with a jolt. And why should it? He wasn't the one who would have to face Jo on a regular basis when they returned home. In fact, from a man's point of view, sleeping with the best friend of the woman who had ditched him at the altar was probably the most perfect revenge he could exact. Hurt stabbed her deep, and she felt like a fool for not seeing the situation so clearly last night. Pam swept her hand toward the bathroom. "Be my guest," she said with as much indifference as she could muster.

When he had closed the door, she strode to the closet, yanked out her large canvas beach bag and started stuffing her personal articles inside. Most of the clothes she could leave here, she decided—since Alan had bought them, he could dispose of them however he wished.

Not relishing another plane ride so soon after their turbulent experience a few days ago, she decided that the bus sounded like the best alternative home—even if it took two days, which she presumed it would. Today was Thursday, so she'd still be back in Savannah by late Friday, or Saturday at the latest. Which would give her plenty of time to decide what—or if—she was going to tell Jo.

She jammed her Elvis paraphernalia into the bag and practiced her speech. "Gee, Jo, you were finished with him and he was just so darned sexy. No, I promise we weren't sleeping together behind your back while you and Alan were an item."

"Pam."

Alan's voice sounded behind her, jangling her already clanging nerves so badly she dropped the bag, and her towel with it. Yanking the towel back in place, she wheeled to find Alan leaning on the doorjamb.

"What are you doing?" he asked quietly.

She retrieved the bag and continued rooting through the tiny closet. "What does it look like I'm doing? I'm packing."

"To go home? Why?"

She turned and leveled her gaze on him.

He did, at least, have the grace to blush. "I mean, I can guess why, but I don't think this is the best way to handle what just happened, do you?"

"You have a better plan?"

Alan shrugged. "Try not to blow it out of proportion. I was lonely, you were lonely. We had a romantic evening—everyone treated us as a couple. We drank half a bottle of wine, then topped it off with good champagne."

He looked contrite. "I owe you an apology—I feel guilty as hell for dragging you down here, and now…"

"Now look at the fine mess we've made," she finished for him, ending with a sigh. "There's no need to apologize, Alan. You didn't exactly hold a gun to my head."

He pressed his lips together in a tight line. "Sleeping together wasn't particularly smart, considering the touchy circumstances, but we're adults and surely we can exercise enough control to make sure it doesn't happen again."

"Oh, it can *never* happen again," she said emphatically.

"Agreed," he said, walking to stop an arm's length away from her. "Since we have that settled, now you can stay."

"It's not settled, Alan," she said, dropping her gaze. "What am I going to tell Jo?"

"We," he said firmly, "aren't going to tell Jo anything. She's married, Pam. She doesn't care about my sex life— or yours. And even if she did, it's none of her business."

"But how will I face her?"

"As if nothing happened," he said simply, affirming her earlier suspicion that their lovemaking had shaken her far more than it had affected him.

"But I can't lie to her, Alan. She's my best friend."

He lifted his hands. "Fine—if we get home and Jo asks you, 'Pam, did you and Alan sleep together?,' you can say, 'Yes, as a matter of fact, Jo, we did.'"

"It would never occur to Jo to ask," Pam said with a wry smile.

"My point exactly," he said. "But you might arouse her curiosity if you went scurrying home early." He gave her a lopsided smile. "So put down your bag and I promise to stay out of your way until Saturday. Hopefully we can still go home as friends.''

He made it sound so simple—they had made a mistake, and they wouldn't do it again. Period. That was Alan— Mr. Practical. She lifted a corner of her mouth. Maybe that's what the 'P' stood for. Even though he obviously wasn't wrestling with the same troubling issues their lovemaking had unearthed in her psyche, perhaps he was right. Maybe they needed a couple of days to get back on a casual footing. Although she would never look at Alan in quite the same way, it would be a shame to lose his friendship because she simply couldn't cope with their lapse.

''I'll stay,'' she said lightly. ''And of course we'll go home as friends.'' She dropped the bag and gave him her brightest smile. ''I'll go shopping today, and do some sight-seeing.''

''And I'll find something to do,'' he said. ''And if you're out late—''

''—or if you're out late…''

''—we'll see each other…''

''—tomorrow,'' she finished.

He nodded. ''Fine.''

She nodded. ''Fine.''

''Do you want to shower first?''

''Sure,'' she said, and walked past him. The pink-tiled room did not seem nearly so electric this morning, although the vestiges of their interlude were scattered throughout: her bikini top, the burnt-down candles, the half-empty bottle of champagne. She closed her eyes for a few seconds and squashed the mushrooming regret when it threatened to overwhelm her.

''By the way,'' Alan said behind her.

She whirled to see him squinting at her from the open doorway, just as something crunched under her foot.

"Have you seen my glasses?"

Pam looked down, picked up her foot, then winced and nodded.

ALAN PUSHED his glasses higher on his nose, frowning when he encountered the bulky piece of masking tape that held the broken bridge of his frames together. He sank lower in the upholstered seat of the nearly empty movie theater and smirked at the corny previews. With a sigh he glanced at the vacant seat next to him and imagined Pam sitting there, munching popcorn and giggling like a teenager.

It was funny how much his perception of her had changed in the last few days. She was still the sexy bombshell who made him a little nervous, but now...now he had glimpsed the warm, funny, smart woman who lurked beneath the showy facade. Sure, her showy side inflamed his baser needs, but it was her squeal of laughter when they'd ridden the Wave Runner and her shining face when he'd filled the moat of her sand castle that stayed with him every waking minute.

The ear-numbing, teeth-jarring, bone-melting, mind-blowing sex was simply a bonus.

He smiled a slow, lazy grin. The sex was a big, fat cherry on top of a sundae more delectable than any he could have imagined as a kid. Which presented an interesting paradox, he noted as the main feature bounced onto the screen. If Pamela Kaminski was such a catch, what was keeping him from pursuing her with gusto?

He imagined Pam counting off the reasons on her brightly colored fingernails. "Because my friendship with your ex-fiancée means more to me than any relationship we could ever have, Alan. Because I have dozens of men waiting for my return, Alan. And most important, because you're not the kind of guy I'd settle for, Alan.''

The flick started, a splashy good-guys bad-guys film with several gorgeous women and just enough one-liners to make it amusing. But his mind wandered from the movie plot to Pamela so often, he lost track of which double agent crossed which federal bureau so when the movie credits rolled, he wasn't quite sure what had happened or who had gotten the girl. But he had the sinking feeling it wouldn't be him.

He sat through another matinee he couldn't follow, at the end of which he had to admit that for the first time in his thirty-odd years, he was completely consumed with, distracted by and besotted over a woman. A woman who was beyond his reach.

When he walked outside, he squinted into the light, even though dusk was already falling. Oh well, he thought as he joined the mingling crowd on the sidewalk, things would be different when they got back to Savannah. He would return to his demanding job running his consulting business, and she would return to the frantic pace of real-estate sales, along with her bottomless pool of boyfriends. They would probably see each other occasionally at charity functions. He would wave and she would smile, and no one would ever know they had made passionate love in a gaudy room in Fort Myers on Valentine's Day.

Determined to stay away from the beachfront area to avoid running into Robin, Alan strolled along the retail district, browsing in music and electronics stores. He wandered by a jewelry-store window and stopped when he spotted a gold sand-castle pendant. He desperately wanted to give Pam something to remember him by, and the pendant seemed to call him. He walked inside and left fifteen minutes later with the pendant and a matching gold chain.

He wasn't sure when or if he'd give it to her, but for now, buying the pendant seemed like the right thing to do.

He bought a couple of CD's by local artists, then stopped at a sports bar and ordered a sandwich and a beer. The ponytailed bartender who served him found a Georgia State basketball game on one of the many TV screens and made small talk while he washed glass mugs.

The barkeep wore a tight T-shirt with the sleeves ripped off to show his many tattoos to their best advantage. Alan tried not to stare, but he must have failed because the guy quirked a bushy eyebrow and asked, "You ever had a tattoo?"

Alan shook his head and pointed to one on the man's arm, squinting. "Is that an ad?"

"Yep—best tattoo parlor in town is just down the street. I get a discount for wearing the ad."

"Human billboards," Alan acknowledged with a tip of his bottle. "Now *there's* an untapped industry." He figured he must be getting a buzz because the idea of someone selling their skin to advertisers, inch by inch, actually sounded plausible. In which case, Pam's body would be worth a fortune, he noted dryly, wondering how much her cleavage would command on the open market. *Location, location, location.*

The bartender leaned on the bar and asked, "Hey, man, are you busy later tonight?"

Alan frowned and deepened his voice. "You're barking up the wrong tree, fella."

"Huh?" The bartender pulled back, then scoffed. "Nah, man, my girlfriend's swinging by and bringing a friend with her. You like redheads?"

"Sure, but—"

"Great! Her name's Pru."

"Thanks anyway, but I'm really not—"

"Saaaaaaaaay." Something past Alan's shoulder had obviously claimed the man's attention. "I could go for some of that," the bartender whispered in a husky voice.

Alan turned on his stool to see Pamela walking toward the bar wearing an outfit of walking shorts and sleeveless sweater that would have been unremarkable on ninety-nine percent of the female population. She seemed intent on finding something in her purse and hadn't spotted him yet. If Alan had been quick—and motivated—he could have thrown some cash on the bar and left. But his reflexes were a little delayed, he conceded, and the sheer pleasure of seeing her after spending the day apart disintegrated his thoughts of leaving.

When she looked up, she did a double take and stopped midstride, then approached him with a wary expression on her face. "Small world," he offered along with a smile. He patted the stool next to him. "Have a seat—I'll buy you a beer."

She leaned one firm hip against the stool and gestured vaguely. "Thanks anyway—I actually came in to find a pay phone. My cell-phone battery died in the middle of a conversation with Mrs. Wingate."

"Is she ready to buy the Sheridan house?"

"Not yet—she's got a priest over there now consecrating the flower beds."

"Don't let me keep you."

"That's all right," she said with a wave. "She probably took getting cut off as some kind of omen and might not come to the phone anyway." Pam glanced at the bartender. "Nice artwork," she said, nodding toward his colorful arms.

Wearing a wolfish grin, the man flexed his biceps and leaned toward Pam. "Thanks."

Jealousy barbed through Alan and he glared at the beefy man. "Pam, what did you do all day?"

She told him about her day of sight-seeing. "There are some beautiful homes here and over on Sanibel Island," she declared. "The real-estate market seems to be very strong—lots of money to be made."

He bit the inside of his cheek as a disturbing thought struck him. "You're not thinking about moving?"

"Not here," she said. "Even though I like it. I always thought Atlanta would be nice—I have lots of friends there."

So she had lovers all over the state, he mused. "Atlanta's a fun city."

She nodded and brushed a lock of hair behind her ear— the ear in which he'd murmured unmentionables only last night. "As long as my mother is alive, I guess I'll stay in Savannah."

"I can't imagine the state my mother will be in by the time I return," Alan said with a wry grin.

"She liked Jo, didn't she?"

He nodded and peeled off the curling corner of the label on his beer bottle. "She thought Jo would make an excellent wife and hostess, an asset to my career."

"She doesn't want grandchildren?"

"My sister has two kids, and my mother thinks that's plenty enough people in this world to call her Granny."

Pam giggled. "Mom doesn't have grandkids—that we know of. Of course, knowing my brothers, who knows how many Kaminskis could be running around."

Alan laughed and tipped his bottle for another drink. Every family, rich or poor, had its dysfunction. "Have you had dinner?"

"I'm not really very hungry," she said, dropping her

gaze again. "Thanks anyway. I'm tired—I think I'll get back to the hotel and turn in early."

Their eyes met and the reason behind her fatigue hung in the air between them. Alan gripped the bottle hard to keep from reaching for her. "Ah, come on," he said. "Why don't you stay for a beer—what's one beer between friends?"

The corners of her uneven mouth turned up slowly, then she relented with a nod. "Okay, one beer."

ALAN STARTED AWAKE, then winced at the sour taste in his mouth. But the movement of his facial muscles sent an explosion of pain to his temples and he groaned aloud, which sounded like a gong in his ears. He closed his eyes and waited until most of the pain and noise subsided before attempting to put two thoughts together.

He was in the hotel room, and he could hear Pam's snore beside him, so it appeared they had slept in the same bed. Straining, he remembered they had consumed large quantities of beer and had left the sports bar, but that's when his memory failed him. Had they gone directly back to the room? And then what?

He opened his eyes one at a time in the early-morning light and gingerly reached up to adjust his broken glasses, which were somehow still on his face. He moved his head to see the reflection in the ceiling. Another gonging groan escaped him when he saw they were indeed naked and intimately entwined.

Not again.

Pam lay on her stomach and the sheet had fallen down to expose the rub-on rose tattoo on her tanned hip. When his scrutiny triggered inappropriate responses beneath his half of the sheet, he pulled himself up a millimeter at a time and stumbled to the bathroom in search of a glass of water.

His hip ached from the unaccustomed lusty exercise, and he rubbed it as he downed the water. But at the sharp tenderness of his skin, he turned to glance in the mirror and smiled dryly. He must have been blitzed because he'd allowed Pam to rub one of her fake tattoos on *his* hip. A wet washcloth and a little soap would take care of it, he figured. Except when he scrubbed at the tattoo, the pain increased and the stubborn design refused to budge. "I must be allergic to the dye," he muttered, and scrubbed harder. But minutes later when he lifted the cloth and saw the tattoo still had not faded, terror twisted his stomach.

"No," he said frantically. "It can't be real!"

He backed up to the mirror for a better look, but he couldn't make out the tattoo. Letters of some kind? It was backward in the reflection, so he snatched up Pam's hand mirror and positioned it to read the reflected word. His eyes widened and his hands started to shake.

Paaaaaaaaaaaaaaaammmmmmmmm!

Pamela jerked awake, unable to pinpoint the origin of the invasion into her peaceful sleep. She swallowed painfully and lifted her head. The sound of breaking glass from the bathroom made her sit up. "Alan," she called, holding her head. "Are you okay?"

The door swung open and he emerged naked, his face puckered and red. "No, I am not okay. In fact, I'm about as far from okay as I've ever been!"

Pam rubbed her tender hip and grimaced. "Don't make me play twenty questions, Alan. It hurts to talk."

"You!" he bellowed, shaking his finger at her. "You talked me into it!"

She sighed. "Did we do it again?"

"Yes!" he roared. "But that's not what I'm talking about."

Her frustration peaked. "Then what *are* you talking about?"

"This!" he yelled, then turned around and pointed to his bare hip.

She leaned forward and squinted. "A tattoo? You got a tattoo?" Laughter erupted from the back of her throat. "You got a tattoo!" Then she stood, twisted to look at her own hip and squealed in delight. "No—we both got tattoos! A rose! Isn't it great?" She strode over to him and glanced down. "What does yours say?" Then she stopped and stumbled backward at the sight of the name etched on Alan's skin, enclosed in a red heart. "P-Pam's?" She covered her mouth with both hands and lifted her gaze to his.

"THERE ARE ALL KINDS of new laser procedures to remove tattoos," she assured him as they moved down the path toward the beach. Alan walked woodenly beside her, occasionally stabbing at his taped glasses.

"But I think we're skirting the bigger issue here," she continued, trotting to keep up with him, even though he was limping slightly, favoring his tender hip. "What happened last night absolutely *cannot* happen again."

"I agree," he said curtly, staring straight ahead.

"We've only got one more day and one more night, so we should be able to stay sober and keep our hands to ourselves."

"Right."

"Let's try to enjoy the time we have left," she said amiably as they stepped onto the warm white sand.

He stopped and turned to her. "How about 'Let's just

try to make it through tomorrow with as few calamities as possible'?''

Pam swallowed and smiled weakly. "That's fine, too."

They rented chaise lounges and Pam couldn't help noticing that Alan waited until she had hers situated, then planted his several feet away. "Safety precaution," he said flatly, then snapped open the newspaper he'd brought to read.

Frowning, Pam turned to her own reading material and tried to blot the disturbing thoughts of Alan from her mind. She had missed him yesterday, and the realization had shaken her badly. So when she'd stumbled across him in the sports bar, she had allowed herself to be persuaded to stay for a drink because she simply wanted to spend time with him. And although the rest of the night remained fuzzy, some incidents she recalled rather clearly.

Such as the fact that she *had* been the one who suggested they get tattoos, inspired, possibly, by the bartender's impressive collection. And Alan had been hesitant, but she had dragged him down the street, and sent him into one booth while she entered another one for her design of choice. Where he'd gotten "Pam's" was less clear to her, and the fact that they'd made whoopee again last night only added to the confusion.

Her heart lay heavy in her chest and she tried to convince herself that things would be better once they returned to Savannah. For one thing, she would rarely see him, if at all, since their connection to each other—Jo—no longer existed. It was for the best, she knew, because she didn't want to be running into him at every turn...didn't want to be reminded of the few days they were together when names, backgrounds and at-risk relationships were irrelevant and all that mattered was the powerful sexual chemistry between them.

"Hello."

Pam looked up and smothered a cringe when she saw Enrico standing over her chair, his lips curved into a sultry smile. Resplendent in orange nut-huggers, the man nodded toward Alan who was still hidden behind a newspaper. "I see your man is neglecting you once again." He wagged his eyebrows. "Perhaps I can remedy that situation."

Annoyed, Pam began rummaging in her bag. "I doubt it."

"Could I interest you in a walk up the beach?"

She jammed on her sunglasses. "No."

"How about a drink?"

She lay her head back. "No."

He leaned close to her and the stench of alcohol rolled off his breath. "You like to tease, no?"

"No," Alan said behind him.

Pam lifted her head and looked up at Alan who stood with his paper under his arm, glaring at Enrico. How like a man to ignore a woman until someone else comes sniffing around. She smiled tightly. "I can handle this, Alan."

His gaze darted to her, then he lifted his hands in retreat and reclaimed his chair.

But Enrico folded his arms and followed him back to his chair. "She is not worth fighting for, *señor?*"

"That is enough," Pam declared, sitting up. "I think you'd better leave, Enrico."

Enrico stood over Alan, taking advantage of the situation. "She is too much woman for you, eh?"

Pam's patience snapped and she scrambled to her feet. "Leave, Enrico!"

He sneered and jerked a thumb toward Alan, who had risen to his feet. "Perhaps your man is weak?" Just as he lunged for Alan, Pam launched herself at the man with an angry growl, climbing his hairy back. She propelled him into Alan and they all went down in the sand. Once the breath returned to her lungs, Pam pummeled the man's back.

Sand flew as they rolled around, scrambling for leverage. Alan splayed his hand over Enrico's face and pushed him back, trying to avoid the man's swinging arms. Pam yelped, clawing the grit out of her eyes while showering Enrico with the blinding stuff. Alan rolled behind the man and grabbed him in a choke-hold. The man grabbed handfuls of sand and threw them in the air.

Somewhere in the background she heard a voice yell for the police. Incensed, she wanted to land one good jab while Alan held him. Pam made a fist, drew back and threw the hardest punch she could through the swirling sand, eliciting a dull groan when she made contact with skin and bone.

She stepped back to blink her eyes clear. But when she massaged her throbbing knuckles in satisfaction, she saw Enrico several yards down the beach, jogging away, and he appeared unfazed by Pam's right hook.

When she glanced back to the site of the scuffle, her stomach twisted. Alan sat in the sand, glaring at her, holding his hand over his right eye.

Whatever apology she might have conjured up was cut short by the arrival of a uniformed officer. "Hello," the cop said, standing over Alan with a tight smile. "Again."

"WELL, look on the bright side," Pam said as she led the way to the double-parked limo the following morning.

Numb from another night in jail and a head full of contradicting thoughts, Alan gingerly touched his swollen right eye and asked, "And that would be?"

"We didn't have sex last night," she said brightly.

Which would have been the only redeeming event of the past twenty-four hours, Alan thought miserably.

"And we're leaving today," she sang, obviously anxious to return home. "I checked us out of the hotel—Twiggy said goodbye. I bought a suitcase and packed your things—they're in the car."

He stopped and stared at two new dents and the Kaminiskiesque parking job that left only two tires of the pimpmobile on the street, but he didn't say anything. Instead, he opened the back door of the limo and climbed in, banging the door closed behind him.

"You're letting me drive to the airport?" Pam yelled from the driver's seat after she buzzed down the divider panel.

Alan clicked his seat belt into place, pulled the strap tight and laid his head back. "Your definition of driving is a loose interpretation, but I'm too drained to argue."

"Okay," she said excitedly, revving the engine. "I'm starved—do you mind if we stop and get something to eat on the way? We've got plenty of time before the flight."

"Go for it," he said, removing his broken glasses so he couldn't witness the driving event.

Of course, he hadn't anticipated she would attempt to take the limo through a drive-through window—they were stuck in a tight curve by a squawking monitor for forty-five minutes. No longer surprised by any stunt she pulled, Alan ordered an ice-cream sandwich to hold against his puffy eye and munched a hamburger in the back seat during the melee. When the scraping sounds became too unbearable, he turned up the TV and watched a rerun of "Laugh-In" until she finally eased the car by the metal posts and the high curbs.

She buzzed down the panel when they were on the

expressway again. "We still have over an hour," she yelled cheerfully. "We'll make it."

He buzzed up the panel and unwrapped the ice-cream sandwich.

Five minutes later they were at a dead standstill. She buzzed down the panel. "It's a freaking parking lot out here—the radio says there's a tractor-trailer overturned and we won't move for at least an hour. Don't worry— we'll still make it." She smiled, then buzzed up the panel.

Alan sighed and picked up the remote control. Then a thought struck him and he buzzed down the panel. "Hey, Kaminski?"

She twisted in her seat. "Yeah?"

"Have you ever gotten naked in a limo?"

Her smile was slow in coming, but broad and mischievous. "No."

"Want to?"

In answer, she buzzed up the panel. Alan sighed again and laid his head back. "Can't blame a guy for asking," he muttered. Especially since she'd go back to her stud stable once they returned to Savannah.

Suddenly the door opened and she bounded inside, toppling over him, laughing like a teenager. She straddled him and kissed him hard, then asked, "Do you think an hour is enough time?"

"We'll have to hit the highlights," he whispered, locking the door.

"What about the lowlights?" she said, pouting.

"In the interest of time," he murmured, pulling at her waistband, "I'll have to give them a lick and a promise."

RUNNING THROUGH the parking lot of the car-rental return, Pam yelled, "That can't *ever* happen again."

"Right," Alan yelled back. "Never."

They rushed into the building. Alan forked over an obscene deposit to a pinched-nose man in case his insurance company wouldn't cover the various damages to the limo, then they sprinted through the airport as fast as his still-aching hip would allow. When they dropped into their seats on the plane, he found it unbelievable that only a few days had passed since they'd left Savannah. It seemed like a lifetime ago—not to mention a small fortune ago, he noted wryly.

After takeoff, he donned a set of headphones, not to ignore Pam, but hoping to put some perspective on the week before they reached Savannah. Indeed, the more distant the Fort Myers skyline became, the more painfully clear the answers seemed.

Instead of trying to dissect the roller coaster of emotions she had evoked in him this week, he simply needed to consider the facts: he had been vulnerable, she had been eager to comfort a friend. Besides, even if the circumstances were ideal—which they weren't—and even if he had the intention of taking a wife—which he didn't—he couldn't imagine any woman more unsuited to marriage than Pamela Kaminski.

Thankfully, their flight was uneventful—the little mishap when Pam sent an entire overhead bin of luggage pounding down on two passengers didn't even merit an eye twitch on his new scale of relativity. Rankling him further, she seemed oblivious to his brooding, chatting with the flight attendants and somehow managing to paint her toenails during the flight.

It was only when they were landing and he glanced over to see her death grip on the padded arms of her seat that he conceded to himself how extremely fond of her he'd become. Alan reached over to squeeze her hand, and the grateful smile she gave him made his heart lurch crazily. He knew in that moment that even if his eye healed, the tattoo was safely removed, the charges were dropped and his car insurance wasn't canceled, he still might never fully recover from his week with Pamela.

She was her usual cheery self through baggage claim and on their way back to her car, reinforcing Alan's suspicion that, for Pam, the week had simply been a casual romp—the woman had no earth-shattering revelations weighing her down. And despite the trouble that seemed to follow her around, he was going to miss her. Perhaps, he decided, after a few weeks had passed and he had shaken this somber, life-evaluating mood, he'd call her, just to see how she was doing.

He offered to call a cab, but she insisted on driving him home, saying she needed to check on some new home listings in his neighborhood, anyway. On the way, she ran two red lights, but stopped traffic on the bypass to let a mother duck and her ducklings cross.

When she pulled onto the long driveway, Alan stared at his imposing home and realized with a jolt that only one week ago, he had anticipated returning to carry his bride, Jo Montgomery, across the threshold. Now he felt almost giddy with relief at the change in circumstances. He and Jo would have been content, but not entirely happy. She had never looked at him the way she looked at John Sterling. And he owed it to himself to find a woman he could care about that much.

"Are you okay?" Pam asked, jarring him out of his reverie.

"Uh, yeah," he said, realizing she was waiting for him to get out. But when he grasped the handle, she stopped him with a hand on his arm.

"Alan," she said softly.

"Yeah," he said, his heart thudding against his chest.

"I'm sorry."

"Sorry?"

"For breaking your glasses and denting the limo and getting the ticket and having you tattooed and blacking your eye and getting you arrested."

"Twice," he amended.

"Twice," she agreed.

Her blue eyes were wide, and her upside-down mouth trembled. She was so beautiful, she was impossible to resist. He inhaled deeply and gave her a wry smile. "Forget it." Her happy grin was worth every misery he'd experienced over the week.

He opened the door and retrieved the dark suitcase she had purchased and packed for him. When he walked around to the driver's side, his mind racing for something to say, he suddenly remembered the pendant he had bought for her. "Oh, I almost forgot," he said, rooting through his gym bag until he came up with the black box. "For you."

"For me?" she asked quietly, taking her lower lip in her teeth. She slowly lifted the lid and stared at the gold sand castle, then ran her finger over the surface. "It's beautiful," she whispered, then raised shining eyes. "But why?"

Because I want you to remember me, to remember us. "Because," he said with a shrug, "I wanted to thank you for keeping me company. It was fun," he lied. It wasn't fun—it was surprising, disturbing, stimulating, stressful and amazing, but it wasn't fun.

"I love it."

She pulled the necklace from the box and fastened the clasp around her neck. The pendant disappeared into her cleavage and Alan swallowed hard.

"Thank you, Alan."

"I'll see you…" His voice trailed off because he didn't want to appear as desperately hopeful as he felt.

"Sometime," she finished for him.

"Right," he said with a nod.

"Fine," she said with a nod.

Alan watched as she rolled up the window, backed over several hundred dollars' worth of landscaping and pulled onto the road directly in the path of a luxury car whose owner stood on the brake to avoid a collision. Then, with a fluttery wave and a grind of stripped gears, she was gone.

11

PAM SLAPPED HER KNEE and laughed uproariously. "That's the best April Fool's gag I've heard today, Dr. Campbell."

Eleanor Campbell pursed her lips and steepled her fingers together over her desk. "It's no joke, Pamela. You're pregnant."

Shock, alarm and stark terror washed over her. Her throat closed and her fingers went numb. "H-how is that possible?"

Dr. Campbell smiled. "Do you want layman's terms or the scientific version?"

"Whichever will make it less true," Pam whispered. "I take my birth control pills faithfully."

"But if you had read the warning brochure for the antibiotics I prescribed for that ear infection a couple of months ago," she said sternly, "you would have known the medication can reduce the effectiveness of birth control pills." She sighed and gave Pam a sad smile. "I take it this is not a happy occasion for you and the father."

Pam closed her eyes and swallowed. "When did it happen?"

"According to the information you gave me regarding your last cycle, I'd guess on or about Valentine's Day."

If she didn't open her eyes, she decided, she wouldn't have to face it. Wouldn't have to face the fact that she was living up to the tainted Kaminski name by conceiving an illegitimate child. Wouldn't have to face the fact that life as she knew it was over. Wouldn't have to face the fact that Alan, whom she'd not seen or spoken to since returning to Savannah—and who *hated* kids—was the father of the baby growing inside her.

"MR. PARISH?" Alan's secretary's voice echoed over the speakerphone.

Alan left what had become his favorite post, the high-backed chair by the window, to push a button on his desk panel. "Yes?"

"I'm sorry, sir. Tickets to the scholarship social are sold out."

He cursed under his breath safely out of range of the microphone. "How about the hospital golf benefit?"

"Sold out."

"The lighthouse-preservation dinner?"

"Gone. The only tickets I could find for this weekend were for the podiatrists' political-action campaign dinner and the bird-watchers' society all-night skate at the roller rink."

Alan frowned. Feet or feathers—not much of a choice. "Get me two of each," he said. He dropped into his leather chair, then flipped to Pam's business card in his Rolodex—as if he hadn't memorized it. Hell, he'd dialed it twenty-eight times in the weeks since they'd returned to Savannah, but he'd always hung up before the first ring. Now he had a good excuse.

Well, maybe not good—but reasonable.

He sighed. Okay, it wasn't even reasonable, but he prayed his ploy didn't come across as desperation...even though it was.

After punching in her number, he cleared his voice, fully expecting to have to leave a message on her voice mail, but to his surprise, Pam's voice came on the line. "Hello, this is Pamela. How can I help you?"

"Uh, hi, Pam. This is Alan…Parish."

A few seconds of silence passed. "Hi, Alan. What's up?"

"Oh, not much," he said, summoning a nervous laugh. "I just called to wish you a happy April Fool's Day."

More silence, then, "That's nice."

He picked up a pen and started doodling on a pad of paper. "So, how have you been?"

"Fine, I guess," she said. "How's your eye?"

"It healed."

"And, uh, the other end?"

"Well," he said, shifting in his seat, "it's a delicate operation—I'm still trying to choose the best doctor."

"Jo told me the two of you talked things through."

"That's right." Not that there were any unresolved issues in his mind. But he knew it had made Jo feel better to explain why she had canceled their wedding.

"She seems really happy being a mom," Pam said.

He tried to concentrate on what she was saying, but he kept picturing her nude in the limo. "Yeah, can you imagine taking care of three kids?"

"Um, no, I can't."

And her breasts—God, he shuddered just thinking about them. "Just the thought sends chills up my spine."

"I remember your view on kids, Alan."

Funny, but right now he could legitimately say the most difficult part about having a baby would be sharing his wife—emotionally and physically. Pam was the kind of woman that made a man selfish. Alan shook his head to clear it. Pam, a wife? What was he thinking?

"Alan, are you still there?"

"What? Sure, I'm here." He cleared his throat. "Say,

Pam, are you free this weekend to attend a business function?''

During her few seconds of hesitation, he died a thousand times. "What kind of business function?"

His mind raced—what the devil had Linda said? "Uh, there's a feet convention at the skating rink."

"Excuse me?"

"I mean, a political fund-raiser for birds."

"What?"

Where was his brain? "Forget business—can we have dinner tonight at the River Plaza Hotel?"

"Is something wrong, Alan?"

She obviously thought the idea of them having a date was so far-fetched there had to be some other compelling reason for them to get together. "I need to talk to you... about Jo," he said, wincing at his choice of subject matter, but it was too late.

"Jo?" she asked.

"Yeah," he said, rushing ahead. "I'm having trouble working through some things and I hoped you could help me."

The silence stretched on.

"Pam?" he urged.

"Sure," she said softly. "What are friends for?"

His heart jumped for joy. "Really? I mean—" he swallowed "—that's great. Uh, seven o'clock?"

"Seven sounds fine."

She didn't sound too happy about it, but he didn't care. He just wanted to see her again. Alan's mind raced for another topic to prolong the conversation. "Have you sold the Sheridan house?"

"Not yet—Mrs. Wingate hired a poltergeist-detection team to spend the night there. We're waiting on the results. Listen, Alan, I really need to run."

"Oh, sure," he said, fighting to keep the disappointment out of his voice. "I'll see you tonight." He hung up the phone slowly, trying to be optimistic, but he'd heard the distance in her voice. Alan looked down at the pad of paper he'd been doodling on and stopped, then jammed his fingers through his hair and sighed.

He'd drawn the outline of a heart and inside, in slanting letters, he'd written the word *Pam's*.

PAM SETTLED the phone in its cradle and blinked back hot tears. How ironic that after all these weeks, he had chosen today to call. Today, when she was wrestling with how to break the news to him that he had fathered a child while on a fake honeymoon with his ex-fiancée's best friend.

How could she face him? How could she present him with the news of a child he did not want by a woman he did not want? Wouldn't the Parish family be proud. She could hear the whispers now, see the sneers on her brothers' faces.

She dropped her head into her hands. How could she face Jo? Since Pam's return, her friend had thanked her profusely for offering Alan a comforting hand during a very trying period in his life. Only it would soon become clear that she had offered Alan more than her hand.

How could she face her child? How could she tell her child that he or she was conceived in lust by a father who had just been jilted and by a mother whose dreams were too outlandish to be realized?

And how could she face herself? She had been careless with her heart, and careless with her body. She had known Alan was in love with her best friend. He'd used her to get over the hurt, and she had let him. She had let him on the slimmest hope that the man who represented everything she wanted in a partner—security, integrity, heritage and nobility—would recognize in her what no man had ever seen and fall in love with her.

Perhaps she had loved him ever since he'd hauled her off Mary Jane Cunningham's back in high school. He had taken up for her, but she'd given him a shin-shiner because she didn't know how else to react to someone in his social class. She couldn't very well act as though she *liked* him.

Since that day, she had found it easier to make fun of him rather than admit he had something she envied. And when their paths had crossed again as adults, she had simply picked up where she'd left off. Only in the wee hours of the morning when she was alone with her thoughts and fears and dreams had she been honest with herself. Only then had she admitted that Alan was the man she wanted but knew she'd never have, so she'd filled her dance card with has-beens and wannabes and never-would-bes.

Just like Alan had filled his dance card with her in the wake of Jo's rejection.

She shoved her hands into her hair. Now what? Pam wiped her eyes and pulled her address book from a desk drawer. After dialing an Atlanta extension, she sniffed mightily, feeling better just at the anticipation of hearing the voice of a dear old friend. Someone with a little objective distance. Someone she could trust to set her straight. Someone with big, broad, undemanding shoulders.

"Hello?"

"Manny? It's Pamela."

"Well, hello, baby doll!" He clucked. "You'd better have a good excuse why I haven't heard from you lately."

She smiled at the laughter in his voice. "Would you settle for a good excuse for calling now?" As much as she tried to maintain control, she could not keep her voice from breaking on the last word.

"What's wrong?" he asked, immediately serious. "Oh, God, it's a man, isn't it?" He sighed dramatically. "The straight ones all seem programmed to seek and destroy."

"I need to get away for a few days," she whispered.

"I'll alert the pedestrians of Atlanta that you're on your way."

ALAN CHECKED his watch for the twentieth time. Where was she? Pam was only a few minutes late, but after he'd talked to her, the rest of the afternoon had crawled. He was impatient to see her, to talk to her. He drummed on the surface of the hotel bar, feeling ready to come out of his skin with anticipation. The bartender slid a shot of whiskey across the bar and he downed it, hoping it would give him the courage he needed.

He loved her. It sounded ridiculous and she'd probably laugh in his face, but he didn't care. The week in Fort Myers, although admittedly fraught with disaster, had given him a taste of her spice for life, and he had become addicted. Every day since returning home, he had told himself the restlessness would pass, that they had simply been caught up in the romance of a beach fling. But he finally had to admit to himself that he wanted Pamela, that he *needed* Pamela in his life.

And he refused to share her with other men—he wanted a commitment. Marriage seemed a bit ludicrous considering he had been standing at the altar with another woman just a few weeks ago. Besides, Pam had made it perfectly clear that she wasn't looking to become any-one's wife. But he hoped she would at least move in with him, a public declaration that they were a couple. Then perhaps someday they would both be ready for marriage…and a family.

Alan stopped and shook his head. He still had to get through tonight—he'd worry about the heavy stuff later. His imminent concern was the risk of her choking from laughing too hard. In his mind he reviewed the Heimlich maneuver, then checked his watch again. She was worth waiting for.

AROUND EIGHT O'CLOCK Pam found a parking place a half block from Manny's apartment building. Her back ached and her feet were swollen from the five-hour drive, an omen of the months to come, she knew. She'd cried off her makeup by the time she'd reached Macon, but Manny wouldn't mind. City sounds greeted her when she opened the door and lifted herself out of the car. Little Five Points was one of her favorite areas in Atlanta, and ablaze with crimson, pink and white azaleas, it was certainly one of the prettiest this time of year.

She rolled her shoulders and stretched her legs, then grabbed her bag. Although it was only a short walk to Manny's building, followed by a brief flight of stairs, her feet felt as though they were made of concrete by the time she arrived at her friend's apartment. He swung open the door before she'd finished knocking and swept her into a huge hug.

When he set her on her feet, he chucked her lightly under the chin. ''Pam, one of these days you simply must begin to age.''

Pam smiled at the tall, fair-haired man she'd met at a club several years ago. They'd hit it off and had maintained contact over the years, visiting at every chance. Manny Oliver was a confirmed homosexual and a world-class good guy. Pam looked at his dancing eyes and sighed. "Manny, if you ever decide to jump ship, I want to be the first to know."

"Darling, you and Ellie would be the only women in my lifeboat."

"How is Ellie?" Pam asked, referring to his former roommate.

"Disgustingly happy," he said, rolling his eyes. "Married less than a year and she and Mark are already expecting a baby." He shuddered. "I ask you—what woman could possibly endure those hideous maternity fashions?"

Pam pursed her lips and dropped her gaze. "Got any dos and don'ts for me?"

"Oh, no," he murmured, sinking into a chair. "Not you, too."

She nodded, her eyes welling with tears.

He simply opened his arms and shooed her inside, then rocked her through another crying jag. Only after she'd blown her nose twice and gotten over the hiccups did he question her.

"Who is the proud papa?"

"His name is Alan Parish."

"Does he know?"

She shook her head.

"Are you going to tell him?"

Pam nodded.

"*Tell* me this guy is husband material."

She laughed dryly. "He had a wedding in February."

"Pam," he chided. "Even *I* don't mess around with married men."

"No, he was marrying my best friend, but she called off the wedding at the last minute."

"Ah. And you picked up the pieces?"

"Something like that. But I don't think he's ready to

make another trip to the altar.'' She laughed softly, then added, ''Not with me anyway.''

''How do you think he will react to the news?''

She bit her bottom lip to stem another flood of tears. ''He hates kids.''

Manny frowned. ''Well, if that's the case, he should keep his pants zipped.''

''It's my fault—my pills failed.''

''That's a moot point. Now you have to make plans for this baby. Are you going to keep it or give it up for adoption?''

''I'm keeping it.''

''And can you expect any help from this Parish guy?''

''I'm not sure.''

Manny squinted and angled his head. ''Pam, is there something you're not telling me?''

''I'm in love with him.''

''The plot thickens. And his feelings for you?''

''Zilch.''

''Not true—he got naked with you, didn't he?''

''Okay, I suppose he's physically attracted to me.''

''It's a start.''

''But he's still in love with my best friend.''

''He told you this?''

''No, but he hasn't called since we were together—until today when he asked me to meet so we could talk about his feelings for her.''

''Sounds like a jerk to me.''

''Oh, no—he's really a great guy. In fact, one of the reasons I admire him so much is that he was so committed to my friend.''

''If the man doesn't scoop you up and count his blessings, he's obtuse,'' Manny insisted.

"He's a little uptight," Pam admitted, smiling fondly. "But when he lets go, he can be very endearing."

Manny handed her a cup of tea and lifted one eyebrow. "And good in bed, I certainly hope."

She nodded miserably.

He sighed. "Promise me you won't wear stripes in the last trimester."

ALAN STRUGGLED to keep his voice calm. "But you don't understand," he explained to the receptionist at Pam's office. "I *have* left voice-mail messages. I've left *fourteen* voice-mail messages."

"Perhaps her cellular phone—"

"She's not answering. Pam was supposed to meet me last night and she didn't show. I'm worried about her."

The receptionist didn't seem particularly sympathetic that he'd been stood up. "Sir, all I can tell you is that Ms. Kaminski said she'd be out of the office for a few days. I can give you her pager number—"

"I called her pager number—she's not answering!"

"Then I'll transfer you to her voice mail."

"Wait—" he yelled, but he heard a click and Pam's voice message, which he'd now memorized. Alan slammed down the phone and cursed. He reared back and kicked his desk as hard as he could, bellowing when the pain shot up his leg.

"Mr. Parish," Linda said, sticking her head through his doorway. "Are you okay?"

Alan inhaled deeply. "I'm fine, Linda." Then he limped to his valet and yanked on his jacket. "Cancel my appointments for the rest of the afternoon."

PAMELA LIVED IN a neat little town house in an artsy part of town—Alan suspected she'd made a good investment, considering her line of work. He had been there only twice to pick her up for some event they had attended together, but he hadn't gone inside. The tiny driveway was vacant, and the shades were drawn. The outside light glowed weakly in the bright midmorning sun, as if to fool someone into thinking she was home.

He walked up the steps and retrieved her untouched morning paper, then knocked on her front door several times before going around to the back and doing the same. After ten minutes, Alan climbed back into his car and pounded his steering wheel in frustration. "Pam, where are you?" he shouted into the cab of his car. "*Where are you?*"

He laid his head back and exhaled, then straightened and turned the key. Within minutes, he was heading toward Jo Montgomery's office, not sure what he was going to tell her, but absolutely certain that he had to find Pam.

As luck would have it, Jo was in a deep embrace with her new husband, John Sterling, when Alan knocked and stuck his head through her open doorway. They quickly parted, although John kept a possessive arm around Jo's waist while she straightened her clothing.

"Alan," she gasped. "What a nice surprise."

"We didn't hear you come in," John said with a tight smile.

"I wonder why," Alan said dryly. "Jo, could I have a word with you?"

"Of course," she said quickly, then glanced at her husband, who wore a wary frown.

"It's about Pam," Alan informed him impatiently.

"Jo, I'll see you at home," John said, dropping a quick kiss on her mouth. He nodded curtly to Alan as he left.

"Do you want some coffee?" Jo asked politely.

Alan shook his head. "I'm looking for Pam and I thought you might know where she is."

Jo averted her gaze and relief swept through him. Jo knew, which meant at least Pam was okay.

"Did you leave her a voice message?" she asked.

"Sure did."

"Maybe she hasn't had a chance to return calls."

"Where is she?"

"Alan—"

"I have to see her, Jo. It's important."

"She asked me not to tell anyone—"

"Jo, there's something you should know."

Jo frowned. "Alan, what's wrong?"

He exhaled noisily, suddenly unsure of himself. "Something happened when Pam and I were in Fort Myers."

"Alan, I don't think this is any of my—"

"I fell in love with her."

Her eyes widened slightly, and a slow smile climbed her face. "What?"

"I fell in love with her." He raised his hands in the air. "Jo, I swear to you on everything I hold sacred that nothing ever went on between us when you and I were together." He pursed his lips and gritted his teeth before continuing. "But when we were in Fort Myers, I saw Pam in a new light. She's warm and funny and smart—" He broke off and shrugged helplessly. "She makes me happy, Jo, and when I'm with her, I understand what you must feel when you're with John."

Jo's eyes were full of unshed tears. "Alan, nothing would make me happier than to see the two of you together."

"I have to find her, Jo, and tell her how I feel. Even if

she doesn't love me, I can't go another day with this on my heart.''

She smiled, displaying a dimple. ''How about five hours?''

''Five hours?''

''She's in Atlanta, staying with a friend for a few days.''

Alan frowned. ''A male friend?''

She nodded, and hurt stabbed him hard in the chest. He laughed softly and shook his head. ''What's the point if she's with another man?''

Jo walked over to him and touched his arm. ''It's a good thing John didn't let that stop him,'' she said quietly. ''For both our sakes.''

12

AFTER A MORNING of hugging the toilet, Pam napped away the afternoon, then dragged herself toward the tub. A shower, she'd discovered, was a heartbroken, pregnant woman's solace because there she could cry freely and it didn't matter.

Not that she didn't cry everywhere else anyway. Throughout the day, Manny pampered her with cool cloths for her forehead, warm cloths for her neck, pillows for her feet, pillows for her back, the latest magazines and nice, bland food when her stomach could stand it. She felt lumpy and frumpy in one of Manny's old sweat suits, but being enveloped in his big, masculine clothes gave her comfort.

When dusk began to fall, he dragged a cushiony chair out onto the fire escape and planted her there while he brushed her hair. The spring breeze was unusually balmy, inspiring Pam to inhale great lungfuls of fresh air. A zillion stars glittered overhead, triggering memories of the night she and Alan strolled along the moonlit beach and the passion that had swept them away.

Well, actually, Alan had been swept away to jail, but that night had been an awakening for her, and she would never forget it. She toyed with the sand-castle pendant that hung around her neck, where it had been since the day they'd returned to Savannah.

"Maybe I need a change of scenery," she said, sipping the cup of peppermint tea Manny had prepared for her.

"You're welcome to this apartment," he offered. "But in a couple of months you'll have to find another roommate."

She twisted in her chair. "You're moving?"

"To San Francisco, in June."

"Why didn't you say something?" Pam demanded.

"Darlin', you've got enough on your mind." He clucked. "I was planning to send you a change-of-address card."

"What's in San Francisco?"

"A career path," he said flatly. "On New Year's I took a glimpse into my future, and believe me, there's nothing pretty about a senior-citizen drag-queen performer."

Pam laughed—Manny hadn't yet seen his fortieth birthday and was an exceptionally handsome guy. "What will you do?"

He bowed. "Concierge at the Chandelier House, at your service, madam."

"Manny, that's wonderful—you'll be a big hit!" Then she made a face. "I'll miss you though."

"You and the *bébé* will have to come out for a visit."

"We will," she declared, grinning at him in the mirror.

Manny cocked his ear toward the apartment and held up a finger. "I think I heard a knock, I'll be right back."

Pam sank deeper into the seat and wrapped her hands over her stomach. *Imagine,* she thought with a little smile, *Alan's baby growing inside me.* And although she wasn't foolish enough to believe raising a child on her own would be easy, she would do what she had done all her life—make the best of her circumstances. This child would be loved, if by no one else, then by her.

"Pam," Manny said from the doorway, "you have a visitor."

She jerked her head around in surprise, then gasped when she saw Alan standing in the living room, his suit jacket over his shoulder and his face grim. To see him after so many weeks was a shock to her senses, and she couldn't fathom why he was here. Standing on wobbly legs, she stepped into the doorway, aware that Manny hovered an arm's length behind her.

Alan straightened when Pam stepped into view. His heart slammed against his chest painfully. She looked beautiful, but different. Softer, perhaps, with no makeup and her hair loose around her shoulders. Wearing her lover's clothes, she looked dewy-eyed and vulnerable. Jealousy ripped through him and he tried not to think about the rumpled covers and pillows on the couch. Seeing their recent sex venue only strengthened his resolve that under no circumstances would he share her with another man.

"Alan, this is my friend Manny—"

"We already met, sweetheart," Manny assured her, but his eyes never left Alan.

Alan's hands twitched at the casual term of endearment, but he tried to focus on the reason he'd come.

"Alan," Pam asked, taking another step toward him. "What are you doing here?"

"Looking for you."

Her smile was shaky. "Obviously, but why?"

Alan glanced to her tall boyfriend, but the man wasn't about to budge from the room. "Would you excuse us, um, Manny?"

The guy poked his tongue into his cheek, then glanced to Pam with raised eyebrows for confirmation. She nodded.

"I'll be in the bedroom," the man said, glaring at Alan. "Yell if you need me, Pam."

"Thanks, Manny."

Alan waited until he heard the bedroom door close before speaking, and then he didn't know where to start. "I waited for you the other night."

"Something came up—I should have called."

"I was worried."

"I'm fine," she said with a nervous laugh. "How did you know where to find me?"

"Jo."

She nodded, lowering her gaze.

"Look, Pam," he said, stepping closer but maintaining a safe distance. "I didn't mean to embarrass you in front of your boyfriend, but—"

"He's not my boyfriend. Manny's gay."

Relief swept through him. "Really? Hey, that's great— I say a man's got to do what a man's got to do, and if that means marching—"

"Alan, what do you want?"

He mentally went down the list he'd made and left in the car. "I didn't mean to embarrass you in front of your boyfriend—"

"You said that already," she said, lifting a corner of her mouth. "Don't tell me you've got a script."

Panic flooded his vocal cords. "I love you, dammit!"

She stood stock-still while he hung out swinging in the breeze, waiting for her answer. Seconds ticked by.

"Say something," he said.

"I'm pregnant with your baby."

He froze and glanced around the room, absorbing her words, but finding them too unbelievable to comprehend. "Come again?"

"I'm pregnant with your baby."

Strange, but the words sounded exactly the same the second time. Alan felt his jaw drop, close, then drop again. Intelligent words to combine into an appropriate response had to reside somewhere deep in his brain, but they didn't seem to be forthcoming.

She waited.

His mind raced. Men became fathers every day—coming up with a reply for the woman he loved couldn't be that hard.

"Gee," he said with a shaky laugh, then felt the room close in around him. "I think I'm going to pass out." But even though the trip to the floor seemed to be in slow motion, the thump of his head against the wood revived him somewhat.

Alan heard Pam scream for Manny, then heard the man tell her to get a pitcher of water from the refrigerator.

Manny slapped him lightly on the cheeks, then a stinging blast of ice water hit his face, taking his breath. His temple throbbed with a new pain.

His eyes popped open and through his water-speckled lenses, he saw Pam standing over him holding a glass pitcher.

"Uh—Pam," Manny said. "You could have taken out the ice first." He handed her a chunk as large as a man's fist, tinged with blood. "He might have a concussion."

"I'm fine," Alan mumbled. "Help me up."

Manny helped him to the couch then gave him a cloth to hold to his bleeding temple. "You're going to have a heck of a goose egg, man."

Alan smiled and shrugged, looking at Pam. "It comes with the territory."

"I hope your insurance is paid up," Manny muttered on his way out of the room.

"Sounds like I'm going to need the family plan," Alan said, locking gazes with Pam.

"Alan—"

"Why didn't you tell me about the baby?" He clasped her by the upper arms. "I've missed you like crazy these past few weeks, and I was nearly insane wondering what happened to you last night."

"When you called, I was trying to decide how to break the news, then you said you wanted to talk about your feelings for Jo—"

"It was an excuse—I didn't think you'd meet me otherwise."

She blinked. "That was dumb."

"I was desperate!"

Pam winced. "How much does Jo know?"

"Everything."

"Oh no."

"And she said she couldn't be happier. In fact, she encouraged me to come after you." His Adam's apple bobbed. "Pamela Kaminski, will you marry me?"

Her eyes widened. "M-marry?"

"You know—you'd be the wife, I'd be the husband."

"Wife?" she whispered, then smiled tremulously. "I hadn't planned on ever being anyone's wife." Then she laughed, her eyes filling with tears. "But I hadn't planned on ever being anyone's mother, either."

He grinned. "I've noticed lately that life is full of surprises."

"Alan, I know you don't like kids—"

"Unless they're mine," he corrected.

"But kids are loud…"

"So are you."

"—and messy…"

"So are you."

"—and the diapers..."

He winced. "You got me there."

"It won't be easy."

Alan curled his fingers around her neck and pulled her face close to his. "Is that a yes?"

Her eyes were luminous as she studied his face, then she dabbed at the blood on his temple. "That's a yes," she whispered, then added, "The 'P' stands for 'papa.'"

THE CHURCH WAS somewhat less crowded this time, Alan noticed from his view at the altar. Which was fine with him, as long as the people who mattered were there.

His parents sat on the front pew, crying happy tears because Pam had enchanted them as much as she had enchanted him. Pam's mother sat on the opposite side, dabbing her eyes. Her two brothers stood next to him, fingering their tight collars, waiting for Pam to make her entrance. Her older brother, Roy, pointed to Alan's bandaged hand. "What happened?"

"A little mishap when we tried on rings," Alan explained with a shrug.

"Sounds like Pam," Roy affirmed with a nod. "You'd better lower your deductible. By the way, where the devil is she?"

Alan tried not to betray the nervousness that wallowed in his stomach. "She must be here, or the director wouldn't have let them start the music."

"They've played that song so many times, I know it by heart," Roy whispered hoarsely.

"Maybe she had a sudden case of morning sickness," Alan said, trying to squelch humiliating flashbacks from the last time he stood at the altar.

"It's two in the afternoon."

"Well, you know women's bodies can be... unpredictable."

Roy grinned. "Not the word I would have used, but whatever."

After another five minutes of "O Promise Me", Alan glanced at Jo, who stood an arm's length away in a simple bridesmaid dress. She chewed on her lower lip and shrugged slightly, then mouthed, "Want me to go check?"

Alan sighed, feeling sick to his stomach. If Pam had changed her mind about becoming his wife, he wanted to be the one to know. He walked down the aisle, trying to block out the concerned murmur that swept through the guests, then marched through the back doors of the chapel.

His hand shook as he opened the door to the bride's waiting room, and his heart pounded when he saw it was empty. He checked the bathroom, but found it abandoned, as well. With a sinking heart, he realized she must have changed her mind. He gritted his teeth, then laughed bitterly. He was zero for two.

His eyes stung with emotion as he walked back toward the chapel once again to tell everyone to go home, but as he walked past the open doors of the church entrance, he heard a familiar beeping horn. He glanced outside in time to see Pam's Volvo jump the curb and come to a screeching halt, mere inches from a stone statue of some important-looking saint.

Dressed in full bridal regalia, with a voluminous veil and enormous train, she took quite a while to extricate herself from the car. When she did, she gathered the skirt in her arms, hiking it up to her thighs to run across the churchyard in bare feet. Carrying her shoes in one hand, she waved when she saw him in the doorway. "I'm coming!" she yelled. "I'm coming!"

"Where have you been?" he demanded when she came to a halt in front of him. God, she was gorgeous, especially with her slightly rounded tummy.

"Mrs. Wingate paged me," she said breathlessly. "Her head psychic told her she had a one-hour window of safety to buy the Sheridan house." She panted for air. "I was already dressed, and I figured I could leave and get the papers signed before anyone missed me." She smiled happily, her chest heaving. "Did anyone miss me?"

He sighed, wanting to shake her. "You scared me to death—I thought you had changed your mind."

She looped her arms around his neck. "Not on your life—you're stuck with me, Mr. Alan P. Parish." She pulled his mouth to hers for a deep kiss.

He raised his head, then bent down and lifted her into his arms. "Let's go make you my wife before anything else happens." Then he turned, carried her toward the chapel and whispered, "I have a confession to make."

"What?"

"I told the guy at the tattoo parlor that the 'P' stands for 'Pam's.'"

Epilogue

ALAN RAISED his hands. "Pam," he said in a soothing voice. "Put down the nail file."

"You!" she yelled at him from the hospital bed. "You did this to me!"

"Honey," he said, "don't you think it was a combined effort?"

He ducked as the vase of flowers flew past his head and crashed against the wall at his back.

"You're right!" he affirmed hurriedly, raising his arms in surrender. He put on a mournful expression and gestured vaguely toward her huge stomach. "It's all my fault—I did this to you and I am the lowest scum on the face of the earth."

Her face contorted with pain and Alan's heart twisted in agony. His beautiful wife was lying in abject misery, and he couldn't even get close enough to the hospital bed to practice the Lamaze they had learned together.

"Do you have your focus point, sweetie?" he called, inching closer.

She lay back, panting, then pinned him with a deadly look. "I'm focusing on a life of celibacy!"

"Honey, you don't mean that," he said in his most cajoling voice, but stopped when she held up the makeshift dagger. "Celibacy is good," he assured her with a nervous laugh. "We can make it work." Alan retreated the few inches he'd advanced. "How about an ice chip?" he asked.

"How about I chip your tooth?" she offered, smiling sweetly.

The door swung open and Dr. Campbell strode in with a smile. "How're we doing?"

Alan, weak with relief to have an ally, smiled broadly. "Just great," he said, then glanced at Pam's murderous expression. "I mean, not very well at all."

"Let's see where you are, Pam." To Alan's alarm, the doctor eased Pam's swollen feet and ankles into the stirrups, giving him a bird's-eye view beneath her hospital gown. He swallowed and cleared his throat. "I think I'll wait outside."

"Oh no you don't," Pam said, ominously. "You're not going anywhere."

Alan nodded obediently and wiped his sweaty hands on his slacks. "Right—wild horses couldn't drag me out of here."

The doctor glanced at the monitor. "Here comes another contraction, Pam. Just try to relax."

"Remember to breathe, sweetie," Alan called. "Hee-hee—"

"Shut up!" she shouted.

"I'm shutting up," he said, nodding vigorously.

"If the pain's getting to be too much," the doctor said to Pam, "I can go ahead and give you an epidural."

"Thanks anyway, Dr. Campbell," Alan said from the wall. "We decided from the beginning to go for natural childbir—"

"Give me the needle, Dr. C.," Pam cut in, "and I'll give it to myself."

"Oh my," the doctor said, moving her hands beneath the gown.

Alan glanced over, then squeezed his eyes shut, muttering thanks to the heavens for the thousandth time today that he was not a woman.

"Forget the epidural," the doctor said, depressing the nurse call button with her elbow. "You're ready to start pushing."

Alan's eyes popped open. "Already?"

"Already?" Pam shrieked. "It's been nine hours!"

But I'm not ready, I'm not wise enough yet to be a father. Perspiration popped out on his hairline and panic rose in his chest, suffocating him.

The nurses rushed in and dressed him in sanitary garb as if he were a kid going out in the snow. He was relegated, happily, to a corner as they prepared Pam for the final stages of labor. Alan had never felt so guilty and helpless in his life. She agonized through two more contractions before the doctor said, "Daddy, you come jump in anytime."

Alan glanced to Pam for affirmation, but her eyes were squeezed shut to ward off the pain. Her hands were on the bed railing, so at least her weapon had been confiscated.

"Pam?" he said weakly, stepping closer. "Sweetie?"

She didn't open her eyes, but she lifted a hand toward him, and he went to her side with relief.

"Alan," she whispered, lolling her head toward him.

"Yes, dear?"

"What does the 'P' stand for?"

"Pam, now doesn't seem like the time—"

She twisted a handful of his shirt and pulled him close to her. "I said, what does the 'P' stand for?"

"Pam, you need to push," Dr. Campbell said. "On the count of three."

"Alan—" Pam said through clenched teeth.

"One—"

"—what does—" Her face reddened.

"—two—"

"—*the 'P' stand for?*"

"—three—push!"

Her face contorted in pain and she screamed. Alan, scared half out of his wits, yelled, "Presley! The 'P' stands for 'Presley!'"

She grunted, bearing down for several seconds, then relaxed on the pillow and opened her eyes. "Presley?" she panted.

He nodded miserably. "My mom was a huge fan."

She laughed between gasping for air, readying herself for another push at the doctor's urging. He held her hand tight and whispered loving words in her ear.

"Here comes the head," said the doctor.

She bore down and squeezed his hand until he was sure she'd broken several bones. His heart thrashed in his chest and he looked around to see what he would hit when he passed out.

"One more push, Pam," the doctor urged.

She took a deep breath and screamed loud enough to rattle the windows. Alan held on, wondering if his hearing would return.

"Here we are," the doctor said triumphantly. "It's a big boy."

Relief and elation flooded his chest and he kissed Pam's face, whispering, "It's a boy. It's a boy."

Pam, exhausted but beaming, held her hands out to accept the wrinkled, outraged infant. Alan's heart filled to bursting as he looked down at his son, whose lusty cries filled the air.

"Do you have a name?" the doctor asked.

"Not yet—" he said.

"Of course we do," Pam said as she raised her moist gaze to her husband. "His name is Presley."

BEGUILED

Lori Foster

PROLOGUE

HARSH WIND THREW icy crystals of snow down the back of his neck, causing him to shiver. He raised his collar, then shoved his hands deep into the pockets of his coat, resisting the urge to touch the gravestone. The grave was all but covered in white, making everything look clean, but Dane Carter didn't buy it. Not for a minute.

He'd missed the burial by almost four months. His family was outraged, of course, but they'd never really forgiven him for past transgressions, so he figured one more didn't matter. Except to himself.

His face felt tight, more from restrained emotion than from the biting cold. The death of his twin was a harsh reality to accept, like losing the better part of himself even though he and Derek hadn't been in contact much lately. Dane had been away from the family, disconnected from the business, for quite a few years now. He deliberately took the cases from his P.I. firm that kept him out of town as much as possible. Though his office was only an hour away, he'd been out of reach when his brother had needed him most.

Though everyone seemed to accept Derek's death as an accident, concerned only with keeping the news out of the media to avoid a panic with the shareholders, Dane couldn't let it rest. He wouldn't let it rest. He had a nose for intrigue, and things had begun to smell really foul. It wasn't anything he could put his finger on, just a gut feeling, but his instincts had held him in good stead as a private detective for several years now—ever since he'd left the family business in his brother's capable hands.

He hunkered down suddenly and stuck one hand through the snow to the frozen ground. "What the hell happened, Derek? This was a lousy trick to play on me. I never wanted this, not the company, hell, not even the family most of the time. You left too damn many loose ends, brother."

The wind howled a hollow answer, and disgusted with himself, Dane drew his hand back and cupped it close to his face, warming his fingers with his breath. "And what about this Angel Morris woman? I got a letter from her, you know, only she assumed you'd get it. Seems she doesn't know you're gone and she wants to pick up where the two of you left off. I believe I'm going to oblige her."

His mind skittered about with ramifications of deceit, but he had to cover all the bases. According to the records he'd uncovered, Angel Morris had been seeing Derek on a regular basis until the takeover of her company. Derek had used information Angel gave him to make the take-over easier, and Angel had gotten fired because of it. She had plenty of reasons to despise Derek, and he certainly deserved her enmity. Yet now she wanted to see him again. After so long, he had to wonder if Angel had as-sumed Derek was dead, but with Dane's return, she felt she had unfinished business. After all, no pronouncements had been made.

As far as the outside world was concerned, Derek Car-ter was still running the business. Only a select few knew of his demise. The family had thought it best if Dane filled in for a while. If he pretended to be Derek no one would start rumors about a company without a leader, or a family with a scandal. All in all, Dane wasn't sure which possibility worried his mother more. The company was her life, and the Carter name was sacred in her mind. She wouldn't want either one damaged. And if Derek had been murdered, if the accident wasn't an accident at all as Dane feared, it would certainly hit the news.

But that wasn't why Dane had agreed to come back, why he was filling in for his brother. No, he wanted the truth, no matter what. And he'd damn well get it.

If Angel knew anything, if she was involved with Derek's death in any way, even peripherally, Dane would find out. He may have disassociated himself from the family, but he could be every bit as ruthless as the best of them.

Dane shook his head. ''I'll be seeing her first thing tomorrow, alone, away from the family as she insisted. I'll let you know how it goes.'' With that banal farewell, he turned and trod back through the snow to the road where his car sat idling, offering warmth, but no peace of mind.

What a laugh. Dane Carter hadn't had peace of mind since he'd walked out on his family, regardless of what he told them, what he insisted to himself. Maybe Angel, if she wasn't an enemy, could prove to be a nice distraction from his present worries. His brother had always had excellent taste in women.

CHAPTER ONE

ANGEL TRIED TO METER her breathing, to look calm, but her heart felt lodged in her throat and wouldn't budge. She hated doing this, had sworn she'd never so much as speak to the man again after his last, most devastating rejection. But she'd been left with little choice.

With her shoe box tucked beneath her arm and one hand on the wall, offering support, she made her way down the hall to Derek's office. She still felt awkward without her crutches, but she knew better than to show him any weaknesses at all. When she reached the open door, she straightened her shoulders, forced a smile, and tried to make her steps as smooth as possible.

Derek sat behind his desk, his chair half turned so that he could look out the window at the Saturday morning traffic. The rest of the building, except for the security guards, was empty, just as she'd planned.

He was still as gorgeous, as physically compelling as ever, only now he looked a little disheveled, a little rumpled. She liked this look better than the urbane business-man he usually portrayed. The only other time she'd seen him relaxed like this was right after he'd made love to her.

That thought licked a path of heat from her heart to her stomach and back again, and she had to clear her throat.

His chair jerked around and his gaze pierced her, freezing her on the spot. Even her heartbeat seemed to shudder and die. Only his eyes moved as he looked her over, slowly and in excruciating detail, as if he'd never seen her before and needed to commit her to memory, then their eyes met—and locked. For painstaking moments they stayed that way, and the heat, the intensity of his gaze, thawed her clear down to her toes. Her chest heaved as she tried to deal with the unexpected punch of reacting to him again. It shouldn't have happened; she didn't care anymore, wasn't awed by him now. Her infatuation had long since faded away, but seeing him with his straight brown hair hanging over his brow, his shirtsleeves rolled up, made him more human than ever. His gaze seemed brighter, golden like a fox, and she tightened her hold on the shoe box, using it to remind herself of her purpose.

She saw some indiscernible emotion cross his face, and then he stood. "Angel."

His voice was low and deep. As he rounded the desk his eyes never left hers, and she felt almost ensnared. She retreated a step, which effectively halted his approach. He lifted one dark eyebrow in a look of confusion.

Idiot. She didn't want to put him off, to show him her nervousness. That would gain her nothing. She tried a smile, but he didn't react to it. Moving more slowly now, he stepped closer, watching her, waiting.

"Can I take your coat?"

She closed her eyes, trying to dispel the fog of emotions that swamped her. When she opened them again, she found him even closer, studying her, scrutinizing her every feature. He lifted a hand and she held her breath, but his fingers only coasted, very gently, over her cheek.

"You're cold," he said softly. Then he stepped back. "Can I pour you a cup of coffee?"

Angel nodded, relieved at the mundane offer. "Thank you. Coffee sounds wonderful." Walking forward, she set her shoe box on the edge of the desk and slipped out of her coat, aware of his continued glances as he collected two mugs from a tray. She didn't mean to, but she said, "You seem different."

He paused, then deliberately went back to his task. "Oh? In what way?"

With one hand resting on the shoe box, she used the other to indicate his clothes. "I've never seen you dressed so casually before. And offering to pour me coffee. Usually you—"

He interrupted, handing her a steaming mug. "Usually I leave domestic tasks to women, I know." He shrugged, gifting her with that beautiful smile of his that could melt ice even on a day like today. "But you insisted no one else be here today, so I was left to my own devices. It was either make the coffee, or do without."

Angel fidgeted. "You know why I didn't want anyone else here. Your family would have asked questions if they'd seen us together."

He nodded slowly. "True." Then he asked in a low curious tone, "Why are you here, Angel?"

Flirting had never come easy to her, but especially not these days. She smiled. "I've missed you, of course. Didn't you miss me just a little?"

He stared a moment longer, then carefully set his mug aside. "Most definitely," he said. He took her coffee as well, placing it beside his, then cupped her face. Strangely enough, his fingers felt rough rather than smooth, and very hot. He searched her every feature, lingering on her mouth while his thumb wreaked havoc on her bottom lip, smoothing, stroking. "Show me how much you missed me, Angel."

Now this was the Derek she understood, the man who always put his own pleasures first, the man who had always physically wanted her. That hadn't changed. Without hesitation, surprised at how acceptable the prospect of kissing him seemed when all day she'd been dreading it, she leaned upward. He was much taller than her, and her leg was too weak for tiptoes, so she caught him around the neck and pulled him down.

When her mouth touched his, tentative and shy, she felt his smile. She kept her eyes tightly closed, mostly because she knew he was watching her and she felt exposed, as if he'd guess her game at any moment. It had been so long since she'd done this, since she'd kissed a man, and she was woefully out of practice and nervous to boot. If necessity hadn't driven her to it, she'd have gone many more months, maybe even years, without touching a man. Especially this man.

But now she was touching him, and shamefully, to her mind, it was rather enjoyable.

Tilting her head, she parted her lips just a bit and kissed him again, more enthusiastically this time, nibbling his bottom lip between her teeth. His humor fled and he drew a deep breath through his nose. "Angel?"

"Kiss me, Derek. It's been so long."

The errant truth of her words could be heard in the hunger of her tone, something she couldn't quite hide. His answering groan sounded of surprise, almost anger, but kiss her he did. *Wow*. Angel held on, stunned at the reaction in her body to the dampness, the heat of his mouth as he parted her lips more and thrust his tongue inside. His body, hard and tall and strong, pressed against hers. It had never felt this way, like a storm on the senses. Her heart rapped against her breastbone, her stomach heated, her nipples tightened, and he seemed to be aware of it all, offering soft encouragement every time she made a sound, every time she squirmed against him. She wasn't being kissed, she was being devoured.

"Damn, Angel."

"I know," she said, because everything was different, somehow volatile. "I didn't plan on…this."

He paused, his lips touching her throat, then raised his face to look at her. He said nothing, but his hand lifted and closed over her breast, causing her to suck in her breath on a soft, startled moan. Oh no. She was so sensitive, and she hadn't realized. "Derek…"

He kissed her again, hard, cutting off her automatic protest, then backed her to the desk. His groin pressed against her, making her aware of his solid erection, of the length and heat of it. Her plans fled; there was no room in her brain for premeditated thought, not when her body suddenly felt so alive again, reacting on pure instinct. His hand smoothed over her bottom, pulling her even closer, rocking her against him. Her leg protested, but she ignored it, an easy thing to do when his scent, his strength, filled her.

"How long has it been, Angel?"

She clutched his shoulders, her head back, her eyes closed, as he kneaded her breast with one hand, and kept her pelvis close with the other. Surely he knew as well as she did, so she merely said, "A long time."

"And you've missed me?" He nibbled her earlobe, then dipped his tongue inside. "Why didn't you call?"

Even in the sensual fog, she saw the trap. "After the way you acted last time?" She was astounded he would even ask such a thing!

He hesitated, then asked, "How exactly did you expect me to act?"

She stiffened as she pulled back. "Not like you couldn't have cared less! And after the way you'd betrayed my trust! You got me fired, you—"

"Shhh." He kissed her again, lingering, and his hand started a leisurely path down her body, measuring her waist, which thankfully was slim again, then roving over her hip. Her thoughts, her anger, turned to mush. She caught her breath with each inch he advanced. His fingers curled on her thigh, bunching her skirt, then moved upward again, this time underneath, touching against her leggings. He cupped her, startling her, shocking her actually. But she didn't move and neither did he. She tried to remind herself that this was what she'd hoped for, but it wasn't true. She'd stupidly hoped for so much more.

His fingers felt hot even through her clothes, but he was still, just holding her, watching her again. "Why now, Angel? Why this secret arrangement?"

She decided a partial truth would serve. "There's been no one but you."

"And you needed a man, so it had to be me?"

"Yes." That was true, too. She didn't know who to trust, who to fear, so for what she needed, no one else would serve. But she hadn't planned on her own honest participation. Her body reacted independently of her mind; she felt shamed by her response to a man she

should have loathed, but overriding that was some inescapable need, swamping her, causing her whole body to tremble. Maybe the pregnancy had altered her hormones or something, but she'd never in her life felt like this, and it was wonderful.

She pressed her lips together and squeezed her eyes shut. Her body felt tightly strung, waiting, anticipating. She dredged up thoughts of the past, of all the reasons she had to despise him, why his touch could never matter...

He seemed a bit stunned as she moaned softly and her fingers dug into his upper arms. He held her close, his own breathing harsh while his mouth moved gently on her temple. In all her imaginings, she had never envisioned this scenario, allowing him to touch her there, with her half-leaning on his damn desk, her face tucked into his throat. His heartbeat drummed madly against her own, and she grabbed his wrist to pull his hand away. "Derek, no."

Her voice shook with mortification, freezing him for an instant.

"Shhh." He dropped her skirt back into place and softly rocked her, soothing her. She bit her lip to keep her tears from falling, but even now she was painfully aware of his scent, his warmth. And the delicious, unexpected feelings didn't leave now that his touch was removed, they only quieted a bit.

She put one hand on his chest and lifted her face. He didn't smile, didn't ask questions. She couldn't quite look him in the eyes. "I'm sorry. I...I don't know what came over me."

"Am I complaining?"

She shook her head. No, he looked pleased, but not really smug. Not as she'd expected. "That's never happened before. I don't understand."

"What's never happened?"

"Between you and me. Usually everything was just so...controlled. And uncomfortable. I've never felt..."

His face darkened, and she hastened to explain. "I don't mean to insult you, but Derek, you know yourself that sex between us was...well, *you* seemed to like it okay, but I was a little disappointed. Not...not that it was all your fault. It's just that I didn't...it wasn't..."

He smoothed her hair, his jaw tight. He seemed undecided about something, and then suddenly he clasped her waist and lifted her off her feet. He sat her on the edge of the desk, roughly spreading her thighs and stepping between them in the same movement. Pain shot through her and she gasped, curling forward, her hand reaching for her leg, wanting to rub away the sharp pounding ache. Her breath had left her and her free hand curled into his biceps, gripping him painfully. Derek froze, then growled, "What the hell?"

Her teeth sank into her bottom lip, but God, it hurt, and with more gentleness than she knew he possessed, Derek lifted her into his arms and headed for the leather couch.

Nothing was going right. "Derek, put me down."

"You're as white as a sheet." He looked down on her as he lowered her to the sofa cushions, and she flinched at the anger in his eyes. "I noticed you were limping a little when you came in, but I didn't realize you were hurt."

"I'm not," she protested, the issue of her leg meant for another day. "Really, I'll just..."

"You'll just keep your butt put and tell me what's wrong. Is it your hip? Your leg?"

Before she could answer he reached beneath her long skirt and caught at her leggings, hooking his fingers in the waistband and tugging downward. "Derek!"

With his hands still under her skirt, his eyes locked on hers, he said, "After what we just came close to doing, you're shocked?"

Flustered was more apt, and appalled and embarrassed and... "Derek, please." But already he had her tights pulled down to her knees. She felt horribly exposed and vulnerable. He explored her thighs, being very thorough, and it was more than she could bear. "It's my lower leg," she snapped. "I broke it some time back and it's still a little sore on occasion. That's all."

He stared at her, and she had the feeling he didn't believe a single word she'd said. "Let me get your shoes off."

She sat up and pushed at his hands. "I don't want my shoes off, dammit!"

"At the moment, I don't care what you want." And her laced-up, ankle-high shoes came off in rapid order, then her tights. As he looked at her leg, at the angry scars still there, his jaw tightened. "Damn."

Angel bristled, her only defense at being so exposed. "It's ugly, I know. If it bothers you, don't look at it."

One large hand wrapped around her ankle, keeping her still, and the other carefully touched the vivid marks left behind by the break and the subsequent surgery. "A compound fracture?"

"So you're a doctor now?"

He ignored her provocation. "This is where the break

was, and this is where they inserted a rod.'' His gaze
swung back up to her face, accusing.

Disgruntled, but seeing no way out of her present predicament, she said, ''I'm fine, really. It's just that when
you sat me on the desk, you jarred my leg and it…well,
it hurt. It's still a little tender. I only recently got off
crutches.''

His gaze was hot with anger. ''And you're running
around downtown in the ice and snow today?''

''I wasn't running around! I came to see you.''

''Because you needed a man,'' he sneered, and her temper shot off the scales.

''Damn you!'' Struggling upward, pulling herself away
from his touch, she pointed to the shoe box still sitting
on his desk. ''I came to bring you that.'' Then she added,
''Whether you wanted it or not.''

He turned his head in the direction she indicated, but
continued to kneel beside the couch. ''What the hell is
it?''

Angel came awkwardly to her feet and limped barefoot
across the plush carpeted floor. She picked up the box,
but then hesitated. She hadn't planned to raise hell with
him, to anger him and alienate him. She had to move
carefully or she'd blow everything. She closed her eyes
as she gathered her thoughts and calmed herself. She
hadn't heard him move, but suddenly Derek's hands were
on her shoulders and he turned her toward him.

''What is it, Angel?''

He sounded suspicious, an edge of danger in his tone.
She'd always known Derek could be formidable, his will
like iron, his strength unquestionable. But she'd never

sensed this edge of ruthlessness in him before. She shuddered.

"I don't mean to shock you, Derek. And I realize you weren't all that interested when I told you, but I was hoping you'd feel different now."

His arms crossed over his chest and he narrowed his eyes. "Interested in what?"

She drew a deep breath, but it didn't help. "Our baby."

Not so much as an eyelash moved on his face. He even seemed to be holding his breath.

"Derek?"

"A baby?"

She nodded, curling her toes into the thick carpet and shivering slightly, waiting.

"How do you know it's mine?"

She reeled back, his words hitting her like a cold slap. After all she'd been through, everything that had happened, not once had she suspected he might deny the child. That was low, even for him. She had to struggle to draw a breath, and once she had it, she shouted, "You bastard!" She swung at him, but he caught her fist and the box fell to the floor, papers and pictures scattering.

"Miserable, rotten..." Her struggles seemed puny in comparison to his strength, but he had destroyed her last hope, delivered the ultimate blow. She wanted to hurt him as badly as she'd been hurt, but he was simply too strong for her and finally she quit. He hadn't said a word. Panting, shaking from the inside out, she whispered, "Let me go."

Immediately, he did. Keeping her head high, refusing to cry, to contemplate the hopelessness of the situation in the face of his doubt, she went to the couch and sat, snatching up her tights and trying to untangle them so she could get them on.

Even though she refused to look at him, she was aware of him still standing there in the middle of the floor, fixed and silent. When he squatted down to pick up the contents of the box, Angel glanced at him. His face was set, dark color high on his cheekbones. He lifted one small photo and stared at it.

All Angel wanted to do was get out. She jerked on her shoes, pulling the laces tight, fighting the tears that seemed to gather in her throat, choking her. She'd humiliated herself for no reason. She'd allowed him to touch her for no reason. He wasn't going to acknowledge the baby.

"I'm sorry."

She glanced up as she shrugged on her coat. Derek still crouched in the middle of the floor, a single photo in his hand, his head hanging forward.

Angel frowned. "What did you say?"

He slowly gathered up the rest of the things and came to his feet. "I said I'm sorry. The baby looks like me."

"Oh, I see. Otherwise, you wouldn't have believed me. In all the time you've known me, I've proven to be such an execrable liar, such an adept manipulator, it's of course natural that you would have doubts. Well, it's a good thing he doesn't have my coloring then, isn't it? You'd never know for sure."

"Angel…" He reached a hand out toward her, and there was something in the gesture, a raw vulnerability she'd never witnessed. In fact, too many things about him seemed different, some softer, many harder edged. Had something happened to him in the months since she'd last seen him?

She shook her head. She would never be drawn in by him again. "Those things are yours to keep. They're duplicates. Records, photos, a birth certificate, which if you notice, has the father's name blank."

"Why?"

He sounded tortured now and she frowned, tilting her head to study him. "You weren't interested, Derek, though I admit I was hoping you'd changed your mind by now."

"I'm interested," he growled.

She thought of the last time she'd called him, the hell he'd put her through. "When we spoke on the phone, you rudely informed me you didn't want any attachments to a baby. You told me I was completely on my own, not to bother you."

He actually flinched, then closed his eyes and remained silent. But she had no pity for him, not after all that had happened. "That's not why the name is blank, though. Remember what you told me about your family? Well, I love my son, and I won't lose him to anyone, not to you, not to your damn relatives."

He looked blank and her irritation grew. "Your mother is a damn dragon, determined that everyone live according to her rules. You said that's why your brother left, why he became so hard. Your family frightens me, if you want the truth. Especially your brother."

His golden eyes darkened to amber. "That's ridiculous."

"You said he was the only one strong enough, independent enough to leave the company without a backward glance, to go his own way and tell the rest to go to hell. You said he was the only one who could make your mother nervous or your sister cry. You said he could do anything he set his mind to.''

''No one makes my mother nervous, and my sister is a younger replica of her. Nothing touches them.''

Angel buttoned her coat. ''You've changed your mind then, but I won't. I won't take a chance that they'll try to take him away from me. I don't want them to know about my baby.''

''Our…'' He stopped and she saw his Adam's apple bob as he swallowed. ''Our baby.''

This was a point too important to skimp on. She went to him, holding his gaze no matter that he tried to stare her down. She pointed at his chest and forced the words out through stiff lips. ''I don't know what new paternal mode you're in, but don't try to take him from me, Derek. I swear I'll disappear so quick you'll never find me or him again. I can do it. I've made plans.''

''No.''

She was incredulous. ''You can't dictate to me! Not anymore. Whatever power you held over me, you gave up months ago when you rejected my pregnancy.''

He didn't shout, but his near whisper was more effective than any raised voice could be. ''Is that right? Then why are you here?''

She had to leave, now, before she tripped herself up. She turned toward the door. ''There's an address in with the papers and photos. A post office box.'' She slanted her gaze his way. ''I'm sure you remember it. You can get in touch with me there.''

''Give me your phone number.''

"I don't think so. But I'll call you soon."

"You're playing some game, Angel, and I don't like it."

She had her hand on the doorknob and slowly turned. "It's not a game." As she stepped through the door, she said over her shoulder, "And I don't like it either. Think about the baby, Derek, what you'd like to do, and I'll call you tonight. We can talk then, after you've gotten used to the idea."

He took two quick steps toward her. "What I'd like to do?" He frowned. "You want me to marry you?"

"Ha!" That was almost too funny for words. As she pulled the door shut, she said, "I wouldn't marry you if you were the last man on earth."

And she knew he'd heard her ill-advised words, because his fist thudded against the door.

Well, that hadn't gone off quite as planned. Actually, nothing like she'd planned. She'd hoped to seduce him, to regain his interest. She needed his help, his protection, and that was the only way she could think to get it. Sex had been the only thing he'd been interested in before, so it was what she'd planned to offer him now.

Only it felt as if she was the one seduced. Damn, why did he have to have this effect on her? Her body was still warm and tingling in places she'd all but forgotten about, and all because of a man she thought she'd grown to hate.

A man who had never affected her so intensely before.

Damn fickle fate, and whatever magic had made Derek Carter into a man her body desired.

CHAPTER TWO

DANE HIT THE DOOR once more for good measure, vexed
with himself and the turn of events. Dammit, he hadn't
meant to touch her. He had intended to get close to her,
but not that close. He'd wanted to learn about her, to
discover any involvement on her part, whether or not she
could provide a clue to his brother's death. But he'd also
planned to keep his hands to himself.

She'd made that impossible.

He'd wanted her the minute he'd seen her. She was
lush and feminine and seemed to exude both determination and vulnerability. He'd also been stunned because
Angel Morris looked nothing like the usual polished,
poised businesswoman his brother tended to gravitate toward.

And then she'd demanded he kiss her.

Without knowing the exact nature of her relationship
with Derek, he couldn't take the chance of turning her
away without raising suspicions. And at the moment,
given everything that had just transpired, he needed to
keep her close, not drive her away.

He'd suspected she was there for a purpose, but God,
he'd never considered a child.

Stalking across the office, he picked up the phone and
punched in a quick series of numbers. His hand shook as

he did so, and he cursed again. He could still feel the tingling heat of her on his hand, still pick up the faint hint of her scent lingering in the office. Angel might have been sexually aroused—her first time with him, to hear her tell it—but he felt ready to burst, not only with lust, but with a tumultuous mix of emotions that nearly choked him.

If not for her injured leg, he had a feeling they'd have both found incredible satisfaction. He'd have taken her and she would have let him. He grunted to himself, disgusted. Making love in his brother's office, on a damn desk, with a woman he barely knew and whose motives were more than suspicious. His own motives didn't bear close scrutiny.

"Sharpe here."

"Be ready," Dane barked, frustrated beyond all measure. "She should be leaving the building any second now." After receiving Angel's note, Dane had gone through her file, learning what he could about her, which wasn't much. When he'd first decided on the tail, he'd been reacting on instinct, his life as a P.I. making decisions almost automatic. Now he was driven by sheer male curiosity, and the possessive need to keep what was his. She had his nephew, and that formed an iron link between them that he wouldn't allow to be severed.

"Description?"

All his agents were very good, but Alec Sharpe, a brooding, almost secretive man of very few words, was the best. Dane trusted him completely.

"Blond, petite, probably limping a little. Wearing a long wool skirt and a dark coat."

"Got it."

The line went dead and Dane sighed, putting the phone

down. Alec would contact him again using the car phone once he was sure of his lead. He figured it would take Angel at least a few minutes to maneuver out of the building. If she was parked in the lot, that would take even more time. If she hailed a cab, no telling how long he'd be left waiting.

Alec knew he was still checking out the circumstances of his brother's death, but no one else did. So far he'd found only enough to raise his concerns, but not enough to form any conclusions.

His brother's home had been discreetly searched, his papers riffled through. And Derek had some unaccounted time logged in his otherwise very orderly date book that made Dane think he'd had meetings best left unnoted.

Dane settled himself back behind his brother's desk and began going through the papers and pictures Angel had given him. The first picture of the baby had shaken him and he stared at it again for long moments. It was a photo taken at the hospital of a tiny red-faced newborn that looked almost identical to the twin photos his mother still displayed on her desk. The shape of the head was the same, the soft thatch of dark hair, the nose. He traced the lines of the scrunched-up face and a tiny fist, then smiled, feeling a fullness in his chest.

The next picture was more recent, and the changes were amazing. As plump as a Thanksgiving turkey, the baby had round rosy cheeks, large dark blue eyes, and an intent expression of disgruntlement that reminded him of Derek. Dane wanted to hold the baby, to touch him, make sure he was real. He was a part of his brother, left behind, and Dane knew without a doubt he'd protect him with his life. He hadn't even met the baby yet, but already the little fellow had found a permanent place in his heart just by existing.

Dane turned the picture over and found the words, *Grayson Adam Morris, November 13, 1997.* A very recent picture, only a week old. And the name, it was respectable, solid, except that it should have read *Carter,* not *Morris.* Dane intended to see to that problem as soon as possible.

There were also copies of the birth records, and the baby's footprints, not much bigger than Dane's nose. He made note of the hospital Angel had gone to, the name of the doctor who'd attended her, and considered his next move. He shook his head, then looked impatiently at the phone. As if he'd willed it, the phone rang and he jerked it up.

"Yeah?"

Without preamble, Alec said, "She's getting on a bus and she has a baby and some tall guy with her."

Dane went still, then shot to his feet. The baby had been here with her? "Are you sure it's a baby?"

"Bundled up in a blue blanket, cradled in the guy's arms. I don't think it's her groceries."

"Who's the guy? Are you certain he's with her?"

"Tall, dark hair, sunglasses. Wearing a leather bomber jacket and worn, ragged jeans. He's holding her arm, they're chatting like old friends. You want me to find out?"

"No." His hand clenched iron-hard on the phone, and Dane decided he'd figure that one out on his own. "Just concentrate on the woman. You can see if he goes home with her, but other than that, ignore him."

"I'm on it. I'll get in touch when we reach a destination."

Again Dane hung up the phone, only this time he used a little more force than necessary. Damn her, had she been lying all along? Why would she bring the baby and a boyfriend with her when she claimed to have missed him—*Derek?* Didn't she think that was a bit risky, considering he could have followed her out?

He seethed for almost a half hour before Alec called him back with an address. The guy with Angel had in fact gone into the same building, and the building was located in one of the less auspicious areas of town. Dane pulled on his coat and put everything back into the shoe box, tucking it beneath his arm. He couldn't risk leaving anything behind where his family might find it. He locked the office on his way out.

Angel Morris thought she knew how to deal with him, but she was judging her moves on how Derek would react. Dane wasn't a game player, never had been and never would be. His family had figured that out too late; the sooner Miss Morris figured it out, the quicker they could get things settled. He intended to explain it all to her this very day.

WITH THANKSGIVING not too far off, many of the houses had Christmas decorations already up. All the shops he passed had their front windows filled with displays. But as he neared the address given to him by Alec, the spirit of Christmas melted away. Bright lights were replaced with boarded-up windows. Graffiti rather than green wreaths decorated the doors. None of it made any sense. Dane knew Angel had lived in a very upscale apartment complex while working for the Aeric Corporation. He knew from her file that she'd lost her job there after Derek had taken information from her to assure the success of a hostile takeover. But surely she wasn't destitute. She'd made a good yearly wage.

Wary of the denizens in the area, Dane parked his car in a garage and walked the last block to Angel's home. The bitter November wind cut through his clothes and made him shiver, but filled with purpose, he easily ignored the cold. When he reached the brick three-family home that matched the address Alec had given him, he gave a sigh of relief. Calling the house nice would be too generous, but it was secure and well-tended, located on a quiet dead-end street of older homes. Angel and his nephew should be relatively safe here.

At least until he moved them.

The front door wasn't barred. He entered a foyer of sorts and looked at the mailboxes. There was no listing for an Angel Morris, and he frowned. Then he saw an A. Morton and his instincts buzzed. Going on a hunch, he figured that had to be Angel. Why would she hide behind an alias, unless she had a reason to hide? He recalled his purpose in first starting this ruse. Though it was obvious she knew nothing of Derek's death, he couldn't discount the possibility that she might have helped set him up for the fall, even innocently. She certainly had plenty of reason to hate him and want him out of her life, and she professed to fear his family, so why then had she approached him today? Because she was surprised he *wasn't* dead? Did she have contact with an insider who had informed her of his resurrection? Very few people were privy to the fact of his and Derek's relationship.

The apartment number listed was on ground level and he went to the door, then knocked, bracing himself for the sight of her again. She'd really thrown him for a loop with her sensual response to him. And he knew in his gut her reaction hadn't been feigned. Just remembering it made his every muscle tense.

"Come on in, Mick."

Dane tightened his jaw and his temper slipped. So the guy who'd been with her, Mick, was welcome in any time? Did she respond as hotly with Mick as she did with him? Dane turned the doorknob and stepped inside.

Angel was lying on a sofa, her injured leg propped up on pillows. She wore only a flannel shirt and loose shorts cut down from a pair of old gray sweats. Thick socks covered her feet. She shoved herself half upright and stared at him in undiluted horror.

Dane looked at her from head to toe, and as a man he appreciated the earthy picture she presented. But he'd use caution from here on out. Angel seemed to vacillate between fear and awareness. Dane decided that either way he'd use her emotions against her to find out for sure what her purpose might be.

Her fair hair was tousled and spread out over the arm of the sofa. Her breasts beneath the worn flannel looked soft and full, without the casing of a bra. Her legs were very long and pale. He saw the vicious scars on her left leg, still angry and red, and his simmering temper jumped in a new direction.

He closed the door quietly and her incredible green eyes went wide and wary. "Derek."

He indicated her cushioned leg. "You're hurt worse than you let on."

Color washed over her face as she started to rise from the sofa. Dane was beside her in an instant. He caught her shoulders, pressing her back down, feeling the narrow bones beneath his hands, aware of her smallness, her softness. "Be still. It's obvious you overdid it today. You shouldn't have been up and around."

He perched on the sofa cushion next to her, feeling her apprehension while he examined her leg, trailing his fingers gently over her smooth skin. Just seeing the scars left behind made him wince in sympathy.

She seemed to gather herself all at once. "Just what are you doing here?"

"Checking up on you."

"How? How did you find me?"

"I had you followed." His gaze swung from her leg to her outraged face. "Why use an alias?"

Angel paled a little. "What are you talking about?"

"Your mailbox."

Rather than answer, she tried bluffing her way with anger. "That's none of your business. And why do you care anyway?"

He was good at lying when it suited him. "Because I have the feeling you'd never have let me get this close. But I second-guessed you, didn't I?" He waggled a finger in her face, bringing back her healthy surge of angry color. "I think I'll keep close tabs on you from now on."

She gasped and he added a not-too-subtle warning. "You can keep your secret, Angel—for now. But when I'm ready, I will know what's going on."

Her lips firmed and her look became obstinate. But beneath it all, he saw a measure of pain. "You're not completely mended yet, are you? Were you hurt anywhere else?''

She gave him another stubborn frown and his attention dropped to her body. Holding her gaze, he asked quietly, ''Would you like me to find out for myself?''

She jerked and her arms crossed protectively over her breasts. ''All right! I also had some bruised ribs and a few cuts and scrapes—all of which are now healed.''

He continued to look at her, and she turned her head away. ''My shoulder was dislocated, too.''

''Good God. What the hell happened to you?''

Even before she spoke, he knew no truths would cross her beautiful lips. Amazing that he could read her so easily after only knowing her such a short time, but he could.

Her chin lifted and she said, ''I fell.''

''Down a mountainside?''

''Down a long flight of stairs, actually.''

Keeping his hands to himself became impossible. He cupped her cheeks in both hands. Whatever had happened, it had been serious, and talking about it obviously agitated her. ''You could have been killed.''

She started, and her eyes met his. For the briefest moment she looked so lost, he wanted to fold her close and swear to protect her. *Idiot*. Then she shook her head and that stubbornness was back tenfold, forcing an emotional distance between them. ''My leg is the only thing scarred. Nasty-looking, isn't it?''

Without missing a beat, he said, ''You have beautiful legs. A little scarring won't change that.'' And it was true. Her legs were long, smooth, shapely. He imagined those long legs wrapped around him while he touched her again, only this time she would climax, holding him inside her

so he could feel every small tremor, every straining muscle. He nearly groaned.

He let his hand rest lightly on her knee and moved his
thoughts to safer ground. "You've no reason to be embarrassed, Angel. The scars will fade."

"You think a few scars matter to me?"

He did, but he wasn't dumb enough to tell her that, not
when she was practically spitting with ire. She hadn't forgiven him yet for Derek's past sins, and for his own, in
questioning the baby's parentage. But she would. He'd
see to it.

He put his hand to her cheek and noticed again the way
her pulse raced, how she held her breath. "I'm sorry you
were hurt." Then he kissed her. As angry as he was, he
needed a taste of her again. She may have decided her
little sampling of lust in the office was enough, but he'd
found only frustration. He'd barely touched her, barely
begun to excite her, and she'd heated up like a grand
fireworks display, perilously close to exploding. He was
still semi-hard because of it and caught between wanting
to bury himself inside her, to see her go all the way,
climaxing with him, and wanting to shake her into telling
him what her ridiculous game was.

At first she froze, but seconds later her body pressed
into his. One small hand lifted to his neck and that simple
touch made him shudder. He pulled back, not wanting to
test himself. Angel stared at him, wide-eyed.

"Nice place," he said, hoping to distract her and himself. His gaze wandered around the sparse room, taking
in the worn wallpaper and faded carpet. He didn't really
mean to be facetious, but she took it that way.

"You don't have to like it, Derek, since you don't live here."

He dropped his gaze back to her flushed face. With one arm above her, his body beside her, he effectively caged her in. He could tell she didn't like it; he liked it a little too much. "I want to know why you're living here. What happened to your apartment?"

Her eyes narrowed. "I lost it."

"Why?"

"Because I hadn't paid the rent."

He sighed. This was like pulling teeth, but she obviously wasn't going to make it easy for him. "Okay, we'll play twenty questions. Why didn't you pay the rent?"

Angel stared at him, then put one arm over her eyes and laughed. "God, you're incredible. Everything is so simple for you."

Wrapping long fingers around her wrist, he carried her arm to her stomach and held it there. He felt her muscles clench. "Why didn't you pay your rent?"

In a burst of temper, she slapped his hand away and half raised herself to glare at him. "Because I had no money, you ass! I lost my job, thanks to you, and no one else would hire me for what I was good at. After you finished, I was considered a *bad risk*. I tried everywhere, and in the process, ran through a lot of my savings. For a short time, I had a job as a waitress, but then I had the accident and was laid up for a while. People won't hire women on crutches, you know. My savings weren't so deep that I could afford to stay in an expensive place, keep up my medical insurance, and pay additional medical bills besides, so I moved here. Satisfied?"

Her shout had awakened the baby, and Dane looked

toward the sound of disgruntled infant rage. Angel groaned. "Now look what you've done. Well, don't just sit there, get out of my way."

Her mood shifts were almost amusing, and fascinating to watch—when she wasn't ripping his guts out with regret for the way his brother had treated her. She started to sit up, and again he pressed her back. "I'll get him."

"No!"

He caught her chin and turned her face up to his. "Now or later, Angel, what difference does it make? I want to meet him. I promise, I'll bring him to you."

She bit her lip and her eyes were dark with wariness, but she apparently realized there would be no contest if they tried to match strength or wills. At least, not at the moment. He had the feeling, on a better day, her strength would amaze him.

Dane stared a second more, wishing there was a simpler way to reassure her, then went to fetch the baby. He followed the sounds of the cries to where Grayson was making his discontent known. When Dane entered the room he was assailed by the scent of powder and baby lotion, soft soothing scents. Grayson's pudgy arms and legs churned ferociously, and with incredible care, Dane lifted him to his shoulder. The baby was soaking wet.

Cloth diapers and plastic pants were on top of a dresser, along with a few folded gowns. Dane scooped up what he thought he might need and went back to the main room and the worried mother. Angel immediately reached her arms out.

"No, he's soaked, which means I'm soaked. No reason for both of us to become soggy. I think if you talk me through it, I can get him changed."

Angel's mouth fell open and she stared at him as if he'd grown an extra nose. He smiled at her reaction.

She looked dumbfounded and utterly speechless.

"I know," he said, grinning, "changing diapers isn't part of my established repertoire, either. But I'm efficient at adapting."

In the short time he'd known her, she'd thrown him off balance more times than he cared to think about; it was only fair that he get a little retaliation when and where he could.

He didn't know a hell of a lot about babies, but he figured now was as good a time as any to learn. "Where should I put him to clean him up?"

Finally managing to close her mouth, Angel fretted, then pointed to a table. "There's a plastic changing pad there. You can put him on that and change him."

"Good enough." Dane shook out the padded plastic sheet with one hand, spread it out on the table, and carefully laid Grayson down. The baby wasn't pleased with delayed gratification, so Dane hurried. With Angel's instructions, he got the baby diapered and dried and redressed, all in under five minutes which he considered a major accomplishment. Grayson had stopped squalling, but he still fussed, one fist flailing the air, occasionally getting caught in his mouth for a slurpy suck or two.

This time when Angel held out her arms, Dane handed the baby to her. The entire right side of his shirt was wet and clinging to his chest.

She looked away, pressing her face against the baby. "He's hungry."

"Do you want me to get him a bottle?"

"No." Angel cleared her throat, then said, "He's...
breastfed. I just...need a little privacy."

"Oh. *Oh.*" Dane looked at her breasts, imagined the
process, and didn't want to take so much as a single step
from the room. He also couldn't bear to hear the baby
whimpering. "I'll, uh, just go in the kitchen and try to
rinse out my shirt."

"You do that. And stay in there while it dries."

He leaned down and caught her chin. Her eyes opened
wide on his and she drew in a deep startled breath. "All
right. But don't always expect me to follow orders, honey.
You're going to have to get used to me being here."
Knowing he shouldn't, but unable to stop himself, he
leaned down and pressed a firm kiss to her mouth. It felt
damn good. He walked out while she sputtered.

He wanted to kiss her again, as a starting point, knowing where they'd finish. He wanted to show her he was
no sloth in bed, contrary to her damn misconception. He
wanted to find out the truth about his brother's death and
her involvement with him, and he wanted to protect her
and take care of her and Grayson. There were a lot of
wants piling up on him too quickly and contradicting each
other.

Christ, what had his brother gotten into?

He pulled off his shirt and rinsed the damp spot under
running water, then wrung it out and hung it over a chair
to dry. The apartment, thankfully, wasn't cold. He
scratched his bare chest and looked around.

Her tiny kitchen was all but empty. The cabinets held
the essentials, but not much else. With further inspection,
he found the refrigerator was in similar shape. Dane

frowned, then began snooping. Hell, maybe he should call her Mother Hubbard.

The conclusion he came to was not a happy one. Damn the little idiot, she should have contacted him sooner, before she got in such miserable shape. He immediately snatched that thought back because if she'd tried, she would have encountered his family, and the mere thought made him queasy. She was right to fear them.

He had wondered what she was after, why she'd come to him if indeed marriage wasn't her goal. Now he assumed sheer desperation had been her motive. She needed financial help, and as the baby's father, he could give it. She was proud, and she claimed to have already suffered several rejections from Derek, a possibility that made Dane so angry he wanted to howl. But pride was no replacement for desperation, especially with a baby to think about. But if that's all it had been, then why hadn't she simply said so? Why come on to him, pretend she still cared?

He sat in a kitchen chair, stewing, listening to her murmur to the baby, hearing the sweet huskiness of her voice. Goose bumps rose on the back of his neck. He called out, "Angel, why don't you use disposable diapers? Aren't they easier?"

There was a hesitation before she said, "I don't like them."

Which he translated to mean they cost too much. His fingertips tapped on the table top, followed by his fist. "Where did you take therapy for your leg?" He hoped it was someplace close, so she hadn't had to travel too far.

There was mumbling that he couldn't decipher, then

she said, "I didn't take therapy. And what do you know about it anyway?"

He stiffened. No therapy? With a lot of effort, he curbed his temper. "I've seen similar breaks. I recognize the incisions on your ankle and knee where they inserted the titanium rod. It was a hell of a break, so I know damn well therapy was suggested."

Silence. He almost growled. He did stand to pace. "How long ago were you hurt, Angel, and don't you dare tell me it isn't any of my damn business!"

Another pause, and a very small voice. "A couple of months ago."

It took him a second, and then he was out of the kitchen, stalking back to the couch to loom over her. She took one fascinated look at his naked chest, squeaked, and pulled her flannel shirt over her exposed breast as much as possible. Grayson's small fist pushed the shirt aside again. But Dane was keeping his gaze resolutely on Angel's face anyway. In a soft, menacing tone, he asked, "A couple of months ago, as in when the baby was born?"

She gave a small nod. "Grayson was early, by a little more than six weeks. The accident started my labor."

His insides twisted and he could barely force the words out. "Who took care of you?" He drew a breath and felt his nostrils flare. "Who helped you when you were in the hospital? When you first came home?"

Her gaze shifted away and she smoothed her hand over the baby's head, ruffling his few glossy curls. The sound of the baby's sucking was loud and voracious. "There was no one, Derek, you know that. No family, no close friends. Grayson and I helped each other."

Without meaning to, without even wanting to, he

looked at the baby. Grayson's small mouth eagerly drew on her nipple while a tiny fist pressed to her pale breast. His eyes were closed, his small body cradled comfortably to Angel's. Dane felt a lump in his throat the size of a grapefruit and had to turn away.

So he'd seen her breast? So what. He'd seen plenty in his day, just never any with a baby attached. He didn't feel what he should have felt at the sight of her pale flesh, which was undiluted lust. Lust he understood, but this other thing, whatever the hell it was, he didn't like.

He snatched up his still-damp shirt and shrugged it on, then grabbed his coat. There were a lot of things he had to do today. "I'll be back in a couple of hours." He looked at her, his expression severe. "Make sure you're here when I get back, Angel. Do you understand?"

She hugged the baby tighter, then waved a negligent hand without looking at him. "Go on. Just go."

"I'll be back."

She nodded, more or less pretending he was already gone. Dane didn't know what to say to her, what to think or feel. He was reaching for the doorknob when a soft knock sounded, and a second later it opened.

It was a toss-up who was more surprised, Dane, or the young man standing in front of him, his arms laden with a large pizza and a wide grin on his face.

That grin disappeared real quick, replaced by a ferocious look of menace. "Who the hell are you?"

Dane, at his most autocratic and not in the least threatened by the rangy youth, lifted his eyebrow and turned to Angel. "I think that may be my question."

CHAPTER THREE

"NO," ANGEL SAID, keeping her voice low and managing to cover herself as Grayson fell asleep and released her breast. He was such a good baby, so sweet. She loved him so much she'd gladly do anything necessary to protect him. "It's not your question because it's none of your business."

She quickly buttoned up her shirt. Mick automatically put the pizza on the coffee table and took the baby from her while Derek stood there, that damn imperious eyebrow raised high, and watched. Slowly, because her leg really was aching, she lifted herself into something closer to a sitting position, resting against the arm of the couch with her leg still outstretched.

"Well." Derek smiled, but it wasn't a particularly nice smile, more a baring of teeth which Mick responded to with a scowl. "I'm not leaving until I know who he is." He sat down and stretched out his own long, strong legs, at his leisure, and waited.

Angel sighed. God, she really didn't need this. First the trip downtown, which had tired her leg terribly. Then the kiss and his naked chest... Her mind was turning to mush.

Mick bristled. "Just who the hell do you think you are, coming in here and demanding answers?"

"The baby's father."

"Oh." Mick straightened, blinked, then glanced at Angel. Derek had said that with so much relish, so much ridiculous pride, she was temporarily stunned herself. His complete acceptance was such a swift turnaround, she was having trouble accepting it.

It took her a moment before she nodded, giving Mick permission. She knew he wouldn't say another word without it and yet Derek wasn't likely to leave unless he got his answer. She knew how incredibly stubborn he could be. And even though he wasn't acting like himself, he could pull out his ruthlessness at any moment. She didn't want Mick caught in the cross fire.

"I'm Mick Dawson, a neighbor." Mick jutted his chin. "And a friend."

"A very good friend," Angel added, thinking of how much help Mick had been to her since she'd first moved here. She surveyed Derek, lounging at his leisure, his shirt tight across his broad shoulders and his hands laced over his flat stomach. She wanted to kick him for looking so damn good. "You asked who helped me. Well, once I moved here, Mick did. He picks up my groceries for me, gets my mail and paper." She waved at her leg. "Until recently I've been pretty much out of commission. Mick lives upstairs, his mother owns the building, and he's been an enormous help."

Mick started to hand her the baby back, still keeping one eye on Derek, and that seemed to galvanize Derek into action. "I can take him," he said, reaching for Grayson. "You should go ahead and eat."

Mick again looked at her for guidance. Derek's willingness to take part wasn't something she'd counted on. It was an awkward situation, but it shouldn't have been—

not if he would just act like himself. But he didn't seem to be in an accommodating mood today, which she supposed was like him after all.

Exasperation made her tone extra sharp. "Really, Derek, weren't you just about to leave?"

He smiled. "I can stay a little longer. Besides, I like holding the baby." He pressed his cheek to the top of Grayson's head, and his expression caused a silly sick reaction in Angel's stomach. "He smells good."

Mick folded his arms and stared. "So you're just now showing up? You waltz in today and pretend to be the happy father? To my mind, you're about two months too late."

Oh no. Angel tensed her muscles in dread of Derek's response. "Mick…"

Derek nodded, cutting off Angel's warning. "I agree. Actually, I'm close to a year late by my calculations. But I'm going to be near at hand from now on." Then without missing a beat, he asked, "How old did you say you were?"

Mick grinned his sinister street-tough grin. "I didn't." Before Derek could react, he added, "But I'm sixteen. And before Miss Morris makes it sound like I've done her any big favors, she's helped me out a lot, too. Without her, I doubt I'd make it out of high school."

Angel couldn't stand it when Mick did that, put himself down, especially since he was such a remarkable young man. Unfortunately, he still didn't believe her about that. "That's not true, Mick, and you know it. You're very bright and you'd have figured out that math with or without my help." She turned to Derek, for some reason anxious for him to understand. "Mick works two jobs, plus school, plus he pretty much runs this place. His mother is often…sick.''

Mick gave Derek a solemn, measuring look. ''My mother is an alcoholic.''

Angel closed her eyes on a wave of pain. Mick had such a chip on his shoulder with everyone but her. He asked for disdain, as if he felt it was his due, then would fight tooth and nail to prove a point. She still wasn't certain what that point might be, though.

With no visible sign of reaction, Derek looked at Mick. Angel knew Mick looked much older, much wiser than any sixteen-year-old boy should look. She also knew, deep down, he was still a kid, a little afraid at times, a lot needy given that his life had been nothing but empty turmoil. Her praise always embarrassed him, but he thrived on it. And she loved him like a little brother. If Derek said anything at all that would upset Mick, she'd manage to get her sorry butt off the couch and kick him out.

But he surprised her by cradling the baby in one arm and offering Mick his hand, which Mick warily accepted. ''I appreciate what you've done for her. Did she move here when she was first hurt?''

''Yeah, not long after.'' Mick narrowed his eyes again, very nice dark brown eyes that she knew all the high school girls swooned over. But Mick didn't spare time for serious girlfriends. He was too busy surviving. ''If I hadn't been here, I don't know if she'd have made it. She was pretty banged up, and Grayson was just a tiny squirt. Even getting herself something to eat was difficult, but she did it, because she had to stay healthy for Grayson. Truth is, I don't know how the hell she managed.''

"Don't be so melodramatic, Mick." Angel didn't want them talking about her and she didn't want Derek to view her as a helpless, pitiful victim. He seemed to be hanging on Mick's every word, analyzing them and drawing his own conclusions. She didn't like the way his intense interest made her feel.

Later, after she figured out what he was up to, then she'd confide her biggest worry and hopefully he'd be able to take care of it. She cleared her throat. "Derek, you can put Grayson in his crib if you'd like. I don't want to hold you up."

He surprised her again by agreeing. After he settled Grayson, he came back in and walked over to her, giving her a gentle kiss on the forehead that made her skin tingle and her breath catch. She frowned at him, but held her tongue. When they were alone, safe from Mick's protective nature, she'd set him straight about his familiarity.

Derek looked at Mick. "Could you walk me out?"

The bottom dropped out of her stomach. "What for? I think you can find your way out the door. It's straight ahead."

Derek grinned at her. "Man talk, honey. Mick understands."

"It's all right," Mick said to her, then followed Derek out despite her protests.

For all of two minutes, she fretted, imagining every kind of hostile confrontation. But when Mick came back in he was shaking his head and almost laughing.

"What? What did he want?"

"A list."

She searched his face, stymied. "A list of what?"

"Everything you might need." Her mouth fell open.

"He also wanted to know if there was anyplace safe around here for him to park his car since he plans to be hanging around a lot. I told him he could use the garage."

"But you don't let anyone use the garage!"

"Yeah, but he has a *really* nice car. I wouldn't want it to get stripped."

She could imagine what kind of car he had: expensive. What was it about males of all ages that made them car crazy?

Mick picked up a huge slice of pizza and took a healthy bite, then went into the kitchen for plates. "You want juice to drink?"

Absently, her thoughts on Derek, she said, "Please." She made it a habit to drink juice, since it was healthier for the baby. Real juice was her one small luxury.

They ate in near silence, and Angel was aware of the passing minutes. When she caught Mick watching her watch the clock, he grinned. "I'm not about to leave until he comes back. He raised hell with me because the door was unlocked when he got here."

Indignation rose, hot and fierce, crowding out her other, more conflicting emotions. "He yelled at you?"

"No, he just told me I should be more careful. I, um, gave him your key. He's having a couple made, so I can have one, and he can have one. That way, he said, you can keep your door locked, and you won't have to get up to let us in if you're resting your leg or feeding the baby or something."

"Didn't you tell him you already had a key and that he didn't need one?"

"It didn't seem like a smart thing to do."

He was still grinning at her. She shook her head. Never

before had she seen Mick take to another person this easily. "Well, I'll tell him. If he actually does come back."

"Oh, he'll be back, all right." Mick tilted his head at her. "Are you going to tell him what's been happening?"

"Not right away. I have to find out first if he's going to get involved with Grayson, if I can count on him to help without having to worry that he'll sue me for custody. I can't risk having Grayson around that family. It's my bet the threats start with them. His mother, according to him, is as far removed from the grandmotherly type as a woman can get, and the stories he shared about his brother don't even bear repeating they're so dreadful. And," she said, when Mick's mouth twitched, "before you start grinning again, I don't need his help with anything but protection and you know it."

He handed her another piece of pizza. "For a little bitty single lady you've done okay. But you know as well as I do that things are getting worse for you. First the job, then your old apartment, then the accident. That bit with your car still makes me sick when I think of it. You can't keep up. You never get enough rest and your leg hurts all the time from overdoing it. You need to let it heal. Hell, you need therapy."

Angel had long ago quit trying to curb Mick's colorful vocabulary. Now she just rolled her eyes. "I'm getting more papers to type up every day. Pretty soon, everything will even out."

He only shook his head. He didn't really approve of the late hours she spent transcribing papers for local businessmen and college students, but he helped her anyway by picking up the papers and dropping them off. Like her, Mick knew she had few options.

They both looked up when they heard the doorknob turn. It was locked as per Derek's instruction. He looked supremely satisfied as he used the key to get in. ''Much better.''

Angel glared at him. ''You're not keeping a key to my apartment, Derek, so forget it.''

He didn't look daunted. ''Mick, you want to help me carry a few things in?''

''Sure.'' Mick was already on his feet, setting the half-eaten slice of pizza aside. He looked anxious, and Angel imagined he was every bit as curious as she was.

Then she remembered herself. ''Now wait a minute! I don't want or need anything from you! I already told you that.''

Derek went out the door whistling. Mick followed him, trying to hide his smile. Angel hadn't seen him grin this often in one day since she'd met him. They returned with several boxes and various brands of disposable diapers. Angel could have wept. Using cloth had been so tiring and so much added work, but the expense of disposables was out of the question.

As they carried them in, Derek explained. ''The woman at the store told me some kids are allergic to some kinds. You can tell me which works best and I'll pick up more of them. But this ought to hold you for now.''

He set the boxes in the living room, a huge wall of them, then tiptoed into Grayson's room where she couldn't see him. The apartment was tiny, only the two small bedrooms, a closet-sized bath, then the open area of the living room and kitchen, separated by half a wall which cornered the refrigerator. Angel seethed, even more so when he came back out carrying the almost filled diaper pail. "Where are you taking that?"

"To the dumpster." He made a face, turning his nose away. "I left the clean ones in there in case you wanted to use them for dust rags or something."

She started to get up, but he was already out the door again and she slumped back in frustration.

By the time he and Mick finished carrying things in, she had full cupboards, a stuffed refrigerator and freezer, a bathroom that practically overflowed with feminine products, and a sore throat from all her complaining, which Derek blithely ignored.

Not only did she now have the basics, but she had luxuries she hadn't recently been able to afford. Had Mick told Derek that she missed conditioning her hair and giving herself facials? That she missed creamy lotions and scented bath oils? Or had he figured it out on his own? She wouldn't ask. He'd simply have to take it all back; she wouldn't be bought. Material things weren't what she wanted or needed from him.

Mick dropped the last large sack behind the couch and straightened. "I've got to get going. I have to be at work in fifteen minutes."

Derek came in and handed him a newly purchased ice-cold soda, holding his own in his other hand. Another luxury she'd avoided. She had milk, water, tea and for health reasons, juice. The soda looked so good, her mouth watered.

Derek propped his hip on the back of the couch, close to her head, and Angel forgot about the soda to scoot away. Derek winked at her, knowing damn good and well she didn't want him that close, before turning to Mick. "Where do you work?"

"Part of the week at the garage on the corner. The weekends at the Fancy Lady. It's a neighborhood bar. I wash dishes there."

Mick had his chin jutted out, his obstinate expression that dared Derek to make a wisecrack. Instead, Derek appeared thoughtful. "Aren't you too young to work in a place like that?"

"I look old enough. No one ever questions it."

"I suppose not." Again, he stuck out his hand. "I appreciate your help today, Mick."

"No problem."

"You know, if you ever wanted to work just one job, for decent pay, I have a friend who's looking for someone."

Mick narrowed his eyes, skeptical. Few things had ever been given to him, and when something good came along, he generally doubted it, and with good reason. "Doing what?"

"Various things. Cleanup, phone duty, running errands. The hours are flexible, but the pay's good."

Silence dragged out while Mick considered the suggestion. Finally he shrugged. "I'll think about it."

"Take your time. The job's not going anywhere." Derek locked the door behind Mick after he left, then turned to Angel. He stared at her until her pulse picked up and her blood raced. "Now."

Startled, she stiffened her shoulders and frowned. "Now what, you...you...? How dare you come barging in here rearranging my life?" She'd been so enthralled, listening to the male bonding taking place before her eyes, and then he'd looked at her with such warmth in his gaze she'd practically jumped when he spoke. Now all her grievances came swamping back. "You can take all this right back out to your car, and you can hand me back my key." She thrust her hand, palm up, toward him. "Right now."

Derek leaned against the door, studying her for a moment, seemingly gathering his thoughts. After a moment, he said, "I like Mick. He's a good kid."

That threw her off guard. Again. Slowly, her hand fell back to the couch. "Yes, he is. I don't know what you were up to with that job offer, but if it isn't legitimate, I'll...."

He grinned. "You'll what? No, don't answer that. The possibilities are too frightening to contemplate." He walked to her and sat down beside her on the couch, then took her hand before she could try to get up. "It's a real job, certainly a better one than what he'll find around here. I thought you'd like to know he was working someplace safer. Hell, I could even get my friend to throw in a car with the job, to make sure he's protected when driving."

Angel was struck speechless. Between his touch and his words, she couldn't seem to draw enough breath. Such generosity had never been a part of Derek, at least not a part she'd seen. "I don't understand you."

His thumb rubbed over her knuckles. She tried to tug her hand away, but he held firm. "I know you don't, and I'm sorry about that. Sorry about a lot of things." He gave her a sideways look, then sighed, the sound tinged with real regret. "I hesitate to make you angry, but—"

"Then don't."

"Here's how it's going to be, honey." His tone was

stern, his expression determined. "You're going to keep everything I've just given you. And you're going to use it, too. And enjoy it, I hope, but I suppose that's up to you. I know you don't like me or trust me right now, and that's okay. I understand it. But I'm not just going to disappear or come visit once a month for fifteen minutes. And I'm not going to sit back and ignore you when I know you need things. I can help you, and you're going to accept my help. God knows, you should have had it all along."

Angel shook her hand free, then kept it held protectively away from him. A glint of amusement brightened his eyes. She felt swamped in confusion, uncertain what to do or say next. She'd never dealt with Derek in this mood, firm but concerned and caring. It was sort of... sweet. *No, whoa on that thought.* She would not be suckered in by him. Never again.

Glaring at him, she said, "Why don't you just tell me now what you're up to and save us both some time?"

"What I'm up to? Well, all right. Let's see. I want to help you. I want you to trust me again—"

"Ha!"

"—and I want to be with you." He said that last part with a small smile, and his fingertips grazed her chin. She ducked her face away. "I want to be a part of Grayson's life and be a father to him. I want to show you that I can be responsible and honorable and that I'm not a total jerk. I want...a lot of things."

She stared at him hard, unnerved. "You're an alien, right? Derek was zapped into space and you were sent to replace him? That's the only thing I'll believe."

He laughed, but his eyes looked sad. "Would you like that, if the real Derek was gone for good?"

None of this, most especially his somber tone, made any sense. Angel dropped her head against the back of the couch and sighed. "I never wished you any harm, Derek. Not even when I thought I hated you, when you suggested we'd both be better off without the baby. I just didn't want to ever see you again."

"But you invited me back into your life. I may be trying to take up more of that life than you're comfortable with, but I won't hurt you again. I promise."

Without lifting her head from the couch, she turned her face toward him. In a soft whisper, she said, "Do you actually believe I'd ever trust you again?"

"Yes." He said it without hesitation. His eyes were dark and sincere and intense, probing into her mind, trying to read her thoughts. "I can get you to trust me again."

The mere possibility scared her half to death. She could never leave herself that vulnerable again; her baby's well-being depended on her strength. "And then what? You'll steal my baby away from me?" Her chest squeezed tight with the thought and she knew her voice shook. She couldn't help it. She'd known the risks involved when she contacted him, but Mick was right. She couldn't handle things on her own anymore. The threat was there and it was real and she was afraid, not so much for herself, but for Grayson. He relied on her, and she had to protect him. That's what mattered most.

If it was Derek's family behind the awful threats, as she suspected, he might well be the only person who could protect her.

Derek stood, giving her his back. His fists rested on his

hips and he looked angry and frustrated and somehow heartsick. "I would never take him from you," he said, the words low and raspy. "I'd swear it to you, but I realize my promises mean nothing—yet. All I want to do is help."

"But you never wanted to help me before. You made it clear you wanted no part of me or the baby."

She heard him swallow, then he turned to face her. He looked angry, and almost confused, a bit desperate. "I was an ass. An idiot and a bastard. *I'm here now, Angel.* Don't shut me out."

She really had little choice in the matter. It was difficult to say the words, but he seemed so different, not at all like the man she'd known. Her reactions, her feelings toward him, were different, too. He touched something inside her that the old Derek hadn't gotten close to. She supposed anyone could change, and she knew how Grayson had affected her life, the impact he'd made on her.

As if reading her mind, he whispered, "Grayson hit me like a punch in the heart. A tiny little person, part of my blood." His eyes narrowed. "You said it yourself. How holding him made you feel."

"But I carried him and went through all the changes the pregnancy caused. I got sick in the mornings, stayed awake at night as he kicked, stayed tired *all* the time. I felt him grow and I saw him born. I saw him take his first breath, give his first cry."

"You think I don't regret missing all that?"

He sounded so sincere, but she just didn't know. Unless he planned to take the baby from her, she could see no reason for an emotional deception. She searched his face,

but it was a futile effort; whatever he felt was well hidden.
Damn, she had so few choices in this. "All right."

He let out a gust of air, ran a hand through his hair,
rubbed his chin, then smiled. "Okay. Shew, I'm glad
that's settled." He looked much relieved, his shoulders no
longer so tense, his eyes no longer worried. "Okay. On
to the next battle. I want to move you someplace else."

Angel could only stare at him in disbelief. "You're
nuts. I give ground on one little thing and you want to
take over!"

"Come on, honey, you can't *like* living here."

She wanted to shove his condescension back into his
face until he choked on it. "I most certainly do like it,"
she lied, knowing Mick to be the only redeeming factor
of her present residence. "I'm close to the downtown
businesses and I do transcription at home for a lot of the
offices and the students. I make enough money to keep
the rent paid and my health insurance active. It's convenient and I enjoy the people and I'm not moving."

He pursed his mouth and studied her, then must have
decided not to push his luck. "I'll let that go for now."

"You'll let it go forever!"

"Now, about therapy." Angel rolled her eyes, which
didn't even slow him down. "I've known people with
compound fractures. It can take months to heal with
proper treatment, and you've not had that."

"I have a very good doctor."

"Who no doubt told you that you needed therapy."

That was true, but it had been out of the question. Not
only did she not have anyone to watch Grayson, but she
had no way of getting back and forth each day to the
therapist and her insurance would have only covered a

small percentage of the bill. She shook her head at Derek, hopeless. "It's been almost two months. It's too late for therapy."

"Nonsense. I know the perfect person. I'll have her come here. What would be convenient for you?"

Angel rubbed her eyes. He was coming too fast and too hard, and suddenly she was tired. He'd invaded her life, her emotions. She'd had such a simple plan, and she'd thought for a while it might work. Then he'd held Grayson, and he'd kissed her and taken off his shirt and bought her disposable diapers and lotion and she just couldn't take it all in. She didn't have it in her to continue fighting him, at least, not right now. "Derek, please. Let off a little. You're here. You've met your son. My apartment is stuffed with new purchases. Isn't that enough for now?"

"I have a lot to make up for."

She certainly wouldn't argue that point with him. "Well, let's save it for another time, okay? Right now, I'm exhausted. I worked really late last night finishing up some papers that were due this morning and Grayson still wakes up during the night to be fed. If you'll take yourself out of here, I'd like a nap."

"What papers?"

With barely veiled impatience, she explained once again. "I transcribe files or notes for the local offices when one of the secretaries is ill, and I do term papers and such for students at the college. I'm sure you remember I have top-of-the-line office equipment, even if my computer *is* getting a little dated."

"You don't have to continue working. I can give you money."

Just like that, he expected her to become totally dependent on him. She wanted to get up and smack him, and she wanted to cry. Neither would have brought about the results she needed. "I'll pretend you didn't say that."

He stood there, obviously undecided, and she waited. But he only smiled, his look rueful. "Come on, I'll help you into bed."

Panic edged into her weariness. She didn't want him touching her again, getting so close. He'd kissed her, and that brief touch had unnerved her, had made her belly tingle. When he'd taken off his shirt, she'd almost groaned. He'd been her first lover, her only lover. And she'd never found fault with his physique. Though their single night together hadn't been great, she knew a lot of the blame was due to her own uncertainty. And now, she missed so much the closeness of being with a man, not necessarily sexually, but with gentleness and concern, a special friendship between two people who know they're destined to be lovers. Or who have been lovers in the past. The intimacy was there for her, whether she despised him or not.

But despising him was no longer an issue. He was too damn different.

"No thank you," she muttered, shaken by her own revelations, afraid of her own weaknesses. But true to form, he wasn't listening and had her pulled up close to his side before she could move away. With one hard muscled arm around her waist, the other holding her elbow, he practically carried her into her room. She could feel his heat, his strength, and it felt too good to be coddled, to have some of the burden lifted, even if in a superficial way.

Closing her eyes didn't help, only made her more aware

of the shifting of muscle, the hardness of his body, his incredible heat and enticing scent. The man even *smelled* different, more welcoming, more comforting. More exciting.

Her bedroom door had been shut until now and when Derek stepped inside he paused to look around. She pulled away from him, her hands shaking, and he took her elbow to assist her to the bed. Her hobbling gait embarrassed her.

"Really, Derek. How do you think I ever managed when you weren't around?"

Her sarcasm was wasted, judging by his frown. "I've been wondering about that myself." He lifted her legs onto the bed and pulled the sheet and blankets over her. "Are you comfortable?"

With him looming over her while she rested in a bed? His shoulders looked hard, his chest broad. When she'd glimpsed him with his shirt off earlier, she'd noticed the remains of a tan. He'd been in warm weather recently, sunning himself.

His hair hung over his forehead, soft and silky dark and a tracing of beard shadow was showing on his face. No, she was far from comfortable. "I'm fine."

"This is a pretty room. It…suits you."

The things he said seemed so strange, as if another man had taken over his body. Derek had never before commented on furniture or even noticed it as far as she could tell. Her belongings were nice, but they weren't picked by an interior decorator as his had been.

Still, they were hers, and she loved them. She'd hated to spend so much of her dwindled savings on movers when she'd left her old place, but she'd been unable to do the work herself, had no friends to call on, and she refused to live on someone else's furniture.

Besides, the familiar objects gave her comfort, as if her entire life hadn't been reorganized by the vengeful hand of fate.

Unable to help herself, she said, "The bed is new."

"Oh?" He looked it over, but she could tell he hadn't realized it.

"I thought about burning the other one, sort of as an exorcism given the hideous memories attached to it, but that seemed wasteful in my financial predicament, regardless of the sentiments attached." She propped a pillow behind her head and smiled at him, enjoying his scowl and the two spots of hot color high on his lean cheekbones. "I sold it instead. Cheap."

Like an animal of prey moving in, Derek slowly approached the bed and leaned over her, his eyes never leaving hers. He braced an arm on either side of her head and lowered his face until only inches separated them. Angel pressed back into her pillow and held her breath.

His voice was low and rough, compelling. "You keep pushing me, honey, practically daring me with those big green eyes of yours."

He looked away from her eyes to her mouth, and she bit her lip. "Derek..."

"Shh." His lips brushed hers, light, teasing. "I told you I'd never hurt you again. You can believe it. Besides, it's too soon for much, but not for this."

That was all the warning she got before his mouth settled warmly over her own, devouring. Angel gasped, clasping the soft blanket next to her hips, tightening her fists to keep from kissing him back. But it was impossible.

Nothing like this had ever happened to her. Surely it hadn't been like this before or she'd have remembered.

Heat exploded, radiating out to her arms and legs in tingling waves; behind her closed eyes, tiny sparks ignited. She squirmed—then felt his tongue at the same time he groaned, giving her the sound, letting her feel it deep inside herself. Wet, warm, he shifted for a better angle and she leaned up to him, anxious for more.

It seemed an eternity before the kiss ended, before Derek was slowly pulling away, taking small, nibbling, apologetic kisses along the way. He breathed hard, but when he lifted his head, there was a gentle smile on his mouth.

Angel didn't trust herself to speak.

"Don't look like that," he chided.

"Like…like what?"

"Like you're afraid, and sorry." His thumb rubbed the corner of her mouth. "One way or another, everything really is going to be okay."

Reality intruded. "Derek, swear to me you won't tell anyone about Grayson."

"You'll believe me?"

Tears filled her eyes. "Do I have a choice? I don't want to run again. I don't—"

"Again?"

He had her rattled, that was the only reason she'd made such a slipup. Shaking her head, she said, "If you tell your family about Grayson, I'll go."

His large warm hand cupped her cheek. "I won't let them bother you, and I won't let you go."

She was afraid they were already bothering her, because she couldn't think of another single enemy she could have. Why they would want to hurt her, she couldn't

guess. Unless they knew of Grayson and were afraid she'd
come to Derek for marriage. She just didn't know what
lengths they might go to in order to protect their son from
a woman they'd consider beneath him.

Her hands shook, as did her voice. "How could you
stop them if they knew? Especially your brother." She
shivered, knowing her fear of the brother was out of proportion, based on Derek's dramatized bragging and her
own wild imagination. But in her mind, he'd become her
nightmare, and she was very afraid. "Out of all of them,
I fear him the most."

He leaned back, watching her carefully. "Angel..."

"No! They can't know. Ever. If that seems selfish of
me, I don't care." Her hands trembled, despite her tight
grip, because she knew if he decided to take her baby
away, he could. And she was already proving how weak
she was against him. "I'm a good mother, Derek, I swear
it."

He sighed. "I never doubted it, honey." He shoved
himself reluctantly from the bed and pulled a pen from
his pocket. Using a notepad on the bedside table, he scribbled down some numbers. "I'm going to give you my
number."

"I already have it."

He stalled, looking harassed for a moment, then shook
his head. "It's hard to reach me at home these days. Here
are the numbers to my cellular and my pager. You can
always reach me with them. If you ever need me, for
anything, call either one of these numbers."

Angel nodded, feeling foolish for her outburst. She was
just so weary, so tired of being afraid. He cupped her
cheek again.

"I'll be back tomorrow." His gaze probed hers, demanding. "You'll be here?"

"Yes."

"Good." He leaned down and kissed her once more, a light kiss that still made her shiver. "Pretty soon, you'll stop looking so afraid, Angel. And you'll start to trust me. I promise."

As he walked out of the room, Angel looked at the paper with his numbers. Somehow, just having someone to call made her feel safer.

She heard the front door close, the lock turn, and she dropped her head back on the pillow, closing her eyes. As she drifted off to sleep, the paper was still in her hand.

CHAPTER FOUR

"I was tailed last night," Dane said the minute Alec had taken his seat. He looked at his closest friend, waiting for his reaction.

"From the woman's place?"

"No, thank God. Later, from my house. It was dark, and I have no idea who it was, but I don't like it. I want you to set up a watch at her apartment. Something is definitely going on and I don't want her hurt."

"The man who was with her yesterday?"

Dane shook his head, again remembering how protective Mick had been. "No, he's a kid and a blessing as far as I can tell. If it hadn't been for him, she'd probably never have made it."

Alec said nothing. It was one of the things Dane liked most about him. He didn't pry. In fact, he was one of the most closemouthed bastards he'd ever met.

"Something about her just doesn't add up. It's like she wants Derek around, but she's forced to it." Then he shook his head again. "No, that's not entirely true. There's something there—but it sure as hell isn't trust or friendship. She initiated things, but now that I'm, or rather Derek's, interested, she's trying to back off. I think she got more than she bargained for."

"You want me to check into her background, the time

she spent with your brother?'' Alec's eyes were almost black, the same as his hair, and piercingly direct. Dane knew he could find out anything he wanted. *How* he found things out sometimes left him curious.

''No.'' He didn't want anyone snooping into Angel's past but himself. He had no idea what clues he might uncover, but they were his business and no one else's. He didn't question his protective attitude. He'd find out what happened to his brother, but he'd find it out his way, and isolate Angel's involvement as much as possible. After all, she was his nephew's mother; for now, that was all the excuse he needed. ''I'll take care of it. In fact, I have Raymond coming in today.''

Alec snorted, shifting his big body uneasily in the chair. He was in his usual jeans and a flannel shirt, his hair pulled back in a ponytail. He looked like a mugger, or the typical bad guy. Dane grinned.

''You don't like him either? Why?''

Alec shrugged, indifferent. ''I don't really know him.''

''Dammit Alec...''

''Something about him just doesn't sit right. You know it yourself.''

''Yes. I know you're also suspicious of just about everyone.'' Dane assumed his own dislike of Raymond was personal. He was engaged to Dane's sister, Celia, and Raymond reminded him too much of his own family, ruthless, business-oriented. He probably suited Celia to a tee.

''I do have some info for you.''

Dane straightened, his thoughts once again in perspective. ''Let's have it.''

''Where your brother's car went off the road, there's an extra set of skid marks. Two cars were going fast that day, and two cars braked. Unfortunately, your brother's was the one that went off the berm.'' Alec handed him a file folder. ''I checked with the police on duty that day. They say that's a dangerous curve and people are always squealing their tires there, that the extra marks don't mean anything and could have been from long ago. I don't think so.''

Dane took the folder, his temper heating as he pondered his brother trying to escape another car. He would find out what had happened.

''There's another thing.''

Dane looked up.

''Your brother had been in a local bar, not the classiest of joints, which is what drew my attention, and he'd been drinking it up right before the accident. The bartender said he'd met someone there, but that nothing seemed unusual about it. He didn't have a description, only that it was a male.''

''Dammit!'' Dane exploded from his seat and paced around his desk. Playing the role of his brother was wearing on his nerves. Using Derek's office, his name, made him edgy. He'd left this life behind long ago and though he hadn't moved far away, he'd still managed to keep an emotional distance from it all; now he was back under the worst possible circumstances. ''Why are the cops blowing this off?''

''You know as well as I do, everyone claims your brother was acting goofy for a month. They just summed this up to stress.''

''Bullshit. My brother could run two companies and not be stressed. He was primed for it, raised to do it. And he thrived on it.'' Unlike Dane, who hated every minute of the corporate business agenda. He wondered why his mother didn't know any of this, why she hadn't pursued the truth.

"I'm not arguing with you."

Pressing a fist against his forehead, Dane muttered, "So what does Angel have to do with all this? I don't believe she was directly connected to Derek's death, but it is possible she helped pave the way for the killer, maybe unknowingly. She could be our only lead to what really happened since she was the last person to be close with him. But why would Derek have treated her so poorly?"

Alec shrugged, not forthcoming with a verbal response.

A knock on the door had both men swinging their heads around. "Come in."

Raymond Stern sauntered in, his three-piece suit immaculate, his hair styled. Dane winced at the sight of him. The man, though pleasant enough, represented everything Dane disliked about the corporate world and his family. "Thank you for stopping by, Raymond."

Raymond looked at Alec, a suspicious frown in place. "No problem. You said you wanted to talk?"

Dane nodded and reseated himself behind his desk. Alec stood. "I'll be going now, unless you need something else?"

Dane shoved the file folder into a drawer before answering. "No. I'll be in touch with you later."

As Alec left, his eyes briefly skimming over everything and everyone in the room, Raymond asked, "A crony of yours?"

"One of my top men."

A look of disbelief, or maybe scorn, passed over Raymond's features. "Is he working on something right now?'' Before Dane could answer, Raymond continued. ''I think this P.I. business is fascinating, regardless of how your sister feels about it.''

''Oh?'' Dane cocked one eyebrow, wishing he could plant a fist in Raymond's face. ''And how does Celia feel?''

He chuckled. ''That you'll outgrow it. She seems to think now that you're enmeshed back in the office, you'll want to stay.''

There was an unasked question in his tone. Dane started to reassure the man that once he married Celia, the business would be his, with Dane's blessing. In truth Dane wanted no part of it. He was already bored with the endless paperwork and the tedium of board meetings. But he decided against it. Let Raymond stew. Let him wonder if the company was part of the marriage bargain.

''Celia has never liked it that I stepped out of the family's affairs.''

''I think it's incredible that you've always been located so close, yet I never met you.''

''My own offices aren't that far away, true, but I've traveled a lot, especially in recent years. Some cases require constant surveillance, and that means you follow all leads, regardless of where they take you.'' He didn't add that he deliberately hadn't kept in touch with his family, hadn't clued them in to where he would be or for how long.

And now his brother was dead and he hadn't even made it to the funeral.

Quickly closing that particular subject in his mind, Dane went on to another. ''I asked you here because I know you transferred over from the Aeric Corporation.''

Raymond straightened with pride. "That's right. Derek was there often once his intent was known, and he and I met. I agreed it was a natural acquisition, combining your family's interests in health products manufacturing with Aeric's research capabilities. When Derek finalized everything, he asked me to join him here."

"You were at the funeral?"

Shaking his head, his eyes downcast in a regretful way, Raymond said, "No, unfortunately I missed it, also." He looked back up, his expression resigned. "I hadn't realized what happened until I reported here a week later. Derek had given me time to tie up my own loose ends and I spent two final weeks at Aeric, then took a break to sell my house and move closer. When I reported to work here is when I was told. That's also the day I really got to know your sister." A small smile now curved his mouth.

"I see."

"When I asked to see Derek, I was referred to Celia. Things were still in an uproar, your mother most upset and Celia constantly on the verge of tears. They couldn't locate you and they needed everything to be kept quiet, contained. Derek's death hit them all very hard…" Raymond stuttered to a halt. "I'm sorry. I wasn't making accusations. I realize it was very difficult for you as well."

"Yes." Dane knew that Raymond had shown up when the company needed him most, his past experience and lack of emotional involvement, along with Derek's written blessing, making him the ideal man to take temporary control. Every effort was made to keep the stockholders from panicking. If nothing else, he owed Raymond his gratitude for that.

But Dane deliberately kept his own dialogue brief in the hopes Raymond would say more. Trying to get information from his sister or mother had proved most provoking. Anytime he mentioned Derek's name, they would turn solemn, overwhelmed with the loss. The entire episode of the takeover of Aeric seemed very hush-hush.

"Anyway, I guess you could say your sister and I hit it right off. I care deeply for her."

And deeply for the Company, but Dane kept those thoughts to himself. His sister was old enough, and certainly wise enough, to choose her own husband.

"Did Derek associate on a regular basis with anyone else at Aeric?"

Raymond shrugged. "Most everyone on the board, the managers, the—"

"No, I mean in a social way."

"Well, there was the woman, secretary to the R&D department."

Research and Development. Dane already knew what Angel's position had been. Somehow, Derek had gotten information from her that had enabled him to take over the company.

And then he'd dropped Angel cold.

"Were they close?"

Raymond shrugged, looking thoughtful. "Everyone thought so. She'd never dated much, and then suddenly she had a steady date. At that time, no one realized Derek was after the company. But I suppose it should have been more obvious that he was using her. She was a mousy sort of person, not real talkative, withdrawn, but apparently good at her job. Good enough that the head of R&D

often sent her top-secret information through a P.O. box to work on at home."

"A post office box? That's unusual." Derek remembered the address Angel had given him, not a home address, but the anonymity of a post office.

Raymond shrugged. "Her supervisor was from the old school and didn't trust the company computers, swearing too many secrets had been stolen. But he trusted the wrong person. Angel got the last of the information, a huge breakthrough worth top dollar that would have offset the takeover attempt, and she gave it to Derek. Of course, we found all this out after Derek dropped her." He laughed. "She got fired real quick. Most everyone else was able to keep their jobs."

"I see."

"Why do you ask?" Raymond straightened. "She's not here asking for a job, is she?"

Raymond looked appalled by the possibility. "No, of course not. I just wondered if I could get in touch with her, to talk to her about Derek."

"Why?" Raymond's eyes narrowed and he shifted forward. "What's going on?"

Keeping his tone smooth and nearly bored, Dane said, "Not a thing. It's just that I hadn't seen my brother for some time. I'd like to talk to the people who knew him." Raymond relaxed and Dane asked, "What happened to her, do you know?"

Dane had to keep his hands beneath the desk. His fingers had curled into fists as Raymond spoke and he imagined Angel's humiliation, her hurt. He didn't like feeling so much anger toward a dead man, especially when that man was his twin. The conflicting emotions ate away at his control.

"I have no idea. I haven't seen her since I left Aeric. And Derek broke things off with her during a board meeting, for everyone to see. He asked her to sit in on the meeting, then deliberately told everyone where he'd gotten his information. That pretty much proved she couldn't be trusted in the company."

"Good God." Sick dread churned in the bottom of his stomach.

Raymond laughed. "Yeah, she was stunned to say the least. But maybe it taught her a lesson about keeping business dealings private. As I'm sure you already know, even though you haven't been involved in some time, there's no room for deceit in the corporate world. You absolutely have to be able to trust your employees. Especially when they're in the position she was in."

Dane could barely see, he was so angry. The rage ran through him, red-hot, and he wanted only to get to Angel, to apologize, to… He stood abruptly, coming around his desk with stalking steps. He went to the coat tree and grabbed up his coat. Raymond quickly stood to face him.

It took two deep breaths before Dane could trust himself to speak without breaking Raymond's nose. This was exactly why he hated the business, why he had to separate himself from his family. Ruthless barracudas, all of them, with no thought for humanity or dignity. It sickened him.

Raymond looked at him warily. "Is that all you wanted?"

"Yes, thank you." He couldn't bear to shake the man's hand. He turned toward the door instead and opened it. "I appreciate your help, Raymond. Unfortunately, I have an appointment at my own offices shortly, so I'll need to ask you to go.''

"Yes, of course.'' He hesitated. "You know, Derek and I were somewhat better than associates before he died. If you'd ever like to talk about him, to know about him, I'd be glad to tell you what I can.''

Dane's smile actually hurt, but he managed it. "Thank you. I'll keep it in mind.''

"Will you be at dinner tonight?''

Damn, he'd forgotten his mother planned a family gathering. He had hoped to eat with Angel, to get to know her better. "Probably,'' he conceded, knowing his mother would demand a valid reason for missing the meal. It was to be a formal dinner in preparation for his sister's marriage, where the duties of the company would be discussed.

"I know it's difficult for you, stepping in here and keeping your own business afloat. If I can help in any way…''

"I'll keep that in mind. Thank you.''

Raymond finally left with a lagging step, looking as if he had more to say but was reluctant to press. Dane knew he sensed where the present power lay, but that was just a fabrication of his mother's fancy. He didn't want the damn company. In fact, he would only stay in charge as long as was necessary to find out what had happened to Derek, to uncover the truth.

And to get things settled with Angel.

ANGEL SLOWLY HUNG UP the phone, her fingers tight on the receiver to keep her hand from shaking. Why wouldn't it stop? She'd never hurt anyone, she held no power. There was absolutely no reason for someone to harass her.

For one insane moment, she wanted to call Derek, but she quickly quelled that absurd thought. She wouldn't rely on him, ever again. For all she knew, he could be behind all this. That thought made her stomach queasy.

Moving slowly, she made her way to the bathroom and splashed water on her hot face, then leaned against the counter and took deep breaths.

When the knock sounded on her front door only seconds later, she jumped, her hand going to her throat. The apartment was quiet, Grayson sleeping soundly in his crib. It couldn't be Mick because he had left for school hours before after dropping off more papers to be typed, and no one ever called on her other than him. Derek would surely be at work and—

The knock sounded again, this time a little harder and she feared Grayson would wake. She hurried to the door, hesitated just a moment, then called out, "Who is it?"

"Ah," she heard in deep, satisfied tones, "much better than just letting anyone in. I see you're learning."

"Derek?" She turned the dead bolt and unlocked the door, swinging it open. "I always lock my door, except when I'm expecting Mick." She looked him over, the casual way he leaned against the doorjamb, his open-neck shirt, so unusual for him. "What are you doing here this time of day?"

His gaze went over her from head to toe. She wore a long caftan of muted gray-and-blue plaid. It was old and worn and the material draped her body softly. It unzipped down the front, making it easy for her to feed Grayson. Right now, the zipper was just low enough to show her cleavage and assure Derek that her breasts were unrestrained by a bra. Typically of late, her feet were bare; since injuring her leg, she seldom bothered with shoes at home.

A long low whistle filled the air between them and Angel felt herself blushing. Self-consciously, she tried to smooth her hair which hung loose, but when she realized what she was doing she dropped her hand and scowled. "Aren't you supposed to be at work?"

"Yeah, but I missed you so I'm here instead."

Before she could move, or even guess what he would do, he leaned forward and kissed her. The touch of his mouth was warm and soft and fleeting, leaving her stunned. Then Derek pushed in past her, taking his welcome for granted. The door closed with a snap.

"Don't do things like that."

"Why not? You like it, and I can guarantee I love it."

She felt her temper rise and he quickly held up both hands. "Okay, okay. You don't like it. You're entirely repulsed."

"Derek…"

"What?" He smiled at her, a beautiful smile and she looked away. "I really do enjoy it, sweetheart. And I honestly did miss you." He stepped closer to her once again, his gaze bright and probing. "You didn't mind yesterday in my office. You asked me to kiss me then."

Angel drew a blank. He was right, she had pushed the issue. But that was when she'd thought he might not be interested, when she'd thought he'd need motivation.

For a single moment she wondered if he was toying with her, but his expression was enigmatic, impossible to read. "This is a bad time," she said, suspicious and determined to resist his classic charm. "I have tons of things to do."

"I can help."

"Derek..."

He came close to laughing, but swallowed it down. "Okay, I'm sorry. I'm pushing again. But damn, I have so much to make up for and I'm anxious to get started."

Nonplussed, she moved past him, removed a large basket of laundry still needing to be folded, and sat on the couch. "The past is the past, Derek. You can't erase it, and since you haven't contacted me in all this time, I have to assume it didn't matter much to you until now."

"You're surprised at my easy acceptance of things?"

More than surprised. She was amazed.

His hands were deep in his trouser pockets, his coat pushed back, and he rocked on his heels as if in thought. Finally, his head down, he sat beside her. Silence hung heavy in the air. He turned to her. "I'm sorry." He shrugged his wide shoulders, his expression earnest. "I have no excuse, nothing, to explain why I was such a bastard. I wish I did, I wish I could pull up some believable tale to help smooth things over, to take away some of the hurt. But what I did to you was unforgivable. I know that. Still, I want you to forgive me." Dumbfounded by this outpouring of emotion, she allowed him to take her hand, holding it when she would have pulled away. "Do you think you can?"

When she merely frowned, he added, "For Grayson's sake?"

Angel stared at him, so many things he'd said clogging in her brain. He wanted forgiveness, even though he admitted there was no excuse for his behavior? And to use the baby's welfare against her…but that was her biggest concern, her reason for contacting him in the first place.

Only he didn't act the way she'd expected, as she'd planned for. She'd expected grudging help in calling off his family—if indeed they were behind the threats. She didn't even want to contemplate the possibility of another enemy.

She wanted only to live in peace, to be able to take care of herself and her son without fear of danger.

His hand was large and warm and again she noticed the roughness, which had never been there before. To buy herself some time, she said, "What have you been doing?" She turned his palm over and looked at it. "You have callouses."

He blinked at her, then looked down at his hand. With a twisted grin, he said, "Chopping wood, if you can believe that."

"It might be difficult."

"I know. I'm not normally the physical type."

She shook her head. "No, you're in shape, always have been. But from a gym, not from physical labor."

She continued to look at his hand and he raised it to her cheek, curling his fingers around her jaw and lifting so that her gaze met his. His eyes were bright, intent. "I'm glad you noticed, but it doesn't matter. Will you try to forgive me?"

His voice had been so soft, so cajoling. She hated herself for wanting to believe in him again, for wanting so many ridiculous things. But she'd been so alone for so long now. Her mind scurried for some response, some way of making him back off.

"We could start over," he said. "I'm different now,

everything will be different. If I start to backslide and I disappoint you or Grayson, then you can toss me out.''

At her skeptical look, he made a cross on his chest. ''I promise. The decision is yours. You're right about my family, they wouldn't make good relatives at this point for Grayson and they'd likely make your life a living hell.''

If Angel was right, they were already making her life hell—and determined that it get much worse. But she kept the words unsaid for now.

Derek smiled. ''And since I plan to be involved, that means they'd make me miserable as well. They don't need to know anything about Grayson, or about you for that matter. At least, not until you're ready.''

As she opened her mouth, he interjected, ''*If* you're ever ready.''

She had no defense against his optimism, his good humor. It was beyond her to remain disgruntled when he was being all she'd ever hoped for—for Grayson's sake. ''All right.''

His grin was wide and sexy and suggestive. ''Thank you. Damn, but you know how to keep a man on pins and needles. I hope this is the last time you test me, because my heart can't take it.''

She snorted, not ready to believe his heart was involved. Then to her disbelieving eyes, he set the laundry basket between them and began folding baby blankets. Angel stared.

''Shocked you, have I? Well, good. God knows you've done me in enough times lately.'' He lifted a small gown, struggled with it for a moment, then handed it to her. ''I think I'll leave the more complicated garments to you, and stick to the blankets and—'' His voice trailed off as he lifted a pair of panties from the basket. They were pink and satiny and her blush was so hot, she knew her face had to be bright red. She snatched them from his hand.

''Not a single word out of you or you can go.''

''I'm mum.'' He continued to fold, now in silence, but she could see his devilish smile.

He was so very different, so unlike the Derek she knew, the man she couldn't forgive or ever care about, not with the way he'd turned on her. This Derek was considerate and warm and somehow, more of a man because of it. In the past, she'd been drawn to his confidence, his good looks and his sophistication. She'd been overwhelmed by his attention, so flattered she hadn't been able to think straight. Then he'd abruptly discredited her in every way possible.

They worked in near silence, other than Derek humming, until all the laundry was done and put away. After Angel had placed her unmentionables in her dresser, leaving Derek to put up the baby's things, she found him standing over Grayson's crib, just watching the baby sleep. When she crept in to stand beside him, it somehow felt right to be there together, sharing the sheer joy of seeing the baby, hearing his soft breathing. When Grayson made a grumbling squeak in his sleep, Derek smiled, a small, proud smile that touched Angel's heart and made her feel too warm and full inside. She turned around and walked out.

She'd barely reached the kitchen before she felt Derek's hand heavy on her shoulder. Her pulse raced, her breathing quickened. Slowly he turned her, and he whispered, ''Angel,'' his tone low and husky and affected by some emotion she couldn't name but understood. Even before she met his gaze, she knew he was going to kiss her. She tried to tell herself it was necessary, that she had to keep him interested to have his help, but she knew she was lying. She wanted his kiss.

And he didn't disappoint her. This was no casual peck as he'd given her when he first arrived. No, this time his mouth devoured hers, without hesitation, hot and hungry, his tongue immediately sliding inside while his hands held her face and kept her close.

Just that, nothing more. He didn't touch her anywhere else, didn't put his arms around her or pull her body into full contact with his. She could feel his heat, crossing the inches that separated them, and she wanted to be closer. But lovemaking was new to her and she wasn't sure how to initiate anything, or if she even wanted to.

Derek slanted his head, his breathing harsh in her ear, and a low groan came from deep in his throat. In the next instant, he pulled his mouth away and pushed her head to his shoulder. "This is crazy. I can't believe how you affect me."

Angel didn't know what to say to that. Crazy? It surely felt odd, but in a wonderful, miraculous way. Her hands were caught between them and she could feel his heartbeat, fierce and fast. "Why is it different this time?" she asked aloud, and all the confusion she felt could be heard in her tone.

Derek laughed, then groaned and squeezed her tight, finally pulling their bodies close together. "Because it just is, because I'm different."

He pushed her back so he could see her face and smiled at her. "I'd like to take you to lunch."

The topic had changed so suddenly Angel was caught off guard. "I...I can't go anywhere. Grayson..."

"We'll take him with us."

She shook her head, not even considering the possibility of them being seen in public together with the baby. "No, I already ate." She pondered all that had happened, all he'd done so far, then suggested, "Why don't you come here for dinner instead." She felt ridiculous, making such an offer, extending the verbal olive branch. But they did need to get reacquainted; she needed to decide if and how much she could trust him. She drew a deep breath and plunged onward. "I can cook us something."

He searched her face, and his continued silence made her wish she could withdraw her offer. Then he shook his head. "Damn, I'd like that. I swear I would. I can't imagine a better way to spend my evening."

"But?"

He released her and turned away. "My mother has this damn dinner planned." He waved a hand, essaying his feelings on the affair. "My sister is getting married soon and it's a sort of celebration dinner. All family is expected to attend."

"I see."

He ran a distracted hand over his face, then laughed. "I doubt you do. But at any rate, I appreciate the offer. Will you give me a rain check?"

"Yes, of course."

He looked at her, *into* her, and she shivered. His hand came up to cup her cheek. "Aw, Angel, you do know how to drive a man crazy."

She didn't know what he meant by that, so she ignored it. "If you're hungry now, I could make you a sandwich."

Like a starving man, he grabbed up her offer. "Thank you. Anything is fine. And while I eat, will you tell me more about Grayson, about yourself?"

That seemed like an odd request. As she pulled lunch meat out of the refrigerator, she glanced at him curiously and said, "You know everything there is to know about me."

"Not true. Tell me about the pregnancy, when you found out—"

Slowly, feeling as if she'd been doused in ice water, Angel turned back to him. She dropped a package of cheese onto the table with a thunk. It was cheese he had bought, so she knew he must like it. "About the pregnancy. Now why would you want details on that?"

Wary now, he shrugged and said, "I'm just curious."

"I see. Are you trying to verify that Grayson really is yours? Is that why you were so awful when I first called to tell you I was pregnant? You thought I was lying about you being the father?"

"Of course not!"

"You doubted me in your office. You had the nerve to ask me if I was certain."

His face tightened, his mouth grim. "It was a legitimate question, Angel." He faltered, looking tormented. "I just wasn't expecting you to…"

"Legitimate? When you were the only man I'd ever been with?"

There was a heartbeat of silence. "Ever?" His eyebrows rose in incredulous disbelief.

She slapped down a knife on the table. "So you thought once you humiliated me, once you'd *used* me, I would just willingly jump in bed with another man? You thought

I found my one experience with sex so titillating I had to race out for more, and since you weren't available, I'd take any man who was?''

As she spoke, her voice rose almost to a shout, but it all came back on her, all the pain and mortification. She laughed, but it wasn't a happy sound. Derek sat staring at her, his expression almost comically blank.

Well, he wasn't used to hearing her yell. She'd always been meek and agreeable with him, so much so she'd made his objective pathetically easy. He'd overwhelmed her with his bigger-than-life persona, but not anymore. Now she'd changed, thanks to the way he'd screwed up her life. And he had changed as well.

"Believe me, Derek, you were the only one. And once with you was more than enough."

It was her sneering tone, meant to show him her loathing, only it didn't work.

She'd started to tremble and Derek was suddenly there, his arms around her, his lips against her temple. "Shh, baby, I'm sorry. So sorry."

"Just go back to work, Derek. Leave me alone."

"I can't do that." He leaned back, keeping her pelvis pressed to his, but putting space between their upper bodies. "You don't want me to do that. For whatever reason, Angel, you contacted me."

She opened her mouth, but she couldn't think of a single thing to say.

"Shh. It's all right. You don't have to tell me now. I'll wait until you're ready."

That he suspected her of having ulterior motives should have alarmed her, but she was just too tired to fight with him. And since she desperately needed his concession, she nodded, relief making her slump against him.

"I was an idiot in the office yesterday. Of course I know you haven't been with anyone else. Sometimes men just say...stupid things." He seemed to be floundering for the right words as his hands coasted up and down her back, soothing. "We won't mention that again, okay?"

Reluctantly, she nodded.

"Good." He stepped back, but rather than sit at the table again, he began compiling his own sandwich. "I do want to hear everything—no matter how insignificant— that's happened to you since we've been apart." He gave her a sharp, assessing glance. "I have a lot of catching up to do. All right?"

"Yes." The distraction of simple conversation would help her regain her balance. She didn't want to confide in him yet, not until she knew she could trust him with Grayson's safety. "Yes, I'll tell you...everything."

He stayed longer than she would have guessed, and he asked more questions than she could answer. When Grayson awoke, Derek changed the baby, cuddled him for long moments, and when Grayson demanded to be fed, he finally took his leave. But he promised to come back the next day.

And though she was annoyed with herself, Angel already looked forward to his next visit.

CHAPTER FIVE

DINNER SEEMED TO LAST forever. All Dane wanted to do was go home and ponder Angel's revelation. *She'd been a virgin.* God, he still felt stunned. And entirely too aroused.

From what she'd told him, she'd only been with Derek once, and that had been a disappointment.

Possessive heat filled him. She hadn't really belonged to Derek, not the way a woman should, not the way she would belong to him. Guilt plagued him as he considered making her his own while knowing Derek had been her first and only. But with every minute that passed, he felt more determined to tie himself to her. There were numerous reasons, none of them overly honest, but still, they served his purpose.

He adored Grayson, already loving him as if he were his own. Dane had never thought to fit the bill of *father*— his chance had been lost to him so long ago. But it was precisely because his chance had been lost, and why, that he wanted to protect Grayson. Angel was right to fear his family; they would take over without giving her a single chance if he let them. But her fear also seemed exaggerated and somewhat pointless. Sooner or later they'd find out about the baby. It was inevitable.

He planned to be there when they did, to soothe her fears.

Angel also deserved his protection, and the luxury the Carter name could supply. Whatever else Derek had become, he'd still been a wealthy man. Grayson had a birthright that would pave much of his way in the world. Derek should have seen that Grayson received his due; for reasons of his own, he hadn't, and Dane was determined to correct the oversight.

He also still believed Angel to be the most likely link in discovering what had happened to his brother. So far, nothing seemed to fit. Derek was capable of some pretty ruthless behavior, but the way he'd treated Angel seemed out of character even for him. Much of the cruelty had been deliberate and unnecessary. Why had Derek done it? And what was the real reason Angel had contacted him again, despite the damn past they shared? There were secrets there, things he had to discover, and that too, was a good reason to stay in touch with Miss Angel Morris.

The biggest reason of all, of course, was the chemistry between them. When he touched Angel, all his senses exploded like never before. And not even the memory of her and Derek's past experiences could dampen her responses; it was driving him insane.

Damn his brother for complicating things so, for hurting her. And most of all for letting himself get killed. What had Derek been up to?

"Dane?"

Startled out of his ruminations, Dane looked up to see his mother frowning fiercely across the table at him. She did it well, he thought as he speared a bite of asparagus and chewed slowly. Her look was so forbidding that most people immediately apologized even before they knew what they'd done wrong. At sixty, she was still a slim, attractive woman with her light-brown hair stylishly twisted behind her head, and her brown eyes sharp with intelligence. She kept herself in top physical shape; her pride would tolerate no less.

Dane stifled a bored yawn. He'd quit playing his mother's games long ago. "Did you want something, Mother?"

She pinched her mouth together at his lack of manners and deference due her. "Where in the world is your attention? You haven't been following the conversation at all."

Celia smiled toward him. "Do you have a big investigation that's got you stumped, brother?"

He sent her a chiding glance. Celia had been teasing him about being a P.I. since he'd walked in the door. She'd had the gall to ask him if he carried a spy kit. His sister seemed different than he remembered, more light-hearted, more playful. He liked the changes.

To his surprise, Raymond blurted, "You aren't still wondering about the Morris woman, are you?"

His mother straightened to attention, jumping on the topic like a dog on a meaty bone. She had plans for Dane, he knew. She'd sat him at the head of the table—a major concession for her, and an indication of what she expected from him in the future. She wouldn't want any threats to her plans, and his interest in anyone or anything other than the company would certainly be considered a threat.

He hadn't yet told her of his intentions, or rather lack thereof, toward the family and the company. He wanted everything settled first before he dropped his news on her.

"What's this, Dane?" Her face was alarmingly pale, her eyes flashing. "What's Raymond talking about?"

"Nothing of any import, Mother. I merely asked Raymond a few questions about Angel Morris. I was curious since Derek had been seeing the woman for a while."

Celia turned quiet and gave her attention to her food. His mother wasn't so reserved. Her hands fisted on the table, yet she managed to keep her tone calm. "He wasn't *seeing* her, for heaven's sake. He merely associated with her to ease the effort of the takeover. She was a secretary of sorts, no one important. Certainly no one important to Derek."

Forcefully keeping his emotions in check, feigning a certain lack of interest, Dane asked, "Do you know what happened to her?"

His mother carefully laid aside her fork, then looked down her nose at him. She sat to his right, Celia and Raymond to his left.

"After she was terminated, you mean? Why would I care?" She made a rude sound of condescension. "You certainly didn't expect us to employ the woman, did you, not after she gave away company secrets."

Celia spoke up for the first time, her voice clipped, her expression stern. "I already told you, Mother, Derek stole that information from her."

Dane felt as though he'd taken a punch on the chin. His mother made an outraged sound and Raymond sat watching them both, his expression somewhat satisfied. He stared at his sister and saw that two spots of bright color had bloomed on her cheeks. "What did you say?"

Celia gave her mother a lingering frown, then turned to face Dane. "Mother persists in making this woman out as a villain, even though I've told her repeatedly that it isn't so. If anything, she was a victim, and we certainly should have employed her in an effort to make amends. Derek explained to me himself that Angel hadn't volunteered the information to him. He rifled through her personal belongings until he found what he wanted.''

Raymond held his fork aloft, using it to emphasize his point. ''Ah. But she should have seen to it that the material was well secured. That was her responsibility. The heads at Aeric trusted her, and she let them down.''

''I suppose part of the blame is hers,'' Celia agreed, her tone snide, ''in trusting Derek too much, in thinking him honorable toward her—''

Dane's mother gasped, coming to her feet in furious indignation. Her hands slapped down on the cloth-covered tabletop while her voice rose to a near shriek. ''How dare you suggest otherwise, Celia Carter? He was your brother!''

Looking belligerent and stubborn, Celia forced a shrug and met her mother's gaze. ''Mother, he *stole* that information from her. He led her on, made her believe he cared for her, and then took shameful advantage. Would you rather I call that honorable?''

Raymond patted Celia's hand. ''Sweetheart, he only did what was best for the company. That was always his first priority.'' His eyes slid over to Dane. ''As is true of any CEO.''

Dane waited, watching while his mother visibly struggled to regain her control. Such an outburst from her surprised him and piqued his curiosity. When she had grudgingly reseated herself, pretending to be appeased by Raymond's words, and Raymond had taken a healthy bite of his braised pork, Dane asked, "Are you saying, Raymond, that you wouldn't have a problem with using a woman that way?"

Raymond promptly choked, covering his mouth with his napkin.

"Really, Dane, enough of this nonsense!" his mother protested. "Raymond has been an enormous help to us and deserves better from you."

Celia looked at Dane, a wicked smile of appreciation curving her lips, then proceeded to pound her fiancé on the back until he'd managed to catch his breath. Dane leaned back in his chair, enjoying the dinner for the first time that evening.

Damn, so much to think about. So Angel was innocent all the way around. That fact twisted his guts, making him feel guilty as hell, as if he were the one who'd betrayed her. He determined to make it up to her somehow. Whether she wanted him to or not.

An hour later as they all gathered in the salon for drinks and conversation, Dane cornered his sister. Raymond was busy schmoozing their mother, and Celia was blessedly alone, staring out a window at the dark night. As he approached, she looked down at his hand and the drink he held.

"I thought you abstained."

He lifted the glass in a salute. "Pure cola and ice. Nothing more."

"It irritates Mother, you know. That you won't have a social drink."

Dane thought of Mick, so defiant as he explained his mother was an alcoholic. "In my line of work, I see too many drink-related cases. Men and women who abandon their families in favor of a bottle. They all started out as social drinkers.'' Shaking off his sudden tension, he smiled at Celia. ''Besides, I enjoy irritating Mother.''

To his surprise, his teasing wasn't returned. Celia turned fully to face him. ''How do you do it, Dane? How do you just turn your back on everything, on all of us?''

A frontal attack. He hadn't expected it of his sister, but he relished a moment to clear the air. He'd missed her in the time he'd been away. Though she was a lot like his mother, her strength and determination not to be underestimated, she was also a woman who thought for herself, who didn't blindly accept his mother's dictates. He'd found that out tonight. In the years he'd stayed away, his sister had evidently come into her own.

Too long, too damn long. ''There's nothing for me to stay here for, Celia. You know that. Mother made certain she drove me away—''

''She's sorry for that, Dane.'' Celia touched his arm. Her eyes, the same hazel shade as his, were dark with concern. ''She realizes now that you really did love Anna, that she shouldn't have interfered.''

He snorted. ''Is that what you call it, interference? She deliberately destroyed my life, accused my fiancée of all kinds of reprehensible things, and just because she didn't approve of Anna's family.''

Celia bit her lip, then forged on. ''You were both so young. Besides, she did take the money, Dane. Mother didn't force it on her.''

''She made Anna feel as if that were the only option, as if she couldn't possibly be my wife. Mother made sure she knew she'd never fit in.'' Even as he said the words, he accepted that he wasn't being a hundred percent truthful with her or himself. "Anna was pregnant, you know. After she ran off, she lost the baby. My baby."

Celia covered her mouth with a hand. "Oh no, I didn't know. I'm so sorry."

"I told Mother. I was angry and hurt and I wanted her to understand exactly what her manipulation had cost me. Do you know what she said?"

Numbly, Celia shook her head.

"She said it was for the best."

Celia lowered her forehead to Dane's shoulder and her voice was quiet, almost a whisper. "Mother's set in her ways, Dane. She means well, and she really does love you. It's just that sometimes she doesn't think."

He had nothing to say to that. It amazed him that his sister would always try to defend their mother, no matter what she did.

"Will you stay on at the company this time? We need you here."

Lifting a hand to his sister's fair hair, giving one silky lock a teasing tug, he said, "You already know the answer to that."

She sighed. "I suppose I do. But I was hopeful."

"It's not for me, sis. I don't feel comfortable there and besides, I love playing detective too much to give it up."

She smiled at his teasing, then turned to face the window again. "I miss him so much."

"Me, too. Even though we hadn't been in contact much lately, I always knew he was here. There were only miles separating us, and I knew we could get in touch if we chose to." Dane wanted to tell her that he suspected Derek had been murdered, but he held back. His sister had enough on her plate for the moment. "I'm proud of how you stood up to Mother."

She made a disgusted sound. "She's hurting. And it angers her if anyone even suggests Derek might not have been perfect. But I can't sit by and watch her persecute an innocent woman."

Dane thought his sister was pretty damn special at that moment, and more than ever, he regretted the amount of time he'd let pass without seeing his family.

"How long are you willing to help out?"

Until I see things settled, he thought, but he only shrugged. "I don't know. We'll see. Right now, I have every agent in my own business maxed out, working on two or more cases at a time. And running between offices isn't getting any easier." Especially while trying to uncover a murderer.

He looked up at that moment to see Raymond watching him while his mother chatted in Raymond's ear, no doubt regaling him with stories of old acquaintances, money and power. It was all his mother knew, all she cared about, and Raymond, with his desire to ingratiate himself, provided the perfect audience. Dane nodded then looked away. "Do you love him?"

Celia laughed. "You say that as if such a thing is unimaginable."

"I just want you to be happy."

"I'd be happy if you stayed on." She quickly raised her hands. "But I understand why you can't. Dane, why were you asking questions about Angel Morris?"

She effectively sidetracked him and he rubbed his chin, wondering what to tell her. Finally he said, "I suppose it just surprises me what Derek did. I don't like to think him capable of such things. Can you even begin to imagine what Angel Morris must have felt like?''

Celia leaned into him, their shoulders touching. ''If it's any consolation, I think he regretted it. He was very distracted those last few weeks. And unhappy. He told me once that Angel would never forgive him, and that he didn't blame her. It was almost like he'd *had* to hurt her, though I never understood why. I planned to ask him, to understand, but then he died.''

Dane didn't understand either, but he felt better for having talked with his sister. His mother he simply hoped to avoid so she couldn't try to nail him down on his intentions. He didn't want anyone to know his plans until he'd figured everything out. At this point, he wasn't certain who to trust, so he trusted no one.

Not even Angel. The more he learned, the more reason he had to wonder why she'd ever contacted Derek again in the first place. She had to hate him for all he'd done to her. But, his thinking continued, Derek had also given her Grayson, and the baby appeared to be the most important thing in her life. Maybe for that reason alone, she'd been able to give up on some of her anger and resentment. Maybe she'd come to the very reasonable conclusion that Grayson deserved a father and all that Derek could provide. It could be only misplaced pride that still made her insist she wanted nothing from him. Heaven knew, he'd had a hard enough time making her accept the essentials, food and diapers and damn shampoo. She also had plenty of reason to hang on to that pride, given the way she'd been treated.

As Raymond and Mrs. Carter joined them, Raymond smoothly slipped his arm around Celia and gave her an affectionate peck on the cheek. Watching them, Dane pondered the idea of starting over. Ever since Anna had abandoned him, allowing his mother to buy her off, he'd avoided relationships. He hadn't met a woman he'd wanted to see more than twice.

Anna hadn't trusted him, had believed his mother's tales over the truths he'd given her. He'd never admit it to anyone, but Anna's actions had proved his mother right; she wasn't the woman for him. He expected, needed, a woman to give him everything, not merely her trust, but her unwavering loyalty. Her soul. Anna hadn't been able to do that, and while he still regretted the loss, it was more the manipulation that he resented. He'd long since gotten over his first love. It had been a lesson to be learned, and he'd learned it well.

This time, he could think more clearly. He'd make certain the same didn't happen with Angel. He'd reason with his brains, not his heart, and sooner or later, he'd win her over. His ruthlessness was an inherent part of his nature. After all, much as he might dislike it on occasion, he was still a Carter.

Angel didn't stand a chance.

"I DON'T LIKE IT. I think you should tell Derek."

Angel was so sick of hearing Mick's refrain. He and Derek got along wonderfully, but then who wouldn't get along with him? Derek was generous and thoughtful and attentive and protective. He'd shown up every day for the past week, helping with everything from bathing the baby to shopping and housework. Twice he had brought over dinner, then cleaned up the mess so Angel could get caught up on her typing. He'd tried to give her money, but after she'd told him exactly what she thought of that idea, he hadn't mentioned it again.

Instead, he asked questions, hundreds and hundreds of questions. Sometimes it made her nervous, though she couldn't say why. He just seemed so...different.

"The job he got me is awesome."

She smiled at Mick's enthusiasm. He'd been with her since six o'clock while they went over his homework. Now it was nine and he'd done little else but talk about Derek in between lessons in calculus and conjugating Spanish verbs. "So you like it?"

"Are you kidding? What's not to like? It's a private investigations office and the people there are so laid back and friendly. It's like a big family."

Angel's heart twisted. Mick had never had much family to brag about. His mother was more absent than not, and even when she was around, she didn't demonstrate any maternal instincts. Mick had pretty much raised himself, and Angel knew what a lonely existence that could be.

"They've been telling me some of the cases they've dealt with. Incredible stuff, like shoot-outs and drug busts and all kinds of stuff. This one guy, Alec Sharpe, he's actually sort of scary, but don't tell Derek I said so."

Angel smiled in amazement. If the man spooked Mick, who wasn't afraid of anyone as far as she could tell, he must be one frightening character. She pretended to lock her lips with an imaginary key. "Not a word, I promise."

"The guy has the darkest eyes and he's real quiet and when he talks, even if it's just to ask for coffee, everyone around him shuts up and listens. I think he's sort of a boss or something."

Angel gathered up pencils and pens and put the calculator away. "What do you do there?"

Mick made a face. "All kinds of stuff, from cleaning and running out for doughnuts to making coffee and putting files away. But they're all real nice about it. They don't act like I'm getting paid, but more like I'm doing them a huge favor and they really appreciate it. And Alec gave me this really cool car to drive. It has the best stereo."

Angel knew Mick would be paid more working there than he had made doing both jobs before. And it had been agreed he wouldn't work past six o'clock on school days, and only until the afternoon on the weekends. She was so incredibly grateful to Derek, seeing the change in Mick. He was more like the average kid now, happy and proud. And he adored Derek.

Of course, Mick didn't know everything that had happened between Angel and Derek in the past. And she'd never tell. Derek was doing his best to prove the past really was over; not for the world would she take away Mick's present happiness.

"Why do you still dislike him so much, Angel?"

"Mick…"

"He could help," Mick said, anxious to convince her. "The phone calls were bad enough, but now the letter—"

She rubbed her head. "I know. The letter proves whoever it is knows where to find me. I've been thinking about this a lot." She hesitated, almost afraid to voice her suspicions out loud. "It's possible Derek is the one behind all this."

He stared at her hard, then got to his feet and paced away. "You don't really believe that."

She didn't want to believe it. But the letter proved her alias hadn't worked—an alias Derek had noticed his first time to her apartment. She didn't want to think he could be so vindictive, but he might have slipped up and told his family, and they were using the information to drive her away. That she could believe only too well.

"I don't know what all's going on between you two, but I do know you're in trouble. You're being stalked, and whoever's been making the calls could have gotten your number from anywhere, maybe even from the ads you ran for typing. But now he knows where you live. The letter proves that. If you keep putting off telling Derek, you could end up hurt."

"Well, I can't do anything about it tonight. Derek had business and couldn't come over. And it isn't something to discuss on the phone."

Mick nodded slowly as he slipped his jacket on. "I'll try to watch out for you, Angel. I wouldn't let anyone hurt you if I could help it, but I can't always be here."

Her blood ran cold with his words. "Mick, if you ever, *ever* hear anything suspicious, or see anyone around the mailboxes, you call the police. Don't you dare try confronting anyone on your own."

He didn't reply to that, merely made his way to the door. "I'll lock this behind me."

"Mick?"

"Call him, Angel. Tell him what's going on. He cares about you and Grayson. I know he does."

It would have been nice if Mick didn't act like the typical domineering, overprotective male. Why were men, of all ages, so blasted stubborn? She sighed. "I'll think about it."

Mick looked at her a moment longer, then nodded. "All right. I'll see you tomorrow?"

She smiled at him. She was very lucky she'd met him when she had. Knowing him, having his friendship, had made her life much easier. "Yes. Get some sleep so you're well rested for that test."

"Yes, ma'am."

After checking that the door was securely locked, Angel peeked in on Grayson. He was sleeping soundly, which would give her a chance to take a quick shower. With all of Derek's help of late, her leg had more time to rest. It didn't hurt as often anymore, but tonight it was sore. She'd sat too long typing at her desk earlier and the muscles felt cramped. A hot shower usually helped.

Leaving the bathroom door open so she could hear Grayson if he cried, she stripped off her clothes and reached into the tub to adjust the temperature of the water. Once the steam started billowing out, she slipped in under the spray.

It felt wonderful to once again wash her hair with scented shampoo, to use all the toiletries she'd given up on due to lack of funds. At first she'd tried returning the things to Derek, but he'd been so sincere in wanting her to keep them, so anxious to *relieve the guilt of his past sins*—his words for his execrable behavior of the past— that she couldn't deny him.

She lingered for a long time, relaxing in the hypnotic warmth of the steam and stinging spray, until she became sleepy and knew she needed to put herself to bed. Grayson still woke during the night for a feeding, and he was usually up with the birds in the morning.

She was just stepping over the side of the tub when the phone rang.

Her first thought was that it might be Derek, and ridiculously enough, her heart leaped. He'd taken to calling her several times a day, whereas before her phone had seldom rung at all. Many times now he'd called to tell her good morning, or good-night, even if he'd spent hours at her apartment.

Wrapping a thick white towel around herself, she hurried out of the bathroom and into the kitchen to snatch up the phone. She was smiling as she said, "Hello?"

A rough, rasping breath answered her, then turned into a growl. Her smile died a quick death.

Shaken, Angel started to slam the phone back down, and then she heard, "Bitch. Give me what I want."

The rasping tones didn't sound human and her blood rushed from her head, leaving her dizzy. "I don't know what you want," she said, her voice shaking despite her efforts to sound unaffected.

"Yes, you do." There was a laugh, taunting and high-pitched. "You're not as innocent as you like to pretend, Angel *Morton*. But your time is up. Do you hear me?"

"I'm hanging up now," she said, determined not to let the caller get the upper hand.

"Did you get my letter? I know where you are now. You better watch your back…"

Angel slammed the phone into the cradle. Her heart was beating so hard, it rocked her body and she quickly wrapped her arms around herself. She was only marginally aware of the water dripping from her hair down her back, leaving a puddle on the floor. Goose bumps rose on her skin, but she was frozen, unable to move.

When the knock sounded on the door, she let out a startled, short scream, jumping back two steps and bumping into the kitchen table. A chair tipped over and crashed to the floor. Grayson woke, his disgruntled wail piercing in the otherwise leaden silence.

She heard Derek call out, "Angel!" at the same time a key sounded in the lock. The door immediately swung open. She couldn't help herself, she gaped at him. How had he known to show up just when she needed him most?

In the next instant, doubt surfaced, and she had to wonder if it was a coincidence, or part of a plan. Was it possible he was working with his family to drive her away? Had she inadvertently stepped into the lion's den?

Derek stormed in like an avenging angel, took one look at her standing there with nothing more than the towel covering her, then crossed the room with long, angry strides. He grabbed her shoulders. "What's the matter? What's happened?"

Angel managed to shake herself out of her stupor. She clutched at her towel with a fist. "What are you doing here?"

He looked nonplussed by her calm question and tightened his hands on her. "I wanted to see you." His head turned in the direction of Grayson's wails and a fierce frown formed. "You're both okay?"

"Yes, of course."

"But you screamed." He turned back to her, raised one hand when she started to speak, then shook his head. "First things first. Go get dried off. I'll get the baby."

She was shaking all over, but he thankfully didn't comment on it. "Thank you. I think the phone disturbed him, and then your knock…"

Derek started her toward her bedroom with a gentle push. "I understand, babe. Go. We'll talk about it in a minute."

Regardless of what he'd said, Angel followed Derek into the baby's room and made certain everything was all right. She never let Grayson cry, and even now, when she was so rattled, she couldn't stand to hear him upset. Derek cradled him close to his chest, rocking him, murmuring to him, and Grayson immediately began to quiet, his yells turning into hiccups as he recognized his father's scent and voice. Derek held his face close to the baby's, nuzzling, kissing his tiny ear, his cheek, smoothing his large hand up and down Grayson's back. Angel's throat felt tight and her chest restricted.

He turned suddenly when he realized Angel had followed him. Slowly, his gaze ran the length of her, lingering, she knew, on the still harsh scars of her left leg. His attention returned to the baby. "Go get something on, Angel, before you catch cold."

She wondered if her leg repulsed him; his voice had sounded unusually gruff and low. It really was ugly and overall she looked like a drowned rat at the moment. "All right. I'll...I'll be right back."

In the bathroom again, she quickly dried off, dragged a comb through her tangled hair, then shrugged into her housecoat. It was long and thick and covered her from head to toe. She hurried back in to Grayson. The baby now had his entire fist stuffed in his mouth, sucking loudly. She knew from experience that would only suffice for so long.

"Let me have him. After I nurse him, he should fall back to sleep."

Derek gave her a long look before nodding. "Let me change him first."

He disappeared into the other room and Angel paced. The letter this afternoon, then the phone call.... It was the first time she'd heard a voice. Usually the calls consisted of heavy breathing and ominous silences. Again, chills ran up her arms and she ducked her head, her brain working furiously. Mick was right; she had to trust Derek, had to tell him of her suspicions. But she wouldn't tell him everything. She'd only confide about the most recent events. After she saw how he reacted to that, then she'd consider telling him the rest.

When he touched her shoulder, she again jumped, whirling about to face him, her hand pressed to her throat. His expression was dark, his eyes narrowed, and she tried a nervous laugh.

"I'm sorry. You startled me."

"Obviously. But we'll talk about that in a minute."

She took the baby, quickly settled herself on the couch and then looked at Derek. He always left the room when she nursed Grayson, giving her the privacy she needed, but this time he stared right back. Slowly, his gaze never leaving her face, he took the chair opposite her. Heat bloomed inside her. "Derek..."

"No more secrets, Angel."

Grayson rooted against her, anxious for his meal, and she knew, judging by Derek's expression, arguing would gain her nothing. She pulled her gaze away from him, deliberately ignoring his very attentive audience, and went about feeding her baby. She felt stiff, unable to relax, so many things racing through her mind.

After a moment, Derek rose from his chair and reseated

himself beside her. The soft, worn cushions of the couch slumped with his weight and her hip rolled next to his, bumping into him. He felt warm and hard, his presence overwhelming. Angel was acutely aware of his undivided concentration on her breast. She kept her visual attention firmly placed on Grayson.

Casually, Derek slipped his arm around her shoulders. She had trouble breathing. She moved Grayson to her other breast, closer to Derek, and as he nursed he began to fall back to sleep. He looked precious, and she couldn't hold back a smile.

"He's beautiful, Angel." Derek's warm breath fanned her temple and she shivered. "You're beautiful."

His voice sounded with awe, and as he scooted even closer, seeming to surround her with his heat and scent and power, she felt herself relaxing. This felt right. Derek was doing nothing untoward, only taking part in what was rightfully his. His left arm moved across her abdomen in an embrace, just below the baby, circling both mother and son. He kissed her temple, a light, loving kiss. Slowly, Grayson released her nipple and a drop of milk slid down his chin. With his fingertip, Derek wiped it away.

They neither one moved. She knew Derek was looking at her, studying her, but there was nothing lurid about his scrutiny. He dipped his head and kissed Grayson on his silky crown. In a low, husky whisper, he asked, "Would you like me to burp him and put him back to bed?"

Angel nodded.

As he was lifted, Grayson stretched and groaned and gave a loud belch, making any further efforts unnecessary. Derek grinned as he hefted the small weight to his shoulder and got to his feet. He looked down at Angel. ''I'll be right back,'' he whispered. ''Don't move.''

Other than covering her breast and nervously shifting, she obeyed.

It was late, now close to eleven o'clock, but she was far from sleepy. So many emotions were pulling at her, fear and anxiety and anticipation, but also a deep contentment. Derek was everything a father should be, and she couldn't quite work up the energy to distrust him anymore. It took all she had as she fought herself to keep from falling in love with him. Despising him was out of the question.

Derek stepped out of the baby's room, softly closing the door behind him. For long moments, he merely stared at Angel across the room. The time of reckoning, she thought.

For the life of her, she couldn't seem to move. Her heart began racing, her palms grew damp. She saw Derek lock his jaw, saw his shoulders tighten and flex, and she knew, without him saying a single word, he was caught in the same inexplicable flow of emotions as she.

What would happen next, she couldn't guess, but she was anxious to find out.

And then the phone rang.

Angel gasped. Both wary and disgusted by the interruption, she stared toward the kitchen where the phone was located.

Derek frowned at her. ''Do you want me to get that for you?''

''No, I'll…'' She shook her head, wiped her palms across her thighs. And still she sat there, staring at the phone.

Sparing her a curious glance, Derek stalked to the phone and snatched it up on the fifth ring. "Hello?" He kept his gaze on Angel as he spoke and she tried to clear her expression, but she could see he'd already read too much there.

"Hello?" he said a little more forcefully. He looked at the receiver, then gently placed it in the cradle. As he walked back to loom over Angel, she could see the questions in his eyes. "What's going on, honey?" His tone was soft, menacing.

She shook her head. "I don't know."

He waited, not moving away, not saying another word. She recognized his stubborn expression, only now there was more of a threat there, more determination than ever.

"Sometimes I get strange calls."

She hadn't meant to make such a bald confession, but it just slipped out. After a deep breath while he raised one eyebrow, encouraging her, she continued. "Sometimes, eight or ten times now, someone has called and just…breathed in the phone. Today I finally heard a voice. He…said things to me." She lifted her gaze and got caught in his. "He called right before you got here."

Derek's eyes darkened, his eyebrows lowered, and suddenly he was crouching there in front of her, his hands holding hers, hard but not really hurting her. It did give her the feeling she couldn't get away, even if she tried.

His gaze was so intense, so probing, she squirmed. "You thought it might be me," he accused.

He didn't sound angry precisely, though she couldn't pinpoint the dominant emotion in his tone. She straightened her shoulders and frowned right back. "I wondered. I have no enemies that I know of, no reason for threats.

You're the only person who ever seemed to despise me, and I've never really understood why."

There, let him deal with that, she thought and jerked away to walk carefully into the kitchen. She needed something to drink, some warm tea. And she needed to escape his close scrutiny.

Out of the corner of her eye, she watched Derek stand, then pace around her tiny living room. He had his hands back in his pockets and his head down in deep thought. She was familiar with that look now, that show of serious introspection. She'd seen it a lot lately, though in the past she couldn't recall Derek ever doubting himself, ever giving so much thought to anything pertaining to her.

She put water on to boil, then asked, "Would you like some tea?"

"Thank you."

After righting the fallen chair, she sat at her small kitchen table, waiting for the water to get hot. Moments later she felt Derek's hands on her shoulders, heavy and warm.

"The problem is," he whispered, "I'm not making the calls. And I don't despise you." His hands slipped up to her throat, caressing, then smoothing her damp hair back behind her ears. "On the contrary, Angel, I want to take care of you."

Anger caused her eyes to narrow. She wanted to believe him, to understand and accept his help. She twisted to face him. "Why? Why now, when you made it plain months ago how you felt? You deliberately humiliated me in front of my supervisors. You didn't just break things off, you tried to break me. *Why?*"

His eyes closed and he turned his head away. "You're

right, of course. I can't undo the past. I can only have regrets, which don't amount to a hill of beans. But I'm here now and I'd like to help.''

Since that was what she'd wanted all along, what her entire plan had been, she should have been relieved. But somehow everything was different than she'd expected. He wasn't the same man, easy to be detached from now. The Derek who'd first hurt her had been more of an illusion to her, an image of strength and power that had seduced her by sheer impression. She hadn't really known the man, other than in the most superficial ways; she'd merely been attracted to his image. But now she genuinely liked and respected him. When she could set the past aside, he was fun, and when he held Grayson, the affection in his eyes filled her with an insidious warmth that expanded her heart. More often than not, she didn't understand what she was feeling.

Only one thing was certain; Grayson could be at risk if she didn't find some sort of protection.

She got up to serve the tea, collecting her thoughts. After she sat his cup near him on the table, she said, ''I've gotten several anonymous calls lately, more than ever before. Usually, it's just breathing and such. They started before I'd moved, when I lived in my old apartment. After I moved here, they stopped for a while and I thought I'd lost whoever it was. But just recently they started up again. It's possible my phone number was taken from one of the posted ads around the colleges. The ads are generic, offering typing, but since I've been transcribing for colleges ever since the accident, it could be my number was relocated that way.''

Derek nodded. "Very possible, I suppose. But the person making the calls would have to be damn determined."

Angel shivered. "He spoke for the first time today. He said, very clearly, that I couldn't hide. He called me a few…choice names and told me to give him what he wanted."

She saw Derek's jaw go hard and knew he was clenching his teeth. He stared at her and she shrugged helplessly. "I don't know what he wants. I wish I did."

"Go on."

"I also got a letter in my mailbox."

"Where is it?"

She pulled an envelope from the basket on top of her refrigerator and handed it to Derek. The letter was now wrinkled from her many hours of examining it, but Derek had no trouble making out the typed message. *"I've found you,"* he read aloud. He was silent for a long time, his face dark, his expression tight. He threw the letter on the table and turned on her.

"You thought I was behind this?" he asked, his teeth clenched, color high on his face. "You thought I would resort to sneaking around and stuffing threatening letters in a woman's mailbox, in *your* mailbox?"

His reaction was genuine and for the first time she felt absolutely positive that he played no part in the harassment.

A little truth now certainly wouldn't hurt. Problem was, as she tried to give it, tears gathered in her eyes, and she couldn't quite work up the nerve to accuse his family, the most likely of suspects. Not yet.

She shook her head. "No," she said, trying to sound sure of herself. "I don't really think you're behind it. But the letter came after I contacted you. Before that, all I'd gotten was phone calls. And you noticed the fake name on my mailbox that day. Now tonight, you showed up right after the call, and it was the first time he'd ever spoken to me. That's a lot of coincidences." She searched his face, hoping he'd understand. "I had to consider you, Derek. I couldn't take any chances with Grayson's safety."

Seconds ticked by, then he reluctantly nodded.

She drew a deep breath of relief. "The whole reason I contacted you again, the only reason I introduced Grayson to you is because deep down, for some incredibly insane reason, I guess I still trust you. Even after everything that happened, I thought… I thought you would help. I *hoped* you would help."

She swallowed, the sound audible, almost choked. "Derek…I've been so scared, and I don't have anyone else to go to."

A stunned moment of silence fell between them. She could feel the waves of emotion emanating from him, anger and regret and need. Then she was in his arms and it felt so good, so right, she curled closer and snuggled tighter, trying to fit herself completely against his long, hard length. His arms wrapped around her, urgently, almost violently, while his mouth nuzzled down her face, giving her small anxious biting kisses until finally he reached her lips and then he was devouring her and she was glad, so very, very glad.

CHAPTER SIX

DANE KNEW HE SHOULD pull back, that he was making a terrible tactical error. He wasn't completely in control, and he should be. But he couldn't put so much as an inch between them. He wanted, needed her, right now. Even two seconds more would be too long to wait. And Angel was so soft and anxious against him, her breasts pressed to his chest, her pelvis cradling his own. She wanted him, too, and that was all that mattered. The deceptions, the worries, could be taken care of in the morning. He'd make it all okay, one way or another, but for now, tonight, he wouldn't say a single thing that would put a halt to her greed.

Growling low, he slid his hands down to her backside and cuddled her even closer. She felt so damn good.

"Angel."

She pressed her face into his throat and shuddered. "I don't understand this, Derek," she said on a near wail. "I've never felt like this before."

How could he possibly explain it to her, when he didn't understand it himself? He knew she would compare him to Derek, and as much as he'd loved his brother, as dedicated as he was to finding out the truth, right now claiming her took precedence over everything else.

He shushed her with more kisses. "I've never felt this

way either, honey. Don't worry about it now. Just let me love you.''

She opened her mouth against him and took a soft, greedy love bite of his throat. Gasping, he quickly picked her up, mindful of her injured leg, and hurried to her bedroom, nudging the door shut behind them until it closed with a secure click. He didn't want to take the chance of waking Grayson. He wanted no interruptions at all.

He didn't put her on the bed, choosing to stand her beside it instead. He wanted her naked, and he wanted to look his fill. It felt as if he'd been waiting forever.

As he grasped the cloth belt to her robe, ready to pull it free, she caught his wrists. His gaze darted to her face and he was amazed to see how heavy and sensual her eyes had become, her thick lashes lowered, the green eyes bright and hot. Her high cheekbones were colored, but with need, not embarrassment. She took soft, panting breaths as she looked up at him.

She licked her lips, and even that innocently seductive sight had him trembling.

''I don't want to disappoint you, Derek.''

He'd never before minded being mistaken for his twin. Through his entire life people had often done it, sometimes even his parents. Before their father had died, he and Derek had often played tricks on him, deliberately confusing him.

But now, he hated it. He had to struggle for breath. He gave her a hard quick kiss, which turned tender and hungry and lingered sweetly. When he pulled away, it seemed to take a great effort on her part for her to get her eyes open. He smiled. "There's no way you could disappoint me, honey."

"My body's changed. The baby…"

Still holding her gaze he tugged the knot out of the belt and pushed the robe off her shoulders. She dropped her arms and the robe fell free all the way to the floor. Angel lowered her head and turned slightly away.

For nearly a minute he was speechless. She was more beautiful than any woman had a right to be, and there was absolutely nothing motherly about her heavy, firm breasts, the stiff dark nipples. Her rib cage expanded and fluttered with her uneven breaths and her belly looked soft and slightly rounded, very pale. He spread one large, hot palm over her stomach and heard her small gasp.

"Derek…?"

"Shhh. I've never wanted a woman the way I want you, Angel. Trust me when I tell you there's not a single thing about you that could disappoint me." Her legs were long and so sexy, even with the harsh scars on her left shin. He immediately pictured those long legs wrapped around him, her heels digging into the small of his back, urging him on, and he groaned as his erection pulsed, demanding release.

Slowly, so he wouldn't startle her, he slid his palm downward until he was cupping her, his fingers tangling in the dark blond curls over her mound. They felt damp and soft under his fingertips, her flesh swollen, and he breathed deeply through his nose, trying to ease the constriction in his lungs. He held still, just holding her like that, letting her feel the heat of his palm, letting the anticipation build.

Angel moaned and stepped up against him. Her hands gripped his biceps, her forehead pressed to his shoulder.

Dane swallowed and smiled grimly. "Do you remember when I touched you in my office?" he asked against her temple.

She nodded her head.

He licked her ear and gently nipped the lobe. "You were so close then, Angel, and I'd barely done anything to you. Little more than kissing." He nearly groaned with the memory.

Her hips jerked, encouraging him. Anticipating her response, he inched his fingers lower, gliding over her warm flesh, opening her soft, plump folds, learning her, exploring. She was already so hot, so silky wet, and it amazed him the way she reacted to his touch. It also made him nearly crazy with a frenzied mix of lust and overwhelming tenderness.

Her body felt frozen against his, very still, waiting. Even her breathing became suspended, as if she was afraid to move for fear of missing something. Determination swelled within him. He had no intention of leaving her with complaints; her views on the joys of sex were about to be altered.

"Open your legs a little more for me, Angel." He could tell that she responded to his words, and he wasn't about to disappoint her. "Let me feel you. All of you."

With a shudder, her face well hidden against his chest, she carefully widened her stance. Immediately he pressed one finger deep inside her, at the same time he braced his free arm around her waist.

She needed his support.

Her body went alternately stiff and completely yielding.

Holding her against him, acutely aware of her broken breaths, her soft moans, the way her fingers dug into his chest, he stroked her. He could feel her tightening, feel the small shudders moving up and down her body. He eased her a little away from him and she allowed the small separation, her head falling back on her shoulders, her still-damp hair trailing down to tickle against his arm. He saw her breasts heaving and dipped his head down to take one plump nipple into his mouth.

"Ohhh…"

He lapped with his tongue, nibbled with his teeth, drew deeply on her. Her hands raised from his chest to his head and her fingers tangled in his hair, tugging, trying to draw him even closer.

"I have to sit down," she moaned.

"No." He blew on her damp nipple, watching it go painfully tight. The pregnancy had no doubt made her breasts extra sensitive, and he intended to take advantage of that fact. "Right here, Angel. We'll get to the bed in a minute."

He switched to her other breast and heard her give a soft sob of compliance. Voluntarily, she parted her legs even more and then thrust against him. He slid his finger all the way out, teasing, then worked it heavily back into her again. "You're so wet for me, honey," he said on a groan, amazed and thrilled and so hot himself he wanted to die.

Forcefully, making him wince, she brought his mouth back up to her own and this time she kissed him, awkwardly but with so much hunger he thought he might burst. He rubbed his heavy erection against her soft hip while he carefully forced a second finger inside her. He found a rhythm that pleased her and went about seeing to her satisfaction. He was playing it safe, not about to remove his clothes or lie with her on the bed, knowing his control was thin at the moment and any little thing could send him over the edge. He wouldn't risk taking his own completion before he'd seen to hers.

Within minutes she was crying, her body tight and trembling, her hands frenzied on his back and shoulders. Slowly, he eased her down to the side of the bed so that her legs hung over the edge, then knelt between them. She dropped back, her hands fisting in the bedclothes, her hips twisting. Dane lifted her legs to his shoulders and before she could object—if indeed she would have given how close she was—he cupped her hips in his hands and brought her to his mouth.

She tasted sweet and incredibly hot and he was beyond teasing her, so close to exploding himself. His heart thundered and her scent filled him as he nuzzled into her, driving himself ever closer. As his tongue stroked over her sensitive flesh, as he found the small engorged bud and drew on it, teasing with his tongue, tormenting with his teeth, she gave a stifled scream and climaxed.

Quickly, wanting to feel every bit of her, he pushed his fingers back inside her. Her feminine muscles gripped him, the spasms strong as she pressed herself even higher, moving against his open mouth and continuing to cry and moan and excite him unbearably. It went on and on and he almost lost control. He was shaking all over when she finally quieted, her eyes closed, her lashes damp on her cheeks, her mouth slightly open as she gulped air.

She never so much as blinked when he lifted her legs gently to the bed and stood to look down at her. Slowly, drinking in the sight of her limp, sated body, he pulled his shirt free from his pants and began unbuttoning it. He forced himself to go slow, to savor the moment of his claiming. Even to his own mind, his thoughts, his responses, seemed primitive, maybe even ruthless. But he wanted her to be his and his alone—a feeling he'd never encountered before, not even with Anna. He wanted to take her so thoroughly, possess her so completely, she'd be willing to forgive him anything, willing to trust him in all matters.

She gave a shuddering sigh, lifted one languid hand to her forehead and pushed her hair away from her face. Dane watched her, so suffused with heat the edges of his vision blurred.

While he tugged his belt loose from the clasp with one hand, he dropped his other lightly to her soft thigh. Her skin felt like warm silk to him, and tempted him more than it should have.

Her lashes fluttered as his fingers trailed higher, and finally her eyes opened. She looked dazed and relaxed, on the verge of sleep. He smiled and carefully worked his zipper down past his throbbing erection. "You scream very well, Angel. I liked it."

"Oh." Her cheeks filled with color and she swallowed. When her gaze dropped to the open vee in his slacks, her eyes opened wide. *"Oh."*

Dane sat on the bed beside her, his hand still on her thigh. "No, don't get up. I like seeing you sprawled there." She relaxed back again and he used the toes of his left foot to work off his right shoe, while at the same time surveying her body. He traced a nipple with his fingertip, around and around until she made a protesting sound. Then he dragged his fingers over her ribs and to her belly. She shifted abruptly.

"Ticklish?"

"Derek…"

Leaning over, he pressed a lingering kiss to her navel. "I love the way you taste, honey."

She made a groaning sound of renewed interest, then tried to turn away from him. He caught her hips, stopping her.

"Derek, you can't expect me to…"

"Yes I do." Once again his fingers slid between her legs, anchoring her in place while he kissed his way up her abdomen to her breasts. "I expect you to let me pleasure you, and I expect you to continue enjoying my efforts."

He raised his head for just a moment, pinning her with a look. "You came, Angel. A nice long, hard climax. And if I didn't miss my guess, it was your first. So don't try to deny it."

She gasped. "I wasn't going to!"

"Good." When he drew her nipple into the heat of his mouth she writhed against him, then fisted her hands in his hair.

"No, Derek."

He jerked upward and pinned her hands next to her head. "Yes."

She said quickly, before he could kiss her, "I want you to take your shirt off. I want to see you, too. It's not fair for me to lie here…exposed, while you're completely dressed."

His grin was slow and wicked. He knew it, but didn't

care. She wasn't denying him at all as he'd first thought. She only insisted on her fair share. "All right."

He pushed himself off the bed. "Don't move, Angel. You inspire me, lying there like that."

He shrugged his shirt off and grabbed the waistband of his pants. He stepped between her legs as he pushed them down, removing his Skivvies at the same time. When he straightened, he was naked.

Angel's gaze roamed over him and her face heated again. He stifled a laugh, delighted with her. Her particular brand of innocence and hot sexuality was driving him crazy. He loved it. He loved... No, his thoughts refused to budge any further in that direction. He firmed his resolve.

Using a knee, he spread her legs even more and lowered himself over her. Propped on his elbows, he smiled down at her. "Hi."

Rather than smiling back, she traced his face, over his eyebrows, the bridge of his nose, the dip in his chin. "You took me by surprise, Derek. Everything is so different..."

"So you keep saying." He didn't want to talk about that right now. Thinking of his brother with her like this was enough to make him howl at the moon.

"What happened was...unexpected."

"But nice?" He again caught her hands and trapped them over her head, leaving her submissive to his desires.

She looked thoughtful as she continued her study of his face. "Very nice. Incredible really. But ever since I saw you again, it's been that way. You look at me, and I get all hot inside. You touch me and I can't think straight. I try to despise you; I have good reason to despise you, but

I can't. It doesn't make any sense. Unless having the baby changed me somehow.''

"Angel." She was killing him with her words, but he didn't know how to tell her that.

"After everything that happened between us, I thought I'd always hate you.''

He groaned. "Don't, babe." He kissed her, hard and long, his tongue thrusting deep, stroking in a parody of the sex act. He rubbed his hairy chest against her sensitive nipples and felt her legs bend, coming up to hug his hips. The open juncture of her legs was a sweet torture, her damp heat against his belly, her soft thighs cradling him. He rubbed against her, his muscles bound so tight he felt ready to break.

She shifted, and then his erection was smoothly pushing against her wet sex. Angel began moving with him, their mouths still fused together, both of them breathing rapidly, roughly.

She jerked and pulled her mouth away, crying out.

Dane was stunned as she quickly climaxed again, shuddering beneath him, her head arched back, her heels digging into his thighs.

His control snapped. Shaking, he grabbed up his slacks and fumbled like a drunk for his wallet. He found a condom and viciously ripped the packet open with his teeth. Angel was still gasping breathlessly and when he turned, catching her legs in the crook of his elbows, spreading her wide and driving into her with one hard thrust, she cried out again.

He couldn't think. His brain throbbed and his vision went blank and all he could do was feel and smell and taste her. She'd invaded his heart, his soul. He was the one who felt possessed and he rebelled against it even as he felt himself spiraling away. He squeezed his eyes shut and growled and pumped and when he heard Angel groan he knew she was with him yet again. It was too much. It felt like he exploded, his entire body gripped in painful pleasure, but it was so damn wonderful he never wanted it to end.

It took him a long time to come back to reality, to hear Angel's soft sniffling, to feel the shudders in her body. Slowly, feeling drugged, he struggled up to his elbows again. Tears dampened her eyelashes and her lips looked swollen. His heart twisted.

Damn, her leg. His arms were still tangled with her legs and he knew she had to be in pain. He'd taken her roughly, almost brutally. That he'd hurt her made him wince in self-loathing. Carefully, he straightened, letting her legs down easy. She groaned and pressed her face to the side, away from him.

He cupped her chin and turned her back. "Angel, honey, I'm sorry."

She shook her head.

"Babe, look at me."

Her eyelashes lifted and she stared up at him. The tears in her eyes twisted his guts. He pressed his forehead to hers and kissed her gently. "I'm so sorry, sweetheart. I didn't mean to hurt you."

She frowned.

"I got a little carried away." He tried a smile but it felt more like a grimace. "You moaned, and all rational thought fled my mind. I'm sorry." He sounded like a parrot, apologizing over and over again.

"Derek…"

Goddammit, he hated having her call him that. "Shh. It's all right." Her hair, dry now and tangled impossibly, lay wild around her head. He tried to smooth it. "Can I get you anything? Some aspirin or something?" He felt like an idiot, having sex with a woman then offering her medicine for the pain.

She shook her head again and her voice, when she spoke, was tentative and as soft as a whisper. "I'm fine, just a little...stunned. Is it always like that?"

Now he felt confused. Buying himself some time, he sat up and carefully moved to the side of her. Her body had been damp and warm from their exertions and combined heat, and she shivered in the cool evening air. He pulled the corner of the spread up to cover her, but left her leg bare. Gently, he massaged her calf and saw her wince.

"Dammit, I'm an unthinking bastard. I—"

She laughed, catching his hand and twining her fingers with his. "No, you're not. I'm fine, Derek."

He forcefully ignored the continued use of his brother's name. "Then why were you crying?"

She sat up and put her arms around him, burrowing close. "Because it was so wonderful."

His heart pounding, Dane hugged her back. "I didn't hurt you?"

She laughed. "Maybe a little, but I didn't notice...until after."

He pressed her back down on the bed and stood. "I'll be right back." With those words, and one last glance at her naked body, he left the bedroom. He wanted to make sure the apartment was secure for the night. There were three windows, one in the kitchen over the sink, but it was too small for an intruder, and one in the living room on that same wall. He checked to make sure it was locked, then realized the window was so old and warped, opening it would be a true effort. He'd be in the bedroom, so he wasn't worried about that window. He'd already locked the front door when he'd first come in. He glanced at the phone, scowled, but put that particular worry from his mind. Right now, he wanted to concentrate on Angel.

He peeked in on Grayson to see the baby sleeping soundly. He'd been afraid their commotion might have disturbed the infant, but Grayson was snuggled warm and comfy in his crib. He lay on his side, and one chubby cheek was smooshed, his rosebud mouth slightly open.

Damn, Dane felt good. He hadn't felt this good in… He'd never felt this good. Angel was the perfect bed partner, wild and abandoned and responsive. She burned him up. She was also sweet and caring and strong.

And she had Grayson, his nephew, the strongest bond he had left to his brother. In his heart, Grayson was his own.

As soon as he set things right with Angel, they'd be able to work together to find out what had happened to Derek. Likely, the threats to her and Derek's death were related. He hated the unknown, hated how ineffectual he felt when dealing with the whole problem. Somehow he had to uncover a mystery and protect Angel at the same time. Thank God the threats to her were so far only abstract, not physical. Long before they got too serious, he intended to have everything resolved. From here on out, he'd double his efforts.

Dane returned to the bedroom moments later with a damp washcloth. He'd disposed of the used condom, and set two more on the nightstand. The night was still young, and he was still hungry.

Angel looked almost asleep and the fact she hadn't been concerned with him roaming her apartment assured him that she was starting to trust him, at least a little. It also proved, to some degree, that she had nothing at all to hide.

She opened her eyes and blinked sleepily up at him when he sat on the edge of the mattress. "What are you doing?"

"I was just going to make you more comfortable." So saying, he swiped the warm, damp cloth over her face, her neck, then down her body. She smiled and arched into his hand with a sigh of pleasure.

"You wore a...a..."

Dane cocked one eyebrow. "A what?"

Pointing down to his lap, she said, "You know. Before you made love to me."

"A rubber? I didn't want to take any chances. Much as I adore Grayson, the last thing you need right now is another pregnancy, what with your leg and—"

"And my financial situation and the threats."

Dane leaned down and kissed her. "I'll take care of the threats. Don't worry about that. And as far as I'm concerned, you don't have any financial worries. I can take care of everything." As quickly as he said it, he raised a placating hand. "I didn't mean that quite the way it sounded."

But Angel was already scowling fiercely. "I've told you enough times now, Derek, I don't need anything from you."

Dane eyed her heaving breasts, her flushed cheeks, and

tossed the washcloth away. "I wouldn't say that's precisely true." In the next instant they were sprawled on the bed again. Angel moaned his brother's name.

As he shoved the spread out of his way so nothing would be between their bodies, he whispered, "I'm spending the night, honey, and in the morning we'll figure everything out. But for now, I want you again."

"Derek."

He'd have to settle things soon. Being called another man's name while making love to a woman who was quickly obsessing his mind couldn't be borne.

In the morning, he thought. He'd clear it all up in the morning. Then Angel could begin accepting things. She could begin dealing with Dane Carter. And he'd be sure to remind her how much more she liked him than Derek.

CHAPTER SEVEN

ANGEL WOKE WITH A GROAN. She felt sore in places she'd never thought about before, her muscles protesting as she stretched, her mind foggy from too little sleep.

She and Derek had made love several times during the night. The man seemed insatiable, yet she wouldn't complain. Everything he'd done to her had been wonderful, if a bit shocking. She smiled as she looked toward the window and saw that the sun was coming up in a blaze of orange light. She loved dawn in the winter, the promise of sunshine when the weather was so bleak and cold.

Turning back to the center of the bed, she reached for Derek, only he wasn't there. Angel frowned, and then her gaze fell on the clock on the nightstand. Eight-thirty. Good grief, she hadn't lain abed so late in ages. She wondered if Derek was in another part of the apartment, but it was then she noticed the note on his pillow. She straightened in the bed and unfolded the slip of paper.

Sorry I had to run off, but I had to be at the office early today. I didn't want to disturb you—any more than I already had through the night.

Angel smiled. She could almost hear the boasting tone of his voice in the teasing words.

A lot to do. I'll call you later. Stay in the apartment and don't worry. I'll take care of things.

D.

Don't worry, indeed. How did he presume to magically "take care of things"? she wondered. She dropped the note as she yawned and stretched once more. Time to get up and check on Grayson. At least Derek had had the foresight to leave the bedroom door open. He'd closed it during the night, against her protests, but true to his word, he'd heard Grayson when the baby awoke, and had even fetched him to her so she hadn't been forced to leave the warmth of the bed. After she'd nursed him, Derek had taken him back to his crib, then since they were both awake, he'd made love to her once more. Even that last time it had turned fast and furious and she'd bitten his shoulder to keep from screaming like a wild woman.

Her face heated with the memory of Derek's satisfied smile. He'd looked at the small teeth marks on his shoulder and grinned with pride.

Unaccountable man. Angel smiled.

It was as she was slipping on her housecoat that the crash sounded. Breaking glass and a loud thunking sound, followed by a low hissing. Her heart leaped into her throat and it took her a moment to unglue her feet, to get herself in motion. She raced out of the bedroom, and was immediately assailed by the smell of smoke. Billows of it poured out of the kitchen into the rest of the tiny apartment.

"Oh my God." Angel stared, then ran for Grayson. The baby had just been jarred awake, and his face was blank for only a second before he began to squall. She jerked him up into her arms, wrapped a blanket tightly around him and then raced to the front door. It took her too much time to manipulate the lock and she was cursing as she finally got the door to open. Once in the hallway she froze, wondering what to do, if maybe the fire had been deliberately set for just that reason, to get her out of the apartment, vulnerable. Shaking, her heart beating too fast, she tried to soothe Grayson even as she ran the length of the hall to Mick's apartment.

She pounded on the door, trying to look around herself, to be aware of any danger. The door opened and Mick's mother stood there, her face ravaged from a long night, her clothes rumpled as if she'd slept in them. She looked unsteady and very put out. Before Angel could say anything, Mick came around his mother.

"What's happened?" He jerked Angel into the apartment and looked her over. She knew her housecoat was only hastily closed and she tried to adjust Grayson to better cover herself.

"A fire. In my apartment. Someone broke a window I think."

Mick stared at her, then started to thrust her aside, determined, she knew, to investigate. Angel grabbed his arm. "No! Just call the fire department, for God's sake."

He shook her off and spared a glance for his mother. "Make the call. I'll be right back."

Mrs. Dawson made no effort to stop her son, frustrating Angel beyond measure. She watched the woman pick up the phone and try to make a coherent call, but it was obvious she was hungover.

Gently, Angel took the receiver from her and gave the details as best she could. The man on the other end told them all to vacate the building and that someone would be there right away. Angel prayed Mick would hurry back. She'd never felt so afraid in her life.

Mick stormed back just as Angel was trying to bundle Grayson up. "It's okay. It was only a small fire and it's out now, but to be safe, let's wait for the firemen outside." He went into his own room and fetched two blankets to bundle Angel in, and then slipped on his own coat.

His mother made grumbling noises and held her head. "I think I'll just go over to Jerry's. You can handle this, can't you, Mick?"

Mick gave a quick, abrupt nod. "Yes." Mrs. Dawson picked up her coat and walked out, one hand holding her head. Mick's face looked set in stone.

He took Angel's arm and started her outside. Already they could hear the sirens. He put his arms around Angel and the baby, trying to lend his warmth and comfort.

Angel wished with all her heart that he was her son. "Thank you, Mick."

He ignored that. "First thing once the place is declared safe, you're calling Derek."

She swallowed. "All right."

"You have to tell him everything now, Angel. No more playing around."

"I know."

She could feel how tense he was, his anger tangible. "Damn, I wish I'd seen whoever it was."

Angel was eternally grateful he hadn't.

It only took the firemen minutes to confirm what Mick had told her. Someone had broken her small kitchen window with a rock, then tossed in a bundle of gas-soaked rags. The result had been more smoke than anything else.

Mick had smothered the flickering flames with a blanket, much to the firemen's disturbance. They lectured him on safety matters, on the importance of walking away from a fire rather than trying to handle it himself. Mick, she could tell, only halfheartedly listened to their speeches.

Endless questions followed, but finally it was all put down to a prank. It was obvious to the firemen that while the fire could have become serious, that hadn't been the intent. More of a lark, they said, their tones edged with anger. Angel didn't tell them about the other threats, the phone calls and the letter. She wanted to talk to Derek first. She had a feeling he'd want to be with her when she spoke to the police.

Mick skipped school that day, opting to stay with Angel instead. He'd already missed his morning classes arguing with his mother, who'd come home drunk once again. Angel felt for him, even as she gladly accepted his company.

The apartment was a mess, the smell of smoke lingering on everything. All of her clothes stank. She could do nothing about her jeans, but Mick loaned her a fresh sweatshirt to wear. They were in the apartment for mere moments, only long enough for her to gather the necessities for Grayson and a few of her own things. She didn't have apartment insurance, and the thought of the expense of replacing several things overwhelmed her. The firemen had suggested she call a professional cleaner to tackle the smoke damage and the singed areas of her kitchen, but she knew she couldn't afford it. She would have to do the cleaning herself.

Mick hovered over her as she settled herself on the

couch in his mother's apartment. He handed her the phone. "Call Derek now. You've put it off long enough."

She sighed, knowing he was right, but not sure how to tell him. He was going to be angry, no doubt about that. And her thoughts still felt so jumbled.

Buying herself a little time, she thumbed through the personal phone book she'd retrieved from her desk. Her eyes closed as she thought of all the papers still to be typed, all of them gray with ash dust. How such a small fire had done so much damage she couldn't imagine. Her world was quickly unraveling around her, her choices falling away one by one until now she had no choices at all—she needed Derek. The idea didn't panic her nearly so much as it had only a week ago.

Deciding not to dawdle anymore, she found Derek's work number and punched it in. A secretary answered.

Angel cleared her throat. "I'd like to talk to Derek Carter please."

A very polite voice regretfully turned down her request. "I'm sorry, ma'am. Mr. Carter can't take your call right now."

Angel drew a calming breath and tried to pull herself together. Yelling at a secretary wouldn't gain her a thing. "You don't understand. I *have* to speak with him. It's an…an emergency."

There was a slight hesitation before the secretary said, "Just a minute please."

But it wasn't Derek who came on the line. Angel didn't recognize the impatient male voice, but at his inquiry, she repeated her request.

Suspicion crept into his tone when he asked, "Who is this?"

Because she was rattled, Angel answered without thinking. "Angel Morris."

Stunned silence followed, then a rough laugh that was quickly squelched. "Well, well. I'm sorry to be the one to break it to you, sweetheart. But Derek Carter is dead." There was another moment of silence where Angel could hear her own heartbeat, and then he added, "Maybe I can help you. What do you need?"

Angel dropped the phone as her heart kicked violently in panic. She couldn't draw a deep enough breath. Mick frowned at her and picked up the receiver. "Angel?"

She shook her head, slowly coming to her feet. She knew her face was white, her breathing too fast. It couldn't be true; it was likely part of the threat, some vicious game to taunt her, confuse her.

A cleansing rush of anger ran through her. First the damage to her apartment, and now this contemptible prank. She absolutely refused to believe it was any more than that.

Mick started to speak into the receiver but Angel snatched it away from him and slammed it down in the cradle. "No. Don't say anything else to him."

"Him? What's going on, Angel?"

She paced in front of Mick, her stride stiff and angry. "He said Derek's dead, but I know it can't be true! It can't be."

Mick frowned. His face turned pale with confusion and concern. "Of course it's not." He looked undecided for only a second, then determination replaced every other emotion on his face. "Come on." He hauled Angel along behind him with a firm grip on her arm.

"Where are we going?"

"To his company. You'll see for yourself that Derek is just fine, and then you're going to tell him everything. This is starting to get too damn weird."

"Yes." Angel nodded, not at all concerned with her mismatched clothing, her tangled hair, or her ash-smudged face. She only cared about seeing Derek, alive and well.

Her reaction was telling, she thought, but she refused to dwell on it. He was okay. She was certain he was okay. Her hands shook with anger and her heart ached as she bundled Grayson into a blanket and followed Mick out the door. Once she knew for certain it was all part of the threats, that Derek was indeed fine, she intended to tell him everything.

She'd never doubt him again.

DANE STARED AROUND at the solemn faces watching him. He knew his mother wanted to protest this little meeting he'd called, but so far she'd held herself silent. That alone confused him, because his mother had never been one for circumspection. She had a tendency to go after what she wanted with the force of a battering ram.

Which made her acceptance of Derek's *accident* all the more suspect. He pushed that aside for the moment.

The meeting wasn't officially with the board; it was a family matter and Dane intended to treat it as such. His two uncles, both older and naturally calm, held positions on the board, but it was their positions as heads of differing departments, as well as the fact they were family, that had guaranteed their presence here now. His mother was again seated to his right. His cousin, an amicable sort in charge of the sales department, was at the end of the

table. They were waiting for Raymond and his sister, who
had each been attending to previous meetings of their
own.

His sister walked in first, looking chic in a stylish business suit, her fair hair loose, her face pale. She knows,
Dane thought. His sister was well aware of how he felt
about playing corporate head; it wouldn't take much de-
duction on her part to realize he was ready to make his
exodus from the company. He hoped his mother would
consider giving the position to Celia instead of Raymond.
It would be his recommendation, with the promise he'd
visit more often if his wishes were met. It was blackmail
of a sort, something his mother could understand and appreciate.

Raymond hurried in right behind Celia, straightening
his tie and tucking his shirt in more firmly. His hair was
mussed, his face flushed. Very unusual for Raymond, who
made a great effort to always look immaculate and com-
posed. Dane had the disquieting thought that the two of
them had been together, possibly playing around rather
than attending to business. What in the world his sister
saw in the man, he didn't know. Dane watched Celia give
Raymond an inquiring glance, saw him quickly smile and
pull out her seat, then take his own beside her. Maybe
they hadn't been together, he thought, seeing his sister's
dark frown, but at that moment his mother cleared her
throat, impatient.

Dane stood. He wanted to get this over with quickly.
He'd been at the office for hours now, anxious to get back
to Angel. He pictured her lying soft and warm and exhausted in her bed and his groin tightened. He should have

been well sated, but he was beginning to believe no amount of time with her would be enough.

He had to tell her everything, to remove all secrets between them. In truth, he should have done so before making love to her, but he hadn't wanted to risk being turned away. Now, he needed her help, both to find the truth behind Derek's death, and the source of the threats against her. In his gut, he knew the two were undeniably tied together, and they needed to share information in order to get to the truth.

Dane now had two agendas, avenging his brother and protecting Angel. He couldn't do either one while playing the role of his twin, with Angel or at the office.

He glanced around the table at the curious expressions of his family. "I have a few announcements to make, then you can all get back to your plans."

His mother stared ahead stonily, her mouth pinched, her eyes hard. For the first time, Dane noticed the signs of her age, the tiredness, the brittleness that suddenly seemed a part of her. He turned to his sister and saw that she was staring down at her hands.

Only Raymond seemed attentive, almost anxious, and Dane wished there was some way to exclude the bastard, to kick him out on his ear. But as Celia's fiancé and his mother's first pick, the man had a right to sit in on any and all business.

"To say I was pleased to step in for my brother would be a lie. You all know I have my own business to run and cases are piling up with me absent so much."

His mother shifted, crossing and recrossing her legs.

"I never wanted to be a part of this company, at least,

not for many years now. Everything is now in order. I think it's past time I—''

A wild commotion in the outer office drew everyone's attention. Dane frowned, staring at the closed door and the raised voices coming through it. His mother came to her feet. ''What in the world?''

Raymond also stood, his eyebrows lowered, his eyes flickering back and forth. ''Would you like me to see what's going on?''

The uncles gave a disinterested glance over their shoulders, and everyone started murmuring at once.

The door was thrown open and Angel, looking ragged and harassed and determined, pushed her way in, despite Dane's secretary's hold on her arm. Dane felt his mouth fall open, his heart lurch. Behind Angel, Mick hovered, Grayson in his arms.

Angel ignored everyone but him, her gaze zeroing in on him, and then her face crumbled and she cried out. She'd obviously strained her leg again, given the awkward way she rushed toward him.

Dane skirted the end of the table and met her halfway, gathering her up in his arms, filled with confusion. ''Angel?'' He stared over her head toward Mick, who looked too grim by half.

She pushed back in his arms, her fingers clutching at his dress shirt. ''They said you were dead!'' She yelled the words at him, and now she seemed more angry than anything else. Her face was smudged, her hair wild, and she began to babble. ''I wanted to talk to you because of the fire, but I was told you were busy and then they came right out and told me you were dead! I had to see for myself. I had to know you were all right. When I got here, they told me Mr. Carter was in a meeting and couldn't be disturbed, but don't you see, I had to have proof." Her hands went busily over his face, reassuring herself, confirming his safety.

Dane glanced around at the stunned faces watching them, aware of the mounting tension, the delicacy of the situation. Everyone was now standing, expectant. Angel's babbling barely made sense and he hesitated to upset her further. Few people knew Derek was dead, so who the hell had told her? But first things first. "What fire?" he demanded, concentrating on the one thing that wasn't guaranteed to get him in any deeper.

Angel drew a shuddering breath. "Oh, Derek. Someone threw a mess of burning rags through my kitchen window! Everything in the apartment stinks of smoke."

His mother gasped and went two shades paler, grabbing the conference table for support. "Dane, what's going on here? Who is this person?"

The muscles in his face felt like iron. "Give me a minute, Mother."

"Oh my God! It's Angel Morris, isn't it?" Celia stepped forward, trying to get a better look at Angel. "What in the world happened to her, and why is she calling you Derek?"

Dane closed his eyes. He heard the conference room door slam and looked up to see Mick standing against it, Grayson held in his arms, his expression so hard he looked more like a man than ever.

Raymond barked out, "I'm calling security!" and reached for the phone. His movements were jerky and frantic.

"No." Dane stopped him with a word, and everyone seemed to turn to stone, frozen and shocked and confused.

"This is insane," Raymond argued. "She's upsetting the women!" And again he reached for the receiver.

Dane released Angel as she slowly backed away from him. "No, Raymond, everything is fine."

"Fine?" Raymond argued, filled with outraged indignation. "The woman is mad, coming in here calling you by your dead brother's name. For God's sake, man, your mother and sister have been through too much already."

His mother did look shaken, pale and drawn and confused, but Celia looked titillated. Her eyes were bright and wide and didn't budge from Angel's face. "You are Angel Morris, aren't you?"

Angel looked around the room at all the avid expressions and she swayed. Dane grabbed her, but she jerked back from him and her expression was so dark, so accusing, he felt it like a blow. Her bloodless lips moved twice before the words finally whispered out. "You're not Derek?"

Again Dane reached for her, firmly taking hold of her shoulders while she tried to shake him off. "Dammit, Angel, sit down before you fall down." Then he looked around the room and ordered, *"Everyone out."*

His mother started to protest and he said, *"Now."*

Grayson chose that inauspicious moment to give one short, protesting cry. Dane thought it might have been Mick's tight hold on the baby that prompted the objection.

Again, everyone froze.

Drawing on lost reserve, Dane again tried to take control of the situation. "Mick, I want you to stay. Please sit down so everyone else can leave."

Obligingly, looking as if he wouldn't have left anyway, Mick went to the leather couch and sat. He whispered nonsense words to Grayson and glared at anyone who tried to get closer to the baby.

Dane took Angel to the same couch, trying to support her weight when he saw how badly she was limping, but she sidled away from his touch as if she found him repulsive. Once she was seated, Dane strode over to the door and held it open. "All of you, wait outside. I'll explain everything in a minute."

One of his uncles shook his head. "Can't wait to hear it."

The other agreed. "Always did say that boy knew how to shake things up." They left together. His cousin gave him an uncertain, wide-eyed look and hurried out.

Raymond stopped, holding Mrs. Carter's arm. "Are you sure you don't require security?" he asked. "I could get them up here, just in case. Or I could stay with you, as a precaution. You can't be too careful with crazy people."

Dane ground his teeth together, sparing only a very brief glance at his mother's angry, drawn face. "Out, Raymond."

Mrs. Carter stared up at her son. "Don't trust anything that woman tells you about Derek."

"Mother…"

"I'm giving you the benefit of the doubt, son. Do what's right, for us and yourself." With that caustic warning, she walked out, Raymond hanging on her arm.

Celia paused in front of Dane. Her lips were trembling, her eyes wet with unshed tears. But she brazenly tried to act in control, unwilling to contribute to the chaos. "I hope you know I'm not budging from this outer office until you give me a full report.''

Dane nodded, appreciating her reserve.

Celia licked her lips nervously, then ventured, "I could hold the baby while you two talk.''

"No!" Angel sat forward on her seat, but Dane ignored her, his attention on his sister.

"Thanks, sweetheart, but Mick can handle things and the baby's already used to him.'' Celia looked so crushed, Dane touched her cheek and added softly, "Get Mother something to drink. She looks ready to faint. And be patient, please.''

Celia nodded at him, offering up a shaky smile. "Good luck.''

As he closed the door, Dane muttered, "I'm going to need more than luck now.'' He drew a long, calming breath before turning to Angel. His mother's warning rang in his ears. Would Derek have seen his actions as a betrayal? Had he felt justified in his treatment of Angel? Things had seemed so simple when he'd first started this. Now he felt mired in conflicting emotions. But one thing was certain, he couldn't lie to her anymore.

Angel's entire posture showed how wounded she felt, both physically and emotionally. She stared at Dane, her expression fixed, her arms crossed belligerently over her chest. As she'd been doing since Grayson's birth, she held herself together by sheer force of will.

Something inside Dane felt like it was breaking apart. Despite his mother's warning, despite his loyalty to his twin, Dane knew he couldn't ever hurt her again. And that meant he had to give her the full truth. "Derek's dead. He died months ago.''

For about ten seconds she looked shocked, then she jerked to her feet. Comprehension dawned in her face and her eyes widened on him, appalled. "Oh my God."

Dane nodded slowly. "Yes, I'm the dreaded evil twin, of course." He took a measured step toward her. "I can explain everything, honey."

Her eyes went wild. "Don't you come near me. I don't want to hear anything you have to say."

"Well, you're going to hear it," he said, tightening himself against her disdain. He was well aware of how she felt about him, and the damn reputation Derek had amplified. But it still hurt as he felt her emotional withdrawal, the separation between them growing. He bit off a curse, knowing if he didn't push now, he'd lose her for good, along with the opportunity to discover what had really happened to Derek.

"Angel…"

All signs of fear were replaced by anger. Her face was flushed, her body practically vibrating with her temper, her scorn. "You miserable lying bastard."

Dane closed his eyes and tipped his head back. He heard Angel's furious whispering, heard Mick grumble a reply, and quickly faced her again. "You're not going anywhere, babe."

"The hell I'm not!" She tried to take the baby from Mick, but he resisted her efforts. She turned her cannon on Dane again. "You can't dictate to me, and I'm certainly not going to listen to any more of your lies. There is absolutely no excuse for what you've done!"

Mick glared at Dane, but spoke to Angel. "Nothing's changed. There's still someone trying to hurt you, and your apartment is still a mess. Think of Grayson. At least hear…'' He looked at Dane, then shrugged in his direction. ''At least hear him out. Whoever the hell he is.''

Dane tightened his jaw. ''Dane Carter.'' The formality of an introduction was ludicrous.

Angel sneered. ''Derek told me all about you. You're the worst of the lot!''

''I was going to explain everything to you today, Angel. In fact, I was just telling my family that I won't work for the company—''

''I don't care what you were telling them.''

''Angel.'' He felt hollow inside. ''Honey, you have to hear me out. The only reason I came back to the company in the first place is because I think Derek was murdered.''

He shouldn't have blurted it out like that, but he knew he had to make her listen. Angel wrapped her arms around her middle and sank back onto the couch, slowly rocking. ''No, no, this can't be happening.''

Dane knelt down in front of her. ''I'm so sorry, honey. At first, when you contacted me, I was suspicious of you, thinking you had more reason than most to hate Derek, to want him dead. I thought you might have had something to do with setting him up and then when I came home, you thought you hadn't succeeded. There's been no official announcement of Derek's death and my family has done everything they could to keep the news quiet.'' He spoke quickly, hoping to get his explanations out while she was still listening.

She laughed, a harsh, broken sound and rocked that much harder.

''It took me only a short time of knowing you to realize how ridiculous that theory was.''

''No, not at all,'' she said, her grin twisted and mean.

Provoking. "I did despise him. Almost as much as I despise you."

"Angel," he chided. "You don't mean that. Not after last night."

He caught her right fist just inches from his face and stared at her in incredulous disbelief. "Dammit, Angel, that wouldn't have been a little ladylike tap! Are you trying to—"

A split second later, her left fist connected with his temple, almost knocking him off balance and making his brain ring. "Goddammit!" Dane caught both her hands and pulled her to her feet, struggling to subdue her. "If you can refrain from inflicting your vicious temper on my head, I think we can get this all straightened out!"

Angel tugged her hands, obviously accepted that he had no intention of releasing her, and went still. "Let me go."

"Not on your life. We have a hell of a lot of talking to do and I think we'll accomplish it more easily if my brain is left intact." He lowered his voice to a mild scold, somewhat amused by her despite his still ringing ears. "I had no idea you were such a fury. Why don't you just settle down and behave yourself."

She growled, anger flushing her face crimson. "Behave myself? *Behave myself!* Do you mean I should try conniving and manipulating and lying!" She jerked against him again, but he held tight. "You and your brother are two of a kind."

Dane grew somber. "No, actually we're not." He let her go and paced two steps away, out of harm's reach. "Angel, this is the first I've seen my family in years. We hadn't been on the best of terms, precisely because I'm not like them. I don't approve of what Derek did to you—''

''What you did was worse,'' she growled, then grudgingly dropped back into her seat.

She looked defeated and he hated it. ''I suppose it was, regardless of what my excuses are. But I want to make things right. That's what I've been trying to do this morning. I want to take care of you and Grayson, and don't shake your beautiful head at me! The threat to you is very real, dammit. Derek is dead, and somehow you're tied to it!''

She gave him a look of contempt. ''You think I don't know how serious it is? Someone tried to run me off the road. That's the accident, you know, that started my labor and injured my leg. I almost died. Obviously whoever did that isn't very happy that I survived.''

Every muscle in his body jerked at the ramification of her words. His heart pounded, his knees locked. *She could have been killed.* And he'd been thinking the threats against her weren't physical? ''Goddammit, why didn't you tell me this sooner?''

Her brow lifted. ''Trust goes both ways.''

He let loose with a string of curses that had Mick chuckling and Angel frowning.

''At first I thought the accident was just that—an accident. I was disoriented for a long time and in a lot of pain after the wreck, not to mention I had a brand-new baby to take care of. There wasn't a lot of room in my thoughts for suspicions. But then, the phone calls started and I got spooked. Then I had to wonder.''

''And finally,'' he said, his voice low and barely controlled, ''you realized you had to have some help. That's when you came back to Derek. Not because you wanted to, but because you truly had nowhere else to turn.''

She nodded. ''I thought if nothing else, he might be willing to check into things for me.''

They stared at each other, and Dane read her thoughts. She'd been willing to try seducing Derek to gain the help she needed, to get protection for her baby.

She had truly despised Derek, and now she felt the same about him. Angel was still very pale, but more collected. Her eyes glinted with raw determination and he knew it was only her concern for Grayson that was keeping her in the same room with him. He had his work cut out for him. ''Derek was run off the road. Unlike you, luck wasn't on his side that day.''

Angel closed her eyes on a sigh. ''You should probably know, someone followed us here today. From the time we rushed out of the apartment until we pulled in the lot, we were followed.''

Dane hesitated only a second, then stalked to his desk phone and quickly punched out a series of numbers. He waited, but then the office door opened and Alec strolled in, holding up his blinking cell phone. ''No need to call me. I'm right here.'' Raymond tried to follow him in, but Alec slammed the door in his face.

Angel sank back against her seat with his entrance, but Mick perked up. ''It's Alec!''

The dark visage merely nodded in their direction. ''I got there too late to find out what was going on until they'd already left the building.'' His look was reproachful when he added to Dane, ''You left earlier than I thought you would.''

Again Angel surged to her feet. "What is he talking about, Der…Dane?"

Satisfaction settled into his bones. Finally, finally she was calling him by his rightful name. "Alec works for me, honey. I'm the one who hired Mick, not a friend. And I've had Alec watching you for several reasons. At first, because I thought you might take off before I could figure out what's going on, whether or not you could give any insight into Derek's death. But then for your safety when I couldn't be there."

Her eyes narrowed. "So you told him you were spending the night with me last night?"

Mick made a choking sound and got up to stroll to the other end of the room, pretending to keep all his attention on Grayson.

Feeling as if a trap were closing around him, Dane tried for a show of bravado. "I didn't have to tell him. Alec's good at what he does or I wouldn't have him working with me. He knew I had gone in your apartment, and he was able to figure things out quickly enough, given I didn't leave right away."

Alec nodded. "That's about it. Only I didn't figure on you rushing off so early today or I'd have been there to cover her."

"That's my fault. I made up my mind on what I wanted to do and saw no reason to wait. I should have contacted you."

Angel threw up her hands. "*Someone* should have contacted me!"

The conference room door crept open and Celia tried peeking in. Her eyes were huge and went immediately to Alec. "Why is he allowed in and I'm not?"

Dane groaned. The last thing he needed added to the mix was his sister's curiosity. Alec merely turned away and headed for the door, while Celia quickly started backing out. "Dane?" she called, but Alec kept going until they were both on the other side of the closed door. Dane could hear his sister's loud and nervous protests.

"I can always count on Alec to know what needs to be done." Dane's smile had no seeming effect on Angel. She glared at him.

"Honey, there's a lot we have to settle." He sat close to her on the couch and pretended not to notice her efforts to move away. "First off, I want you to know that last night was genuine."

"Spare me your diatribe on last night, Der—Dane. I won't believe anything you have to say about that."

Dane had to trust she'd eventually change her mind, but now wasn't a good time to push her. Instead, he concentrated on what had to be done. "Tell me about the fire."

She did, in totally detached tones that made Dane want to shake her. Didn't she care about last night? Hadn't it affected her at all? The way she was behaving now, last night might as well have not happened. The timing was unfortunate, but he'd been counting on it to soften her some when presented with his truths.

Mick filled in some of the details on the fire, apparently more concerned with it than Angel was at the moment.

Dane decided he'd make a quick trip by there to check out the apartment himself. Maybe there was a clue that the others had missed. "I'll pay for the damages and the cleaning, Mick, so that the apartment will be as good as new."

"You don't need to do that. It's my mother's building. We'll handle it."

Dane's respect for the youth doubled. "It's the least I can do, given all you've done to keep her safe." Seeing that Mick's pride would force him to argue further, he added, "Angel, you and Grayson can come to stay with me."

She snorted. "Not on your life."

Inconspicuously drawing a fortifying breath, Dane took his last shot, and prayed she wouldn't fight him too hard. He knew things were happening too fast, for him as well as her. Without hesitation, he'd gladly taken over his brother's life, his role in the company. He'd consoled himself with the fact he was trying to find his brother's killer. Even as he'd walked through his brother's office and gone through his desk and personal notes, he'd been empowered by the fact that he had a mission, a purpose. But now he was taking Derek's woman and son, too, for no other reason than he wanted them. Despite all the very real motives he had justifying his actions, he knew the truth, and it was tough to swallow.

Regret that he hadn't taken the time to make his peace with Derek squeezed his heart. Still, he had to think Derek would approve of what he was about to do. Regardless of how he'd treated Angel, Dane refused to believe he'd want Angel terrorized, or his son abandoned. Grayson deserved the family name, and the power and protection that came with it.

With renewed resolution, Dane said, "It seems like the best solution, honey."

"How do you figure that?"

"Because as soon as I can manage it, we'll be married."

CHAPTER EIGHT

ANGEL STARED AT DEREK…no, *Dane*. She had to remember that. This man—a man she'd slept with—was a total stranger. He'd betrayed her, used her, and as far as she could tell, despite all his assurances to the contrary, he was no different from his family. *But everything about him had seemed different.*

No, she didn't trust him, and she'd been right to fear him all along.

"We could make it a Thanksgiving wedding," he said, sounding absurdly enthusiastic. "Not very romantic, I know, but there you have it. I really do think the sooner the better."

Angel could only shake her head. "I'm not marrying you."

"Have you forgotten my family, honey?"

What a joke. As if she could ever forget such a thing. "It's not likely, not when I've suspected them most from the start."

"Suspected them?" Dane sounded confused, his eyebrows slowly drawing down.

"They, more than anyone, have reason to want me gone. After all, I know firsthand just how unscrupulous Derek could be, when they're bound and determined to make him out a saint. If I chose to go to the papers…"

"Being snide isn't going to help anything."

"It's making me feel a damn sight better!"

"Angel, my family wouldn't try to physically harm you."

"Ha!"

He sighed. "Okay, look at it this way. It's obvious whoever tried to run you off the road, succeeded with Derek. Now surely you're not going to suggest my family could be responsible for that? The two incidents are too closely related to not be done by the same person or people."

He was right, and that made the peril even worse. When she'd thought she knew who was after her, it was bad enough. But not knowing…

"I just found out about Derek today. Before now, my reasoning seemed sound."

"Possibly. I had my own suspicions about why my mother has been so accepting of Derek's death. Normally, she'd be looking for a person to blame, and you could have been a target. But I think you may have hit the nail on the head. She knew he was unscrupulous, knew the way he'd treated you lacked any sense of professional honor. Could be she just didn't want any reporters getting wind of the story and embellishing on it."

Angel's brain felt stuffed to overflowing with problems, and she needed to get away from him so she could think. She looked toward Mick, but Dane quickly regained her attention.

"You still need my protection from the family, honey, just not in the way you thought. Look at yourself. You haven't made the best first impression on any of them, and believe me, they'll use your little show today to their advantage. They'll call you a crazy woman running in here all mussed and smelling of smoke. Just the fact of the danger involved is enough to give them an edge. They'll gladly use anything they can to cow you. My mother would love to claim you unfit, taking into consideration your financial predicament, your insecure life, compared to everything their money and influence can provide—''

''All right!'' Angel stood and began pacing. It seemed her options were sorely limited, and by her own design, she'd put herself in his family's righteous path. She couldn't, wouldn't lose Grayson, not to anyone, not for any reason.

Dane slipped up behind her, not touching her, but his warmth did and her stomach gave an excited little flip. *Fool*, she thought, disgusted with herself and her feminine responses to him.

Well, she'd wondered many times why things were different now, why she would be more attracted to Derek now after the way he'd used her. She had her answer of sorts, the mere fact that it wasn't Derek, but his brother instead. Again, she shuddered with the humiliation of it. Everything Derek had told her of Dane had scared her spitless. He'd been like a dark, silent enemy, someone she'd wanted to avoid at all costs. But now, she didn't really fear him at all. On the contrary, she was madder than hell.

''As my wife, they couldn't touch you, Angel. Grayson would be safe, and you would be safe, from them and the threats.''

''Why?'' Angel whirled around to face him, his motivations very suspect given everything she now knew. It had seemed strange enough that Derek would be interested in her, but then she'd found out he only wanted to use her. What could possibly be driving Dane? "Why would you want to marry me, damn you?"

Dane's eyes lifted briefly to where Mick hovered in the corner. Then he leaned down until their foreheads nearly touched. He didn't look at her face, choosing instead to stare at her mouth. "Grayson is my nephew, but I care about him as if he were my own. I'd gladly kill, or die, for him. And we're good together, babe. Last night proved that." His fingers touched gently on her cheek, then dropped away. "I think we could make a go of things. It's the only logical solution."

Weary defeat dragged her down and she rubbed her forehead. He hadn't said anything about caring for her. His reasoning was so far from love as to be laughable. But then, she didn't love him either. *She didn't.* How could she possibly love a man she didn't even really know? She felt boxed in and almost desperate, as much by the circumstances as her own emotional needs. "I'd want a marriage of convenience."

Dane straightened with a short, curt laugh. "Hell no."

"Dane—"

"I love how you say that, Angel. You have no idea how damn difficult it was being called by another man's name."

He was impossible and she couldn't deal with him. She felt caught between a good cry and a hysterical laugh.

Dane took her shoulders and gently shook her. "Let me take you home. To my house. You look exhausted and we need to talk without the threat of my family bursting in any minute. You need to tell me everything this time;

no more secrets. And Grayson needs to get settled down. We have a lot to take care of today.''

Since she didn't know what else to do, she finally nodded. Dane let out a long breath of relief and smiled at her. ''Don't look so glum. Marrying me won't be nearly the hardship you're imagining. I promise.''

Her look of intense dislike was rudely ignored.

The outer door opened then and Dane's sister marched in, looking militant for all of three steps—until Alec's long arm appeared, grabbed her by the shoulder, and tugged her back out again. The door closed quietly on her outraged complaints.

Dane chuckled. ''I think my sister is anxious to meet the baby.''

It was almost impossible to beat down her panic. ''Dane…''

''Shh. I won't let anything happen to him, honey. You're going to have to trust me on this.''

Before she could tell him she had no intention of trusting him ever again, he continued. ''Let me do the talking, okay? I don't want my family to know everything yet. My mother might want to start her own campaign to find Derek's killer, and that could put you at risk.''

''Then what will you tell them?''

He shrugged. ''As little as possible.''

He went to the door and opened it. Angel could see Dane's sister standing on her tiptoes, one manicured finger poking at Alec. Angel marveled at how the woman stood up to him, as scary as he appeared, so cold and hard. But Alec seemed to ignore her, arms crossed over his chest, his black gaze pinning Raymond across the room. Dane's mother sat quietly beside Raymond, her hands clasped in her lap.

''Celia, would you like to meet your nephew?''

Halting in midcomplaint, Celia squealed, loudly, which caused Alec to wince. ''Then he really is Derek's son? I wasn't wrong in that?''

She looked so anxious, so excited, Angel felt her heart twist. Dane laughed. ''Yes, he really is.''

Casting only a quick triumphant glare at Alec, Celia rushed in. Alec shook his head and chuckled behind her.

As Celia cooed over the baby, Mick willingly gave him up to her. Seeing her baby in Celia's arms made Angel begin to shake. This was exactly what she hadn't wanted to happen, what she had always feared the most.

There was more chaos as Dane's family started their interrogation. He gave an edited version of how they'd met and when. He managed to make it sound romantic while excluding any suggestion of suspicions, and explained about Grayson in the process. He told them of the fire and why Angel had appeared looking so harried. They waited to hear why she'd called him Derek, but Dane ignored that and Angel realized he had no intention of explaining. It seemed he didn't care what his family thought, and given his closed expression, they were just as reluctant to question him.

''How do you know the baby is Derek's?''

Silence fell as every face turned to Mrs. Carter. Feeling stiff from the roots of her hair all the way to her toes, Angel met the older woman's glare and refused to look away or give any sign of defense. Mrs. Carter could think whatever she wanted; Angel had no reason to be ashamed.

But Dane laughed. ''Excellent, Mother. If you don't

believe the baby is his, then I don't have to concern myself with your interference.''

Raymond looked at Grayson over Celia's shoulder. ''I don't remember Ms. Morris ever dating anyone else. In fact, it caused a buzz in the company that she was dating at all, especially that Derek had shown an interest. But the baby is…what? A couple months old? That's cutting it close.''

Dane narrowed his eyes, and he suddenly looked near violence. ''He was born six weeks early.''

''Ah. Then the timing fits, doesn't it?''

Celia beamed. ''Of course it does. He looks just like Derek and Dane. Mother, I don't have a single doubt.''

Angel had always heard what a formidable dragon lady Mrs. Carter was, but now, she looked so vulnerable it pained even Angel. As she approached the baby, she breathed hard, her nostrils quivering as she tried, and failed, to find some measure of control. Her hand came up to touch the baby's head. ''He does have a family resemblance.''

Celia smiled and rocked the baby.

Dane's tone was very gentle, but firm, and only Angel seemed to notice the way he watched his mother. ''I don't mean to rush off, but we have a lot to do today and we'd better get to it.''

Stepping forward, Raymond looked at each family member in turn. He wasn't a scary-looking man, like Alec, but he did appear rather cold and calculating.

''I'd be glad to help you out around here, Dane. It does seem you have your hands full at the moment, and as you'd been saying before the…ah, interruption, you have your own business to run.''

Angel wanted to deny her familiarity to Dane, but the truth was, she could already read him, and what she saw in his complacent gaze was a sort of evil anticipation. He didn't smile, but she could see the satisfaction in his gaze as he faced the other man. "Thank you, Raymond, but I was going to suggest Celia take over. The board will, of course, have to approve her, but with my mother's backing—" he glanced toward his mother, who gave an imperial nod of her head, but withheld any verbal comment "—and of course my own, I don't think it should be a problem. Anyone who wants to fight it, would have to fight me. And I assure you that's not a pleasant prospect."

Angel noticed that Dane had just made his sister a very happy woman. Like her mother, she kept still, but as she kissed the baby again, Angel could see a small exuberant smile on her face.

With that apparently settled to his satisfaction, Dane glanced at his watch. "We have to get going. I need to get Angel and Grayson settled down in my house."

"In your house?"

"Yes, Mother. I've asked Angel to marry me as soon as I can arrange it, and she's agreed."

Dane's announcement started a new flurry of comments and Angel wished there was some way to remove herself and Grayson. They all deserved to fight among themselves; she just didn't want to take part in it. Mick sidled up beside her, and she had the feeling he was as disoriented by the Carter family as she.

"I can keep the baby while you go on a honeymoon."

Angel's heart skipped a beat at Celia's anxious offer, but Dane easily covered her reaction. His arm slipped around her shoulders and gently squeezed, offering her reassurance, she knew. But with him so close, she felt far from comforted.

"Thanks, but we're not going to even think about anything like that for a while. And Grayson is too young to be left. If you want to visit him, you can come to the house and sit with Angel sometime." His arm squeezed again, and he added, "Call first, though, and clear it with Angel. I know you wouldn't want to wake Grayson from a nap or interrupt his feeding."

Celia looked at Angel, and there didn't appear to be any animosity in her expression. "You'll join us for Thanksgiving? Please? I realize it's short notice, but then all of this is, and we're very anxious to get to know the baby better." Tears welled in her eyes and she snuggled Grayson closer. "He's all that's left to us of Derek, now."

Angel licked her lips, feeling cornered. Celia's sincerity smote her, made her feel petty and mean. But she was still afraid, and she refused to trust any of them. "I... Dane and I will discuss it."

Dane gave her an admiring glance for her tact. "Yes, we'll let you know, sis. It may be we'll have our wedding by then, if I can get a wedding together in two days. I really have no idea how these things are done."

"I can help."

"No thanks. Angel and I can handle it, I'm sure, once we have a chance to sit down and put our heads together."

Regaining her aplomb, Mrs. Carter said, "This is absurd! I've just discovered my grandson, but you're refusing us any rights. You can't simply cut us out this way. I won't have it."

Dane smiled at his mother. "Watch me."

"You've always been deliberately difficult, but this

time I insist you be reasonable! We're talking about Derek's son, his heir, and you want to whisk him away?''

''No one is stopping you from visiting, Mother, as long as you check with Angel first.''

Her face flushed darkly. It was apparent to Angel that Mrs. Carter wasn't used to asking permission for anything. ''Check with her? Don't be outrageous! We have as much right as anyone to be with the child. In fact, more.'' Her eyes narrowed. ''And frankly, I think it's unconscionable that she's dared to keep this a secret.''

Dane stared at his mother, his eyes narrowed. ''I'm sure you can understand her reasons.''

''Dammit, he's my grandson!''

Having heard enough, Angel stepped forward, away from Dane's side. She lifted her chin and spoke firmly. ''But I'm his mother.''

The two women stared at each other, and Angel had the feeling they were coming to an understanding. It wasn't easy to face the older woman down, but she couldn't allow Dane to continue shielding her. Now that they knew about Grayson, they were bound to have regular contact.

Mrs. Carter looked undecided on how to react, but Celia interceded and smoothed the waters. ''The important thing is that you're going to be family, Angel. I hope you'll let me know if there's anything I can do to help you get settled.''

Angel didn't want to be a part of this family; the very thought appalled her. But Celia was so sincere, Angel didn't have the heart or the energy to tell her that. ''Thank you.''

Raymond took Mrs. Carter's arm and consoled her, as

if she'd been horribly victimized. Dane rolled his eyes, then began making plans.

"Alec, could you take Mick with you to the apartment and pick up whatever Angel or Grayson might need?"

Alec nodded and Angel noticed a look passing between them. She started to question Dane, but Mick looked thrilled for the excuse to be with Alec and Angel couldn't disappoint him by countermanding Dane's order.

Then Dane handed Alec a credit card. "And stop at the store to buy whatever needs to be replaced."

Angel glared at him. It was time she stood up to Dane, too. She went on tiptoe to look him in the eye, then whispered low, "Don't press your luck."

He grinned, but quickly removed the sign of humor. "Uh, did you have a better suggestion to make?"

"No. But you've been steamrolling me and I don't like it. Stop treating me like I can't make my own decisions."

"Is that what I've been doing?" His words were soft, intimate. He totally ignored the rapt faces of his family.

"Yes, and I don't like it." She tried to sound firm, rather than affected by the tender way he watched her.

"I'll try to reform." His sincerity seemed doubtful, but then, right in front of his whole family, he kissed her. "It won't be easy though, honey. I like taking care of you."

Bemused, Angel wondered if this was part of his plan to convince his family they were marrying by choice, rather than need. Before she could completely sort her thoughts, Dane took control, settling things to his satisfaction.

WITHIN AN HOUR they were ensconced in his house, a spacious ranch out in the middle of nowhere with a wrap-around porch and too many windows to count. It sat about a quarter of a mile from the road and was surrounded by gently rolling hills and huge, mature trees.

Angel had shivered at the isolation of it; her life would be irrevocably changed now, but then, that had been true of so many recent events: meeting Derek, being dismissed from her job, the car accident. Grayson's birth. Because of the baby, she couldn't truly regret her ill-fated relationship with Derek.

And if she hadn't met Derek, she'd never have met Dane.

That thought shook her, and made her face her own feelings. Lately, she'd been so busy surviving, getting through one day at a time, she'd almost underestimated how precious life could be. Not once had she ever considered that Derek might be gone. What if it had been Dane? What if the murderer had finally reached her?

Life was too short to carry grudges or pass up chances. The awful fact of Derek's death was just starting to sink in, making her tremble all over again. If she put her emotional hurt aside, she could understand Dane's behavior toward her. It hadn't been unconscionable as Derek's had been, but rather motivated by the strong need to find a killer.

Angel intended to help him in his efforts.

She glanced around the house without much interest. It was open and airy, the colors bright and clean. It had been professionally decorated and seemed impersonal to Angel, not at all suited to Dane.

She fed Grayson while Dane grilled her on a dozen questions and she did her best to answer them to his satisfaction. Dane was antsy, pacing around her as he tried to find out exactly when her accident had occurred, when the phone calls had begun. Angel had contacted Derek for the last time when she was five and a half months pregnant. He'd turned her away. Shortly after that, he'd died. Two months later, her own car was run off the road, starting her labor. The timing made Dane even more agitated.

Angel put Grayson down for his nap in an empty guest room. Dane lit a fire in the family room then called Alec at her apartment. Unfortunately, though Alec was very thorough, there were no additional clues to be found there.

Angel was tired, but she had no idea what the sleeping arrangements would be. She assumed they would share a certain amount of intimacy. Dane had certainly been insistent, and with her new revelations, she wasn't averse to the idea. She wanted him; in the middle of all the crisis they'd managed to find something very special. Dane made her feel things she'd never felt before, things she hadn't even known existed. She had no idea how much time they might have together so she didn't intend to waste any of it.

Which meant she needed to clear the air first. "Dane?"

He had just hung up the phone and now he lifted his head to stare at her.

"I never wished Derek any physical harm. I'm so sorry for what happened to him."

Just that quick, the distance between them was narrowed. Dane strode to her, stopping a mere inch in front of her. "I don't know if it means anything honey, but Derek regretted what happened." His gaze was searching, warm and direct. "Celia claimed he was almost sick with remorse, and that he knew you'd never forgive him. She said he seemed preoccupied by it all in the time before his death."

Angel nodded, thinking that was at least something, though she wasn't certain she believed it.

Dane laid his large warm hands on her shoulders and gently squeezed. "When I think of all the time we could have saved if either of us would have simply been honest, it sickens me." He drew a deep breath and let it out slowly. "You've been at risk all this time, and I didn't know it. If anything had happened to you—"

Angel gently laid her fingers against his mouth. He was trying his best, even willing to sacrifice himself to marriage to keep her safe. The least she could do was be totally honest with him. He was right about that.

She tipped her face up to him and had to catch her breath at the tender look in his eyes. Somehow, despite the fact he was the mirror image of Derek, her heart had always known he was different. She still didn't appreciate the underhanded way he had manipulated her, but knowing she hadn't been taken in by the same man twice was a balm to her pride.

He lifted one finger to caress her cheek, unnerving her, sending her thoughts in scattering directions. She smiled. "Dane, if you'd admitted who you were when I first contacted you, I'd have taken off."

He frowned at that possibility.

"I was so afraid of you," she explained, "of all the Carter family, but especially you." His eyes darkened to golden amber, and her stomach muscles constricted in reaction. She had to force herself back on track.

"Derek had told me so many horrible stories of how ruthless and unforgiving you could be."

He pulled her close, pressing her head to his shoulder and rocking her. She had the feeling he was comforting himself as much as her. "Derek and I had major disagreements on the family, and on the company. He felt challenged by all the games, while I was sickened by them. I suppose he didn't like it much that I walked away." He hesitated, then whispered, "And now he's gone."

Needing to reassure him, Angel pushed back and smiled up at him. "He always spoke of you with admiration, making you out to be bigger than life, and twice as frightening. I didn't trust anyone in your family, and there was only a marginal amount of trust for Derek. But deep down, despite everything, I thought he'd do the right thing for his son."

Dane pulled her close again. "So you're saying it's actually a good thing I didn't introduce myself up front?" He kissed her chin, featherlight, then her temple. "If I had, you'd have taken off and who knows what might have happened to you?"

He shuddered roughly with the thought, and then he kissed her. All her turbulent emotions of the day seemed to swell and heat into one overwhelming need. She wasn't used to the sexual demands of her body and didn't know how to temper them. All that they'd done the night before, all the ways he'd touched her and pleasured her, came swamping back. Heat pounded beneath her skin and her legs suddenly felt weak and shaky. She wanted to lie down beneath him, she wanted him inside her again, making her shudder with nearly painful pleasure. She wanted him to help her forget—at least for a little while.

"Let me make love to you, Angel."

The quiet plea was whispered into her ear, his warm breath a caress on its own. She wanted him, and that single focus drowned out everything else.

He'd asked her to marry him so he could protect Grayson. He was noble enough to go to any lengths to make sure the baby was taken care of. And now he needed her, if only in a physical way.

It was such a huge risk, letting her heart get involved when he'd made his motivations crystal clear. But she found she had no choice. She'd used up all her energy for the day, and for now, nothing seemed more right than making love with Dane. "Yes."

DANE WANTED TO SHOUT like a conqueror when Angel went soft and willing against him. God knew, after the turmoil of the day, he needed a distraction and he couldn't think of a nicer one than sinking himself into her warm body.

He did nearly shout when her small hand suddenly snaked down his chest and cupped over his fly. He choked and got an erection at the same time.

"Angel?" Her name was a harsh groan, but he couldn't help that. Too many emotions were slamming into him. He'd planned on wearing her down slowly, using the advantages he had: her love of Grayson and her need for protection, combined with their compatibility in bed. Loving Grayson wouldn't be a hardship; the baby was adorable and had owned Dane's heart from the first moment he'd met him. And even before he'd known Angel had no part in Derek's death, he'd felt compelled to protect her. He'd die before he let her suffer the same fate as his brother.

No woman had ever affected him so strongly.

He didn't understand her sudden submission to his lust, not when she'd been outraged only an hour or so before, but he wasn't fool enough to question her on it. He covered her small, soft hand with his own and pressed hard, catching his breath at the exquisite feel of her holding him. He watched her bright green eyes widen, saw her lips part on a deeply indrawn breath, and he kissed her again. He wasn't gentle. He possessed her mouth with his own, giving her his tongue and groaning when she sucked on it. Her fingers curled around his erection, stroking, proving what a deft learner she could be.

His revelations of the day, the fear he felt for her, his frustration in being unable to solve the mystery of his brother's death, all clamored inside him. He needed her, her comfort. Being with her overrode everything else.

He lifted his fingers to her breast and teased. Already her nipples were peaked, thrusting against the worn material of the sweatshirt she wore. Dane moved his mouth down to her throat, over the sensitive, ultrasoft skin beneath her chin, then to her ear. When he took a breath, he noticed the smoke smell still clinging to her and wanted to pull her into himself, to make her a part of him and forever keep her safe. She and Mick had claimed the fire to be a mere threat, without the intent of burning her out, but he wasn't so sure and the idea that someone could have gotten to her so easily filled him with an ice-cold rage. He *would* protect her.

Ruthlessly, hoping to banish the disturbing thoughts, he backstepped her up to the brick wall beside the fireplace and pinned her there with his hips. His hands jerked up her sweatshirt and he covered both plump, tender breasts with his rough palms. "You're mine now, Angel."

She moved against him, inciting him, encouraging him, and he reacted to her on a primitive level. He jerked back, lowered his head and carefully closed his teeth over one erect nipple. Angel cried out. He knew her breasts were sensitive; he'd found that out last night, taking extra care with her then. But now, he wanted to dominate her, to make her beg, to make her admit that she needed him, and not just for convenience and the safety he afforded. It was disquieting to feel such depth of emotion with this one particular woman. He hadn't wanted to ever again care so much, not like this. But now he had to admit, especially to himself, that what he felt for Angel had no comparison. It was crazy, given the short amount of time he'd known her, but he couldn't fight it—didn't even want to try. He wouldn't feel guilty about it, either. Derek had thrown away his chance to have her. Dane felt guilty for a lot of things, but not for this.

"Dane," she cried, digging her fingers into his back, and he relished the small pain for bringing him a measure of control.

"Say my name again," he told her as he began unfastening her jeans.

"I want you, Dane."

"Now, Angel, right here."

Her eyes widened, but he tugged her jeans down to her knees and turned her. "Brace your hands on the wall."

"Dane?" Eyes wide with confusion, she looked at him over her shoulder.

"Do it, honey." Not waiting for her to comply, he took

her wrists in his hands and flattened her palms on the wall, wide on either side of her head. "Now don't move."

He could hear her frantic breaths, her small whimpers, a mixture of excitement and uncertain anxiety. Grimly he smiled as he released himself from his slacks. He was rock hard and throbbing and more than ready to explode. When his arms came around her to ply her breasts, his fingertips plucking at her nipples, his erection just naturally nestled in the cleft of her rounded bottom. Angel gasped, pressing her head back, and at the same time, pushing her hips more closely to him.

He moved his pelvis, stroking her, teasing. He felt blind with lust, but also determined to accomplish his goals. "I want to get married tomorrow, no later than Wednesday."

"Yes."

A startled squeak escaped her when his arms squeezed her tight, but his relief was a living thing and there was no way to get close enough. He hating rushing her into marriage after everything else she'd been through. She deserved a proper courtship, with moonlight dates and flowers and gentle promises, all the things she hadn't had, all the things women wanted. But he had to do what he thought was best for both of them, and right now, tying her to him was his first priority.

Slowly, making himself as crazy as she, he dragged his palm down her ribs to her belly, and when she held her breath he bit her shoulder, a soft, wet love bite—then cupped her fully, taking her by surprise, loving the sound of her startled pleasure as she jerked and moaned.

His fingers gently pressed and found her ready for him, her feminine flesh swollen, the soft petals slick and hot. His middle finger glided over her, barely touching until her hips began moving in a counterpoint. He kept the pressure light and easy, teasing. She tried to hurry him, to encourage him to give her what she now needed, what she desperately wanted, but he resisted. Once, she started to drop her hands but he quickly repositioned her as he wanted her, vulnerable to him, submissive. Judging by the sounds of her panting breaths and raw moans, she loved it as much as he did.

"Dane, please…"

Just as he'd plucked at her nipples, he used his fingertips now to torment her again, but this flesh was so much more sensitive, the feelings so acute, she cried out and almost jerked away from him. His free arm locked around her, holding her in place for his sensual torment.

"You're mine, Angel. Mine." His words were harsh, commanding, breathed against her temple as he thrust against her, his fingers unrelenting.

To his satisfaction and deep pleasure, she came.

Her arms stiffened, her head dropped forward and her body jerked and bucked as her hips pressed hard against him. Dane groaned with her, encouraging her, continuing the gentle abrasion of her most sensitive flesh. As she quieted, he praised her, telling her how crazy she made him, how special she was. He had no idea if she heard him, and she gave no reply other than her gratified groans.

He'd never before resented the use of protection, but now, as he fumbled in a rush to get the condom in place, he cursed the use of them.

Angel was barely staying upright, her body now slumped fully against the wall, her arms no longer stiff and straight. Her cheek pressed to the warm brick and he feared the abrasion against her soft skin, so he pulled her away and lowered her to the carpet, entering her at the same time.

Her tight jeans restricted his movements, but it didn't matter. He simply needed to be inside her, like he needed his next breath and the occasional sunshine and a few hours' sleep. *He needed her.*

Riding her hard, pushing errant thoughts of the danger from his brain, he concentrated on the pleasure. Angel didn't join him again, but chose to watch him instead, her eyes soft in the firelight, her body pliant to his urgent thrusts. One hand lifted and she smoothed his shoulder, smiling gently.

Knowing she watched his every move, that she witnessed every emotion to pass over his face, knowing she could see his explosive pleasure as he came, made it all that much more powerful. He didn't disappoint her, and let himself go completely. He ground his teeth together to keep from shouting and strained against her, knowing she had just taken his heart. His body went rigid and he took his own orgasm with a low, endless growl of blinding pleasure.

He loved Angel Morris, he thought as he slumped against her. He loved her more than he'd ever thought to love anyone or anything. He loved her enough to give his life for her, to do anything to keep her bound to him.

Well damn, he thought, the effort almost painful to his muddled brain. That sure shot a hole in his altruistic plans of merely offering protection. It was also enough to scare ten years off his life.

CHAPTER NINE

"WELL, THAT DIDN'T go quite as I had planned it."

The words, so softly spoken, drifted around Dane, but it took considerable effort on his part to lift his head. He felt not only physically appeased, but emotionally full, and he didn't want to move, not yet, maybe not ever. He didn't want to lose the feeling, the closeness, and he didn't want reality, with all the present problems, to intrude. But he finally managed to struggle up onto his elbows.

Angel, tender and warm and womanly beneath him, looked at him with gentle, shining eyes, a tiny satisfied smile on her mouth.

God, he loved her. The profound acknowledgment shook him. He'd been careless with her, and just as he'd lost his brother, he could have lost her, too.

He tenderly tucked a pale curl behind her ear. "What didn't go as you planned? Did I disappoint you, sweetheart?" He asked the outrageous question to give his brain a chance for mental recovery. Looking at her now, with the realization of how easily she could crush him, was going to take some getting used to. He wasn't accustomed to feeling fear, but what he felt for Angel scared him down deep in his bones, clear to his masculine core. It also made him feel near to bursting and kept his male flesh, still buried tight inside her, semihard. Nothing would ever be enough with her.

Feeling the way he did, realizing just how special she was, made him doubt what he knew about Derek. His brother couldn't have used Angel as vindictively as everyone thought. No man could possibly spend time with her and not appreciate how special, how unique she was.

Her smooth brow puckered as she frowned at him. He had to laugh, and luckily that lightened the moment for him, at least to the point he could talk coherently without fear of professing undying love. Angel had been badly misused by his family, and he hadn't done much better by her, though that would quickly change. He fully intended to rush her headlong into marriage. Burdening her now with his excess of emotion before she'd had a chance to get used to the rest would be grossly unfair.

And besides all that, he was suddenly a horrible coward. He simply didn't want to lay his heart on the line, not when the odds were she'd disdain his love. She wanted him on a physical level, there was no denying that, not with the heated scent of their lovemaking still thick in the air. And they had the mutual love of Grayson, a binding responsibility for them both. He'd have to build on those things, and hope it would suffice.

Touching his fingertips over one tightly drawn eyebrow, he grinned. "How can you look so embarrassed after what we just did? Your pants are around your knees, I can feel your nipples hard against my chest, and you're still holding me inside you." He leaned down and brushed his mouth over hers. "So tight, Angel, like you never want to let me go."

"Dane." Unconsciously, she lifted her hips into his and he groaned.

"What didn't go as you planned?"

She looked shyly away, charming him anew. That she could be so wild one minute, and yet timid the next, kept his lust on a keen edge, and sharpened the emotional needs he felt to tie her to him, to keep her safe.

"I wanted this time to be different."

He laughed again. She never ceased to surprise him. "More different than making love against a brick wall with your—"

"Dane, hush!" She pressed her hand against his mouth and he kissed her palm, silently laughing.

"I'm sorry," he said, the words muffled until she drew her hand away. "You're too easy to tease."

"This time, I wanted to do stuff…to you. It doesn't seem fair the way you always give so much and I just take."

Those overwhelming emotions washed over him again in a wave of heat, stealing his thoughts and turning his body iron hard. He crushed her against him, burying his face against her throat. He was reminded of the near-fire at her apartment by her smoky scent, and the fact that someone was trying to hurt her, and had likely killed his brother. The events that had brought them together were never far from his mind. Because those same events could tear them apart.

Gently pulling away from her, he sat up. Angel started to do the same, looking at him uncertainly, but he stopped her by lifting one of her feet to his lap and removing her shoe. "You need a shower and some sleep. And Alec and

Mick should be here soon." He caught her pants and stripped them the rest of the way off.

"I don't need sleep. I need to see the rest of your house."

"And you will." *Later, after she was rested up.* She may be doing a good job of holding herself together, but he was still running on adrenaline, and a compelling need to ensure her safety. Their lovemaking had only served to blunt the edges of his urgency a bit.

Once he had her naked from the waist down he caught her under the arms and lifted her with him as he stood. He pulled the sweatshirt free, surveyed her naked body with a deep satisfaction, then cupped her face in his hands. "You listen to me, Angel Morris." His thumb coasted over her bottom lip and she nodded.

"We have plenty of time to play sexually. The rest of our lives in fact because I intend to keep you. For better or worse, for richer or poorer. Eventually, we'll both get to do some exploring. But don't ever think you've disappointed me. For one thing, it's not possible, not when you go so wild when we're together. Not when I know that wildness is only for me. That's more of a gift than most women ever give, and most men ever deserve. We're being forced into this marriage, but the perks, to my way of thinking, are damn enticing."

His gaze traveled from her mouth to her breasts, then down, lingering on the damp curls over her mound. His tone dropped, rough with renewed arousal. "As far as I'm concerned, I don't have a single complaint. As your husband, I'll have you on hand day and night, and the way I see it, that's a hell of a bargain. All right?"

She nodded, but her eyes had gone dark and soft again

and he knew what he'd said had turned her on, that his words of explanation had put visual images in her mind. Seeing her reaction put them in his mind as well. He hadn't been this horny or insatiable since high school, and he had to wonder just how much of it was based on a desperate need to reaffirm what they had, before it was taken away. "Come on. While you're showering I'll keep an eye on Grayson and get us something to eat." He eyed her pale naked body as he led her into the hall bathroom, unable to keep his hands from patting her rounded behind, smoothing over her waist and belly. He drew a deep breath and chastened himself to behave. "I'll also find you a robe to wear until your other stuff gets here."

"It feels strange, Dane. Being naked with a man, not being the only one to keep an ear trained for Grayson." She drew a breath, watching him closely. "Not having to be so afraid."

He hoped that meant she felt a measure of trust for him. "I'm not going to let anything happen to you, babe. You can rest a little easier now."

She turned to face him as he pulled two thick towels out of the cabinet and set them close to hand.

"It feels strangest of all to be in your house. That's going to really take some getting used to."

"It's our house," he said firmly, wanting her to feel comfortable, determined to get her fully enmeshed in his life, so much so she wouldn't be able to help but love him back. "When I took over Derek's office, my mother wanted me to move into his house as well. But I drew the line at that. The memories there are too sharp, too suffocating. I feel enough like an interloper as it is, usurping his office, his files…his woman."

Angel shook her head. "I was never that, not really. Derek and I had a brief fling, but it ended long before he got possessive. I'm not sure if he intended to use me all along, or if he just jumped on the opportunity when it presented itself. But almost from the first, I felt more for you than I ever did for him." She looked around, then smiled. "I'm glad this is your house, not his."

He, too, looked around. "I paid to have it decorated because I was clueless and didn't have the time to worry about it anyway, not traveling as often as I did. It's a home base of sorts, but it's always felt kind of...cold to me. So if you get in the mood and want to change things, go right ahead. Just don't ever let anyone in unless I'm here with you."

"I'm not an idiot."

He nodded agreement. "Far from it. But right now, I'm not willing to trust a single soul with your safety. The house is secure, but only if you use the security system correctly. There's an intercom for the front and back door. Don't take any chances, okay?"

She gave a grave nod. He didn't want to frighten her again, but they both knew just how much danger she was in. Hopefully living with him would keep her out of harm's way while he continued his investigation of Derek's death. He would probably bring the police into it shortly, once he'd had a chance to go over things with Alec.

The future stretched out before him, and for the first time that he could remember in too many years to count, he saw more than an endless, empty void. He wanted a future with Angel, with Grayson.

And he wouldn't let anything stand in his way. Not even a murderer.

MOTHER NATURE conspired against them.

Looking out the kitchen window, Angel sipped her coffee and then sighed. Finally the sun was shining again, though she knew the weather wouldn't clear for a while. Record-breaking lows were predicted for the rest of the week.

She also knew Dane was frustrated, that if it had been up to him, they would have been married already. But the most horrendous snowfall of the season, a good twelve inches, had all but canceled Thanksgiving and confined everyone indoors, making a wedding impossible. It had also stalled his investigation, putting personal queries on hold.

Dane had improvised Thanksgiving, forgetting the plan to meet with his family—to Angel's relief and Celia's disappointment. For lack of a turkey, he made a superb pork roast and surprised Angel with his culinary talents.

It had felt right somehow to spend an evening in the kitchen with Dane, bumping hips and sharing chores, working together. Grayson sat in his pumpkin seat watching them, and the setting would have been picture perfect if it hadn't been for the fact that someone evil was still out there, still a threat, keeping them both edgy despite their efforts to the contrary.

The weather provided the ideal excuse for them to linger in bed, forcing away the dark cloud of menace with an overload of sensuality. Just a few hours ago Dane had awakened her from a sound sleep with warm hands and a warmer mouth, gently encouraging her higher and higher until she'd had to muffle her shouts with a pillow. It amazed her that every time with him seemed better, more intense. She wasn't certain how much more she could take, but was anxious to find out.

He'd left her limp and exhausted in the bed. He had kissed the tip of her nose, told her he'd be home in a few hours, and then lovingly cupped a breast before turning away and hurrying out. Dane often hurried away from her, as if he were afraid if he lingered, he wouldn't go at all.

Angel had never felt so pampered, or so loved. Only he'd never said anything about love.

It worried her, how easily she had adjusted to being with Dane. He was the perfect father to Grayson, the perfect companion to her, even if he was overly autocratic on occasion.

She understood his worry because she shared it. No matter how many times they went over it, they couldn't come up with a single reason for someone to kill Derek and try to kill her. The idea of never knowing, of always having to be on guard, made her angry.

She had just come up from the basement with a large load of laundry when the phone rang. Expecting it to be Celia, who'd made a habit of calling daily, she balanced the laundry basket on one hip and used her shoulder to hold the phone to her ear. "Hello."

There was no reply, and within a heartbeat the fine hairs on the back of her neck stood up and gooseflesh rose on her arms. *No.* She forced a calm tone and said again, this time more firmly, "Hello?" but still received no answer and she quickly hung up the phone.

Frozen, she stood there, trying to convince herself that it was an accident, a coincidence. Not once since she'd

moved in with Dane had there been a threatening call.
There was no reason to think this was one of them. She
drew a deep breath and tried to convince herself she was
right.

At that moment Dane came in. Snowflakes glistened in
his hair and his mellow golden eyes were warm with welcome.

When he saw her just standing there, he hurried to take
the basket from her. "Angel, are you all right? Have you
hurt your leg again?"

She swallowed hard and automatically repeated the
words that had become a litany. The man was too overprotective by half. "Quit pampering me, Dane. It's getting
annoying."

"I have a cleaning woman for this—"

"Who hired on to do your laundry, not mine and Grayson's. Besides, I'm perfectly capable of taking care of
myself. I don't want a stranger muddling through my
things. And," she added when she could see he was con-
triving more arguments, "the maid hasn't been able to
come here in this weather. Grayson has laundry that needs
to be done every day."

"Oh." He looked distracted for just a moment, then
suddenly drew her into his arms and swung her in a wide
circle. "All right, I'll let that go for now, but only because
I have a few surprises for you and I don't think you'll be
properly appreciative if you're angry."

"You've found out something?" she asked, her entire
body tensing in hope.

Dane lightly kissed the bridge of her nose in apology.
"No, I'm sorry, babe. There's nothing yet, but we're
working on it. I contacted a few personal friends in the

police department and they're doing some checking for me, looking things over again. Something will turn up soon, I promise.''

Angel bit her lip as disappointment swelled inside her. She didn't think she could take much more waiting. And she knew it was even harder on Dane. He felt compelled to avenge his brother, and to protect her and Grayson. He'd taken on a lot for her sake, and she worried constantly about him. If he got hurt because of her…

''Hey, no long faces now, honey.'' He kissed her again, this time more lingering. ''I want to see you smiling, not frowning.''

She considered telling him about the phone call, but at the moment, his expression so expectant and happy… There would be plenty of time to talk about that later—if it was even important, which she was starting to doubt. The last phone call she'd received had been verbal, and this one had been silent. Likely there was no connection at all, just a wrong number.

''Where did you rush off to this morning?'' she asked, shaking off her eerie mood.

Backstepping to a kitchen chair, he sat and pulled her into his lap. His heavy coat was damp in places and he struggled out of it, then laid it on the table next to the laundry basket. One rough fingertip touched her cheek. ''My sister is dying to get back out here and see Grayson. And you. She's overflowing with questions and curiosity.''

Celia called at least once a day, and she was always cordial and inquisitive, but cautiously so, as if she were taking pains not to be pushy. Angel couldn't help but like her. The rest of his family had been ominously silent.

"How would you feel about having her and Raymond to dinner? The roads are much better today, and with no more snow predicted, by Tuesday they should be fine."

Angel wondered at his reasons for the sudden invitation, but said only, "She's your sister, Dane. If you want to have her over, that's fine." She hesitated, then added, "Maybe you should invite your mother, too. It might help to smooth things over with her."

"Not yet." He said it easily, but Angel was aware of his sudden strain.

"Dane, what ever happened between the two of you? I know Derek told me once that you just didn't see eye to eye, but—"

His laugh, a sound bordering on sarcasm, interrupted her. "A difference of opinion, huh? Well, Derek was right about that. But it's past history honey, and I don't want to bore you."

"Shouldn't I know what's going on, since the past probably plays a part in the tension now? What if your mother says something? I don't like to be kept in the dark."

"It doesn't concern you."

And that, she thought, was the crux of the problem. She wanted everything about him to concern her. "I'm sorry." She tried to get off his lap, but he made a rough sound at her movement and hugged her close.

"Dammit, I didn't mean that quite the way it sounded." He gave her a frustrated look, then shrugged. "All right, you want me to bare my soul, I suppose I can live through it."

He was in such a strange mood, teasing one minute,

then solemn, then teasing again. "I don't mean to push you."

"Ha! All right, I'm sorry." He tightened his hold on her. "Don't rush off."

Angel gave him an impatient look.

"All right, dammit, but as soon as I finish this stupid tale of woe, we're moving on to your surprise, okay?" After a brief hesitation, he said, "I was engaged to be married once." His hands looped around her and he looked off to the side, staring at nothing in particular, merely avoiding her gaze.

"Mother didn't approve, of course, but then I'd already started bucking her on almost everything. Derek went to the college of *her* choice, I went to a state college. Looking back, I realize how infantile I acted, opposing her just for the sake of opposition, but she was so damn controlling about everything, it just naturally rubbed me the wrong way."

Angel couldn't begin to imagine anyone attempting to control Dane. The very idea was ludicrous.

"Both Derek and I had gotten our business degree in the same year my father died. He and Mother had always planned for us to take over, but not that soon. His heart attack took everyone by surprise. Mother, never one to grieve for long, wanted us to jump into the company together. I wanted to get my MBA. Derek was born to run a corporation, was anxious to get started, but I resisted her. I was glad to let Derek handle things, and despite all her carping and complaining, I went back to school."

A heavy silence fell and Angel felt him shift slightly, as if he were uncomfortable.

"I met a woman while I was in school, and I wanted

to get married. Since that didn't meet with Mother's plans, she did everything she could, including disowning me so I couldn't touch my inheritance money, as a way to discourage me. But the more she did, the more determined I became. When I told her I fully intended to go through with the wedding, she...she bought Anna off.''

Angel had no idea what to say to that. She waited, hoping he'd elaborate. And finally he did.

"I don't like to think it was the money that enticed Anna. She wasn't from the same background as me, and my mother intimidated the hell out of her. She spelled out this grandiose life Anna would be expected to live up to and it spooked her. When Mother offered her the money, she took it and walked away.''

What a fool, Angel thought. She knew Dane had money, but he didn't flaunt it. His house was very nice, but it wasn't ostentatious. Everything about him was casual and comfortable and understated. Anna must not have known him at all to believe such idiocy. Or maybe it just hadn't mattered to her. "I'm sorry.''

Dane shook his head impatiently. "The worst part was, she was pregnant with my baby.''

Angel stiffened, seized by a mingling of jealousy and confusion. Where was the child now?

As if he'd read her thoughts, Dane gave her a squeeze. "By the time I'd caught up with Anna, she told me she'd lost the baby.''

He looked so troubled, Angel curled down against his chest and hugged herself close to him. She'd never before seen Dane like this, and she didn't like it. Derek's death had filled him with calculating determination, with a purpose. His mother's disdain had only seemed to amuse him. But now he sounded hurt deep inside. She preferred his arrogance any day. And at that moment she'd have given a lot to ease his pain.

His large hand settled against the back of her head and he idly tangled his fingers in her hair. "I've never admitted this to anyone, but to this day, I'm not sure Anna didn't have an abortion. I blamed my mother because it was a hell of a lot easier to blame her than to accept that I might have been wrong about Anna, that I might have made a colossal mistake marrying a woman who didn't care enough about me to believe in me. She told me, rather tearfully in fact, that she'd been afraid and taking my mother's bribe seemed her only choice."

Angel could feel his pounding heartbeat, a little faster now, and she slipped her hand inside his shirt, smoothing her fingers over his warm, hair-rough skin. Dane went still even as his breathing changed, grew a little rougher and quicker. Angel pulled his shirt from his pants and pushed it upward, kissing his chest, his small tight nipples. Dane groaned and quickly yanked the shirt over his head.

Whispering against his chest, Angel said, "She could have come to you, and that's what bothers you most?"

Dane tilted his head back against the chair. "She didn't trust me."

"I trust you. I've been trusting you with not only my life, but Grayson's." He started to speak and she straightened, cupping his jaw with her palms, holding his head still as she attacked his mouth. Dane groaned again and Angel used that as her cue. With their lips still touching she breathed, "I'm not like her, Dane. Your mother can't send me away. Only you could do that now."

Rather than answer, he kissed her again, and there was

hunger in the way he held her, the way his mouth moved heavily over hers. He might not love her, but he needed her, and from that, love could grow.

He pulled himself away from her with a harsh sound of impatience. "Damn woman, you distract me."

"I'm glad."

Laughing, he avoided her mouth as she tried to capture his again. "Your surprise, remember?"

"We could do that later?"

"Insatiable wench. Stop that!" He caught her hands and pulled them away from his belt. When she pretended to pout, he grinned. "Show just a modicum of patience, okay? Now, first off, Mick got your apartment rented, so you can stop worrying about that."

That wasn't at all what she'd been expecting. Dane had insisted, against her and Mick's protests, on keeping up the rent until Mick found a new tenant. Angel knew Mick and his mother needed the money, and she'd felt bad leaving as she had, without notice, but Dane wouldn't hear of her paying the rent herself, and Mick hadn't wanted either of them to pay. He was such a proud young man.

"Who is it?" Angel still worried about Mick. She talked with him often, but she missed their daily school lessons together. As soon as the weather permitted, she intended to start them back up again. Dane was all for the idea.

"You'd never guess so I might as well tell you." He took a moment to build the suspense, but when she gave an impatient growl, he grinned and said, "Alec."

At her look of surprise, he nodded. "Yep, I showed him the apartment myself. It's not too far from the office, and Mick is a fantastic manager, especially for a kid."

"And you wanted Alec there to keep an eye on him, to make certain he was okay?"

"Not at all. I knew you would worry, and I figured this would put your mind at ease for the most part. But Alec really was looking for a new place, and he likes it there."

Angel smiled at him. "It's a wonderful surprise. Thank you."

"That's only part of the surprise. Now don't get angry before you hear me out, okay?"

Like a red flag waved before her face, his words had the effect of putting her instantly on guard. She stiffened. "What have you done?"

"We've agreed that it's best to get married, and that means I want to do what I can to ensure you and Grayson are taken care of. I know how you feel about money, but it's silly. Thanks to my inheritance—"

"I thought your mother took that!"

He shrugged. "She gave it back, sort of another bribe to bring me back into the fold. It's been sitting in a bank gathering interest because I had no use for it until now."

"I don't want you going against your principles for me, Dane Carter!"

He laughed. "It wasn't a principle. It was plain stubbornness and the fact that I like to prick my mother's temper whenever possible. But since we'll be married Tuesday morning—"

"Whoa!" Angel held out her hands, astounded by having so much information thrown at her at one time. She needed a few minutes to assimilate it all. "What do you mean we're getting married Tuesday morning? Since when was this decided?"

He had the grace to look sheepish. "Ah… Actually just

today. That was another part of your surprise. I talked with my doctor and the lab will do the blood tests tomorrow. As soon as we do that, we'll head downtown and pick up the license. A pastor from my sister's church has agreed to do the deed on Tuesday.''

There was a brief struggle as Angel tried to remove herself from his lap and he was just as determined to keep her in place.

Dane won.

''You agreed to marry me, honey.'' He held her securely, his eyes never leaving hers. There was a look of challenge on his face, and something else, something not so easily defined. ''We've made the deal, you and I. Grayson needs me, and I'm not about to turn my back on him, not now, not ever. If you're thinking about changing your mind, it's too late.''

Realization hit, knocking the breath from her. He wanted things confirmed, he wanted a guarantee, and he was afraid to leave it up to her because he thought she might back out. Knowing he felt such an obligation for Grayson, and that he was afraid of losing the baby, was a revelation. But she couldn't merely condone his autocratic behavior. He'd become a tyrant in no time if she let him.

She scowled darkly, and grumbled, ''Next time, check with me first before you set things up.''

His eyes widened and the arrogance was immediately back in his gaze, along with a healthy dose of relief. ''There won't be a next time, honey. I told you, regardless of why we're getting married, it's still forever.''

As he said it, he leaned forward, then kissed her long

and slow and deep. When he pulled away, he whispered, "I suppose I should get the rest of it over with."

"There's more?"

"I'm afraid so." He drew a deep breath, then blurted, "I paid off your and Grayson's medical bills."

She should have expected it. But with all that had happened the last few days, her accumulated bills had been the last thing on her mind. In a way, it was almost a relief to be rid of that particular burden, except that she didn't want their relationship to be about what material things he could give her. She wanted more than that.

When she only narrowed her eyes at him, he continued, evidently encouraged by her silence. "I also opened an account in your name. You can add your own money to it if you like, but there's a hefty sum already deposited. Only your name is on the account, so you can do whatever you want with it. Understand, Angel, this isn't for household stuff. If you want to redecorate the house—which by the way, I was thinking Grayson's room could really use some color..."

"Dane."

"Come on, honey, don't get all prickly on me." He ran a hand over his head and his frustration was almost palpable, forcing her to hide a grin. "As far as I'm concerned, what I have is already yours, only you're being too pigheaded about it to let me take care of you."

"Pigheaded? Gee, you smooth-tongued dog, you. You sure do know how to win a gal over."

"Dammit, Angel, I am not my damn brother! You don't have to worry about any hidden motivations on my part."

"And I'm not Anna," she said, just as firmly. "I won't

be bought off. You're trying to make sure I have money so if or when your mother offers it, I won't be tempted."

He looked away, his entire body drawn tight, his shoulders rigid, which to Angel was as good as an admission of guilt. When he turned to face her again his eyes were diamond hard and probing. "Would you be tempted?"

"No!" Trying to calm herself, and at the same time, sort through the words that needed to be said, she took a deep breath, and then another. It didn't help. "Dane, we need to talk. There's something I really need to tell you."

He stiffened, as if bracing himself. "I'm listening," he said, but his expression remained fierce.

Grayson chose that unfavorable moment to give his patented, *I'm awake and I expect some attention* yell, effectively diverting them both. Angel gave Dane one long last look before hurrying out of the kitchen. She heard his soft curse behind her.

It was almost a relief to get sidetracked. She loved him, and he deserved to know that. But he already had so much on his mind, it might be easier for him to not be burdened with her love. He wasn't marrying her for that reason, so he might not even welcome her affections.

She needed to give it more thought before she made any grand declarations. After the threats were resolved would have been ideal, but with him pushing for marriage so soon, that was no longer an option.

She changed Grayson's diaper as the baby cooed at her, impatiently waiting to be fed, then pulled up the rocking chair in his room. She had just settled the baby against her breast when Dane spoke.

"He's such a little glutton."

Dane stood propped in the doorway, more handsome

and appealing than any man had a right to be, especially now, with that boyish look of wonder on his face as he watched the baby greedily suckle. He'd put his shirt back on and had it all buttoned up, the sleeves rolled to his elbows.

At her silence, he walked the rest of the way into the room and knelt on the floor beside her chair. ''I feel so much guilt, Angel, when I think about what Derek will miss.''

Angel silently watched him as he smoothed one finger over Grayson's cheek. ''Aside from the way he treated you, which I really don't understand, he was a good man, and he was a damn good brother. He never gave up on me, never sided with the family against me. Most of the time when we were growing up, we were inseparable, best friends as well as brothers. I loved him a lot, but I can't help but be damn glad that I'm the one here with you and Grayson now.''

''Oh, Dane.'' Angel felt tears gather in her throat. She could just imagine the hell he was putting himself through, and there was no way for her to help him.

He squeezed his eyes shut, his jaw tight. ''I have to find out what happened to him. It's the very least I owe him, for having my life when his is gone, for taking over where he left off.''

''Derek chose his own paths, Dane. You can't blame yourself.''

He looked away, his face grim. ''If I'd have come back instead of being so stubborn, I might have been able to help him. He might still be alive.''

And we wouldn't have found each other. Angel shivered with the thought, then felt her own measure of gripping guilt.

The baby, recognizing Dane's voice, released Angel's nipple to turn his head. He stared at Dane, his blue eyes alert. Dane smiled, though his expression was still sad. "I love him, you know."

Angel nodded, a lump of emotion gathering in her throat.

Dane came to his feet and dug into his pocket. "I bought you this today. At least this time you can grant me the traditional rights of the groom to spend my money." He handed her a small black box, then gave his attention back to Grayson. The baby stared at him a moment longer before going back to his feeding. Some things were simply more important than others.

Awkwardly, Angel managed to open the small box. Her hands shook and it was difficult maneuvering with the baby in her lap. Inside the box, nestled in cream velvet, was the most beautiful diamond engagement ring she'd ever seen. It was large, but not *too* large, an oval diamond surrounded by rubies. Breathlessly, she whispered, "It's incredible."

"Then you like it?"

"Dane..." She reached for him with her free arm and somehow he managed to embrace them both, making Grayson squirm in protest.

"Why don't you finish what you were going to tell me before I have to go out again."

Surprised, she asked, "Where are you going now?"

Dane took the ring from her and slipped it on her finger. He seemed pleased by the snug fit. "I'm going to close out your post office box. It's too far from here to do you any good and besides—'' his gaze met hers in a challenge ''—with the threats against you, I want anything and everything that concerns you to come by me now, at least until things are resolved.''

Angel curled her fist tight around the ring. ''That's fine. I haven't used that box in ages anyway, not since I left Aeric. Take the key from my key ring. It's hanging by the phone in the kitchen.''

Dane couldn't quite hide his satisfaction. She saw no reason to fight him on this, not when she didn't use the post office box anyway. ''Now what were you going to tell me?''

She needed more time, she thought. Tonight, over dinner, without interruptions or the distractions of wedding dates or suffocating guilt, she'd tell him she loved him. But not now, not when they both felt confused and he was ready to head back out the door.

''Angel?''

''I don't want Grayson to be an only child.''

Dane blinked at her, his gaze sharpening. ''What did you say?''

Heat rushed into her cheeks, but at least she was giving him a truth. ''I never had any brothers or sisters and it was awful. I…I know we'll be married for practical reasons, but I want another child. I thought you deserved to know that before we marry. Just so you're…prepared.''

Dane searched her face in silence for several moments, looking more shocked than dismayed. Slowly, a smile broke over his face. He looked at Grayson and chuckled as the baby made grunting, squeaking noises while he nursed. ''Nothing would make me happier, honey. As long as we wait a while so you're not overburdened. I want your leg to heal completely and I don't want Grayson to be cheated out of being a baby. Just as you had no siblings, I had one that got half of all my parents' attention. I'm not complaining, but I think there must be a happy medium. And keep in mind, you run the risk of having twins with me. Three in diapers would be a bit much for even the most determined parent.''

He hadn't refuted their reasons for marrying, but she wasn't discouraged. The practical reasons did exist, but there was also the love she felt. And tonight, she'd tell him so.

CHAPTER TEN

DANE STOOD BENEATH the post office overhang while the freezing wind whistled around him, blowing open his coat, pelting his face with a dusting of snowflakes caught in the frigid gusts. Nothing could penetrate the heat of his rage.

With deliberate movements he uncurled his fist and stared again at the name on the large manila envelope. His brother had sent Angel one final message.

The overwhelming urge to tear the envelope open was difficult to resist, but Dane knew in his heart he had to bring the letter to Angel. Not only was it a violation of her privacy to look inside, but she might take it as a measure of distrust as well. It could be a love letter—or it could be the information, the missing link to the threats, that they'd been looking for.

He didn't want her hurt.

He didn't want anything his brother might have put in the letter to cause Angel more heartache. And he didn't want to suffer the sweltering jealousy he now felt that was enough to ward off even the worst winter had to offer. *Damn it.* He didn't want his brother eulogized in Angel's heart with a final farewell.

Conflicting feelings of grief, guilt and possessiveness jumbled his thoughts.

The postmaster had watched with a jaundiced eye as Dane tossed out the majority of the mail unceremoniously stuffed into the large mailbox. Dane had only briefly glimpsed the numerous sale ads and magazines and offers before Derek's letter caught his notice. Now, with stiff steps and an anxious stride, he headed for his car. He couldn't understand his own urgency; he just knew he wanted to be with Angel and Grayson. He needed to know they were okay.

It took him all of five minutes to realize he was being followed. Using his cell phone, he impatiently dialed Alec's number.

"Sharpe."

"I'm being trailed," Dane said, no other explanations needed.

"I'm on it."

Over the past few days Dane had been aware of being followed. He couldn't get close enough to figure out who it was, so he'd alerted Alec to watch his back. Dane had told Angel he didn't want her out in the cold, but in truth, he wasn't willing to take the risk that whoever it was might be able to get to her. He preferred keeping her at home, safely behind locked doors and away from any threats.

This morning, he'd specifically opened the account in her name so she'd be protected financially if something happened to him. She'd accused him of not trusting her, but that was no longer true. He simply wasn't willing to leave her future to chance. Though he'd told her the sum in the account was hefty, he knew she couldn't begin to guess the amount. And he wanted it that way. Angel had a prideful tendency to fight him on every little thing he tried to give her. When she saw the bank records, she'd hit the roof. He smiled in anticipation. In some perverse way, he enjoyed arguing with her as much as he enjoyed loving her. Things would never be sedate between them, that was a certainty.

Alec shouldn't be very far behind, and now with Dane's signal, he'd close the gap and they would trap the driver between them.

"Dammit!" Dane muttered the curse into the open phone line as he saw the car swerve away.

"That him taking the entrance ramp to the highway?"

Dane watched his suspect speed away and knew, whoever the man was, he'd been on to them. "Yeah, that was him. How did he figure us?"

There was a shrug in Alec's tone. "Maybe he didn't. Maybe he was going that way all along."

"Nope. He was following me, I know it."

"Want me to go after him?"

Dane considered it, then shook his head to himself. "No, there's no point. I'm heading home to Angel and staying there. Though I doubt it'll do us any good, run a quick check on the plates, just in case we can get lucky for a change." Dane didn't for a minute doubt Alec had the plates memorized. Not much ever got by him.

"I'll get right back to you."

Less than three minutes later, Alec had his news. Both he and Dane had cultivated contacts in every facet of the police force. The information they received, and how they received it, wasn't always on the up and up. But it was generally beneficial to all, so the cops tended to work with them. "The license plate shows a newly rented car."

"*Dammit.*" Dane thumped his fist against the steering

wheel, his frustration level high. "That means the name it's registered under is likely false."

"Yeah, 'fraid so. You want me to go check into the rental agency where the car came from?"

"There's no point. Whoever it is, he's covering his ass. I doubt he'll make any mistakes this late into the game." With an irritated sigh, Dane suggested, "You might as well take the rest of the day off. I'll let you know if anything comes up."

"All right. I do have a few personal things to take care of."

The line went dead before Dane could question that cryptic comment. It was the first time in the history of their acquaintance that Alec had ever alluded to a personal life. Though Dane was certain he must have one, he'd never mentioned it before.

It only took Dane another fifteen minutes before he pulled into the garage. As per his instructions, Angel kept the alarm on, and all the doors and windows locked. It was a hell of a way to live, constantly being on guard, but maybe with the help of Derek's letter they would be able to put the past, and the threats, to rest.

After turning off the car he used his remote to close the garage door. As he came in through the kitchen by the door that attached to the garage, he heard Angel laughing. Following the sound, the manila envelope still clutched in his hand, he found her sprawled on the family room carpet before the fireplace. Grayson was held over her head, and each time the baby gurgled, she laughed and lowered him for a tickling nip of his pudgy belly.

Without intruding, Dane watched their antics, a small smile on his face. Damn, but he loved her. The feeling was starting to settle in, not so scary now, more like a necessary part of him was finally working as it should. He pictured Angel with a baby girl, as well, his daughter, a child that would look like her mother, have her bright green eyes. He'd missed being a part of her pregnancy with Grayson, but this time, he'd be here. *I'm sorry, Derek. But she'll be my wife.*

''When did you come in?''

Dane hadn't even realized she'd turned to him, he'd been so caught up in the comforting images of baby and home and hearth, images he'd long ago given up on. ''Just a minute ago.'' He strode over and sat cross-legged beside the two of them, reaching out to take Grayson into his own lap.

''What do you have there?''

Angel looked at the envelope, her expression inquiring. ''It's for you, honey.'' He let her know by his tone the seriousness of the envelope. ''Derek evidently sent it to you. It's postmarked some time ago, from before his death. Haven't you checked your box at all?''

Angel stared at the envelope like it was poison. ''There was no reason. I only used it for the information my supervisor wanted me to work on at home. Files he wanted me to prepare before he made a presentation. He didn't trust very many people, or the regular mail. He figured a locked post office box was the most secure way to go. No one knew the number except the two of us.''

''And Derek.''

She nodded. ''I usually kept those files locked up. But I was…anxious to see Derek one day, so I just stuck them in a desk drawer when he called to say he was coming over. I never considered that he might go through my personal things. He must have taken the box number off the envelope.''

Dane hated hearing about her and Derek together. He didn't regret loving Angel, he couldn't, but he sometimes felt as if he'd stolen everything good from Derek. Forging his place in the family had never mattered to him, but it had been everything to Derek. Now Dane had taken Derek's place in the family, and in the office.

He'd gladly give up both those dubious perks, but he'd never give up Angel or Grayson.

He knew the night Derek stole the information from Angel was the same night he'd taken her to bed. For that reason, more than any other, Dane had hesitated to discuss it with her. The thought of Derek with her, how he'd hurt her, was almost too difficult to contemplate.

''I was asleep when Derek went through my desk,'' she said, her tone flat. ''We were never…intimate after that, and a month later, he dropped me.''

Several silent moments passed, then Dane tried to hand her the envelope. ''Go ahead and open it.''

With a shudder, Angel pulled back. ''No thanks. I'd rather you did it.''

''Are you sure?'' Even as he asked it, Dane was laying Grayson aside on the blanket. The baby turned his head and directed an intent gaze at the bright flames in the fireplace. Dane slid a finger under the flap of the envelope and pulled it open.

There were several printouts inside, and Dane scanned them quickly. ''These are details outlining industrial espionage at Aeric.'' His blood surged with the ramifications. He lifted one paper after another, finally coming to a personal note addressed to Angel.

"What?" Angel scooted around to peer over Dane's shoulder. She picked up the discarded printouts and studied them.

Dane laid the last paper aside and stared at Angel. When she felt his gaze, she looked up.

"I'm sorry, honey."

"What is it, Dane?"

He touched her cheek. "Derek was trying to protect you." Dane lifted the sheaf of papers, holding them out to her. "He sent you these as an explanation of why he'd gone to so much trouble to alienate you, why he specifically did it so publicly. He wanted everyone to think your relationship was over, that you meant nothing to him. He suspected some level of danger after he'd discovered several discrepancies in various Aeric research files, shortly after stealing that information from you. He wasn't certain what was happening, but when he investigated further, small accidents started to happen to him. He was afraid you'd be in danger too, by association." Dane touched her cheek, then forced the words out despite the tightness in his throat. "Derek had no problem doing what needed to be done for the takeover, he saw that only as good business, part of the corporate game. But he hadn't deliberately planned to hurt you in the bargain. He cared for you, honey."

Angel squeezed her eyes shut and swallowed hard, clutching at Dane's hand. Dane knew, without asking, the regret she felt because he felt it, too.

The sound of a gun cocking seemed obscenely loud in the silence of the room. Both Angel and Dane jerked up their gazes, and there stood Raymond. The forty-five in his hand made an incongruous sight with his three-piece suit and immaculate presence. "Well, I commend your investigative skills, Dane. Of course, your damn brother pretty much spelled it out for you, didn't he? I knew he was too thorough not to have something written down. And Ms. Morris was the likely person to have the info."

Dane quickly tried to cover his shock, to act calm and in control. He was very aware of Angel sitting frozen beside him. "So that's the reason you've been harassing her?"

Raymond shrugged. "I lost her for a while there, you know, after she moved. It was tedious finding her phone number again, but I had no idea where she'd gone. Unlike you, I don't have connections in these matters. It was rather frustrating, never knowing when she might resurface, if she'd try to discredit me with that damn information your brother put together.

"I tried to hedge my bets a bit by telling your mother, regretfully of course, what a bitch Angel was, how she'd used Derek, how she was likely to come sniffing around with blackmail in mind. I had half hoped she'd find Angel for me, but your mother is getting old and has no taste for revenge. She only hoped to avoid a scandal. Luckily for me, you're not nearly so derelict in your familial duty." Raymond grinned. "You led me right to her."

"*Bastard.*" Dane came smoothly to his feet and deliberately stepped in front of Angel and Grayson, shielding them both with his body. "You killed Derek."

"Now that," he said with a shrug, "was an honest accident. I knew he'd been playing detective—funny that the two of you were even more alike than you knew. But he proved to be rather proficient at it. I tried a few minor scare tactics, and for a while there I thought they'd worked. But the bastard was just biding his time, letting months go by, waiting for me to make another move. He was careful not to call in the authorities, not wanting to scare me off.'' Raymond held up two fingers, a millimeter apart. ''He came that close to nailing my name to his damn discoveries after I thought the coast was clear again.''

''My brother was no idiot. And he would have taken any theft from a company he owned as a personal insult.''

Raymond laughed. ''He was a wily bastard, I'll give him that.''

It almost sounded as though Raymond had respected Derek, had maybe liked him. Dane felt sick with disgust.

''Needless to say I had to up the pressure to get him to back off, but the fool didn't drive quite as well as Ms. Morris.''

Dane had to fight the urge to lunge at Raymond. Only the fact that doing so would put Angel in more danger kept him still, but he didn't like it. Every muscle in his body twitched with the almost unbearable need to do physical harm. ''How did you get in here?''

''I beat you home. Yes, that was me following you. Of course, as soon as I realized you had sicked your watchdog on me, I veered off. Mr. Sharpe really is a nasty-looking fellow. He gives me the creeps.''

''Alec's good at what he does.''

''It doesn't matter now, does it?'' Raymond smiled his perfect artificial smile. ''As I was saying. It was easy enough to swing around and with a heavy foot on the gas pedal, I was able to get here before you. I hid in the bushes. Not very dignified, but then, you gave me little choice. When you started to close the garage door, I

slipped a small wedge underneath it, and rather than closing tight, it reopened on its own. I waited just long enough
to see if you'd double-check it. But you were in too big
a hurry to see your ladylove. Such a hurry in fact, that I
believe the two of you will elope.'' He grinned, his expression taunting.

Dane tried to calm his racing heart and his anger. He
needed a cool head to deal with Raymond. He only
wished he'd trusted in his instincts earlier and not given
Raymond the benefit of the doubt. He should have beat
the details out of him when he had the chance.

Determined to keep Raymond talking, he asked, ''Was
that you in the bar with Derek the night he died?''

Raymond looked briefly surprised. ''You are good. And
yes, that was me. I offered to take Derek out slumming,
just because he'd become so maudlin with all his investigations and his regret over Ms. Morris. That's how I
knew it wasn't over between the two of them. Women
threw themselves at your brother, and he turned them all
down.''

Angel made a small sound of distress, but Dane ignored
her. He didn't want Raymond's attention to waver to her.

''I had hoped he'd confide in me, but he was keeping
his secrets to himself that night, no matter how much
booze I poured down him.''

Dane suppressed a growl. ''Alec was the one who discovered Derek had been to a bar that night. He also dis-
likes you on instinct. If I disappear, he'll be all over you.''

Raymond looked briefly alarmed by the prospect, then
he visually shored up his confidence again. ''Once I'm
married to Celia, he won't dare touch me.''

Dane narrowed his gaze, trying to figure ahead. "My sister isn't an idiot. She'll never marry you."

Raymond laughed. "She's anxious to be married." His gaze flicked to Angel and quickly back again. "And your mother, now that you've defected to the enemy camp, is anxious to turn the company over into my capable hands. In fact, I believe your mother would give me control whether Celia married me or not. But I've decided I want Celia. It seems like nice insurance if anyone should ever discover you didn't elope."

"I'll kill you."

Raymond merely laughed at the threat. "Not that your mother will question it, will she, Dane? After all, this won't be the first time you've walked away from your family without a backward glance—both times over a woman. You know, your mother has been trying valiantly to keep her mouth shut, to avoid just such a situation, hoping to make amends. Ah, you didn't know that did you? But I've become something of a confidant for her, and she's told me all about how she regrets the past. Too bad you won't have a chance to forgive her, to put her poor old mind to rest. She'll have to spend the rest of her days with regrets."

Angel staggered to her feet beside Dane and when he would have pushed her behind him again, she forced her way forward. "You've set yourself up a small problem, Raymond."

"What's that?" he asked with a touch of amusement. Obviously he believed he had everything well in control.

"I'd already suspected you. And I told people. The police have it on record that I thought someone was trying to kill me."

"They didn't believe you though, did they?" Raymond's smile was smug. "You didn't have enough proof. And I was careful, even with the smoke-fire, to keep the threats from being too serious, gaining too much attention." He laughed at Angel's comprehension. "Yes, that was a nice touch, wasn't it? Running you out of your apartment and then intercepting your phone call at the office. You reacted just as I planned, showing up at the company like a wild woman, demanding answers. I had hoped once you knew the truth, that Dane was only using you, you'd have enough pride to walk away from him. That would have made you more vulnerable. But no, you decide to marry the bastard."

He looked briefly beyond anger, almost enraged. Dane braced himself, but Raymond shook off his anger, his smirk once again in place. "I have everything planned. And unfortunately for you, both Celia and Mrs. Carter will back up the theory that you ran off together. Thanks to the information I sold at Aeric, and your sister's cut in the family coffers, I should be able to live rather comfortably from here on out."

Dane took a small step forward. "You're an idiot, Raymond. Will anyone believe I abandoned my company? Think about it. I walked away from my family, but I never shirked my own responsibilities."

Raymond shrugged again, totally unconcerned. "So now you're in love. Who's to say what you'd do?"

Grayson made a cooing sound and for the briefest moment drew Raymond's attention. Dane started to move, but the gun was quickly leveled at his head. "Ah, ah. I really don't want the mess of it here in the family room."

Angel shifted beside him and Dane grabbed her arm.

"You're not going to hurt my baby," she said, her voice low and fierce as she pulled away from Dane.

"I really hesitate to. After all, I'm not a monster. And the child seems to have softened Mrs. Carter quite a bit. But I see no way around it."

Angel stiffened. When she spoke, her tone was so mean even Dane blinked. "You can't kill us both at the same time," she taunted. "Try it, and one of us will be on you before you can take a second aim." She slipped further away from Dane, spreading out, making it more difficult for Raymond to maintain control.

Pushed past his composure by her goading, Raymond lifted his arm, taking point-blank aim. His eyes narrowed and his mouth drew tight. Dane felt Angel tensing beside him and realized in horror what she intended. She would attack Raymond, giving Dane the upper hand. The little idiot would sacrifice herself. Panicked, Dane prepared to beat her to it, ready to leap on Raymond full force. He could only hope Angel would use the moment to grab the baby and run.

In the next instant, a shrill screech filled the air, loud and outraged. Dane instinctively leaped toward Angel, pushing her behind him as he stiffened for the additional threat. But they weren't in danger.

Raymond, wide-eyed and frantic, tried to turn. He wasn't fast enough.

Celia lunged around the corner from the kitchen to the family room, still screaming and viciously swinging a heavy crowbar. Raymond ducked, but the length of iron connected with his elbow with satisfying force. There was a sickening crunch as bone gave way, and the gun fell to the carpet. Raymond screamed in agony, his arm hanging at a grotesque angle by his side.

"You miserable worm!" Celia yelled, the perfect epitome of a woman scorned. She hit Raymond again as he tried to roll away, this time thumping the bar against his thigh and eliciting more screams. Dane had no doubt the man's arm was broken, and he couldn't be all too sure of his leg. Celia would have delivered a final blow to his head, ignoring Dane's curses as he reached for the gun, but Alec came storming in and grabbed her from behind. She struggled, and Alec had a time of it subduing her, but finally she calmed.

Alec still held on, his arms circling her, making soft hushing noises in her ear until the tire iron fell to the carpet by their feet. Celia turned in his arms, weeping.

Dane looked at Angel. He was breathing hard, the adrenaline still rushing. "Are you okay?"

She had Grayson squeezed tight in her arms, gently rocking him, kissing him. Tears rolled down her pale cheeks. The baby and Raymond seemed to be vying for the loudest cries, Raymond out of pain, Grayson out of upset. Angel's watery gaze met Dane's and she nodded. He could see her body shake as she drew in jerky, uneven breaths. "Yes. We're fine."

Dane pulled her close and tried to comfort her as best he could, but he himself was shaking with residual fear. Never in his life had anything ever terrorized him like knowing Angel could be shot and even killed. He kissed her full on her trembling lips, verifying her safety, her vitality and warmth. Then he turned to his friend, Angel still tucked safely to his side. He didn't know if he'd ever let her go again.

"Damn, but I'm glad to see you, Alec." It didn't matter that his voice shook, that his eyes felt glazed and moist. All that mattered was the feel of Angel beside him, safe and sound.

Alec smoothed his big hands up and down Celia's back. "I followed her. I don't know how she knew what was going on, but I could tell she was upset."

Celia pushed back from him. "You followed me?"

Alec looked down at her, pushed her head back to his shoulder, and said, "Yeah."

Dane grinned. In the midst of all the chaos, he found Alec's actions incredibly humorous. "Well, I'll be."

"I already called the cops," Alec said, ignoring Dane's laughter. "They should be here any minute. Dammit, will you shut up?" he said to Raymond, while maintaining his tight hold on Celia. "You're lucky I didn't let her kill you."

Again Celia pushed back. "Why didn't you? He deserves it."

"It would have complicated things, especially for you."

"Oh."

Angel stepped away from Dane, then cautiously around Raymond, who was obediently silent. When she reached Celia, she touched the woman's shoulder. "Thank you. You saved our lives."

Celia sniffed and pulled away from Alec's masculine embrace while still standing very close to him. She wiped away her tears and then frowned at Alec, as if some of the drama was his fault. With an obvious effort she returned her attention to Angel. "I caught Raymond making a phone call today, but he hung up real quick when I came in.''

Angel gave a quick peek at Dane and he frowned. Had she gotten a call and not told him? ''Angel?''

She shrugged, but he could tell the careless effort cost her. ''He didn't say anything, Dane, so I thought it was just a wrong number. I was going to tell you, but we got…distracted.''

Dane would have had more to say about that, but Celia sniffed again. ''Several times now Raymond's not been in his office when he should be. He was acting funny the last few days. I thought he was cheating on me. I knew he was up to something, but I thought it was just another woman, not…not this!'' She indicated the entire mess with a wave of her hand.

Alec grunted. ''Why the hell would he be after another woman?''

''How should I know?'' she snapped. ''He was sneaking around, showing up late. But then I had his letter of recommendation from Derek checked and found out it was forged.''

Alec looked livid. ''So you just decided to follow him and could have gotten yourself killed as well!'' He bent down so he could stand nose to nose with Celia. ''What the hell did you ever see in him in the first place?''

Angel grinned at Dane while the other two continued to argue. Dane shook his head and pulled Angel close again. He was almost afraid to stop touching her, reassuring himself she was truly okay. ''If this isn't the most bizarre thing that's ever happened, I don't know what is.''

As Dane spoke to her, Angel turned her gaze on Raymond. He wouldn't be walking any time soon. Angel shivered, and that made Dane furious all over again.

"I'd like to kill him with my bare hands."

Angel touched his mouth. "Shh. Don't say that, Dane. It's been awful, and you've lost so much, but I want it to end now. For all our sakes."

Grayson gave a last shuddering sob and snuggled close.

Dane pressed his lips to the baby's forehead. "Me, too. God, I was afraid for you and Grayson."

Angel sighed. "Oh, Dane. I feel awful. Your brother wasn't the villain after all. He was trying to protect me."

He smoothed her hair back from her face. "That'll be a comfort to my mother, I think."

"Your mother!" Angel blinked up at him. "Raymond said she was sorry, that she wasn't ignoring us because she was mad, just being careful not to say anything that might drive you away again. You need to talk to her, Dane. When I think of her suffering…"

Police sirens sounded in the distance. "I'll settle things with my mother, honey, just as soon as we get things taken care of here. And then," he added, cupping her face and holding her close, "you and I are going to talk. I have a few things to say to you, Angel Morris, and no matter how angry you get, you're going to listen."

ANGEL WATCHED DANE pace around the bedroom as Grayson began to doze in his strong arms. Dane wore only his slacks, and those were undone. His bare feet left impressions in the thick carpet and the flexed muscles of his forearms left an impression on her.

Love swelled, making her warm and shivery at the same time.

It had been a long day, filled with police interviews and questions and confrontations. Grayson had a difficult time settling down, too many strangers invading his small world at one time. But he charmed the detectives who'd run the investigation, as well as Dane's mother once she showed up. Angel smiled again. She was actually beginning to like Mrs. Carter. How could she not when the woman obviously adored her son and grandson as much as Angel did? Oh, she tried to hide it, but tonight her defenses had cracked just a bit, and Angel had seen the woman beneath the iron.

"Do you think it's okay to put him in his crib now?" Dane whispered, not halting in his even strides around the room. Grayson nestled close against the warmth of Dane's broad, naked chest, one small fist clutching his chest hair.

Angel smiled and laid her brush aside. She was freshly showered and in her nightgown, exhausted, but at the same time elated. Everything was over, all the fear and bad feelings and hurt put to rest. Her confession had been on the tip of her tongue when Grayson had begun fussing. "Do you want me to take him?"

"No, I can do it." Dane gave her a long, sizzling look. "Why don't you get under the covers? I'll be right back."

Her heartbeat picked up its pace and she slid into bed. When Dane returned, he removed his slacks, laid them over the back of a chair, then faced her with his hands on his naked hips.

Angel smiled. "If you ran a board meeting like that, you'd be sure to have everyone's attention."

He looked chagrined for just a moment, then dropped his arms and started toward her. "Right now, I only want your attention."

Angel eyed his naked body. "You have it."

"*Angel...*" He growled her name as he climbed into bed beside her.

"Your mother is a proud woman, Dane. It hurt me to see her so upset."

He stilled his hands, which had been in the process of removing her nightgown. "I know what you mean. It nearly broke my heart to hear her admit to so much guilt. She said it was so hard losing Derek, and the only solace she could find was that maybe I'd finally forgiven her."

Angel stroked his head, knowing what his mother's confession had done to him. "I'm proud of you for how you handled it."

"I wish I'd known how she felt long ago. Maybe it wouldn't have gone on for so long."

"You're both too proud for your own good. But your mother is making the attempt to accept me."

"Ha!" Dane pulled down the right strap of her nightgown and cuddled her bare breast in his rough palm. "My mother adores you. She hides it well, but that's just how she is. I think she sees you as a link, a way to soften our reassociation even though I told her all was forgiven. And there were tears in her eyes when she finally got to hold Grayson." He kissed the slope of her breast, his mouth warm and gentle. "That's the first I've ever seen her cry. You know, she's going to spoil him rotten."

"Thank you for refusing her and Celia's offer to keep Grayson. I'm not ready to be separated from him yet. Not after being afraid for him for so long."

"Me, either. Maybe when I'm old and gray I'll be ready to let him out of my sight. But for now, they can visit him here, and we'll make a point of visiting them often.''

They were both silent for a moment, Dane busy in his minute study of Angel's skin, caressing her, kissing her, Angel trying to formulate the words she knew she needed to say.

''My sister is holding up well.''

Diverted, Angel asked, ''Did you get a chance to talk alone with her?''

''Yeah. I don't think she ever would have gone through with the marriage to Raymond. She was as suspicious of him as I was.'' Angel felt him tighten and knew he was reliving the horror of the afternoon. He pulled her close and buried his face in her breasts. ''You could have been hurt. I don't think I've ever been so frightened in my life.''

Angel kissed his temple. ''Thank God for your sister.''

''Alec wants her.'' He lifted his head and there was another grin on his face. ''Damn, but I can't get over it. Alec and Celia. Somehow it just doesn't fit.''

''You know, Celia does have some say about it. Right now, she told me she's in no hurry to get involved with any man again. Raymond really hurt her.''

''Mostly her pride. But she's tough. She'll get over it.''

''And Alec wasn't speaking to her when he left.''

Dane shrugged. ''He's always quiet. It's just his way.''

She wasn't convinced. ''Don't get your hopes up, Dane. I can tell you'd like to see the two of them together, but all things considered, a romance between them would be difficult.''

''That's what I thought about us. But look how much I love you.''

Angel would have fallen off the bed if Dane hadn't been sprawled on top of her, anchoring her in place. "What did you say?"

"Don't look so shocked." He tugged the other strap of her nightgown down, baring her to the waist. "I know I deceived you from the start, that I was pretty ruthless at times to get what I wanted."

"When were you ruthless?" Angel felt both numb and cautiously elated. She couldn't quite believe what he was saying.

"I convinced you we needed to marry because you needed protection. But I could protect you without marriage. I lied to get you where I wanted you."

"You did?" Angel shook her head, trying to clear it. "I mean, you said you wanted to marry me so Grayson would have a solid home."

"I have enough money to insure Grayson would be happy and well cared for without marrying you. That just seemed a convenient way to trap you."

Her heart rapped against her ribs, threatening to break something. "I don't feel trapped."

His eyes darkened, turned warm and probing. "Good, because I still want you to marry me, but with no more secrets between us. I love you."

Angel licked her suddenly dry lips. "You know, you beat me to the punch. I was going to tell you the same thing tonight."

Very slowly, a slight, pleased smile tilted his mouth and Dane leaned down and kissed her. "Is that right?"

"Yes." Her breathing accelerated with the touch of his warm breath. "I knew ages ago that I loved you."

"You didn't know me ages ago, honey. Hell, our entire courtship has taken only a heartbeat."

"Well," Angel said, wrapping her arms around him and hugging him tight, "it was long enough to make me irrevocably and madly in love with you."

Dane grinned as he began tugging up the hem of her nightgown, groaning at the feel of her soft naked belly against his abdomen. "It's a damn good thing, because I have no intention of letting you go."

"Your mother did mention to me what an intelligent businessman you are."

His hand slid over her ribs, then lower, his fingers probing, and he closed his eyes when he found her warm and ready. "I know a good deal when I find it. You, Angel Morris—soon to be Carter—are a very good find."

EPILOGUE

"MICK, MICK!" Grayson came barreling around the corner of the house, chubby arms pumping the air, and threw himself around Mick's long legs. Mick was always greeted with the same amount of verve when he came over after school. He was one of Grayson's favorite people, a surrogate big brother.

Mick swung the seventeen-month-old toddler up into his arms. "Hey, buddy."

"Mick, Mick!"

Angel came in on the heels of her son and dropped onto the couch. "Thank God you're here. He's been screeching your name all day. I can't tell you how glad I am that school's almost over."

Mick, devastatingly gorgeous at eighteen, topping a few inches over six feet, grinned his killer grin at Angel while he tossed Grayson into the air, encouraging the screeches of berserk joy. "You look exhausted, Angel. Is this little monkey wearing you out?"

With a serene smile, Angel said, "I think it's his little brother or sister that's actually doing the trick."

Dazed by her news, Mick tucked Grayson under one leanly muscled arm and staggered into a chair. "You're pregnant?"

She smiled happily, pleased with his reaction. Now to

get Dane's reaction. She heard the front door opening and leaned toward Mick. "I was hoping to have a few minutes alone with Dane, if you—"

"I'll take short-breeches here out to the swing."

"Mick, Mick!"

But as Dane stepped into the house and called out, "I'm home," Grayson launched himself from Mick's arms. Angel gasped, but Mick, quick on the draw, managed to juggle the toddler until he could get both feet on solid ground. And like a shot, Grayson was off again.

"Daddy! Daddy!"

Mick laughed. "To think, he used to be such a peaceful baby."

Dane entered with Grayson perched on his shoulders. He went directly to Angel, who dutifully lifted her face for a kiss. "My mother said you had something to tell me."

Angel glared. "She promised!"

"Promised what?"

Mick lifted Grayson from Dane's shoulders. "The squirt and I are going out to the swing."

"Wait a minute, Mick. I have something for you." Dane reached into his pocket and pulled out an envelope.

"What is it?"

As usual, Mick was still hesitant at the sign of a gift. But Dane, who delighted in trying to spoil Mick as much as he did Angel, only laughed. "I know the academic scholarship you got doesn't pay for everything, so this will help pick up some of the tab."

Mick merely frowned until Dane gave an exaggerated sigh of impatience and opened the envelope. He waved the paper under Mick's nose. "It's from the company. We have our own set of tax deductible donations, and this year, my mother decided to expand into scholarships. The two combined ought to take care of most of your schooling expenses. And let me warn you, if you even think of refusing it, you'll have to deal with Mother. Since Celia left the company and Mother's taken over again, she's more autocratic than ever. I believe she actually missed it. And she's taken to singing your praises, so don't even think to fight her on this.''

Mick looked ready to faint and with a numb expression, took the paper from Dane and read it. Silently, Angel retrieved her son, who promptly planted a sloppy kiss on her cheek, then laid his head on her shoulder. With everyone else he was a dynamo of constant motion. With Angel, he loved to cuddle.

Very slowly, a grin settled over Mick's face. Then with a loud whoop, he jumped up and slapped the ceiling. Angel felt like crying every time he acted like the young man he was, rather than the old man he'd been forced to be. Since his mother's death, he spent more time than ever with her and Dane, and they were as close as a family could be.

After a gentle hug to Angel, and a bruising bear hug to Dane, Mick swung Grayson up and headed out the door.

''He's something else, isn't he?''

Angel smiled at Dane. ''You've been a good influence on him.''

He grunted. ''If only I could say the same for my sister.''

''Oh no, what did she do now?'' About six months ago Celia had decided she'd had enough of the corporate world, and following in Dane's footsteps, she was determined to become a P.I. Dane was horrified, but didn't know how to stop her. In an effort to keep an eye on her, he gave her a job at his office, which rankled Alec no end. Just as Angel had predicted, nothing had come of a romance between them, and instead, their constant bickering kept Dane on the brink of insanity.

Dane gave Angel a telling look. "She almost got shot, that's what she did. She was supposed to *locate* that little chump who jumped bail, not try to bring him in. I don't remember the last time I've seen Alec that mad."

"Why was Alec mad?"

"Because he *did* get shot." Dane quickly grabbed her when she paled. "Now, Angel, he's all right, just a flesh wound. The bullet grazed his thigh. But he's been raising high hell for the past two hours, and Celia, that witch, has steered clear, which means I've had to listen to it all."

It was too much, and Angel fell into a fit of giggles. She'd been so worried about Celia, who'd become reclusive after her emotional hurt with Raymond. But now Celia was determined to experience everything life had to offer, and there was no one who could stop her, not even Alec. And heaven knew, he tried hard enough. Grown men might walk a wide path around him, but Celia continually tried to go through him.

"I'm glad you think it's so funny. Between Mother constantly working to reel me back into the company, and Celia's antics, I'm ready to go hide under my covers." He grinned at Angel. "Want to come with me?"

"Maybe. But first I need to talk to you."

Dane groaned. "Tell me this won't be bad news, babe. I can't take any more bad news."

Angel drew a deep breath. "I told your mother I'd need

a leave of absence in about six months." Angel had agreed to fill in for vacationing secretaries, which she thought would be a week's worth of work a month, and instead it was turning out to be more like three weeks' every month. Something always seemed to come up so that she was required. Luckily her mother-in-law didn't mind when she did most of that work at home, so she could be with Grayson. On the days she had to be in the office, Dane adjusted his schedule. Or sometimes Mick, or Celia, or even Alec...

"Is my mother wearing on your nerves? I thought the two of you were getting along pretty good?"

"It's not that. Dane, do you remember when we first talked of getting married?"

He sat down and pulled her onto his lap. "If you're thinking of backing out now, it's too late. You signed the marriage certificate ages ago."

Angel playfully punched his shoulder. "I'm pregnant."

He froze for a heartbeat, then a gorgeous smile spread over his face. "Pregnant?"

She nodded. "Almost two months now. I waited to go to the doctor so I could be sure."

His large hand opened over her abdomen, and as usual, she quickened in response. "It's not twins?" he asked, looking at her body.

"The doctor doesn't think so, so you can relax."

He did, then he grinned some more. His hand on her belly turned caressing and he kissed her throat. "This time will be different, babe. I'll take care of you."

"Dane, I don't regret anything about my pregnancy with Grayson. If things hadn't happened as they did, I